D1520037

Whispers On A String

Kathleen Stone

"Important encounters are planned by the souls long before the bodies see each other."
~ Paulo Coelho

For Ken, who made my lifelong dream of being a full time writer a reality

2011

It was the kind of headache you get when you've been out in the sun all day... the heat emanating off your skull and the dull throbbing of drums that causes your stomach to go all queasy. I could hear the buzzer for my apartment going off, then my phone started ringing. I could barely focus my eyes as I poked my head out from under the covers to see it was my friend Lonny trying to video chat with me. I wasn't in the mood to talk to anyone, so I ignored it. Then the buzzing from outside and my phone ringing started all over again. I decided that whoever was buzzing my apartment could only be bad news, so I answered my phone instead.

"Hey Rooster," Lonny said with his crooked toothed smile, his eyes hidden behind a pair of aviator sunglasses.

"Lonny," I groaned, barely opening my eyes. "What time is it?"

"Seven o'clock."

I wanted to strangle him. He rarely woke up before nine in the morning... why was he calling me at seven?

I could hear the buzzing to my apartment door continuing in the background and knew it was bad news. Everything was bad news lately.

"Come on Rooster, wake up. I have a surprise for you."

I opened one eye to look at Lonny smiling at me from my phone. "Oh yeah? What's that?"

"I'm standing outside your door. Don't you hear me buzzing to get in?"

I jumped out of bed and grabbed my head, the throbbing so intense it was as if someone hit me with a hammer. I stumbled to the door and buzzed Lonny into the building, then began searching blindly for some clothes. I managed to throw on a pair of shorts and a t-shirt before he tapped on my apartment door.

I opened the door to see my best friend standing in front of me, wondering how he managed to get to New York from

1

California without telling me. I put on a smile and pulled him into my arms, hugging him as tightly as I could.

"What are you doing here?" I asked as I finally pulled away.

"I'm picking up a car for my daughter," he chuckled, sitting on a kitchen chair. "And driving it back to Vegas for her."

"Why didn't you tell me you were coming?"

"I wanted to surprise you. Surprise!"

I searched in the cabinet over the kitchen sink for a bottle of aspirin, dumping four into my hand and swallowing them down with water from the tap. I wasn't in the frame of mind to explain things to Lonny, and I could already see he was quickly figuring out that I hadn't been completely honest with him the last couple months.

"What's going on, Roo? The shop downstairs is closed up, your apartment is nearly empty—"

"Lonny please," I begged. "I can't do this right now."

"You look like shit," he said, standing. He opened the door to the refrigerator, but made no comment about seeing that it was practically empty. Instead he smiled and said, "Let's get some breakfast. I'm starving."

1975

I met Lonny Winter when we were both fourteen and just starting high school. We seemed to be shoved together at every opportunity, not only having the same last name, but the same birthdate as well. Our names were bound together, attached at the hip, from the day we met, standing in line to get our yearbook photos taken. I giggled as his name was called when it was his turn... *Leonard Winter!* He turned and glared at me; I was so painfully shy I immediately regretted it. I could feel my face burning as the redness took over.

He was the most beautiful boy I'd ever seen.

Lonny was still in the room when they called my name... *Ruby Winter!* I could hear him cackling like a kid who just heard the funniest joke of his lifetime. I deserved it, I knew, but it was hard to ignore him. I was so embarrassed, I wanted to run home and crawl into my bed. Instead I joined my friend Molly and some of her girlfriends, and we walked uptown to get something to eat when we were finished.

When we walked into McDonald's, Lonny was already there with a group of his friends. I wanted to die. I told my friends I needed to head home and walked out. They were used to my odd, shy disappearances so never questioned me. I didn't realize Lonny was right behind me on his bicycle.

"Where you going?" he asked.

"Home."

"Why?"

"I have to."

I was so embarrassed by this cute boy that I just wanted him to go away. I almost started to cry. My heart thundered in my chest as I wondered if that's what it felt like to be in love. I was fourteen... what did I know about love?

"Ruby." He continued to speak as he rode his bicycle slowly beside me. "Sounds like an old lady name."

I stopped walking and glared at him with my eyes burning. "*Leonard!*" I hissed. "That's my grandpa's name!"

3

He stopped riding his bike and put his feet on the sidewalk. We stared at each other silently for what seemed like hours to me. All of a sudden we both started giggling, which turned into hysterical laughter. It was that moment the spirits aligned to bring us together. The moment we became the Winter twins; looking nothing alike but having everyone convinced we were siblings living in different houses. The very moment I became Roo... but only to him. He was the only one I ever allowed to call me that; the only one who would ever get away with it. When he was feeling particularly funny he called me Rooster, which he knew I hated. He claimed it was a combination of my name and my auburn hair, and it became a term of endearment between us.

2011

I plopped myself into the booth across from Lonny in the diner a couple blocks away from my apartment. I never understood why he loved it so much; to me it was just another greasy spoon, but I obliged him whenever he was in town. He smiled as the waitress came to our table, ordering coffee for both of us. I stared at my menu, not really reading anything, all the words just a jumble of letters taunting me.

The waitress brought our coffee and I was still staring blankly at my menu. I could hear Lonny speaking; he knew me better than anyone and ordered my breakfast for me — two eggs sunny side up, english muffin, a side of bacon, hash browns, and a small orange juice. He gave the menus back to the waitress and after she walked away, I finally looked up at him. He was grinning at me. I couldn't help but smile back.

"Come on, Roo," he said, poking my hand with his finger. "What's going on?"

"Billy left me," I managed to croak.

"Left? When?"

"Two months ago. The divorce was final yesterday."

I could tell he wanted to scold me for not telling him, but he didn't. "We talk twice a week… why wouldn't you tell me?"

The throbbing in my head continued as I tried to answer my friend without bursting into tears. I closed my eyes and rubbed my temples, hoping for some relief, but none came.

"I was too ashamed."

"Rooster," he whispered. "I'm so sorry."

I went on to explain how my husband of nearly 30 years was having an affair with one of the young tattoo artists in our shop, right under my nose. Eight weeks earlier he closed up the shop, left me, and took her to Arizona to start a new life.

"I'm behind on the rent. I've been selling everything he left behind, everything I own, hoping to go back home." I spoke just above a whisper. "I have nothing left."

The waitress deposited our food plates in front of us and I dug in, unable to remember the last time I had a decent meal. I tried not to look like a homeless person Lonny had pulled in off the street, but I was so hungry.

1979

Lonny was on the short side for a teenage boy when I met him, but had a growth spurt between sophomore and junior year that brought him to about five foot eight. I always seemed to be two inches shorter than Lonny at any given time. He was always skinny, always funny, always pretty quiet and shy. Most of the girls at school thought he was a silly twerp, but he wasn't too keen on high school girls anyway. He despised their giggling and screeching, and he really hated the way they seemed to stab each other in the back at the flip of a coin.

Lonny preferred music over anything. He was a genius on the guitar and would rather spend his time away from school playing or writing music. He was never comfortable playing in front of anyone, so he never joined a band or played for an audience. He was perfectly happy playing in his room or for his friends and mother, but that was it.

Until senior year, when Billy Downey transferred to our school. Billy and I hit it off immediately when we met in English class his first day, and started dating that weekend. Lonny let me know right away that there was something about Billy he didn't trust. I knew Billy loved to embellish the truth a bit, but didn't see that as a reason not to date him.

Right before graduation there was a student talent show put on by the seniors, and Billy, who claimed to be the greatest guitar player our school would ever see, signed up to perform. Lonny and I snuck into the theater after school one day when they were having rehearsals and Billy's guitar playing was abysmal at best.

As we tried to sneak back out of the theater, Ms. Cooke, the choir director, caught us and threatened to assign us detention the following day. Lonny stared at the ground, kicking at imaginary rocks with his foot as I tried to think of something to say. He finally looked up at her and asked, "Got any open spots for the talent show?"

Ms. Cooke's face lit up like a neon sign, a smile spreading over her face so large it was almost clownish. "I'll see you at rehearsal tomorrow, Mr. Winter," she replied.

7

"Nope. Tell me what time I'm going on. I'll be there."

Ms. Cooke wrinkled her nose, but for some reason, chose not to argue with him.

Word spread quickly that Lonny was going to be doing something in the talent show. Rumors ranged from magic to gymnastics to juggling bowling pins set on fire. I sat in the theater's front row watching the different talent acts perform, impressed by what our student body could do. Even Billy sounded better during his actual performance than he did at rehearsal, but he had no idea what was to come. Ms. Cooke added Lonny at the very end of the show, and introduced him as the last act of the evening. I held my breath.

Lonny walked onstage carrying his electric guitar and a small amp. He looked directly at me and winked, then closed his eyes and let his fingers do the talking. He played that guitar like a man who had been doing it for three lifetimes. He played a medley of genres covering blues, pop and rock. The intensity on his face as he played brought tears to my eyes. I could hear the gasps all around me as people were realizing what a talent goofy Lonny really was.

It was because of his unexpected performance that evening I eventually lost him.

2011

I looked up at Lonny when I finished eating every morsel on my plate, and he was holding a piece of toast with butter and grape jelly close to his lips. He hadn't even taken a bite of his breakfast, but I was already finished with mine. He grinned, the mischievous grin I knew so well. His grin quickly turned into his famous crooked-toothed smile that I adored our entire existence together. I wiped my mouth with a napkin and leaned back, crossing my arms in front of me.

It had been almost a year since I saw him last, on our forty-ninth birthday. Even though we talked at least twice a week, we only saw each other once a year on our birthday. It was something we had always promised we would continue, no matter what the circumstances were in our lives.

Even though he hated people gawking at him, Lonny was good at the staring game. I watched his face intently as he ate his breakfast, not a word spoken between us. He never broke eye contact; it was a game he always liked to play with me, ever since we met. Whoever laughed first, lost.

Lonny had beautiful brown eyes that were more copper than anything else, but when the sun hit them, they almost looked gold. He had the kind of eyes that drooped on the outside edges and when he laughed, his eyes almost completely disappeared. I loved it when he laughed. He had dimples in both cheeks and his teeth were far from perfect, but they were perfect for him.

The day I met Lonny, he had short brown hair with awesomely crooked bangs that rested about an inch above his eyebrows — something he blamed on his mother, who insisted on cutting his hair. She agreed, however, once he got into high school she would leave his hair alone and I don't think he had it cut once while we were there. He was one of those guys who grew into his look when he let his hair grow; he fancied the shaggy look with the feathered layers that went off to the side, his bangs long enough that he could have them or not, depending on his mood.

9

I sat staring at Lonny and he stared right back at me, never flinching. At that moment I just wanted to see his eyes light up the way they did when he was about to laugh. For a guy so close to his fiftieth birthday, he didn't look a day over thirty. The only telltale signs were a few laugh lines by his eyes and a few strands of gray hair, but even that was barely noticeable. People had said the same about me, but I never believed them. And this day, sitting in the diner playing the staring game with Lonny, I felt about eighty.

I opened my mouth to speak but Lonny wagged his finger at me. I had forgotten the staring game rules... no talking. He winked, continuing to eat his breakfast. I knew I would win this round, as I was so depressed and without hope that I couldn't imagine breaking into laughter. I was suddenly overwhelmed by feelings of dread, my chest getting tight and my head about to explode. I don't know what I looked like, but it was severe enough to get Lonny to break his own staring game rules.

"Hey," he whispered, "it's going to be all right."

He put down his fork and wiped his hands, then slid into the booth next to me, pulling me into his arms and letting me sob against his chest.

1979

Lonny walked off the stage after his performance in the senior talent show to something he never expected — adoration from nearly everyone in school. As he fought his way through the crowded theater to get to me, he was stopped by everyone in his path. People shaking his hand, teachers patting him on the back, and girls trying to hug and kiss him. *Girls.* He definitely wasn't used to that. He'd had a few girlfriends in high school, but here he was being fawned over like a rock star.

I hugged Lonny, who had a smile on his face wider than I'd ever seen before. It was almost as if he wasn't expecting to play as well as he did; that even he was surprised by his own performance. I was in the middle of telling him how amazing he was onstage when Billy found me, tugging on my arm.

"Gotta go," Billy said. He shook Lonny's hand and congratulated him on an amazing performance.

My parents were strict when it came to curfew, so Billy wasn't being pushy when he said it was time to go. As I always did, I told Lonny to call me when he got home, then said goodbye and walked outside to Billy's car.

On the ride home I was gushing over Lonny's performance. "Wasn't he dynamite? I can't believe he finally played in front of an audience!"

"Yeah," Billy agreed. "He's pretty good."

"Pretty good? He's the best!"

"And you're so experienced you've heard every guitar player on earth? Don't be stupid."

"You're stupid."

"If you like Lonny so much, why don't you go out with him?"

I started laughing hysterically then made gagging noises. "Ew! He's my *brother.*"

"He's not really your brother."

Maybe not technically, but Lonny *was* my brother. It's the only way we ever thought about each other. *Siblings.*

Billy parked in my driveway and leaned in for a goodnight kiss. We made out like high school kids did, but I kept looking at the clock, knowing that if I was in the house one minute past ten o'clock, I would be grounded. As he kissed me, I felt his hand slide under my shirt and squeeze my breast. I was so shocked, I slapped his hand and got out of his car as quickly as I could, running into the house.

I made it into the house by the skin of my teeth, kissing my mom and dad. They asked me how the talent show went, and I gushed about Lonny, which surprised them, because as well as they knew him, they'd never seen him play the guitar. I got ready for bed and waited for Lonny's call. It never came.

The next morning, Billy picked me up for school, and as was the routine, swung by Lonny's house next. He honked, but Lonny never came out. Lonny's mother Joanie came out in her nightgown and I heard Billy grumble, "Have another drink, Mrs. Winter."

I rolled down the window and said, "Hi Mom."

"Lonny's not here. He never came home last night."

I wrinkled my forehead. That wasn't like Lonny.

"You tell him he's in big trouble," his mother said, before stumbling back toward the house.

Joanie was an alcoholic, and everybody knew it. Lonny was embarrassed by her at times, but he loved her dearly. She was the only one he had in his life after his father took off the summer before sixth grade. Lonny's mother and my parents were part of the story we made up about being siblings; my parents adored Lonny and Joanie loved me. We were the craziest, perfect mixed family.

We were a few blocks from school when I spotted Lonny walking alone, carrying his guitar case and his amp, and I urged Billy to pull over. Lonny looked like he hadn't slept much, and was still in the clothes he was wearing the night before.

"Are you okay?" I asked, worried.

He nodded, but said nothing.

"Your mom is worried sick about you."

Normally, Lonny would have something sarcastic or witty to say in response, but he remained quiet. He wouldn't even look at me.

2011

"Let's get out of here," Lonny said after paying the bill.

Lonny took my hands in his and said, "Why don't you stay at the hotel with me tonight? We can eat junk food, drink from the mini-bar and watch stupid movies."

This did not sound appealing to me. "Thanks, but I think I'd rather just stay home."

"And do what?"

"I still have a few books."

"Come on, Roo," he said with a grin. "I'm leaving tomorrow; don't you want to spend time with me?"

The truth was, I didn't want to burden Lonny with my depression or my destructive thoughts. I just wanted to crawl back in my bed and sleep forever.

"We're spending time together now," I whispered, almost unintelligibly.

Lonny glanced at his watch and pulled a face. "Exactly two hours. All right then, I'll be on my way."

My stomach lurched as I watched him get up and walk out of the diner without giving me a hug. I knew I'd made a big mistake because Lonny didn't like games, and we never parted company without a loving hug. I was in self-destruct mode and I could only focus on my own misery.

By the time I hit the sidewalk outside he was getting into a taxi and driving away. I didn't even know where he was staying. I wiped tears off my face as I walked back to my apartment, stopping at the empty storefront below it that used to be our tattoo business. I stared at the soaped-out windows and the "Out of Business" sign crookedly hanging at the front entrance. I didn't know anything about business, or tattoos for that matter, but Billy was a tattoo artist like no other. He was an artist like a painter takes to canvas, and he was very well known in the area. I managed the shop — answered telephones, made appointments, cleaned up, and all the other grunt work he didn't want to be bothered with. And I was okay with that; I had my place and I knew what needed to be done every day.

14

I went upstairs to my apartment and searched the medicine cabinet for anything that would help with the raging migraine I couldn't get rid of. I assumed if I could just stop crying that would help, but it didn't seem to be in the cards. I found a bottle of pain killers from my appendectomy and took two. I crawled into my bed, pulled the covers over my head, and went to sleep.

1979

High school in the seventies was a different time than high school now. We had so many more restrictions, but there were certain freedoms you don't see these days, like outdoor smoking areas for the students and open campus. If you didn't have a class, you could leave school and go uptown and do whatever you wanted, as long as you came back. Lonny and I shared the same lunch period, so the day after the talent show I went to the smoking area — nicknamed the Pit Stop — looking for him. One of his buddies told me I just missed him, so I tried to find him.

I finally caught up to Lonny walking uptown smoking a cigarette, still looking as strange as he did that morning when we picked him up on the way to school.

"Are you okay?" I asked.

"I'm fine. Just tired."

"Where were you last night?"

He turned to look at me, and I didn't like the expression on his face. "Nowhere."

"I need to talk to you about something," I said. "Something important."

Lonny took a detour into the park and we sat on a bench, facing each other. "What's up?" he asked, taking a drag off his cigarette.

"Billy grabbed my boob last night."

Lonny started laughing, nearly choking. "That's it?" he managed to ask through bursts of laughter.

"It's not funny," I grumbled. "He keeps pushing me harder and harder to have sex and I'm not ready."

"Then don't do it. If you're not ready, don't do it."

"But he keeps pressuring me."

Lonny threw his cigarette on the ground and stomped it out ferociously. "Do you love him?"

"Well, I—"

"Do you love him?"

I love you.

16

"I don't know. He's my first boyfriend and I feel like I love him."

"Look," Lonny said, putting a hand on my shoulder. "Guys are assholes. They're gonna say and do anything they can to get in a girl's pants. It's what we do."

"Is it what *you* do?" I stared at him with wide eyes waiting for a response, but he just looked up at the sky and let out a heaving sigh.

"You're a good kid," Lonny finally answered. "Don't give it up for any guy who pays you a compliment or claims to love you... don't be one of *those* girls."

I certainly didn't expect an answer like that out of Lonny. I opened my mouth to speak, but couldn't find any words.

"We better split," Lonny remarked, lighting another cigarette and starting to walk away.

"Were you with one of *those* girls last night, Lonny?"

He stared at me for a while before answering, "No. No I wasn't."

2011

I had to be dreaming. My apartment doorbell was buzzing and my phone was ringing at the same time.

Isn't this how I woke up this morning?

Lonny was trying to video chat with me again. I accepted the call and there he was, just like that morning, wearing his aviator shades with a goofy grin on his face.

"Let me in, Rooster."

I hung up on him, dragging myself out of bed and buzzing him into the building. He entered the apartment talking.

"Do you have a suitcase?"

"What time is it? What?"

I couldn't even focus my eyes. I sat on a kitchen chair and watched as he went into my bedroom, opened the closet door and grumbled. He pulled out an old box-style suitcase and showed it to me. "Is this all you have?"

I nodded.

He disappeared back into my bedroom. I gathered all the strength I had in me and followed him, shocked to see him pulling what clothes I still owned out of the closet and from my dresser, and neatly packing them in the ancient suitcase.

"What are you doing?" I asked.

Lonny gently sat me on the bed, holding my face in his hands.

"How much weight have you lost?" he asked.

"Don't you know never to ask a woman about her weight?" I tried to joke. "Is that why you go through so many girlfriends?"

He rolled his eyes, grunted, then leaned over and pressed his forehead against mine. "You're coming with me, and I won't take no for an answer."

"But Lonny, I—"

"No. No excuses. You have *nothing* left here. Billy's gone, your business is gone, you can't pay your rent, and you have no food. You've never liked living here, so why would you want to stay?"

18

I felt foolish as the words left my mouth, but I said them anyway. "Billy might come back, and I want to be here when he does."

Lonny apparently had enough, and he didn't lose his cool very often. "Why would you *want* him back?" he yelled. "He left you here with *nothing* so he could start another life with some young piece of trash he was screwing behind your back! You deserve better than that. Stop feeling sorry for yourself and move on."

I felt as though Lonny just punched me in the gut. I curled up into a ball and pulled the pillow over my head to hide my hideously ugly sobbing. I couldn't understand why Lonny was being so cruel during the lowest point in my life. I wanted him to go away and never come back, but at the same time I needed him so desperately.

I heard him snap the latches shut on my suitcase, then felt its weight leave the bed. I lifted the pillow just enough to peek out at him with one eye. He was standing there holding my suitcase, watching me.

"Let's go," he said.

"You don't understand," I cried.

"I don't understand how you've been using a toothbrush that's nearly bald, but we'll stop and get you a new one."

I stared at him, dumbfounded. I was having a meltdown and he was scolding me for the condition of my toothbrush.

Lonny removed the pillow from my face and tossed it on the bed. "Let's go," he said again.

"Exactly where are we *going*, Lonny?"

"To my hotel."

"And then what?"

He grabbed my hand, pulling me off the bed, onto my feet. He tried pulling me out of the room, but I slapped his hand away. He picked up my suitcase and grabbed my hand again, but this time I shoved him away from me with both hands. He didn't move, he didn't flinch, he let me do my thing and watched without emotion.

"Are you on drugs? What the fuck is wrong with you?" he yelled.

19

I realized how violent I'd become and collapsed to the floor, continuing to sob. Lonny sat on the floor next to me, taking my hands in his.

"Listen," he whispered. "Billy isn't coming back. And if he does, so what? He doesn't deserve you. This person you've become, this isn't the Ruby Winter I've known all these years. This isn't *my* Roo. I want my Rooster back, and I'm going to find her. But you have to let me help you."

I watched his face, so serious and still like the teenage boy I first met at fourteen. "How can you even begin to help me?" I asked.

He shrugged and with a smile replied, "I don't know, but I'm willing to try."

"Just for the record, I'm not on drugs."

We had a good chuckle and he squeezed my hands. "The rest of your life starts right now. You're coming with me to Vegas, and we'll figure things out as we go."

"I have no money," I argued.

"I'll take care of everything. Besides, I don't want to drive cross country by myself. Just you and me, like old times. *Before* Billy came into our lives."

I wiped the tears from my face and nodded, agreeing to go with Lonny on his road trip. I threw my apartment keys on the kitchen table and followed him out the door, never to look back again. When we reached the street, Lonny unlocked the passenger door of a mint condition 1965 Mustang convertible. Red. My dream car.

"This is the car?" I asked, smiling from ear to ear. I couldn't wait to get in it.

I sat in the passenger seat and as Lonny started the engine he said, "Yep. This is the car."

1979

Senior prom is supposed to be a rite of passage for teenage girls; that end of the year dance where you dress up like a princess and your prince puts a flower on your wrist with the expectation of a night filled with romance, dancing and the promises of a blissful summer. Mine went from one nightmare to another.

My best girlfriend Molly and I helped each other get ready for the big night, doing each other's hair and applying the little bit of makeup our parents would allow for the evening. We helped each other put on our frilly dresses and waited anxiously for our dates to arrive at my house. Both sets of parents were fussing over us, taking photographs and acting more nervous than we were. We giggled like high school girls do, thinking our parents were such nerds.

Lonny begrudgingly agreed to be Molly's date because I didn't want to go alone with Billy. He hated dressing up, and he especially hated dances, but he did it for me. Billy had amped up the pressure on getting me to have sex with him, and I just wasn't ready. I was of the belief that if he really loved me, he would wait until marriage, because that's what I wanted. And everyone knew prom night was the time of year a lot of high schoolers lost their virginity. I had no intention of becoming another statistic in that category.

Lonny arrived promptly with his mother, and he looked so handsome in his tuxedo. I watched as he nervously put the corsage on Molly's wrist, all our parents snapping photo after photo, clearly making him uncomfortable. If there was one thing I knew about Lonny, he did *not* like being the center of attention. I paced back and forth, trying not to chew on my beautifully painted fingernails, looking out the window, wondering where Billy was. He was late, and he was our ride to the dance.

It was nearing the time that if we didn't leave immediately, we were going to be late to the dance and if you were late, they closed the doors and didn't let you in. Had Billy been in an accident? Did he decide to back out at the last minute? I didn't know what to do. Molly took me by the hand and dragged me to my bedroom.

"What are you going to do?" she asked.

"I guess I'll stay home," was my numb response. "You and Lonny go, I'll be okay."

But I was *not* okay. I wanted to burst into tears for being stood up on my senior prom night. Stood up by my boyfriend. My boyfriend for all of senior year. How could he do this to me?

We joined Lonny and the parents back in the living room and Molly's mother said, "You guys really need to be going."

"You guys go ahead," I told them. "Have fun."

Lonny's eyes grew large and I knew he was silently freaking out.

Molly's father agreed to drive Molly and Lonny to the dance, while I disappeared to my room to change clothes. Lonny was right behind me.

"You have to go," he insisted. "I only agreed to do this because of you."

"I can't go by myself," I replied, my eyes filling with tears. "You just don't go to prom by yourself. How embarrassing."

This was 1979… you *didn't* go to prom without a date.

"The three of us can go together," Lonny said with a smile. "Come on, it'll be fun."

"Everyone will make fun of me."

"They won't, I promise. *Please*."

Lonny was only going to prom because of me; how could I say no to him?

Relieved, he pulled me back into the living room and announced that the three of us were going together. I wasn't sure what the expression on Molly's face meant, but I climbed into the front of the car with her dad, while she crawled into the back with Lonny.

I felt foolish, but I wasn't going to let Lonny down. He never turned his back on me and I wasn't about to turn mine on him. When we entered the school gym, people looked at me strangely, but no one said anything. Molly and I sat down while Lonny went to get us drinks.

"Did you know?" Molly asked.

"Know what?"

"Did you know Lonny was going to ask me to prom?"

I wasn't quite sure where she was going with this, but I was thankful when Lonny promptly returned and I didn't have to answer her question. How would she feel if she knew Lonny only asked her to prom because I begged him to?

Molly put her drink on the table and grabbed Lonny's hand, dragging him onto the dance floor. I giggled as he looked like he was being led to slaughter. I certainly owed him; God only knew what I would have to do in return.

I watched the two of them dance and tried not to laugh when Lonny was facing me. He had his hands on her hips and hers were on his shoulders, as they seemed to just step from side to side, standing an arm's length apart. I wasn't about to make fun of them as I was not a dancer either, and at least they showed up with each other.

As I was watching Lonny and giggling at him like a goof, I felt someone sit on the chair next to me. It was Seth Brown, Billy's best friend. He asked where Billy was, and I told him I had no idea. He chatted about classes, which I thought was strange, because we had no classes together. I noticed Lonny watching us, and wondered what he was thinking.

As soon as the song was over, Lonny let go of Molly and walked back to where I was sitting with Seth. Lonny didn't say anything to him, but gave him a dirty look.

"You three all together?" Seth asked.

"Yep," Lonny replied, taking a drink out of his cup and glaring at him.

"Not exactly," Molly corrected him with a giggle. "Lonny's here with me."

Seth just nodded and smiled, getting up and walking to the other side of the gym to join his friends.

"What did he want?" Lonny asked me.

"I'm not sure," I laughed.

We were soon interrupted by Ms. Cooke, who was a chaperone for the dance that evening. "Lonny, I have some really exciting news, if I could talk to you in private please?"

23

I watched as Lonny reluctantly followed Ms. Cooke to another part of the gym to talk privately. Her face was lit up like a Christmas tree as she spoke, her lips never stopping to take a breath, her hands dramatically doing their own talking.

"This is a great band," Molly said.

I was too busy watching Lonny to hear what she said. "What?"

"This is a great band," she repeated. "They need to play more slow songs though."

I nodded as if I cared, then continued watching Lonny with Ms. Cooke. He never seemed to say much, but nodded every once in a while. What on earth could she be talking to him about?

When Lonny rejoined us, he never said a word. Molly and I looked at each other and shrugged, knowing if he wasn't interested in talking, no amount of begging would make him change his mind.

The band changed gears and started playing one of my favorite songs, "You Take My Breath Away," by Rex Smith. Molly smiled brightly, happy a slow song was being played, but her smile disappeared quickly as Lonny grabbed my hand and pulled me out to the dance floor.

We danced pretty much the same way I watched him dancing with Molly, his hands on my hips and my hands on his shoulders, standing an arm's length away from each other. I assumed he dragged me out there to tell me what Ms. Cooke wanted, but he didn't say a word. He just stared at me with a faraway look in his eyes; a look I'd never seen on him before. I decided that if he wasn't going to say anything, I was going to start singing. We both knew I couldn't sing to save my life but if anything, it would get him to start talking just to shut me up.

"You, you take my breath away, and I don't know what to say," I sang.

Lonny just busted out laughing, which caused me to laugh as well. He finally said, "You're not supposed to be talking while you're dancing to a love song."

"Oh? I didn't know that. I'll shut up then," I laughed.

"Nah, don't. I like it when you sing."

24

That made me laugh even harder, which caused the couples dancing near us to yell at us to be quiet.

"You can't sing a note," Lonny said, "but at least you do it from the heart."

I smiled. The song ended quickly and I thought our dance would be over, but the band went right into "Lady," by the Little River Band, and Lonny made no moves to leave the dance floor. I was surprised when he put his hands on my shoulders and pulled me closer; close enough that our bodies were almost touching. My arms hung awkwardly by my side, unsure what I should do with them.

He leaned close to my ear and said, "Livingston Monroe."

Livingston Monroe was our favorite rock band. I assumed he'd heard they were coming to town on tour, so I was really excited.

I jumped up and down a bit to show my excitement, smiling like a fool, and he wrapped his arms around my waist and held me against him. He rested his chin on my shoulder, putting his mouth close to my ear.

"Ms. Cooke's cousin is dating their manager," he continued. "She wants me to audition for them."

My whole body became stiff with shock. "Lonny!" I whisper shouted. "How?"

"Joey Buckingham split a couple days ago."

I pulled my head away from him so I could see his face. It was expressionless, but I covered my mouth with my hands to conceal my excitement from those around us.

"Please don't tell anyone," he begged.

I promised I would keep his secret, but inside I was screaming. He never said whether or not he was considering the audition.

Livingston Monroe!

When the song finished, we walked back to where Molly was talking to another girl and they immediately stopped speaking as we approached. Lonny said he was going outside for a cigarette, and I stayed behind. The girl Molly was talking to disappeared, and it was then I noticed it looked like my friend had been crying.

"Are you okay?" I asked Molly.

25

"Lonny is *my* date and you're ruining it," she said.

"What? How?" I was honestly surprised.

"You just danced two slow dances with him!" she scolded. "Slow dances are supposed to be for your *date*."

I didn't understand why she was so angry with me. "I'm sorry. He just wanted to talk."

"Oh yeah, sure," she huffed. "You're the one without a date, so you're trying to take mine."

I couldn't understand why she was getting so upset with me. Then it dawned on me.

"Do you *like* Lonny?" I asked.

She pouted at me, but didn't answer.

"Molly, you never told me you *liked* him!"

"And I thought he liked me too, since he asked me to prom," she spoke quietly, as if she were ready to burst into tears.

"We're just friends, I promise," I said. I'm not sure she believed me, but she smiled and nodded anyway. She saw Lonny returning and said she was going to the bathroom to clean up her smudged makeup.

I waited until I was sure she couldn't hear me and I told Lonny that Molly really *liked* him, and then I apologized for putting him that position.

"It's okay," he assured me. "I could have a worse prom date."

"So what about the audition?" I couldn't keep it in any longer.

"I don't know."

I was stunned. "You don't *know*?"

"I don't wanna talk about it, okay?"

I understood the look he gave me all too well and agreed that I wouldn't mention it again. Lonny was a genius on the guitar, but he didn't think so. He never wanted to be in a band; he never thought he was good enough. The only reason he agreed to play in the talent show was to piss Billy off. He hated playing to an audience.

Molly soon returned and told us there was nobody waiting to have the photographer take their photos, so we all decided it was time to get that done. I was glad to see she was no longer angry

26

with me for trying to take her date away. I stood to the side as Molly and Lonny posed awkwardly for the traditional prom photos that everyone looks so silly in, but I was surprised when she pulled me in for the three of us to have photos taken together. Molly explained that I didn't get any photos taken back at the house, and she wanted me to have a memory of prom, too. We had fun with it — we made funny faces, posed in silly positions, and the photographer was laughing and enjoying that we chose to make it different. He had clearly been bored out of his mind up until then. When we were done, Molly stepped to the side and insisted Lonny and I take some photos together. And we posed just like a brother and sister would — arms around each other's shoulders or giving rabbit ears behind the head, and me putting Lonny in a headlock.

When the dance was over, Lonny's mother picked us up and drove me home first, which surprised me. I thanked her for the ride, and turned in my seat to say goodbye to Lonny and Molly who were sitting in the back seat, holding hands. This stung me a bit, I had to admit. Lonny offered to walk me to my door and got out of the car with me. When we reached the front door, Billy was sitting on the stairs.

2011

We entered the hotel room and I immediately flopped onto one of the soft, cushiony beds. The room was bright and smelled so fresh, unlike the musty old apartment I'd been living in for the last twenty years. My arms and legs were splayed out across the bed as I closed my eyes and smiled. It felt good to be treated to a bit of luxury, and I couldn't remember the last time I'd stayed in a hotel.

Being a fairly well-known tattoo artist, Billy would travel for business a few times a year, going to conventions or trade shows. Sometimes he would make an odd appearance at a comic convention or something similar, where people would pay him ungodly amounts of money to have their favorite superhero or fantasy character tattooed somewhere on their body. He always had great stories to tell from those experiences. I was never able to travel with Billy as I had to keep the shop running since I was the only one he trusted. I started to realize there were probably ulterior motives in his reasons for wanting me to stay home.

In high school Billy was tall and athletic with blue eyes and beautiful, white-blonde hair. By the time he reached thirty, however, he had lost almost all of his hair. He insisted on keeping it long in the back, constantly wearing a hat or bandana of some sort over the top of his head, because the whole top of his head was bald as a baby's bottom. By the time he reached forty, he had developed quite a sizable beer belly. He blamed it on my cooking, which was impossible, because I only cooked Sunday dinner when the shop was closed and all our employees were invited to spend it with us. Other than that, we ate on the fly because we were always working. It didn't matter that his looks had changed so drastically; he was a smooth talker and everyone loved him. His incredible ego and ability to embellish everything won over the toughest critics. Throughout his life, he rarely heard the word no.

Lonny placed our suitcases on the floor and tossed his sunglasses on the table. He kicked off his signature Chuck Taylors and threw himself on the other bed in the room. Coming in from a hot June day, the air conditioning was a welcome relief.

"Twenty-five pounds," I said out loud.

"Huh?"

"I've lost twenty-five pounds since Billy left."

"I wasn't really expecting an answer to that."

"Well you got one."

He turned on his side to face me, and I did the same. "How have you been able to afford to keep your phone?"

I was a bit embarrassed to admit it, but I said, "Your calls were the only thing I had left. I made sacrifices to keep it."

"Like food?"

"Like food."

I could feel tears threatening to spill and I didn't want to go there again, so I jumped off the bed and went into the bathroom. I closed the door and stood in front of the mirror, trying to figure out whose reflection was looking back at me. My skin was pale, and the freckles covering my face were hideous. My auburn hair was lackluster in color with a few gray hairs peeking out near my temples that I promptly pulled. My blue eyes looked lifeless and tired, having already given up on inner peace and happiness. The one positive was I had hardly any wrinkles, thanks to spending almost my entire existence indoors and away from the sun. We were always in the shop early, and home late, rarely spending much time outdoors. That was odd for me, because I was always an outdoor girl. I loved riding my bike, camping and hiking, and never wanted to be stuck inside. The weather never mattered; I hated being cooped up inside. I needed fresh air to breathe, the sun warm on my face, and nature at my fingertips. Now, I had no idea who I was.

By the time I came out of the bathroom, Lonny had fallen asleep. I didn't blame him as it had been quite an exhausting day, and my eyes were feeling a bit heavy themselves. I crawled back onto my bed and stretched out on my side, watching Lonny, my savior. He was always saving me, and always seemed to know exactly when I needed saving. It wasn't long before I fell asleep as well, comforted by the fact that I was no longer alone, and for at least a short time, my life had a plan.

1979

"Did you go to prom with *him*?" Billy slurred. He was drunk.

"And what if I did?" I was angry. He stood me up for our senior prom because he was drunk!

"Seth told me… he told me… you were dancing together. *Slow* dancing. And he was… whispering in your ear."

"You stood me up!" I hissed. "I had to go with Lonny and Molly! Do you know how embarrassing that was?"

Lonny turned and walked away, leaving me alone with my drunk boyfriend. I didn't mean for it to come out so horribly, but I knew I hurt his feelings.

"How did you get here?" I asked Billy.

"Dunno."

I walked past him and went into the house where my mom and dad were watching the news, waiting for me to get home. Before they could even ask how the dance was I asked my dad if he would drive Billy home, explaining he was outside and he was drunk. My dad went into the kitchen and picked up the telephone, calling Billy's father.

I watched from the kitchen window and my dad sat outside with Billy until his father arrived. When Mr. Downey got out of his car I immediately knew he was livid. I saw him shake my father's hand then he grabbed Billy by the front of his shirt and practically dragged him to the car, slapping him in the head the whole way there. He shoved him into the back seat and took off, his enraged words heard all the way down the street.

I went upstairs and changed into my pajamas, washed my face, then crawled into bed. Even though I was devastated Billy stood me up for my only prom, I had to admit it was fun. I regretted the evening had to end with drunk Billy sitting on my doorstep, and me hurting Lonny's feelings with my stinging words.

It wasn't long before I heard a pebble tap my bedroom window. I got up and looked outside to see Lonny standing down below, so I put on my robe and snuck out to the back yard where he met me at the picnic table. We both sat on top of it, neither of us saying a word. I finally got up the nerve to look at him and he stared at me with such sad eyes.

"Are you okay?" he asked.

"I'm sorry, Lonny, I didn't mean what I said."

"Yes you did."

"Okay, I did, but it had nothing to do with you or Molly. I had fun, and I'm glad you talked me into going."

"You know if Billy wasn't around it would've been just me and you at prom like we always planned."

"I know."

He lit a cigarette and asked, "What happened to Billy?"

"His dad came and got him. He's probably getting the crap beat out of him." It was a very real possibility and I was worried for Billy's safety. I changed the subject, asking, "So did you kiss Molly goodnight?" I smiled when I looked at him, and an embarrassed grin slowly crept across his face.

He took a long drag off his cigarette and chuckled. "My mom was there, so no."

"Did you want to?"

Lonny lay on his back, looking up at the sky. "I'll never tell."

I knew I was being nosy, so I just laughed and said, "Okay, okay."

"How do you see your future after graduation?"

I lay on my back next to Lonny, putting my hands behind my head. "Not sure. I'm not going to college, so I guess I'll get a job."

"What about Billy?"

"I don't know," I admitted.

"He's a jerk, Roo."

I knew he was a jerk; Lonny didn't need to state the obvious. "It's not like boys are ringing my phone off the hook," I chuckled.

"You can do better."

"How do you know that? I don't know it. I'm not exactly pretty and popular."

"Stop it, Rooster."

Tell me you want to be my boyfriend.

31

"You brought it up," I argued. I didn't want to talk about Billy anymore. "Molly really likes you."

"She does?"

I laughed as I told Lonny how Molly was so upset with me, thinking I was trying to steal him away from her at the dance. "I know you asked her to prom because of me, but if you like her too, you should tell her."

Lonny rolled off the picnic table, grabbing my hand and helping me up. "Gotta split," he said. "I'll talk to you tomorrow."

"Call me when you get home."

I watched him walk away into the night, wondering how he really felt about Molly, and how I was going to handle the situation with Billy. If he truly cared about me, he would never have stood me up on prom night, the biggest event of a girl's high school life. I was happy that I got to spend it with Lonny, even if he didn't originally want to be there.

The next morning at the breakfast table my dad was reading the newspaper, as he did every day. He said, "Liverwurst Monster... isn't that the band you and Lonny like so much?"

My dad thought he was so funny, changing the names of everything to be goofy. It was even worse when I had friends over.

"What Dad?" I wasn't really paying attention.

"Liverwurst Monster... says here their guitarist just quit."

So it was true. Joey Buckingham quit Livingston Monroe

.

2011

I opened my eyes to see Lonny sitting on the bed, concentrating intently on his phone. I stretched my weary bones, letting him know I was awake.

"You hungry?" he asked, never looking up.

I looked at the clock and couldn't believe it was already six o'clock.

"We can go downstairs to the restaurant or order a pizza," he suggested.

"Pizza," I replied dreamily. It had been so long since I'd had pizza!

"Playlist for our road trip is all set," he said with a big smile, finally looking up from his phone. He called to have a pizza delivered, then suggested we go downstairs to the bar for a drink while we waited.

The bar was fairly empty, middle of the week slow time most likely, so we sat down and ordered our drinks. The bartender set a tequila sunrise in front of me, and a scotch on the rocks in front of Lonny, then a shot of Jack Daniels in front of us both.

Lonny held up his shot glass and said, "For old time's sake."

I held up my shot glass and said, "To new beginnings."

"Cheers!"

We clinked glasses and threw back the shots.

"So tell me what the deal is with this car you're driving back to Celia," I urged, curious to know why he was driving a mint condition 1965 Mustang convertible cross country for his twenty-five year old daughter.

A smile as bright as the sun crept across his face, but before he could respond, some woman with bleached blonde hair, badly in need of a touch-up, interrupted us.

"Aren't you Lonny—"

"No." He wouldn't even let her finish. He was actually quite rude, which caught me completely off guard.

"Aw come on," the blonde woman insisted. "I know it's you, Lonny."

Lonny took a swig of his scotch, then faced the woman. "Can't you see I'm with somebody?"

She glanced at me with a disapproving look and said, "Your sister, yeah, nice try."

Lonny was clearly uncomfortable, but grumbled that he would be right back, taking the woman by the arm and guiding her to a private part of the bar. I tried to watch without looking like a busybody, or worse yet, a jealous girlfriend, but I couldn't help myself. She kept trying to touch him and he would push her hand away, or she'd try to get close to his face and he'd nearly fall over trying to lean the opposite away. It was actually quite comical. I couldn't wait until he came back so I could tease him mercilessly.

Lonny sat back down next to me, grumbling expletives under his breath.

"Your rock star is showing," I teased.

He gave me the side eye, never turning his head, but he did smile.

"That one needs to hang up her groupie shoes," he remarked.

"Yeah, she looks like she was rode hard and put away wet."

Lonny almost choked on his drink and we both got a great belly laugh out of it. I loved Lonny's laugh — it was as if it started in his toes and burst out of him like a rocket, loud and full of life. There was a time I didn't think I'd ever hear him laugh again.

1979

I wanted to spend a quiet, lazy Sunday with my parents, but I could hear my phone ringing upstairs. I chose to ignore it, but it kept ringing. Finally, the phone rang in the kitchen, and when my mom answered it was Billy. I didn't want to talk to him, so I made my way into the kitchen at a snail's pace, picking up the receiver.

I'm not exactly sure where it came from, but as soon as he started speaking I interrupted and said, "I don't want to see you anymore."

Billy was stunned. "Are you breaking up with me?"

"Yeah."

"That's it?"

"Yeah."

He started talking again and I hung up the phone. I was done with his excuses, done with feeling insignificant, done with his lies. I returned to my favorite chair in the living room and continued watching the baseball game. I just wanted to be left alone.

About thirty minutes later, someone was ringing the front doorbell. Thinking that it was probably Billy, I ignored it. My mom grumbled but got up and answered it, letting Molly into the house.

"Why aren't you answering your phone?" she scolded.

She grabbed my hand and dragged me off the chair, all the way up to my room, closing the door behind her.

"Is it true?" she asked, out of breath. She must have run all the way to my house.

I sat on my bed. "What?"

"Did Billy break up with you?"

"What? No...."

"Oh thank God! I told Jenny it wasn't true!"

"Jenny? What... wait... I broke up with *him*," I corrected her. "I broke up with Billy."

She was shocked. "But everyone is saying he dumped you."

Of course.

35

"Everyone? It happened half an hour ago!"

"Everyone is saying it's because you cheated on him."

"Cheated on—"

"With Lonny!"

"*Lonny!*"

Molly started crying. "Please tell me it's not true, *please!*"

I couldn't even form words. Billy was now telling everyone that he broke up with me because I cheated on him... with *Lonny!*

"Are you crazy?" I yelled. "Shut up!"

"Why are you yelling at me?" Molly cried.

"Because you're being stupid!"

Molly ran out of my room in hysterics and I was left staring into the hallway like an idiot. I didn't even notice Lonny standing there.

"What's her problem?" he asked innocently.

"Did you hear?"

He shrugged his shoulders and held up his hands, looking completely baffled.

"I broke up with Billy, but he's telling everyone *he* broke up with *me* because I cheated on him with *you!*"

Lonny started laughing.

"It's not funny!"

"Yeah, it kinda is," he insisted.

"Now Molly is upset with me because she likes you!"

I knew how much Lonny hated girl drama, and now he was right in the middle of it.

"Okay," he said, throwing his hands in the air. "While you're doing your freak out girl thing, I'm gonna watch the game with your dad."

And with that, he disappeared.

I wasn't typically a girl who did the whole drama thing, which is one of the reasons Lonny and I got along so well. I hated the way girls in school giggled and screeched and went mental over boys. And now I was not only having my first official "freak out girl thing" as Lonny called it, I was also experiencing my first break up. With no one to talk to.

I wasn't sure what emotion to feel. I was sad that I broke up with Billy, but I was furious with him for spreading lies about me

36

and Lonny. I was upset with Molly for believing Billy's lie, and angry at her for deciding she liked Lonny. I really needed to talk to Lonny, but he wouldn't come near me with all the drama spilling out of me, and I was upset that he'd rather be watching the baseball game with my dad than listening to me.

I decided to suck it up and go downstairs where I found my dad in his chair, my mom on the couch knitting, and Lonny spread out on the floor with a pillow, all watching the game as we usually did on Sunday afternoons. I curled up in my favorite chair and quietly watched with the rest of them.

When the game reached the seventh inning stretch, my mom cleared her throat and said, "You two are awfully quiet today." Lonny said nothing and I just looked at my mom and shrugged. I could tell she wanted to know more, but instead got up and went to the kitchen to make popcorn.

Lonny and I were quiet throughout the rest of the game, and I knew my mom was staring me down, wondering what happened. How could I even begin to tell her everything? I couldn't wrap my own head around it and it was all happening to me. And it was all so embarrassing.

Lonny went home after the game, declining my mom's offer to stay for dinner. He said he'd see me in the morning and that was it. I knew I would be interrogated when we sat down to eat.

"Did something happen at the dance last night?" my mom asked as soon as I put food in my mouth.

The only significant thing that happened at the dance was Lonny finding out about an audition for Livingston Monroe, but I wasn't allowed to talk about *that*.

"Nothing," I answered. "We had a lot of fun."

"Then what was with all the silence between you and Lonny today? You two are *never* quiet."

I rolled my eyes and my dad scolded me for disrespecting my mother. I looked at my dad, then looked at my mom. They weren't going to let it go.

"Billy showed up here drunk last night, that's what happened," I finally answered.

"What was Molly so upset about? She ran out of here crying and almost knocked Lonny down the stairs on the way out," my dad said.

I sighed heavily and stopped eating, which bummed me out because I really loved my mother's mashed potatoes and didn't want them to get cold.

"I broke up with Billy today," I explained, waiting for their shocked gasps to end before I continued. "Molly is upset because Billy is telling everyone that he broke up with me."

"Typical teenage boy," my mom grumbled.

This made no sense to my father, who asked, "Why would that be so upsetting to Molly?"

"Because Molly likes Lonny," I replied. I looked up to see my parents both staring at me like I grew two more heads. I knew it didn't make any sense, but I was too embarrassed to tell them everything.

"Ruby Marie," my mom scolded lightly. "What on earth is going on?"

"Fine," I grumbled, folding my arms in front of me. "Billy is telling everyone that he broke up with me because I cheated on him. With *Lonny*." Seeing the shocked looks on their faces I added, "I danced with Lonny, is that cheating? I didn't do anything else, I swear!"

My mom reached out to take my hand as my dad tried to hide the fact he was laughing. "Honey," she said, "dancing with Lonny is not cheating."

"Did Lonny kiss you goodnight?" my dad teased. "If he did, then that could be considered cheating."

"Dad!" I was utterly humiliated. "That's just gross!"

My mom slapped my dad in the arm, but I could tell she was trying not to laugh. They assured me that I didn't do anything inappropriate with Lonny, and that Billy was just being a jerk. What they really wanted to talk about was the revelation that Molly liked Lonny, you know… like *that*.

2011

We returned to our room, settling on one of the beds with the pepperoni and garlic pizza and sodas from the mini bar. As soon as we saw the opening scene from *This Is Spinal Tap* on the television we both screamed, "HELLO CLEVELAND!"

We polished off the entire pizza and enjoyed the movie, and again I decided to ask Lonny about the car he was driving to his daughter, without fear of interruption by some random groupie this time.

His face lit up like the sun whenever he talked about Celia, and he was more than eager to tell me about the car. Apparently Celia was a bit of a classic car junkie, and just like me, her dream car was the red, 1965 Mustang convertible. She was one year from completing medical school and he wanted to do something special for her. At twenty-five, she still had a year of school to go, but the car she currently drove was on its last legs, and she couldn't afford to buy another one. She knew he was coming for a visit, but she had no idea he was bringing her such an extravagant gift.

"Why this car?" I asked. "Why not a car on the west coast, where you both live?"

"I'm not sure," he chuckled. "This is the one that spoke to me. Purchased new and has been sitting in a garage under a cover since 1965. Ten original miles."

Lonny was a big believer in fate and spirits, and if this was the car they led him to, it made perfect sense. I wasn't about to argue with him; I had no reason to.

"It's a beautiful car," I told him. "She's going to love it."

"And this car put me on your doorstep just when you needed me most," he said with a wink.

"I'll thank the car in the morning." I laughed, then went into the bathroom to get ready for bed. When I came back out, he was sitting on his bed in a pair of sweatpants and nothing else.

I crawled into my bed and pulled the cool sheet up to my chin. I watched Lonny, who was staring at his phone. I could see the scar that started at the palm of his left hand and snaked under his arm, stopping just under his armpit. It had faded some with time, but was still a grim reminder of not so rosy days.

1979

I was sitting in English class Monday morning when Billy came in late, taking his assigned seat next to me. He had a black eye and a fat lip and he caught me staring at him, my mouth agape. I felt my eyes burn, knowing his father did this to him after picking him up at my house after prom. I felt a tear fall down my cheek and wiped it away quickly hoping he hadn't noticed, but he smiled at me and nodded, letting me know he was okay.

I couldn't concentrate on anything in class, thinking about the way Billy's dad beat him up, thinking about how Molly was still upset with me, and thinking about the quiet walk to school I had with Lonny. It was like we were both in another world, thinking about different things, and not wanting to verbalize any of it. That was odd for us, because we were always chatting and bouncing things off each other, no matter what it might have been.

I was so thankful when the bell finally rang, gathering my books and leaving the classroom as fast as I could. I just wasn't fast enough, soon feeling a hand on my shoulder and finding it belonged to Billy.

"Can I talk to you later? Maybe after school?" he asked.

I hesitated, but agreed. I didn't want to talk to Billy. The only person I wanted to talk to was Lonny, and I wouldn't see him until lunchtime. I went to my next class and sat at my chemistry station where Molly, my lab partner, was already seated. She gave me the stink eye and said nothing. I wasn't in the mood to deal with her, either.

All of a sudden Jenny, the high school gossip, and the one spreading Billy's lie about me cheating on him, burst into the classroom and headed right for Molly and me.

"Did you see Billy?" she asked us, much too loudly for my taste. "Did you see what Lonny did to his face?"

I knew what happened to Billy's face, and it had nothing to do with Lonny.

"Lonny didn't do that!" I argued.

"Everybody knows Billy dumped your ugly ass," Jenny said. "Because you cheated on him with that twerp Lonny."

"You're so *stupid*," I argued. "Lonny is my *brother*!"

She laughed at me. "Everyone saw you dancing with Lonny. And where was Billy? Home, nursing his broken heart."

I was dumbstruck. There was no arguing with this girl. I knew what the truth was, but she kept throwing the lies back in my face. It upset Molly so much, believing it was all true, that she ran out of class and never came back. It was only second period and I was already believed to be the senior slut, and Lonny was believed to have bloodied Billy's face because of it.

The rest of the day dragged on, with people whispering behind my back and giving me dirty looks in the hallway or in class. I was so relieved when lunchtime finally rolled around I could hardly get out of the classroom fast enough. I ran to my locker, threw in the books I no longer needed, grabbed my lunch and grabbed the books for my afternoon classes. I slammed my locker shut and Billy was standing there. My heart fell into my stomach.

"Can you talk now?" he asked.

"Now? You have class now."

"I'll cut it so we can talk."

"I don't have anything to say to you." I started to walk away, but his words stopped me in my tracks.

"But I love you."

I turned to face him and said, "You told people you dumped me because I cheated on you. With *Lonny*. Do you know how sick that is? And people believe it! And now you're telling them he's the one who beat you up?"

Billy chuckled. "I didn't start *that* rumor."

"You don't tell lies about people you love," I said softly.

I walked away from him, rushing as fast as I could to find Lonny. I didn't see him anywhere, which was unusual, because he was always in the Pit Stop before I was. I sat on the grass and leaned up against the fence, eating my lunch and studying the chapter in my history book for next period. It wasn't long before I saw Lonny walking toward me, and he wasn't alone. He was with Molly, and they were holding hands.

I can't even begin to explain why, but seeing the glorious smile on Molly's face as they approached made me angry. I felt as

42

though someone had just stabbed me in the heart and it would soon stop beating. I didn't know if it was betrayal I felt, and the worst part was I didn't know which of my friends I felt most betrayed by.

Molly giggled and blathered on about how excited she was to be a head camp counselor that summer, and Lonny just smiled and nodded. I pretended to be studying my history book, saying nothing. I was still upset with Molly and the way she believed the lie about me and Lonny, and here she was acting as if it never happened. And why didn't Lonny tell me he was going to ask her out? Ever since prom, our entire friendship was turned upside down and I didn't know which end was up.

Molly suddenly remembered she was supposed to get extra help from her math teacher during her lunch period, and stood up quickly to leave.

"Will you walk me home after school?" she asked Lonny. He said he would and she quickly kissed him on the cheek and ran off.

I couldn't even look at him. I kept my nose in my book, trying to avoid eye contact with him. He poked my foot with his toe and I ignored him. He plucked a dandelion out of the grass and tossed it onto my book and I still ignored him.

"Aw come on Rooster, what's the matter?"

I slammed my book shut as I felt the tears burning my eyes. "People are whispering behind my back and calling me a slut. Everyone believes the lie and now you're holding hands with Molly, who has been treating me like *shit*, and acting like nothing ever happened."

"Are you mad at me?"

I felt stupid for crying, wiping the tears off my face. "Why didn't you tell me you were going to ask her out?"

Why don't you love me?

"I didn't plan it," he admitted. "It just sort of happened."

I pulled a face. "Lonny, just stop, okay? *Stop.*" I gathered my books and stood up, staring down at him. "Don't you start lying to me, too."

I walked away but I could hear him calling after me. "Roo, wait!" I didn't want to talk to Lonny anymore. I wanted to go to the nurse and tell her I was sick. I just wanted my mom to pick me up and take me home.

I went back inside to the cafeteria and was walking as fast as I could, until someone grabbed my arm. I was about ready to go off on Lonny, but it wasn't him. It was Billy, and he was smiling at me. He took everything I was carrying and put it under his arm, then held my hand and walked me to an open table. As I sat down I saw Lonny looking for me and when our eyes met, there was a look on his face I couldn't figure out. He continued walking and didn't try to talk to me again.

"Ruby, I'm sorry," Billy said, still holding my hand. "I'm sorry about getting wasted before prom and blowing you off. I'm sorry about starting the lie. It's just that I love you so much, and I thought maybe you did like Lonny, but he's with Molly and—"

"People are calling me a slut," I replied, tears choking me as I spoke.

"Please give me another chance. I'll make sure everyone knows the truth."

Billy was saying everything I thought I wanted to hear, but it wasn't making me happy. Deep down I just hurt, and thinking about Lonny with Molly made everything even worse. My best friend with my best girlfriend... now who was I going to talk to?

"Ruby?" I snapped back into reality and looked at Billy, who was smiling at me. He squeezed my hand and said, "Whattya say? Can we get back together?"

I lost my best friend to Molly, so I felt like I didn't have anything more to lose. I said okay, even though the thought just made me feel like crying. At least Billy was interested in me; nobody else wanted to go out with me. He was all smiles, pulling me onto his lap with a giant hug.

The rest of that week dragged on like one continuous Monday. Studying for finals was bad enough, but I was trying to finish my final project in Home Economics class — the dress I planned on wearing to graduation. Lonny and I had drifted apart and weren't speaking much to each other, and we never saw each other unless it was in passing at school. I missed him more than I cared to admit, and it was breaking my heart.

2011

Lonny set his phone on the bedside table and crawled into his bed.

"Still sleep in the pitch black?" he asked.

"Yep."

He turned off the light and we both settled down in the blackness of the hotel room. Without the distraction of talking to Lonny, watching a movie, or running into bleached blonde bimbos, my thoughts turned to Billy. Every time I closed my eyes I saw him. Or I saw him with *her.* Zoe was a sweet girl, and I was the one who talked Billy into hiring her. He thought she was too young and inexperienced for a coveted artist position in his shop, but I had seen her work and I knew she was exactly what we needed, especially in such a male dominated field. We were on the cusp of our shop's tenth anniversary, and we were desperate for another tattoo artist as we were busier than we could manage. She was only twenty years old, but I pushed hard for her. I knew she had the talent, but I also loved her personality, and I really needed another woman to spend my work days with. Billy reluctantly agreed to hire Zoe for a three month trial period and she never left.

Zoe may have been twenty years younger than me, but we became very good friends. Being the only two women in the shop helped, but she was like the daughter I never had. In the ten years she worked for us, I helped her through the death of her mother, the fatal heroin overdose of her brother, and various romantic hookups and breakups. I worried about some of her destructive decisions, but she had the right to make her mistakes just like everyone else. Her personal life aside, she was nothing but professional and on top of her game while at work. The first nine years we were closer than any two women could be without literally being family. Then things began to change; Zoe became distant, confiding in me less and less. The girl who spent holidays and weekly Sunday night dinners at our house didn't come around anymore. She no longer wanted to go out to lunch with me, or have our weekly girls' night out. I thought I had done something wrong, but Billy convinced me it had nothing to do with me, that he

45

noticed she had become withdrawn from everyone. He was suspicious she was moonlighting behind our backs and might be looking for another job, suggesting she was acting guiltily.

I kept waiting for her to tell us she was leaving, but she never did. Then I began to notice that the only one she was withdrawing from was me. I watched her with the customers and the rest of the employees, and she was exactly the same as when we hired her. Obviously I had done something to cause this, and I was determined to make things right, as I desperately missed the relationship I had with Zoe.

Before I could approach her, however, I ended up in the hospital for an emergency appendectomy. I didn't recover from it as well as I should have, and ended up being gone from the shop for two weeks. Billy said things were a bit rough without me, but insisted I follow doctor's orders and stay home. I was stuck in the apartment alone, bored out of my mind with nothing to do. I was so thankful for my video chats with Lonny, and I found myself smiling in the dark thinking about it.

One night I woke up and it was dark outside, so I knew I missed dinner. Billy was nowhere to be found, and he promised we'd have Chinese that evening, as I'd been craving it since my surgery. I looked at the clock and was shocked to see it was just after midnight. I called the shop but there was no answer, so I put on my shoes, grabbed the keys and slowly made my way downstairs. The shop was closed, as it should have been, so I let myself in and let my eyes get used to the dark. I knew my way around the shop with my eyes closed, so I made my way through to the back, where our office was. I turned on the light and saw them… together.

I didn't realize I'd been crying, silent tears rolling down my face and into my ears. I gasped out loud at the memory, briefly forgetting where I was.

Lonny asked me if I was okay, but didn't turn on the light. I wiped the tears from my face and cleared my throat, pulling myself together.

"Not at the moment," I replied honestly.

"You have to move on, Roo. You've grieved long enough."

I wasn't grieving for the husband who left me; I was grieving for the thirty years I lost spent married to a man I never loved.

"Have you ever had a truly broken heart, Lonny?"

He was quiet for a while, then shocked me with his answer. "Yes."

I didn't know if I should say anything in return, so I remained silent. Lonny had never mentioned anything to me about being brokenhearted over a girl. Ever. He always acted so nonchalant when it came to girls, like he really didn't care if they existed or not.

"It was a long time ago," he broke the silence.

1979

Graduation day finally came and before I ran out of the house to Billy's car, my mom stopped me to say, "Lonny and Joanie are coming over for dinner after graduation tonight."

I nodded numbly.

"What's going on with you two? I haven't seen him in a week."

"He's going out with Molly," was all I could say.

"You guys can see Molly and Billy on your own time. This dinner is for family only."

I smiled. "Okay, Mom."

I kissed her on the cheek and raced out the door. I hopped into Billy's car and he gave me a quick kiss.

"I love your dress," he said. "You did a great job."

I felt my cheeks flush. I was really proud of the dress I made, even though my fellow classmates thought it was sadly outdated. I created it to look like my mother's dress from 1959 and I absolutely loved it. It was light green silk and sleeveless, with a zippered back and an A-line skirt that fell just above the knees. I embellished the neckline with pearls from a broken necklace my mom lent to the project, and added a tulle underlay to make the skirt fluffy and bouncy.

I felt beautiful for the first time in my life. I couldn't wait for everyone to see me in my dress, mainly to eat their words. Billy kept looking over at me and smiling during our drive to school, making me feel even more beautiful. Once Billy and I got back together and people saw Lonny with Molly, the rumors about me cheating seemed to fade away quickly. They started blaming Jenny for starting and spreading it for no reason.

The students were organized alphabetically in two separate lines outside the gym to make the grand entrance inside, where we would sit in our assigned seats for the graduation ceremony. Ms. Cooke was one of the teachers making sure everyone was in the right place in line, and that our graduation caps and gowns were on straight. She noticed Lonny wasn't standing next to me and frowned.

48

"Where's Lonny?" she asked.

I looked around and replied, "I don't know."

"You didn't come together?"

"We don't live together," I reminded her.

"Oh there he is!" She pulled him into line in front of me, adjusting his cap.

After she walked away he looked at me and rolled his eyes. I couldn't help but laugh.

"Mom says we're invited to your house for dinner," he said.

"Yep. My mom said it's family only, so Billy and Molly aren't allowed."

We both laughed.

Before either of us could say anything else, the line began to move toward the gym and we marched until arriving at our assigned seats. It was hard to believe this was it… high school was over and we were moving on to the next stage of our lives. I had no idea what my future looked like; I couldn't even imagine what the summer held. I knew I had to get a job and where was the fun in that?

After the ceremony was over, kids gathered with their friends and families to take photos and say goodbye to their teachers, none of us knowing what the future would bring to everyone in our graduating class. As I was getting ready to leave with my parents, I noticed Ms. Cooke talking to Lonny. More like talking *at* him as he said nothing, only nodding his head.

We picked up pizza on the way home, with Lonny and his mom meeting us at the house. We had a nice meal spending time together with no outsiders, enjoying each other's company as we always had in the past — two families who had become one by the chance meeting of two teenagers as they began their freshman year of high school.

When we were finished eating dinner, Joanie presented a beautifully wrapped box to both of us. Lonny and I were extremely proud of her; she hadn't had a drink all day, and we knew how difficult it was. She was so beautiful and so funny when she wasn't drinking, but those times were few and far between.

"We all went in and got you both a graduation present," my dad explained.

Lonny and I looked at each other and grinned. Being the kind boy he was, he let me open the gift. We both peered into the box, where an envelope with our names on it sat beside magazine photos of different places in Europe. We looked at each other, a bit confused.

My mom explained, "We're always hearing you talk about your dream to backpack around Europe one day, so we decided you both deserved it now. This summer."

Joanie had tears in her eyes as she struggled to speak. "You were both good students, you never got into trouble, and... dammit... you're just good kids!"

My dad concluded with, "We know how it is to make plans for the future and never see them to fruition. It happens; life gets in the way. We wanted you to experience your dream now, before your lives take you to different places."

Lonny and I were speechless. He opened the envelope, which contained an unknown amount of cash. My eyes burned with tears as I glanced at Lonny, who looked the same way.

Lonny said, "But Mom, you—"

"We'll not hear another word," my mom interrupted.

Lonny and I were both in tears as we jumped up to hug all of our parents. Neither one of us knew how they came up with money for such an amazing gift, but we were more than grateful.

Lonny said he would be right back and ran out to the car. His mother pulled me into her arms and cried, hugging me tightly. "When Lonny's dad left, he was never the same boy. He was always so sad and quiet... not the happy, funny boy he had always been. Until he met you, Ruby. You gave me my boy back."

This made me cry, and when Lonny reappeared with his beat up acoustic guitar, he had a worried look on his face.

"I was just telling Ruby how much I love her," his mom explained. "Are you going to play for us?"

It always made me happy when Lonny played guitar, which he did a lot, but only in the safety of his own bedroom. My mom cut the cake and we moved into the living room where Lonny got comfortable in my favorite chair and began to play for us. He had never played for my parents before and they watched in amazement.

Lonny played some blues, some fifties rock and roll for my parents, and a bit of classical for his mother. I watched his face, so intense, and with his eyes closed. He couldn't stand knowing people were watching him play, so he'd close his eyes, unless his hair was long enough, then he let that fall in his face when he played. He had agreed to get his hair trimmed before graduation, so his hair wasn't quite long enough to cover his eyes that night.

I watched his fingers as he played, so fluid and smooth, like he'd been playing for fifty years. He never had a single lesson; his father gave him the beat up guitar when he was five years old and the rest was history. He never stopped playing. He couldn't read a bit of music, but he could play anything after hearing it once. I knew he was secretly writing his own songs but I wasn't allowed to say anything about it, and I would never break that trust.

The phone rang, disturbing our wonderful, musical evening and my dad came back saying it was Billy. I didn't want to talk to Billy; I wanted to continue listening to Lonny create magic on his guitar. I excused myself to answer the phone and could hear my parents praising Lonny's talent behind me.

"When can I pick you up?" Billy asked.

I hesitated, then told him to come over in an hour, assuming Lonny would be done playing for us by then. I quickly hung up the phone and returned to the living room, sitting on the couch in between my parents.

What came next surprised me. Lonny cleared his throat and said, "Okay Roo, I've been working on this one for you. I hope you like it."

He closed his eyes and began playing my favorite song, "Drift Away," by Dobie Gray. But it wasn't the song choice or the fact he was playing it for me that brought me to tears, it was that he actually sang the words. We would always sing along to our favorite songs together, but he never sang while he played guitar. And on this special day he not only learned to play my favorite song, he sang it to me as well.

Lonny sang, "And when I'm feelin' blue, the guitar's comin' through to soothe me... thanks for the joy that you've

51

given me," and I thought of what his mother told me, completely losing it. Everything that happened since dinner was so unbelievably emotional for me, I wasn't quite sure how to process it all. I realized then how much I missed Lonny the last week when we weren't communicating with each other, and I couldn't stop crying.

Lonny finished the song and I jumped off the couch and pulled him into my arms, guitar and all, crushing him against me. I think I may have blown out his eardrum by trying to talk but sobbing instead, as he pulled away to look at my face. He was just about to say something when the doorbell rang. I cursed under my breath, which was rare for me, and he started laughing.

I heard my mom saying hello to Billy and I was angry that he came right over instead of waiting an hour like I asked him to. I was even more furious that he interrupted such a wonderful evening with Lonny and his mom.

"Sorry I'm early," Billy chuckled. "I just couldn't wait to see Ruby."

"Are you going to see Molly tonight?" I asked Lonny.

"No. She has family in from out of town. I was done here anyway."

I wrapped my arms around him and whispered in his ear, "That was the most beautiful thing anyone's ever done for me. Thank you."

He just smiled, looking embarrassed.

I kissed my mom and dad, then Joanie, thanking them for dinner and the wonderful gift. Lonny stood up and put his guitar in its case so I took the opportunity to hug him properly, not caring that Billy was watching. I hugged him tightly and he cautiously hugged me back, his body stiff and robotic.

"I'll see you tomorrow," I whispered. "We can start planning our trip."

He smiled and nodded, watching me as I left with Billy.

As we got in the car Billy said, "Looks like you and Lonny patched things up."

"Yeah, well, he's family."

"Wanna go to a party?"

I was a bit uncomfortable as I wasn't a party kind of girl, but I smiled and nodded. I was still wearing the dress I made, and as soon as we walked into the party at Seth's house, all eyes were on me like I was some kind of freak. Jenny the gossip queen was there and I heard her laughing loudly and whispering as I walked by. Someone handed Billy a beer but he declined, taking my hand and leading me out to the back yard. We sat with some people I knew in passing at school, but had never talked to before.

Some girl said, "That's an interesting dress."

Before I could respond Billy said, "It was her final project in Home Ec class. She aced it!"

I smiled at the way he was protecting me from what he thought was going to be someone making fun of me.

"It's cool," she said with a smile.

"I styled it after my mom's graduation dress," I explained. "She graduated high school in 1959."

The girl I was talking with took a hit off a joint and replied, "Maybe you should go into fashion then."

Fashion? The thought had never entered my mind. I liked to make my own clothes and had fun recreating styles from photos of my mother, but I had no desire to do it for a living. Besides, I wasn't that good I realized, noticing a loose hem on the dress I was wearing.

Seth drunkenly plopped himself next to the girl and took the joint from her, taking a hit himself. He narrowed his eyes as he stared at me, but he stayed quiet. He offered the joint to me and I waved him off but Billy took a hit and gave it back to him. Billy then put his arm around me and held me as close to him as he could without pulling me on his lap. I was growing increasingly uncomfortable but I said nothing.

"So," Seth finally spoke, still staring at me. "What's the deal with Lonny? He's your brother, he's not your brother... it's weird."

"Lonny is like my brother," I answered. "Our families are very close."

"Didn't his dad take off with some stripper?"

"Wouldn't you?" the girl laughed. "Have you *seen* his mom? Falling down drunk every time I see her."

"Shut up," I said softly.

"What's that Roo?" Seth said, mocking me.

"I said shut up."

Billy tightened his hold on me. "It's okay Ruby, they're just being jerks."

"I saw you dancing with Lonny at prom," Seth continued. "Saw him whispering in your ear—"

"Shut up!" I wasn't going to sit there and let Seth make fun of me, let alone Lonny, who wasn't even there to defend himself.

"Knock it off, Seth," Billy groaned.

"You should've brought Lonny," the girl said. "He's cute. And I saw him wail on that guitar at the talent show… man, he's better than Hendrix!"

I smiled. It was refreshing to hear someone say something nice about Lonny. And she was right… Lonny *was* cute, and he *was* better than Hendrix! I suddenly wished I was back home with Lonny and our parents, listening to him play guitar for us in the living room.

"Yeah, he rocked that talent show," Seth agreed. "Maybe he can get the hell away from his drunk mom."

I stood up and shoved my finger in Seth's face. "You shut up! You don't know anything about Lonny's mom, so stop talking about her!"

Seth began laughing hysterically. He was laughing so hard he had to hold his stomach. I was waiting for Billy to stand up for me, but he remained silent. Seth stood up and glared down at me, trying not to spill his beer. He laughed and giggled, swayed a bit, then placed his free hand heavily on my shoulder for balance.

"I don't know what Billy sees in you," he grumbled. "You follow Lonny around like a lost puppy, your face makes me sick, and you're not cool enough to hang with our friends."

Before I could respond, Seth spilled his beer down the front of my dress. I gasped in shock as Billy jumped up from his seat and pushed Seth to the ground.

The girl sitting with us said, "Seth, you're such an asshole."

I stormed off, heading back into the house and out the front door. Billy was running to catch up, grabbing my hand and stopping me in the driveway.

54

"Take me home," I insisted.

"Seth's drunk," Billy said. "Don't let him ruin our night."

"Too late," I cried, trying to smooth out my soaked dress.

"Come on, Ruby, don't do this."

"Take me home!"

"What if I take you home to change, then we can go to the lake or something?"

At that point I didn't want to be with Billy. I just wanted to be with Lonny, my best friend, the one I could trust, the one who would never hurt me. And it was Friday night… the night Lonny and I always watched *The Midnight Special* together. We would watch it in my living room every week, then he would sleep on the couch and go home the next morning after breakfast.

Lonny.

I started bawling. "I just want to go home."

"Please," Billy begged. "I'll make it up to you, I promise. I'm hungry, are you hungry?"

"A little bit."

Billy drove to McDonald's and ordered some burgers, fries and drinks from the drive-thru, then headed to the lake. I had calmed down by this time, no longer crying, but still upset about my beer-soaked dress. My parents wouldn't be happy I went to a party where people were drinking and doing drugs. And they certainly wouldn't be happy with Billy for taking me there.

Billy grabbed a blanket from the trunk of his car and we walked down to the beach. Graduation night always found its way down to the beach, where students made a bonfire and enjoyed the end of the evening. I realized we were significantly early and I was okay with that, not really wanting to engage with anyone else at that point. Especially if Seth found a way there.

Billy and I were quiet as we ate our food, and I enjoyed the silence. I loved the sound of the waves as we sat on the beach, but my mind drifted to Lonny. I wondered what he was doing at that moment, and wondered if he was thinking about me at all. My thoughts of Lonny were disturbed when I felt Billy touch my cheek.

"Would it be okay if I kissed you right now?" he asked, smiling.

I nodded and he leaned over with a quick peck on the cheek, then a quick peck on the lips. I smiled, letting him know I was okay. As we kissed, I felt his hand touch my leg and I flinched. Normally when I would flinch, which was sadly quite often, he would remove the offending hand and it would be over. This time he didn't remove his hand, instead slowly moving his fingers up my leg, closer to my thigh. I continued kissing him, but slapped at his hand. I cursed myself for not going home to change my clothes. If I had been wearing jeans he wouldn't have had such easy access.

"Billy, please stop," I whispered.

"Come on Ruby," he said, continuing to kiss me. "We're adults now. We can do adult things."

"I'm still seventeen," I reminded him.

I thought about Lonny and wondered if he'd been doing "adult things" with Molly. She never told me a thing, avoiding me at all cost, so I had no idea how far their relationship had actually gone. I realized how ridiculous I was being, making out with my boyfriend and thinking about Lonny. I let Billy lay me down on the blanket and we continued to kiss as his hands groped me. I assumed if I let him grope me on top of my clothes he would be satisfied, so I didn't stop him. He was satisfied with that for a while, but then his fingertips grazed my thigh, hesitated, and slid their way up toward my panties.

I squirmed underneath Billy, but I couldn't do much to stop him. I knew I wasn't ready for sex, and when he slid his hand in my panties I clamped my legs shut and tried to push him off me.

"Ruby, relax," he scolded. "There are things we can do and you'll still be a virgin. Trust me."

But I didn't trust Billy. I wanted to go home.

"I want to go home," I begged. "Please."

"Why?" he asked. "So you can be with *Lonny*?"

"What? No!"

"I saw the way you were hugging him before we left your house. You like him, don't you?"

I love him.

"What a stupid thing to say!" I defended myself. "I don't want to have sex with you so it's because I like Lonny?"

56

He sighed heavily. "Do you love me?"

I hesitated before I said, "Sure." I don't know why, but I didn't want to hurt his feelings.

"Why don't you ever say it?"

Because I love Lonny.

"Why don't you ever say it?" he asked again. "I love you, Ruby. I want to show you how much."

I agreed to let his fingers do the walking if he promised not to do anything else, and it got me out of saying I loved him. We continued kissing and things were going further than I was comfortable with, but I believed Billy when he said I wouldn't lose my virginity that night. His hand began fumbling with something and I soon realized he was unzipping his pants. I protested by pounding on him with my fists and trying to escape from underneath him, and he stopped.

"I promise, Ruby, I won't put it all the way in," he gasped, out of breath. "I *promise*."

"No, don't," I cried. "I don't want to do this anymore."

"If you don't do this," he warned, "it just proves you like Lonny."

"No," I argued. "I don't like Lonny, not that way!"

"Everybody thinks you do," he insisted. "Prove it."

I stopped fighting him and gasped in pain when he shoved himself inside me, crying until he was finished. He stood up and closed his pants, holding out his hand to help me up. He picked up the blanket as I collected our garbage and we headed back to the car, just as others were beginning to arrive.

We were both quiet in the car, and when he pulled into my driveway he said, "Get out."

I stared at him in shock. "Get out?"

"You're so stupid, Ruby," he laughed.

"I don't understand."

"Seth bet me twenty dollars I couldn't get in your pants tonight. And now I'm going back to the bonfire to collect."

I couldn't speak because I couldn't breathe. I felt so foolish as the tears streamed down my face. I didn't want this in the first place, but I let him talk me into it, and all because he kept accusing me of liking Lonny.

57

"You said you loved me," I cried.

"Yeah, well, I'd say anything to be the one who broke Ruby Winter, the most virgin girl in high school."

I sat there choking on my tears. I was paralyzed, but he kept insisting I get out. Billy finally got out of the car, came over to my side and opened the door, trying to pull me out. The next thing I knew he grabbed my dress and pulled as hard as he could, ripping it at the zipper. I didn't even fight as he pushed me into the grass and reached to tear off my panties for proof of what he did to me.

I lay there on my front lawn staring at the sky in my ripped dress. I realized my shoes were still in his car, but I didn't care. I cried over my stolen virginity, feeling like the biggest fool on earth. I could see the lights were still on in the house, meaning my parents were still up, and I couldn't go in there looking like I did. They could never know what happened.

I pulled myself off the ground and started walking, barefoot, to Lonny's. I needed him so badly I was going to get there no matter how long it took. I snuck up to his first floor bedroom window and lightly tapped with my finger. I had no idea if he was even home, but I tapped again. The light was off, so I assumed he wasn't there. I pulled myself together and started to walk back home. I reached the street when Lonny ran out of his house to catch up with me.

"Why are you walking by yourself in the dark?" he asked.

"I need to talk to you," I cried.

"Are you okay?"

I started bawling and shook my head.

Lonny started noticing things. "Where are your shoes?" I heard him gasp loudly before he asked, "What happened to your dress?"

I was so numb I could only respond with tears.

"Did Billy do this?" he asked, raging.

When I didn't answer he started running. Billy only lived two blocks away. I don't know how I did it in bare feet, but I caught up to Lonny and tackled him on someone's front lawn.

"Please don't," I cried, rolling onto my back. "Please, just don't."

Lonny got up and pulled me to my feet. We walked back to his house and went inside, where his mother was fast asleep on her recliner. We went into his room and he closed the door.

"What happened?" he asked, sitting on his bed.

I sat across from him, too embarrassed to look him in the eye.

I explained what happened when we were at the party, making sure I let Lonny know some girl thought he was cute and better than Hendrix, and then how Seth insulted me and spilled his beer down my dress. I told him how Billy and I ended up at the beach, and how he kept trying to talk me into having sex with him.

"Roo," Lonny whispered. "Did he...?"

I finally looked into Lonny's eyes and saw tears forming there. I told him how Billy kept pushing me and telling me he wouldn't go all the way, that he would make sure I stayed a virgin.

"It was all a trick," I cried. "He went all the way and I'm not a virgin anymore."

"Aw Roo," Lonny said, taking my hands in his. "It's okay."

"That's not even the worse part."

"There's more?"

I told him about Billy's bet with Seth and how he ripped my dress pulling me out of the car and pushing me on the ground.

"He took my underwear." I nearly choked as I spoke the words.

"Why would he do that?"

"Proof."

Lonny's face turned red as he tried to control his anger. "What a piece of shit," he hissed. "I want to kill him right now."

"Lonny," I cried. "Do you hate me?"

He looked shocked. "Why would I hate you?"

"Because now I'm nothing but a piece of trash."

Lonny put his hands on my face and pulled it close to his, our noses touching. "Don't ever say that again. You're *not* trash, do you hear me?"

But do you love me?

I nodded as I continued to cry, thinking the tears would never stop. I closed my eyes, wishing he would kiss me. I needed

59

something to replace the memory of Billy that replayed over and over in my mind.

Lonny got up from the bed and said, "Let's get you home. I have a jacket you can wear so your parents won't see the dress."

"Got any underwear?" I managed to joke through my tears.

"I don't wear them."

"Oh my God, stop." We were both laughing at this point. I knew I could count on Lonny to make things better in my world. If only he had the power to give me my virginity back.

I knew Lonny was worried about me, protectively holding my hand the entire walk to my house. I was tired of talking about myself, so I asked him how things were going with Molly, since she wasn't talking to me anymore.

He hesitated before answering. "I broke up with her."

"You did? Why?"

"Does it matter?"

"I guess not."

We walked in the front door of my house where my parents were in the living room waiting. Lonny distracted them as I quickly ran upstairs to change my clothes. By the time I came back down, my parents had already gone to bed and Lonny was waiting with popcorn and sodas and *The Midnight Special* about to start.

"Journey is hosting tonight!" he announced excitedly.

I turned off the lights and we sat on the floor as we did every Friday night, ready to watch our favorite music program. I was completely exhausted and when Journey began to perform "Lovin', Touchin', Squeezin'," I thought about Billy and the night's events and began crying all over again. I felt like a tramp whose reputation was being trashed all over town that night because of Billy's lies.

Lonny put a pillow on his lap and patted it, where I buried my face as I curled up next to him. He didn't say anything, but I had a feeling he had a lot that he wanted to.

When the song was over Lonny sighed heavily and said, "I'm not a virgin either."

I rolled over onto my back so I was looking up at him. "You're not?"

"Did you think I was?"

60

"I didn't know for sure."

He looked at me with great sadness in his eyes and said, "It happened the night of the talent show."

I remembered how Lonny never went home that night, and how Billy and I picked him up walking to school carrying his guitar and amp the next morning.

"But you've had girlfriends before. I thought you were doing it with all of them." I wasn't trying to make light of his announcement, but he was a guy, and it was perfectly acceptable for teenage boys to have sex.

"My mom didn't make it to the show because she was too drunk to drive, so I had no way home. You and Billy were already gone, so I started walking. Ms. Cooke stopped to give me a ride but asked if I could help her with something at her house first."

My eyes grew large as I realized what Lonny was telling me. I sat up quickly, waiting for him to continue.

"She had some boxes she needed moved from her garage so I thought it was no big deal, just returning the favor for the ride home. The next thing I knew she had me pinned against the kitchen counter and was trying to open my pants."

I covered my open mouth with my hand, unable to find words. I'm sure my eyes looked like they were going to pop out of my head. Ms. Cooke wasn't ugly, but she was nearly forty years old, plump, and wore far too much makeup. The kids often snickered behind her back about the amount of makeup she wore, as if she were ready to go onstage at any moment.

"I tried to get away from her," Lonny continued, "but she was doing things that felt good and then she got naked and took me to her bedroom...."

I stood up and paced the length of the living room with one hand on my stomach and the other covering my mouth.

"Lonny," I whispered. "You never went home that night."

"I was there all night," he said, looking embarrassed. "In the morning she kicked me out and told me to walk to school."

I quickly sat on the floor next to him and asked, "Are you okay? I mean... it's not okay for a teacher to do that."

"Yeah, I'm okay. It was just sex. But I couldn't stand the way she was always looking at me after it happened. Big dreamy eyes like she wanted to do me right there at school."

I shuddered at the thought. "Creepy." Then the magnitude of everything hit me all at once. "Wait a minute… is that why she told you about the Livingston Monroe audition before it was even announced?"

"Probably. Now it looks like I'm getting that audition because I did it with her."

"But nobody knows you did it with her."

"*She* does, and she held it over my head every single day after it happened."

"Well, she's the one who looks bad by doing it with a student, whether you take the audition or not."

"I can't have her in my life anymore. I *can't*. Everything about that audition is everything to do with *her*."

I couldn't believe what I said next. "Then don't do it. Nobody knows about it anyway. We'll plan our summer trip, and Livingston Monroe will find a new guitarist."

He looked into my eyes and I thought he was going to say something else, but he just smiled and nodded.

"Thank you for singing for me tonight," I whispered. "It meant the world."

"Anything for you, Roo."

"I love you, Lonny."

He grinned, embarrassed. "Yeah, me too."

2011

The smell of brewing coffee woke me, and I stretched my arms and legs before opening my eyes. As I focused my eyes I saw Lonny, who was sitting at the table opening various pill bottles and washing their contents down with a glass of water. He saw that I was watching him and smiled.

He pointed at each bottle as he described its contents, "Blood pressure, cholesterol, thyroid."

"You're a mess," I teased.

I threw off the covers and went to use the toilet. When I reemerged, Lonny said, "Take your time. We're not in any rush on this trip."

"Good to know."

"I see you still sleep like the dead."

"My best quality." I laughed. "It's how Billy managed to sneak around behind my back for so long."

Lonny grabbed my hand as I passed him. "Hey, no more talk about that asshole. Your life starts *today*. This is the first day of the rest of your life."

I rolled my eyes. "Thank you, Hallmark."

He playfully pushed me away and I grabbed my tattered old suitcase, tossing it on the bed. I opened it to see what Lonny had actually put in there, since he was the one who packed it. I searched under my clothes, and mixed in with my panties were the remaining pain killers from my surgery, and an entire bottle of prescription sleeping pills. I wasn't sure he would take those, and while I was relieved he did, I was hoping I didn't need them.

I took a long, hot shower, hoping to wash away every day that happened before that moment; every memory, every tear, everything Billy had ever done to me. I knew it wouldn't be easy, but I was willing to do what I could to find myself again. And there wasn't anyone better than Lonny who could help me do that.

I emerged from the bathroom dressed in a pair of shorts and a tank top, ready for the hot day ahead. I slipped on my flip-flops as Lonny was just coming back into the room. He was holding a bag that he immediately handed to me.

"I bought you a present," he said, a goofy smile covering his face.

"You've already done too much, and it's only been a day."

"Just open it."

I pulled a brand new digital Nikon camera out of the bag, speechless.

"You sold your camera, didn't you?" he asked.

How would he know that? I didn't remember telling him, but maybe he assumed it since I told him I had to sell most of my stuff.

"Lonny, you really shouldn't—"

He pulled me into his arms, hugging me tightly, and I melted into him, feeling safe and loved for the first time in many years.

"You're not you without a camera," he said against my hair. "And we should document this trip, don't you think?"

I nodded, not knowing whether he understood me or not, but I didn't want to move from that position. I didn't want to leave his arms, or his embrace. I wanted to go back to high school and do so many things differently; things that may have changed the course of my life thirty odd years before. But unless someone invented a time machine that wasn't going to happen, so I chose to enjoy the moment I was living in right then. And it felt so good.

Lonny suggested we go downstairs and eat breakfast before we checked out of the hotel, and in the elevator on the way down I asked, "So who was that blonde woman in the bar last night?"

I could see his face flush and an embarrassed grin appeared. "Let's just say I knew her in a time of drunken weakness. Once or twice."

"Knew her in the biblical sense?" I teased.

"Oh my God, shut up."

We laughed all the way down in the elevator and into the restaurant, until the hostess seated us and gave us menus. I continued to giggle behind my menu, peeking over it at one point only to see Lonny doing the same. That sent us into another fit of laughter until the waitress appeared to ask us if we wanted anything to drink. It was the bleached blonde woman who recognized Lonny in the bar the night before.

64

"Hey Lonny," she said, a bit sheepishly.

"Hey Windy. We'll both have a bloody Mary to start, thanks."

She walked away and I asked, "Windy... or Wendy?"

"Windy. Like blowin' in the wind," he laughed.

"Am I interrupting a tryst you had planned with her or something?"

"What? No... why would you think—"

"We've run into her twice since we got here."

Lonny's face got serious as he set down his menu. He looked at me so intently I thought my face would start burning. "I haven't seen or talked to her in over twenty years. It's just a coincidence, trust me."

"Okay, okay. I was just going to say I'd get out of the way if you wanted some alone time with her."

Lonny rolled his eyes so hard I thought they'd be stuck like that forever. Then a sly grin appeared on his face and he asked, "Are you jealous?"

I didn't mean to, but I laughed loud enough for everyone in the restaurant to turn and look at us. I covered my mouth, a bit embarrassed.

Windy returned with our drinks and she smiled at me. "I'm Windy," she introduced herself.

"Nice to meet you. I'm—"

"You're Roo, I know. Lonny used to talk about you all the time. It must have been fun growing up with him."

"It's Ruby," I corrected her politely, "but yeah, Lonny is the best brother I could have ever hoped for."

Windy took our food order and disappeared.

I noticed Lonny's face looked a bit flushed. "So you talked about me all the time?"

He dismissed it with a wave of his hand and a farting sound from his mouth. "No big deal, you know, everyone knew who you were."

I could tell he was a bit flustered, so I chose to let it go. The last thing I wanted to do was get into an argument with Lonny on the first day of our road trip.

"So how old *is* she?" I asked with a wicked grin.

65

"Sixty at least."

My eyes grew large and I animatedly mouthed, "Wow!"

Lonny quickly changed the subject, telling me our first stop of the day would be the Baseball Hall of Fame in Cooperstown, which was about a four hour drive. He planned to spend the night there, then we would head to Niagara Falls the following day. I was all smiles as I'd always wanted to go both places, but never had the opportunity. Leave it to Lonny to make it happen. I wondered what other surprises he had in store for this trip.

1979

A week after graduation, Lonny and I were sitting in his room planning our backpacking trip when his mom knocked and entered. She looked angry, which made us both a bit nervous.

"Lonny, I just got off the phone with Ms. Cooke."

Lonny paled and I thought for sure he was going to faint. He stared at her, terrified, but said nothing. I could feel him trembling just by sitting next to him.

"She's on her way over. You had better have a good explanation for your behavior."

She walked out of the room and I grabbed Lonny's hand tightly, probably cutting off all circulation.

"Please don't leave," he managed to whisper, terror written all over his face.

"I won't," I replied. We stood up and I linked my pinky around his, saying, "Pinky swear."

"My mom is gonna kill me."

"Not if I'm here."

We were sitting in the living room when his mom invited Ms. Cooke into the house. She was all smiles and makeup as usual, but I saw how she looked at Lonny and it made me cringe, knowing what happened between them. I felt like I was going to throw up.

Joanie offered Ms. Cooke some lemonade, but she declined. "I'll only be here a few minutes," she said. "Lonny, I don't understand why you haven't told your mother about the offer I made you."

I watched him closely and he looked like he was about to vomit. His face literally turned green.

She continued, "Mrs. Winter, because of personal connections, I was able to offer Lonny an audition with the band Livingston Monroe. They're in need of a guitarist, and after seeing Lonny play at the senior talent show I thought it was something he should explore."

Lonny must have been holding his breath since his mother announced Ms. Cooke was on her way over, because I heard him exhale loudly as his color returned.

"I've made arrangements for an audition in July," Ms. Cooke continued, "but Lonny hasn't gotten back to me about whether or not he's interested."

Lonny couldn't even respond before his mother was scolding him. "Lonny, how dare you? Ms. Cooke has gone out of her way to make this happen for you, and you didn't even acknowledge her with a response?"

"Mom, I—"

"There's no excuse! Of course he's going to do it," his mom answered for him. "He's not going to college and what's he going to do around here? Bag groceries? Wash cars? Lonny, how could you not tell me about this?"

"Because I—"

Ms. Cooke wasn't about to let Lonny decline. "The audition is in Los Angeles next week." She handed Lonny's mom an envelope. "Arrangements have all been made."

"But Mom, me and Roo are planning our backpacking trip," he argued. "You know, the one you helped pay for?"

"Lonny, watch your mouth," she hissed. "This is a once in a lifetime opportunity!"

I understood where Lonny's mom was coming from. Since his dad walked out, she'd had to work several jobs in order to pay the rent and put food on the table. She didn't want Lonny to keep living that way, and thought this audition could lead to bigger and better things. A career. Money.

Joanie opened the envelope and pulled out two plane tickets. "Two tickets?" she asked.

Ms. Cooke chuckled and said, "Well, yes, I assumed you'd want to accompany Lonny on the trip."

"I have two jobs," she said. "I can't just take a few days off."

I could see the wheels turning in Ms. Cooke's head, and I knew exactly the moment Lonny realized it as well.

"Well," Ms. Cooke chuckled. "I suppose it doesn't matter since he'll be eighteen by then. I'll be making the trip as well, so Lonny will be in good hands."

Lonny's mouth fell open, but no words came out.

"I'll go," I blurted.

Ms. Cooke glared at me, but as I watched a relieved grin cross Lonny's face, I saw his mom clasp her hands together in excitement. She said, "Ruby, that would be perfect!"

"If my parents are okay with it," I added.

"Well of course, Ruby, why not?" Ms. Cooke said with a forced smile. "The ticket is already paid for, so why let it go to waste?" She stood to leave, and as she headed for the door told Lonny she would be in touch early next week with all the details.

Everyone was quiet until we were sure Ms. Cooke was long gone.

"Lonny!" his mom yelled. "Why wouldn't you tell me about something like this?"

"Because I don't want to do it," he answered honestly.

"Then why didn't you tell Ms. Cooke that?"

"You didn't give me a chance!" he yelled back.

She swung her hand back and slapped Lonny across the face. "Don't you ever raise your voice to me!"

Lonny got up and went outside to the back yard, sitting on one of his old swings. I followed him and sat on the swing next to him. He didn't want me to see that he was crying, looking down so his hair covered his face.

I slowly reached my hand out and hooked my pinky with his. He looked at me with a tear-stained face and tried to laugh. My heart broke for him, but I had no idea how to fix the situation at hand.

"Don't do it," I whispered, afraid his mom's radar ears would hear me. "Let's run away."

"What's wrong with washing cars? I like cars. What's wrong with bagging groceries? I like food." He laughed as he wiped the tears off his face. I wasn't sure if he was crying because of the audition, or because his mom slapped him in front of me. I'd never seen her do that before, and now I wondered if it was something she did regularly or if this was an isolated incident.

"Lonny, we have all that money for our trip… let's take it and go."

I watched him chew on his lower lip and noticed his hands were shaking. I'd never seen him this upset before.

"I could just screw up the audition," he whispered. "Make them not want to hire me."

"Why don't you want to audition?"

He was silent for a long time before he said, "I don't want to be onstage with people watching me. You know I hate that. I love music, but I like to keep it to myself."

"I'm not trying to talk you into anything, but you're so amazing. You *are* better than Hendrix!"

"I don't know what I'm worried about," he chuckled. "There's gonna be so many guys auditioning who are much better than me."

"Then let's go back to planning our trip."

2011

We checked out of the hotel right after breakfast and got in the car around ten o'clock. My family never traveled or went on vacation when I was a kid, but we did do car trips to visit my grandparents on their farm in Iowa every summer. I loved road trips and couldn't wait to get this one started. Lonny had some sort of adaptor he hooked up to the car's cigarette lighter so we could hear the playlist from his phone through the speakers. I was so amazed and in awe of technology most days!

Lonny put the top down on the car and we were off. I felt like some weight was finally lifted off my shoulders, breathing a bit easier as he drove. I was going to be leaving New York City for good, and I hoped never to return. Billy and I had success there, but mostly I was homesick for my family, and we were tied to a business that gave us no room to enjoy the money we brought in. And then he left and took it all away from me.

The first song to explode from the speakers was "Band On The Run" by Paul McCartney and Wings, and we both shouted at the top of our lungs to the lyric "I hope you're having fun!"

I reached into the backseat and pulled up the bag with the new camera, carefully taking it out of the box. I loved my beat up old Nikon and it killed me to have to sell it, but it was worth it to be able to talk to Lonny. I handled the new camera as if it were made of glass, so afraid I might drop it and break it.

"It's pretty durable," Lonny chuckled. "You don't have to be so gentle."

I looked over to see him smiling at me, his eyes hidden by his sunglasses. I began taking photos of him and he immediately turned his head.

"Dammit, Rooster," he groaned.

"You're part of this trip, aren't you? Shut up and smile."

He made a face, which I snapped a photo of, then gave me the biggest phony smile he could manage, and I snapped a photo of that, too.

I always had some kind of camera in my hands growing up. My grandfather gave me my first camera when I was ten years old

— a used Kodak Duaflex — and it just progressed from there. Like Lonny with his music, I kept my love of photography to myself; it wasn't something I ever wanted to make public. I took all the photographs that were on Billy's shop website, but that was out of necessity for the business, not photographs I enjoyed taking.

As we put the city behind us I said, "Promise I'll never have to go back there."

"It's all up to you, Roo. You're free to go wherever you want now."

He was right. I didn't have to answer to anyone else ever again. I was finally free of the city I hated, the marriage I regretted, and the man who had been hurting me since I was seventeen years old. Relief rushed over me like a wave and I began to laugh, which turned into tears of joy. I unbuckled my seatbelt and got on my knees, leaning far over to hug Lonny and thank him for saving me. Cars driving beside us weren't happy with my display, but I held his face in my hands and kissed his cheek several times before he told me my hair was getting in his eyes. Before I got buckled back in, I stood up and held on tightly as I threw one arm in the air and screamed as loudly as I could, thankful for my freedom.

We were exhausted by the time we reached the hotel in Cooperstown. We entered the room and there was only one king-size bed. He explained, "There's a huge baseball tournament going on and all the rooms are booked."

"It's okay," I laughed. "It's not like we haven't shared a bed before."

"Just keep your hands to yourself," he teased.

I burst into bellowing laughter and he soon joined in. It felt good to enjoy belly laughs with Lonny again. I never realized just how much I missed him in my life, and how much I truly needed him.

1979

Lonny and I turned eighteen on July 4, 1979 and a week later we were on a plane with Ms. Cooke to Los Angeles for his Livingston Monroe audition. Neither of us had been away from our parents before, and neither of us had ever been on a plane. We were both expectedly nervous, but more so because of Ms. Cooke. I could see the way she looked at Lonny, like he was some piece of dessert for her after dinner enjoyment. He was worried sick that because he decided to go through with the audition, she would take that as him wanting to have a continued sexual relationship with her. Our parents trusted her with our safety and well-being on this trip, but if they had any idea what happened between her and Lonny, they would never have allowed us to go, and Joanie would never have insisted he go through with it.

Ms. Cooke's cousin Louise picked us up at the airport and brought us to our hotel, where Lonny and I would be staying in a room next to hers, with a door that opened to both rooms. Each room had one king-size bed, which meant Lonny and I had to share. We were both too nervous and out of our element to care, but as long as Ms. Cooke didn't think Lonny was staying in her room, everything was fine.

"We don't have a lot of time to spare," Louise told us. "Your audition is in an hour. Do you need anything before we head over to the studio?" Lonny shook his head numbly, unable to speak. I'd never seen his eyes so large before; he was in a perpetual state of shock ever since we walked onto the plane. I don't remember him saying much after we said goodbye to our parents.

We all piled back into Louise's car as she drove us to the Village Recorder studio, where Livingston Monroe was holding their auditions that week. Lonny's guitar case sat between us in the back seat, but I managed to snake my arm around it to lock pinkies with him. I wanted to tell him to breathe, but both of us were too nervous to say a word.

Louise led the way as we followed her into the studio, Lonny holding onto my hand tightly. She introduced us to Howard

Hammond, her long-time boyfriend and the manager of Livingston Monroe.

"So this is Lonny," Howard said with a grin. "I've heard a lot about you."

Lonny smiled, unsure what had actually been said about him. Howard seated us behind a pane of glass where we would watch the men auditioning for the coveted guitarist spot until it was Lonny's turn. The guy we were watching looked almost like Joey Buckingham, the guitarist who quit the band and caused an uproar in the music world. He had long blond hair halfway down his back, with a beard and mustache, just like Joey. If we didn't know better, we would have sworn we were watching Joey Buckingham performing before us.

The Joey lookalike was just jamming for a while until Howard instructed him to play certain Livingston Monroe songs. He would call out a song title and the guy would play it. He'd call out the next one, and the guy would play it. Sometimes he let him play for a while, some songs he stopped him after only a few seconds. Lonny and I looked at each other, reading each other's minds — how could he possibly compete with guys like this?

Howard made his way back to where we were sitting and told Lonny he was up next. He stood and I got up to give him a hug. I whispered, "You're gonna be great." I kissed him on the cheek and he was gone.

I sat back in my seat and could see Ms. Cooke glaring at me out the corner of my eye. I wondered if she thought I was now Lonny's girlfriend, and if she did, it made me smile inside. Maybe if she thought Lonny and I were involved, she'd leave him alone. I pulled my camera out of my bag, hoping to get a few shots of Lonny during this once in a lifetime experience, but Louise put a gentle hand on my arm.

"Howard will throw you out if he sees a flash," Louise said.

I nodded understanding, knowing full well I hadn't planned on using a flash, and unless Howard was watching me instead of Lonny, he'd have no idea I was even taking photographs. I quietly took photos as Howard explained the process to Lonny while he took his guitar out of the case and tuned it. I chewed my fingernails waiting for him to start playing, still having no idea if he was going to sabotage the audition as he originally planned.

I heard Howard say, "Okay Lonny, show us your personal repertoire," and I held my breath. He was making mistakes here and there at first, which made me wonder if he was just nervous, or actually going through with his plan of sabotage. I soon got my answer as I watched Lonny transform into the musician I knew him to be. His eyes were closed and his face took on the emotions his fingers were playing, as if he were home alone in his bedroom. He wasn't sabotaging anything; I don't think he knew how.

Lonny played a variety of genres to showcase his talent, and as I quietly snapped photos I felt tears burning my eyes. I was so proud of him, and so happy he was given this opportunity, even if it came from sinister beginnings.

Howard stopped Lonny after about twenty minutes to give him a break. He asked him if he needed anything and Lonny laughed, saying, "I could use a cigarette."

Howard laughed loudly, pulling a pack of cigarettes from his jacket pocket and tossing them to Lonny, along with his lighter. While they shared a cigarette break Howard made small talk, putting Lonny at ease and actually getting him to converse and smile. I assumed Howard had been in the business a long time and knew how nervous Lonny was, trying to make things as comfortable as possible.

It came to the part of the audition where Lonny would have to play Livingston Monroe songs. Howard did the same thing with Lonny as he had the last guitarist, shouting out a Livingston Monroe song he wanted to hear, then listening for a few minutes, sometimes only seconds, before shouting out the next song.

Lonny's fingers flew so fluidly that his guitar became an extension of him, part of his body, part of his soul. I looked over at Ms. Cooke and her cousin Louise, both sitting there with their mouths hanging open in shock. Ms. Cooke turned to look at me and smiled brightly, putting an arm around me for a quick hug.

The next thing I knew Mitch Monroe, the lead singer for Livingston Monroe, entered the room and picked up a microphone. I gasped, but Lonny, who still had his eyes closed, had no idea he was there. He was magnificent, and even better looking in person, with his wild mane of curly blond hair framing his face. Howard shouted, "Take Me Home!" which Lonny began to play instantly, but when Mitch began singing along with him, his eyes flew open to see the lead singer standing in front of him. Lonny never missed a beat, playing the song better than Joey Buckingham himself. I realized I was now the one sitting with my mouth hanging open in shock. To witness Lonny playing alongside a member of our favorite band was something I could never put into words, and it was more emotional than I ever would have imagined.

Lonny and Mitch performed the entire song and when they finished, Mitch was smiling from ear to ear, reaching out to shake Lonny's hand. They conversed for a bit, Mitch doing most of the talking with Lonny smiling and laughing. I put a new roll of film in my camera and kept taking photos. There was no way I was going to miss documenting this once in a lifetime experience for Lonny!

Mitch joined in on several more songs, and there were times where he stopped singing just to sit back and watch Lonny play. I watched Howard, but he sported a continuous poker face, making it unable to tell how he was feeling about Lonny's skill level.

Then just like that, it was over. Howard and Mitch both shook Lonny's hand and he packed up his guitar. He was brought back to where we were waiting, Howard quickly kissing Louise on the lips. Louise ushered us out of the studio and back to her car, where she announced she was going to treat us to dinner. I looked at Lonny, who was white as a ghost and sweating. He leaned back against the headrest and closed his eyes.

"Can we just go back to the room?" I suggested. "I don't think Lonny is feeling very good."

Ms. Cooke turned from her seat in the front to glare at me. "Ruby, you're being quite rude," she scolded.

I didn't dare say another word, but I saw Louise look at Lonny through the rearview mirror. "He really doesn't look well," she said. "It's all right, Cookie."

In order to keep from laughing at Louise's nickname for Ms. Cooke, I focused on Lonny, who really didn't look well at all. I was beginning to get worried.

76

"You two probably want to catch up," I spoke carefully. "You can just drop us off and go to dinner without us. I promise we won't get into any trouble."

I know Ms. Cooke didn't want Lonny and I to be alone. She wanted to keep her eye on him every chance she could. She turned in her seat to look at Lonny, and frowned.

"He doesn't look well," she admitted. "But I'm responsible for these kids. I really shouldn't be leaving them alone."

"It's okay, Ms. Cooke," I said. "Lonny will probably just sleep, and I brought a book I'm really excited to get back to."

"They're eighteen, Cookie. Come on," Louise urged. "We haven't seen each other in so long."

Ms. Cooke agreed to drop us off at the hotel and continue on to dinner with her cousin. I carried Lonny's guitar case into the hotel and up to the room, as he could barely carry himself. No sooner had I closed the door, he was running to the bathroom to vomit. I felt terrible because I had no idea what was wrong with him, or how to help him.

As promised, I made a collect call to my parents to let them know how the audition went. I explained that Lonny wasn't feeling well and would probably call his mother later in the evening. We only talked for a few minutes so as not to run up their phone bill, but it was nice to hear my mom's voice, even though we'd only been gone since that morning.

I went into the bathroom to check on Lonny, who appeared to be passed out on the floor. He was drenched in sweat and wasn't moving. I put my finger in front of his mouth to make sure he was still breathing; relieved that he was, I folded up one of the towels and placed it under his head.

"Thanks," he managed to say.

"Are you okay?"

He never opened his eyes, barely nodding his head. I wet a washcloth with cold water and sat on the floor with him, pushing his hair away from his face and gently wiping off the sweat. I was amazed he let me take care of him, because generally he couldn't stand anyone fussing over him for any reason.

"Can you make it colder?" he whispered.

77

I told him I'd be right back, and went out to get some ice. I returned to the room and he hadn't moved, but I managed to get him out of the bathroom and onto the bed, where we'd both be more comfortable. I sat down and he rested the back of his head on my leg while I held the ice wrapped in the washcloth on his forehead, moving it every few minutes.

He still hadn't opened his eyes, but smiled, whispering, "Wasn't that dynamite?"

"You blew Joey Buckingham out of the sky," I whispered excitedly. "And when Mitch Monroe came out, I almost peed my pants!"

He chuckled, the dimples in his cheeks ever present. "Did I do okay?"

"Lonny, you were amazing, and I'm not just saying that. You were on fire. Louise told me I'd get thrown out if Howard saw any camera flashes, but she didn't realize I can do it without the flash. I took a lot of pictures for you."

"Thanks, Roo." I moved the washcloth to his temple and he whispered, "As soon as we walked outside I felt like my head was gonna explode," he explained. "The stress got me."

"Don't talk, just relax."

About an hour later I heard the adjoining door to Ms. Cooke's room being opened. She walked in with Louise and looked as though she was expecting to find us in an embarrassing situation, but there was nothing explicit to see. I was still icing Lonny's head and he was sound asleep.

"Is he okay?" she whispered.

"He threw up a few times."

She took a few steps back. "Flu?" I began to wonder if she had an aversion to vomit, and it gave me an idea.

"It might be," I answered.

Louise set a bag on the table and said, "We brought you some sandwiches and drinks in case you get hungry later."

"Looks like you're taking good care of him," Ms. Cooke whispered. "We'll be next door if you need anything." I thanked Louise for the sandwiches and they went back into her room, closing the door behind them.

I saw a grin cross Lonny's face and knew he heard the whole thing. He opened his eyes for the first time since we got back to the room and looked up at me.

"Molly broke up with me," he said.

Where did this come from?

"I didn't break up with her, she broke up with me," he admitted.

I pushed a piece of wet hair from his face and said, "It doesn't matter."

"She got mad because I didn't make any moves."

I tried so hard not to laugh, but it ended up dribbling out of my mouth as a muffled giggle. "You were together a whole week, and you didn't make any moves?"

"Ha ha, very funny." He continued to rest his head on my leg, looking up at me. "I only went out with her so people would leave you alone."

"Whattya mean?"

"The whole prom thing... people thinking you cheated on Billy with me, calling you a slut."

"You did that for me?"

"Well, yeah."

"So you didn't like her even a little bit?"

"She was okay, but you and me... I didn't like that we weren't talking. It's like losing my arm or something."

"Aw Lonny," I grinned. "I'm so happy to be considered one of your body parts."

He laughed and sat up, running his hands through his wet hair. "I'm starving."

We took the sandwiches and drinks Louise brought us and went out onto the balcony to eat. By this point the sun was beginning to set and after only half a day in Los Angeles, we saw the airport, Louise's car, the studio, and our hotel room. It was a shame we couldn't do some sightseeing, but we had to be up early the next morning to head back to the airport for our flight home. It wasn't long before Ms. Cooke entered the room and found us outside.

"Glad to see you're feeling better, Lonny," she said from behind us. "You should both get to bed soon, since we have an early flight tomorrow."

"Thanks, Ms. Cooke." Lonny was always so polite.

She went back to her room as we slowly made our way back into ours. Lonny locked the balcony door as I dug in my suitcase for my pajamas. I went into the bathroom to change, wash my face and brush my teeth, and when I came back out Lonny was already in his shorts and t-shirt, talking to his mom on the phone. I noticed, however, that Ms. Cooke left the adjoining door to her room wide open.

Lonny hung up the phone and asked, "Do you want under or over?"

"Do I want what?"

"Under the covers or over the covers?"

"Come on Lonny, we don't need to do that." He rolled his eyes toward Ms. Cooke's room and I understood. "I'll go under."

I climbed into the bed and watched as Lonny pulled some sort of notebook out of his suitcase. He sat on the edge of the bed and started writing in it.

"What's that?" I asked.

He grinned, a little embarrassed. "My journal."

"I thought only girls had diaries."

"I started after my dad left," he explained. "I want to get today in there before I forget anything."

I poked him with my foot from under the covers and when he looked at me, said, "I think it's great."

I watched Lonny while he wrote, hunched over his journal, his hair covering his face. He seemed to write forever, but considering the day he had, I shouldn't have expected any less. I fell asleep while he was still writing, waking with a start when he turned off the light and lay beside me on top of the covers.

"Lonny—"

He put his fingers against my mouth to stop me from talking, then scooted as close to me as he could without touching me.

"She left the door open," he whispered.

"Does she think we're gonna do stuff?"

80

"I guess so."

"She's crazy."

He giggled then whispered, "I hate the way she looks at me."

"She gave me a dirty look when I kissed your cheek before the audition. She probably thinks we're… you know… *together*."

"Good. Maybe she'll leave me alone."

"I should'a kissed you on the mouth."

"Maybe you should've."

I was silent, wondering if Lonny just told me he wanted me to kiss him on the mouth. My heart thundered wildly in my chest as I wasted time analyzing our conversation.

"Thanks for coming with me," Lonny whispered.

His face was so close I could feel his breath on my mouth, and I'd never wanted to kiss someone so badly in my life. But this wasn't just anybody, it was *Lonny*. And Ms. Cooke, who was dying to get her hands on him, was in the next room, probably listening to everything that was going on.

I slowly moved my head forward until my nose touched his, then pressed my lips against his. Neither of us moved, frozen in place until the phone rang in Ms. Cooke's room and scared us half to death. We both burst into laughter, unable to control ourselves until she came in and scolded us, and then Lonny accidentally rolled off the bed onto the floor.

Lonny returned to the bed and I rolled over so my back was facing him. We said goodnight to each other, but continued to giggle on and off until we finally fell asleep. It was a long, exhausting day, and we needed all the sleep we could get because morning was going to come too fast.

And come fast it did… Ms. Cooke didn't get our wakeup call in time and we were all rushing around to get ready. It felt like we were in a Beatles movie, running behind Ms. Cooke to check out of the hotel, then Louise running into the lobby like a lunatic, yelling that there was a change in plans and rushing us to her car. As she careened onto the street we were all holding on for dear life as she tried to catch her breath.

81

"Howard called right before I left," she explained. "Auditions are over, but the band is insisting on a few callbacks today, and Lonny is one of them."

"But what about our flight?" Ms. Cooke croaked, unsettled with anything that changed her always organized schedule.

"I'll take care of everything," Louise replied, darting in between cars as she sped through the streets of Los Angeles. I reached over and grabbed Lonny's hand. He was stressed about the audition he *knew* about; I couldn't imagine what he was feeling hearing this news. I looked over at him, his eyes hidden by the sunglasses he was wearing due to the headache he suffered the day before. He seemed calm and unaffected, or maybe he was sleeping. I let go of his hand and quietly pulled my camera out of my bag, snapping pictures of him. I noticed a slight grin appear, but he never turned to look at me. I even snapped photos of Louise and Ms. Cooke for posterity's sake. Mostly I got the back of Ms. Cooke's head, which was just fine.

Lonny handed me his sunglasses as we entered the studio and I put them in my bag. We were ushered to the same seats as the day before, having no idea how many people were included in the callback, and which order they would be auditioning. This day, however, we were all there at the same time, as it was a last minute decision by the band; something Howard had not planned on, according to Louise.

Lonny and I were silent as we watched Mitch Monroe, Benji Livingston, and Adam "Fuzzy" Livingston enter the studio. The Joey Buckingham lookalike was the first to audition, and of course he was a perfect fit. He looked just like Joey, and matched his movements and sound note for note. It seemed to me he was the wise choice, as fans of the band were distraught over Joey's unexpected departure.

Lonny was the last callback to audition, and for some reason, I made no moves to show him any affection before he walked out of the room, other than squeezing his hand as he passed me. I watched as he entered the room and was greeted by the band, all smiles and each of them shaking his hand. Mitch Monroe was the last to greet Lonny, patting him on the back and conversing with him as he pulled out his guitar and got set up. I snapped photos of everything, just as I had the day before, thankful I brought lots of film. I had assumed we'd do some sightseeing after the audition was over, but things didn't turn out that way.

The audition played out more like a band rehearsal of sorts, with the band deciding which songs they wanted to play, then stopping for a bit after each to talk with Lonny. At one point, they played "Lonely Girl," one of their biggest hits with one of the most talked about guitar solos in the music world. I felt as though this was a test for Lonny, and I had no doubt he would ace it. I held my breath as the solo approached, and watched Lonny dive into it as if it was his daily routine. Not only did he play the famous solo, he put his own twist on it, bringing it up to date and grittier than originally played by Joey. Mitch Monroe looked stunned, and I wasn't sure if that was a good or bad thing. I felt tears running down my cheeks as I watched Lonny play. He wasn't a showy musician who danced around and had to be constantly moving; his hands and fingers did that for him, a show in themselves.

When the audition was over, Lonny packed up his guitar and had a brief conversation with the band before leaving. Howard walked all of us out to Louise's car where he told Lonny, "Thanks for coming back on such short notice. Please don't take this the wrong way, because you were impressive in there, but we're looking for someone with a little bit more experience in the business."

Lonny shook his hand and thanked Howard for the opportunity. Then Howard turned to me and said, "And you young lady, have something for me." I had no idea what he was talking about until he said, "The film. Hand it all over."

My face burned with embarrassment as I reached into my bag and pulled out all the used film, handing it to Howard. I apologized, but I don't think he heard me. He quickly kissed Louise goodbye and we were back in her car on the way to the airport. Everyone was quiet in the car, the excitement of the morning a quickly fading memory. I silently cried all the way to the airport, not only for Lonny, but because the sting of embarrassment was still fresh and burning, and I wouldn't be able to give him the photos I'd taken of his Livingston Monroe experience.

2011

Lonny and I spent a wonderful afternoon at the Baseball Hall of Fame and Museum, walking amongst the memorabilia of baseball greats such as Babe Ruth, Cy Young, Carlton Fisk, Ty Cobb, Lou Gehrig and Fergie Jenkins. The best part of the museum was seeing the Ebbets Field Cornerstone, one of the few items visitors are actually allowed to touch. It was a granite block set into the field's wall back in 1912, measuring four feet by three feet, and one foot thick. Ebbets Field was home to the Brooklyn Dodgers before they left for Los Angeles after their 1957 season. Until that time it had hosted forty-five years of baseball, and now the historic granite stone has spent more time in the Baseball Hall of Fame and Museum than it did at the actual ballpark. I was a big history buff, and pairing that with my favorite sport I had the most amazing day.

Famished, we walked to an Italian restaurant for dinner before heading back to the hotel. Lonny ordered a bottle of Chianti and a calamari appetizer to start. As I perused the menu I began giggling.

"What's so funny?" he asked.

"Are we going to run into another one of your groupies here?"

"Doubtful, but if we do, I'll let you handle it."

I laughed. Actually, it was more a guffaw. "I'll tell her to take her groupie ass back to Skankville."

Lonny didn't laugh and I felt bad, peeking over my menu at him. He glared at me like I said something horrible about someone he loved.

"Groupies are people too," he said. "They have feelings."

"Lonny, I didn't mean—"

"I don't keep bringing up your past."

"My past hasn't interrupted us."

I was expecting him to laugh and say, "Gotcha," but he never did.

The waitress returned with our appetizer, then took our dinner orders. Lonny ordered the grilled salmon and I ordered the

Chicken Scarpariello, and as she walked away I quickly drank my glass of wine. I could tell the evening was not going to be as pleasant as our day was. We ate in silence, which only caused me to drink more wine. By the time we left the restaurant I was pretty drunk, stumbling down the sidewalk toward our hotel.

Lonny kept trying to catch up to me, but I was still upset with the way our conversation had turned before dinner. I just wanted to get back to the hotel and watch television so I didn't have to deal with him anymore.

He unlocked the door to our hotel room and I fell onto the bed, grabbing the remote control off the bedside table. I turned on the television and flipped through the channels, not really watching any of them. I watched Lonny out of the corner of my eye, pulling his laptop out of his suitcase. He sat quietly at the table working and I just watched him through blurry eyes.

"Whatcha doin'?" I asked.

"Checking my email. Want some more wine?"

"Want some cheese to go with your whine?" I asked, thinking I was hilariously funny.

He went into the bathroom and I yelled, "Can I check my email?"

"Go ahead."

I stumbled over to the table and fell onto the chair, then typed my email carrier into the browser and waited. My email was mostly a spam collector, but sometimes there were things of importance. I scanned the many emails for stores I'd shopped, or music sites I frequented. Then I saw it. An email from Billy's tattoo shop. He must have forgotten to remove my email address from their customer server. I opened it to see an ad announcing the new shop location in Arizona, with a picture of Billy and Zoe smiling together, their collective tattoos and piercings mocking me from two thousand miles away. He changed the name of the shop as well, and even though I was drunk, I could make it out easily… B-Z Tattoos. Was that supposed to be text speak for busy, as in Busy Tattoos, using their initials?

I tried to stand up but tripped over my own feet and fell on the floor. I picked myself up and managed to walk into the hallway, closing the door behind me. I got in the elevator and took

85

it down to the first floor, finding the indoor swimming pool area. I sat on the edge and dropped my feet in, crying and blubbering like a drunken idiot. I rolled into the pool, but I don't quite remember what happened after that.

I could hear muffled voices talking above me, but I just wanted to sleep. Why was I soaking wet? Someone was touching me and I struggled against them, but was too weak to fight.

"Where's my flip-flops?" I grumbled drunkenly. "I lost my flip-flops."

"They're in the room."

Lonny.

I tried to open my eyes, but everything was blurry. I could hear Lonny thanking someone as he tried to wrap a towel around me. I kept pushing it away for some reason, and he stopped fighting me. He held me against him with one arm while he pushed the wet hair away from my face with his other hand. I lifted my arm and touched the top of his head, finding his hair was wet. I slowly slid my hand down his face, down his shirt, all soaking wet.

"I'm sorry," I cried.

"Let's go back to the room, okay? Get into some dry clothes."

"Why doesn't anybody love me?" I blubbered.

"Come on Rooster, you know that's not true."

"Billy didn't love me... why did he marry me? I hated him... why did I marry *him*? No one else wanted me. Not in high school, not ever. *You* didn't love me." My crying was now out of control, and if there was one thing Lonny hated it was an overemotional, crying, drunk woman.

I heard someone ask, "Is she okay? Should I call an ambulance?"

Lonny chuckled and said, "She's fine. Just drunk."

Lonny stood up and helped me to my feet, wrapping the towel around me. I stumbled and he caught me before I fell, keeping his arm around me all the way to the elevator, and back to our room. He put me in the bathroom, then brought in my suitcase.

"Can you manage changing into dry clothes, or do you need help?" he asked, somewhat angrily.

"I can do it," I hissed.

He slammed the door shut, then burst back in, pointing an angry finger at me. "And don't you *ever* tell me about *my* feelings!" He grabbed a towel and slammed the door again.

I slid to the floor and opened my suitcase. What was he so angry about? I managed to peel off my wet clothes, dry myself, and put on a pair of shorts and a t-shirt. I went back into the room and Lonny was sitting on the bed in a pair of dry sweatpants working on his laptop.

I fell onto my side of the bed and immediately passed out. When I opened my eyes again, I looked around the room and realized I was alone. I figured Lonny had enough of my antics and left me there, continuing on his way to Vegas without me as extra baggage. I looked at the clock which read eleven-thirty. Checkout time was eleven o'clock.

I dragged myself out of bed and into the bathroom where I did my business and brushed my teeth. Lonny came back into the room and said, "Hurry up — if I get you out of here by noon they won't charge me for an extra day."

I changed my clothes, put my hair in a ponytail, and followed Lonny out to the car. He put my suitcase in the trunk and handed me a food bag from McDonald's. I ate while he drove, neither of us having anything to say. Lonny didn't even put on his road trip playlist, instead turning on the radio. I wasn't even sure why we were so angry with each other, trying to remember what happened the night before.

"How long to Niagara Falls?" I asked.

"About four hours."

I finished my food and unbuckled my seatbelt. Lonny looked a bit panicked as he glanced at me.

"Wake me up when we get there," I grumbled, crawling into the backseat and curling up into a ball.

"Roo, we've been on the road for a day... why are we fighting?"

"Because you didn't like it when I called your groupies skanks."

"You know that's not how I spent my time," he argued.

"I know the awful things they said to me when you weren't there to hear them!"

87

"And where were *you*?" he shouted.

"Shut up," I whispered, knowing he couldn't hear me over the wind with the top down.

"When I needed you, where were you, Roo? You were always with *Fuzzy*!"

Even though I was in the backseat, I felt like Lonny had reached back and slapped me in the face. His argument was so unfair.

"I don't want to talk about Fuzzy," I grumbled.

Lonny decided not to say anything further, and I closed my eyes and went to sleep.

1979

Life went back to normal after returning from Lonny's audition; I got a job uptown at Vinyl Horse, the local record store, and Lonny started working across the street fixing people's bicycles. We continued planning our backpacking trip, but decided we'd go in the fall when everyone was back in school. This gave us a little more time to plan the trip we really wanted to experience.

Livingston Monroe hired the Joey Buckingham lookalike, as I had a feeling they would, and they went into the studio to record their new album. It's all anyone in the record store talked about, and I just smiled, never telling anyone about Lonny's audition.

About a month after returning home from L.A., I walked in the house after work and my mom told me there was a package on the kitchen table for me. I opened the battered envelope and pulled out a stack of photographs with a note attached to the front of them. The note read, "You're good. Louise."

One by one I gazed down at the photographs I had taken at Lonny's auditions. Howard must have developed the photos and had Louise mail them to me. I hopped on my bike and headed toward Lonny's house, meeting him halfway, as he was on his way to see me. He didn't want to talk in the middle of the street, so we headed back to my house, to the safety of my bedroom.

I handed him the envelope and he looked at all the photographs with a smile on his face. "Wow, Roo," was all he could say.

"Come on, what's your news?" I was squirming in my seat waiting to hear.

"I just talked to Louise," he said, looking up from the last photograph so I could see his face. "Livingston Monroe fired the Joey Buckingham guy. They want me."

I was speechless, unsure how Lonny felt about this news, until a huge smile covered his face. I screamed a loud, teenage girl scream and hugged him as hard as I could. "What did you tell her?" I asked.

"I said I'd call her back. I wanted to talk to you first. I guess the band wanted me from the beginning, but Howard thought I was too young. They've been working on the new album, and this guy is trying too hard to *be* Joey. Louise said they want someone who isn't already in the business, someone like me, with no experience but who can play."

"What are you going to do?"

Lonny cracked his knuckles. "I know I didn't want to do the audition at first, but after being there and playing with them… it was the coolest thing I've ever done."

I covered my mouth to hide my excitement, saying, "You're gonna be a rock star!" Then I screamed like a teenage girl again, this time prompting my mom to come running upstairs to see what was wrong. When she entered my room Lonny and I were laughing and hugging and I didn't want to let him go. I should have never let him go.

2011

A clap of thunder woke me from my hangover nap and I shot up in the backseat. The rain was falling in sheets and it was hard to see the road ahead. I looked at my phone and realized we should have been in Niagara Falls at least an hour earlier. I climbed back into the front passenger seat and buckled myself in.

"You missed all the excitement," Lonny said. "Got a flat, then the rain started. We're behind schedule."

"You said we weren't in a hurry," I joked.

"I did say that."

I turned in my seat to face him. "I'm sorry, Lonny. What happened to us?"

"Life happened to us, Roo. We both lost our innocence in shitty ways to shitty people, and it just progressed from there."

"But why are we taking it out on each other?"

"Good question."

I faced forward again, watching the windshield wipers pounding back and forth trying to keep up with the rain. I had an unsettled feeling in my stomach about the night before, and it had nothing to do with my drinking. Bits of memory were flashing in my head, but I didn't know if they were things that really happened, or if I had dreamt them.

Lonny pulled into the parking lot of our hotel and turned off the car. We decided to stay put until the deluge of rain slowed down a bit. I unbuckled my seatbelt and turned to face him, resting my cheek against the back of the seat.

"What happened last night?" I asked.

"You got drunk, that's what happened."

"You know what I mean," I grumbled.

Lonny released his seatbelt and turned to face me. He explained that he heard the door to our room close, and when he came out of the bathroom I was gone. He saw Billy's website up on the laptop and came after me, even though he had no idea where I went. He stopped at the front desk to ask if they'd seen me, and the girl pointed to the pool area. He rushed in just as I rolled into the water, but he didn't jump in right away; he knew I was a good swimmer and waited to see what I'd do. Apparently I floated to the top but I wasn't swimming, and I was face down, so he came in after me, dragging me across the water and up the pool stairs.

"You should've let me drown," I joked.

"Roo, just stop. I would never do that."

"Did anything else happen?"

His eyes looked past me, out the window at the rain that seemed to be letting up a bit. He shrugged and replied, "Not really. I brought you back to the room, we changed our clothes and you went to bed and passed out."

I felt like he was keeping something from me, but didn't press him further. I watched him from where I sat, saying nothing. The way his long hair framed his face and fell perfectly on his shoulders, the tiny lines that appeared near his eyes when he laughed, his golden brown eyes that have probably seen more things than I ever wanted to know, and that smile. It wasn't the same innocent smile I knew so well when we were teenagers, but it was still his, and I loved it more every time I saw it. I loved that he was here, with me, at that very moment. He realized I was staring at him and started laughing, causing my insides to go wobbly. Feelings I worked so hard to bury were clawing their way to the surface again and I couldn't let that happen.

"Rain stopped!" I shouted excitedly.

We got out of the car, grabbed our suitcases and headed into the hotel to check in.

1979

Reality hit hard for Lonny's mother when he agreed to join Livingston Monroe. She didn't count on the fact that he would have to leave home; somehow it never entered her mind. She cried for days after he told her he was offered the job and would have to go to L.A. to work on the album they were already in the process of recording.

On Lonny's last day in town my mom made a special dinner for him, and our two families ate together as we always did on special occasions. Lonny played guitar for us and we all enjoyed each other's company. Joanie had a few breakdowns during the evening, but she was so proud of her son, and made sure she told him so. Lonny was just as proud of her, as she hadn't had a single drink all day. Lonny still hadn't told anyone he was going to L.A.. He figured they'd find out soon enough, and then he wouldn't be around for everyone to hound him about it. I teased that he wouldn't be around, so they'd all be hounding *me*. I didn't mind though; I was so proud of him, I would be happy to talk about his success to anyone who asked.

When it came time for Lonny and his mom to head home, I was overcome with emotions I wasn't expecting. I hugged him at the front door and burst into tears, unwilling to let go of him. He didn't seem to want to let go of me, either.

"Ruby," Joanie said. "Why don't you stay with us tonight? I'm sure your parents won't mind."

My face was still buried in Lonny's hair and I refused to pull away to see my parents' reaction to that idea. Lonny had spent every Friday night on our couch, but I'd never spent the night at his house before. And while he was on our couch, I was upstairs in my bed.

"Ruby's eighteen now," my mother's voice croaked. "It's her choice."

"We're all driving to the airport together tomorrow anyway," my father added. "We'll just pick you up on the way."

I ran upstairs to pack some things in my overnight bag, quickly returning and kissing my parents goodbye as I headed out the door. As soon as we got to Lonny's house, his mother got comfortable in her recliner with a whiskey and turned on the television. Lonny and I went into his bedroom and he closed the door.

"We won't see her again tonight," he grumbled.

"I have something for you." I pulled an envelope out of my bag and handed it to him.

He looked inside and immediately shoved the envelope back at me. "No way. No."

"Lonny, you're gonna need money while you're gone. And we don't know how long that's gonna be."

"I'm not taking your money."

"It's *our* money."

Lonny threw himself on his bed and covered his eyes with his arm. "I'm sorry we're not going on our trip."

"Don't be. This is your big chance… we can go some other time."

"Promise?"

I sat on the bed next to him and linked my pinky around his. "Promise."

Lonny and I stayed up listening to records, flipping through old magazines where Livingston Monroe was prominently featured, and laughed. We laughed a lot. It was one of the things we did best together.

Around midnight we decided it was best to go to bed, and I went to the bathroom to change into my pajamas. I poked my head into his bedroom and said goodnight, then turned to head toward the living room.

"Hey," he called. When I returned to his doorway he said, "You can stay in here. My mom doesn't care."

"Door open or closed?"

"Closed."

I walked toward his bed and asked, "Over or under?"

"Cookie's not here!"

We both laughed as he turned on the television, turned off the light and we crawled into his bed. We lay facing each other, the light from his little black and white television bright enough that we could see each other.

"I'm really scared," he whispered.

"You're gonna be great," I tried to assure him. "They obviously thought you were dynamite… the band wanted you from the beginning!"

"I don't know anything about recording music, or being in a studio… or being away from home."

"They know all that; that's why they liked you so much. I'm sure the guys will take good care of you."

He was quiet for a few minutes before saying, "I don't want to leave you."

I could see his eyes getting moist, and mine followed right along. "I don't want you to leave either, but… you'll call me, right? Or write letters?"

He nodded. "Promise."

"Stay away from drugs."

"Stay away from Billy."

We both laughed and I said, "I'm never speaking to Billy again. I don't care what he says."

"He'll be going to college anyway, so that's a good thing."

"I don't even want to see his stupid face."

"I don't know what you ever saw in him."

I made a face. "I guess because no one else paid any attention to me, and he did. He's the only one who ever asked me out. No one else liked me."

"Other guys liked you," he replied. "You just didn't pay attention."

I was shocked. "Who liked me?"

Lonny looked like he wished he'd kept his mouth shut. "Come on, Rooster, it doesn't matter now. High school is over."

I wanted to know who liked me.

"If anyone liked me," I argued, "they never asked me out."

"Well it's their loss. Their own fault for being stupid."

"Yeah," I agreed. "Yeah. It's their own stupid fault. Look what they're missing!"

We both chuckled at that and after a few minutes I whispered, "I'm gonna miss you, Lonny."

"I'm gonna miss you, too."

"Lonny, we're best friends, right? Nothing will ever come between us?"

"Never."

"Can I ask a favor?"

He grinned. "Sure."

"Will you kiss me?"

Lonny stared at me, wide-eyed. "I'll be right back," he said, getting out of bed and leaving the room. Thinking I'd made a terrible mistake, I hopped out of his bed and followed him, only to find he had gone into the living room to cover his mother with a blanket and bring her empty whiskey glass into the kitchen. I suddenly realized how much Lonny took care of her, and wondered what would happen once he was gone. I snuck back into bed before he saw me, closing my eyes and pretending I was asleep. I felt stupid asking Lonny for such a ridiculous favor.

I felt Lonny get back into bed and squirm around, then fight with his pillow. I tried not to laugh and give away my sleeping ruse. I could feel his warm breath on my face and it smelled like the lasagna we had for dinner. He pressed his mouth against mine and I opened my eyes, causing him to smile.

"Faker," he whispered.

I laughed then whispered, "I promise to take care of your mom."

He made a farting noise with his mouth and said, "She'll be fine."

"She's gonna be wrecked after you go."

"We should get to sleep."

I smiled. "Thank you."

He kissed me again, this time opening his mouth slightly, but never invading me with his tongue. We closed our eyes, his lips covering my bottom lip, my lips covering his top lip. The memory of that sweet, innocent kiss would get me through some of the darkest days of my life.

Neither Lonny nor I slept much that night, both of us anxious about his leaving for L.A. in the morning. My parents picked us all up and nobody said a word on the drive to the airport. I sat in the back with Lonny and his mom; Lonny sat in the middle with his mother gripping his left hand like she'd never see him

96

again. My left pinky was hooked with his right, hidden between our legs so no one would see our hands.

Lonny held my hand as we all walked through the airport together until we reached his terminal. Our parents tried to make small talk until he had to board the plane, but I could tell by the look on his face he was terrified. I wished there was something I could do to put him at ease, but I was no help. I couldn't imagine what my life would be like without him there every day; just that one week in school when we didn't speak to each other was agony.

All five of us took in a collective gasp when Lonny's flight was called to start boarding. My mom hugged him tightly, my dad shook his hand but ended up hugging him anyway, and his mom started crying as she pulled him against her and nearly squeezed the life out of him. She was blubbering indecipherable phrases as she sobbed, and I knew it was because she started drinking the minute she woke up that morning. My mom finally pulled her off of him, and our parents walked away to give us some privacy.

I smiled at him and said, "You're gonna be great, Lonny. I'm so proud of you."

He tried to smile, but the terror was written all over his face. "I feel like I'm gonna barf."

I pulled him into my arms and we hugged each other tightly as I buried my face in his hair. It was soft against my skin and he smelled so good. My heart was about to explode into a million butterflies of love, but I could not bring myself to tell him I loved him. He was already agonizing over his choice to leave; I didn't think it was fair to burden him with a declaration of love in the airport.

Tears stung my eyes as I said, "Don't forget about me, okay?"

"I could never forget you, Roo."

Another announcement was made for passengers to board and I pulled away from Lonny. "You better go."

"I left some things on my bed for you."

I smiled and nodded, the tears threatening to spill at any moment. He hugged me one last time, then kissed me. Not on the cheek as I expected, but on the mouth, in front of everyone. He turned to wave to my parents and his mom, kissed me again then walked away. He waved one last time before he disappeared from sight.

We were all quiet on the way back to the car, but once I hit the backseat I burst into tears. Lonny was gone and I had no idea when I would see him again. It was ugly, guttural sobbing, and it was something my parents had never seen me do before. I don't think they quite knew how to respond, but Joanie, who was in the backseat with me, pulled me down so my head was in her lap, caressing my face and my arm to comfort me as the silent tears ran down her face.

My crying hadn't stopped by the time we reached Lonny's house, but I ran in quickly to get what he left for me in his bedroom. It was the envelope of money, the photographs I took at his audition, and his favorite Livingston Monroe t-shirt. There was a note that read, "Keep the money so you can come visit. Keep the pictures so you can remember me. Keep the shirt because I know it's your favorite. Love, Lonny."

2011

I followed Lonny into our room and he said, "Since we got here so late, I'm thinking we can grab some dinner and just chill out tonight. Then we can see the Falls tomorrow. Maybe stay an extra day?"

Seeing as I was penniless and homeless, I would obviously go along with whatever Lonny suggested, but I knew he was doing so much of this for me. I doubted very much that he would have been making all these stops if he was alone. He would have picked up the car and driven straight back to Vegas. I knew how anxious he was to see Celia, as they didn't see each other very often.

I smiled at my dearest friend and said, "That would be wonderful."

We went out to get some Chinese food and brought it back to the room, playing tunes from Lonny's phone as opposed to turning on the television. The first song that played was Humble Pie's version of Eddie Cochran's "C'Mon Everybody." I hadn't heard the song in decades and danced like a fool and sang out of tune, as I always did.

"Gotta pocket full of money, and you know I'm gonna spend it right," I sang at the top of my lungs.

Lonny laughed but he jumped right in with the next line, "Been doin' my homework all week long...."

I sat back down at the table and said, "Hard to believe we didn't even know each other when this album came out. Seems like we've known each other our whole lives."

"I think we have," he replied, digging into his cashew chicken.

"What do you mean?"

"We may have physically met when we were fourteen, but I feel like we've been together spiritually forever."

Lonny amazed me at times, saying things that completely blew me away. He was always a deep thinker, and smarter than anyone ever gave him credit for. Even in high school, people assumed because he played guitar and had long hair he had no brains. That couldn't have been further from the truth, seeing as he graduated near the top of our class.

Lonny's phone rang and he laughed. It must have been someone video chatting with him because he watched his phone as he spoke. "Hey man, I'm just eating dinner, can I call you back later?"

"Sure, kid, yeah."

"Look who's here!"

Lonny turned the phone to face me just as I put food in my mouth. I covered my mouth with my hand as I saw Fuzzy Livingston smiling at me.

"Is that Ruby? Hey doll!" Fuzzy said.

I nodded, trying to chew and swallow before I choked.

"Hey Fuzzy!" I finally managed to say.

"Where are you guys?"

"Lonny came and saved me from my shitty life, and now we're headed to Vegas to see Celia," I answered.

"Well you guys finish your dinner, I'll talk to you later."

Lonny hung up the phone and continued eating.

"Fuzzy looks great," I said.

"Yeah, he's doing really well."

Fuzzy was the guy who took Lonny under his wing when he first joined the band. Fuzzy was one of the good guys, which is rare in the music business. As Lonny and I edged closer to fifty, it was hard to believe he was now sixty-two years old. Talking to Fuzzy, even for only a few seconds, brought back memories and emotions I wasn't prepared to deal with. The pain of spending nearly thirty years of marriage to Billy was almost preferred over the memories of losing Lonny to rock and roll.

After we finished eating Lonny handed me my fortune cookie. He opened his and read, "Nothing is impossible to a willing heart." He made a face and laughed.

I opened mine and read, "Big journeys begin with a single step." I chuckled and said, "Ain't that the truth."

"Do you mind if I call Fuzzy back?"

"Go ahead... I think I'm going to soak in the bathtub."

I could hear Lonny talking and laughing the entire time I was in the bathroom. I was glad to see they were still such good friends; the only true friend I ever had was Lonny. Once I married Billy, I was cut off from my friends, and after we moved to New York I had nobody. I wished there was an invention that would erase most of my memories... they were almost too much for me to handle at the moment. I tried to imagine that my best days were in front of me ready to be discovered, but at my age I was too tired to even dream that reality.

When I came out of the bathroom, Lonny was sprawled out on his bed watching some program about tattoos. I rolled my eyes.

"Why don't you have any tattoos?" Lonny asked.

"Maybe I have one you can't see," I teased.

"Do you?"

I laughed. "Nope."

"Why is that? You were married to a tattoo artist and not one tattoo?"

"Billy didn't trust anyone else to tattoo me, and he wouldn't do it himself." Hearing myself say it out loud made it sound even more ludicrous.

I could see the wheels turning in Lonny's head just by watching his face. I had a feeling I wasn't going to like where this was headed.

"He didn't want other men looking at you," he said.

"What are you talking about?"

"He didn't want to decorate you because he didn't want you to get attention from other men. Men who would be looking at your tattoos, if you had them."

"You could be right."

"He didn't want you for himself, but he certainly didn't want anyone else to give you attention."

My heart dropped into my stomach. I knew Lonny was blunt and to the point, but why was he insisting on pushing the knife deeper?

I was trying hard not to cry, but I was so emotionally fragile I didn't think it was possible. And I certainly didn't want to fight with Lonny. *Again.* So I crawled into my bed and pulled the covers over my head.

"You going to bed already?"

I grunted.

101

"Don't you want to watch a movie?"

I ignored him.

I heard the channels on the television changing and just wanted to go to sleep. I wanted to leave the real world and escape to my dreams, where people like Billy didn't exist and I was young, tall and gorgeous.

"Come on, Roo, look! *My Cousin Vinny* is on!"

I continued to ignore him until he lifted the covers and I looked up to see his face smiling at me. His smile disappeared quickly when I started crying again. All I wanted was to be loved by a man who thought I was everything in the world to him; someone who would love me for who I was, baggage and all, without conditions.

"Move over," he said.

I moved to the other side of the bed, and he climbed in next to me. He leaned against the headboard and pulled me into his arms, kissing the top of my head.

He continued to hold me as he chuckled at the movie, and when I finally stopped crying I focused my eyes on his scar. I touched the starting point in the middle of his palm with my finger, lightly and slowly tracing it to the end, just under his armpit.

"Does it hurt?" I whispered.

"Not anymore. The memory is more painful than the actual scar."

I woke up the next morning with my face smashed against skin and tried to remember where I was. I opened my eyes and looked around without moving. My eyelashes must have tickled Lonny's back because he squirmed away from me and groaned, "We have to stop meeting like this."

I watched as he sat up and swung his legs over the side of the bed, running his fingers through his hair. I pulled the covers up to my nose because I wanted to be able to see him, but I didn't want him to see my goofy smile. As promised, he never left my side during the night, even though I ended up taking up most of the bed. He stood up, adjusted his shorts and went out onto the balcony for a cigarette.

I got up and went to the bathroom, and when I returned he shouted, "You've got your passport, right?"

102

"I think you threw it in my suitcase," I said, joining him on the balcony.

"We're going to Canada. We're going to see the Canadian side of the Falls and we're spending the night there."

Who was I to argue? I smiled and nodded, then said, "Thanks for not leaving me last night."

He pulled me into a loving embrace. "I promise I will never leave you again."

1979

Life was not the same with Lonny gone. He called the night he arrived in L.A., and a couple times later that week, but he was so busy he barely had time. The times he was available to call was usually the middle of the night and he didn't want to wake me up, and he really didn't want to charge up a long distance phone bill. He was staying with Fuzzy and his wife Marilyn, and said they were taking really good care of him. Since he didn't want to call me in the middle of the night, he would write me letters instead, which I received several times every week. I missed him so much I would cry after reading them.

Lonny sounded happy. He was enjoying being in the studio and learning the recording process, as well as what it meant to be part of a band, which is something he'd never done before. He was really excited to be included in some songwriting, even though most of the songs they planned to record had already been written before Joey Buckingham left. They decided to scrap the songs Joey had participated in writing, and wrote a few new ones with Lonny instead.

I would always write a letter in response to Lonny, but in each one I begged him to call me, even if it was the middle of the night. I didn't care what time it was, I just wanted to talk to him and to hear his voice. To hear for myself that he was happy and doing well. But every morning I would wake up and realize the call never came and I'd be heartbroken all over again.

Sometime around Halloween I was pulling last month's magazines out of the racks at the record store to replace with the new batch and pulled out the new stack of *Creem*. I screamed at the top of my lungs and kept screaming until my boss, Ricky, came to see what was wrong with me. There, on the cover of the magazine, was a photograph of Lonny with the headline, "Livingston Monroe's New Golden Boy."

Ricky grabbed my shoulders as I jumped up and down, staring at me with his mouth wide open. "Lonny? *Lonny?*" he kept saying.

"Lonny!" I shouted.

"Did you know?"

I nodded with the biggest smile across my face.

New magazines were always stocked on Tuesday, and once school was out that day people were flocking into the store to get their hands on a copy of Lonny's *Creem* debut. Ricky and I stashed a few copies away for ourselves, thankful we did, because those magazines didn't last five minutes.

I was manning the cash register when the last of the magazines was plopped on the counter, and I looked up to see Ms. Cooke standing there.

"Did you know about this?" she asked coldly.

"I did."

"I arranged that audition, and this is the thanks I get? I'm not even told he ended up getting the job?"

"Are you buying the magazine, Ms. Cooke?" I asked.

"Yes, of course."

I took her money, gave back her change, and placed the magazine in a bag. Before handing it to her, I said, "I know what you did to Lonny."

Her face paled. "I don't know what you're talking about."

"I know what you did, and you better leave him alone."

She snatched the bag out of my hand and disappeared quickly. I was so angry I wanted to scratch her eyes out. The way she looked at me with such contempt, and acted as if Lonny was supposed to call her after what she did to him? I had half a mind to tell his mother what she did, but knew that wouldn't solve anything.

Ricky knew I was excited to get home and let me leave early. I raced to Lonny's house first, letting myself in with the key. I knew his mom wasn't home from work yet, and left a copy of the magazine on her kitchen table. I got back on my bike and rode home, running into the house excitedly yelling for my parents. They were just sitting down to eat dinner when I put the magazine on the table for them to see.

My dad said his usual, "Well look at that," while my mom screeched and hugged me.

"Makes sense why the phone has been ringing off the hook for you," my mom said.

I frowned and asked who'd been calling for me.

"All your friends from high school. They didn't say why, but all of them want to talk to you. Must be because of Lonny's magazine."

I had gotten my own phone line for my sixteenth birthday, and after Lonny left for L.A. I had my number changed. I wanted to know that when my phone rang, it was Lonny on the other end. Seemed people could no longer reach me that way, so they were calling my parents' line instead. All my friends… people I hadn't heard from since graduating high school.

"Have some dinner," my dad said. "Those people can wait."

I was too excited to eat, but I knew how much my parents enjoyed eating dinner as a family, so I joined them. My work hours didn't always allow me to eat dinner with them anymore, so I was happy to oblige.

I sat down at the table and as my mom dished up dinner on my plate, I glanced at the list of people who had called while I was at work. Names of people who were never my friends or who never spoke to me at school, and then there they were. Molly and Billy. I tore the paper off the pad, crumpled it up and threw it in the garbage.

"Users," I grumbled, sitting down to eat and praying Lonny would call me that night.

"Honey, we're worried about you," my mom said.

I looked up from my plate and saw my parents watching me carefully. "Why?"

"Ever since Lonny left you go to work, you go to his mom's, and you come home," she replied.

"You don't go out with your friends, you don't have any fun," my dad added.

I chuckled and swallowed my food before responding. "I work all day, so I'm tired when I come home. Just like you, Dad," I teased. "Besides, I don't want to go out. I like staying home."

"Don't you want to date?" I couldn't believe my mother was asking me that.

"Not really," I laughed. "Are you in a rush to get me married and out of the house?"

"Don't be silly," my father said. "We just want you to be happy."

At that moment I could hear my phone ringing upstairs. I took off running and managed to answer it on the fourth ring.

"Lonny!" I yelled.

"I was afraid you were still at work!" It was so great to hear his voice.

"Ricky let me leave early today — Lonny! *Creem* magazine? Why didn't you tell me?"

He laughed and said, "I wanted it to be a surprise."

"Kids came in after school and bought them all!"

"So what did you think?"

"I love the photo of you on the cover... I'd rather see you smiling, but I understand why they made you look like a serious musician."

He laughed again. "The article was more an interview with the other guys, so I didn't get to say much."

"Lonny, it's dynamite. I brought a copy to your mom."

"How is she?"

I was honest with Lonny, explaining that his mother was lost without him there, and probably drinking a lot more than she normally did, but I assured him that I visited her regularly, and my parents always had her over to the house. None of us were going to let her be lonely if we could help it.

Lonny did most of the talking, and I was happy to listen. He was so excited and sounded truly happy, and that made me happy. He talked about the recording process, writing music, the interviews he'd been doing, and the photo shoots with the band. He raved about what a great guy Fuzzy was, and how his wife Marilyn looked over him like a mother. He said Mitch and Benji were great too, but he really seemed to bond with Fuzzy.

Fuzzy and Marilyn set up a bedroom especially for Lonny, giving him free reign to do as he pleased. Depending on their schedules, Marilyn would take Lonny around L.A. to get him acquainted with the area, and introduce him to people they knew. He felt I would really like Marilyn if I had the chance to get to know her.

"How are the girls?" I found myself asking.

107

"Girls?" he laughed. "Who has time for girls?"

I felt stupid for asking. "They make it sound like rock stars have girls hanging around all the time, so I figured—"

"Fuzzy is married, Benji is married with a kid, and Mitch has a girlfriend. We're in the studio so it's not like I'm out partying and picking up girls."

"I'm sorry."

"Nothing to be sorry about, Roo. Just facts."

"Do you know when the new album will be out?"

"Nah, I have no idea. But we might take a break and I can come home for Thanksgiving."

I had never heard any sweeter words. "Oh Lonny, I hope so!"

"So what have you been up to?" he asked.

"Working and visiting your mom. That's about it."

"You should go out and have fun, Roo."

"You sound like my parents."

"They're not wrong."

What was happening here? Was Lonny having so much fun forgetting about me that he wanted to make sure I was doing the same?

"Well, you know," I sighed. "There was a list of people who called me today after seeing your magazine cover. People who were never my friends, but I suppose I could call them all back."

"Like who?"

I rattled off the names I could remember and let that sink in for a bit before adding, "Oh, Molly and Billy too."

"You stay away from Billy," he ordered.

"I'm not calling Billy," I groaned. "But thanks."

"I mean it Rooster, stay away from him."

"He's at college and I hate him. Besides, what can you do about it? You're not here either." What was I doing? I couldn't wait to talk to Lonny, and now I was being a complete jerk.

"I gotta go Roo," he said quickly.

His line went dead and I immediately burst into tears. That was not how I wanted our conversation to go, but especially not how I wanted it to end. I buried my face in my pillow and screamed as loud as I could.

My phone rang again. "Lonny, I'm sorry!"

"I miss you, Roo."

"I miss you, too," I cried.

I love you.

He hung up again and I sobbed into my pillow. I had so many feelings coursing through my veins, combined with confusion and heartbreak, I didn't know which end was up. Lonny and I were leading two completely different lives now; how could we ever connect on the same level again?

My mother came up to check on me when I never went back downstairs after my phone call with Lonny. She sat on the side of my bed and pushed the hair away from my face.

"Honey, what happened?"

I wiped the tears from my face, and looked up at her from my pillow. "I miss him so much."

"I know you do, but honey, you have to live your own life. You can't sit around here waiting for him to call. He has a completely different life now."

I know my mom was trying to be helpful, but she was only making things worse, and I burst into another fit of tears. She pulled me into her arms and rocked me like she used to do when I was little.

"How is he?" she asked. "Does he sound happy?"

"He's really happy," I cried.

"I know you don't want to hear this, but you have to start thinking about your future. You can't work in a record store forever. And you need to start going out. Meet new people, make new friends."

I continued to cry saying, "Lonny is the only friend I want."

"But Ruby, he's meeting new people, making new friends, probably meeting lots of girls."

And just like that, the ugly, guttural sobbing I experienced after taking Lonny to the airport erupted again. It was that moment my mom figured it out.

"Ruby, do you *like* him?"

109

"I love him, Mom. More than anything in the world."

"Does he know?"

"No," I cried. "But it doesn't matter, because he doesn't feel the same way. And now he's gone. And probably meeting all kinds of beautiful girls."

My mom did everything she could to soothe me, but nothing helped. I just wanted to go to sleep and escape real life, and I finally convinced her I would be all right and she went down to watch television with my father. I turned on the light, flipping through Lonny's magazine and reading the article over and over again. I was so happy for him, as he deserved success more than anyone I knew, but inside I felt nothing but agony for myself. And that upset me even more, because I knew I was being selfish. Lonny would be so disappointed in me.

I set my alarm for the morning, turned off my light and fell into a deep sleep. I'm not sure what time it was, but I knew by the way the moon shone through my bedroom window it was probably around three in the morning when my phone rang.

I answered on the first ring.

"I just wanted to say goodnight, Roo."

I smiled in the dark. "I love you, Lonny."

"Yeah, me too."

2011

As we crossed over the Rainbow Bridge into Canada, I couldn't take enough photographs of the Falls. It was the most magnificent thing I had ever seen! I snuck in some photos of Lonny as well, but he had no idea. Getting through border control was entertaining though, as the guard recognized Lonny and chatted with him for a while before letting us through. I took a photo of them together and promised to email it to him when we got to our hotel.

"People still love you, Lonny," I remarked.

He laughed me off with a wave of his hand, and I knew that was my clue to end that line of conversation. We pulled into a parking lot where he parked and put the top up on the car.

"Ready for an adventure?" he asked, smiling at me.

"I'm not sure." Lonny knew I wasn't an adventurous person, so I was a bit nervous.

We were at a place where you zip-line two hundred feet in the air along the Falls to an observation deck about two thousand feet away. I wasn't afraid of heights, but I wasn't keen on floating in the sky that high above the ground. Lonny was so excited to do this, but I felt sheer panic as we got closer to the launch area. We were wearing protective helmets, but if anyone fell from that height they weren't going to survive. There were four parallel zip-lines, all facing the American and Canadian Horseshoe Falls, with a breathtaking panoramic view. Lonny and I were next to each other, but far enough away that we couldn't touch or get tangled. I'd heard about people having panic attacks, and though I never experienced one myself, I could understand how they begin. My heart thundered in my chest and I began to sweat, fearing I'd just made the worst decision of my life. I wanted to get off, but I was already flying through the air and terrified. Lonny managed to get ahead of me and I watched him, his arms stretched out as if he were flying all on his own like a bird. I was about to close my eyes and spend the rest of my flight blind, but I looked out at the scene before me and was completely awestruck by the beauty. I didn't realize until that moment how free I finally was; so free I was soaring through the Canadian skies with my best friend, on a road trip that would undoubtedly decide the next path in my life.

When we reached the landing area and were free from our secured flying chairs and helmets, I fell into Lonny's arms, shaking.

"Wasn't that amazing, Roo?"

"It was amazing and scary as hell," I managed to reply. "I need a drink."

We walked to a nearby restaurant for lunch, and I was still shaking when I sat down. I immediately ordered a tequila sunrise with a shot of tequila on the side. Lonny laughed at me, but he had no idea how badly I was shaking until I lifted my hand and he saw it for himself.

"I've never felt so free... or so terrified," I said. "But thank you, Lonny, that was amazing."

"You have to get out and try new things," he said, perusing the menu. "Live a little."

I laughed. "You might get me killed."

"I know you, Rooster. You've never been one to take chances, step out of your comfort zone, do anything crazy."

"That's not entirely true."

"Name one thing."

The waitress brought our drinks and I immediately threw back my shot of tequila. All three of us laughed, and she left us alone to decide what we wanted to eat.

I could list off several things, but he wouldn't understand. And I was too embarrassed to remind him, because he may not have seen my actions with the same eyes I did. I thought kissing him in the hotel in L.A. when he went for his audition was stepping out of my comfort zone. Or asking him to kiss me the night before he left to join the band. Or the countless times I told him I loved him and he just didn't get it.

"You're right," I conceded. "I've never done a daring thing in my whole life. I went from my parents' home to my husband's home, and spent the rest of my life under his thumb."

Why was it whenever I started to feel good about things, or think I was getting closer to happiness, something Lonny said always brought me back to ground zero? Back to Billy, back to my worthless marriage, back to me wanting to end it all?

"We were going to plan something epic for our fiftieth birthday this year," he changed the subject. "It's coming up quick."

"You mean this road trip isn't it?"

"Hardly," he laughed.

"Well, since I'm not very adventurous, what did you have in mind?"

"Ouch, okay, I get it. I'm sorry."

"Look, you're not going to get many ideas from me, because I have no money. I'm not comfortable planning something when I can't pay my own way."

Lonny leaned back in his chair and folded his arms in front of him, staring at me. "I told you not to worry about that."

"Lonny—"

"Just stop with the poor me shit, okay? It's tiring."

"You don't understand."

"I don't understand?" he nearly shouted. "I understand perfectly. I lost *everything*, but I didn't refuse help when it was offered. As humiliating as it was, I embraced it with open arms and *never* made the same mistakes again."

The waitress returned and we placed our food orders, and I ordered another drink. As she walked away I said, "Well, you can bet I won't be making the same mistakes again."

"I think we should take our backpacking trip."

"What? To Europe?"

"Yeah. We never got to take it and I think we should."

"Well, if you think we should," I said nonchalantly, shrugging my shoulders. "And since you've actually *been* to Europe now, it'll be a lot easier to plan."

Lonny winked at me and said, "That's my girl." He always called me his girl... if only he had the slightest idea what that did to me. It was loving and painful all in the same breath.

We spent lunch talking about our parents and Celia, which was still hard for me to wrap my head around. I'd never had the pleasure of meeting Lonny's daughter, and it was hard for me to believe he was a father. I didn't know anything about Celia's mother, except he refused to talk about her. One of many items on

113

Lonny's list of things he wouldn't discuss. He talked about me and my comfort zone!

It comforted me that Lonny not only called his mother once a week, but my parents as well. He would visit home twice a year, spending equal time with my parents as his own mother. He was a much better son to them than I was a daughter. I hadn't seen my parents or his mother in five years, and it was nobody's fault but my own. Business was booming and Billy wouldn't let me leave, but I was too afraid to tell him I was going whether he liked it or not.

"Are we going home?" I asked.

Lonny smiled the smile that brought out the dimples on both sides of his face. "We'll be there to celebrate our big 5-0 with the family."

I was so overcome with emotion I couldn't form words. I laughed at myself as I wiped the tears from my face.

"But our parents don't know. I wanted it to be a surprise," he added.

I was so happy knowing I was going to see my parents soon. I thanked him with tears and a hand over my mouth because I couldn't speak. He reached across the table and placed his hand over mine and I stared at it. He had the most beautiful hands I'd ever seen on a man, soft, with long, slender fingers and perfectly trimmed nails. They were perfect hands for a guitar player; I remember many times watching his hands as he played and paying attention to nothing else. He thought it was a bit strange, but he didn't see them the same way I did. To him they were just hands; to me they were instruments of musical genius.

After lunch we were on to our next adventure, a boat cruise that takes passengers as close to the Falls as possible without drowning them. Lonny told me to leave my camera locked in the trunk of the car, and had his phone double wrapped in plastic bags, which I didn't understand. We had to wear rain gear, which I also didn't understand. Lonny was taking all kinds of pictures with his phone, which aggravated me at first, because I should've been taking amazing photographs with my camera. He took pictures of us together with the Falls behind us, and the closer we got to the belly of the beast, I understood why he had me leave my camera

114

behind, and why we had to wear rain gear. Even with the rain gear on, we ended up soaked to the bone from the bottom of the Falls spraying us. The sheer force of the falling water was impossible to describe; I could feel it thundering in my chest like God beating on a drum. The water was cold on my face but it felt like I was being washed clean of my past; everything that happened before that moment was a memory that I could think of if I wanted to, but wasn't chained to.

As the boat headed back to where our journey began, I turned to continue watching the Falls, awestruck by its enormity and beauty. Lonny stood behind me and wrapped his arms around me, resting his chin on my shoulder. He softly sang the words from Johnny Nash's "I Can See Clearly Now" in my ear, ending with, "Here is the rainbow I've been prayin' for." Chills covered my body as I looked up to see a rainbow appear in the mist.

We spent the rest of our beautiful day wandering around town, taking lots of photographs, eating ice cream, popping into shops, and buying souvenirs for our parents. We headed to our hotel around dinnertime, and as we walked toward its massive structure from the parking lot, I noticed there was a casino attached.

"Lonny, there's a casino here," I mentioned, as if he couldn't possibly have noticed.

"Yeah, I know. Don't worry, it's okay."

I wasn't so sure, but said nothing further. I followed Lonny into the hotel where he checked in, then up to the room where he had me close my eyes before he opened the door. I could hear him set the suitcases on the floor, then he covered my eyes with his hands and maneuvered me through the room. When he pulled his hands away and I opened my eyes, I was greeted with a floor to ceiling, wall to wall window with the most breathtaking view of the Falls. Like a child, I pressed my nose against the window to take in the beauty that greeted me.

"Lonny," I said breathily. "It's gorgeous!"

"I knew you'd like it."

"I don't even know what to say."

"Don't say anything, just enjoy it."

I immediately pulled my camera out of my bag and started snapping photographs of the view. I turned around and snapped Lonny as well, even as he protested. "Come on, cover boy," I teased. "Your face has been all over every magazine known to man… now you're camera shy?"

Lonny laughed, hesitated, then began posing like a model, making me laugh. He was still an attractive man, and I was amazed some hot, young girl hadn't snatched him up by now. He started making goofy faces, but I didn't stop. The beauty of digital cameras — no running out of film! He eventually threw himself on one of the beds in the room and sighed heavily.

"I'm exhausted," he said. "We should take a nap, then have a late dinner. There's something really cool we need to see later tonight."

I thought that sounded like a splendid idea, and crawled on top of the other bed to stretch out. Lonny set his alarm and we both fell asleep quickly after such a busy, exciting day.

When I started waking up, I realized Lonny was lying next to me, taking all kinds of goofy selfies with me while I was asleep. "I didn't hear the alarm," I grumbled.

"I was awake so I turned it off." I covered my face with my hand and he said, "Open your eyes and look at me."

I opened my eyes and his nose was practically touching mine, he was so close. "What's up?"

"I know I say things that come out hurtful sometimes, but it's just because I care about you," he answered. "I don't mean to upset you."

I patted the top of his head. "I know, Lonny. I appreciate it."

"Let's go eat. I'm starving."

We freshened up and changed our clothes, heading to the steak restaurant downstairs. Lonny seemed fidgety at dinner, drinking a lot more than I'd seen him on this trip. By the time he paid the bill he was drunk. I hadn't seen Lonny drunk in many years.

As we walked out of the restaurant Lonny was a little wobbly, so he put his arm around my shoulder for balance. "What should we do now?" he bellowed, his voice echoing through the hotel foyer.

"Let's go back to the room," I urged.

"No, let's party!"

He started pulling me toward the entrance to the casino and I stopped walking, causing him to almost fall on his face. "We're not going in there."

"Come on, Roo, just a few minutes."

"No."

"Roo, I promise, I can do it for just a few minutes. It's okay."

"No, Lonny, it's *not* okay. I'm not letting you go in there." He pulled away from me and stumbled toward the casino. I grabbed his arm and turned him to face me. "I'll do anything," I begged. "Please, Lonny, whatever you want."

He looked at me, barely able to open his eyes, a sly grin crossing his face. "Anything?"

I knew I was going to regret it, but I couldn't let him go into that casino. He lost everything to gambling and I wasn't about to let him destroy his life all over again. "*Anything.*"

He put his arm around me and walked toward the front desk. He told them he wanted a bottle of champagne delivered to our room and gave them the number. We walked to the elevator and stumbled in, quiet all the way up to our floor. I watched as he leaned his head back against the wall with his eyes closed. I caught him as he fell out into the hallway and we managed to make it back to our room without injury.

Lonny fell into a chair before I had a chance to close the door, and when I turned around a man was standing there with the bottle of champagne he requested, and two champagne flutes. Lonny fumbled around with his wallet, pulling out a twenty dollar bill and handing it to me. I thanked the man and sent him on his way, closing and locking the door behind him.

"Okay Lonny, your champagne is here," I chuckled.

He wanted me to give him the bottle, which he struggled to uncork. I was laughing so hard I almost peed my pants. When he finally popped the cork, it flew across the room and hit the wall, bouncing off and pelting me in the head. I hit the ground, feeling

117

like I'd been shot, but I continued laughing. Lonny was drinking the spillage straight from the bottle as I lay on the floor in pain, but laughing about it.

Lonny handed me the bottle and pulled his phone out of his pocket. He intently searched for something, his eyes nearly crossing at whatever he was looking at. "Okay," he finally said, "I found it."

I looked past him as I saw fireworks going off outside and walked straight to the window. "Lonny, look!"

There was a spectacular fireworks show going on over the Falls, and I sat on the floor in front of the window to watch. Lonny fell on the floor next to me and said, "That's what I wanted you to see tonight!"

"It's beautiful!"

Lonny leaned closer to me, resting his head on my shoulder. "Sorry I shot you in the head," he slurred. We both burst into a fit of laughter.

"Better a cork than a bullet," I reasoned. More laughter.

Lonny stretched out on the floor laughing, resting his head on my leg. He looked up at me and asked, "How long since you had sex?"

"Lonny!"

"It's been a year for me," he laughed.

"A year!" I was stunned. "How is that possible? You're…."

"I'm what?"

"A *guy.*"

He burst into another fit of laughter, holding his stomach. "Rooooooooo," he hollered. "Rooooooooo." For some odd reason this made him laugh even harder, with tears streaming down his face. I soon followed suit, his laughter making me laugh harder.

"Let's play a game," he giggled. "Truth or Dare."

"No way."

"I already started, come on," he groaned.

"Okay, fine."

"Truth or Dare?"

"Truth."

"When's the last time you had sex?" he asked again.

118

I found myself hoping this was the "anything" he had in mind for keeping him out of the casino that night. He was really drunk and silly, and I had no idea where things were bound to end up.

"Two years ago," I answered honestly.

Lonny shot up from the floor to a sitting position and stared at me in shock. "Two years! I heard after one year your virginity grows back," he said, causing both of us to start laughing again.

"Then I guess we're both virgins again!" I shouted.

He grabbed the bottle of champagne and took a swig, shouting, "To virgins!" He pushed it toward me and I took a swig, knowing this might be a long night. I knew I needed to stay in control; I couldn't let Lonny slip out on me and end up in that casino.

We enjoyed the fireworks show for the most part, but Lonny was so drunk he couldn't sit still or concentrate on anything for very long. He stood up, almost falling on the bed, and held out his hand. "I still have something for you," he said, trying to help me to my feet. He grabbed his phone and I heard "Lady," by the Little River Band start to play. "Remember prom?"

I laughed loudly. "How could I forget?"

"We were dancing to this song when I told you about the audition. I think we should do that dance the right way."

"You want to dance?"

He nodded with his eyes closed, waving his hand for me to come closer. I stood in front of him and he pulled me into his arms, resting his head on my shoulder. I swore he fell asleep, but then I felt his hands on my back, sliding down toward my backside. He stopped at my waist.

We danced slowly, because any faster and he would have fallen over. I could feel his breath on my neck and then I heard him say, "Do you remember when my mom dropped you off at your house, and I walked you to your door?"

I smiled at the memory. "I remember."

"And then drunk Billy was sitting there," he grumbled.

"Yeah, Billy. He ruins everything," I tried to joke.

"Do you know why I walked you to your door?"

"Because you were a sweet boy?"

119

Lonny pulled away to look at me. He could barely keep his eyes open, but said, "I walked you to your door because I wanted to kiss you goodnight."

I couldn't believe what I was hearing. I just stared at him, unable to find words. My heart raced as I continued to watch his face. He turned and walked toward the window, picking the bottle of champagne up from the floor. He stood staring out the window and all I could think was, *that's it*? I was slapping myself internally because I couldn't think of anything intelligent to say. Was he expecting me to say something? What an idiot I was!

"My turn!" I shouted. When he turned to look at me, I said, "Truth or dare."

He grinned. "Dare."

This was my chance, but I sucked at this kind of thing. And would I be taking advantage of Lonny because he was drunk? I knew he probably wouldn't remember any of this in the morning.

"I dare you to kiss me. Like you would have on prom night." There, I did it. The ball was in his court.

Lonny walked toward me, setting the bottle of champagne on the table. Every thought I'd ever had about him was fighting for prominence inside my head and they were making me dizzy. He put his hands on the sides of my face and smiled, his eyes wide open. He pressed his lips against mine and held them there for a few seconds, then pulled away. He grabbed the champagne and took another swig.

"That's it?" I asked. "That's how you would've kissed me on prom night?"

"I was seventeen and clueless," he laughed. "That's probably the way it would've happened."

I realized how ridiculous I was being and started laughing. I could feel my face burning and covered my cheeks with my hands. But the way he looked at me when he placed his hands there….

I grabbed the champagne from him and took a long drink. So long, I emptied the bottle. "All gone," I informed him.

He picked up the room phone and ordered another bottle, plus some sandwiches. He definitely needed some food to soak up all the alcohol he'd been drinking. I wasn't even sure how he'd be able to drink another bottle… I'd certainly had my fill.

The next song that played was "You Take My Breath Away," by Rex Smith, the other song Lonny and I danced to at prom. He took my hand and pulled me close, but I wasn't sure if we were dancing, or I was just holding him up. He was pretty far gone at this point, and I was about ready to put him to bed.

There was a knock on our door, and the same man who brought us our last bottle of champagne was there to deliver another bottle, plus the sandwiches we ordered. Lonny just handed me his wallet, unable to pull any money out of it on his own, and I pulled out another twenty dollar bill for a tip. I thanked the man and closed and locked the door after he left.

I sat on my bed and patted it with my hand, hoping Lonny would sit down and eat. I opened the tray which contained a large bunch of grapes in the middle, with all sorts of finger sandwiches surrounding them in a circle. There were meat sandwiches, egg salad, chicken salad, and tuna. After complaining how hot it was in the room and peeling off his shirt, he fell onto the bed next to me, grabbing an egg salad sandwich. I think he ate five sandwiches as I finished my first. He struggled to uncork the second bottle of champagne and I took it away from him, afraid I'd end up shot in the face this time. I went into the bathroom and managed to open it without any spillage and returned to the bed, where Lonny had eaten another five sandwiches. I started wondering if he got drunk to keep himself from wandering down to the casino; it made sense, as he probably would never have made it down there anyway, and if he did, they probably wouldn't let him in based on his level of inebriation.

I pulled a handful of grapes off the stems and reached out to hand them to Lonny. "Here, have some fruit," I chuckled.

He held onto my wrist and pulled my hand toward his mouth, eating two. He looked at me with slits for eyes and grinned devilishly. He kissed the top of my hand, then slid one of my fingers in his mouth, sucking on it. I immediately yanked my hand away from him, even though parts of me I believed long dead were definitely responding and very much alive.

Lonny slid his finger under the strap of my tank top, lightly touching my skin. "Why did we never end up together, Roo?" he slurred, his eyes closed. "Because there's too much love."

We each grabbed one of the last two sandwiches. I was amazed at how much food one person can consume just because they're drinking alcohol. I got up and placed the empty food tray on the table and took a swig of champagne. What the hell was Lonny going on about? Too much love? I didn't know how much longer I could handle drunk Lonny; he was exhausting. He wasn't even drunk anymore... he was *wasted*.

Lonny took the bottle from my hand and took a drink. "Okay, my turn!" he shouted. "Truth or dare?"

"Lonny, it's late. Let's just go to bed."

"No, no, no. My turn. Truth or dare?" He couldn't even open his eyes.

"Truth," I sighed heavily. I had no interest in what he might dare me to do at that point.

He tried to open his eyes and look at me as he quietly asked, "Why did you marry Billy?"

"Please don't," I whispered, holding back tears I was so tired of crying.

He lay down on his side, patting the bed next to him. I followed suit, stretching out next to him so we were facing each other. I wiped a tear off my cheek and watched him struggle to open his eyes.

"Why did you marry him?" he whispered.

I almost couldn't speak the words. "Because you didn't love me," I cried.

"That's not true," he said, pushing a strand of hair off my face and behind my ear. "I've always loved you, Roo."

"Please don't do this."

He touched the tip of his finger to my lips and brought his face close to mine, his eyes drunkenly fixed on my mouth. I was frozen, waiting to see what he would do next, and he slid his hand behind my neck as his lips pressed against mine. He was sweet, just like any kiss we had shared in the past, including the one earlier when I dared him. Then he crawled on top of me and placed his hands against my face, leaning over and kissing me again, only this time there was nothing sweet about it. It was hot and wet and hungry, and I felt truly alive for the first time in many years. My body was so desperate for a loving touch that Lonny's physical attention caused an aching that haunted me.

Out of breath he sat up, straddling me. I reached out and pressed my hand against his bare chest, but he moved it over his heart, where I could feel it thundering under my touch. I took a moment to admire how physically fit he was for his age, lean but not skinny like he used to be. I slid my hand slowly down his chest to his unbelievably flat stomach, and stopped. Looking at his jeans I could see he was aroused, and I smiled.

I managed to squirm out from underneath him and switch positions, straddling him instead. He grinned at me, trying to keep his eyes open. I unbuttoned his jeans and watched his face. He sat up quickly so that we were face to face and I wrapped my legs around him. He kissed me hard, then kissed his way down my neck and across my shoulder, where his hands reached under my tank top and groped my breasts. I ripped my tank top off and threw it on the floor and he stared at his hands covering my bra. His mouth was open, as if in shock, and he finally lifted his eyes to look at my face.

"Are you sure?" he slurred.

I kissed him softly, letting him know I was never more sure of anything in my life. I got off the bed and he leaned back on his elbows to watch me as I slid my shorts off and kicked them across the room. I looked at Lonny, and his eyes were closed.

"Lonny?"

No answer.

I walked closer and poked his shoulder. His arms gave out on him, and he landed flat on his back.

"Lonny?"

I grabbed one of his hands and patted it lightly. Nothing. I leaned over and kissed his mouth and he started snoring. He was passed out cold.

I smiled. While I was disappointed things didn't go further, I was happy for the attention I did get, and that it was from Lonny.

I made sure to flip him over, then climbed into the other bed and went to sleep. When I woke up in the morning, he was still

123

passed out. I took a shower and put on some fresh clothes, then called room service and ordered breakfast. I sat in front of the window and just marveled at the magnificence of the Falls. I could hear Lonny stirring behind me and turned to see him trying to focus his eyes through the mop of hair covering his face.

"I ordered breakfast," I said, laughing. "You have a *lot* of alcohol to soak up."

Lonny slowly got up and swung his legs over the side of the bed, setting his feet on the floor. He held his head with both hands and groaned.

"What happened last night?" he croaked.

"You got wasted to avoid wandering down to the casino. I helped."

Lonny got up and stumbled to the bathroom, where I could hear him urinating for what seemed like fifteen minutes. I was scrolling through the photographs on my camera when he finally reemerged.

Breakfast arrived and Lonny tipped the man, and we sat at the table to eat. He lifted up the empty sandwich tray and wrinkled his forehead.

"Late night sandwiches," I explained.

"Two bottles of champagne?"

I poured us each a cup of coffee and asked, "Don't you remember anything?"

He pulled a face, trying to remember the slightest thing about the night before. We ate quietly as I started realizing any attention I received from Lonny was alcohol-induced, and I should be thankful he couldn't remember any of it.

"Roo, did we...?"

"Did we what?"

He looked at me wide-eyed and confused. "Did we—"

"You got wasted," I explained. "Passed out on the bed."

I could tell he wanted to say something else, but kept his mouth shut. He kept looking at me strangely, and I knew it was because he couldn't figure out whether what actually happened between us was a dream or not.

"So we didn't... you know...?"

"Nope." I chuckled. "Did you have a sex dream about me?"

124

We both burst into laughter and he replied, "Almost…?"

"Damn. I was hoping you could tell me if I was any good."

He ate silently for a moment before saying, "Well, the bits I remember were really *hot*."

I thought about the reality of what nearly happened and felt my face flush. "Oh good," I teased, "because it's been two years and I've probably forgotten what to do."

He stopped chewing and looked at me strangely. He wrinkled his forehead and started chewing again, very slowly, never taking his eyes off me. I suddenly realized I said something similar the night before during our game of Truth Or Dare, but he didn't question me. He did keep looking at me strangely, however. I just smiled.

Lonny finished his breakfast and stood up, and I noticed his eyes fixed on something that I soon realized were the tank top and shorts I was wearing the night before, still on the floor where I flung them. He disappeared into the bathroom for a shower and as soon as I heard the water running I jumped up and grabbed the offending articles of clothing and tidied up the rest of the room while I was at it.

When Lonny emerged from the bathroom he was brushing his teeth, but all I could focus on was the towel wrapped around him, hanging low on his waist. I mentally slapped myself and looked up at his face and noticed he was pointing at me. He still said nothing, going back into the bathroom to finish his business. Lonny knew me better than anyone, and I had a feeling he knew I was lying about what happened. Or what *almost* happened. Why was I so insistent on letting him think it was a dream? Why not tell him the truth? Because I knew it was a drunken tumble that was nothing to him but hormones and abandoned inhibitions, and I was willing to live with that small piece of physical attention from Lonny, tucked neatly away in my heart forever.

We checked out of the hotel and when we reached the car he tossed me the keys. "You mind driving?"

"Are you sure? I haven't driven in a long time."

"It's insured."

"Very funny."

We got settled in the car and he punched in our destination on his phone's GPS. "I'll probably fall asleep, so just listen to the voice."

"No map?" Living in the city, we didn't own a car; we took public transportation everywhere we needed to go. I had no idea how GPS worked.

He turned to face me, his eyes covered by his sunglasses, and chuckled. "Oh Roo… you have so much to learn."

Once we made it across the border back into New York, Lonny reclined his seat back as far as it would go and joked, "Last time I was that drunk I ended up with a daughter."

My heart shattered into pieces so tiny, I didn't think it could ever be mended. And I only had myself to blame.

1979

My job at the record store was a blessing and a curse. A blessing in that not only did I love my job, but I had first pick of any new albums, magazines, or posters that came in, but a curse in that people were constantly coming in just to ask me questions about Lonny. Since his *Creem* cover debut, people in our small town and the surrounding areas flocked to the store to find any information they could about him. Girls from miles away would come in giggling, asking if I knew where Lonny lived. I was becoming a local celebrity in my own right because people from school knew how close I was with Lonny, and they'd flippantly tell their college friends, "Oh Ruby knows him."

It was kind of cool at first, but it started becoming a drag because I didn't have a single day at work without someone asking me a million personal questions about Lonny. I loved talking about him, but people wanted to know personal things I wasn't willing to divulge. Things about his family life, or his love life, or things I just couldn't answer. It got to the point where Ricky and I had no idea if someone walking into the store was a paying customer, or a Lonny Lurker. We had fun with it though, calling the Lonny obsessed girls The Lonny Lurkers, Lurkers for short. I was amazed at how nobody paid any attention to Lonny at school, and now everyone wanted a piece of him.

I was disappointed when Lonny broke the news he wouldn't be able to come home for Thanksgiving. We were all hoping he'd be able to spend the holiday with us, but it wasn't to be. They were nearly finished with the album, spending every hour possible in the studio to have it complete for a Christmas release. He called me late Thanksgiving evening telling me about the nice dinner he had with Fuzzy and Marilyn and their families. I was happy that he really did have someone looking after him while he was there; when he left I was fearful he'd be wandering around alone in L.A. being taken advantage of by everyone looking for fresh meat. Fuzzy had no idea how thankful I was to him and Marilyn for showing him the ropes, and keeping him safe.

Lonny sounded down, which worried me. "Are you okay?"

"I'm just tired," he said. "I'm loving this, but it's exhausting. And I was really hoping to come home for Thanksgiving."

"We missed you," I replied. "But we understand. Just think... the new album will be out soon, and I'll be the first one in town to buy it!"

He laughed. "The tour starts in March. That's the part I'm worried about; playing live in front of all those people."

I assured Lonny that he would be dynamite and he had nothing to worry about. I reminded him that he got the job because he was such a phenomenal guitar player, and that the band threatened to break up if Howard didn't fire the Joey Buckingham guy and hire Lonny. How many established rock bands threaten to break up if they don't get the inexperienced, eighteen-year-old guitar player they want from the midwest? Apparently this one, and they got their way.

"And Lonny, when you play in Chicago I'll be able to see you!"

"Do you think my mom will come?"

"I'm sure she will. My parents want to."

"I'm really scared."

"Remember how scared you were to do the audition? Then go to L.A.? You survived all of that and you're loving it. You're gonna love this, too."

"I wish you were here," he said with a sigh. "I miss your laugh."

"I miss your face," I laughed. "But if you keep showing up in all these magazines, I'll be able to wallpaper my bedroom!"

He laughed so hard I thought he hurt himself. "We've been doing a lot of interviews, and a lot of photo shoots, so be prepared."

"The Lonny Lurkers will be happy to hear that," I teased.

I explained who the Lonny Lurkers were, and he couldn't believe girls were coming into the store on a regular basis asking about him. I informed him that he was quite the popular subject in town, and he seemed embarrassed. I told him he better get over that quick, because if his *Creem* debut was any indication, he was going to be quite famous, and soon.

128

I hung up with Lonny, thinking of how drastically our lives had changed in just a few months. Lonny's poor mother had no idea how to handle her son's new local fame; once girls found out where he lived, they were constantly ringing her doorbell and bothering her. It got to the point where she wouldn't answer the door most of the time. I felt terrible for her, having to deal with this all alone. She was fragile to begin with, and I worried this would push her over the edge.

I went to work the next day excited about the new Livingston Monroe album that would be coming out, and getting my hands on it before anyone else in town could. I couldn't wait to lose myself in the new music knowing Lonny was part of making it, and seeing what the album cover would look like. I couldn't wait for the tour to be announced so I would know exactly when I would be seeing Lonny again, even if it was only from a distance as a member of the audience.

I was just coming out of the back room when I saw Billy walk into the store. My heart jumped and my stomach fell. I ran back into the office where Ricky was having a smoke break.

"Please go out front," I begged. "My ex-boyfriend is out there and I don't want to see him."

Ricky smashed out his cigarette and headed into the store, no questions asked. I could hear them talking, but I couldn't tell if Billy had seen me or not. I was hoping he'd think I wasn't there and leave, but no such luck.

"I just want to see Ruby," he said.

"She's not here right now," Ricky told him.

"I'll just hang out until she comes back."

It wasn't Ricky's fault Billy was such a jerk. I swallowed my nerves and walked back into the store.

"Hey Ruby," Billy said. "Can I talk to you?"

As much as I hated Billy, I was one of those people who couldn't find it in me to be rude. "I don't have time," I replied. "I'm working."

Billy made it obvious he was looking around an empty store. "I'm the only one here."

Ricky nodded, letting me know I could talk to him if I wanted to. He went behind the counter and I walked to the back corner of the store with Billy.

"What are you doing home?" I asked.

"Thanksgiving break. That's some news about Lonny, huh?"

I nodded and smiled, crossing my arms in front of my chest. "Can I help you find something?"

"Did you know Lonny auditioned for Livingston Monroe?"

"Since when are you so interested in Lonny?"

"Just trying to make conversation," he answered.

"Of course I knew," I conceded. "I went with him to the audition."

Billy looked surprised. "How have you been?"

"I really have to get back to work. Lots of boxes in the back to unpack."

"Can we have lunch or something before I go back to school?"

I swallowed hard and said, "No, thank you."

"You look great."

I didn't respond, heading into the back room to calm my nerves. As much as I hated him and what he did to me, there was always an odd sort of yearning when it came to Billy. I attributed it to him being my first and only boyfriend, but it was something I certainly didn't understand. Or enjoy.

When I got off work all I could think of was going home to enjoy Thanksgiving leftovers for dinner, and hopefully talking to Lonny later on, but when I walked out of the store Billy's car was parked at the curb waiting for me. I pretended I didn't see him and started walking toward home, the opposite way he was facing. He got out and ran after me, standing in front of me to block my path.

"Will you have dinner with me tonight?" he asked.

"I'm really tired and I just want to go home."

"Can I give you a ride?"

"No, thank you."

I walked around him and kept going. I didn't want him to think I had any interest in him, which I didn't, but I also didn't want him to think he could persuade me otherwise.

130

He ran to catch up to me again, standing in front of me. "Ruby, I know I was an asshole. I know what I did was wrong, and I don't blame you for hating me. But I'm sorry. I'm really, really sorry I hurt you like that. I just wanted you to know that."

He seemed to be sincere, but with Billy it was always so hard to tell. And even if he was, I was through with him. I ignored him and kept walking. He finally gave up and went back to his car and drove off.

When I got home about twenty minutes later, my cheeks pink from the cool November air, Billy's car was in the driveway. Now I was angry. I stormed into the house and he was sitting in the living room with my parents! I tried to comprehend what they were thinking, inviting him inside when I wasn't even there. On top of that they knew I hated Billy, so why would they even let him in to wait for me?

"Why are you here?" I asked him.

"I just came by to say hello to your parents."

"I asked him to stay for dinner," my mother announced.

I felt like I had fallen down a rabbit hole and my parents were the ones holding me prisoner there. "I'm not hungry," I grumbled and ran upstairs to my room.

My mom was right behind me, closing the door when she entered. "Why are you being so rude?"

I was stunned. "Rude? Billy is a horrible person, and I don't want anything to do with him!"

"His mother is *dying*," she whispered.

I shook my head. "What? So what?"

"Just be nice to him while he's here. I'm not asking you to date him."

"But Mom, you don't—"

"You're living in my house, and you will do what I say."

I was shocked at my mother's insistence on the matter. "Mom, Billy—"

"Get downstairs. It won't kill you to miss one phone call from Lonny."

With that, she opened the door and went back downstairs. I stood in shock, seeing a side of my mother I'd never experienced before. If my parents had any idea what Billy did to me, they

131

would be singing a much different tune. Maybe it was time to tell them exactly why I wasn't dating him anymore.

I slumped down the stairs angrily, taking my seat at the dinner table. Billy was in the process of telling my parents that his mother's breast cancer had spread to other parts of her body, and she was giving up treatment. They had no idea how much time she had left, but she wanted to live it her way. I tried to imagine what my life would be like without my mother and even though I was angry with her, I didn't want to lose her.

"I'm sorry about your mom," I spoke quietly.

"You realize how important people are when you're waiting for someone to die. I've hurt a lot of people, and I'm trying to apologize to whoever I can. And Ruby, you're one of them."

I suddenly felt like the most horrible person on earth. I had no idea Billy's mom was dying, but did that mean I had to be nice to him? I suppose his apology could have been sincere; it seemed as though it was.

I spent dinner eating and listening to the rest of the conversation. I really didn't have anything to contribute, but my parents were all full of questions about college and Billy's sister Gina's first year of high school. Then I heard my phone ring, and I caught my mother glaring at me. Normally I would've shot right out of my chair and run upstairs to answer it, but this time I didn't dare move. Inside I was raging because I couldn't talk to Lonny, and I had no idea if he would be able to call me back later.

My mother offered up pumpkin pie after we were finished eating dinner, which Billy gladly accepted. A brilliant idea suddenly came to me, and I waited until the perfect moment.

As Billy put the last of the pie in his mouth, I said, "Mom, did Billy tell you why we broke up?" I smiled inside as his face paled.

My mom stared at me, wondering why I would even bring something like that up. I looked at her, then at my father, then back at Billy, who looked like he was getting ready to make a fast exit. No matter how much I wanted to humiliate him in front of my parents, I couldn't do it. I couldn't be that person. I would end up regretting that decision the rest of my life.

"He accused me of loving Lonny," I numbly explained. "And he was right."

Billy quickly thanked my parents for their hospitality and gave my mother a hug for asking him to stay for dinner. He practically ran out of the house and I followed him.

"If you come back here again," I warned, "I'll tell them what you did to me."

"You're so stupid," he laughed. "If you think Lonny cares anything about you… especially now that he's a rock star—"

"Shut up! I'm not in love with Lonny! I just said that because I couldn't tell them the truth."

"Why do you have to ruin everything?"

"I ruin everything!" My blood was boiling.

"All I wanted to do was apologize for what I did, and—"

"And stop calling me stupid!"

"Face it, Ruby… Lonny is big time now. You're small town trash, just like the rest of us."

I ran back into the house crying, slamming the door behind me and racing upstairs to my bedroom where I slammed that door, too. I thought my mom would be right behind me, but she didn't follow. As upset as I was with her, this made me feel worse. I sat on the floor next to my stereo, put on my headphones, and played the last album by Livingston Monroe, "Tide Is Turning." With tears streaming down my face, I lost myself in the music and shut out the rest of the world.

Billy's mother died three days later, with her husband and children at her side. My mother informed me of the news, and I did get a bit emotional as his mother was always kind to me. She was a good person, even though her son was a rat. I thought about my own mom and what it would be like to lose her; what it would mean for me and my father.

Ricky let me have the day off to attend the funeral, and I rode along with my parents, wringing my hands in the back of the car. Nobody likes funerals, but they made me incredibly uneasy since fainting at my grandpa Leonard's service five years earlier. He was the person I was closest to in my life, and when he died, part of me went with him. The stress of losing him caused me to hyperventilate during the service, which eventually led to me sliding off my chair onto the floor in a dead faint.

As soon as we entered the room where her funeral was taking place, I tried to sneak off to a chair in the back, but my mom grabbed my arm and gently pushed me toward the casket, where the family was being greeted by mourners. I was thankful the casket was closed, but I did not want to talk to Billy. I had no idea what to say, and even though he lost his mother, I still hated him. Her death changed nothing.

My mother and father greeted Mr. Downey with hugs and handshakes, and did the same with Billy and his sister. I stood behind my father chewing my fingernails, the anxiety rushing through my veins like fire threatening to burn me alive. I saw Billy, his face red with grief and stained with tears. The anguish he exhibited was almost too much for me to witness. I was about to turn and flee, but he saw me and started bawling. He pulled me into his arms and sobbed on my shoulder, gasping for breath as he did so. My arms hung awkwardly at my sides because I didn't want to touch him. I didn't want him to think anything had changed between us, that I still hated him as much as I did before his mother died.

A piece of my heart broke for him. I thought about how much I missed Lonny, and what it would feel like if I never saw him again, and I cried with Billy. When he finally pulled away from me, I followed my parents to the other side of the room and sat down. But my tears didn't stop there. I thought about Lonny living and working in L.A., meeting new people and probably lots of pretty girls. I thought about never seeing him again; I thought about how Billy said we were just small town trash to Lonny now and that he didn't care about me anymore. Tears stung my eyes as I tried to remain calm, but being in a funeral home nobody thought my behavior was strange. Not even my parents.

I was glad when the service was over and we were finally on our way home, but my mother informed me we would be heading over to the Downey house with food trays to continue the grieving process. I said nothing, knowing any protest would just cause problems for myself and I was having enough of those. We returned home to pick up the food trays, and just as we were about to head back out to the car I heard my phone ring. I stopped dead in my tracks and my mother glared at me. I fought hard with myself, trying to decide whether it was more important to talk to Lonny, or to respect my mother. My poor father was stuck in the middle, giving me a look of helplessness in trying to keep the peace.

I turned to run upstairs and my mother said, "Ruby Marie, let it go."

"But I haven't—"

"Get in the car," she insisted.

"All Billy's friends will be there. I went to the funeral, isn't that enough?"

"Get in the car," she said again.

I walked back to the car, silently raging at my mother who was slowly pushing Lonny and I further apart, whether she realized it or not. I didn't understand why she insisted I accompany her and my father to the events of the day. I was eighteen; I was an adult who could make her own decisions, but my mother still ruled my life.

I cried silently in the back of the car, simultaneously hating my mother and Billy. Then I cursed myself for not telling my parents the truth about what Billy did to me. If I wasn't so worried about upsetting everybody, I would have been home talking to Lonny right then, instead of being dragged to Billy's house where his friends would use me as their verbal punching bag.

We entered Billy's house carrying our food gifts, and it was already crowded with people. I didn't see Billy or any of his friends, but his sister Gina informed me they were all downstairs in the basement. I had no intention of going down there, so I tried to fade into the crowd and become invisible. I noticed Gina disappeared into her room, so I followed her.

"Are you okay?" I asked, poking my head through the door.

She shrugged as she sat on the floor next to her bed. "I'm just really tired right now."

I sat on the floor across from her. "It must be hard."

She burst into tears and I didn't know what to do. I had no idea how to comfort a fourteen year old girl who just lost her mother. I reached out and took her hand in mine, and we just sat

135

there as she cried. After several minutes she wiped the tears from her face and looked at me with a tired smile.

"Is it true you know Lonny?" she asked.

I smiled and nodded. "He's my best friend."

"He's so cute."

We both started giggling and I said, "He is, isn't he?"

I stayed in Gina's room for a good part of the day, comforting her, talking with her about high school, about boys, about Lonny. She was a sweet, innocent girl who was nothing like her brother. She didn't have very many friends and was thankful I was spending time with her. I understood exactly what she was going through and told her all about meeting Lonny for the first time, and how we were together every day until he left for L.A..

"Do you miss him?" Gina asked.

I didn't want to cry in front of her, as her heartache was so much more severe than mine, but I could feel the sting of tears in my eyes. "I miss him more than anything," I replied. "It's hard not being able to see him every day like I used to."

Billy barged into the room, looking surprised to see me there. "Dad wants you to come out and eat something. Hey Ruby." He left as quickly as he entered.

"Will you come with me?" Gina asked.

"Sure."

Gina and I walked out of her room together, into the kitchen where there was enough food to feed an army. Neither one of us was very hungry, but put some food on our plates and went into the living room where Billy and a few of his friends were eating. Gina looked uncomfortable, so I made sure we sat on the love seat together.

"It can't be!" I heard a familiar voice shout as he entered the room. "Ruby Winter!"

Seth Brown.

My stomach lurched forward, but I managed a smile as an acknowledgment.

"So Lonny, huh," Seth continued. "Looks like the twerp hit the big time."

I could see Gina clenching her teeth, guessing she wasn't a big fan of Seth's. Who could blame her?

I didn't say a word, pretending to eat something off my plate.

"Cat got your tongue, Ruby?" Seth continued.

"Nope," I said. "I just don't talk to assholes."

Everyone in the room started laughing hysterically. I don't know why I said it; I think it was to show Gina that she should never let anyone push her around. I spent my whole life being pushed around because I was too afraid to speak up for myself.

"You're still an ugly slut," Seth growled.

"You shut up Seth!" Gina yelled.

"Yeah," Billy chimed in quietly. "Shut up."

Seth just laughed, and way too loudly for such a sombre occasion.

I stood up and said, "Come on Gina," and she followed me out to the deck. It should have been cold on that November day, but temperatures hovered in the high sixties, and we both needed some fresh air.

"He's such a jerk!" Gina shouted.

"Want to go for a walk?"

Gina smiled and off we went. Just two teenage girls taking a walk, talking about teenage things, and what the future could possibly hold for us. Gina was a sweet girl and I was suddenly feeling very protective of her. I never spent much time at their house when Billy and I dated, so I never got to know her very well. He never wanted to stay home, so we would drive around or go see one of his friends. I was strongly regretting that, wishing we had developed a relationship while I was dating her brother.

When we returned to the house, Billy was sitting out on the deck waiting for us. "Can I talk to Ruby?" he asked Gina.

She went into the house and left us alone.

"Seth is such—"

"I don't wanna talk about him," I said.

"I'm sorry."

"It's not your fault."

"Thanks for coming today. It's been really hard."

I shrugged. "Thank my parents. They forced me to come."

He looked like I just stabbed him through the heart. "I know you hate me," he spoke softly. "And I don't blame you. I should never be forgiven for what I did."

"You got that right." I was feeling no mercy for Billy.

Billy burst into tears. "What am I gonna do without my mom?"

I didn't know how to answer him. Assuming it was a rhetorical question, I said nothing.

"I love you, Ruby," he cried.

"You don't love me," I replied bitterly. "You love controlling me."

"I'm sorry, Ruby. That's all I can say."

With that, he walked into the house and left me outside alone. I decided this was a good time to head home; I'd been there long enough, insulted one time too many, and was tired of Billy. I went into the house to tell my parents I was going to walk home and they didn't argue. I stuck my head into Gina's bedroom to tell her I was leaving.

She jumped off her bed to give me a hug and said, "I know my brother's a jerk, but all he ever talks about is you. It's kinda gross."

We both laughed loudly and I said, "I'll tell Lonny you said hello."

She was all smiles when I left.

By the time I got home, I was exhausted and headed straight for my bedroom. I fell on my bed face first and instantly fell asleep. I heard someone knocking on my door and tried to focus my eyes in the dark. My mom walked in and I could see her silhouette from the light in the hallway.

"There's someone here to see you," she said softly.

Still half asleep I groaned, but then I wondered if it might be Lonny coming home to surprise us. It was a bit early for Christmas, but maybe he would be staying home until they had to go on tour? I jumped off my bed and ran down the stairs, but when I reached the living room I saw Gina sitting there. Not wanting to disturb my parents and their television time, I led Gina into the kitchen where we sat at the table.

"Are you okay?" I asked.

"I wanted to give you something." She handed me a necklace made of yellow beads with a tiny heart charm hanging from it. "I made it for you."

I put it on, the heart falling right at the notch in my neck. "I love it, thank you."

"You're the only one who's ever been nice to me," she said.

"Your brother has some pretty jerky friends," I tried to joke. Seeing that it was already nine o'clock, I asked how she got to our house.

"Billy drove me. He's waiting for me outside."

"Did he put you up to this?" I asked.

"No, I swear! I begged him to bring me here, honest!"

I assured Gina that I believed her and thanked her for the gift once again. I walked her out to the car and went to the driver's side, where Billy rolled down his window.

I leaned over and whispered, "She's a good kid; tell your friends to be nice to her."

He laughed and promised he would take better care of her, especially now that their mother was gone. As I tried to straighten up, Billy put his hand behind my neck and pulled me toward him, kissing me quickly on the mouth. I jerked away from him and walked back to the house. He got out of the car and followed me, grabbing my hand before it reached the doorknob.

"I'm sorry Ruby," he said, anguish written all over his face. "I'm sorry. Please don't hate me, *please*."

"Billy, I don't—"

"I just buried my mom," he cried. "I don't know what to do."

"You'll figure it out," I replied. "It'll just take time."

"Please don't shut me out, Ruby. My friends are assholes, and you're a good person. You're good for *me*."

"No, Billy. Please leave me alone."

I tried to pull away from his grasp and go inside, but he stood there bawling. He looked so pathetic, but his emotions were raw and painful and there was no faking the devastation he was experiencing. He put a hand on my shoulder and wiped the tears from his face with his jacket sleeve.

139

"I love you," he whispered. "I swear to God it's true."

I stood there frozen as he inched closer to me. I wanted to run to my room and lock the door and be far away from where I stood, but something held me there. Billy leaned over and kissed my cheek, then kissed my mouth. I couldn't explain why I didn't pull away, but when I didn't, he took advantage of my brain lapse and kissed me longer. It felt so good to have someone giving me attention.

As quickly as it started it was over. He turned around, walked back to his car, and drove away. I went back into the house and got ready for bed; I just wanted this day to be over. I lay there crying, and for so many reasons. The main reason was that I hadn't spoken to Lonny in a week, and the two times that I knew he called, my mother prohibited me from answering the phone. Everything had changed and my whole world was crashing down around me. My mother's relentless attempts at keeping me from Lonny and pushing me toward Billy made no sense, and it was causing my relationship with her to crumble. I had always respected and admired my parents; they were my heroes. Never before had things been this strained. My father was stuck in the middle, usually staying out of the arguments I had with my mother, but I saw the way he looked at me. He was on her side, he just wouldn't voice it in front of me. But what *was* her side? What was her problem with me? Why all of a sudden couldn't I do anything right?

I heard a knock on my door and my mom entered. I turned to face the wall, making it known I wasn't speaking to her. She sat on my bed and put her hand on my arm.

"Honey, there's something you need to know."

My heart jumped into my throat. Was my mother going to tell me she was dying now?

"Lonny has a girlfriend," she said.

I whipped around to face her, even though all I could see was her shadow. "Who told you that?" I demanded.

"His mom."

"When did she tell you that?"

"A few weeks ago."

I turned my back on her again, facing the wall. This time so she wouldn't see the tears I couldn't hold back.

"Honey, I just want you to have your own life," my mom said. "I don't want you pining for a boy that may never come back. Especially if he doesn't have the same feelings you do."

She kissed my head and left, closing the door behind her. I buried my face in my pillow as the sobs choked me. My mother knew Lonny had a girlfriend for all this time and never told me. For that matter, why didn't his mother tell me? It certainly explained my mother's odd behavior. So that was it then. Lonny had a girlfriend.

I thought about Billy kissing me earlier and gagged. Everything was going so horribly wrong I couldn't think straight. I cried so hard for so long, I eventually ended up running to the bathroom to vomit. When I finished I brushed my teeth, watching myself in the mirror as I did so. I knew then that Lonny would never have the same feelings for me that I had for him. My face was ugly and covered in freckles and I barely had any boobs. I thought about Billy kissing me again and used my toothbrush to scrub my lips raw. I scrubbed as hard as I could until I made them bleed. I had a headache from all the crying I'd done and took a few aspirin before heading back to bed.

I pulled the covers over my head and continued to sob, my entire body shaking from spasms caused by my uncontrollable tears. Life as I knew it was over, and I didn't care if I ever got out of bed again.

My phone rang. I almost didn't answer it, but after the fourth ring I picked it up. "Hello?" I was so numb I didn't answer in my usual excited, "Lonny!"

"Roo? Is that you?"

"Yeah."

"Are you okay?"

I never wanted Lonny to know I was upset or had been crying when I talked to him. I never wanted him to feel bad about me, or feel guilty about leaving. This time, I didn't care. He had a girlfriend, so what difference did it make?

I told him about Billy's mom dying, and the funeral, but I never filled in any details. I explained that I wasn't feeling very

141

well, that I had a headache. So I listened while he talked about the album coming out the week before Christmas, about how he and Fuzzy had been writing all kinds of new music together, and other things I wasn't really paying attention to. I was trying so hard not to let him hear me crying that I didn't say much in return.

At one point I just wanted to hang up the phone, but instead interrupted with, "Are you coming home for Christmas?"

He hesitated before saying, "No." A gasp caught in my throat, but I said nothing. "We're in such a writing groove, we don't want to lose it."

"I thought the album was finished." I didn't understand how the whole business worked.

"This is for the next album."

When was he going to tell me about his girlfriend? Or was he just going to hide it from me forever? I didn't want to talk to Lonny anymore. I told him I had to go, and quickly hung up the phone. He called right back.

"Roo, what's the matter?"

"Nothing," I lied.

"I don't believe you."

"Everything's great," I said, holding back my tears. "Honest."

"Roo...."

"Honest Lonny, but I have to go. I just... I have to go."

I hung up and he didn't call back.

The next morning was robotic and routine for me, getting up and taking a shower, then eating breakfast and walking to work. I didn't sleep much the night before, spending most of it crying and thinking about Lonny having a girlfriend he wouldn't tell me about. My swollen eyes gave me away, but my mom said nothing and Ricky didn't ask.

Ricky had the local Chicago rock radio station playing overhead in the store, and we both froze when we heard the disc jockey announce they were going to be playing the world premiere of Livingston Monroe's new song, "Just Say Yes" after the next commercial break. My heart raced like a train, knowing I was finally going to hear what Lonny had been working on all this time. I couldn't contain my excitement, pacing back and forth until the song started with its opening drum beat, followed by a guitar riff that sent shivers to my soul. Ricky and I were silent as the song played, both with smiles a mile wide plastered on our faces.

When the song ended the disc jockey said, "And that's the new single by Livingston Monroe, with their new guitarist, Lonny Winter. The kid is only eighteen, and... dare I say it... better than Hendrix? Let's open the phone lines and see what you think about the new song!"

I didn't realize I was holding in a squeal until Ricky said, "Let it out! Let it go!"

I screamed loudly, jumping up and down for several seconds until I heard the bell sound as someone entered the store. I pulled myself together and the woman asked if I was Ruby Winter, to which I said yes. She reached out and shook my hand, introducing herself as Theresa Brooks, a reporter for a local Chicago newspaper. She wanted to interview me about Lonny and gave me her card so I could call her when I was ready. She said she'd love to interview Lonny's mother as well, if I could set that up. She left quickly and I stared wide-eyed at Ricky, but Theresa immediately took a backseat as callers to the radio station were beginning to voice their opinions about the new Livingston Monroe song.

Overall, listeners were more than excited about the new song, some saying it was the best thing they've produced in years, others saying they didn't believe Lonny was only eighteen because he played like a seasoned veteran. One guy said he was a wannabe hack, and the disc jockey quickly put him in his place, explaining how he was the genuine article and he had never heard *anyone* play like Lonny in all his years in the music business.

I was floating on air the rest of the day, so happy for Lonny and excited that people were loving the new song. I couldn't wait until the album was released so I could sit in my room with my headphones on and listen to it over and over again, knowing that was *my* Lonny playing guitar. It didn't matter if Lonny had a girlfriend in L.A., he was still *my* Lonny. I just wished he'd be upfront and honest and tell me about her.

Later that afternoon when school let out Gina visited me at the store, absolutely giddy about hearing the new Livingston

Monroe song on the radio. I was a bit surprised when Billy followed her in, but he shrugged his shoulders and pointed at his sister, letting me know it wasn't his idea. Gina flitted around the store, looking at albums and posters and magazines, off in her own little world. It was nice to see her smiling, considering they just buried their mother the day before.

Billy whispered, "So my sister is in love with Lonny. Go figure." He laughed and I smiled in response.

"Isn't everybody?" I teased.

"Thanks for yesterday... hanging out with Gina."

I shrugged and waved him off, uncomfortable with his praise.

"Ruby," Gina called. "Will you save Lonny's album for me when it comes out? I've been saving my babysitting money and I don't wanna miss it!"

I promised I would save her a copy, and she smiled and clapped happily. Billy urged Gina to move along, that she had homework to do, and she reluctantly met him at the front of the store. Billy asked if I needed a ride home, but I told him I had two hours left of work. He smiled and led Gina out the door. I was impressed that Billy seemed to be taking care of his sister, taking more of an interest in her as a person than the bother he always made her out to be in the past.

I clocked out and when I left work, Billy was parked at the curb in front of the store. He rolled down the passenger side window and said, "It's cold, and it's dark... let me give you a ride."

I wasn't afraid of walking home in the dark, but it was bitterly cold and I gladly accepted his offer. Neither one of us said anything during the fairly short ride, and I was thankful for the heat of his car. The best part of the ride was several blocks from my house, the new Livingston Monroe song came on the radio and my heart swelled. I was so incredibly proud of Lonny.

Billy pulled into my driveway and I didn't even wait for the song to finish, opening the door to exit quickly. I thanked him for the ride, and he left without another word. I thought it was strange that he didn't try something... ask me to dinner, try to kiss me... but I was grateful. I didn't want to end up in that position again. I ran into the house talking, telling my parents how I heard Lonny's new song, that they played it on the radio all day long, and how everybody just loved it. My parents smiled, as they were happy for Lonny, but I could tell my mother was looking at me with sadness in her eyes.

I was going to pull some leftovers out of the fridge for dinner, but heard my phone ringing. I ran upstairs two at a time and answered on the third ring. My mother had no excuse to keep me from talking to Lonny this time.

"Lonny the song is out of this world!" I screamed into the receiver.

He laughed loudly... oh how I missed his laugh and his smile... "Thanks, Roo!"

"They played it on the radio all day long," I told him. "Everyone loves it! And some reporter came into the store today... she wants to interview me about you!"

"Wow, that's great."

"Why would she want to interview me?" I honestly didn't understand.

"She probably found out how close we are and thinks she can get a juicy story."

"But I have no juice!"

We both laughed hysterically for several minutes before Lonny said, "I miss you."

This melted my heart. "I miss you, too. Which is why you should come home for Christmas." It was the perfect opportunity to try convincing him.

"Yeah, that's not gonna happen. I'm sorry."

I was deflated, but I understood. Lonny asked about my parents, about my job, and about whether his mother was really doing as well as she made it sound in their conversations. I assured him that she was having a rough time without him, but it was getting easier for her, and how me and my parents were always looking out for her. We made sure she was never lonely, and I spent as much time with her as I did with my own parents. He seemed relieved, but in a guilty way. What I didn't understand was if he felt so guilty leaving his mother, why didn't he want to come and visit for Christmas? I wasn't going to go there again.

145

"Billy's sister Gina is crazy over you," I changed the subject. "I told her I would say hello to you for her."

"Billy's sister?" I could tell by the change in his tone that he wasn't happy.

"I spent a lot of time with her yesterday after the funeral. She's a freshman this year... pretty shy and awkward. Reminds me a lot of myself."

"Tell her I said hi."

"She's been saving her babysitting money for the new album. She's a good kid."

"And Billy?"

"What about Billy?"

I could hear him lighting a cigarette. "Are you staying away from him?"

"I'm trying. It's hard when my mom keeps pushing him in my face."

"What does that mean?"

I cursed myself for opening that can of worms. I should never have said anything, but I couldn't take it back now. I explained how Billy showed up at the house the night after Thanksgiving and my mom asked him to stay for dinner. I assured him it was because Billy's mother was dying and she felt sorry for him. Then I told him about how I didn't want to go to the funeral, or to his house afterward, but my mom forced me to do that as well.

"Does your mom *like* him?" he asked.

"I think she just feels bad for him."

"Stay away from him."

"Lonny, it's not like I'm out looking for him. He just keeps showing up."

"What does *that* mean?" He was angry again.

"Nothing. I don't wanna talk about Billy, okay?"

"Roo, are you going out with him?"

"No!" I shouted.

"Don't lie to me."

Who was Lonny to lecture me about telling the truth? He had a girlfriend that he still hadn't mentioned, but he was grilling me about Billy?

146

"Lonny, what about you? Are you telling me the truth about everything? Anything you're not telling me?"

"Why are you acting like a jealous girlfriend?"

I felt like Lonny had just punched me in the gut, and it took me a moment to catch my breath. "What did you say?"

"Nothing. Forget it."

"I'm acting like a jealous girlfriend?" I threw back at him. "You're the one getting all pissed off about Billy."

"I'm just trying to protect you from that asshole!" Lonny rarely raised his voice, but when he did it got my attention.

"Well you're not here, are you? You can't protect me from anything."

"Roo, I'm sorr——"

"At least Billy isn't afraid to say how he feels about me!"

"What did he say?"

I instantly regretted our entire conversation. "Nothing."

"Roo, what did he say?"

I was quiet, chewing on my knuckle. "He said he loved me," I whispered.

"He always says that!"

"He's different now, Lonny. Since his mom died... he's changed."

"Are you fucking serious!" Lonny was furious, and I can't say I blamed him. "How can you be so stupid?"

That was the last straw. I was making an observation; I never said I wanted to go out with Billy! "Don't you *ever* call me stupid again."

"Roo, I'm sorry, I didn't mean it like that."

I nearly choked on the words I spoke next. "And don't you *ever* call me again." I slammed down the phone and burst into tears. My world had officially come to a screeching halt. My phone rang and I picked up the receiver, slamming it down over and over again before hanging up and unplugging it from the wall. I never wanted to speak to Lonny again.

2011

I had been driving for about two hours when we crossed the border into Pennsylvania. In need of fuel, I pulled into a rest stop and parked the car at a gas pump. I gently poked Lonny to wake him up, asking if he could pump the gas while I went to the bathroom. When I came back outside, he had moved the car to a parking space and was sitting on top of a picnic table nearby. I sat next to him and he handed me a can of soda and a bag of chips.

"How you feeling?" I asked with a grin.

He lowered his head and peeked out over his sunglasses. "Hungover."

"Why would you stay in a hotel with a casino?"

Lonny popped a chip in his mouth and chewed slowly, staring straight ahead. He wiped some crumbs off his pant leg and shrugged. "It was the hotel with the best view of the Falls."

"So what? We went down *into* the Falls... you can't get a better view than that."

"Roo, I'm just trying to give you everything you deserve."

"By putting yourself at risk?" I didn't understand what he was trying to prove. "Being with you is enough."

Lonny stretched out on his back and lay his head on my lap. I couldn't see his eyes through the sunglasses, and he couldn't see through mine either, and for the moment I was glad. My eyes were fixed on his mouth, where I so badly wanted to kiss him.

"Roo," he said, licking his lips. "I want you to experience great adventures, good food, nice hotels... and yeah, the perfect view. We missed out on so much being apart, I guess I'm trying to make up for it. I should have never left you behind."

I didn't know what to say. I ran my fingers through his soft hair, pulling it away from his face. I noticed a few strands of gray, but even after the life he had, Lonny still looked youthful.

"Why didn't you ever get married?" I asked, finger combing his hair.

He blew air out of his mouth, then laughed. "No matter who I was with, there was always something missing."

"But you were with Veronica for a long time."

148

"Five years. And last year she finally kicked me out because I wouldn't marry her."

"I didn't know that."

"You can love someone without being *in* love with them. Does that make sense? I've always felt that if you weren't crazy in love with someone, you shouldn't marry them."

I continued to finger comb his hair, something I knew he loved from the time we were teenagers. I would always do it when we were watching television, and it started because I needed something to do with my hands. I could have taken up knitting or something, but I chose to play with Lonny's hair. It was much more enjoyable for me.

"What do you think crazy in love is?" I had to know.

He grinned. "Well to *me,* crazy in love means you can't imagine living without the other person. You feel like you would just stop breathing if they were gone, because they're part of your heart and soul; the very fiber of your being. The women I've had relationships with, I could always imagine my life without them."

I felt myself getting choked up, and covered my mouth with my hand. "You should write a song about that."

"I did. 'Love In Slow Motion.'"

It was one of Livingston Monroe's biggest selling hits, and one of the most covered songs in music history. Not only did Lonny sing lead vocals, he was the sole songwriter, and royalties rolled in on a daily basis.

I pretended I had a leg cramp and gently pushed him off me so I could stand up. I limped around, acting like I was trying to work it out. The truth of the matter was that I got choked up every time I heard "Love In Slow Motion" and now hearing Lonny's backstory on what it was about made it even worse. I told him I had to go to the bathroom again and walked away, tears burning my eyes. I knew I didn't love Billy when I married him. I knew I was settling because I didn't see a future for myself, and my mother made it clear I had no skills and needed to be taken care of. But I did know what crazy in love was, according to Lonny's definition. I knew what it was to feel like I'd never breathe again because Lonny wasn't there. I was crazy in love all by myself; the loneliest place a person could ever be.

149

When I returned to the car, Lonny was in the driver's seat. "You sure you're okay to drive?"

"I'm fine," he said with a grin.

"I noticed on the GPS we were headed to Mill Run. What's in Mill Run?"

"Fallingwater."

I couldn't believe Lonny remembered how much I loved Frank Lloyd Wright, and had always dreamed of visiting one of his historic homes. I squealed with excitement, kissed him on the cheek and buckled my seat belt.

Lonny scrolled through his phone and started the music. As he pulled out of the rest stop, "Find Your Way Back," by Jefferson Starship was playing. Lonny had done a really great job with our road trip playlist, finding songs we both loved and I had nearly forgotten about.

"Leave a message with the rain," Lonny sang.

He knew I couldn't sing, but I especially couldn't reach the high notes like Mickey Thomas. We both laughed as I screeched out, "You can find me where the wind blows!"

1979

I hadn't spoken to Lonny in over a week, never plugging my phone back into the wall. I was so angry with him for calling me stupid, I didn't care if I ever saw him again. He tried calling my parents' phone, but I would take the receiver and immediately hang it up. My parents never asked why I had such a sudden change of heart where Lonny was concerned, and I didn't volunteer any information.

On Friday night after work I walked out of the store to find Billy waiting in his car at the curb. He rolled down the passenger side window and said, "It's cold. Want a ride?"

I thanked him as I got in and closed the door. "Want to go grab some dinner?" he asked.

"Sorry, I already have plans."

He was visibly shocked. "With who?"

"I spend Friday nights with Joanie."

"Who?"

"Lonny's mom."

"Why?" he chuckled.

I gave him the side eye and replied, "Because she's my mom, too."

He raised his hands in concession and said, "Okay, that's cool. I'll drop you off there, then."

"Thank you."

During the drive I asked how Gina was doing, and Billy told me she was struggling in school. He said the only time she wasn't crying about their mom was when she talked about me, or Lonny. She listened to the Livingston Monroe single "Just Say Yes," so often he was afraid she'd wear the grooves out of the record.

"Tell her she can come and see me anytime," I told him.

"She'd like that."

As he pulled up to Joanie's house, I asked, "When are you going back to school?"

"After Christmas break. Hey listen... would you want to catch a movie?"

"Billy, I'm not—"

"Look, I know you love Lonny but—"

"I do *not* love Lonny," I grumbled.

"Okay whatever, can I take you to the movies or something?"

"Sorry, Billy, I'm just not interested."

I thanked him for the ride and got out quickly, walking to the front door and letting myself in with the key. It was eight o'clock, so Joanie was already sitting in the dark in her recliner and had been drinking for about two hours. I could smell the whiskey as soon as I walked in the door.

"Hi Mom," I sang, leaning over and kissing her on the cheek. "Want me to order the pizza now?"

"Hello my beautiful girl," she slurred. "Yes, please." I threw my coat and purse on a dining room chair and asked if she'd heard from Lonny. "He kept telling me you won't talk to him, but I know that can't be true."

I picked up the phone and ordered our Friday usual, a large pepperoni pizza with garlic and extra cheese. I sat on the couch and tried to figure out how to respond to her comment. I knew she wouldn't remember anything I said, but I didn't want to upset her.

"What else did Lonny say?" I asked instead.

"The record comes out next week and he's really excited. You're going to save me a copy, right?"

"Yes, Mom, of course."

"Something's wrong with Lonny," she said, her head lolling back and forth. "I'm worried about him."

"Why? What happened?"

"He doesn't… he just… he doesn't sound like my boy."

"He's got a lot going on, Mom. He's probably just nervous about the record coming out, and then the tour."

"Did he tell you that?"

"Yeah. I'm sure he's fine."

"Turn on that island show," she said.

I giggled and changed the channel so we could watch *Fantasy Island* together. It was the same routine every Friday, and I now understood what Lonny went through with his mother on a daily basis. She was exhausting when she was drunk.

152

I paid for the pizza and went into the kitchen to dish it up on plates. I returned to the living room and turned on the light, which she scolded me for, then yelled at me for trying to make her eat.

"Mom, you have to eat something or you'll get sick." It was really pointless trying to reason with a drunk person.

"I'm not hungry," she growled.

"I'm going to tell Lonny you're not taking care of yourself," I threatened.

"Okay okay." She looked at me through slits for eyes and ate one pie-shaped piece of pizza, then two more. Typically when she refused to eat, she ended up vomiting all night long and I was satisfied that wouldn't happen this night.

"Mom, would it be okay if I slept in Lonny's room tonight?"

"Oh sure, sure, of course."

As per our usual Friday night, Joanie was passed out drunk by eleven o'clock, which left me to watch *The Midnight Special* without interruption. I covered her with a blanket, brought her empty whiskey glass into the kitchen, and got comfortable on the couch. The Village People were hosting *The Midnight Special* that night, and the Little River Band was one of the bands performing on the show. My chest tightened, remembering how Lonny and I danced to "Lady" at prom, but when the show was over, they never played that song. They did play "Cool Change," which was my favorite song of theirs, and I cried until I had no tears left to shed.

Normally I slept on the couch so I could be close by if Joanie needed me for anything, but I really needed a personal connection to Lonny. I turned off the television and made my way to his bedroom, which looked exactly as we left it the day he flew to L.A.. I knew his mother changed the bedding every Friday morning before she left for work, in the hopes that Lonny would surprise her with a visit and he would have clean sheets. I crawled into his bed and buried my face in his pillow, which still smelled like him. I didn't have a chance to get comfortable, however, as the phone started ringing.

Lonny knew I spent Friday nights with his mom, and even though I knew the phone wouldn't wake her, I rushed into the

153

living room to answer it. I held the receiver to my ear, but said nothing.

"Roo, please don't hang up," Lonny begged.

I hung up and went back to his bed where I cried myself to sleep.

The following week was a blur. Between my job, taking care of Lonny's mom, and offering to help Gina with her schoolwork, I barely knew which end was up. The day the Livingston Monroe album was released, there was a line several blocks long before we even opened the store. We were prepared for an onslaught of people, but had no idea fans from neighboring towns would come to our store to purchase the album simply because it was where Lonny frequented when he lived there.

Ricky and I stayed well after closing the night before to open all the boxes and set up the album display. He held back his copy, and I held back three — my own, Gina's, and Joanie's. They, along with the free poster that came with every album, were secured in a locker in the back office just to be safe. Ricky wondered what it might be like to have Livingston Monroe come to his store to do a record signing. Seeing the line stretching for blocks as we got to work, we knew it would probably be mayhem.

Ricky and I took turns manning the cash register, while the other handed out the albums and the free poster that went with it. The album played over the speakers, but there was so much chatter and excitement in the store, nobody could really hear it. I did notice at one point, however, Theresa Brooks milling about the store taking notes, while a male companion took photographs. I never did call her back, so angry with Lonny I was afraid to talk to anyone about him, especially a reporter. She never did talk to me that day, doing whatever she came to do and leaving without a word.

We sold out of all the albums we had, and there were a lot of disappointed girls leaving the store in tears. Girls whose parents let them skip school in order to stand in line for hours. I was astounded by their level of anguish over not getting a copy of the album. Livingston Monroe fans were generally men and women in their twenties and older, not typically girls in junior high and high school. Were they truly huge Livingston Monroe fans, or was it all over Lonny?

As I put my coat on to leave work, all I wanted to do was go home and lose myself in the new album and talk to Lonny about it, but I was still so angry with him. I was tired of being called stupid and when it came from him, it hurt more than anything else in the world. I grabbed my bag of albums, said goodnight to Ricky and headed out the door.

It was so cold, and it started to snow. I used to love watching the snow fall, but that was when I had a full, warm heart. Now it just made me sad. I clutched the bag of records tightly, afraid I would drop them and they'd shatter. I held it so tightly I lost feeling in my fingers. I was halfway home when Billy pulled up alongside me, offering me a ride. I gladly accepted, unable to feel my feet.

"Big Livingston Monroe day, huh?" he asked.

"Huge! We had to turn people away. Middle school girls were crying because they didn't get their copy today."

"It's all Gina's been talking about."

"I have her copy right here. Tell her it's an early Christmas present from me."

"You didn't have to do that."

"I know I didn't. I wanted to."

"You hungry?"

I hesitated, then said, "Yeah, actually I am."

Billy's face lit up, surprised that I finally agreed to have dinner with him after being shot down so many times. I couldn't believe it myself but I was tired, heartbroken over Lonny, and very lonely.

After eating at the local burger joint Billy drove me home, parking in the driveway. "Thanks for dinner," I said, pulling Gina's album and poster out of the bag and setting it on the seat beside me.

"Thanks for finally letting me take you out," he chuckled.

I suddenly felt awkward. "Thanks again," I said, getting out of the car and rushing to the door.

Billy got out of the car and followed me, reaching for my coat sleeve and turning me around before I opened the door. I

155

could see his breath in the cold air, waiting for what he was going to say or do.

"Can I see you again?" he asked.

"You see me almost every day," I joked.

"I mean... on a date?"

"I don't know, Billy, I just—"

He didn't let me finish, pulling me closer to him by my coat sleeves and pressing his mouth against mine. It was all lips and tongues and it left me weak in the knees and so very confused.

He pulled away and said, "Think about it." I watched as he walked back to his car and drove off. I stood there for a few minutes cursing myself for letting him kiss me.

I walked into the house and my mom said, "You're later than usual."

"I went out to dinner with Billy."

My mom and dad smiled. I'm not sure why, but it upset me. It seemed as though they'd been pulling for Billy all along, not caring at all about my feelings. I ran upstairs to my room, changed into my pajamas and sat on the floor next to my stereo. I tore off the plastic wrapping from the album and slowly slid the record out of its protective paper sleeve, careful only to handle it with my fingertips at the edge. I placed it on side one, put on my headphones and set the needle down to play.

I don't remember how many times I listened to the album that night, but it was many, over and over again, listening to Lonny wailing on guitar the first time through, then listening for his background vocals, then the album as a whole. Over and over I listened, over and over I flipped from side two back to side one, never getting enough of the masterpiece they had produced. And over and over again I cried, for the beauty of the music Lonny was part of, for missing Lonny so badly, and for letting Billy kiss me.

The album cover was interesting — a guitar amp that was on fire, with the flames spelling out the name of the album, "Fire In The Sky," and the band's name made to look like the amplifier brand logo, melting from the heat. It was cool, but I spent my time staring at the photo on the back of the album, where all four band members were silhouetted in their own picture frame from the shoulders up, each dressed in snazzy black suits. None of them

156

were smiling, of course, trying to look like the serious musicians they were. And Lonny was *hot*. The look on his face could only be described as what I'd always heard of as that "come hither look," which I never understood until seeing that photo of him. I traced his photo with my fingertip, wondering what he was doing at that very moment. Was he celebrating the release of the new album with his bandmates? Was he celebrating with his girlfriend? Was he thinking of me at all?

I carefully removed the album from my turntable and slid it lovingly back into the paper sleeve, which I turned upside down before placing it back in the album cover. I didn't want to risk it ever falling out and getting scratched, or worse yet, broken. I crawled into my bed and stared at the ceiling in the dark, shadows of the tree branches near my window dancing in time to the wind blowing outside. I suddenly became so overcome with emotion, I jumped out of bed and plugged my phone back in, hoping and praying it would ring. It never did.

2011

Lonny and I were switching off the male and female vocals on Roxette's "Dressed For Success," when I felt my phone buzz in my back pocket. I ignored it.

"Whatcha gonna tell your brother?" Lonny sang.

"Oh oh oh."

"Whatcha gonna tell your father?"

"I don't know!"

"Whatcha gonna tell your mother?"

"Let me go...."

I loved that Lonny enjoyed singing with me, even though I couldn't hold a tune to save my life. He always got a kick out of it, and never made me feel bad that he sang like an angel and I just ruined everything we sang together.

My phone buzzed again and I decided to see what it was all about. I rarely got calls or text messages, but maybe one of my parents was trying to get in touch with me. I hadn't talked to either of them in some time. I pulled my phone out of my back pocket and stared at it in disbelief.

Billy: WTF?!

My heart raced in panic, having no idea why he would be sending me a message like that. I didn't say anything to Lonny, listening to him sing his heart out to George Harrison's "What Is Life." And oh how I loved listening to him sing.

My phone buzzed again and I saw that Billy had sent me some photos. My hands trembled as I opened the message to get a clearer view of what he sent me. There was a photo of Lonny and I on the boat at the base of the Falls, hugging each other with huge smiles on our faces. Across the bottom of the photo were the words, "Thanks, asshole!" and a smiley face. The second picture was a photo of me laughing hysterically with my mouth wide open and my eyes squeezed shut, with Lonny sticking his tongue in my ear. I could feel a lump in my throat, trying to figure out where Billy would have gotten such pictures.

"Lonny, you need to pull over."

"What?"

"I need you to pull over. Now, please!" I couldn't breathe and my chest felt heavy.

Lonny pulled off at the next exit and parked in the empty lot of an abandoned restaurant. "What's wrong?" I handed him my phone and he read Billy's message. Then he slid his sunglasses on top of his head to *really* look at the message. He didn't say anything for a long time, then asked, "Did you send him these?"

"No! You took all the photos on the boat! And when did you take that other picture?" I could feel myself getting hysterical.

Lonny grabbed his phone and looked at his text messages. "Well I didn't text him. I don't even know his number."

"Lonny, how did he get those photos?" I was frantic.

I watched as Lonny poked at his phone, scrolled, poked some more. Then a grin slowly crept across his face. And then he began laughing loudly, having to get out of the car so he could double himself over in hysterics. He walked back to the car and handed me his phone, where I saw an email he sent to Billy through his tattoo shop's website the night before. He must have done it when he was plastered, because neither one of us remembered it.

I got out of the car and paced frantically, asking Lonny why he would do such a thing.

"I guess I thought it would be funny," he replied. "And it was!" He continued laughing hysterically, trying to control himself but failing. He wiped the tears from his eyes, but continued laughing.

"It's not funny," I scolded. "Now he thinks——"

"Who cares what he thinks, Roo?"

"But he's furious!"

"I don't understand the problem."

"Lonny! He thinks we're *together*."

"Again, so what? He's the piece of shit who cheated on you and took off with another woman. Never mind the fact he left you with *nothing*. You're acting like you cheated on *him* last night. Why can't you see the humor in this?"

I continued pacing frantically. "I can't believe you did that," I growled. "Why would you do that?"

"Get in the car," Lonny demanded.

"What?"

"Get in the car. I'm not going to have this argument with you."

"You just don't get it!" I yelled. "Billy always knew... I mean... Billy always thought I had a thing for you."

Lonny got back in the car and started the engine. "Get in now, or I'm leaving without you." He plugged his phone back into the car and put his sunglasses on.

I got in and buckled my seatbelt and he took off quickly, spraying rocks behind him. As he drove I looked at Billy's text again, staring at the photos Lonny sent him. He was thanking Billy for letting me go; thanking him for the time we could now spend together. And we looked gloriously happy in the photos. I can't remember the last time I was that happy. I suddenly realized how ridiculous I was being and started to giggle. My giggling turned into hard laughter as I began to understand why Lonny thought the whole thing was so funny. Billy was always jealous of Lonny, knowing how I truly felt about him, and now he was furious because he thought I finally "got" him. It didn't matter that Billy no longer wanted me, but it pissed him off to think Lonny did. Once I realized the true humor in what Lonny did, I couldn't stop laughing. I was doubled over with my face in my lap from laughing so hard. It didn't take long before Lonny was laughing with me and all was forgiven.

1979

I held out hope that Lonny was going to surprise us and come home for Christmas, but he didn't. I spent most of the morning crying in my bed before getting up to join my parents and open presents. Even after plugging my phone back in, I never heard from him again. And he stopped calling my parents' line as well. We were all disappointed, but his mother had a really hard time with it. She started drinking as soon as she got up Christmas morning and my dad had to pick her up and bring her to our house for dinner, because she was in no shape to drive. She was falling asleep at the table as we ate, and my heart broke for her. Before we even had dessert, I walked her to the couch and set her down for the night, covering her with a blanket and a kiss on the forehead.

We were watching *It's A Wonderful Life* on television when the phone in the kitchen rang. I raced to answer it, only to find Billy on the other end.

"Merry Christmas," he said.

"Merry Christmas. How are you guys holding up?"

"First holiday without my mom, so it's been tough. Trying to stay positive for my dad and Gina, but it's hard."

"I can't even imagine."

"I know you're with your family, but would you mind coming over? I think Gina could use your company for a little while." I didn't answer right away and he said, "I'll pick you up. You don't have to stay long, I promise."

"Yeah, okay."

"I'll be right there."

I hung up the phone and went to the hall closet, pulling out my coat and putting it on.

"Where you headed?" my mom asked.

"Going to Billy's for a few minutes to see Gina."

"Only Gina?" my dad teased.

"Don't get any ideas," I playfully scolded. "I'm not going out with Billy."

"But you're not talking to Lonny," my dad said.

161

I stared at him, but didn't respond. As soon as I saw headlights in the driveway I walked out to Billy's car. We made small talk until we got to his house, and as soon as I walked inside Gina ran up to me and gave me a big hug.

"Look what I got!" she shouted excitedly, handing me a black and white photograph of Lonny that he personally autographed and mailed to her so she'd have it in time for Christmas.

"That's great!" I cheered. Lonny went out of his way to make this young girl happy during a difficult time in her life, and I felt like a jerk.

We went into the living room where Billy's father was watching television and I said hello, wishing him a Merry Christmas. I then followed Billy and Gina into the den where we could talk without disturbing him.

"Ruby, do you think Lonny will ever come back home? If he does, do you think I could meet him?"

"Gina, stop," Billy scolded her.

"If Lonny ever comes home, I'll make sure you get to meet him. Maybe Billy will take you to their concert when they go on tour."

"Maybe we could all go together," he suggested.

Gina was very excited over that prospect. "Oh I hope I hope I hope!"

We heard the phone ring and their father yelled, "Gina! Phone!"

Gina looked confused, surprised that anyone would be calling her. She ran into the living room and a few seconds later we heard a blood curdling scream, causing Billy and I to rush to see what happened.

She was crying and trying to talk, but mostly listening. We had no idea who she was talking to, and could only hear her end of the conversation. "Yes, thank you. Merry Christmas. I miss her so much. Will you be back home soon? Ruby said when you come home maybe I can meet you."

Lonny!

My face began to burn.

162

"Okay, thank you. Thank you so much for calling. Ruby's here, do you want to talk to her? Okay, thank you. Goodbye." She hung up the phone and screamed at the top of her lungs. "Oh my God that was Lonny!"

I smiled, but inside I was dying. I wanted to be home with my parents, watching *It's A Wonderful Life*. Instead I was at Billy's house, where Lonny just called to talk to Gina, and he knew I was there.

Gina jumped into my arms and squeezed, thanking me over and over again for making it all happen. I had nothing to do with the autographed photograph, or the phone call; that was all Lonny. I tried to explain that, but she wasn't listening.

"So Gina," Billy said, rubbing his ear. "Lonny didn't wanna talk to Ruby?"

I could feel my face flush as she answered, "He said he had to go."

"Hey Billy, can you please take me home? Lonny's mom is there, and I felt bad for leaving."

We put our coats on and Gina gave me a hug, thanking me for the best Christmas ever. I said goodbye to Mr. Downey and we were on our way. I was quiet during the drive, knowing that I got what I wanted. Lonny was never going to talk to me again.

"You okay?" Billy asked. I nodded. "Do you even talk to Lonny anymore?"

"Not really," I said. "I had nothing to do with that autographed photo or the phone call. That was all Lonny."

"It was nice of him to do that for Gina."

"Lonny's a good guy." Tears stung my eyes as I realized what I lost by turning my back on him.

Billy pulled into my driveway and thanked me for coming over. I smiled, and as I reached to open the door, he took my left hand in his. I turned to look at him and I knew he could see the tears welling up in my eyes.

"I'm sorry for all the bad things I've ever done to you," he whispered, getting choked up. "I know I don't deserve another chance."

I fought to keep the tears from falling, but lost. I could feel one slip down my face, then another. I didn't want to be in that car

163

with Billy. I wanted to be in my room, listening to the new Livingston Monroe album with Lonny. I wanted Lonny home, and I wanted everything to go back the way it was before Ms. Cooke got him that audition. Before Ms. Cooke stole Lonny's innocence, and before Billy took mine.

"I really want to kiss you right now," he whispered.

I looked up at the roof of the car, wiping the tears off my face with the sleeve of my coat. I began to think that Billy was my lot in life; that I was meant to be with him, even if I didn't love him. That my love for Lonny was childish, only a high school crush, and I needed to grow up. Lonny was living in an adult world now, and maybe I needed to do the same.

I turned toward Billy, leaning closer, and let him kiss me. He held my hands in his as we kissed, and he never attempted to touch me anywhere else. He made no moves other than with his lips and tongue, and I was relieved, allowing myself to get lost in his affection. After a few minutes I pulled away and opened the car door.

"So does this mean…?" he asked.

"Maybe. I don't know."

I got out of the car and went into the house, leaving Billy as unsure as I was about our relationship status. He would be going back to school soon, so it wasn't like he'd be around for me anyway. I hung up my coat, kissed my parents goodnight and went to my room. I sat on my bed and flipped through the scrapbook I started for all the newspaper and magazine clippings I could find of Lonny. The reviews of the new album were all positive, and Lonny was known as the Golden Boy who saved Livingston Monroe. Music journalists actually went on record saying he was better than Hendrix, Clapton, Page, Beck and Van Halen. His photo appeared in all the rock magazines, and he was starting to show up in the teen idol magazines like *Tiger Beat, 16* and *Teen Beat*. I bought copies of the rock magazines for Gina, and she bought copies of the teen magazines for me. Lonny was becoming more famous by the minute, and I knew with each passing day he thought about me less and less. Soon I would be nothing more than another girl he went to high school with.

The article Theresa Brooks ended up writing was based more on the frenzy of the day "Fire In The Sky" was released. She interviewed fans standing in line, but she never spoke to Ricky or myself because we just didn't have time. There was a photo of the first fan to purchase the album from our store, and a photo of the first fan in tears who was turned away because we were sold out. And there was a photo of me smiling like I'd just won the lottery, placing an album and poster in someone's hand. The caption underneath the photo read, "Lonny Winter's twin sister Ruby, working the frenzied crowd on album release day."

Two days after Christmas I was in the office taking my break when Ricky poked his head in and said, "There's someone out front looking for you."

"Who is it?"

"I don't know," he whispered, "but she's gorgeous!"

I smirked and headed out to the store where I saw her flipping through our magazine selection. She was tall like a supermodel, with blonde hair in a Farrah Fawcett style, and huge sunglasses covering her eyes. She chewed a piece of gum and smoked a cigarette simultaneously, and she definitely looked out of place in our small midwestern town.

"Can I help you?" I asked, a bit intimidated by her stature and beauty.

She slid her sunglasses to the top of her head and smiled, her red lipstick accentuating her perfectly white teeth. "The elusive Ruby Winter."

"The... what?"

"Tell your boss I'm taking you to lunch."

I stood staring at the woman, having no idea who she was or why she would be taking me to lunch. "I don't... what?" I cursed myself for not being able to form words.

"Surely Lonny has told you about me."

My heart fell into my toes. "Are you Lonny's girlfriend?"

"Lonny's girl— no doll, I'm not his girlfriend." She laughed, as if being Lonny's girlfriend was the most ludicrous idea in the world. She reached out her perfectly manicured hand and said, "Marilyn Livingston."

165

Fuzzy's wife! What on earth was she doing in our store? And why was she specifically seeking me out?

I swallowed hard and asked, "Is Lonny okay?"

"Yeah doll, he's fine. But we need to talk."

In a complete daze, I introduced Ricky to Marilyn and he was over the moon with excitement. He reminded me that we were in the after holiday slow time at the store, and to take as much time as I needed. I followed Marilyn outside and got into the Corvette she had parked at the curb. She popped the new Livingston Monroe cassette into the dash and blasted it as she drove off. She drove to our burger joint, as it was the most popular in the area, and parked the rental car.

"Is that not *the* most groovy rock record you've ever heard?" she asked, turning to smile at me.

I nodded, still in shock that I was with Marilyn Livingston, and she was taking me to our burger joint in a Corvette. We walked into the restaurant and every eye in the place was on her. Nobody was sure who she was, but they knew she was out of place and not a local. We were seated immediately and I waited for her to tell me the purpose of her visit.

"I'm not happy to be here," she told me, looking at the menu. "It's too damn cold and I'm freezing my tits off."

"Why are you here?"

She lit a cigarette and concentrated on the menu, not answering me. Our waitress returned, we placed our orders, and she popped a fresh piece of gum in her mouth. I didn't want to be rude, but she was making me extremely nervous.

"You're coming back to L.A. with me for New Year's Eve."

I wrinkled my forehead, unable to comprehend what she just said to me. "I don't understand."

"Look doll, I love Lonny like my own family. Hell, he *is* family. But he's miserable. Whatever this thing is between you, you're killing him. I can't let that continue. They've got interviews and television appearances coming up to promote the tour, and he needs to be on top of his game. I realize this is all new for him, but he can't have all this outside anguish you're causing him."

I felt like she slapped me across the face.

166

"I'm causing *him* anguish?"

"Doll, Lonny is always smiling, always upbeat, always positive. He's a good kid. But we talk. I don't know any details, but I know you guys aren't speaking to each other."

I was blown away. Here was this woman I'd just met, telling me I was killing Lonny. She didn't know anything about me, or about my history with Lonny. She had some nerve.

"I have a job. I can't just leave, you know."

"I already talked to your boss. He said he was fine with it."

My hands balled into fists in my lap. "I have responsibilities here," I tried to explain, thinking about Gina and Joanie. "And besides, I don't have the money for a plane ticket."

She rifled in her purse and handed me an envelope. "Here's your ticket. We leave tomorrow morning."

"What's wrong with Lonny?"

She took a drag off her cigarette and blew the smoke above her head. "Nothing's wrong with him. He's living the dream, doll. Playing in a rock band, number one album in the charts since day one, living in L.A., sunshine and pretty girls. I just know *you* are an important person in his life, and if there's turmoil there, it brings my boy down. I don't want Lonny down. Ever."

I stared at her with a blank look on my face. I had no idea how to take this woman, liking her and hating her at the same time. She was blaming me for something she didn't understand; she had no idea what happened between me and Lonny. Would she be so forgiving if he had called her stupid? I highly doubted it.

I didn't even realize tears were welling in my eyes until Marilyn handed me a napkin and said, "Oh doll... you're in love with him."

I wiped my eyes and growled, "He's my best friend, but I am *not* in love with him!"

She patted my hand and said, "You keep telling yourself that."

I jerked my hand away from her and said, "You don't know anything about me, and you don't know anything about me and Lonny. You know *nothing*."

"I didn't mean to get you all upset. But it looks to me like you really need to see Lonny."

I was embarrassed when I burst into tears, covering my face with my hands. I wasn't even sure why I was crying; was it because I was so upset about how my relationship with Lonny had disintegrated, or because Marilyn handed me a plane ticket and I had the possibility of seeing him the next day?

"I miss him so much," I bawled.

"Then I guess I arrived just in time."

"Does he know you're here?"

She wagged her finger and shook her head. "Fuzzy sent me. Nobody else knows. We wanted Lonny to be surprised."

"What if it just upsets him instead?" I couldn't fathom the thought.

She took my hands in hers from across the table and smiled. "I don't think that's possible. Doll, he misses you just as much."

My parents were furious when I told them I was going to L.A. with Marilyn. They couldn't believe I would follow her like a puppy, having no idea who she was or where she could really be taking me. I tried to explain that I knew exactly who she was, and how Lonny had been living with her and Fuzzy since he moved there. They didn't budge on their opinion even after Marilyn came to the house to meet them. They were surprised when I stood my ground, insisting I was an adult now and they couldn't stop me from going. Marilyn did everything she could to assure my parents I would be safe, insisting I would be home in less than a week.

Marilyn went back to the hotel and I ran upstairs to pack my suitcase. I had no idea what to pack... it was freezing at home, but I assumed it would be warm in L.A.. Marilyn said to bring a bathing suit, but I didn't even own one. Lonny and I used to bum around at the lake, but we'd jump in with all our clothes on and dry off on the walk home. My mother came into my room while I was trying to pack and sat on my bed.

"Please don't do this," she begged. "I don't like the sound of it."

"Mom, I'm going to see Lonny! I haven't seen him in four months!"

"I know honey, but I don't like the idea of you going there. Why can't he just come home to visit?"

168

"Because everything he needs to do is happening in L.A.. They have interviews and television appearances, and rehearsals for the tour."

"It's just that... you finally started getting over Lonny and living your own life, and you've been seeing a lot of Billy...."

I stopped what I was doing to look at her. "Get over Lonny? He's my best friend, Mom."

Just then my father yelled up the stairs that Billy was on the phone. I hadn't even thought about telling Billy about going to L.A.. My mom and I went downstairs and I took the receiver from my dad.

"Ruby, what are you doing for New Year's Eve?" Billy asked.

"I sort of have plans," I said.

He didn't answer right away, then said, "You do? With who?"

"I'm going to L.A. tomorrow to visit Lonny."

The phone went dead.

Well that was easy.

I shrugged and went upstairs to finish packing. I flitted around my room like I had wings, my feet never touching the floor. It was short lived, however, when my mom called up the stairs that Billy was at the door.

Crap.

I took my time before slowly heading down the stairs to the living room, where Billy sat on the couch talking to my father. As soon as he saw me, he pulled me into the kitchen.

"Can we go for a ride? Just a few minutes, I promise," he said.

"I'm trying to finish packing."

"Please."

I grabbed my coat and told my parents I would be right back. Billy drove around saying nothing and I wondered why he was wasting my time. "Just Say Yes" came on the radio as he pulled into the secluded wooded area where all the kids went to make out. I was about to protest that we were a little bit old to be hanging out at high school make out spots, but he parked the car and pulled me closer, kissing me. When he finally came up for air, I was breathless.

"Marry me," he said.

I couldn't believe what I was hearing. "*What?*"

"Marry me. I love you, Ruby. It doesn't have to be right away, but I want to spend the rest of my life with you."

"I'm only eighteen," I argued, trying not to laugh at him.

"I don't want you leaving tomorrow without knowing how I feel."

"Come on Billy, you're being silly."

"L.A. isn't a place for girls like you. It'll hurt you."

"I'm only gonna be gone a few days."

"Promise you'll… promise you won't…."

"This is about Lonny, isn't it?"

He looked away from me, out the window, then grasped my hands tightly in his. Looking deep into my eyes he said, "I want us to be together without anyone else getting in the way. I love you. I want to be the only one in your life."

"And you're going back to college, doing whatever it is you'll be doing there without me."

"I'm not that far away. I can come home on weekends."

"Take me home."

"Ruby, all I'm asking for is a commitment before you leave tomorrow. I didn't ask you not to go."

"I can't give you something I'm not even sure I want."

Billy looked like I ripped his heart out. "So what's all this been? I thought I was getting somewhere."

"I told you I didn't know. I'm still trying to forgive you for what you did."

Billy put the car in gear and drove off, straight back to my house. "Have fun in L.A.," he said. "Call me when you get back."

I rolled my eyes as I got out of the car and headed for the front door. Billy followed me and pulled me into his arms, giving me a huge hug.

"Just remember who loves you," he whispered against my face. And then he kissed me with such fire I could feel it all the way down to my toes. I pulled away, said goodnight and went back to my room to finish packing. At that moment nothing else mattered, because I was going to see Lonny!

2011

As we got closer to Fallingwater, I noticed Lonny rubbing his temples and looking a bit peaked as he drove. I asked him if he was okay, but he smiled and waved it off as being hungover. I knew he suffered from migraines ever since the first one he experienced right after his Livingston Monroe audition. They didn't happen often, but when they did, they were brutal.

Lonny drove straight to our hotel and when he parked the car said, "I'm sorry Roo, we'll have to wait until tomorrow for Fallingwater."

"It's okay. You stay here, I'll see if we can check in early."

He handed me his wallet. We were hours early for check in, but I could tell Lonny was fading fast. I needed to get him into a room where he would be comfortable, and soon. I knew that's where we'd be spending the rest of our evening.

I went to the front desk and said, "Reservation for Winter. We're really early, I'm sorry, but is there any chance we could check in? My friend isn't feeling well, and I need to get him out of the car and into some air conditioning."

The girl smiled and said she'd see what she could do. Lonny had reserved a room with two queen beds, but there were currently none available at the moment. I thanked the girl for trying and turned to leave, but she called me back.

"I have a room with a king available," she said. "It's just a little bit more, but it'll get your friend inside."

"We'll take it," I said. "And make it for two nights. We're obviously not going anywhere else today." I wasn't used to taking charge of things that way, and it was liberating.

I walked back out to the car and told Lonny we were good to go. He put the top up on the car and we each grabbed our suitcase from the trunk. He was starting to sweat and put his arm around me for guidance. I knew at this point his eyes were probably barely open, trying to keep all sources of light out. I managed to get him to our room and as soon as I put my suitcase down I went for a bucket of ice, caffeinated soda, and snacks. By the time I got back to the room, he was in the bathroom throwing up. I made sure the curtains were closed and the air in the room was cold. I went into the bathroom to wet a washcloth, turned off the light and sat on the floor with Lonny, wiping the back of his neck and the parts of his face I could reach. When he was done hovering over the toilet, I repositioned myself so he could rest his head on my lap, and I began my ice routine. I hadn't done it for him in many years, but I never forgot it.

"I'm sorry, Roo," he croaked.

"Don't be sorry. You don't *choose* to get these headaches. Just relax."

We sat on the bathroom floor for a couple of hours as I iced Lonny's head in accordance with the way he switched positions. Just me, Lonny and the bucket of ice, sitting in darkness and silence as we had done so many times before.

I knew Lonny was beginning to feel better when he whispered, "I didn't pay for a king."

I chuckled and said, "Well... it was the only room they had available when I tried to check in. And we're staying an extra night."

"Yes, ma'am." Lonny sat up and patted my leg, thanking me. He got up and walked into the room where I heard him open one of the soda bottles.

I wrung out the wet washcloth and hung it up to dry, dumping the watery contents of the ice bucket in the sink. I told Lonny I was going to get more ice, but he motioned for me to join him on the bed instead. I climbed onto the bed next to him, where he pulled me into his arms and kissed the top of my head.

"Promise you'll never leave me again," he whispered.

"I promise."

Lonny and I had fallen asleep and when I opened my eyes I had no idea what time it was, as the curtains were still closed and the room was dark. His arms were still wrapped tightly around me as my face was pressed against his neck. He smelled like a putrid combination of sweat, vomit and sugary soda, but I didn't want to move. To be held so tightly in his arms was all I ever dreamed of, but Lonny began to move, kissing my forehead and groaning loudly. He unraveled himself from around me, stretching his arms and legs.

173

"What time is it?" he asked.

I turned to look at the clock on the bedside table and said, "Almost seven o'clock. Are you hungry?"

"Starving."

We both freshened up and changed into clean clothes before heading to the restaurant downstairs for dinner. After a quiet meal, Lonny wanted to go back up to the room but I begged him to go outside and watch the sunset. He smiled and agreed as I took him by the hand and led him outside to the pool area, where we settled into two pool chairs that I pushed close together. It was a beautiful mountain view and the sky was aglow with varying shades of pinks and purples, with shocking splotches of orange and red mixed in. It was surreal, more like a painting than real life. We certainly didn't get sunsets like this back home, or in New York City. Lonny and I were silent as we stared ahead at nature's beauty, but I reached over and interlocked my pinky with his, our super secret signal since we were fourteen years old.

"Do you think Celia will like me?" I broke the silence.

"She's gonna love you."

"How do you know?"

"Because she's just like me," he chuckled.

"Why don't you ever talk about her mother?"

I turned in my chair to face him, but he continued facing forward. "She's not a person worth wasting any breath on."

"Obviously you saw something in her—"

Lonny quickly turned to look at me and said, "No, Roo. Get any romantic ideas out of your head, because it was just a drunken night when I was lonely and feeling sorry for myself. It was that or put a bullet in my head."

I felt sick to my stomach. I had never known Lonny to be the type who felt sorry for himself, let alone suicidal.

"Do you ever blame me?"

Lonny pulled his hand away from mine and lit a cigarette. "Roo, I'm not having this conversation."

"That's your problem," I scolded. "You force me to talk about Billy and relive my nightmares, but you refuse to talk about *yours*."

He took a long drag off his cigarette, slowly blowing smoke rings out of his mouth. Without looking at me he replied, "My nightmares are *real*, Roo. Unlike yours, where you married the class asshole and spent your life tied to a tattoo business."

I stopped breathing. I couldn't even look at him. I turned forward in my chair once again and stared straight ahead, unable to form words. I wanted to go back to the room, but I was frozen to my seat. I was shocked when Lonny got up and walked away, leaving me there alone.

I shouted after him, "I hope Celia isn't just like you, because you're a fucking asshole!"

I half expected him to come back and chew me out, but he kept walking. I was too angry to cry, sitting in that pool chair for I don't remember how long, but Lonny would never get away with talking to me like that again. Once we reached home, my journey with him would be over. I had no intention of continuing on to Las Vegas with him; I was going to stay with my parents and figure out what to do with my life. Start over... start fresh, without either of the men who caused every ounce of heartache I ever experienced. It was time I lived my life on my own, without either one of them. Thirty-six years was long enough.

I slowly made my way back to the room, knowing I didn't have a key with me. I knocked on the door and Lonny let me in, quickly returning to his position on the bed where he was watching a movie I didn't recognize. I opened my suitcase and spotted the bottle of sleeping pills. I popped two in my mouth and headed into the bathroom to change, drinking them down with water from the sink. I didn't even want to be in the same room as Lonny, but there was nothing I could do about it.

As I walked out of the bathroom in my shorts and tank top, the cold air from the room took my breath away, and I crossed my arms over my chest. I crawled into the bed and pulled the covers up to my chin, turning my back on Lonny. As far as I was concerned, Lonny was now in the same category as Billy — someone I would never allow to hurt me again.

I fell asleep pretty quickly and when I woke up again it was seven the next morning. As I headed to the bathroom to take a shower, I stopped to look at Lonny, who was sound asleep. His beautiful face, the face I had loved since I was fourteen years old, the face who broke my heart so many times over, and the face I never wanted to see again.

Lonny was still asleep after I showered and dressed, but I was hungry. I had no money of my own and normally would have waited for him since he was paying for everything, but I was still so angry I didn't care. I went down to the restaurant and ordered a full breakfast, reading the complimentary newspaper I grabbed from the lobby on my way. Just as my breakfast arrived, I noticed Lonny taking a chair several tables away from me.

So this is how it's all going to end.

The waitress gave me my bill just as I finished eating, and I promptly stood up, walked over to Lonny, and dropped the bill on his table.

"We should just head for home today," I said. "I'm done."

"Yep."

1979

I was a ball of nerves as I sat in the back of the taxi with Marilyn as we headed toward her house in suburban Los Angeles. The sun was shining and the weather was warm, but I didn't notice much as I kept trying to talk myself out of throwing up. I rehearsed over and over again what I would say to Lonny, praying he wouldn't be disappointed when he saw me. I didn't know what I'd do if he turned me away.

I followed Marilyn into their bright, beautiful home, still decorated to the hilt for Christmas, my heart beating so hard in my chest I thought it would crack a rib. I could hear Lonny playing guitar and my eyes immediately teared up. We walked through the living room and she told me to be quiet as we peeked our heads over the balcony to the level below, where Lonny was playing guitar and Fuzzy was sitting behind his drums. They were talking and joking around, and Lonny looked so happy. We watched them for a few moments before Marilyn pulled me back but leaned over the balcony and yelled, "Hey guys, I'm home! Lonny, I brought you a present!"

I could hear their voices getting closer as Lonny and Fuzzy made their way upstairs to where we were waiting for them. I turned just as Lonny hit the top of the stairs and set eyes on me. He ran at me so fast I didn't have time to react, his body slamming into mine as he wrapped his arms around me. We held onto each other tightly, our faces buried in each other's hair.

"I'm so sorry Lonny," I cried. "I miss you so much."

"No, it was my fault. I'm sorry."

We stood there holding each other for what seemed like forever. He pulled away first so he could see my face, and it was then I realized he was crying, too.

"Lonny," Marilyn broke the silence. "It was Fuzzy's idea to bring her here. Ruby, this is my husband, Fuzzy."

He shook my hand and said, "It's nice to finally meet you, doll."

Did everyone in L.A. call everyone doll?

"Lonny, why don't you and Ruby go catch up?" Marilyn suggested.

Lonny grabbed my hand and dragged me through the house until we were outside by the swimming pool.

"I can't believe you're really here," he said, still holding my hand. "How long are you staying?"

"I'm leaving on the fourth."

He pulled me in for another embrace, and I was thrilled that he was so happy to see me. "I missed you so much," I cried.

We sat together on a lounge chair and he wiped the tears from my face. "No more crying," he said.

I looked around the beautiful property with its tall, shady trees and plethora of colorful blooms and said, "I can see why you didn't want to come home."

"We've been super busy," he said, still holding tightly to my hand. "This is the first week we've had to relax. And what are we doing? Jamming."

We both laughed, and I pulled him into my arms and hugged him tightly. I had a feeling Marilyn and Fuzzy were watching us, but I didn't care. I wanted to thank Lonny for everything he did for Gina, but that might have led to discussing Billy, and I didn't want to go there.

I looked at his face and he couldn't stop smiling. His dimples were huge because his smile took up his whole face. I'm not sure I remembered seeing him that happy before.

"You look great, Lonny. So happy and perfectly suntanned."

He grinned, a bit embarrassed. "So… what do you think of the album?"

I shrieked. "Oh my God, Lonny, it's out of this world!"

We talked about the album, our parents, my job, and the upcoming tour, Lonny holding my hand tightly the entire time. Time passed so quickly as we talked the next thing we knew, Marilyn was calling us in for dinner.

I was quiet through most of the meal unless asked a specific question, because I was enthralled with the conversation between Lonny and Fuzzy. They talked music, they talked business, they talked about the tour, and I couldn't get enough. I

178

still couldn't believe I was sitting inside Fuzzy Livingston's home, let alone listening to him talk shop with Lonny, who was now part of his band.

After dinner I helped Marilyn clean up as Fuzzy and Lonny went outside by the pool. I could hear Lonny strumming on his guitar through the open window.

"Wow," Marilyn sighed. "I thought I knew what happy was on Lonny. I had *no* idea."

"What do you mean?"

"He's a completely different person with you here. You're his true happy."

I grinned as I felt my face flush.

We joined Lonny and Fuzzy outside, where we all got comfortable as Lonny played guitar while he and Fuzzy sang random songs that came to mind. Lonny seemed so at ease playing and singing in front of others now; I was glad to see it, because I worried about how he would manage having to perform onstage in front of thousands of people each night.

At the end of the evening Fuzzy and Marilyn said goodnight and Lonny took my hand, leading me to the opposite end of the house. I had no idea where I would be staying while I was there, as nobody ever mentioned it. I assumed Lonny was leading me to a spare bedroom somewhere, and my suitcase would be there waiting for me.

Instead he led me to his bedroom, where my suitcase sat on the floor next to his guitar case.

"I'm staying with you?" I asked, surprised.

"Well... yeah."

"What about your girlfriend?"

"What?"

"Won't your girlfriend get upset?"

"Girlfriend? I don't have a girlfriend."

"Your mom told my mom you had a girlfriend."

He began laughing hysterically, almost doubling over. "My mom is so drunk when I talk to her, she keeps thinking Marilyn is my girlfriend!"

I stood there stunned for a minute before I found the humor in it, then I was laughing along with Lonny. It made so much sense!

I went into his private bathroom to change into my pajamas, and when I came back into the room he was already in bed. I felt a bit awkward, not really sure what I should be doing.

"Come on," he teased. "I won't bite."

Lonny moved over to make room in the bed for me, and I climbed in beside him. He turned off the light beside the bed, but the glow of the television helped us see as we lay facing each other. We just stared at each other for a while, neither of us believing that I was actually there.

"Do you really like the new record?" he whispered.

"Lonny, it's the greatest record of all time, and I'm not just saying that because you're my best friend. It really is!"

"I'm not sure about the whole Golden Boy thing...."

"All the articles are saying you saved the band... it's a good thing. People are saying you're better than Hendrix... or even Jimmy Page!"

"I don't know about that...."

"Just don't get a big head," I teased. We both laughed, and I was so happy to see him laughing. I was just overjoyed to see his face again.

Morning came too quickly as Lonny and I joined Marilyn and Fuzzy for breakfast. "I don't usually go all out for breakfast," she said, "but I wanted to make a good impression."

Pancakes, eggs, toast, coffee and orange juice waited for us on the table, and I realized how hungry I actually was.

"We're usually okay with a bowl of cereal," Lonny replied.

"We have a special guest," she said with a smile. "And while you guys are at rehearsal today, I'm taking her shopping."

My stomach fell. I hated shopping. I was definitely not the typical American girl. "You don't need to do that," I said quietly.

"You need something to wear for the New Year's Eve party," Marilyn said. "It's gonna be fun!"

I suddenly felt uncomfortable in my own skin. I was never one for parties to begin with, but a New Year's Eve party in Los Angeles? I wanted to take Lonny by the hand and run away.

Fuzzy must have sensed my trepidation, chiming in with, "Don't worry, doll, it's just a small party here with some close friends."

I smiled and nodded, suddenly remembering I was in Fuzzy Livingston's house! He was really cute in person for an older guy, and I didn't even mind the full beard and mustache. He had always been my favorite member of Livingston Monroe, but things were so personal now. He was always smiling and took such good care of Lonny, he had easily become one of my favorite people.

Fuzzy and Lonny were off to rehearsal, while I got into Marilyn's Corvette for a day of shopping. I felt so out of place, and I really didn't know what to say to her. It was okay, though, because she did all the talking. She was always talking. Talking, smoking and chewing gum, all at the same time. I don't know how she did it.

I had to admit it was fun hanging out with Marilyn, driving from shop to shop, trying on fun, fashionable and expensive clothes, but at some point I had to put my foot down. I didn't have the money to pay for such extravagances. She told me not to worry about anything, that she was taking care of it all. We tried on clothes together, laughed like best friends, and moved on to the next shop. We eventually agreed on matching outfits we knew were the day's winner — for Marilyn, a red sequined mini-dress with a halter top and a low-plunging neckline, and for me, the same outfit in emerald green sequins, with shorts instead of a mini-skirt. We purchased platform shoes to match, and we were back out into the sunshine.

As she drove with the top down, Marilyn asked, "Could you see yourself living here?"

I didn't really answer her question, saying, "I can see why Lonny doesn't want to come home."

"Wanna check out the rehearsal?"

I looked at her with a smile on my face. "Really?"

"Hell yes, doll!"

Marilyn drove to a giant warehouse where she needed to check in with a guard at the front gate.

"Hey, Marilyn," the guard greeted her.

"Hey, doll! Meet Lonny's girl, Ruby. She's in from Chicago."

He smiled and said hello, and I returned the greeting.

Marilyn parked the car and I followed her through the front door and down a maze of hallways until we reached a door with a sign reading "Livingston Monroe." I followed her inside and there they were... Fuzzy, Fuzzy's brother Benji, Mitch and Lonny, playing the hell out of their classic song, "Take Me Home." Joey Buckingham sang the lead on that song, so I assumed Mitch would take over in his absence, but I was wrong. There was Lonny, playing and singing a song that we had listened to hundreds of times at home, and he made it his own, and he rocked it.

Marilyn and I sat off to the side without disturbing anyone, and I was in pure heaven. Not only sitting in on Livingston Monroe's rehearsal, but watching Lonny as part of the band.

When they were finished with the song they decided it was time for a break, and Fuzzy greeted Marilyn with a kiss. Marilyn introduced me to Mitch and Benji, again referring to me as Lonny's girl from Chicago. Lonny, however, greeted me with a smile and nothing else, and I noticed the strange looks from Mitch and Benji. Nobody could begin to understand my relationship with Lonny, and I didn't expect men in their early thirties to get it either.

"How did it sound?" Lonny asked.

"Lonny... you're incredible!"

"It's getting easier."

I poked him in the shoulder and whispered, "You're a rock star."

He laughed as they quickly got back to rehearsal. Marilyn and I stayed for a few more songs and she decided it was enough. As I followed her out the door, I looked back sadly at Lonny, so badly wanting to stay. I waved goodbye and he smiled, because we knew we'd see each other later in the day.

As we got back into Marilyn's car she said, "You've seen one rehearsal, you've seen them all."

That may have been true for her, but not for me. I wanted to stay and experience the entire thing. I didn't want it to end. I

182

wanted to absorb every note, every word, every emotion going on in that room.

"Did you bring a bathing suit?"

"I don't have one," I admitted sheepishly.

"One more stop before heading home."

Marilyn had me trying on the most ridiculous bathing suits and bikinis I'd ever seen. None of them looked good on me, and I felt extremely over-exposed.

"It's okay," I tried to assure her. "I'm not here that long. I don't need a bathing suit."

"Please don't be like Lonny and swim in your cutoffs."

This made me laugh, because that's exactly how we would swim in the lake at home. I agreed to try on one more suit, and it actually wasn't bad. It was a two-piece that covered more than the bikinis did.

"Oh doll, I like that one," she said, examining me. "Covers all your insecurities... even your barely visible boobs." She saw my face fall and said, "Doll, I'm only teasing!"

After dinner that evening, the four of us sat around the living room where Fuzzy played music on his stereo. I was sitting on the floor with Lonny lying in front of me with his head in my lap. As we listened to music and talked, I did what I always did, finger combed his hair. I noticed Marilyn watching us closely.

Pointing at us and sipping a martini, she finally said, "You guys can't do that in public."

Lonny didn't move, he just looked at me and rolled his eyes, which she couldn't see.

I was curious. "What do you mean?"

"The fans can't know Lonny has a girlfriend. It'll ruin everything."

"Marilyn, stop," Fuzzy lightly scolded.

I pulled a face. "But I'm not—"

"I'm just saying," she defended herself. "The girls are crazy over Lonny, and if they think he's unavailable we'll lose that fan base. I know it sounds crazy, but trust me. I've seen it happen."

"Don't worry, Marilyn," Lonny spoke up. "We'll keep our hands off each other in public." We both giggled.

The only question I had at that moment was when would we ever be seen in public together? Marilyn's concern made no sense to me.

"Back home everyone thinks I'm Lonny's sister," I explained.

"His sister?" Fuzzy chuckled.

"In high school we had everyone convinced we were brother and sister," Lonny said. "Same last name, same birthdate."

"And now, Lonny, a newspaper labeled me as your twin, so it must be true!"

"Twins!" Lonny roared.

"We could really mess some people up," I teased.

We laughed as Fuzzy stood up. "You guys feel free to stay up as long as you like, but I'm going to bed."

"Yeah, we'll probably hit it too," Lonny agreed.

We all said goodnight and I followed Lonny back to his bedroom. When he closed the door I asked, "Who do they think I am, Lonny?"

"Whattya mean?"

"Everyone's acting like I'm your girlfriend or something."

He shrugged. "I don't know. Does it matter?"

"No, but what Marilyn said—"

"Don't listen to her. She talks to hear herself talk sometimes."

"I don't want her to not like me."

Lonny took my hand and sat me on the bed. "She loves you. She told me after we got back from rehearsal."

"You promise?"

"I swear! I would never lie to you."

Lonny and I wanted to spend as much time together as possible, and we didn't want to spend it sleeping. We sat on the floor of his room as he strummed his guitar, and we talked about anything and everything. It was just like being back home, like old times.

"Thank you for what you did for Gina," I said.

"No problem. I just wanted her to have a nice Christmas."

"They all thought I had something to do with it, but I told them it was all you. That you're a good guy."

184

"You were there when I called."

Here we go.

"I was. I went over to see Gina."

Lonny played around on his guitar, not looking at me, only watching his own hands. After a few minutes, he looked up and asked, "So what's going on with Billy?"

He was looking right into my eyes, into my soul, and I was afraid he could see what I'd done with Billy. "He's still trying to convince me he loves me," I admitted.

"And you believe him?"

"He really is different since his mom died, but—"

"Aw, Roo, come on!" he scolded.

"Let me finish! He really is different, but I'm not going out with him. Gina has become attached to me, so I've been helping her out when I can. That makes things harder, because he's always there, either giving her a ride, or being at the house. But he's going back to school soon, so I won't have to see him anymore. He's trying really hard to get me back, but I'm not interested."

"Did he kiss you?" He looked back down at his own hands, plucking the guitar strings.

"Aw Lonny, why does it matter?"

He shrugged. "It doesn't. I'm just asking."

I sighed heavily. "Lonny, I don't want to spend our time together talking about Billy."

He still wouldn't look at me but said, "I just remember you telling me when you first went out with him what a great kisser he was."

I felt my face burn. "I did?" He nodded, still not looking at me. "Gross."

"Yeah, gross."

"I've been lonely," I admitted. "He kissed me a few times."

I could see the muscles in Lonny's jaw tighten, then he looked into my eyes. "There's girls everywhere," he said. "Everywhere we go, there's girls ready to mob me. It's like a prison sometimes, being in this house, but at least I'm safe here. I'm lonely, too."

I took Lonny's guitar out of his hands and gently set it on the floor, crawling to where he sat. Facing him, I wrapped my legs

185

around his hips as I pulled him close to me and held him tightly, our bodies and faces pressed against each other. I wanted to hold him forever and never let go. I dreaded having to go back home without him.

The next day, the day before New Year's Eve, was spent lazily around the pool at the house. All the band members were there, including Mitch and his girlfriend Hattie, and Benji came with his wife Wanda and their one-year-old son, Calvin.

I was terrified of being seen in the bathing suit Marilyn bought for me, staying in Lonny's room arguing with myself. I threw on a t-shirt to cover myself up, then took it off. Put it back on, then took it off. I hadn't worn a bathing suit since I was a little kid, and I wasn't used to having so much skin showing. I nearly hit the ceiling when Lonny knocked on the door, asking if he could come in.

He peeked his head into the room before entering, smiling as I quickly held the t-shirt up to keep him from seeing my body.

"Everyone is wondering where you are," he said, grinning.

"I can't go out there like this."

"Why not? Let me see."

He was the *last* person I wanted to see me. "No!"

"Nobody is gonna be looking at you."

"They will now," I croaked. "I've been in here way too long."

Before I could bat an eye, Lonny reached out and grabbed the t-shirt I was clinging to, tearing it away from my body. I gasped loudly as he checked me out. And there he stood, in his cutoff shorts and nothing else.

"You look fine," he said, poking me in the shoulder. "You should see what the other chicks are wearing. I call them barely-suits." He rolled his eyes and laughed.

I grabbed my t-shirt away from him and threw it on, then followed him outside to the pool. Lonny was right… the bathing suits the other three women wore barely had enough material to cover their lady parts. I looked overdressed compared to them.

"There she is!" Marilyn yelled from her pool chair, her hair piled on top of her head with huge sunglasses covering her eyes.

She tossed a bottle of suntan lotion at Lonny and said, "Make sure you lotion her up good. She's as pale as my ass."

Lonny turned white and quickly flipped the suntan lotion my way. I didn't need him to put it on me; what was she thinking?

"Come sit by me, doll," Marilyn said, patting the pool chair beside her with a cigarette hanging out of her mouth.

I slathered lotion on my arms and legs and the front parts of me that were visible, but struggled to reach my back.

"Sit down, I'll get your back," Marilyn said. "Fucking Lonny... you'd think touching a girl would cause his dick to shrivel up and fall off."

I laughed loudly, and quickly covered my mouth when everyone turned to see what was so funny. Marilyn had a mouth like a truck driver, and she never minced words. If you wanted the truth, she was going to give it to you straight, without ribbons and bows. I continued to giggle uncontrollably as Marilyn rubbed suntan lotion into my back.

When she was done, I turned to face her and whispered, "That's not funny," as I continued giggling.

"Yes it is."

"Yes it is," I giggled.

"I love shocking that kid. You'd think he never heard a woman swear before he met me."

Neither one of us grew up with parents who used foul language, so neither of us used it often. It probably was a shock for Lonny to hear Marilyn's potty mouth on a regular basis. Though after living with her for four months, you'd think he'd be used to it.

Late in the afternoon Marilyn, who had been drinking all day, took my hand and said, "Doll, what's the deal with you and Lonny?"

"What do you mean?"

"I mean... I'm just so confused." She was slurring her words. "You touch, but not really. The most physical you've been is when you first got here, then nothing. There's never any kissing... not even on the cheek. I just don't understand." I squeezed her hand and as I opened my mouth to speak she shrieked, "Oh my God!" scaring me half to death. "It's so obvious!"

I stared at her wide-eyed, waiting for her to explain her epiphany.

She leaned close to my face and whispered loudly, "You're both virgins!"

I thought for sure everyone heard what she said, but looking around it seemed that wasn't the case. I did notice Lonny glance my way with a questioning look on his face, though.

"Shhhhh Marilyn, that's not it, I swear," I whispered.

"You two are so sweet!" she bellowed. Everyone heard *that*.

Fuzzy strolled over to where we were sitting and asked if everything was all right.

"Yeah, we're fine," I said, shrugging.

"Fuzzy!" Marilyn shouted. "I figured it out!"

"Marilyn, shhhhhh, no... *please*," I begged. I didn't care if she wanted to out me as a virgin, but I had no idea if that would embarrass Lonny, and my guess was he'd be mortified. Even though neither of us were virgins, nobody needed to know our business. Or why we weren't doing it with each other.

Fuzzy lifted Marilyn out of her chair and threw her into the pool, cigarette, sunglasses and all. She surfaced sputtering and cursing him out like a machine gun firing bullets.

"You okay, doll?" he asked me.

I nodded, wondering why he felt that was the only way to diffuse the situation, but as Marilyn got out of the pool, she cursed him all the way into the house and we didn't see her again.

Fuzzy sat in the chair Marilyn involuntarily vacated and said, "There's no shutting her up when she's drunk, so whatever that was, I'm sorry."

I was still shocked at what happened, but replied, "You didn't have to... it's okay."

Marilyn's disappearance seemed to signal the end of the gathering for everyone who wasn't sleeping under their roof. Everyone left and Fuzzy went into the house to check on his wife. I dove into the water and met Lonny at the edge of the pool where he was just about to get out.

"What was all that about?" he asked.

I bit my lip. "You really want to know?" He nodded, so I said, "Marilyn thinks we're both virgins and was going to announce it to everyone."

"There's nothing wrong with being a virgin," he replied.

"I know that. I wish I still was."

"So you haven't... I mean... you haven't done it again?"

"Ew, no! Have you?"

He grinned and said, "No."

Fuzzy came back outside to tell us he ordered some pizzas for dinner, so we got out of the pool to dry off and get changed.

Dinner was quiet without Marilyn. I knew she was passed out in her bedroom, but I missed her. She was definitely the one in the room everyone noticed first. In a way, it was a relief she wasn't there so I didn't have to worry about her bringing up mine and Lonny's sexuality.

Fuzzy talked about how there would be a film crew with them on the tour, and that one of their rehearsals at the warehouse the following week would be filmed from beginning to end. Apparently there was going to be a movie or documentary to come out of it at some point, and possibly a live album. It sounded very exciting, and I was so happy that Lonny was going to be part of it all.

I was curious about the warehouse where they had their rehearsal space, asking, "Do you need to get permission from the warehouse to film in there?"

Fuzzy chuckled and answered, "Marilyn and I own the warehouse, so we can pretty much do what we want."

"That's so cool!"

"It's good to have other business ventures," he said. "And it gives Marilyn something to do besides shop."

"How did you two meet?" I asked, hoping to hear some far out romantic tale.

"Marilyn's mother is Howard's secretary. Hey, don't you two have a connection to Howard?"

"Louise," Lonny answered. "The chorus teacher at our high school is her cousin."

"Ms. Cooke got Lonny the audition," I said.

189

"Because I slept with her."

I froze, stunned that Lonny would ever tell anyone that, but then he started laughing and Fuzzy roared, thinking it was the funniest thing he'd ever heard. I laughed too, even though I didn't think it was the least bit funny.

"You should come on tour with us," Fuzzy said to me. "I'm sure Lonny wouldn't mind having you around."

Lonny and I looked at each other, wide-eyed. Lonny then sat bolt upright in his chair and tugged at my arm. "Do it, Roo! Come on, it'll be fun!"

I was speechless. "I'm sure they don't want another person taking up space and getting in the way."

Fuzzy chuckled. "They? They would be us... and Howard."

"Come on, Roo!" Lonny cheered, unable to sit still.

"I'm sure we can find something for you to do," Fuzzy teased. "We're all bringing our old ladies; no reason Lonny shouldn't bring you."

I could feel my smile get bigger as Lonny hugged me excitedly, but all I could think about was having to quit my job and telling my parents. They weren't happy about me coming to visit Lonny in L.A., I could just imagine what their reaction would be when I told them I was going on tour with him.

Fuzzy was really good at reading people, and sensing my non-committed response said, "I'll talk to Howard, see what he thinks."

"If Howard is okay with it, then yeah, count me in!"

Being careful not to disturb Marilyn, Lonny and I lightly stomped our feet on the floor and pumped our fists in the air with our mouths screaming silently, thrilled with this turn of events.

We headed down to Fuzzy's game room where I watched the two of them engage in a very competitive match of billiards. It was comforting to see them get along so well, like brothers, and that Lonny had a level-headed man to be his mentor. I knew as long as Fuzzy was in the picture Lonny would be safe, and that's all that mattered to me.

The next day was spent with a bright-eyed Marilyn giving us all our assignments for the day in preparation for the New Year's Eve party that evening. I spent most of the time in the

190

kitchen with her chopping or stirring or mixing whatever she threw my way. She was a whirlwind at all times, never still for very long and always talking, smoking and chewing gum. It was a wonder the ash from her cigarettes never made their way into any of the food we prepared.

"Lonny is my angel," she said to me as I chopped vegetables. "He saved the band, and he saved my marriage."

"He saved your marriage?" This was a shocking revelation.

"Yeah… well… things were a bit rocky with Fuzzy and me, and when Lonny came along it was a breath of fresh air. He gave us something else to focus on, you know?"

I smiled. "I'm glad to hear it."

"And if you want that boy for yourself doll, you better make a move quick."

"Make a move?" I could feel my face burning.

"Has he made any moves on you?"

"No, but—"

"Exactly. You have to make the first move doll, before rock and roll sucks him up and you're left out in the cold. He needs you to keep him grounded."

"Keep him grounded, or innocent?" Fuzzy's voice appeared out of nowhere, startling both of us. He popped a piece of cauliflower in his mouth and said, "Come on Mare, leave 'em alone. They're just kids."

Marilyn rolled her eyes at me, causing me to giggle, but her words about rock and roll sucking Lonny up disturbed me. What did she mean by that? And what could I do to prevent it from happening?

Fuzzy disappeared again and Marilyn paused briefly to stare at me with squinted eyes. "Are you and Lonny really eighteen? You look about sixteen, which would explain a *lot*."

"We're eighteen," I assured her.

"Don't worry doll, I've got it all planned out. You and Lonny are gonna end up together before the night is through, I guarantee it."

"Marilyn, I don't think you understand my relationship with Lonny. He's my best friend… I'm not interested in having sex with him."

Marilyn immediately stopped what she was doing and smashed her cigarette out with such force the ashtray nearly flew off the table. She glared at me for a long time, making me uncomfortable. She was never that still at any given time that I'd ever seen.

"You think I don't see the way you look at him?" she whispered.

"You're wrong. I don't want to have sex with him," I argued quietly.

"That's only because you don't know anything about sex," she said with a grin.

"I'm not a virgin." As soon as I said it I wished I kept my big mouth shut.

"Then you can teach Lonny what it's all about." She was enjoying this way too much.

"Lonny's not a virgin either."

She held a perfectly manicured hand to her chest, feigning a heart attack. "Lonny's been with a girl?" she whispered, shocked.

I nodded, silently cursing myself.

"Doll, you've got me. I'm so confused right now, I'm not sure which end is up."

"What's so great about sex anyway?" I definitely showed my age and inexperience with that question.

"Oh doll," Marilyn cooed as she sat next to me and took my hands in hers. "It can be such a beautiful thing, especially if you're with someone you really love."

I tried to laugh but I could tell by the way she looked at me she could see right through me.

"I take it your first time wasn't so great?"

"My boyfriend sort of—"

"Wait... you have a boyfriend?" she gasped.

"Not anymore."

"I'm sorry, go on."

"It was after graduation, and my boyfriend sort of pushed me into it. Then he took me home and told me it was all to win a bet with one of his stupid friends."

"What a shitty boyfriend!"

I chuckled. "Yeah, he was. And I don't ever want to have sex again."

She smiled at me. "You say that now, but you'll change your mind. Now tell me about Lonny."

"No."

"Oh come on, you can trust me."

"No."

"So he's really a hot stud underneath that innocent, boyish exterior?" Marilyn teased.

"He's just like me," I said, biting my lip. "Only once."

Marilyn seemed utterly shocked to be in my presence at that moment. As if Lonny and I were some sort of circus sideshow she'd never encountered before, and wasn't sure how to deal with.

"I'm sorry for being so pushy," Marilyn said. "I just love Lonny to death, and I care about you, too. And the two of you belong together, for so many reasons." She gave me a hug and finished with, "I'll keep my nose out of it, I promise."

Marilyn and I spent the couple hours before the party holed up in her bathroom getting dressed and prettied up for the occasion. I was having second thoughts about the outfit she bought for me to wear — every time I moved, my breasts, small as they were, kept popping out from the low-cut halter. I'd have to sit in a chair and not move the entire night in order to keep that from happening. But Marilyn had the answer to everything, pulling out a roll of double-sided tape and taping the material straight onto my nipples. I jumped up and down and shimmied from side to side, and everything stayed in place.

After setting my entire head of hair in curlers, then putting a few curlers in her own hair, she sat me down to do my makeup. She knew that I never wore makeup and promised not to make me look like a hooker, which was my biggest fear.

Fuzzy popped his head in and said, "Why are there catering vans pulling in the driveway?"

"To feed our guests, obviously," Marilyn answered, applying a light coating of mascara to my eyelashes.

"I thought we were only having a few people."

"Well... yeah... but then I didn't want to hurt anyone's feelings so I invited a few more."

193

I could see Fuzzy wasn't amused as he asked, "How many, Mare?"

She didn't answer right away and he began drumming his fingers on the door. "I don't know, fifty maybe... hundred if they all bring someone."

He cursed under his breath and walked out, closing the door behind him. I knew right then and there Fuzzy was furious, but didn't want to explode on Marilyn in front of me.

"Big party," I chuckled.

"Hey, it's the end of the seventies... what better reason to party than that?"

Marilyn applied a light coat of pink lipstick to my mouth and stood back to admire her work. She gently pulled the curlers out of my hair, tousled it with her fingers, and presented me to the mirror. I stared at the person looking back at me, not believing it was my own reflection.

"Whattya think, doll?"

I stared at myself with my mouth agape. "I'm beautiful," I gasped.

"Yeah, you are." Marilyn had a huge smile on her face, more than satisfied with her work. She grabbed her Polaroid off the counter and took two photos of us through the mirror, smiling and posing like models; one copy for her, and one for me. When the photos were dry, she stuck her copy up in the mirror as a memento.

"Are you ready to make your grand entrance, doll?" she asked, taking my hand. I nodded excitedly and we skipped out of the bathroom, through her bedroom and down the hall until we reached the kitchen, where Fuzzy and Lonny were trying to make sense of all the food trays the catering company had delivered. Marilyn cleared her throat loudly to get their attention, and when they turned to look at us Fuzzy had a huge smile on his face, his anger seeming to have faded, and Lonny stood with his mouth open, speechless.

Realizing we were both still barefoot, Marilyn said, "Oh! Doll! We forgot our shoes!"

"I'll stay barefoot until I need to put them on," I said, staring at Lonny who was still staring at me.

"Lonny, you should get changed," Marilyn suggested. "People will start arriving soon."

Lonny walked past me, grabbing my hand and pulling me along with him. We went to his room, where he closed the door and sat on the bed.

"So what are you wearing?" I asked.

He pointed to the outfit hanging on the back of his door — a white flared disco suit, reminiscent of John Travolta's outfit in the movie *Saturday Night Fever*.

"That's dynamite!" I squealed.

He laughed. "I guess it's a 'Best of the Seventies' party. Everyone has to dress up."

"You're gonna look so handsome," I said. "What does Fuzzy have to wear?"

Lonny covered his mouth with his hand, trying to hold back laughter. He patted the bed next to him, so I sat down. As if Marilyn and Fuzzy could hear everything we said, he pressed his lips against my ear and whispered, "Han Solo." He didn't pull away immediately, and I swore he sniffed my hair. Surely I was imagining it… or was I?

"I bet he'll be handsome," I whispered.

"He's pissed. He didn't want a huge party like this, but now she's making him wear a costume."

"She's hard to say no to."

"You should probably… I need to change so…."

"Okay, just let me find my shoes." I went into his closet and pulled out the green sequined platform shoes that matched my outfit, then sat on his bed to put them on. I buckled each of them around my ankle and stood up, their three-inch wedge nearly toppling me over. I grabbed the top of Lonny's shoulder for balance as he made sure his hands were far enough away from me that he didn't accidentally touch anything he wasn't supposed to.

As I walked out the door Lonny called, "Rooster!" I poked my head back into the room and he said, "You look really pretty."

I think I floated all the way back to the kitchen, because I don't remember my feet touching the ground. I interrupted Fuzzy and Marilyn just as she was running her fingertips through his beard and kissing him on the lips. I skidded to a halt trying not to disturb them, but as my shoes stopped, my forward motion propelled me into the air and I landed flat on my face. They were both quick to reach me and help me back to my feet.

"Are you okay, doll?" she asked, nearly out of breath.

"Just not used to these shoes," I explained, laughing at myself.

"Are you hurt?" Fuzzy asked. It was then I realized he was wearing his full Han Solo costume and it made me smile, because he really did look handsome.

I assured them I was fine, but gladly took the chair Fuzzy offered me. Marilyn pushed a glass my way and said, "Try this."

Fuzzy disappeared when the doorbell rang and I smelled the frothy red liquid in the glass Marilyn wanted me to drink from. It smelled fruity, so I tasted it. It was sweet, but it was good.

"Like it?" she asked.

"Yeah, it's pretty good. What is it?"

"My special punch."

Lonny joined us in his snazzy white suit and asked how he looked. Marilyn and I whistled our praise as an exasperated Fuzzy popped in asking, "Mare, where do you want the DJ?"

"Doll, fix Lonny's collar," Marilyn told me as she and Fuzzy disappeared to deal with the DJ.

I stood up and adjusted Lonny's lopsided collar and he smiled at me.

"What?" I asked, grinning.

"I'm just so happy you're here."

"Me, too." I brushed his bangs away from his eyes so I could see them clearly, and he seemed to lean forward as if he wanted to kiss me, but Fuzzy tore into the kitchen grumbling under his breath and grabbed a beer out of the refrigerator. Marilyn soon followed, but realizing we were standing there, just smiled and asked if Lonny could help her with the disco ball.

I studied Fuzzy's face as he took a swig of beer and even though I barely knew him, I could tell he was furious. "Are you okay?" I asked anyway, hoping to ease some of the tension.

He looked at me sideways never moving his head, and said, "I'm pissed and that woman drives me insane, but I can't live without her."

"She's hard to say no to," I whispered, smiling.

"I know she means well," he sighed. "I just don't like being blindsided all the time."

"But then your life would be pretty boring."

He laughed and said, "You got that right."

Sounds of the seventies soon started pumping throughout the house and we knew the DJ was set for the evening.

"You look really handsome by the way," I told Fuzzy with a grin.

The doorbell rang and we could hear Marilyn screech as she greeted their first guests.

Fuzzy rolled his eyes and smiled, saying, "Time to go slay some Wookiees or whatever it is I'm supposed to be doing."

"Chewbacca is a Wookiee! He's your friend!" I corrected him, laughing.

He winked at me and replied, "Thanks for having my back, doll."

It seemed that hundreds of people showed up for this party once things started swinging, and Lonny was the pet of the evening. Record executives, music media bigwigs, musicians of all kinds, models, actors, actresses and everyone in between wanted to meet the Golden Boy who saved Livingston Monroe. There were so many people there, I kept getting lost in the crowd without knowing a soul I bumped into. One such person was a beautiful guy with long, shaggy brown hair I recognized immediately as English teen idol Peter Summersby. He immediately apologized for bumping into me, then asked if I wanted a drink.

I followed Peter to the punch bowl where he poured each of us a drink and then we went outside by the pool to get some fresh air. Sitting on the same large pool chair he asked, "Are you new in town? I've never seen you around." His English accent and piercing blue eyes melted me.

"I'm just visiting." I was seriously tongue-tied.

"I'm Peter."

"Ruby."

"Nice to meet you, Ruby. Who are you visiting?"

"Lonny."

"Ah yes, Lonny is quite popular this evening."

197

I laughed. "Tell me about it."

"Is he your boyfriend?"

"No... more like my brother."

He smiled. A perfectly beautiful mouth of pearly white teeth.

"So what are you up to?" I asked.

"Well," he sighed. "I'm going into the studio soon for my next album, but I just finished filming a new weekly television series where I play a superhero who also has singing talent. Rubbish, actually, but my agent thought it was a good idea. I might need to fire him."

"So what's your super power?"

He smiled brightly and touched the tip of my nose with his finger. "If I told you, I'd have to kill you."

"I can wait."

After we both stopped laughing he asked, "So you think you'll tune in?"

"Sure, why not?"

"You'll have to let me know what you think. If nothing else, it was fun to do."

I took a sip of the punch he gave me and realized it was spiked. It didn't taste bad, but I wasn't a drinker and wanted to stay that way.

Noticing Peter was dressed in a pair of tight jeans covered with patches, a belt with a giant turquoise buckle, a long-sleeved silk shirt, and a shell necklace, I asked who he was supposed to be dressed as.

"David Cassidy," he said. "Not obvious enough?"

"Yes!" I shouted. "I knew it!"

"I'm not very creative when it comes to costumes."

"Marilyn dressed me. I have no idea what I'm supposed to be," I joked.

"A seventies disco queen, obviously. And a very beautiful one."

I felt my face flush and announced I was hungry, going into the house in search of some food. I realized he was right behind me and I drank the contents of my cup in one swallow. When we reached the food table I felt light-headed and grabbed a sandwich, chowing it down like I hadn't eaten in weeks. I didn't even care that it was tuna.

"You okay?" Peter asked.

I nodded as I chewed. He asked if I wanted more punch, and I smiled, chewed and swallowed. I must have looked like a damn animal. Marilyn was soon at my side asking if I was all right.

"Just hungry," I told her.

Peter returned, handing me another cup of punch, and I watched Marilyn as she eyed him curiously. She greeted him with a kiss on the cheek and asked, "How's your mother?"

"She flew back to England last week. I think the California sunshine was too much for her cranky personality."

They shared a laugh and then she said, "David Cassidy called. He wants his clothes back."

Peter laughed and began unbuttoning his shirt. The next thing I knew he was shirtless and I was speechless. When he began unbuttoning his jeans, she threw a hand up and teased, "Okay, stop trying to impress Ruby. I think she's seen enough."

"Not really," I giggled.

What did I just say?

For the first time since meeting Marilyn, I think I said something that truly left her without a response. I reached out and touched Peter's perfectly sculpted chest, then recoiled as if I had been burned. Part of me felt guilty, but why? I was a single girl and I was just having some fun for a change.

"Okay Peter, put your shirt back on," Marilyn insisted. "Be a dear and get me some punch?" Peter disappeared and she immediately began scolding me. "What are you doing? You're supposed to be making the moves on Lonny, not Peter!"

"Making the moves... I'm not—"

"Peter will fuck anything that moves," she whispered. "You're just the fresh face in town."

Ouch!

"Lonny's too busy for me tonight," I pouted. "I can't even get near him. Besides... he's not interested in me that way."

"Doll, when that clock strikes midnight you better make sure he's with you and not somebody else."

199

I nodded, feeling like it was a hopeless cause. Marilyn grabbed me by the hand and pulled me onto the makeshift dance floor under the twirling disco ball so we could dance to the Village People's "Y.M.C.A." together. I laughed more than I danced, but Marilyn always knew how to have a good time. Before the song was even over, I saw a disgruntled look cross her face and once again she was taking me by the hand and pulling me somewhere else. We stopped where some large breasted woman dressed like Marilyn Monroe was getting very cozy with Lonny.

"He's just a kid you old bat," Marilyn hissed. When the woman gave her a dirty look she said, "It's a best of the seventies party, didn't you read the invite? Beat it!"

Lonny and I were shocked at Marilyn's behavior, but he looked relieved when Marilyn Monroe rolled her eyes and made her way to another part of the house. I noticed she was a lot older in reality once I saw her up close, and wondered what she wanted with Lonny.

Marilyn took us both by the hand and pulled us outside by the pool for fresh air, making us sit down. She ordered us not to move until she and Fuzzy came back with plates of food and a cup of punch for each of us.

"You need to eat," she insisted.

"They don't need alcohol," Fuzzy quietly scolded.

"There's barely any alcohol in that punch," she retorted.

I accidentally burped out loud, and smelling it Lonny said, "Rooster, have you already been drinking?"

"What did you call her?" Marilyn asked.

"Rooster."

"Rooster? What the hell is that?"

"It's one of his nicknames for me," I explained.

"It's terrible! She's a woman, not a farm animal! Don't ever call her that again!" she demanded.

Lonny's face paled at being scolded by Marilyn, and I did everything I could not to burst into laughter.

"Come on Mare, leave 'em alone," Fuzzy said softly, taking her by the elbow and leading her back into the house.

Once he was sure they were out of hearing distance, Lonny whispered, "What's her problem?"

I couldn't hold in my laughter any longer. "That was hilarious!" I bellowed. "I'm a woman, not a farm animal!" I was laughing so hard I could barely breathe.

I knew Marilyn was frustrated that her plan of getting Lonny and me together kept getting interrupted, but she had also promised to stay out of it. If things couldn't happen naturally because we both had feelings for each other, then I didn't want anything forced on him. And I certainly didn't want alcohol to be a factor in anything that happened between us. So I decided to have fun that evening, and not worry about whether or not Lonny loved me like I loved him.

"She's coming back," Lonny whispered, panicked. "Eat your chicken."

We started eating like we were starving when Marilyn stood in front of Lonny, her hands on her hips. "Lonny, can I please have a word?"

Lonny looked like he'd just been given a death sentence, his eyes wide with fear, as Fuzzy made his way back outside shouting, "Mare! Where's the corkscrew?"

Marilyn huffed angrily as she turned on her heel and marched into the house. Fuzzy shrugged and mouthed, "I'm sorry," letting me know he knew exactly where the corkscrew was.

"I'll be right back," I told Lonny, "stay here."

I set my plate on the chair and walked back into the house to the kitchen where Marilyn opened a drawer and pulled out a corkscrew, waving it viciously at Fuzzy.

"Marilyn, can we talk somewhere private?" I asked nervously.

Marilyn pointed at me with the corkscrew and said, "Doll, you're gonna need this to pry Lonny's mouth open later, because I don't think he's tongued a girl in his life."

Marilyn was starting to scare me, and Fuzzy sensed it. He gently took the corkscrew from her hand and whispered, "Ruby would like to speak to you privately."

Marilyn smiled, took me by the hand, and led me to her bedroom where we sat on the big, cozy bed. "What's up, doll?"

"I feel like you're not having fun at your own party."

"What makes you say that?"

201

"You seem so mad."

She laughed loudly and said, "Mad? If I was mad, you'd know it."

"Can you leave Lonny alone? He hasn't done anything wrong, and you were really tough on him out there."

"Doll, Lonny is afraid of his own shadow!" she laughed. "He needs to grow a set of balls."

"Please," I begged. "Stop trying to push us together. If it happens, that's fine, but if it doesn't, that's fine too. He's my best friend, and I love him no matter what."

"Aw doll, I'm sorry." She crossed her heart and promised to leave us alone.

"Lonny is a sweet boy," I said, feeling a bit emotional. "And I love him just the way he is."

"Even if it means you never get him for yourself?"

I wiped a lone tear from my cheek and nodded. "I want him to love me because he loves me, not because someone else thinks he should."

Marilyn pulled me into her arms for a big hug and whispered, "I love you, doll. I just want you both to be happy."

"I love you, too."

"Fuzzy's right… maybe you are just kids." She hopped off the bed and took my hand, pulling me along and saying, "Let's go find Peter. He's always good fun."

We passed the sliding glass doors out to the pool where I left Lonny sitting, but he was no longer there. Marilyn led me back to the dance floor where "Knock On Wood" by Amii Stewart was blaring throughout the house. I had no idea what time it was but the party was in full swing, and the dance floor was swarming with bodies. Peter soon found his way to where we were dancing, and I was relieved to see he had redressed himself and wasn't half naked. I craned my neck looking for Lonny, but I couldn't find him anywhere.

We had just begun to do a line dance to Michael Jackson's "Don't Stop 'Til You Get Enough" when Mitch Monroe playfully slapped me on the backside and told me Fuzzy was looking for me. He took me by the hand and pulled me away from the dancing mob and I followed obediently, leaving Marilyn and Peter dancing

202

together. I wondered what Mitch's costume was because he looked a bit like Peter Frampton, but he looked a bit like Peter Frampton all the time, so maybe he wasn't dressed up at all. He took me outside by the pool where Fuzzy and Lonny were talking with Howard, and I noticed Lonny giving me the side eye when he saw Mitch holding my hand.

"Hello Ruby," Howard said, "it's nice to see you again."

I smiled. "Hello. Is Louise here?"

"Unfortunately she's out of town." Not one for small talk, Howard got right to the point. "Fuzzy tells me you're interested in joining the tour."

I didn't know how to respond, considering it wasn't my idea to begin with. "Well, I... um..."

I was feeling a bit giddy as I listened to Howard drone on and on, not really paying attention. I think the small bit of alcohol I'd consumed had gone to my head, and I stood there smiling like a fool.

"We were talking about closing down the fan club since it was never very productive anyway, but since Lonny joined the band membership has skyrocketed and we're getting hundreds of new members every week. I was impressed with the photos you took during Lonny's audition... if I provide all the film, would you take photos of the band exclusively for the fan club? I'll give you pre-stamped envelopes and you can just pop the film in the mail back to me."

With my hands on my hips, I pulled a dramatic thinking face and hesitated. I could see Fuzzy and Lonny staring at me like I was insane, then asked, "Will you send me copies of every photo?"

Fuzzy visibly cringed. It was obvious nobody ever asked Howard for much. He reached out to shake my hand and said, "Deal. Welcome aboard."

I thanked him with a huge smile on my face, then leapt into Lonny's arms as I jumped up and down with excitement. Then I hugged Fuzzy, who was the orchestrator of the entire idea. I excused myself and ran back into the house to find Marilyn to tell her the fantastic news. This time it was me grabbing her hand and dragging her away from what she was doing.

203

When we reached the kitchen I was out of breath, saying, "Howard just said I could go on tour!"

"You're coming with us?" she asked, wide-eyed. I nodded wildly and we hugged each other tightly, jumping up and down with excitement. "We can be bus buddies!" she cheered.

We both screamed like teenage girls and continued jumping excitedly until Peter interrupted us, handing us each a cup of punch.

"Save some excitement for midnight," Peter laughed.

"Ruby will be going on the road with us when the tour starts," Marilyn told him. "Now I'll have my doll to keep me company!"

"What fun!" he replied.

I was starting to get hot, and no longer tasting the alcohol in the punch, I chugged it.

"Doll, slow down," Marilyn warned, taking the empty cup away from me. She shoved a giant roll in my face and said, "Eat."

I ate the roll as commanded, but as soon as I was finished, Peter took me by the hand and led me back for more punch, and then onto the dance floor. I was in another world and I was having the time of my life. Peter and I shared the cup of punch he was holding and he was getting quite touchy-feely, which was something I wasn't used to from a complete stranger. Not only a complete stranger, but a famous teen idol.

Peter leaned close to my ear and asked, "How old are you?"

It was hard to hear over the loud music, so I shouted, "Eighteen!" He smiled, seemingly satisfied with my answer.

"How old are you?" I asked, half joking.

"Twenty-five," he spoke directly into my ear, not pulling away. I could feel his breath on my neck as his lips brushed against it, and my skin went all tingly at his touch. I thought he was a bit old to be a teen idol, but then judging by the recent television series he finished filming, he was probably on the downhill slide of his teen idol stardom. It didn't matter much to me, because after the party I would never see Peter Summersby again.

"I Feel Love" by Donna Summer began to thump through the speakers and as the inebriation level of the guests was quite high by this point in the evening, men and women began pairing off, their bodies writhing against each other. Peter was dancing behind me and I could feel him press himself against my back, his hands gently caressing my bare shoulders. He wasn't being inappropriate in any way, and I was enjoying his attention. He rested his chin on my shoulder and wrapped his arms around my waist, entwining his fingers through mine. As he started kissing my neck, I noticed Marilyn filling a cup of punch and handing it to Lonny. He drank it down quickly and she filled it again. He turned and made eye contact with me so I smiled and waved, hoping he would join us, but he just gave me a quick head nod and turned back to focus on Marilyn. She turned to look at me, and I couldn't read her facial expression at all. I couldn't tell if she was scheming, or if she was staying true to her word to leave us alone.

The next thing I knew, Peter took my hand and led me away from the dance floor in search of somewhere in the house a little more private. My head was foggy and I was giggling, tripping over my own feet as my limbs felt like wet noodles. Along the way I took off my shoes and tossed them somewhere, feeling I was in better control with my bare feet touching the floor. We ended up in a small hallway bathroom where Peter put his hands on my waist and lifted me up to sit on the sink. He was a beautiful man with his long, feathered brown hair and bright blue eyes. He flashed a smile showing his perfect teeth and said, "I'd really like to kiss you."

I could no longer feel my face and just giggled, showing my immaturity and inexperience. Thanks to many make-out sessions with Billy, I at least had some experience in the kissing department. Peter placed his hands gently on either side of my neck and leaned in slowly, giving me the option to stop him if I changed my mind. He lightly kissed my right cheek then my left, then brushed his lips against mine before sweetly parting them with his tongue. As we kissed, I wrapped my legs around his waist and pulled him as close to me as possible. He kissed my neck and worked his way down the middle of my chest, and back up again. He was making all the right moves and I was falling deeper and deeper under his spell.

Suddenly the bathroom door opened and Marilyn came stumbling in. "It's time to pass out the hats and horns, doll! Fuzzy's already passing out the champagne!" She left just as abruptly, acting as if what she walked in on was completely normal.

"I should have locked the door," Peter joked.

"Duty calls," I said, hopping off the sink and catapulting into the wall.

We laughed at my drunken clumsiness and he asked, "Can I kiss you at midnight?"

I smiled and nodded, saying, "I'd like that." I exited the bathroom first and found Marilyn near the punch bowl separating the top hats from the tiaras. I knew better than to disturb what she was doing, so I drank another cup of punch.

"So doll," she said, smiling at me. "Is Peter as delicious as he looks?"

"Even better," I laughed, following her with the stack of hats and horns she dumped into my arms.

It was fifteen minutes until midnight as we rushed to give everyone the appropriate hat and a horn to ring in the new year. I strapped a tiara to my head and everything was starting to get a bit blurry. I had no idea where my shoes were, and I suddenly realized I didn't recognize a single face around me. For a brief moment I panicked, not remembering where I was until Marilyn appeared out of nowhere right in front of my face.

"You okay doll?" she asked.

I nodded numbly. "Where's Lonny?"

"Last I saw he was chatting up some hottie dressed like Cher. Can't miss her… she's got the giant Indian headdress on. Countdown is about to start, gotta find my man!" And in an instant she was gone again.

I could see the headdress in the distance and debated whether or not to try and find Lonny. What would I do when I found him? What would I say? Neither one of us was making much of an effort to spend time with each other that evening. My decision was made for me when Peter grabbed my hand and pulled me onto the dance floor where the DJ was getting ready to start the countdown.

10… 9… 8…

Peter is going to kiss me and everyone will see it.

7… 6… 5…

Will Lonny care? Or will he be kissing Cher?
4... 3... 2...

Just then someone grabbed my arm and turned me away from Peter. It was Lonny. As the DJ announced the arrival of 1980, Lonny pressed his lips against mine and smiled. "Happy New Year, Roo."

I wrapped my arms around his neck and pressed my face against his, my heart beating like a runaway train. "Happy New Year, Lonny." Nobody was happier than I was at that very moment.

The DJ announced he was going to slow things down a bit and began playing "Everything I Own" by Bread. I pulled my head back to look at Lonny's face and a million dollar smile covered it.

Lonny sang, "The finest years I ever knew... were all the years I had with you."

We sang the words to each other while we danced, laughing at my horrible voice, which was only worse with the addition of alcohol. When the song was over, Lonny held my hand and took me into the kitchen, both of us in desperate need of food. He took off his white jacket and vest and hung them over a chair, then fixed us both a plate with chicken and potato salad.

As we were stuffing our faces, Peter joined us and said, "Ruby, it was nice meeting you. I'm going to head out."

I jumped up so I could say goodbye and told Lonny I'd be right back. I walked Peter to the door where he kissed my cheek and said, "If you're ever back in town, let me know. Maybe we could have dinner." And with that, he disappeared.

When I returned to where Lonny was finishing up his food he asked, "So what's with that guy?"

"Just having fun," I answered. "Lonny, I'm really tired. Can we go to your room?"

He smiled. "Sure. You done eating?"

I nodded and he threw away our garbage, then took my hand and led the way to his bedroom. We sat on his bed and I found myself leaning hard into him, my head pressed against his shoulder. I could barely keep my eyes open and I just wanted to go to sleep, but I kept giggling. I knew how much Lonny hated giggling teenage girls, and it made me giggle all the more.

207

"I can't find my shoes," I mumbled, laughing.

"They're probably with my jacket. Where's my vest?" he asked, looking shocked that he was missing two pieces of his costume. We both started laughing hysterically, unable to control ourselves.

We could still hear the music blaring through the house, and when "Crazy Horses" by the Osmonds started playing I lost my mind. I jumped off the bed and started dancing like the Osmonds did whenever they performed, and Lonny had tears rolling down his face he was laughing so hard.

I was singing Merrill Osmond's line, "What a show, there they go smokin' up the sky," so loud and so horribly that Lonny covered his ears with his hands. This made me laugh so hard I was doubled over, which in turn threw me off balance and sent me stumbling head first into his lap. I quickly righted myself, but in doing so sent my head spinning. I grabbed his shoulders to keep from falling, and his hands rested on my waist to steady me. I straddled Lonny's lap, wrapping my legs around his waist and looking into his eyes, smiling like a fool. I placed my hands on his cheeks and said, "You'll always be my sweet faced boy."

He smiled and I was suddenly overcome with courage I'd never known before, pulling his face toward me and kissing his mouth. I kissed the left side of his neck, then the right side, and leaned back to look at him. I could barely focus my eyes and tried to read the expression on his face, but it was all a blur. I bit my lower lip as I began to unbutton Lonny's shirt, and when I was done he took it off and threw it on the floor. I reached behind my neck and unsnapped my halter top, letting the straps fall. I watched as Lonny looked down, but the expression on his face quickly turned from hope to confusion. I looked down to see the front of the halter still attached to my nipples with double-sided tape and howled with laughter.

I laughed so hard I fell off Lonny's lap and landed on the floor. He was laughing so hard he kept reaching for my hand and missing it. I opened my eyes as he stood over me trying to help me up, and he began spinning. The whole room began spinning and I asked Lonny to please make it stop, as if he could do anything about it. It wasn't long before I was stumbling to the bathroom to throw up. I ended up lying with my cheek on the cold tile floor as Lonny ran in to throw up after me. Neither one of us had ever consumed alcohol before, and we were paying the price.

When I woke up the next morning, I was face down in the shag carpet of Lonny's bedroom. I could barely open my eyes because of the blinding sun shining through the window, and without moving a muscle I tried to figure out where Lonny was. Somehow he made it onto his bed because I could see his arm hanging over the side of it. At least I thought it was Lonny's arm. Unable to form words, I groaned and saw the arm move. I soon saw Lonny lift his head and turn it my way, his hair covering his face.

There was a light tapping on the door and I heard someone enter. I soon saw Marilyn kneeling on the floor beside me, bending way over so I could see her face. "Oh doll, are you okay?" I could tell she was trying not to laugh. She stood up to check on Lonny and I watched as she smoothed his hair lovingly away from his face.

"What time is it?" Lonny croaked.

"Noon," Marilyn laughed. "You guys need to eat."

Lonny and I both groaned in disgust as he crawled out of bed and went into the bathroom. Marilyn and I could hear him urinating and she called out, "Classy Lonny, real classy."

Marilyn helped me sit up and started laughing when she saw my loose halter straps dangling in front of me, the front of my top still taped to my nipples. "I can see nothing much happened in here last night," she whispered. She snapped my halter around my neck and helped me to my feet just as Lonny came out of the bathroom. We obediently followed her to the kitchen and sat at the table where she plopped a bag of McDonald's in front of us. We both gagged, but she insisted it was the best remedy for a hangover and we weren't going to argue since she was obviously more experienced at these things.

Fuzzy popped in saying, "Ziggy Stardust just left. That's everybody." As soon as he saw our pathetic bodies sitting there he started chuckling. "Congratulations kids, you just survived your first Marilyn Livingston party."

Marilyn dumped cheeseburgers and fries onto plates that she shoved at each of us, ordering us to eat. Reluctantly we both ate everything she gave us, and it did seem to help a lot. Lonny was holding his head and I worried that he might be having one of his headaches. Marilyn produced aspirin and orange juice and we obediently ingested that as well.

I closed my eyes and lay my face on the table, searching for Lonny's hand underneath with my own. I finally found it and linked my pinky around his. He stretched his arm out in front of him and buried his face against it. The phone rang and sent us both moaning, causing Marilyn and Fuzzy to laugh at our ridiculous condition.

Marilyn answered the phone in her singsongy voice and then she said, "She's face down on my kitchen table." I opened my eyes to look at her and she mouthed, "Peter." I scrunched up my nose and closed my eyes again.

Lonny and I didn't stick around long after eating, heading back to his room and crawling into bed where we spent the rest of the day sleeping.

The next day was the big rehearsal that was being filmed at the warehouse, so Fuzzy and Lonny were off early while Marilyn and I would join them a bit later in the morning. I sat quietly eating a bowl of cereal for breakfast when the doorbell rang. Marilyn soon returned with a vase filled with a dozen red roses.

"Those are beautiful!" I gasped. "Fuzzy is so sweet."

"These aren't from Fuzzy," she said, reading the card.

I was shocked, wondering who on earth would be sending Marilyn roses if it wasn't Fuzzy.

"And they're not for me," she added, handing me the card.

I silently read the card which said, *Ruby, I thoroughly enjoyed our time together on New Year's Eve. Cheers, Peter*

"I saw Lonny pull you away from Peter to kiss you at midnight," she said.

I grinned, feeling my face flush. "Yeah, he did."

"Anything happen once you disappeared to his room?"

I wrinkled my forehead trying to remember. "No, I don't think so."

"So my plan *half* worked."

"Plan? What plan?"

"Is that the time?" Marilyn screeched. "We need to get to the warehouse. Filming starts in an hour!"

We rushed out the door and hopped into her Corvette, speeding off to the warehouse, but I wasn't going to let her comment go.

"What plan, Marilyn?"

As the wind whipped our hair against our faces, she lit a cigarette and sighed heavily. "I asked Peter to show you a bit of extra attention at the party, hoping it would make Lonny jealous."

My hands balled into fists on my lap as my face burned fire. "You promised to stay out of it!"

Marilyn opened her mouth to speak, but I turned up the radio so I couldn't hear anything she had to say. Robert Palmer's "Bad Case Of Loving You" was deafening even with the top down, but I didn't care. I had nothing further to say to her and I wasn't interested in any explanation she would try to give for not staying out of my business as she promised. True friends don't break promises, and I now felt even Marilyn had betrayed me. What a fool I was, thinking someone like Peter Summersby would have any interest in a boring, small town girl like me! I was never more humiliated in my life and I just wanted to get away from Marilyn, who kept glancing at me but chose to stay quiet. I knew how difficult that must have been for her, and it showed me she understood how upset I truly was.

When we got to the warehouse I followed Marilyn inside, promising myself I wouldn't make anyone else uncomfortable that day. This was a big day for the band, and especially for Lonny, and I would keep my anger toward Marilyn to myself. As Marilyn greeted Fuzzy with a hug and a kiss, I waved to Lonny and made my way to a seat where I had a good view, but away from the cameras. It looked like it was going to be a huge production based on the cameras and people milling about, and my stomach quivered with excitement. Lonny deserved every bit of this, and I was so proud of him.

Marilyn decided to sit as far away from me as possible, and while I was glad, it made me wonder if it was her way of letting everyone in the room know there was tension between us. She was always fawning over me, and now she wasn't even sitting next to me. Judging from the odd looks I received from Lonny and Fuzzy, they knew something was up. The more I thought about what she did, the angrier I got. Not only did she force a man's attention on me, but she plied Lonny and me with alcohol the entire night in the hopes we'd end up having sex with each other. Who does that? And what kind of man was Peter to go along with it? Billy was right when he said L.A. wasn't for girls like me.

I sat entranced as I watched the band play, talk, and joke around, as if there wasn't an entire film crew there documenting everything they did. Even Lonny seemed to be comfortable in his surroundings, smiling and laughing along with everyone else. I guessed his time in front of cameras for photo shoots and doing endless interviews helped break him out of his shell quite a bit since coming to L.A.. At least it was good for one of us.

Before the band and film crew took a break for a catered lunch, they played "Take Me Home" with Lonny on lead vocals, and he watched me during the entire song as I mouthed the words right back at him. When the song ended he had a smile on his face a mile wide, winking at me and nodding. It made my heart swell to see him so happy.

Benji's wife Wanda and their son Calvin arrived as everyone took a break, but that didn't mean the cameras were turned off. Everything the band did that day was being filmed, even something as simple as eating lunch. I wasn't comfortable with that, and made sure I was nowhere near a live camera.

While everyone else was in the food line, Fuzzy took me to the side and asked, "Is everything okay?"

I shrugged. "Sure."

"What did she do?" he asked, rolling his eyes.

"If you knew anything about what she did, then I'm pissed at you, too."

Fuzzy was visibly shocked. "Shit... what did she do?"

"Ask her."

I walked away and joined Lonny, where he was talking and eating with Benji. I sat on the floor and played with Calvin, the cutest little bald headed baby I'd ever seen. Out of the corner of my eye I could see Fuzzy talking to Marilyn at the back of the room, and she was animated as always as she smoked, talked and chewed gum with her hands doing a lot of the talking. He looked frustrated, his arms folded across his chest and simply nodding.

A few minutes later, Marilyn was standing over me. "Ruby, may I please speak with you privately?"

I didn't even look at her, saying, "No." I wasn't sure if it was my imagination, but I swore the entire room audibly gasped when I refused her.

"Doll, please."

By now every eye was on me, which I hated more than being angry with her. I stood up and followed her outside. I leaned up against the building and folded my arms angrily across my chest. She put her hands gently against my cheeks to make sure I was looking at her.

"Doll, I'm *so* sorry. Please forgive me."

I stared at her, saying nothing.

"Doll, I was wrong. I promised to stay out of it, and I didn't. I hate that you're angry with me."

I stared at her beautiful but sad face and knew she was being honest. I had a feeling she didn't apologize to very many people.

My eyes burned with tears and I cursed myself for getting so emotional. "It's embarrassing," I said, wiping the tears from my face. "You pushed Peter on me, then got me and Lonny drunk!"

For the first time since meeting her, I saw tears welling in Marilyn's eyes, threatening to spill if she wasn't careful. "I just love that kid so much," she said, her voice cracking. "And I love you, too. And maybe I'm wrong, but you and Lonny… you belong together."

"But you can't force something that he doesn't want," I cried.

"I know, and I'm sorry. Please forgive me. I can't live with myself if you stay angry with me. And I certainly won't be able to live with Fuzzy. He's furious."

This made me chuckle. "Good. You deserve it."

She laughed and wiped the tears from her eyes, careful not to smudge her perfectly applied makeup. "I just know that you're Lonny's true happy, and it breaks my heart that he's so oblivious."

"Not as heartbroken as I am."

She gave me a sad smile and pulled me in for a tight hug. She pulled away and smiled, saying, "So Peter…"

"God!" I yelled. "How humiliating!"

"Doll, I didn't ask him to send you flowers. *Roses*, no less."

"What are you saying?"

"I may have asked Peter to pay attention to you at the party, but apparently he ended up fancying you on his own."

"I don't believe you," I pouted.

"Doll, I didn't ask him to send you flowers!" she insisted.

I wanted to stay mad at Marilyn for being so humiliated, but I found the tiniest of grins creeping across my face. "I'm leaving in two days," I reminded her.

"So what? Enjoy yourself! And if that means seeing Peter one more time, what's the harm?"

"I came here to see Lonny."

"Well if the little shit is so blind he can't see you're in love with him, maybe he needs to lose you."

It was an interesting concept except Lonny never stepped up where Billy was concerned, and if he had ever loved me, that would've been the time to do it.

"So you think Peter really likes me?" I asked, chewing on my knuckle.

"He sent roses, didn't he?"

"But you told me he screws anything that moves!"

She pulled a face and said, "Yeah, well, it doesn't mean he's not a nice guy. Or maybe you can get laid before you go back home."

"Marilyn!"

"Just kidding doll, let's get back inside."

We walked back into the rehearsal room arm in arm, much to the relief of Fuzzy and Lonny. Lonny pulled me to the side and asked if everything was okay.

"Yeah," I assured him. "Just a misunderstanding."

"Good. Fuzzy was worried."

"I love you, Lonny."

He grinned, embarrassed, then gave me a hug before returning to his spot behind the microphone and picking up his guitar. How many times could I tell him I loved him and get a response like that before I realized the feeling wasn't mutual?

The rest of the day was spent enjoying the live music, experiencing the filming process, loving how tight the band sounded musically, watching them joke around and have a good time, and see them interact as a cohesive unit that was going to be spending a lot of time together when the tour began in two months. All four guys genuinely liked each other and enjoyed playing together. From what I gathered getting to know Fuzzy and Marilyn, that wasn't always the case with Joey Buckingham in the band. He was a bit of a narcissist and loose cannon and Lonny was his polar opposite, which was a refreshing change for the band, according to Marilyn.

At one point during the rehearsal, one year old Calvin, who was sound asleep in his mother's arms with a sturdy headset over his ears for protection, woke up and squirmed to be put down. He immediately wobbled over to Fuzzy, wanting to be picked up. Everyone laughed as Fuzzy stopped what he was doing to pick up his little nephew, holding him on his lap while he leaned far over to bang on the drums.

"He's better than I am!" Fuzzy cheered playfully.

They were in the middle of playing "Fire In The Sky," and even though Calvin interrupted them, the band continued the song for fun. Benji brought Wanda up to sing into the mic with him, and Marilyn joined Mitch on lead vocals, and I sat back laughing and clapping at the scene before me. The film crew was getting a kick out of it as well, and I noticed Lonny motioning for me to join him. I shook my head violently, not interested in being in front of the camera. He wouldn't take no for an answer, leaving his spot behind the microphone and pulling me out of my chair, dragging me to join the others. He strapped his guitar onto me and played it while standing behind me, pressed as close to my back as he could get. I could feel his breath on my neck, his face so close to mine as he leaned forward to sing into the microphone and I tried so hard not to laugh. I decided to go with the flow and enjoy the moment, knowing in just two days I would be heading back home to the dead of winter and no more Lonny. But instead of singing I animatedly mouthed the words while holding the microphone close

215

to Lonny, not wanting my horrible voice to be heard by anyone other than him when we were in private.

Marilyn and I decided to head home as the band and crew began wrapping things up in the early evening, and before we left Lonny hugged me and brushed his face against my cheek whispering, "I'm so glad you're here."

He smelled so good and his face was so soft against my own, I closed my eyes and smiled, saying, "Me too."

As I followed Marilyn out the door I kept turning back to look at Lonny, who was smiling and waving goodbye. I loved him so much it hurt, and I just didn't seem to be able to find a way to tell him that. Maybe it was time I asked Marilyn for advice instead of begging her to stay out of things.

"Let's have ice cream for dinner!" she announced gleefully, pulling into a local ice cream shop. She ordered a pint of Rocky Road for herself, and I ordered a banana split. We sat outside at a picnic table and enjoyed our tasty treats, and I finally got up the nerve to ask for help.

"What do I do?" I asked helplessly. "How do I get Lonny to understand my feelings for him?"

"I'm glad you asked," she said, licking her spoon. "Lonny is very complicated. It's like he's this little kid who's afraid of his own shadow, but then you see him playing guitar and he's a veteran rock god."

"His guitar is where he feels safe."

"I suppose you could dress up like a guitar and ask him to play you."

We burst into laughter and I almost choked on a piece of banana.

"What are we going to do about Peter?" Marilyn asked.

"Whattya mean?"

"Well, he sent you those beautiful roses. You have to thank him."

"I really do."

Marilyn was silent for a while, staring at me. I knew the gears in her brain were in full motion. We headed back to the house and she promised she'd come up with something. The first thing she did when we walked in the house was dial the phone, tell

216

me it was Peter, and hand me the receiver. Panic ran through every inch of me as I listened to the phone ringing on the other end.

"Hello?" I was too shocked to speak and again he said, "Hello?"

"Hi Peter, it's Ruby." I felt like such an idiot.

"Ruby! Hello!"

"I just wanted to thank you for the roses. They're beautiful."

"You're welcome, love. I'm glad you like them." I couldn't think of another thing to say to him and could feel my face burning as Marilyn watched me intently. "Was today the big rehearsal day?" he asked.

"Yeah, it was amazing. Lots of fun."

"Is Marilyn there?"

I was blowing it big time and handed Marilyn the phone. "Hey sweets," she said. "Yeah, film crew and everything. Things are *huge*."

She continued making small talk with Peter for several minutes, and just before hanging up the phone said, "Come by around eight, we'll have a nightcap. The boys should be home by then." She hung up the phone and smiled at me.

"He's coming here tonight?" I asked.

She nodded. "Let's go float in the pool."

We changed into our bathing suits and relaxed in floating chairs, enjoying the silence. I think we probably both fell asleep because the next thing I knew, Lonny and Fuzzy were jumping into the pool and flipping us off our chairs. Once I regained my bearings I jumped onto Lonny's back and pushed his head under the water. I tried to swim away and as he grabbed for me, he accidentally unhooked the top of my bathing suit which ended up in his hand. I screeched, crossing my arms over my chest, embarrassed.

Lonny's face flushed beet red when he realized what he was holding in his hand. Marilyn and Fuzzy were silently watching the scene play out before them, all of us wondering what Lonny was going to do. Everyone seemed to be frozen in place.

"Let's order Chinese," Fuzzy suggested out of nowhere.

Fuzzy and Marilyn got out of the pool, leaving Lonny and I alone in our awkwardness. Lonny stared at me, his mouth open. I could tell he didn't know whether to throw my top at me, bring it to me, or flee. I stood frozen in my spot against the wall of the pool refusing to move.

"I'm sorry," Lonny croaked.

"Well don't just stand there," I scolded.

Maybe this is my chance.

He slowly made his way through the water, getting closer, but not close enough. "I won't bite you," I told him, getting impatient.

He got close enough to lean far over and tried to hand me my top, but I grabbed his wrist and pulled him closer to me. I wrapped my arms around his neck and pulled his bare chest against mine, smiling. He looked traumatized and his entire body was stiff as a board. I brought my face close to his and kissed his mouth.

Marilyn poked her head out the door and shouted, "Hey doll, Peter's—oh shit, I'm sorry!"

Lonny pulled away from me and got out of the pool, grabbing a towel and disappearing. I managed to get my top back on before climbing out of the pool and wrapping a towel around myself, then sitting in a pool chair. My head was spinning in so many different directions. I didn't know which end was up, and I certainly didn't understand Lonny's response to me.

I didn't have a chance to dwell on it for too long because I soon felt a kiss on my cheek as Peter greeted me with a big smile on his face. At least someone was happy to be with me.

"Thank you so much for the roses," I said, blushing. "You shouldn't have done that."

"Did they make you happy?"

"Yes."

"See?" He flashed his perfect smile, which automatically brought a smile to my face.

I stood up and told Peter I was going inside to dry off and put on some clothes. I passed Lonny in the hallway on the way to his room and he stopped briefly as if he wanted to say something, but kept walking. I hung my bathing suit in the bathroom to dry and threw on a pair of jeans and a t-shirt, then headed into the kitchen where Fuzzy was sorting out the Chinese food containers.

Marilyn pulled me into her bedroom and closed the door. "I'm *so* sorry. I had no idea you were... well... whatever you were doing."

"It doesn't matter," I frowned. "I threw myself at him and he wasn't interested."

"Aw doll, I'm sorry." Marilyn gave me a motherly hug and said, "Let's go play with Peter then."

She always had a way of making me laugh, and this time was no exception. We went back into the kitchen and sat down at the table to eat with the guys. Lonny was extremely quiet, barely looking up from his plate, and I was exhausted from trying so hard with him. Fuzzy, Marilyn and Peter talked about the upcoming tour and I listened politely, smiling when it seemed appropriate.

"Ruby, do you like horses?" Peter asked.

Not wanting to speak while I was chewing, I nodded.

"Would you like to go riding tomorrow?"

I swallowed my food and struggled for the right words. "Thanks, but tomorrow is my last day here, and I'd like to——"

"Go ahead, Roo," Lonny said.

Lonny was doing everything he could to push me away and it broke my heart, but I couldn't force him to love me the way I loved him. And here in front of everyone, he was announcing that I should spend my last day in town with Peter instead of with him, which is where I preferred to be.

I smiled and said, "Sounds great, Peter."

The rest of the evening was spent lounging listening to Peter tell stories of growing up in England, with Marilyn and Fuzzy filling us in on their childhoods as well. I found it difficult to believe Marilyn was a shy overweight girl throughout high school, but she reluctantly pulled out a photo album to prove it.

When Peter was ready to go home I walked him to the door and Lonny went to bed. He gave me a quick kiss on the lips and said he'd pick me up at eight o'clock. Whatever Lonny's problem was, Peter was certainly giving me crystal clear messages, and there was no guessing what his intentions were.

I headed to Lonny's room, wondering why I should still be sharing a bed with him. I closed the door behind me, changed into my pajamas and crawled into bed beside him. I turned my back on him, unable to comprehend why he would rather I spent my last day in town with Peter instead of with him. I felt him turn over and wiggle closer to me, pressing his face against my back. I just couldn't figure him out, and I didn't know if I had the strength to try anymore.

I was up at seven o'clock, showered and ready to go, and when I entered the kitchen Peter was conversing with Marilyn while waiting for me. He told me to bring a bathing suit, so I headed back to Lonny's room to fetch mine from the bathroom. Lonny poked his head out from under the covers as I came out of the bathroom.

"Roo, about yesterday…."

I waved him off with the hand holding my bathing suit. "It's okay, I get it."

"But you don't."

"It's okay, Lonny," I said with a smile. "I'm sorry for pushing myself on you."

I left before he could say anything else, rejoining Marilyn and Peter in the kitchen where she told him, "We have dinner reservations at Dan Tana's at seven-thirty, so make sure you get her back here by six-thirty."

Peter agreed and I happily followed him out to the jet black Camaro parked in the driveway. He explained that he owned a couple of horses that he boarded at a friend's stables, and we would be heading there first. I hadn't been on a horse in a long time, and the thought of reconnecting with such a beautiful beast made me smile.

Peter introduced me to his friend Glen, the owner of the stables, then held my hand as he led me toward the beautiful black and white Appaloosa horses waiting for us. He told me the story about how he rescued the mare siblings from someone who could no longer care for them. He came upon them on a drive through a rural area and seeing their skin and bones condition, immediately drove up to the house and made an offer the owners couldn't refuse.

"I was lost," Peter said. "I had no idea where I was when I saw these beautiful girls. After that experience, I've never gotten upset about getting lost again. I feel like it always happens for a reason, even if we never know why."

"That's a good way to look at it. They're beautiful."

Peter helped me onto the mare named Calliope, and he climbed atop her sister, Aphrodite. I mentioned the Greek mythology connection and he told me how much he loved it, which was one thing we had in common. We rode the trails for a couple of hours, stopping at a secluded spot to eat the lunch Peter had prepared for our day. He secured the horses and set out a blanket for us to sit on, then unpacked the food from the picnic basket hanging off the side of his horse. He had sandwiches, an assortment of cheeses, fruit, and what looked to be homemade chocolate chip cookies. He handed me a bottle of Perrier and clinked his against mine.

"You've thought of everything," I said, popping a grape in my mouth.

"It's not my first time," he chuckled.

"Ah, I see." He placed a hand on my shoulder and I stiffened.

"You seem a bit distant today."

"Peter, I'm not the person you met at the party. That was the first time I'd ever had alcohol, and I know Marilyn asked you to pay special attention to me."

"Is that what you think I'm doing now?"

"I don't know."

Peter sighed and said, "I will admit I fancied the idea of playing a role for Marilyn that night, but the more time I spent with you I realized I liked you. You're beautiful, you're funny, and even though you can't sing or dance to save your life, you're a hell of a lot of fun."

I placed a hand on my blushing cheek and asked, "Are you trying to get in my pants?"

"Is it working?"

"No."

"I kid," he insisted. "And I know you're leaving tomorrow, but I just wanted to spend a little time with you."

I grinned, a little embarrassed at his glowing words. "Thank you."

"I think what's attracted me to you is that you're different."

"Different?" I chuckled.

"The girls I meet are generally pretentious starlets or girls only interested in money, or what my money can buy them. You don't seem to be like that."

"Money comes and goes, you know? But if you treat people like crap, all the money in the world isn't going to make you a good person."

He smiled, then leaned forward to kiss me softly on the lips. "See? Different." After eating a bit he asked, "So what's the deal with Lonny? You said he's like your brother, but Marilyn wanted me to make him jealous."

"Marilyn had this funny idea that Lonny and I belong together," I replied. "She doesn't understand that we're best friends, and not interested in each other that way." It was partially true, but Peter didn't need to know the whole sordid story.

"But he made sure he was the one kissing you at midnight," he teased with a grin.

"Tradition," I lied. "And he's very protective of me. He doesn't know you, so...."

"I see. Well good. I'm glad you have a friend like him in your life."

I sighed, putting on a smile instead of crying, which is what I felt like doing when I thought about my embarrassing display with Lonny the day before. "Yeah, he's my very best friend."

We finished our lunch and Peter packed everything back up, but before helping me back on Calliope he put his hands on my cheeks and leaned in for a kiss. It started out sweet and slowly escalated to smoldering, his tongue warm in my mouth, sending a shockwave through my body that caused my toes to curl. My body experienced tingling in areas I'd never experienced before, and I wanted to explore them further.

We rode back to the stables and I watched as Peter and Glen brought the horses into the barn to get them settled. When they reemerged, Peter patted Glen on the back and shook his hand and we were back in his Camaro driving to our next destination, which happened to be his house. It was a modest home compared to others in the area, but it was still four times larger than my parents' house. He held my hand as he guided me inside, then showed me where the bathroom was so I could change into my bathing suit.

I closed the door and stared at myself in the mirror. Who was I looking at? I had no idea. I came to L.A. to visit Lonny for a few days, and here I was on a date with a celebrity who sent me into another world with his kisses. This couldn't be real, I reasoned. I had to be dreaming the entire thing. I stripped off my clothes and put on my bathing suit and looked at my body. I was still built more like a boy than a girl, with my barely-there breasts and skinny arms and legs. But Peter thought I was beautiful… at least that's what he said. I found it so hard to believe staring at my reflection, yet my face was lightly sun-kissed and my blue eyes popped brighter than I'd ever noticed before. Maybe the California air and sunshine had something to do with it. Or maybe it was being in the company of Peter, who was not only a beautiful man, but seemed to have a beautiful soul.

I must have been taking too long, because he tapped on the door and asked if I was all right. I groaned quietly, not really wanting him to see me in my bathing suit, but asked if he had a towel. He opened the door a crack and I saw his hand slide in, trying to hand me a towel without looking. I thanked him, then wrapped the towel around me and made my way out into the hallway. He was dressed only in a pair of red swim trunks and he looked heavenly. If he was a regular swimmer, it would explain his lean and toned body.

He jumped into the pool first and promised to cover his eyes as I took off my towel, but as soon as I threw the towel on a chair he whistled at me. He was so adorable I couldn't be mad at him, so I jumped in right beside him. When I surfaced, Peter was right there to pull me into his arms and kiss me quickly on the cheek. I wrapped my arms around his neck as we looked into each other's eyes and he smiled. He had such a beautiful, heartwarming smile. I hesitated a moment, then brushed my lips against his. Something gave me courage, and it wasn't alcohol this time, so I kissed him hungrily and he reciprocated.

223

Peter pulled away and asked if I wanted to race him, and I gladly accepted the challenge. We started at the shallow end of the pool against the wall, and when he gave the call we were both racing through the water to the opposite side and back again. He only beat me by a few seconds, and was impressed that I was able to keep up with him.

"Have you always been a swimmer?" he asked, wiping his wet hair away from his face.

"I love the water. I almost drown when I was a little kid, but my mother made sure to put me right back in the water so I wouldn't be afraid. I'm glad she did."

"That sounds frightening."

"It was. I don't get to swim anymore, so it's been nice doing it while I've been here."

"We never swam in England. It just wasn't something we did. Once I came here though, I loved it instantly."

"Is that how you keep in such good shape?"

He smiled, almost looking embarrassed. "I swim every day, yes. And thank you."

Peter and I got out of the pool and climbed onto a hammock to dry off in the warm sun. He got on first, then I followed, ending up cuddled next to him with his arms wrapped around me. We were silent as the hammock swayed slowly, enjoying the sounds of nature around us. I closed my eyes, enjoying the feeling of his fingertips caressing my arm. I'd never felt so peaceful and safe in the arms of a guy before. Not surprising, considering Billy was my only reference point, but it spoke volumes in everything I was missing whenever he and I were together.

"Do you ever get lonely, Ruby?" Peter asked.

"All the time."

"People think celebrities have it made, and in so many ways we do. But I think we're probably the loneliest people in the world."

"Why?"

"It's hard to trust people. Hard to know what their intentions are. I never know if people are interested in me, Peter Summersby, boring guy from England, or Peter Summersby, singer, actor, celebrity. Especially women. Most of them are only interested in the celebrity and don't care much about anything else."

"I don't think you're boring. You're very sweet and kind, and you love Greek mythology and animals. And you're a great kisser."

He laughed, covering his face with his hands. "Have you enjoyed the time we've spent together?"

"Very much."

"I have, too. You helped ease the loneliness, even if it was only for a little while."

"What happens for you next?"

"I go into the studio and start my new album. Maybe someday one of my goofy love songs will actually be true," he chuckled.

"Don't ever give up on love. We all want it so badly, thinking we'll never find it, but I believe we all have our true love out there somewhere."

Peter put his finger under my chin and lifted my head so he could see my face. "You're a bright light, Ruby. Don't ever let anyone steal it away from you."

I smiled and he kissed my lips softly. Announcing he was parched, he took my hand and led me into the house where he poured us each a glass of lemonade. I sat on the couch and he disappeared, telling me he'd be right back. He returned holding a small box.

"I want you to have this," he said, handing it to me.

I opened the box to see a stunning silver necklace with a beautiful turquoise pendant hanging from it. I had no idea what to say.

"It was my grandmother's," he explained.

"Peter, I can't take this."

"Why not?"

"We only just met, and it's your grandmother's."

He looked perplexed. "Don't you like it?"

I assured him I thought it was beautiful and his gesture was very much appreciated, but I couldn't accept the gift.

"But I thought all girls expected gifts."

I placed the box on the table and smiled at him. "I'm not one of those girls. Besides, you already sent me roses!"

"So you're truly content just spending time with me?"

I nodded and smiled. "Yeah." I noticed the clock on the wall said four. "And we don't have much time left together."

He flashed a huge smile, looking almost relieved. He took my hand and led me to a gorgeous, white baby grand piano. He sat on the bench and pulled me down next to him. I sat in awe as his fingers fluidly ran up and down the piano keys as if it were no effort at all.

He sang, "No longer a little girl, not yet a woman, she lights up my life with her smile and her charm, and all I want is to hold her in my arms."

"Is that one of your new songs?" I asked.

"I just made that one up. For you."

I grinned, embarrassed, holding my hands against my blushing cheeks.

He continued to play and sing other songs of his that I knew, and then decided to play several different classical pieces that were absolutely breathtaking. I had no idea he was that talented on the piano, or any instrument for that matter, and he took my breath away. That was all the gift I would ever need from Peter. He serenaded me for about an hour, then took my hand and kissed the top of it, leading me to the couch where he stretched out on his back, and pulled me on top of him.

"I almost didn't go to Marilyn's party," he said. "But I'm so glad I did."

I looked down at him and said, "Me, too."

We began kissing and his hands slid down my back and stopped on my backside, where he playfully squeezed. I pulled my face away from his to look at him, and he grinned.

"I have no intention of doing anything you don't want me to," he said.

The problem was, I enjoyed everything he was doing and I wondered how far I was going to let him go. We continued kissing and he slid his hands inside my bathing suit and squeezed my behind and I didn't protest. In fact, I kissed him harder. He was causing feelings I'd never experienced before and my body was

226

reacting accordingly. I was beginning to understand what Marilyn meant about sex being a wonderful thing, unlike what I experienced with Billy.

Peter sat up and placed his hands on my neck as he continued kissing me sweetly, then switched positions so he was lying on top of me. Our bodies moved in synch with each other, and I began to feel a fire between my legs I'd never known before. My breathing became labored, I felt lightheaded, and all of a sudden Peter stopped what he was doing and sat up. I looked at him bewildered as he ran a hand through his hair.

"Sorry Ruby, I just… we should stop."

I sat up and said, "I'm gonna put my clothes back on."

"Yeah, good idea."

I disappeared to the bathroom and peeled off my bathing suit and put my clothes back on. My face was flushed and I grinned, thinking about what almost just happened with Peter. When I rejoined him in the living room, he was dressed in a pair of jeans and button down shirt, with most of the buttons undone. He was definitely a sexy man, and a truly nice guy to top it off. He pulled me into his arms and kissed the top of my head.

"I know you're not that kind of girl," he said. "And I don't want to be that guy."

I lifted my head to look up at him and smiled. "I might not have stopped you."

"If circumstances were different… well, let's get you home. Marilyn will never forgive me if I bring you back late." We both laughed, knowing how true his statement was. He grabbed the box with the turquoise necklace inside it and said, "Can I please give you this gift? Something to remember me by?"

He was so sweet and sincere I felt accepting his kind gift wouldn't do any harm. I nodded and his face lit up. He took the necklace out of the box and fastened it around my neck, where it fell just below the beaded necklace Gina made for me. I thanked him and gave him a quick kiss as he patted me on the bottom and gently pushed me toward the door.

Peter pulled into Marilyn's driveway and removed his sunglasses to look at me. "I'm going to kiss you goodbye now," he said, "but I'm going to walk you to the door."

227

"Such a gentleman," I gushed.

"It was lovely meeting you, Ruby," he said with a smile. "You helped ease my loneliness, at least for a little while."

"Thank you for everything."

He leaned forward, kissing me softly on the mouth. "Maybe one day we'll meet up again."

"I'd like that."

Peter walked me to the door, ringing the bell. He decided to give me a deep goodbye kiss while he waited for someone to answer. Marilyn flung the door open and said, "Hey doll."

Peter walked me into the house, kissing Marilyn on the cheek and thanking her for introducing us. We walked into the living room where we leaned over the balcony to see Lonny and Fuzzy below.

"Lonny!" Peter shouted from above. "Thank you for letting me spend the day with Ruby!" He kissed the top of my hand and whispered, "Thank you for indulging me. I will think of you often."

I smiled as he hugged me goodbye, then he kissed me quickly on the lips and walked out the door. Marilyn was immediately at my side whispering, "Doll, did you...?"

I looked at her and grinned, walking off to Lonny's bedroom to take a shower and change for dinner. When I joined the others in the kitchen afterward in my new sundress, Marilyn was putting a tie around Lonny's neck and I smiled. He looked miserable, but so handsome.

"Come on doll," she gently scolded Lonny. "Fuzzy's wearing a tie, too. Don't you want to look nice for Ruby's going away dinner?"

It suddenly hit me that in the morning I would be headed home, and my time in L.A. would be over. I would have to say goodbye to Fuzzy and Marilyn, and to Lonny, who I hadn't really talked to all day. I was silently cursing myself for getting so caught up in Peter, as my time with Lonny was growing shorter.

Lonny and I hopped in the back of Fuzzy's car and we were off for our last dinner together. I watched Marilyn from where I sat, always so elegant and put together. She was so beautiful, and I loved seeing her and Fuzzy together. They were so perfect for each

228

other, even though they were vastly different. I looked over at Lonny who was staring out the window, and wondered what he was thinking about. I reached out and took his hand in mine, intertwining my fingers through his. He looked at me and smiled, squeezing my hand.

When we got out of the car at the restaurant, Fuzzy handed his keys to the valet and we were suddenly taken aback by the sound of a loud, shrill scream. Two young girls recognized Lonny and started running toward us, shouting his name as we were quickly ushered inside.

Lonny looked petrified as Fuzzy slapped him on the back with a laugh and said, "Get used to it kid, it's only going to get worse."

We sat in a booth and Marilyn said, "It's hard to believe you're leaving us tomorrow, doll."

"I know, I can't believe it."

"I'm going to miss having you around," she said.

"It's only for a little while," Fuzzy reminded all of us. "The tour starts in two months and we'll all be back together then."

"Stay here," Lonny said. I smiled at my best friend, who looked hopeful that I would consider his suggestion. "Don't go home. Stay here until we leave for the tour."

I smiled and replied, "My parents would kill me. It's going to be hard enough to tell them I'm going on tour, and I have to do it face to face. And I have to tell Ricky I'm quitting my job." Lonny looked disappointed and I said, "Why don't you come home with me until the tour?"

"No can do, doll," Marilyn said. "Too much to do here. Plus, we have a surprise we've been waiting to tell you about."

I squirmed in my seat, waiting to hear about the big surprise.

"Lonny, I think you should do the honors," Fuzzy said, winking.

A huge smile crossed Lonny's face as he looked at me and said, "We're gonna be on *The Midnight Special* in three weeks."

I gasped, covering my mouth with my hands. I was so excited I practically jumped into Lonny's lap trying to hug him. I couldn't think of anything intelligent to say, continuing to gasp and cover my mouth with my hands. Lonny was going to be on television! I would definitely need to make sure his mom stayed sober and awake so she wouldn't miss him.

We had a delicious Italian meal and I was thoroughly enjoying being in the company of Fuzzy and Marilyn, and of course, Lonny. I didn't want to go home. Not that I didn't want to see my parents, but being in L.A. was surreal, and I didn't want to go back to my regular, boring life. Granted, it would only be for a couple of months, but the midwest is so dreary in the dead of winter, and I didn't want to spend a single day away from Lonny.

Lonny held my hand as we left the restaurant, and as soon as we walked outside, it was as if chaos began raining down from the sky. It started out slowly but the sound of screaming girls soon filled our ears and an onslaught of teenage bodies appeared like an army out of nowhere. The screaming was deafening and I found myself getting knocked backward as Lonny was seemingly ripped from my grasp. I could see Fuzzy struggling to gain control of the situation, but he was losing the battle quickly. The next thing I knew something smacked me in the face and I hit the ground hard, and all I could see was mass hysteria above me. Every time I tried to stand, I'd get knocked down again by someone trying to get close to Lonny, wherever he was.

All of a sudden Marilyn appeared out of nowhere, grabbing my hand and screaming at a girl standing over me, "Get out of the way, you stupid bitch!"

She pulled me to my feet and before I could gain a sense of balance, she was shoving me into the back seat of Fuzzy's car, and as soon as she was securely in place, he drove off quickly. I was wide-eyed and shell shocked and turned to look at Lonny, whose hair was sticking up all over, as if girls were trying to rip it out of his head. He had a long scratch across the side of his face, and his shirt was completely ripped open. His tie was gone, and every single button on the front of his shirt was missing.

Visibly shaken, Lonny turned to look at me, his eyes huge with terror and his mouth agape. He reached out and lightly touched the skin next to my left eye and I recoiled in pain. He pulled me next to him on the seat and put his arm around me, where I rested my head against his shoulder. I began to wonder

230

how Lonny was going to handle the crazy fans from now on; he was just a kid who shot to superstardom seemingly overnight and he had no idea what he was in for.

When we got back to the house, Marilyn was nursing Lonny's facial wounds as I went into the bathroom to see why my face hurt so badly when Lonny touched it. I looked in the mirror and saw a cut over my left eyebrow, and a brilliant shiner beginning to form. I went into the kitchen as Lonny was leaving to go change his clothes, and Marilyn sat me down to nurse the cut over my eye.

"It could've been worse," she said, examining my eye. "I thought I'd never find you at the bottom of that pile."

"Is that what it's going to be like for Lonny? All the time?"

She gave me a motherly smile and whispered, "Probably for a while. But at least on tour there will be bodyguards and security. It'll get better, I promise."

"That was terrifying."

Cleaning the cut over my eyebrow she whispered, "So Peter…."

"What about Peter?" I knew what she wanted to know.

She grinned. "I'm sorry doll, it's none of my business."

"Peter is a nice guy," I told her. "And you were wrong. He doesn't screw everything that moves."

She lovingly put her hands to my cheeks and kissed my forehead.

Lonny returned in a pair of shorts and grabbed a soda from the refrigerator. "You okay Roo?"

"My parents are going to freak when they see this black eye," I joked. "But I'm okay."

Marilyn took an ice pack out of the freezer and handed it to me, ordering me to the couch to relax. I obeyed her orders and sat on the couch to ice my eye as Lonny sat next to me with his guitar. He and Fuzzy sang to us and I tried not to feel down because I was leaving in the morning. I savored every last moment I had with them, knowing that in just two short months we would all be together again.

Lonny eventually set his guitar on the floor and I stretched out next to him, resting my head on his leg. As I iced my eye he looked down at me and smiled, finger combing my hair like I always did to him. I thought about the mass of girls that swarmed Lonny and giggled. Then I burst into uncontrollable laughter.

I pointed at Marilyn and said, "I'm on the ground and all of a sudden here you come, throwing girls out of the way like the Incredible Hulk!"

She shrugged and smiled, and we all laughed loudly. "I didn't want you to get swallowed up, doll."

Fuzzy stood up to give a reenactment of the event, acting like he was tossing bodies across the room, then speaking in a high pitched woman's voice, "Get out of the way, you stupid bitch!"

We were all in stitches and Marilyn just grinned and took the ribbing we gave her.

I closed my eyes and basked in the attention Lonny was giving me until my ice pack was nothing but cold water and Marilyn took it from me. At that point Lonny said he was tired and wanted to go to bed, so he took me by the hand and I followed him.

We got comfortable in his bed, facing each other, and he said, "I'm sorry you got hurt because of me."

"It wasn't your fault."

"What's it going to be like on tour?"

I smiled and said, "You'll have bodyguards and security on tour. At least that's what Marilyn said."

"Are you sure you still want to come?"

My heart sunk. "Don't you want me to?"

"Well yeah. But I don't want you getting hurt."

"I'll be okay."

Lonny got quiet, but never took his eyes off me. After a long silence he whispered, "Do you like Peter?"

I wrinkled my nose and said, "He's a really nice guy. But he's not my boyfriend or anything."

"He's better than Billy," he teased. We both got a chuckle out of that.

"Nothing happened, if you're wondering. I'm not that kind of girl, Lonny."

"I know. But I know what Billy did and—"

"Peter was a gentleman. He's one of the good guys."

232

"Am I one of the good guys?"

A huge smile crossed my face as I replied, "You're the only good guy that matters."

Lonny reached his hand up to push a strand of hair out of my eyes and I sensed that he wanted to say something, but he remained quiet. I just smiled.

"Why do you put up with me?" he asked.

What a strange question.

"Because you're my best friend and I love you."

"But I'm a stupid jerk."

"You're not. Don't say that."

"Don't leave," he whispered. "Please stay here."

"I don't want to go home," I admitted. "But I have to. And I'm out of clothes."

"You can wear mine."

I giggled. "It's only for a couple months."

"Will you think about it?"

"Lonny, I—"

Lonny pressed his lips against mine and held them there. My heart raced as he opened his mouth slightly and we just took in each other's breath. Time seemed to stop, and I didn't dare move. I tried to read the look in his eyes, but simply waited to see what he would do next. His fingertips gently touched my cheek as he inched his body as close to me as possible, his lips never leaving mine. He gently searched my mouth with his tongue, sending me over the moon. I closed my eyes as I touched my tongue to his, entwined in our first physical expression of love. He continued to kiss me softly, almost as if he was afraid he might hurt me. I melted under the spell of his kisses, finding it hard to believe it was actually happening. It wasn't hard and hurried, and it wasn't all tongues. Lonny was sweet and gentle, just like the boy I always knew. And it was the best kiss I'd ever been a part of; one I never wanted to end. Lonny and I were both inexperienced when it came to physical love, but the raw emotion and innocence of our relationship made everything that much more powerful. His mouth was soft, like an artist's brush just barely grazing its canvas, warm and gentle and leaving me aching for more.

He pulled away to look at my face and smiled, wiping a tear from my cheek that I didn't remember crying.

"Please don't stop," I whispered.

"Stay with me."

"I'll think about it."

He kissed the tip of my nose then pulled me into his arms, where we lay silently until he fell asleep. I don't think I slept much that night, completely comfortable being held in his arms, but at the same time not really sure what it meant. Did Lonny profess his love for me by kissing me the way he did, or was he trying to figure out the best way to convince me to stay?

I snuck out of bed early to take a shower, knowing Lonny would be disappointed in my decision to go home as planned. There were too many loose ends to take care of before I left for the tour, and he was going to be busy with countless interviews, photo shoots, rehearsals and any number of tour preparations. I truly didn't want to leave him, but I had no choice.

I tried to be quiet while packing my suitcase, not wanting to wake Lonny up, but I soon heard him ask, "Why?"

I looked up to see him watching me, and he was visibly disappointed.

"I have so much to do," I explained. "And you're gonna be so busy anyway."

He got out of bed and went into the bathroom to do his business, then I heard him turn on the shower. He didn't even bother closing the door. I decided to give him some privacy and went into the kitchen where Marilyn was preparing breakfast.

"Oh doll," she sniffled, smashing her cigarette out in the ashtray. "I can't believe you have to leave already."

"I know," I frowned. "Lonny *really* doesn't want me to go." I looked around to make sure Fuzzy and Lonny weren't lurking nearby and whispered, "He kissed me last night. *Really* kissed me."

Marilyn held a hand to her heart and gasped audibly. "My sweet boy," she whispered, dabbing at pretend tears. "Did his tongue fall out?"

234

I laughed and assured her Lonny's tongue was just fine. Marilyn pulled an envelope off the counter and handed it to me. "A little gift."

I opened the envelope and pulled out handfuls of Polaroids Marilyn took while I was there. There were a lot of photos of me with Peter, which made me smile. Somehow she got a photo as Lonny quickly kissed me at midnight, and I clasped my hand over my mouth.

"How did you manage to catch that?" I asked.

"Just lucky I guess."

"Thank you so much."

"Anything for you, doll. I'm gonna miss you."

"Don't make me cry."

"Okay okay," she said, waving her hands in the air. "Breakfast. Where's Lonny?"

"Shower."

I took the envelope of photographs Marilyn gave me and went back to Lonny's room to put them in my suitcase. He was just zipping his jeans as I entered. Lonny's kiss the night before had me seeing him with new eyes as he stood in front of me in just a pair of jeans, his hair wet and brushed away from his face.

"Break... fast is almost ready," I stammered. I tossed the envelope into my suitcase and when I turned around he was already gone. I went back to the kitchen where Lonny and Marilyn were laughing and smoking, and I sat next to him.

"Look at you two," Marilyn cooed. "My little bruisers."

My black eye was grossly purple, and the scratch on Lonny's cheek looked like something out of a horror movie. We were definitely a pair that morning.

Fuzzy soon joined us and in his always jovial way, laughed loudly at us and said, "Whoa! Who won that fight?"

Lonny and I both said, "Marilyn," and everyone was in stitches.

The entire time we ate breakfast, Lonny sat as close to me as he possibly could, and held my free hand under the table. This was so unlike the Lonny I was used to; I had no idea if our relationship had progressed beyond the friendship stage, but I was enjoying it.

235

It wasn't long after I helped Marilyn clean up after breakfast that we heard Fuzzy telling us my taxi was outside. My heart jumped into my throat and I went to Lonny's room to grab my suitcase. We all walked outside where Marilyn was taking photos of everyone. She especially wanted to make sure she got a photo of Lonny and I with our battered faces, which we made sure to ham it up for.

I didn't realize saying goodbye was going to be so hard. Not just for me, but for all of us. Fuzzy gave me a huge bear hug and almost didn't let me go. He whispered, "Love you doll, see you soon."

Marilyn turned her back on me, not wanting to say goodbye at all. Fuzzy reminded her the taxi was waiting and she finally turned to face me, tears streaming down her face. She pulled me into her arms and cried against my cheek, which didn't help the emotions I was having a hard time controlling. If it was this hard saying goodbye to Marilyn, how would I ever say goodbye to Lonny?

Fuzzy finally pulled Marilyn away from me so I could say goodbye to Lonny. By this time I was a complete mess, wrapping my arms around his neck and bawling against his face. He hugged me so tightly I could hardly breathe, and I didn't care because without Lonny I had no use for breath.

"I'm sorry," I cried. "I should've stayed."

He gently pushed me away so he could look at my face. "It's only a couple months," he reminded me with a smile.

I couldn't stop crying, and part of that was because I didn't know how to say goodbye to Lonny. Should I kiss him? Should I let him make the first move? My head was so messed up and I was kicking myself for making the responsible choice to go home.

"I love you, Lonny," I whispered, wiping the ugly tears from my face.

He smiled and gave me one last hug, then pulled me in for a long kiss that I wasn't expecting, especially in front of everyone. The sound of the taxi's horn pushed us apart, but before I turned to get into the vehicle Marilyn ran up to me for one last hug.

"I love you, doll."

"I love you, too. Please take care of him," I whispered.

"I promise." She handed me the dry Polaroids she had taken outside and I got into the taxi. We all waved to each other as the taxi pulled away, and I saw Marilyn pull Lonny into her arms and kiss the top of his head. Why did I feel so guilty for leaving?

2011

I was rearranging my suitcase when Lonny returned to the room. He tossed his suitcase on the bed with such force that it knocked mine on the floor, spilling its contents in the process. I glared at him and he mumbled a barely audible apology. I sat on the floor and repacked my suitcase, wondering how long the drive was going to be all the way back home. It was going to be agonizing, no matter how long it took.

Lonny's phone rang and he answered it quickly. "Hey Fuzzy."

I found it interesting that two men video chatted with each other as often as Fuzzy and Lonny seemed to. And I could hear their entire conversation.

"Hey kid, have you had a chance to look at those contracts yet?"

"Sorry man, not yet. I'll look at them tonight when I get to Chicago."

"Mare wants to know if she's going to see Ruby soon."

"Not sure," Lonny grumbled. "Ask her."

Lonny tossed his phone at me, hitting me in the shoulder. I tried not to look angry when I saw Fuzzy, but it was a bit hard to disguise.

"Hey doll," he said, looking a bit concerned.

"Hey Fuzzy."

"Mare wants to know if she'll be seeing you anytime soon."

I frowned and said, "Probably not. I'll be staying with my parents once Lonny drops me off."

"Aw doll, don't say that. It's been too long."

"I know, but—"

"Think about it."

I assured him I would and threw the phone back at Lonny, where it ricocheted off his chest and hit the floor.

I heard Fuzzy say, "You two are making me dizzy."

238

"Sorry man, I'll call you tonight." Lonny ended his call and tossed his phone on the bed. "It's about an eight hour drive," he announced. "Depending on the traffic."

Eight hours! I didn't want to be stuck in a car with Lonny for another eight hours. I could certainly sleep through some of it, but the rest would be a nightmare. I found myself longing for my crappy apartment in New York... but only briefly. Soon I would be home with my parents and I could think about the next phase of my life. Without Billy and without Lonny.

As Lonny pulled out of the hotel parking lot he asked, "Do you need anything?"

"Nope."

And with that we were off. Neither of us speaking, only the radio filling the awkward silence. Two hours into our silent trip I felt my phone buzzing in my back pocket and pulled it out to take a look.

Billy: Are you fucking him?

"What do you care!" I screamed at my phone, throwing it on the floor of the car.

"Billy?" Lonny asked.

"Doesn't matter," I grumbled. I closed my eyes and fell asleep, only to be woken about an hour later by the sound of something seriously wrong with the car. I tried to focus my eyes as Lonny was pulling off to the side of the road, steam billowing out the front of the car. He parked and got out to lift the hood, poking around the engine for a bit before getting back in the car and calling for a tow truck. We sat there for another agonizingly silent hour before we were finally rescued.

Once the tow truck driver had the car hooked up, we got into the front of his truck for a ride to the mechanic's shop. It just so happened the driver was a big Livingston Monroe fan and recognized Lonny immediately. Lonny introduced me as his sister and I just smiled and nodded. I stared out the window as Lonny politely answered questions about his days in the band, and the driver talked about a couple of shows he attended back in the day.

He was a nice guy, and it helped that Lonny had someone to talk to instead of the dead silence we were giving each other.

Lonny and I sat in the waiting room flipping through magazines or pacing the floor for an hour or so until a mechanic joined us to tell him there was a hole in the radiator and it would need to be replaced. He would have to order the replacement, and since it was already so late in the day he wouldn't have it until the next morning.

"Sorry Roo," Lonny said. "Looks like we'll be spending the night."

"Where *are* we?" I asked.

"Cleveland," the mechanic answered. He kindly called us a taxi and gave us the names of some hotels in the area. The last thing I wanted was to spend another night in a hotel room with Lonny, but I bit my tongue as we both thanked the man and waited for our ride.

We walked into the hotel Lonny decided on and I said, "I want my own room."

"Fine," was his response.

Lonny handed me my key card and we each disappeared into our separate rooms. I was exhausted and just wanted to sleep, but I flopped onto the bed and found myself staring at the ceiling. I wanted to call my mom, but then I would have to explain everything that happened and I preferred to do that in person. And I didn't want to ruin the surprise, since she had no idea I was coming home with Lonny.

I pulled the tattered copy of *Jane Eyre* from my suitcase and tried to read, but even my favorite book couldn't keep me focused. I opened the texts I received from Billy, looking at the photos he sent of me and Lonny. I smiled, remembering everything that happened in Niagara Falls, and how much fun we had together. I thought about what almost happened between us, and wondered how different things would be had Lonny not passed out. What on earth was wrong with us? Why were we always so on edge and ready to bite each other's head off? I read Billy's last text to me and threw my phone across the room, hitting the door. My phone lit up with another text and I didn't even want to look at it.

I thought about what my life had become since agreeing to move to New York with Billy. He promised things were going to be great, promised we would have a wonderful life together. I left my parents and Joanie behind, I left my friends, a job I loved, everything that was familiar and comfortable. He used that to control me, cutting me off from everyone I was in contact with and quickly making it so I was completely dependent on him for everything.

I thought about what a weak and easily manipulated person I was my entire life and my heart ached. I was so tired of being angry, and the loneliness was just too much to take. I didn't know how it was possible to have any tears left, but there they were, the one thing in my life that was not only constant, but a reminder that I was still alive.

I crawled off the bed and walked to the door, picking up my phone. I sat on the floor and leaned against the door, wiping the tears from my cheeks. I was so tired of crying. I looked at my phone and saw a text from Lonny.

Lonny: Are you hungry?
Me: No.

I dressed for bed and crawled in, pulling the covers over my head and hoping to shut out the world, even though it was still light outside. It worked, because I didn't wake up again until the next morning. I opened my eyes, expecting Lonny to be in the bed next to me, but of course he wasn't.

I slumped to the bathroom and took a shower, wondering how I was going to spend my day. God only knew how long it would take to get the car fixed, and how long we'd be stuck at the hotel. I hated fighting with Lonny, but in this circumstance he was wrong. He had no right saying the awful things he did to me about how his nightmares were real and mine were just petty annoyances.

As soon as I was dressed, there was a knock on my door. I looked through the peephole to see Lonny sticking his tongue out at me. I opened the door and he asked if I wanted to go to breakfast.

241

"No thanks," I said, getting ready to close the door on him.

"Wait." He handed me a wad of cash and said, "I don't know how long it'll be before the car is ready, so I'm going to stay here and work today. Feel free to do whatever you want."

I glanced at the cash in my hand then up at him. I thanked him and closed the door. At least I didn't have to spend my day stuck in the hotel. I decided to go to the Rock and Roll Hall of Fame, which was a big deal for me because I never went anywhere alone. I needed to do something for myself for a change, and even though I would have preferred seeing it with Lonny, I knew it was something I had to do on my own.

I was mesmerized as soon as I walked in the door. From the birth of rock and roll I was treated to the sights and sounds of music from every generation and every genre. Elvis, Jerry Lee Lewis, Little Richard... all the greats were represented and my heart swelled when I thought about how music had always been such a huge part of my life. At one point I was in the teen idol section and I found myself smiling like a fool. There before my eyes were stage costumes worn by Donny Osmond, Rick Springfield, the Bay City Rollers and the one I was immediately drawn to, Peter Summersby. Hanging there were his famous red satin pants and matching baseball jacket with "Summersby" embroidered on the back. A huge smile crossed my face as I remembered Peter fondly, knowing in a world of ugliness he was truly one of the nice guys. Memories of him made my face flush and I moved on.

The museum was truly a magical place where I saw a collection of David Bowie's stage costumes and the Beatles' Sgt. Pepper outfits. There was a room dedicated to Jimi Hendrix, with artifacts donated by his late father that had never been seen before. I was in awe during my entire visit, overwhelmed by the enormity of the collection available. And that didn't include the parts of the collection that were in storage. It was definitely a place I felt at home.

My stomach was growling loudly, so I went to the cafe to get a sandwich and a drink for lunch. I watched all the people passing by and wondered where they all came from. Every once in a while someone would see me sitting there alone and smile, and I

242

would smile back and say hello. I was definitely in my element there, and I half joked to myself that I should apply for a job. Maybe getting stranded in Cleveland was part of my destiny.

I finished my lunch and went back to the museum, enjoying the homage paid to MTV and its legacy, remembering the first time I watched the station when Ricky insisted on playing it in the record store instead of playing records. I loved the Motown exhibit, chills covering my skin as I listened to the sounds of The Jackson 5, The Spinners, Stevie Wonder and so many more. My heart broke when I stood in front of the exhibit for Jeff Buckley, who sadly died in a bizarre drowning accident at the age of thirty. His version of Leonard Cohen's "Hallelujah" brought me to tears every time I heard it.

I was trying to make sense of the museum map I held tightly in my hands when it happened. I looked up and saw the name Livingston Monroe and my heart raced. I walked into the small side room and was overcome with emotion I couldn't even begin to describe. An entire room dedicated to Livingston Monroe... why had Lonny never mentioned it? I started at one end and went through every item, every piece of memorabilia slowly, as if my very life depended on memorizing every detail. There were photos and albums of the band with Joey Buckingham, which I glossed over. On the wall in protective cases were lyrics handwritten by Lonny, and tears burned my eyes as I read them. There were cracked cymbals from Fuzzy's drums, a favored stage outfit worn by Benji, a microphone stand and microphone that Mitch took everywhere with him, and Lonny's favorite pair of faded jeans... the ones he and I doodled all over while we were riding on the tour bus. I had a matching pair at home packed away with all my other mementos of that time. Then I saw Lonny's prized Gibson Flying V guitar that was smashed to bits. I stood staring at it, tears falling down my face and thinking of the horrors Lonny had been through after his accident. He was right; his nightmares were real and mine were silly and stupid.

I wiped the tears from my face as I tried to look at the other artifacts in the room with clear eyes. There were copies of the Livingston Monroe fan club newsletter that was revitalized after Lonny joined the band, and they included my photos from the tour.

243

I had copies of all the newsletters in a box in my room at my parents' house, and I had forgotten all about them. I stood in front of a wall of photographs and my mouth dropped open when I realized they were mine. Black and white photos of all the band members that I took during Lonny's first tour. I was so overcome with emotion I could only cover my mouth with my hand and hope nobody else entered the exhibit while I was there.

I hadn't noticed there was music playing until I reached the end of the exhibit and saw a video screen playing the movie that was filmed during rehearsals and Lonny's first tour. I caught it just as the ending credits were scrolling on the screen and took a seat in the middle of the room to see if it would play again. It apparently played on an endless loop and I sat there watching the entire thing.

The film was two hours long, and I was frozen in my seat. Even though I had seen the film when it was released, I forgot so much of it as the years passed. I certainly didn't remember how often I actually appeared in the film, even though I remembered trying to avoid the cameras at all cost. I watched us goofing around at the rehearsal that day Calvin interrupted everything and I laughed out loud. Everyone was so happy and it reminded me of how everything had drastically changed. I continued watching, but mostly watching Lonny, in awe of how young he was and the magnitude of everything that weighed on his shoulders. I watched as Lonny was being interviewed in Chicago and how the other band members did everything they could to distract him. Throwing things at him, walking behind him and doing bunny ears behind his head, but it was all in good fun. He ignored them and continued on as if none of it was happening. When the interview was finally over he looked at the camera and said, "Gotta go find my girl." That night on the tour would change my relationship with Lonny forever.

By the time I returned to the safety of my hotel room, I was a wreck. I collapsed as soon as I closed the door, knowing I was the most horrible person who ever lived. I hated how selfish I was and how Lonny was so easy to blame for everything that ever went wrong. I had ruined every relationship I ever experienced with Lonny for over thirty years. It was no wonder he never loved me the way I loved him… I expected way too much and every time we came close, I did something irrational to push him away. I knew I deserved everything that happened to me, and because of that I deserved to be alone. I wasn't capable of loving anyone else because I spent my life loving Lonny. I wasn't capable of loving Lonny because he was too good for me and he deserved someone who was smart, strong and independent. I would always be the sister he left behind, and now it was time for me to go back home. Home to my parents where I would... would what? Move back in at fifty, get a minimum wage job in town and start all over? Then everyone who always knew who I really was could laugh and say "I told you so."

But there was no worse feeling than knowing how I'd hurt Lonny for so many years. He was always there to protect me, to save me, and I was selfish and ungrateful. I didn't blame him for being angry with me, and I needed him to know he didn't have to worry about me anymore. That he could continue on to Vegas and he would not have the burden of my life hanging around his neck.

I curled up on the bed and closed my eyes. The silence of being alone was too much to endure. I contemplated calling Marilyn, but I hadn't talked to her in so long it wouldn't be right to call out of desperation. And I couldn't bear telling her that after all these years Lonny and I were still fighting. I thought about Billy and a pain stabbed my heart. I spent almost my whole life with him knowing I didn't love him, and he only loved controlling me. It was a slap in the face to realize that I was turning fifty and I had never been truly loved by a man. Despair and hopelessness consumed me and the guttural sobs started at my toes and exploded out of me like a train wreck. I sobbed so hard I had to go to the bathroom to throw up. I filled a glass with water and went back to the bed, setting it on the table. I opened my suitcase and searched through its contents for the bottle of sleeping pills. I just needed more sleep and I would feel better. I swallowed two pills and set the bottle on the table. I curled up on the bed but sleep didn't come. My head ached from crying and my stomach lurched. I looked at the texts from Billy again and knew that Lonny would only touch me in a drunken stupor, and not only that, Billy was with Zoe now, so why was he so concerned about who I may or may not be sleeping with? It didn't matter anyway, because nobody was interested in sleeping with me. And I had nothing to offer.

I swallowed two more sleeping pills and stretched out on the bed, staring at the ceiling. I listened to see if I could hear anything coming from Lonny's room next door, but there was nothing. I entertained the thought that perhaps he got the car back and left without telling me.

I pulled out my book and started reading but became bored and tossed it on the floor. I went to the bathroom to get more water then came back and sat on the floor next to the bed. I looked at my phone to see if Lonny may have texted or called, but he hadn't. I grabbed the bottle of sleeping pills and swallowed a handful. My head started to feel funny, but despair and hopelessness consumed me. Tears burned my eyes as they slid down my face and I swallowed two more pills. I was so close to finishing the bottle I decided I couldn't quit now. After swallowing down the last pill and feeling that sleep would overcome me soon, I picked up my phone and tried to focus as I sent a text to Lonny.

Me: imm sorrry

I woke up feeling like someone had hit me in the head with a baseball bat. I tried to focus my eyes and had no idea where I was. The lights were so bright they hurt my eyes. I tried to lift my arm and realized I couldn't move it. I tried to lift my other arm and it was the same. I looked around the room and realized I was in the hospital, and not only was I hooked up to an IV and other monitors, my wrists were fastened tightly to the side rails of the bed. I was alone and had no idea what was going on. I called for Lonny, but nothing.

Then I panicked. "Lonny!" I shouted.

Lonny came into the room carrying a cup of coffee. He looked exhausted, but I said nothing. I waited for him to explain why I was cuffed to a hospital bed.

"Why do you do this, Roo?" he asked. "Why?"

"Do what?"

"Do you think killing yourself is the answer?"

"Killing… what are you talking about?"

"The sleeping pills! What were you thinking?"

I leaned my head back and closed my eyes, trying to remember. I was tired… I just wanted to sleep… despair and hopelessness….

"You always do this!" he yelled. "The smallest thing you can't handle, and you jump head first to the worst possible solution!"

Was this how Lonny talked to a person he thought just tried to commit suicide?

"You need to leave," I said, not wanting him to see me lose my mind.

"Where would you like me to go?"

Before I could tell him exactly where he could go, a nurse entered the room. "Hi Ruby," she said with a smile. "How are you feeling?"

I tried to move both of my arms to let her know exactly how I was feeling.

"That's just a precaution," she explained. "We don't want you trying to hurt yourself."

I glared at Lonny, knowing he was the reason I was cuffed to a bed I couldn't get out of. I was quiet as the nurse took my temperature and checked my vitals.

"I don't know what he told you," I said to the nurse. "But I didn't try to kill myself."

"Can you tell me what happened?"

"I was tired and I couldn't sleep. I just wanted to sleep."

She smiled at me and left the room.

"What time is it?" I asked.

"Ten o'clock."

"Did you get the car back?"

"Yeah."

I noticed I was in a hospital gown and asked Lonny where my clothes were.

"In the closet."

I closed my eyes, trying to get rid of the sick feeling in my stomach, but reality cut like a knife. How long was I going to be poked and prodded and analyzed in the hospital before they'd let me leave? And how long was I going to remain a prisoner in a bed I couldn't escape from?

My stomach lurched and I began vomiting all over myself. Unable to escape the bed I was helpless, throwing up in my lap. Lonny exited the room quickly, rushing back in behind a nurse, who was a bit too late to help at that point. A nurse's assistant came in to help clean me up, and Lonny waited out in the hallway. I was humiliated as they removed my wrist restraints, then stripped me and my bed. Once my bed and I were both cleaned and redressed, I was again restrained to the side rails.

"Is that necessary?" I asked, on the verge of tears.

"Sorry Ruby, but it's protocol until we hear different from the doctor."

The nurses left and Lonny slunk back in. I didn't want him to see me cry, but I was so humiliated I couldn't control my emotions and the tears silently made their way down my face.

Lonny pulled a chair next to the bed and sat down, placing his hand over mine. Due to the restraints I couldn't even pull my hand away from him. This upset me even further.

"I'm sorry Roo, but I didn't know what else to do. I got your text and you wouldn't answer the door... I panicked and called the front desk."

I was so ashamed I couldn't even look at him. I cried silently, angry that I couldn't even wipe my own face. Lonny got up and paced the length of the room, running his hand nervously through his hair.

"When they let me into your room and I saw you on the floor... I thought I'd lost you," he croaked. "They called 911 and as soon as the paramedics got there they pumped your stomach. Then they did CPR and you weren't responding... it was horrifying."

I could see how visibly shaken Lonny was and I felt guilty for causing him even more pain. I wanted to cover my face with my hands, but my punishment prevented me from even doing that. Lonny sat back on the chair next to my bed and placed his hand on mine. He rested his forehead on the bed and burst into tears. I could see his entire body trembling as he cried, and the guilt ate me alive.

248

"I didn't want you to worry about me anymore," I whispered. "I wanted you to be free."

He lifted his head to look at me, his eyes red from crying, his face stained with tears. "So you *were* trying to kill yourself?"

"I'm not sure," I cried. "Maybe."

Lonny stood up and wrapped his arms around my shoulders, holding my head against him. Neither of us said anything as we cried and I wanted to hug him so badly, but my restraints wouldn't allow it.

"I'm sorry, Roo," he cried. "I'm sorry I hurt you. So many times I've hurt you, and now I almost lost you because of it."

"It wasn't your fault."

"Why have we spent our lives doing this to each other?"

I remembered something Lonny said when he was drunk in Niagara Falls. *Because there's too much love.*

He audibly gasped and buried his face against the top of my head. "I'm so sorry, Roo. I'm so, so sorry."

"I don't want to die. I'm just so lonely. Please get me out of here," I cried. "*Please*, Lonny."

I tried to lift my arms again, only to be reminded that they were tied to the side rails of the bed. I became enraged, grasping the rails with my hands and shaking them violently as I screamed at the top of my lungs.

Lonny tried to comfort me, petting my hair and whispering, "It's going to be okay Roo, I promise. I'll get you out of here and we'll go home."

Two nurses entered my room and one of them asked Lonny to step away from the bed. She said, "Mr. Winter, it's probably best if you leave now so Ruby can get some rest."

"No!" I shouted. "Lonny, don't leave me!"

Lonny stood there frozen, not sure what he was supposed to be doing. "Roo, I'm not going anywhere," he tried to assure me.

"Mr. Winter, please."

"Lonny, don't leave me here!" I begged. I struggled with my wrist restraints, trying to magically squeeze my hands free, but nothing worked. I saw one of the nurses coming toward me with a syringe and I immediately panicked, kicking my legs.

"Ruby, please just relax," the nurse said. "You've had a rough day and we just want you to get some rest."

"No," I cried. "Please don't. I'll behave, I promise."

Lonny covered his mouth with his hand, looking like he was going to have a nervous breakdown. I could see the guilt in his eyes when he looked at me, as if he made a terrible mistake. I found myself feeling angry with him, even though I knew it wasn't his fault.

"I'll behave," I whispered. "Please don't make him leave."

"I'm sorry, Ruby, but it appears he's the cause of some of your anguish," the nurse replied.

"No, he's not! I swear he's not!"

She plunged the syringe into the line of my IV and I screamed, "Lonny, please don't leave me here!"

I began to feel drowsy almost immediately, trying to focus on Lonny's face. There was pure torture there as one of the nurses tried to escort him out of my room.

"Lonny, don't leave me," I begged, just before I lost consciousness.

1980

To say my parents were distraught when I returned home with a black eye is an understatement. I explained how it happened and they immediately became concerned about Lonny's safety. When I told them I was asked to go on tour, however, their tune changed. My mother said I was absolutely *not* going on tour with a rock band, even if it was with Lonny, and my father said no daughter of his was going to be living on a tour bus. I told them I was leaving in March and they had plenty of time to get used to the idea. I was eighteen, could make my own decisions, and was going to be the fan club photographer during the tour. I tried to get them to understand that I was going to be doing a job, not just clinging to Lonny the entire time.

I returned to my job at the record store and Ricky tried not to laugh when I explained how I got the black eye.

"Living the dream," he chuckled. "Did you have a good time?"

"I had the best time! It was hard to leave."

"You look great," he said. "Blissfully happy."

I couldn't help but smile when I thought of everything that happened during my visit to L.A..

"I have some bad news," I said, not wanting to tell him I would be quitting my job. "I'm going on tour with the band in March. I'm going to be their exclusive fan club photographer."

Ricky looked stunned. "I'm sorry to lose you, but what a fantastic opportunity!"

I was relieved that he saw it for what it was, unlike my parents who refused to acknowledge that it was actually going to happen.

"So anything you want to tell me about your trip?" he asked, handing me a copy of a tabloid paper. "I was grocery shopping when I saw this and I almost shit myself."

I stared at the rag's cover with the headline, "L.A.'s Mystery Girl" that was accompanied by two photographs — one of me with Peter in our bathing suits by his pool, and one of Lonny

251

holding my hand just before the mob of girls attacked him outside the restaurant.

I realized my mouth was agape as I looked up at Ricky who was laughing hysterically. "You're famous."

"What the… who could've…."

"Paparazzi, baby. They're *everywhere.*"

"Does it really look like me?"

"Um… yeah. So you and Peter Summersby?"

I struggled for what to say. "It's not what it looks like."

Ricky opened the paper to show me even more damaging photographs. There I was kissing Peter in his pool, lounging with him in the hammock, holding his hand as he led me back into the house… in our bathing suits. The accompanying article really didn't say much, only questioning who I was, and why was I seen with two different celebrities on the same day? The paper didn't seem to be interested in the story about Lonny being attacked by the mob of fans that evening.

I had to sit down, feeling lightheaded. "My mom is going to see this. Everybody is going to see this!"

"What's the big deal?" Ricky asked. "You didn't do anything wrong."

"My parents will never see it that way."

"Can I have your autograph?" Ricky laughed as I slapped his arm. "So how's Lonny?"

"He's great," I gushed. "He's nervous about the tour, but I don't think he has anything to worry about. He plays like a god."

I dreaded going home after work that night. My mother never purchased the tabloids, but she read all the headlines while she waited in line with her groceries. I entered the house cautiously, knowing my parents were already in the kitchen eating dinner, and I sat down as if nothing weird had happened. They both eyed me suspiciously and remained silent. My mother got up and pulled a paper off the counter and I knew what was coming. She plopped it down on the table in front of me.

"That's not me," I lied.

"I think I know my own daughter," my mom growled.

"I mean, that's me with Lonny, but that's not me with… who is that? Peter Summersby? Definitely not me."

The phone rang and my father got up to answer it. "Hi Billy. She'll have to call you after dinner." He hung up the phone and sat back down.

I rolled my eyes, knowing how my evening was going to play out.

"Don't lie to your mother," my dad said.

I exhaled loudly and said, "It's me. I met Peter at a New Year's Eve party and we spent the day together, but that's it. Nothing happened. He's a nice guy."

"I can see nothing happened," my mom shrieked. "I can see you weren't kissing him in the pool, or laying with him in a hammock, or—"

"Mom, stop. I'm eighteen years old, and kissing guys is no big deal."

"Does Lonny know about this?"

"What? Why does... oh forget it. I'm not a slut, Mom!"

"I can't even begin to imagine what's going to happen on tour with that rock band," my mom said, fanning herself.

"I already told you I was hired to do a job. I'll be *working*, Mom."

"I don't like it," she hissed. "I don't like it one bit."

"Well I guess you'll have to get used to it, because I'm going whether you approve or not."

I snatched the tabloid off the table and went upstairs to my room where I closed and locked the door. I hopped onto my bed and looked at the photographs, my cheeks flushing at the memory of the day I spent with Peter. I wondered if Marilyn had seen the paper yet, knowing how much she loved reading the gossip rags. If she'd seen it, I knew Fuzzy and Lonny would have seen it, because she would have been parading it in their faces. Lonny knew I'd spent that day with Peter, but he had no idea *how* I spent it.

I thought about my last night with Lonny and how he kissed me the way I'd always hoped he would, and how he kissed me before the taxi took me away. But I had no idea what our relationship was... were we the same as before, or was he claiming me as his own? He never verbalized it, but I didn't think he would have kissed me like that if he wanted us to stay in the friendly relationship we'd always had. Or would he?

253

I didn't know if Billy ever called back, because I didn't want to talk to him. I went to bed early and my phone woke me around midnight.

"Lonny!" I answered after the first ring.

"Hey Roo," he said.

"Hey doll!" Marilyn's voice interrupted. I could hear her wrestling the phone away from Lonny and chuckled. "Did you see the rag? You're famous!"

"I saw it. My parents saw it. They're not happy."

"Oh what's the big deal?" she asked. "You were having some fun, no harm done!"

"They don't see it that way."

"Lonny's giving me the evil eye. I'll talk to you later."

Lonny was soon back on the phone and said, "The phone's been ringing off the hook here, people wanting to know who you are."

"I'm sorry."

"It's not your fault. Marilyn has been messing with everybody that calls." He imitated her voice when he said, "She's my sister! She's Fuzzy's sister! She's Lonny's sister!"

"So I'm everybody's sister."

"Pretty much."

It was the perfect opportunity for me to ask Lonny if he still thought of me as his sister, but my tongue was tied.

Say something! Anything!

"Did you talk to Ricky?" he asked.

"Yeah, I told him today. He's really happy for me."

"Have you seen Billy?"

"No, I haven't seen him. He called, but I didn't talk to him."

"Please stay away from him," Lonny said.

"I don't want to see him."

"Promise me you'll stay away from him."

"It won't be hard. He's going back to school."

"Roo, promise me."

"Why, Lonny?"

I wanted him to tell me it was because he loved me, or at least tell me it was because I was *his* girlfriend now, but all he said was the usual, "Because he's an asshole and I don't trust him."

"That's it?"

"Yeah, why else?"

So I got my answer.

At work the next day, I was surprised when Billy came in looking for me. He asked Ricky if we could speak in private so I took him into the back office.

"What happened to your eye?" he asked.

"Lonny got mobbed by a group of girls and I got smacked in the face." I laughed, but he didn't seem to find it funny.

"Why haven't you called me back?"

"I've been busy."

"Ruby, I wanted to tell you that I'm not going back to school."

My heart sank. "Why not?"

"I can't concentrate on school, and Gina really needs me at home."

"What about your dad?"

"He's no help. He's drowning in his own misery."

"Okay, well... thanks for letting me know."

"That's it? That's all you have to say?"

I started to feel trapped and turned to go back into the store, but he put a hand on my shoulder and turned me to face him. He tried to kiss me and I leaned as far away from him as possible. He gave me a strange look and said, "What's the matter?"

I shrugged. "Nothing."

"This is about Lonny, isn't it?"

"Why do you make everything about him?" I hissed.

"Am I wrong?"

"No, not this time," I said, feeling emboldened. "He's my boyfriend now."

Billy didn't flinch. "Are you sure about that? You seemed to have a good old time out in L.A. with Peter Summersby."

I shouldn't have been surprised. He obviously had an agenda when he came to see me, already having seen the tabloid.

"I don't have to explain anything to you," I told him. "And it doesn't matter anyway, because I'm leaving in March."

"Leaving?"

"I was hired as the fan club photographer for Livingston Monroe, and I'll be going on tour with them."

Billy's expression fell, and it made me happy that I had something wonderful to slap him in the face with.

"Wow, that's... what a great opportunity for you," he stammered. I knew he was trying to find something negative to say about it, but he wasn't coming up with anything. I had blindsided him with something he truly wasn't expecting.

After that, Billy kept his distance from me and only got in touch when it had to do with Gina. It was so nice that he finally understood I didn't have any intention of getting back together with him. I should have told him Lonny was my boyfriend long before; it would have prevented a lot of heartache.

Time moved at a snail's pace waiting for Livingston Monroe's appearance on *The Midnight Special*, and Lonny's mother promised she wouldn't have anything to drink before I got to her house that night so she could stay awake to watch them. When I got to her house that night after work, the front door was wide open and I could hear her screaming at someone. I followed her voice to Lonny's bedroom where she was slamming the window.

"Mom, what's going on?"

She turned to look at me, panic written all over her face. "I came home from work and there were girls in here! They were going through Lonny's things!"

"Did they take anything?"

"I don't know!"

I called the police and while we waited for them, we went through Lonny's room to see if anything had been stolen. I couldn't believe teenage girls would break into Joanie's home to get into Lonny's bedroom. The police arrived promptly and I listened as Joanie explained that she had to work late, and when she went into the house she could hear sound coming from Lonny's bedroom. When she entered there were three teenage girls looking through his things. They had broken in through his

256

bedroom window and as soon as she busted them, they took off running through the house and out the back door.

"Ruby," she said, "you'd know if anything was stolen."

She was right. If anyone would know if something was missing from Lonny's room, it would be me. I noticed immediately that his pillow was gone, and a few old Livingston Monroe posters had been ripped off the wall, their torn corners still taped in place. I looked in his closet where I knew he kept his journals hidden, and they were still there.

I told the police what I knew had been taken, and they said she probably caught them right after they broke in. I was so glad she was still sober, because she was able to give the police a pretty good description of the girls she'd seen. She was such a wreck she was visibly shaking, and once the police finally left I said it would be okay if she had one drink. I ordered our pizza and we talked about what we could do to prevent another break-in from happening.

Joanie started crying. "What am I going to do when you're gone?"

"You'll be fine, Mom, but right now we have to think about protecting Lonny's things."

I suggested we pack all his stuff into boxes and bring it to my house where it would be safe, at least for a little while. She thought that sounded like the most reasonable solution, and we agreed to start bringing his stuff to my house in the morning.

"Why would they take his pillow?" she laughed, wiping the tears from her face.

"Girls are weird." We both laughed, but I was disappointed that I wouldn't have Lonny's pillow to sleep on that night. Let them have his pillow, as long as they didn't steal his journals. I had no idea what was in them, but having his personal thoughts and feelings out there for the world to see would be a nightmare for him. Some unscrupulous person would pay ungodly amounts of money to get their hands on those, and I had to protect them with my life.

Joanie only had a few drinks by the time *The Midnight Special* came on, and she sat on the couch with me as we cuddled together under a blanket and waited patiently. I was chewing my knuckle raw, and I don't think I was breathing. When they announced that the next act was performing live for the first time with their new lineup, we knew immediately it was Livingston Monroe. Joanie was squeezing my hand so tightly I lost all circulation, but I didn't care.

I watched as the band came into view playing their new song, "Just Say Yes," and I squealed. The camera focused on Mitch a lot because he was the lead singer, but they made sure to concentrate on Lonny, the new kid, and that made me very happy. The audience was made up of mostly young teenage girls, which was a completely different demographic than the band was used to. I watched Lonny, hiding behind his hair as he played, but never missing a note and sounding perfect on his backing vocals. I could tell he was nervous, but nobody else would have noticed. I felt tears falling down my cheeks because I was so proud of him and so happy for him. When the song was over several girls in the audience screamed Lonny's name when the camera happened to be focused on his face and he looked up and smiled, waving at them. This caused the audience to go berserk and Joanie and I were screaming at the top of our lungs because we were so excited.

"That's my boy, Ruby! That's my boy!"

"He's so beautiful."

Joanie gave me a squeeze and kissed my cheek. "I'm so proud of him."

"Me too, Mom. He looked happy, don't you think?"

"Absolutely. I wish he'd cut his hair so we could see his face."

"But that's his thing," I joked. "Maybe once he gets more comfortable playing in front of crowds."

Joanie laughed and said, "You like the long hair, don't you?"

"Yeah, I'm a sucker for long hair," I admitted.

Even though it was late, Joanie and I polished off the rest of the pizza while we were waiting for the band's next performance. I was so happy and relieved she held back on her drinking so she could enjoy Lonny's first television appearance, and I was glad we could experience it together. Gina had asked if we could watch it together and it broke my heart to tell her no, but

258

I wasn't about to break tradition with Joanie. She was my mom, too, and I promised Lonny I would take care of her in his absence.

The band came on for their final performance and I held my breath, wondering what song they would be singing. I was more than surprised to hear the beginning bass line of "Take Me Home," which meant Lonny would be singing on live television during his very first performance with the band. And the fans in the audience had no idea that he had taken over lead vocals for this particular song. The camera focused on Lonny almost the entire length of the song, and even though he spent most of it hiding behind his hair, he did shake his head a few times to reveal his eyes, which were sparkling with life. He played his heart out and his vocals were spot on, making the song his own. He looked visibly relieved when the song was over, but the smile on his face spoke volumes. He winked and blew a kiss to the camera, then someone from the audience shouted, "Lonny I love you!" and he laughed, saying, "I love you." The girls screamed like maniacs and I jumped off the couch and screamed along with them.

"Did you see that, Ruby! That was for you!" Joanie shouted.

"I don't know Mom, I think it was for you."

We smiled at each other as I jumped up and down for joy. I knew we wouldn't be hearing from Lonny that evening but I couldn't wait to talk to him the next time he called.

The next day my mom and dad helped Joanie and me pack up all of Lonny's personal belongings and brought them to our house, safe in my bedroom closet. Her landlord was none too pleased that he had to fix the broken window, but made sure it was secure before the end of the day. I made a call to Theresa Brooks, the reporter who wanted to interview me about Lonny, and told her about the break-in, hoping she would do a story to get the word out that his belongings were no longer in the home so Joanie could live in peace. She took the bait. She came to the house to interview Joanie the next day, and I made sure to be there to run interference if Theresa stepped over any lines. Thankfully it was early in the day so Joanie hadn't started drinking yet and had a clear mind. Theresa was extremely professional and sympathetic, and I felt she really cared about Joanie and the way she and Lonny were violated.

Lonny called late that evening after a long day of rehearsal interrupted by magazine interviews. It was then I told him about the girls breaking into his mom's house and how we packed up his belongings and they were now safe.

"How's my mom?"

"She's fine. Lonny, she stayed sober so she wouldn't miss you on TV. She's so proud of you."

Lonny laughed. "And you?"

Not wanting to wake my parents, I squealed quietly. "You were amazing! It was like I was dreaming seeing you on TV!"

"When I had to sing my song I almost passed out. I was so nervous."

"You were perfect," I gushed. "And you looked great."

"I wish you were there."

"Me, too."

Lonny was quiet for a bit then asked, "So do you have my journals?"

"All your stuff is packed up and safe in my closet."

"You can read them if you want to."

"Oh no Lonny, I'm not doing that."

"It's okay, I want you to."

"I'll think about it."

He laughed. "It's not the same without you here. Marilyn and Fuzzy said the same thing."

This made me happy. "I miss you guys, too."

We both laughed and then Lonny said, "Peter says hi."

I felt my cheeks flush and I wasn't sure how to respond since it was coming from Lonny. "Oh... okay. Tell him I said hi back."

"I will."

"So... are you guys friends now?" I wasn't sure I wanted to know.

"He feels really bad about your picture ending up in the rag. He might sue them... he said he's used to it when he's in public, but they had no right invading his privacy like that. He's pissed."

260

"Is he getting calls about me like Marilyn and Fuzzy are?" Part of me wanted him to say he was getting bombarded with calls about his mystery girl… the rest of me just wanted it to go away.

"He didn't say, and I didn't ask."

I could tell Lonny was tired as his lulls in conversation became more frequent, so I told him he should hang up and go to bed. I never wanted to get off the phone with him, but I understood he needed his sleep.

"I love you, Lonny," I said, as I always did.

"Yeah, me too."

2011

Sometime in the middle of the night the nurse came in to check my vitals and I asked, "Where's Lonny?"

"He left."

"He promised he wouldn't leave me."

"Ruby, does he make you feel unsafe?"

Is this a trick question?

"I don't understand," I grumbled.

"What is your relationship with Mr. Winter?"

I chuckled and she didn't find it amusing. "It's complicated."

"Ruby, does he abuse you?"

"The only one abusing me right now is *you*." I was angry. "You're treating me like some suicidal maniac when all I did was take a few too many sleeping pills because I needed to sleep."

"The paramedics saw things differently."

"Well the paramedics don't know me but Lonny *does*, and you made him leave."

"The doctor will see you in the morning. Until then, try to get some sleep."

My blood was boiling. "Or what? You'll give me a sedative and knock me out again?"

The nurse did not respond to my outburst and left the room. Lonny promised not to leave me and that's exactly what he did. I had no more tears to shed because I was furious. If Lonny ever followed through on one of his promises the shock would kill me.

I slept in fits and starts the rest of the evening. I hated sleeping on my back, and with my wrists restrained I had no other choice. All I wanted was to go home and see my parents and end this nightmare. Lonny and I could go our separate ways and move on with the rest of our lives.

Sometime after the sun came up a nurse's assistant came in my room with a menu to ask what I wanted for breakfast. She held the menu open in front of my face so I could read it and I grumbled something about eggs, toast, bacon and orange juice. As she turned to leave I asked, "Are you going to feed it to me?"

She looked at me strangely and I rattled the bed rails with my restrained wrists. She said she'd have to ask my nurse, and hopefully they would remove the restraints so I could feed myself. I thanked her and she left the room. Unfortunately they would not remove my restraints and the nurse's assistant was forced to feed me my breakfast. I knew it wasn't her fault and tried not to take it out on her.

"I'm sorry you have to do this," I said, embarrassed. "This is all a big misunderstanding."

She just smiled and continued doing her job, not getting involved in what I thought may or may not have been a misunderstanding. I could tell she was uncomfortable and just wanted to feed me and get out. She had just put a bite of eggs in my mouth when Lonny walked in.

"Hey Roo," he said, a sheepish smile on his face. "How you doing?"

My eyes grew large and I said, "Being fed like an invalid, thanks."

It was probably a good thing my wrists were restrained because I wanted to lash out at Lonny something fierce. As I slowly chewed a piece of bacon, I noticed the rolling table holding my food tray was almost close enough to touch with my foot. Hoping not to be obvious, I shifted my body to bring my foot within striking distance.

"Lonny," I said, "I want to go home."

"The doctor will be here soon to talk to you," he replied.

"Lonny, you promised you wouldn't leave me here. I want to go home *now*."

"Just a little bit longer, I promise."

"Your promises are bullshit!" I shouted. "Maybe if you ever followed through with something you promised me I wouldn't be here right now, tied to a hospital bed!"

"Roo, that's not fair."

I glared at Lonny. What did he know about fair? I knew we were making the nurse's assistant uncomfortable, and as she held a piece of toast in front of my mouth I turned my head away. My hands balled into fists as my chest heaved with anger. I kicked the table with such force it slammed against the wall, sending the food tray crashing to the floor. It took several seconds before I realized how badly my foot was stinging from the impact.

"Roo, what the fuck!" Lonny scolded. As the nurse's assistant cleaned up the mess he apologized profusely, giving me a look that could kill. When we were finally alone he said, "What the fuck is your problem?"

"You promised not to leave me and you left. You promised to get me out of here and take me home, and I'm still tied to the bed. Your promises mean nothing, and they never have!" Lonny turned around and walked out. I knew I went too far, but I didn't care. He wasn't the one tied to the bed like a prisoner.

About an hour later, Lonny was taking full responsibility over me and signing me out of the hospital against medical advice. We both signed all the paperwork and when they removed my wrist restraints, I cried. I went into the bathroom to put my clothes on and when I came out, a security guard was there to escort us to the front door. Lonny put his arm protectively around me as we made our way out of the room, through the halls, down the elevator and out the front door.

He opened the car door for me and said, "It's about five hours to home, depending on traffic."

I crawled into the back seat so I could go to sleep. The next thing I knew, Lonny was nudging me to wake up.

"We're here," he said, opening the car door.

I sat up and waited for several minutes so I could wake up and get my bearings. I was overcome with emotion as I got out of the car and saw my parents' house, my safe place. Lonny told me to stand behind him so they couldn't see me right away, wanting to keep the element of surprise.

The front door opened and I heard my mom say, "Lonny! Oh my gosh, it's really you!"

I could see her arms as they wrapped tightly around him. He walked into the house and said, "I have a surprise for you."

He stepped to the side and presented me to my parents, who looked like they were seeing a ghost. My mom wrapped her arms around me and immediately began sobbing, which in turn caused me to do the same. It had been so long since I'd been in my mother's arms and I didn't realize how much I missed her until that moment. When she finally let me go I ran to my dad's arms, and even though he was a man of very little emotion, he might've been crying too.

A few minutes later I heard Lonny say, "Mom, look who I brought with me."

I looked to see Lonny pushing his mother into the living room in a wheelchair. She gasped and raised her hands a little bit in excitement, unable to do much more. I knew she'd had a stroke a couple of years earlier and moved in with my parents, but I had no idea she was in a wheelchair, or that she couldn't speak.

I pulled her into my arms and she moaned her happiness in seeing me, as she couldn't verbalize it. She couldn't lift her arms to hug me the way she wanted to, but I could hear her crying against me. I screamed about being an invalid when I was in the hospital and those words choked me as I thought about them.

When we finally ended our tearful greetings, we all sat in the living room and my mom asked, "Ruby, why didn't you tell us you were coming home with Lonny?"

"We wanted it to be a surprise," I replied. "Surprise!"

Sitting next to me on the couch my mom held my hand, as if I would disappear if she let it go.

"Where's Billy?" my dad asked.

I looked hopelessly at Lonny, who nodded and smiled. "Billy left me about two months ago," I told them, hearing gasps from all three parents. "We're divorced." It was the first time I wasn't reduced to tears when mentioning my broken marriage. "Lonny happened to be in New York and stopped by the apartment… so here I am."

"Oh honey, I'm so sorry," my mom said.

"Don't be. It's the best thing that could've happened." I looked at Joanie, who had tears on her face, and said, "It's okay, Mom. I never should have married Billy anyway."

"Why on earth would Billy leave *you*?" my dad asked.

I hesitated and Lonny said, "He was cheating on her with one of their tattoo artists."

Thanks, Lonny.

"You'll stay for dinner, won't you?" my mom quickly changed the subject. "We can order pizza."

"I'm not going anywhere," I chuckled. "I'm home for good if you'll have me."

"As long as you need," my dad said.

During dinner I watched as Lonny lovingly helped his mom eat. It broke my heart to see her in such bad shape, but it really bothered me that I had no idea how she had deteriorated. Had I become so detached from my parents and Lonny that they didn't want to tell me?

Lonny stuck around for a little while after we were finished eating, then announced he was heading to his hotel for the evening to catch up on some work. He brought my suitcase into the house and said goodbye to my dad with a handshake, hugged and kissed my mom, then gave his mom a kiss and a long hug.

"Thank you for bringing Ruby home," my mom said with tears in her eyes.

Lonny looked at me, and I wondered what he was expecting. I was exhausted and waved at him sluggishly, saying, "Thanks for bringing me home. I'm going to soak in the tub."

Lonny wrinkled his forehead, said a final goodbye to our parents and walked out. I grabbed my suitcase and headed upstairs to my old bedroom, which my mom had turned into a spare room and sewing room. I opened the closet door and saw she hadn't removed any of the boxes I had stored in there — Lonny's things we saved from the teenage thieves back in the day, and all of my Livingston Monroe mementos. I didn't dare bring any of that with me when I got married because I knew Billy would have found a way to make it all disappear. I knew it would be safe in my old room until I was ready to reclaim it all again.

After soaking in a luxurious bath until my skin began to prune, I threw on some shorts and a t-shirt and went downstairs where my mom was the only one still awake, watching a DVD of her favorite movie, *The Wizard Of Oz*. I stretched out on the couch next to her and rested my head on her leg. She caressed my head like she used to do when I was a little girl and needed comforting.

"Honey, why didn't you tell us about Billy?" she asked.

"I was too ashamed."

"Did Lonny know? Is that why he went to New York?"

"No, I didn't tell him either."

"You should never have to suffer alone. We would've told you to come home right away."

We watched the movie together in silence, my eyes heavy from the exhausting events of the last couple days. I was almost sound asleep when my mom's voice snapped me awake.

"Is everything okay with you and Lonny?"

"Yeah, why?"

"You just seemed irritated with him."

"Lonny is selfish and only thinks about himself."

My mom was quiet for several minutes before she said, "Lonny is the most selfless person I know." I stared at the television with glazed eyes as she continued. "He paid off our mortgage when he was twenty, and he pays our property taxes every year. When Joanie had her stroke and couldn't live alone anymore, he paid for the addition on our house so she would have a comfortable place to stay where she felt safe. He refused to put her in a home, and we would never have let that happen. I do what I can, and a caretaker comes in a few times a week to make sure she's bathed. He pays for everything. He has her favorite hairdresser come in once a week to do her hair. He even bought the van I use so we have an easy way to drive her around in her wheelchair."

I knew none of this. He paid off their mortgage when he was twenty? Why wouldn't he have told me?

"And when that Furry guy's wife—"

"Fuzzy."

"When Fuzzy's wife wanted out of their warehouse business, or whatever it was, Lonny bought her out and became his business partner."

I stared at the television, trying to figure out when I fell down the rabbit hole. I cleared my throat and said, "Well that's all fine and good, because Lonny would do anything for the people he loves. I'm not one of those people."

She exhaled loudly. "Ruby, he tried to stop your wedding."

267

1980

I could barely contain my excitement as I sat in the back seat of the taxi, heading to Fuzzy and Marilyn's house. Even though I was more in the dark than ever about my relationship status with Lonny, I was anxious to see him. I couldn't wait to put my arms around him, breathe him in, and never let him go again.

I ran to the front door where Marilyn threw it open before I even had a chance to ring the bell. I dropped my suitcase as we screamed at the top of our lungs and gave each other a long hug.

"Okay okay, give the rest of us a chance," I heard Fuzzy say. He pulled me into his arms and gave me a bear hug. "Welcome back, doll."

When Fuzzy released me I saw Lonny standing in the distance, grinning. He waved shyly, as if he wasn't sure how he should be greeting me. I didn't give him a chance to think about it, running to where he stood and wrapping my arms around him. His hair was so soft against my face and he smelled so good, I wanted that moment to go on forever. He was the first to pull away.

"How did the parents handle it?" he asked.

"Oh… you know," I said with a shrug. "They're happy for *you*, but they don't think it's the right thing for me."

Fuzzy roared. "We're going to corrupt you, doll. You just wait!"

I followed Lonny as he carried my suitcase to his bedroom, and I noticed he had a suitcase of his own sitting open on the floor.

"I hate packing," he said.

I laughed as I peered into the empty suitcase. "You haven't even started."

"I have a couple days."

I got the feeling he was holding back or keeping something from me. I had no idea what it was but he seemed guarded, and it made me question why he kissed me the way he did the last time I was there. Awkward and shy Lonny was standing in front of me, and I didn't know what to say.

"Look what I got!" I exclaimed, excited to show him my new toy. I opened my suitcase and pulled out the brand new

268

Polaroid camera I purchased just before I left. "I have to send all the film to Howard, but I can keep the Polaroids."

He smiled and nodded, but said nothing.

Marilyn called down the hallway, "Time to go!"

As I followed Lonny out of the room I asked where we were going.

"Last rehearsal," he said, never turning back to look at me.

As we all piled into Fuzzy's car Marilyn said, "Sorry we're whisking you off before you had a chance to catch your breath, doll."

"No way, it's cool!" I was excited for the whole experience to begin. I looked at Lonny, who was staring out the window with a blank expression on his face. I chalked his odd behavior up to nerves, realizing he was probably a wreck with the first show coming up the next day. The first two sold out shows were going to be at The Forum just outside of Los Angeles. I knew it must have been weighing heavily on Lonny's mind, and I couldn't fault him for being a bit distant.

As we reached the first security gate at the warehouse, Fuzzy grumbled an expletive under his breath as Marilyn shouted, "Lonny and Ruby, get down!"

Not asking any questions, both of us dove as low as we could in the back seat of the car. We soon heard the deafening roar of screaming girls, but when it appeared they could only see Fuzzy and Marilyn in the car it stopped, and we were able to drive through without incident. Lonny was silent and far out front as we all went into the warehouse and walked through the maze of hallways to their rehearsal room.

Mitch and Benji greeted me with hugs, then Marilyn and I got out of their way so they could get down to business. I brought my camera and started my job as official fan club photographer.

"What's wrong with Lonny?" I whispered.

"I don't know, doll. He's been weird the last two weeks."

The rehearsal became one nightmare after another. Mitch singing off key, Lonny breaking strings, Lonny forgetting the words to "Take Me Home," and Lonny seeming to be on another planet. After the first hour Fuzzy called for a break and took Lonny outside.

269

"That kid better get his head out of his ass," Mitch grumbled.

I looked at Marilyn, who was biting her bottom lip. She turned to face me with wide eyes and simply shrugged. This wasn't the Lonny we knew.

Fuzzy and Lonny returned about fifteen minutes later, Lonny with a cigarette hanging out of his mouth and Fuzzy slapping him heartily on the back. Lonny looked at me briefly, and I didn't even recognize my best friend. His eyes were vacant and I had no idea who was looking at me.

"Maybe we should leave," I whispered.

Marilyn insisted we stay put. She said whatever was going on with Lonny, it had nothing to do with either of us. I wasn't so sure, wondering if he really didn't want me to go on tour with him.

Fuzzy, Benji and Mitch pulled Lonny into a group hug so tight, we couldn't hear a word they were saying. We could hear whispers, laughs and low male grumblings, but they were a team, and they seemed to be taking Lonny's struggles seriously, trying to put him at ease. I was so concerned about Lonny I almost forgot I had my camera with me, but managed to get some shots of the group hug before they separated. Lonny didn't look any better, but the rehearsal improved.

I was nervous about asserting myself as a photographer, but decided I needed to get over my apprehension and do my job. I left my seat and got close to the band, snapping shot after shot and they didn't seem to mind at all. I tried not to focus too much on Lonny, who was really the one I wanted to photograph, but I had a job to do, and it wasn't to be Lonny's personal photographer.

It was fairly late when we got back to the house and while Fuzzy, Marilyn and I went into the kitchen to eat because we were starving, Lonny headed straight for his room and never came back out. As we picked off a meat and cheese tray Marilyn pulled out of the refrigerator, I was even more worried about Lonny. I'd never seen him so distant before.

"Ladies," Fuzzy sighed. "He'll be okay. He's got the world on his shoulders right now and he's probably feeling a bit weighed down."

"So what happens now?" I asked, having no clue how a tour like this even worked.

"First gig tomorrow night," Fuzzy replied. "Second gig the next night, with an after party at Howard's. All the industry bigwigs and asses we have to kiss will be there, but it's usually fun. Next morning we get on the bus and head out."

"Are we sleeping on the bus?" I asked.

Fuzzy smiled. "Sometimes. Mostly hotels."

"Where am I sleeping?"

"Come on doll," Marilyn teased. "Do you really have to ask?"

My cheeks burned. I guess that meant I was sleeping with Lonny.

"Fuzzy," I whispered. "Are you sure he's okay?"

He smiled and pulled me into a protective hug. "Once he gets the first gig under his belt, he'll be fine. Think about it… the kid has been under a microscope since he joined the band. It'll get easier, I promise."

He kissed my forehead and I said goodnight, heading to Lonny's room. I entered quietly, not wanting to disturb him if he was already asleep. I closed the door and tiptoed to the bed, where his back was facing me and I could already hear his heavy, sleep-filled breathing.

I didn't even bother going into the bathroom to change, sliding off my jeans and t-shirt and slipping into a pair of shorts and a tank top. I climbed into Lonny's bed and lay on my side, staring at his back. I hesitated then slowly wiggled as close to him as I could get, pressing my forehead and my hand against his bare back. I had to let him know I was there for him, somehow, and I just wanted to feel his skin.

A few minutes later he whispered, "Did you read my journals?"

What a strange question after the day we'd had. "No. I thought it was too personal."

"I really wanted you to read them."

I had no response. He said nothing else, didn't turn to look at me, and went back to sleep. At some point during the night I could hear him vomiting in the bathroom. I listened for a while,

271

waiting for an indication that he was finished, then went to check on him. I walked into the brightly lit bathroom to find Lonny on the floor leaning against the wall next to the toilet, drenched in sweat.

"Are you having one of your headaches?" I asked.

"No," he cried. "I can't do this, Roo, I just can't."

I sat next to him on the floor and took one of his hands. "Can't do what?"

"This tour... this life."

"I saw you on television Lonny, and you were happy. You knocked it out of the sky. What happened?"

"It's worse since being on television. I can't go anywhere... girls show up everywhere and mob me. They try to rip off my clothes, they pull my hair. Fuzzy and Marilyn are always trying to protect me, and I know they're frustrated. This isn't what they signed up for."

"It'll be different on the road. You'll have a bodyguard to protect you. You can't back out now, Lonny, the tour starts tomorrow."

He ran his hands through his sweat-drenched hair and whispered, "I'm glad you're here."

I smiled. "Me, too."

"It's my mom," his voice cracked.

"Your mom?"

"I try to call her when she's not drunk, but with our schedule I can't always do that. You know how she is when she's drunk...."

"Lonny, what happened?"

Lonny went on to tell me how his mother blamed him for the fights I was having with my parents about going on tour, how it was his fault I wouldn't commit to a relationship with Billy, and that being in a rock band was a pipe dream that would soon disappear and he'd be right back where he came from.

"I'm sorry, Roo," Lonny sobbed.

I was furious with Joanie. How dare she say all those horrible things to Lonny, especially since they weren't true!

I grabbed Lonny's hands and forced him to look at me. "Hey, don't listen to your mom. She doesn't know what she's talking about. I argued with my parents because I insisted on coming. I didn't *want* a relationship with Billy, and this band is the greatest thing that ever happened to you. Your mom talks shit when she's drunk, you know that."

He nodded, but continued crying.

"There's more, isn't there?"

"My dad… she said my dad…." He couldn't even continue, sobbing so uncontrollably his entire body shook.

"What about your dad?"

"She said… she said he left because of me. He never wanted me and I was the reason he took off."

As furious as I was that Joanie would tell Lonny such nonsense, my heart broke for him. "Lonny, you know that's not true."

"How do I know?"

"He left because your mom is an alcoholic."

"Then why does he ignore me?"

I had no good answer for him. How was I supposed to know why his dad ignored him? I stood up and held out my hand, saying, "Come on, let's go back to bed."

Lonny took my hand and let me help him up, and we walked silently back to his bed where we crawled in and got comfortable. I pulled him into my arms and caressed his hair as I whispered, "Whatever your dad's problem is, it has nothing to do with you. You're a good guy with a sweet soul. It's the adults who have the problem here. Your parents, my parents… they'll never understand."

"Promise you won't leave," he whispered.

"I promise I won't leave."

The next morning at breakfast Lonny seemed to be back to himself, but I knew the things his mother said to him still weighed heavily on his mind. I had half a mind to call her and tear her apart, but I knew that wouldn't do anyone any good. And it would only come back to haunt Lonny, and I was not about to do anything that would harm him.

"I'm glad to see that smile back on your face," Marilyn told Lonny.

"It's all Roo," he said with a laugh.

273

After breakfast Marilyn said, "Lonny, Fuzzy and I wanted to give you something before the tour. Something from the heart, but something you can use."

Lonny was stunned when they presented him with a brand new, red Gibson Flying V guitar. It had been his dream to own one some day, and here it was in his hands.

Lonny hugged each of them, saying, "Thank you, but I really don't deserve—"

"Nonsense," Marilyn interrupted.

"Let's go try it out," Fuzzy said, and both men disappeared in a flash.

Once she was sure they were out of hearing range, she turned to me and said, "So you were able to fix his funk pretty quickly."

"He's having a hard time with all the girls trying to attack him... but it was really about his mom. She said some pretty awful things to him."

"Why would she do that?"

"She's an alcoholic. He calls her when he can, and sometimes she's already drunk. She can be really mean."

"I'm sorry to hear that. Lonny's so sweet... I hate to see him like this."

"His dad left when he was eleven... I guess his mom decided to tell him it was his fault and that his dad never wanted him."

"What a stupid bitch."

I didn't want to talk about Lonny's mom anymore. "That guitar... it's amazing. He's always wanted one."

"His old guitar is fine but he needed an upgrade," Marilyn chuckled.

The sound of Lonny tuning and wailing on his new guitar exploded through the house and we both smiled. "You guys... you're the best friends he could have ever hoped for. Thank you for taking care of him."

Marilyn touched my cheek. "We're always here for both of you. You're family."

The day flew quickly and before we knew it we were being whisked away to The Forum in a limousine. Lonny was white as a ghost and I worried a headache might hit him before he even set foot onstage. His stress level was out of control and I wished there was a way I could take some of the weight from his shoulders, but it was a burden he had to carry on his own. It was something he needed to figure out how to deal with if he was going to be part of this band.

Backstage, Howard introduced me to the guys who would be filming during the tour, and the professional photographer who would be doing the live stage shots. He explained that I was exclusively the fan club photographer and I would not be getting in their way. I was relieved when they were happy to meet me and said they looked forward to working with me on the road. It was the first time I actually felt like someone who was *supposed* to be with the band.

Marilyn appeared out of nowhere and grabbed my hand, dragging me along behind her as she ran to the dressing room. "You have to fix this," she shouted.

As we entered the dressing room, Fuzzy, Benji and Mitch all pointed to the bathroom. I knocked to let Lonny know I was coming in, and closed the door behind me. He was leaning against the wall with his eyes closed. I held one of his hands and said nothing. I leaned against him and wrapped my arms around his waist, comforting him the only way I knew how.

"You can do this," I whispered. "You're in this band because of your talent. Don't let anyone make you think differently."

He put his arms around me and buried his face against my shoulder.

"You need to get changed," I said. "It's almost show time." I pulled away to look at his face. My sweet Lonny, legally an adult, but still a boy afraid of the world. "I'll be right where you can see me the whole time, I promise."

He leaned over and kissed my mouth whispering, "Thank you."

I let Lonny walk out first and everyone in the dressing room who wasn't a band member left to give them some privacy. Marilyn looked at me with pleading eyes and I smiled, letting her know Lonny would be just fine. She put an arm around me and squeezed my shoulder, heaving a sigh of relief.

Before we knew it, the band was being led to the stage as the crowd let out a deafening roar when the house lights went off. My stomach was in my throat as I watched Benji run to his spot onstage, then Fuzzy behind his drums, and Mitch center stage... and when Lonny walked out and picked up his old electric guitar, the audience went berserk. The screams were so loud I thought my eardrums were going to burst. Fuzzy counted in the beats of their first song and they were off... Lonny was like a statue, never moving from behind his mic stand, but his playing was explosive and on the mark. Mitch's voice was smooth as honey, never sounding better, and he made it a point to engage Lonny onstage as often as possible.

As was typical for Lonny his face was hidden by his hair, but his vocals were spot on and his performance was beyond stellar. I watched with my hands in a praying position, my fingers against my mouth the entire time, and at one point Marilyn stood behind me and wrapped her arms around me. We stood frozen in place, finding it hard to believe the moment we'd all been waiting for was finally here.

At one point someone threw a bra at Lonny and it got stuck on the neck of his guitar. He ignored it and continued to play as his guitar tech tried to get it untangled, but Fuzzy and Benji noticed and began laughing. Mitch finally realized what was happening when he saw people in the crowd laughing and turned to see what was going on. He stopped singing and said, "Need some help there, Lonny?" This caused Lonny to laugh and I knew he was finally feeling a bit more confident.

When the song was over Benji said, "Hey Mitch, remember when you were the one getting the bras?"

Fuzzy laughed so loudly we could hear him without the microphone. When Lonny's tech took the guitar away from him in order to properly remove the bra, he picked up his brand new Flying V and after playing a few test chords, they launched into "Take Me Home." Lonny played every note and sang every word as perfectly as possible, sending the crowd into meltdown mode. The veteran Livingston Monroe fans seemed a bit shaken at first by the screaming young girls who came aboard because of Lonny, but everyone in that audience was mesmerized by his performance. When it came time for his guitar solo, he actually stepped out of his comfort zone behind the mic and walked to the front of the stage, causing concert goers, music journalists and critics to ask, "Joey who?"

Tears fell down my cheeks as I watched Lonny onstage, so talented, so in his element, and so beautiful. He was never more sure of himself than when he had a guitar in his hands. I knew then and there he was going to make it. He was meant to be in this band all along and nothing was going to take that away from him.

The band quickly ran offstage for their break before the encore and they were all drenched in sweat, but exhilarated. Lonny looked a bit peaked and I asked if he was okay. He pulled me to the side and said he was starting to get one of his headaches. I told him not to panic and reminded him that they only had two more songs to do and I would take care of him after the show.

I put my face close to his and whispered, "You were phenomenal."

He smiled and nodded, admitting that he thought he did a pretty good job.

The band was off again, heading back to the stage to perform "Just Say Yes" and "Lonely Girl." The crowd went wild as Fuzzy jumped down from his drum riser to join the rest of the band with their arms around each other for their end of the show bow. They all waved to the sold out audience as they walked offstage, but as soon as Lonny reached me he collapsed. As Fuzzy helped him up and walked him toward the dressing room, I noticed the angry look on Howard's face.

As soon as we got to the dressing room Howard shouted, "Is that kid on drugs?"

"He's not on drugs!" I yelled, angry that such an assumption would be made. As I wrapped some ice in a towel I explained, "He gets these headaches… he'll be okay."

Lonny sat next to me on the couch, resting his head on my lap as I began icing his head.

"I hired you to take photos," Howard grumbled, "not play nurse."

I gave him a dirty look and said, "Don't worry, you'll get your photos."

A few minutes later Lonny was running to the bathroom to vomit. I then picked up my camera and began taking photos, just as Howard hired me to do.

"Poor kid," Marilyn said. "He really blew that audience away tonight."

"Joey never sounded that good," Fuzzy added.

"What the hell with all those screaming girls?" Mitch asked. "Where did they come from?"

"You haven't seen what Lonny's had to deal with," Fuzzy said. "Poor kid can't go anywhere without getting mobbed."

"Definitely not the crowd we're used to," Benji said.

When I knew Lonny was done throwing up, I went into the bathroom with ice and towels and proceeded to take care of him as I always did with these headaches of his. After about an hour Marilyn poked her head in and asked if Lonny was able to get in the car and go home.

Lonny and I got up off the bathroom floor and went back into the dressing room. I pulled his sunglasses out of my bag and told him to put them on. Before everyone left I made sure to get some after show shots of him with the rest of the guys so no one would question why he wasn't in any of the photos. Lonny managed a smile and the guys hammed it up to make everything look legitimate, which I was grateful for.

As we headed out of the dressing room Fuzzy handed Lonny the bra that was thrown at him. "Your first of many, I'm sure," he laughed.

Lonny threw it in the first garbage can he saw.

As soon as we got home, Lonny headed straight for bed and I was right behind him. It was a long, exhausting, fantastic day, but his headaches always took the life right out of him. I knew his headache was probably caused by the stress of the first show, but I hoped he wouldn't have to spend the entire tour suffering.

Facing each other in his bed Lonny whispered, "Thank you for everything."

"Anything for you."

"Did I do okay?"

"Lonny, you were out of this world. You heard the crowd… they were blown away. They love you."

"I almost freaked when that bra came flying at me. I didn't know what to do so I kept playing, but I think that's why it got stuck."

I asked him why he threw the bra away.

"Gross," was his answer, and we both laughed.

I woke up early the next morning, sneaking out of bed so Lonny could sleep. I threw on some clothes and went into the kitchen where Marilyn was grabbing her purse and pulling away from Fuzzy, who seemed to be reaching for her arm.

"Everything okay?" I asked, not wanting to interfere.

"Oh hey doll," Marilyn said. "I have to go… it's my mom…." Without another word she ran out the door.

Fuzzy looked like he just woke up and I stood staring at him. "Is her mom okay?" I asked.

"She's… I don't know."

Fuzzy walked away, running a hand through his mane of curly hair. I wasn't sure what to think, but it sounded pretty serious. I went back to Lonny's room to see if he was awake, and since he was still sound asleep I crawled back in bed and curled up next to him, my face pressed against his shoulder.

Marilyn hadn't returned home that day and when the limousine arrived, Fuzzy insisted we leave without her, that she would make it on her own later. While Lonny was feeling much better, Fuzzy looked really worried and seemed out of sorts. It was odd to see Fuzzy in such a state and I prayed everything with Marilyn's mother turned out for the best.

While the guys did their soundcheck, I wandered through the venue taking photographs of anything that interested me. Making sure to stay out of anyone else's way, I took photos of the band as I could, sometimes just laying my camera on the stage and pressing the button, having no clue what the final photograph was actually going to look like. I had no idea what Howard would think of my experimentation, but I knew I'd find out eventually.

The dressing room was crawling with people about an hour before showtime and Marilyn was nowhere in sight. I felt like an outsider as celebrities and journalists talked to each of the guys, but I used that time to do my job and take photographs of everything going on around me. I only hoped Howard would like what I was giving him, fearful he could send me home at any point during the tour if he saw fit.

At one point I climbed onto a chair in the corner of the room so I could get a bird's eye view of everyone, and I was able to get some amazing shots that way. I was in my own little world when I saw Howard walk into the room with someone behind him. I was hoping it was Marilyn but it turned out to be Peter. My heart raced at the sight of him and since I was standing higher than anyone in the room, he noticed me right away. His big, bright smile lit up the room as he waved and made his way through the bodies to get to me. I leaned over as he gave me a big hug and told me how happy he was to see me.

"Can we talk later, when it's not so noisy?" he asked.

I nodded and he was off to talk to the band as I resumed my position on the chair. I watched closely as he greeted Lonny, who shook his hand vigorously, then looked my way, wondering if I'd noticed Peter was there. I gave him a thumbs up and a smile, then took a photograph of them together. I knew Lonny was thinking the same thing I was… what were Peter's intentions where I was concerned? But more importantly, where was Marilyn?

By the time the band was ready to hit the stage, Marilyn still hadn't arrived and I was getting worried. Fuzzy did a great job of hiding it, but I could tell he was concerned. Peter stood next to me as the guys made their way to the stage, and Lonny shocked me with a quick kiss on the lips as he passed me. I could feel my face flush and pressed my hand against my cheek.

Peter leaned close to my ear and said, "Claiming his territory?" I turned to look at him with a goofy grin on my face and he smiled. "Glad I could help."

Lonny seemed a bit more at ease onstage this time, coming out of his shell somewhat. He wasn't as wooden, his body looking more relaxed and flexible. Several bras made it onstage during this show, but Lonny was able to dodge them like an expert. Everybody got a laugh out of it, and even Lonny was grinning.

"Where's Marilyn?" Peter asked.

"Something happened to her mom," I shouted.

The next thing we knew, a young girl managed to get onstage and ran directly at Lonny, latching onto his neck so tightly it took two security guards to get her away from him. He continued to play as if nothing happened and his bandmates looked more astounded than he did. The offending fan was sent back to her seat and the show continued as normal.

Later in the show Lonny was halfway through "Take Me Home" when a handful of girls made it onstage and rushed him, knocking him to the floor. Peter and I couldn't understand how these girls were making it past security and onstage. As soon as Lonny hit the floor the band stopped playing and Mitch ran over to start dragging girls away from him. Security reacted immediately, but Lonny struggled under that pile of girls for quite some time before he was free.

As shocked as I was I managed to snap some photos from offstage, feeling guilty that I was doing a job instead of trying to help Lonny. Once the girls were removed and tossed back into the crowd, Mitch helped Lonny to his feet and walked him offstage, with Fuzzy and Benji following quickly behind. They made a beeline for the dressing room, with Peter and I in tow. I snapped photos as I could, but we were running to catch up.

"What the fuck!" Mitch was screaming as we reached the dressing room.

Howard rushed in soon after, demanding they get back onstage immediately.

"Lonny almost got killed out there! Look at him!" Fuzzy looked sick and I could see his hands trembling. That scared me more than anything else.

Lonny's shirt was ripped to shreds and he had blood trickling out of his mouth. I stayed out of the way and did my job, but I was afraid for Lonny. He couldn't even be onstage without girls mobbing him.

Howard stormed out of the dressing room leaving everyone stunned and silent. Lonny went into the bathroom to look at his face, cleaning the blood off and coming back out asking if anyone had a shirt he could borrow. This eased the tension a bit and everyone started to laugh.

Howard returned a few minutes later and said, "They're making an announcement right now that if the show has to be stopped again, you're not coming back out."

Lonny asked Howard if he could borrow his tie. Howard pulled a face, but gave the red tie to him anyway. Lonny proceeded to remove his tattered shirt and threw Howard's tie over his head.

"That's what you're wearing?" Howard asked.

"Yep." It was all Lonny needed to say.

I took more photos as the band laughed and headed back out the door, and as soon as they were gone I shoved Lonny's tattered shirt into my bag and followed Peter back to our spot offstage.

The audience erupted into a deafening roar as the guys cautiously made their way back onstage. Mitch got on the microphone and announced, "You ready for us to finish this thing?"

On Mitch's nod Lonny started "Take Me Home" for a second time and sounded more confident singing than I'd ever heard him before. Maybe it was defiance, I wasn't sure, but he wasn't going to let anyone ruin their show that evening. I only wished Marilyn had been there to witness the melee... she wouldn't have believed it with her own eyes.

The rest of the show went off without a problem and the guys were all smiles as they ran offstage when it was over. Seeing that Peter was still standing next to me, Lonny put his arm around my shoulders as he led me back to the dressing room with the others. This was highly unusual behavior for Lonny, and I couldn't help but think that Peter's presence probably caused it.

Back in the dressing room the guys were happy and loud and giving Lonny an extra hard time about being the teen idol of the group, causing hysteria among all the young girls. I stood back on my chair in the corner to take photos and Peter joined me.

"Are you going to the after party?" he asked me.

"Yeah, you?"

"Wouldn't miss it."

The room was quiet for just a moment and Mitch burst into song, singing the opening lines from Grand Funk's "Bad Time."

"I'm in love with the girl that I'm talking about," Mitch sang.

"I'm in love with the girl I can't live without," Fuzzy sang.

"I'm in love but I sure picked a bad time," Lonny sang.

And the entire room sang, "To be in love."

I smiled as I continued to snap photos, loving every bit of this life so far. I hoped this impromptu singalong made it into the final version of the movie when all was said and done. It was too perfect not to make the cut.

As we headed out to the limousine the band was quickly surrounded by a group of fans that had been patiently waiting for them to leave the venue. Lonny's face showed every fear he was experiencing, but these fans didn't mob anyone. They were older and just wanted an autograph or a photograph with their favorite band member. Lonny soon relaxed and seemed to enjoy talking to fans who weren't there to rip his clothes off or tear out his hair. I stayed in the background and took photo after photo, hoping I was getting the kind of shots Howard was interested in. He certainly wouldn't be able to complain that I wasn't getting enough.

As we finally piled into the limousine Fuzzy told Lonny, "You better put a shirt on. Howard won't want you at his party half naked."

This caused me to roar with laughter and for some reason it sent Mitch into hysterics. He wrapped his arm around my shoulders and said, "I love this kid," then kissed me on the cheek.

Benji dug in his bag and pulled out a t-shirt that he threw at Lonny. "It's probably too big, but at least it's a shirt."

Lonny took Howard's tie off and slipped it over my head with a smile. Oddly enough, with Peter nowhere in sight, he made no attempt to touch me in any way. I noticed, however, that Mitch never removed his arm from around my shoulders.

The party was in full swing as we entered Howard's house, and he immediately pulled the guys to the center of it all. Peter found me, which I was thankful for, because I didn't know anyone else there. I continued to take photos as Howard talked about how the future of Livingston Monroe was up in the air after Joey Buckingham left, and how even though he wasn't interested in hiring Lonny, the band insisted they would break up if he wasn't in

283

the band. Howard went on to admit that the band knew what they were doing and they couldn't have hired a better guitarist to fill the spot, even though he was so young and inexperienced. Lonny looked embarrassed as the other band members cheered for him, tousling his hair and slapping him on the back.

"I see you're still wearing the necklace I gave you," Peter said.

I looked at his smiling face, which caused me to smile in return. "Because it's very special."

Servers passed champagne flutes to the guests and Howard raised his glass, saying, "To the best lineup Livingston Monroe has ever seen, and here's to a successful tour… their biggest and most expensive production yet!"

Peter held my champagne glass so I wouldn't miss photos of the toast, and then the band members split up to mingle with other partygoers. Lonny was immediately surrounded by people who wanted to talk to him, and it made me happy. He was important; he was the reason this band was thriving and embarking on their biggest tour ever.

Peter handed me my champagne and clinked his glass against mine saying, "To Lonny."

"To Lonny." I had such a huge smile on my face I thought it might break.

"Ruby, I'm so sorry about that tabloid. If I had known…."

"It wasn't your fault."

"I've made some changes to my property, I can promise you that."

Howard made his way over to me and as I tried to give him his tie he said, "It's okay, you can keep it."

"Is Louise here?" I asked.

He hesitated before saying, "It isn't really public knowledge yet, but we aren't together anymore."

"I'm sorry."

He waved me off and changed the subject, asking where Marilyn was.

"Something happened to her mom," I answered.

Howard looked concerned and walked away, not stopping until he found Fuzzy. I watched them as they conversed until Peter distracted me.

"So the bus leaves tomorrow?"

"Yep! First stop San Francisco."

Peter opened his mouth to speak, but we were interrupted by a funny little man in a three-piece suit who smelled like cheese.

"Excuse me miss," he said, "aren't you the mystery girl from the tabloid?"

Peter and I laughed loudly and I said, "No, not me."

"But you're here... with Peter Summersby," he replied.

"She just flew in from Chicago. Different girl entirely," Peter said. "I'm a bit of a scamp."

The little man shook his head and walked away, Peter and I clinking our glasses and drinking down the champagne. Before we could blink an eye our glasses were once again filled and I laughed.

"This stuff is too good. I have to stop."

"Not much of a drinker?"

"New Year's Eve was the first time."

"Rookie."

I pointed to myself and said, "Eighteen."

"I keep forgetting," he teased.

I looked around the room to find Lonny, flanked by a few older women who couldn't keep their hands off him. They seemed to take turns touching his hair, sliding a finger down his arm, or stroking his chest with their hands. The odd part was I couldn't tell if he was enjoying it or not, but he certainly didn't look uncomfortable. I suppose it was different when hysterical fans were trying to tear off a piece of him, when these women probably wanted a completely different piece of him.

I excused myself, telling Peter I had a job to do, and walked right up to Lonny and his harem to take several photographs. "Smile ladies!" They were all too willing to pose with Lonny and let me know it. Through my lens I saw one of the women slide her hand into the front pocket of Lonny's jeans, causing him to flinch. I made sure to zoom in on it and took a photo. I thought it would be interesting to see if Howard noticed after he had the film developed.

"Thanks, ladies," I said. "Please, continue groping Lonny."

Lonny's face lost all expression as he realized I saw what the woman did to him. I continued on my way, doing my job, taking photos of all the band members. When I met up with Fuzzy, he put a loving arm around me and kissed the top of my head.

"You doing okay, doll?"

"Yeah, sure," I said. "Watching old ladies grab Lonny's crotch."

He nearly choked on the champagne he was trying to swallow. He found Lonny with his eyes and said, "The three amigas. Always ready to feast on the new blood."

"I don't want them feasting on Lonny," I grumbled, embarrassed that I actually said it out loud.

"Then you need to do something about it."

"But Lonny isn't supposed to have a girlfriend."

"Well doll, I don't know what to say."

I knew if Marilyn had been there, those women wouldn't have been able to get that close to Lonny. "Have you heard from Marilyn? Is her mom okay?"

"Um… yeah, I think everything is fine."

"I miss her."

"Me too, doll."

I left Fuzzy and headed to the food table, realizing how hungry I was. It wasn't long before Peter was standing next to me, asking if I wanted to go outside for some fresh air.

"I'd love to, but I have a job to do in here."

"Surely you're allowed to take a break. Where's my fun Ruby?"

Peter was so charming it was difficult to say no. He took my hand and led me through the house, deliberately past Lonny and out the back door. We sat on a love seat and put our feet up on the accompanying ottoman.

"Be honest with me," I said. "Will I end up being lonely on tour because Lonny will be surrounded by girls all the time?"

286

"I guess you have to look at why you're going on tour. Are you there because you're with Lonny, or are you there because you have a job to do?"

"Howard gave me a job to do because Lonny wanted me to go with them."

Peter turned to look at me and said, "You and Lonny need to figure this out, whatever it is... I mean, is he your boyfriend?"

"No."

"Do you want him to be?" When I didn't answer he said, "You can't be the girl pining away for Lonny while he's doing his job... being a rock star. Girls are part of the deal, and if that's something you can't handle you should reconsider going with them."

I suddenly felt sick.

"That being said, it doesn't mean you can't have your fun, too."

"I'm not like that!" I protested.

Peter chuckled. "I know you're not. And honestly, I don't think Lonny is either. You two are like the virginal twins that fell out of heaven or something."

I began laughing hysterically and Peter soon joined in. He always knew how to make me laugh. Leaning back against the seat we turned our heads to face each other as Peter took my hand in his.

Kissing my knuckles he said, "You can always call me and I'll come save you."

"You're very sweet."

He leaned forward, touching his nose to mine and smiling. Just as his lips grazed mine Lonny appeared out of nowhere saying, "We're heading out. Oh... sorry."

"She's all yours," Peter said, standing and helping me to my feet. Lonny was long gone, so he pulled me into his arms and hugged me tightly. "Remember what I told you," he whispered against my face. "You're a bright light. Don't let anyone take that away from you. Not even Lonny."

He kissed me quickly on the mouth and I left him there, heading outside to the limousine. As I stepped in, Lonny was

287

already sitting between Benji and Mitch, so I sat opposite them next to Fuzzy. Lonny wouldn't even look at me.

Fuzzy put his arm around me and said, "Well doll, you survived tonight's craziness like a champ."

"Lonny's the champ," I politely argued, hoping he would look at me. "Attacked onstage by those girls, then getting groped by those old ladies at the party."

Lonny shot me daggers as the other guys howled.

"Hope you got that on film," Mitch cackled.

"Sure did."

"Our very own paparazzi," Benji teased.

"Don't worry," I said, glaring back at Lonny. "I'll only sell Lonny out to the highest bidder."

Again, the guys howled with laughter. Fuzzy, however, picked up on Lonny's body language and, hearing "My Maria" by B.W. Stevenson on the limousine's radio sang loudly, "Sweet Maria the sunlight surely hurts my eyes... I'm a lonely dreamer on a highway in the skies...."

Mitch and Benji sang the chorus, "My Maria... Maria I love you...."

Lonny folded his arms angrily across his chest and stared out the window. I listened to the other guys singing heartily, wondering what I was getting into by going on tour with them.

We walked into the house and I told Fuzzy to let Marilyn know I missed her that evening, assuming she was already in bed asleep. I nervously followed Lonny to his room and wondered what was going to happen once we got there. He went in the bathroom to change, slamming the door behind him. I quickly changed into my shorts and tank top and jumped into bed before he came back out.

Lonny said nothing as he crawled into bed and turned his back on me. I did the same, rolling over and turning my back on him.

"Did you like it?" I asked the air.

"No, I didn't like it. It was embarrassing."

"I would never sell you out."

"Promise me something." I waited for him to tell me what he wanted. "Promise you'll always be my girl."

288

I hesitated then said, "I don't even know what that means."

"I need you on my side, Roo. I need to know you won't ever turn your back on me."

I rolled my eyes in the dark, seeing he and I had very different ideas of what being his girl actually meant. "I've always been on your side, Lonny. You know that."

"Please promise me."

"I promise."

It was quiet for a long time and I thought Lonny had fallen asleep, but he whispered, "Do you love him?"

"Aw Lonny, why are you bringing Billy—"

"Peter."

"I don't think so."

"Don't you know?"

"Goodnight, Lonny."

Morning came all too quickly as Lonny and Fuzzy busied themselves packing their suitcases, and since Marilyn hadn't made an appearance, I took it upon myself to make breakfast. She deserved a break, and I wanted to help in any way I could. When the guys finally emerged, they sat down at the kitchen table and dug in.

"Is Marilyn getting up soon?" I asked.

"She didn't come home last night," Fuzzy said.

"Is everything okay?"

"I'm not sure, doll."

"Is she leaving with us today?" Lonny asked.

Fuzzy looked a wreck. "Probably not today, but hopefully she'll meet up with us in a few days."

My stomach fell. Things just weren't the same without Marilyn. How would I survive if she wasn't there? She looked after all of us; took care of us in ways nobody else could.

"Sounds serious," Lonny mused.

Fuzzy tried to smile, but I could tell by his reaction that things were more dire than he was letting on. My heart broke for them as I couldn't imagine anything happening to one of my parents, or to Lonny's mom.

"We'll get through it," Fuzzy said. "Thanks for breakfast, doll."

Everyone met at the warehouse where the tour buses waited for us. Even though we took a taxi there, Lonny and I still had to dive as low as we could go in the back seat when we approached the first security gate at the warehouse. The crowd of girls had increased enormously knowing the band was leaving for their tour, and it would be the last glimpse they'd get of Lonny until he returned.

Once inside the safety of the warehouse property, I marveled at the activity going on around me. I took photos of everything — the semi trucks being loaded with all the stage equipment, pyrotechnics and light show necessities, and the buses that would carry the band, roadies and their security team. I took photographs of the band's sacred instruments being loaded into the back of the bus we would be traveling in, quivering with excitement and ready to get on the road.

The guys let me do an impromptu photo shoot posing next to their tour bus, then in front of the bus where the marquee jokingly read, "Lonny's First Tour 1980." I was able to get family photographs of Benji with Wanda and Calvin, but apparently Mitch's girlfriend Hattie was also going to be absent when we left later that day.

Howard arrived, introducing us to his brother and business partner Randy, who would be acting as tour manager while we were on the road. I gave Howard all the film I'd gone through already and he looked stunned at the volume.

"You hired me to take photos," I said with a smile.

"I'll have to make sure I send more film," he said. He went on to explain that there would be a package waiting for me at each hotel, containing the film I needed, and prepaid envelopes to send the used film back to him. I smiled like a goofball, not believing that after all the preparation and waiting we were finally hitting the road.

We all piled onto the bus and picked our seats, Lonny and I sitting all the way in the back. My stomach was in knots, a mixture of nerves and excitement of the unknown. As the bus neared the security gate where all the girls were screaming and crying, the guys put the windows down and hung their heads out to wave goodbye to them. While there were shouts for Fuzzy, Benji and

Mitch, the loudest screams were for Lonny. They ranged from, "Lonny, I love you!" to "Lonny, will you marry me!" to "Lonny, I want to have your baby!" I took photos of the hysterical crowd as we passed them, plopping back in my seat once we were on the road.

Lonny slid down in the seat and pressed his knees up against the back of the seat in front of us, and I did the same. He held my hand in his, intertwining his fingers with mine, then turned his head to look at me.

"I'm glad you're here," he said.

"Me, too."

He leaned closer and kissed me softly on the mouth, then touched my nose with the tip of his finger as an adorable grin crossed his face. My insides turned to mush and Lonny still continued to confuse me.

Six hours later we rolled into San Francisco.

When we pulled up to the hotel, there was a group of girls standing outside who immediately flew into hysterics when they saw the bus. It boggled my mind how they knew where we'd be staying, but perhaps they had a lucky hunch. Butch, the head of our security team, was the first to exit the bus, telling the crazed girls they could meet the band and get autographs if they controlled themselves. This seemed to satisfy them, and one by one the guys hopped off the bus, Lonny being the last. I remained on the bus to take photos, hanging out the window for the best vantage point.

The girls crowded around Lonny and behaved themselves, even though some of them couldn't stop crying. He was still signing autographs and posing for photos when the rest of our group went inside the hotel. After all the girls had been satisfied, Butch told them Lonny had to go and to please move along.

I hopped off the bus and walked toward the hotel entrance, surprised to hear someone yell, "Who's she?" The next thing I knew someone stuck their foot out and tripped me, but Butch managed to catch me before I hit the ground. As Butch was distracted by me, two of the girls latched onto Lonny and pulled him back and forth in a fight. The rest of the band's security guys immediately sprang into action, pulling the girls away from Lonny and rushing both of us into the hotel.

"We can't take you two anywhere," Fuzzy teased.

"Oh Lonny," Mitch cooed in a high pitched girl's voice, "can I have a kiss?"

Everybody was laughing, but I was disturbed by the girl who decided to trip me. "You okay, Roo?" Lonny asked, putting his arm around me.

"Yeah, I'm fine."

Randy handed out keys and we all made our way upstairs to the block of rooms reserved for the band and its staff. Lonny and I dropped our suitcases at the door and he flopped onto the bed, exhausted from the journey. I pulled my camera out of my bag and snapped some shots of him, then grabbed my Polaroid to take some photos I wouldn't have to send to Howard. As tired as he was, he indulged me and didn't protest too much. I set the Polaroids on the table to dry and stretched out on the bed next to Lonny.

"I'm starving," he whispered, "but I don't wanna move."

He wiggled as close to me as he could get, resting his mouth on my forehead. I closed my eyes and two hours later, someone was knocking on our door. Lonny got up to answer it, but I never opened my eyes.

"You guys wanna grab some dinner?" Fuzzy asked.

Lonny came back and nudged me, so I opened my eyes and groaned. Fuzzy sat on a chair in the corner of the room as I got up from the bed and stretched.

"Have you talked to Marilyn?" I asked.

Fuzzy rubbed his beard and said, "Yeah, I let her know we made it okay."

"How's her mom?"

Fuzzy shook his head. "Still not sure what's going on."

"I need to brush my teeth," I said, breathing into my palm.

"You're fine, taxis are already waiting for us."

We followed Fuzzy out the door and met up with Butch, Randy and Mitch. Benji and Wanda had already eaten because of Calvin's schedule, so we headed down to the lobby. As soon as we walked out of the elevator, a mob of girls who were waiting outside for a glimpse of the band stormed the doors and pushed their way inside. We ran back into the elevator and Fuzzy pushed the button for the floor below our rooms. We got out and ran into the stairwell then raced up one flight to our floor. As we did this, we could hear the mob of screaming girls getting closer. We all ended up in Fuzzy's room, where he quickly closed and locked the door.

We were all quiet and wide-eyed until we were sure it was safe.

"Howard told me about the girls, but I didn't quite believe him," Randy said, rubbing the side of his face.

Mitch tousled Lonny's hair and teased, "That's our golden boy."

Randy picked up the phone and called the front desk. "This is Randy Hammond. Do you have the mob of girls under control?" He listened for several minutes before saying, "There are two taxis outside waiting for us. Can someone please tell them we aren't coming? Thank you."

"Room service it is," Fuzzy chuckled.

"I'm really sorry," Lonny said.

"Lonny, it's not your fault," I lightly scolded him. "Those girls are crazy."

Randy and Butch left and Fuzzy said, "Should we all just order from here?"

The four of us ordered our dinner, then Fuzzy pulled out a deck of cards and we sat down to play some poker while we waited. We didn't bet any money, just kept a paper tally of the staggering millions each of us was winning and losing. By the time our food arrived I was ahead of them all with a million dollars.

"Remind me not to play against you with real money," Mitch told me.

"Beginner's luck," I lied with a sneaky grin, knowing my dad taught me everything I knew.

We stayed in Fuzzy's room and ate dinner together, talking about the show at the Cow Palace the next evening and how we were going to combat the crazed fans keeping Lonny a prisoner everywhere he went. After we were finished eating, Lonny grabbed his acoustic guitar from our room and played for us. I sat on the bed with Fuzzy, who leaned against me with his head on my shoulder. Mitch and Lonny switched off on vocals, depending on what he decided to play. I pulled both of my cameras out of my

293

bag and snapped away. Lonny hijacked both cameras at one point and took some of his own photos, then Mitch did the same. I hated having my picture taken, but I couldn't really say anything since I was the one taking pictures of them every time they turned around. We mostly joked around and made light of the fact that Lonny was in danger every time he tried to go outside. I was seriously worried for his safety, even with security guards to protect him.

Lonny and I headed back to our room when it started getting late, knowing the band had a big day coming up. Howard had set up a media day at the venue for early afternoon, then band interviews for the film, soundcheck, and finally the show. I sat at the foot of the bed as Lonny closed and locked the door, then put his guitar back in its case. He stood in front of me and put his hands on my shoulders and I looked up at him.

"I'm so glad you're here," he whispered. "I couldn't do this without you."

"You could," I teased.

He leaned over and kissed me, but quickly pulled away to look at me. I smiled and he leaned back in to kiss me again. He put his hands on my cheeks and someone knocked on the door. He grumbled something under his breath and I rolled my eyes as he got up to look through the peephole. He opened the door and Wanda walked in holding Calvin, whose head was lolling as he tried to stay awake.

"Ruby, would you mind keeping an eye on Calvin for a little while? He's almost asleep and shouldn't be any bother. Benji and I have some things we need to discuss."

"Sure, yeah," I said, even though it made no sense to me. Why couldn't they talk after he was asleep, when he was so clearly almost there?

Wanda gently placed Calvin on the bed where he closed his eyes and went to sleep. She thanked us and ran off, Lonny locking the door behind her.

"What are we supposed to do now?" he asked.

"Watch him sleep?" I had no idea.

It wasn't long before we heard exactly what Wanda and Benji needed to discuss, as their room was right next to ours.

Calvin opened his eyes to see neither of his parents were in the room and immediately began to cry and call for mama.

"What do we do?" Lonny asked, panicked.

I picked Calvin up and walked around the room with him trying to comfort him, but he was having none of that. He continued to blubber as we could hear them next door. Lonny made a face out of frustration that caused Calvin to laugh briefly.

"Maybe he likes peek-a-boo," I suggested.

Lonny started doing peek-a-boo with his hands, then progressed to pillows and whatever else he could find in the room to hide his face behind. This seemed to settle Calvin down, which was a relief. From there Lonny decided to play hide and seek, so I set the baby down on the floor. Not that there were very many places to hide, but since Calvin was still wobbly on his feet it made for some great entertainment. And it gave Calvin something to do.

At one point Lonny had gone into the bathroom to hide, closing the door behind him. Calvin looked all over for him, giggling and laughing as he'd raise his shoulders as if to shrug out of baby frustration. About ten minutes later I walked behind Calvin to the bathroom door and opened it, finding Lonny sound asleep propped up against the wall.

Calvin charged him, laughing as I said, "Thanks a lot, Lonny."

"What's that smell?" Lonny asked.

"Oh God, he pooped! She didn't leave us any diapers!"

The smell began to permeate the bathroom and Lonny was quickly on his feet, visibly turning green.

"How long does it take to have sex?" I grumbled naively.

"How long did it take you?" he teased, laughing as he left the bathroom.

"I don't know, a few minutes maybe. Isn't it the same for everyone?"

Lonny stared at me with his mouth open. "I don't know."

"Well how long did it take you?" I was genuinely curious because I was clueless after having only one experience to navigate from. "I'm sorry, never mind." We laughed nervously, knowing how inexperienced and clueless we both were when it came to matters of sex.

Things seemed to have quieted down next door, but it didn't really matter. I took Calvin by the hand and walked him to Benji and Wanda's room, knocking on the door. Benji opened the door looking disheveled, and Calvin walked right inside.

"He needs a diaper change," I said, then walked back to our room where Lonny was already fast asleep.

In San Diego, there was a short note from Howard in my package at the hotel. *"No crotch shots!"* I laughed, remembering the photo I took of the woman sliding her hand in Lonny's pocket at the after party.

Tucson was next, then on to Denver, where Lonny and I walked into our hotel room after the show to find Mitch already there having sex with a girl he picked up backstage. Lonny and I quickly exited the room and stood outside the door in complete shock.

"I thought he had a girlfriend," I whispered, trying to erase the vision of what I'd just seen.

"He broke up with her before we left," Lonny whispered. "I guess that's what he does before the band goes on tour."

"Everything okay?" We saw Fuzzy standing in the doorway of his room across the hall smiling at us.

Lonny and I both fumbled for words, unable to say anything coherent. My face was on fire and Lonny couldn't even look at me. He took the key from my hand to see if it opened the door to Mitch's room, and it did. We said goodnight to Fuzzy and disappeared, embarrassed, into Mitch's room. We had no alternative but to sleep in our clothes since our suitcases were still in our room.

I was exhausted but stared into the darkness wide-eyed, unable to go to sleep. "Lonny?"

"Yeah?"

"I've never seen a penis before."

We both burst into uncontrollable laughter.

296

"What about Billy?" he asked.

"Nope… he shoved it in then zipped it back up."

"I wish I didn't see Ms. Cooke," he said. "I saw *everything*."

"Maybe the next time will be better for both of us." I said goodnight and rolled over to try and get some sleep, knowing we had to be up early for a long travel day in the morning.

In Ft. Worth Mitch destroyed his hotel room before we left for the show because he called Hattie, only to find out she was already seeing the singer from another band. I didn't understand his reasoning, considering he broke up with her so he could screw around on the road. I was learning new things every day and some of them were not pleasant. That night Mitch stomped offstage halfway through the show, screaming at Randy that it wasn't his personal microphone stand they set up. As they argued offstage Lonny, Benji and Fuzzy jammed, giving this audience something none of the others had seen. Randy finally yanked the microphone stand out of Mitch's hands and showed him the engraving down the side. Mitch didn't even apologize, just stormed back onstage and continued where he left off.

In Houston Fuzzy saw me watching Calvin again, which had become a regular occurrence on the tour. Wanda would ask if I could keep an eye on him for a little while and she would disappear. At the hotel, at the venue, it didn't matter where.

"Where's Wanda?" he asked as I handed Calvin a bottle in the dressing room.

"I'm not sure."

"You're not here to play babysitter."

"I know, but I don't mind."

Fuzzy disappeared and returned a few minutes later with Wanda. "Take your kid," he told her. "Howard gave Ruby a job to do and it's not watching Calvin."

Wanda took Calvin from me and stormed out of the dressing room.

"I don't want to cause any problems," I insisted.

"You know what she was doing? Hitting up the roadies for coke." When he realized I didn't understand the big deal he added, "Cocaine, doll."

I immediately covered my mouth with my hand, shocked.

The next morning as we hit the road toward New Orleans, Wanda headed to the airport with Calvin, claiming he had become sick overnight and they couldn't stay on the tour. I couldn't help but feel guilty and that Wanda and Benji might be thinking I complained about having to watch Calvin, which wasn't true.

Sitting in the back of the bus with Lonny, he knew I wasn't feeling right about the whole situation. He took out a pen and drew a goofy looking face on my jeans, which made me smile. He stuck a finger in the hole ripped at my knee and caressed my skin underneath. I looked at him sadly and he put his arm around me saying, "It's okay, Roo. Benji didn't want them on tour anyway."

"I feel like Wanda blames me."

"Who cares? She's gone."

"And Fuzzy...."

"What about him?"

"He just seems so sad without Marilyn here. And I miss her, too."

"Maybe we'll see her soon."

He smiled and I nodded, hoping he was right. He leaned close to my face and pressed his lips against mine, holding them there as he stared into my eyes.

As we got closer to our hotel in New Orleans, Benji asked Lonny to move to a different seat on the bus so he could talk to me. Benji looked just like his brother Fuzzy, only blond and with no facial hair. He put his arm around me and smiled.

I burst into tears as the guilt had been eating me alive.

"It's not your fault," he said. "Wanda has a problem."

"But she left with Calvin," I cried. "Who's taking care of him?"

"Her parents are meeting them at the airport and they're taking care of everything."

I was relieved but the tears continued to burn my eyes.

"You're a good kid," he told me. "Calvin loves you. We all do."

I wiped my face and smiled, thanking him. He kissed my cheek and got up to give Lonny his seat back. As we pulled up to the hotel we noticed there were no girls waiting outside. We all

298

breathed a collective sigh of relief, grabbed our things, and jumped out quickly because we knew word would soon spread.

No sooner did we step inside the safety of the hotel, the skies opened up and a torrential downpour furiously pounded the ground. It continued to rain into the evening and nobody wanted to venture outside. We spent another night ordering room service and going stir crazy inside the hotel. Fuzzy seemed especially down so we all crammed into his room to watch *Jaws*. We ate pizza, drank beer and freaked out over the enormous shark, even though we'd all seen the movie before. Fuzzy and Benji were sitting on one of the queen sized beds, while Lonny and I sat on the other with Mitch sprawled out at our feet. Lonny sat with his arm around me which was bold for him, never showing any affection to me in front of people, especially the band. Halfway through the movie Benji went back to his own room so I hopped off the bed and took his place next to Fuzzy, making room for Mitch on the other bed. Lonny gave me the side eye, but said nothing.

With half an hour left of the movie, Fuzzy was sound asleep and Mitch went back to his room. I was lying down and way too comfortable to move, but Lonny took my hand and said, "Let's go."

"I want to finish watching the movie," I whispered.

"You can watch it in our room."

"I'll be there as soon as it's over."

Lonny let go of my hand and walked out. When I woke up the next morning I was right where he left me, next to a sleeping Fuzzy. He woke up as I jumped off the bed, then he stretched and started laughing.

"Lonny probably didn't sleep all night," he teased.

I tip-toed into the hallway and closed the door but when I turned around, Randy was standing there. He shook his head and kept walking. I lightly knocked on Lonny's door and he opened it right away.

"I'm sorry," I said. "I fell asleep before the movie ended."

"Obviously," he grumbled, crawling back in the bed and pulling the covers over his head.

"Randy just saw me leaving."

"Yeah, well, that's your problem."

299

He was pissed and he stayed that way for most of the day. I knew it wasn't because I spent the night with Fuzzy; it was because he had to spend the night alone, which I knew he hated. Lonny was becoming more and more a prisoner on the road, and while the other guys had groupies at their disposal at every stop, he had uncontrollable teenage girls.

It's a good thing I was on the tour with Lonny, because he would have been isolated and lonely without me. Somehow girls would always find out which hotel we were staying at and show up to get a glimpse of him. The numbers seemed to increase at each stop and it got to the point where Butch would have to sneak Lonny and me out through a back door as the rest of the guys were heading out the front. The rest of the guys were able to go out after a show and blow off steam at a bar or club but Lonny and I were too young to join them, so we'd be shoved in the back of a nondescript car and brought back to the hotel.

In the dressing room before the show that night, a gift of top shelf whiskey was opened and shot glasses were passed around the room. Mitch toasted to the greatest crew a band could ever ask for, and everyone threw back the liquid, including Lonny and me. My entire head was on fire and I tried not to cough as it burned my throat all the way down to my belly. I took photos of the toast and the shots being thrown back, then everyone headed to the stage. I lagged behind, wanting to avoid causing Lonny any more grief. I took photos of the band as they walked ahead of me, but tried not to focus on their backsides for fear I'd get another note from Howard... *"No asses!"*

After the incident at the Forum where Lonny's shirt was ripped to shreds and he went back out wearing only Howard's tie, it became his thing to go out for the encore of every show dressed the same way. When the band returned to the dressing room for their break before the encore, I presented him with his tie for the evening.

Lonny laughed as I handed it to him and asked, "Where do you find all these ties?"

I shrugged and replied, "There's always some guy walking around with a tie... I just ask if I can have it. No one's ever said no."

Lonny ripped off his sweat drenched t-shirt and threw the tie over his head. We all threw back a couple more shots and as the band headed back to the stage, Lonny held me back in the dressing room until we were alone. My head was swimming.

"I'm sorry," he said. "You didn't do anything wrong. I'm just an asshole."

"You're not an asshole. I should've gone with you."

Lonny smiled. I'm not sure what came over me, the alcohol most likely, but I wrapped my fingers around his tie and pulled him toward me, so close I inhaled his breath. I kissed him softly and whispered against his mouth, "You have to go."

Lonny pressed himself against me, pinning me between his body and the door. He kissed me hard, as if he would never have the chance to kiss me again, and my knees almost gave out on me. Then he whispered against my mouth, "I have to go."

We had to run to catch up to the guys and Lonny ended up being the last one back onstage, but he picked up his flying V and performed the encore with such swagger there was no fear there, no hiding behind the microphone stand, no hiding behind his hair. He flipped his sweaty head of hair back and his face — his eyes — were visible to everyone in that venue. That had never happened before.

We had no problem getting back to the hotel after the show that night, as the rain, thunder and lightning were quite ominous and there were no fans hanging out in that weather. It was a relief but I had other things on my mind, like Lonny's arm around me in the limousine, and what might happen once we got back to our room.

As soon as he closed and locked the door to our room he started kissing me and walking me backward toward the bed, where I hit the edge and fell onto my back with Lonny climbing on top of me. His mouth was soft and wet against mine, his breath hot on my face as his hand slid underneath my t-shirt. There were things going on inside me that felt good and Lonny was the reason. He must have been having a similar experience because he groaned as he kissed me, his body pressed down hard against mine. Just as he slid one of his hands underneath my bra, someone began

301

pounding on the door. We ignored it at first, hoping they'd just go away, but whoever it was persisted.

Lonny grumbled an expletive and got off the bed, his hair sticking out in all different directions, and flung open the door.

"Poker game, Fuzzy's room," Mitch said. "Did I interrupt some—"

Lonny slammed the door in his face and walked back to the bed, running his hands through his tangled hair. I sat up as he sat down and we were both quiet.

I said, "Maybe we should...."

"Yeah, okay," he agreed.

We waited a few minutes to collect ourselves, then I grabbed my camera and we went to Fuzzy's room where Fuzzy, Mitch and Benji grinned at us as soon as we walked in. There was plenty of alcohol, snacks and a box of cigars. I took the deck of cards out of Fuzzy's hand and said, "Pour us some drinks and let's get started."

There was always plenty of alcohol on the tour, and while Lonny and I didn't partake most of the time we did on occasion, and it was definitely building up both of our tolerances and I found I enjoyed it. I was tired of everybody treating us like we were twelve years old; I was an adult and I wanted to be treated like one. As Mitch put a cassette in the tape player blasting Queen, I unwrapped a cigar and put it in my mouth, never lighting it.

"Since you so rudely interrupted us," I said, glaring at all of them with a sneaky grin, "strip poker, my rules."

At first Lonny looked like he'd seen a ghost, but then he smiled. He knew how well I played cards and he realized we'd be back in our room soon, where we could continue where we left off.

"No way!" Benji protested. "No, no, no."

"Come on you pussy," Mitch teased him.

"Lonny, you in?" Fuzzy asked.

"You bet."

We all threw back a shot of whiskey before we started, and the guys lit up their cigars. Benji lost both socks and both shoes right off the bat, rolling his eyes in knowing he didn't want to play in the first place. Mitch, Fuzzy and Lonny all lost their shoes and socks, and I was still completely dressed.

302

With Queen's "Fat Bottomed Girls" playing in the background, Mitch folded, singing, "I've been singing with my band...."

Fuzzy sang, "Across the wire, across the land...."

Lonny chimed in singing, "I seen every blue eyed floozy on the way...."

Suddenly the tides turned and I lost both socks and both shoes. We all took another shot and everybody folded. I wondered if I was off my game because I'd been drinking and wasn't playing with a clear head.

Benji lost his shirt and quit, saying there was no way he would ever take off his pants. He disappeared back to his room and it was down to the four of us. Everybody was barefoot, but Mitch had just lost his shirt. I tried not to stare because he had the body of a god, with the perfect amount of blond hair on his chest and the trail that went from his bellybutton to the top of the jeans that hung low on his hips. Then Mitch lost his pants. He slid them off quickly, revealing his bikini underwear, which left nothing to the imagination. I tried not to look at him but my eyes kept drifting. Fuzzy and Lonny both lost their shirts and I knew Lonny didn't wear underwear, so he was down to his last piece of clothing.

Then I lost my pants.

"Roo, don't," Lonny said.

"No, no," I laughed. "It's only fair." I slid my jeans off and threw them on the clothes pile.

I beat Mitch with a four of a kind and thought he was going to go back to his room like Benji did, but he didn't. He stood up and stripped off his underwear, standing there completely naked. I marveled at his physique but kept looking away, embarrassed.

"Game's over," Lonny announced. "Let's go, Roo."

"Game's not over," Fuzzy teased, his eyes glassy. "There's still three of us."

I lost the next round and reached underneath my shirt to unsnap my bra, then slid my arms out of its straps and miraculously pulled it out one of my sleeves. All three guys looked like they'd just seen the most sophisticated magic trick and I laughed.

"I'm done," Lonny said. "I'm going back to my room."

303

And with that, he left me there.

"You should go doll," Fuzzy said. "You don't want to be in a room with Mitch when he's naked."

"He's right, you don't," Mitch said.

I got off the bed to stand up and fell on my hands and knees. I didn't realize I had gotten that drunk. I crawled to the door, down the hall, and to Lonny's room. I knocked and he let me in, locking the door behind him. I crawled onto the bed and flopped on my back.

Standing next to the bed he looked down at me and said, "You've seen your first dick. Are you happy now?"

I screwed up my face and looked up at him, asking, "Are they all that big?"

Lonny rolled his eyes and said, "Uh… no."

"Oh thank God," I said with relief. Lonny crawled under the covers and I said, "What are you doing?"

"Going to sleep. I'm tired."

"But what about before?" I bellowed, trying to sit up. "Don't you wanna finish?"

"Not in the mood."

"What's your problem?"

He gave me a dirty look and answered, "I don't like you like this."

"Like what?"

"Drunk… and half naked."

I laughed. "A lot of guys would be happy with a half drunk naked girl. I mean… half naked drunk girl." I leaned over and tried to kiss him but he pushed me away. I stared at him blankly and asked, "Lonny, are you gay?" I wasn't doing it to be mean; I was seriously beginning to wonder.

"What? No!" He jumped out of the bed and said, "You wanna see my dick? Is that what you want?"

I knew it was the alcohol talking but I just couldn't shut up. "A little while ago you were ready to bang me like a groupie, and now you won't even kiss me."

"Because now you're acting like one!" he yelled.

It would have been less painful if he'd ripped my heart out with his bare hand. "Screw you, Lonny. You think you're a man

304

now, a big famous rock star, but you're still a scared little kid. You need to grow up."

I crawled into the other bed and turned my back on him. He got back in his bed and turned out the light.

The next morning we were headed to Florida, over a nine hour drive, which I knew was going to be brutal. I got on the bus and winked at Mitch with a teasing grin and he said, "Hey baby." I saw that Lonny took his usual seat in the back, so I sat in the middle and stretched my legs over the whole seat to keep anyone from trying to sit with me.

Fuzzy stopped at my seat and asked, "What's going on?"

"Nothing."

"Why are you sitting by yourself?"

"Because I want to."

"Come on doll, I'm not stupid."

I smiled. "I'm gonna catch up on my sleep."

"He's pissed about last night, isn't he?"

"You'd have to ask him that."

Fuzzy rolled his eyes and grumbled, "Just like talking to Mare," before walking away and finding his own seat.

It was a quiet ride the first half of the trip, everyone tired, their heads in their own worlds. I was enjoying a nice nap when someone lifted my legs, sat down, then dropped my legs in their lap. I opened my eyes to see Mitch sitting there smiling at me. I grumbled, curled my legs toward myself and closed my eyes again. Mitch wasn't about to be ignored, leaning over and resting his chin on my knees. He was absolutely gorgeous. And all I could think about was seeing him stark naked.

"If you want Lonny," he whispered, "you better do something about it now. He's pretty isolated from the girls on this tour, but once it's over he's going to start meeting them, and eventually he's going to find one he likes."

"Lonny and me are always one step forward, two steps back. It's never gonna work."

"You're a tease." I opened my mouth to protest and he said, "Okay, okay, you both are. I see you toying with each other all the time. One of you has to pull the trigger."

"He rejected me last night."

305

"Before or after the poker game?"

"You interrupted us *before* the poker game, and he rejected me *after*."

He looked pained. "He rejected you when you were drunk and half naked?"

"Yeah," I replied, sighing heavily.

"Something's wrong with that kid." We both chuckled, then he got up and went back to his own seat.

I pulled out my copy of *Flowers In The Attic* by V.C. Andrews and started reading where I left off. A few minutes later a paper airplane landed in my lap. I unfolded the airplane to see a cartoon Lonny had drawn of himself crying, with a word bubble over his head saying, "I'm sorry." I smiled, but decided to let him sweat it out for a bit and ignored his gesture, folding the paper back up and putting it in my bag. I continued reading my book and a few minutes later, another paper airplane landed in my lap. I unfolded the paper to see a drawing of Lonny handing a daisy to a cartoon version of me, and my eyes were huge hearts. I covered my mouth with my hand so he couldn't hear me giggling. He was trying so hard and it was difficult to stay angry with him. I folded up the second drawing and tossed it in my bag along with the book I was reading, then got up and walked to the back of the bus. Lonny was sitting with his back against the window and his legs crossed in front of him. He bent his knees and pulled his legs inward so I could sit down.

Hugging his legs to his chest he whispered, "I'm sorry. I don't know what's wrong with me."

I turned in my seat to face him, crossing my legs in front of me. Unable to look at him, I picked at a thread on the hem of my jeans and said, "I think we should just go back to being friends."

"Is that what you want?"

I still couldn't look at him. "I don't know... you pushed me away last night, then made me sound like a slut. It's too much."

Lonny leaned forward and took my hands in his, touching his forehead to mine. "I'm sorry... it's not how I hoped things would happen. You being drunk reminded me how much I hate my mom's drinking. Then you lost your pants... and Mitch standing there naked... and you *liked* it."

306

"We're in a different world now," I whispered. "And all I know is being rejected by you hurts more than anything."

"I wasn't rejecting *you*, I was rejecting the situation. It just wasn't right. It wasn't right for *us*."

"What do you mean?"

He pulled away so I could see his face. "It's me, and it's *you*. It's *us*. If it's gonna happen, I don't want it to happen like that."

I smiled. "Last night I said you were a scared little kid who needed to grow up. I was wrong and I'm sorry."

"Maybe we're not ready for… you know…."

"Maybe not." I held my pinky finger out to him and said, "Friends?"

He hooked his pinky finger around mine and replied, "Friends."

I pushed Lonny's hair away from his eyes. "Your hair is getting so long."

"You like it?"

"I love it… but I like to see your eyes, too."

He watched me for so long without saying anything that I could feel my face getting flushed. "I've met a lot of people since I've been in this band," he finally said. "A lot of girls, a lot of women. And nobody has ever looked at me the way you do."

I grinned, embarrassed. "Because I love you. I always have."

Lonny smiled, kissed me softly on the mouth, then pulled me into a loving embrace.

We stormed through Florida then on to Atlanta, where I received a note from Howard that read, *"No orgies! Or whatever THAT was!"* I laughed, remembering our strip poker game. Next Myrtle Beach, Greensboro, Lexington, and Hampton, Virginia, where I accidentally walked in on a girl giving Benji a blow job in the dressing room before the show. He tried to explain to me later that blow jobs weren't considered cheating and when I didn't want to talk about it, he made sure I was aware that the girl in question was only blowing him to get to Lonny. There were so many factors of being on the road that really turned me off, and I was beginning to think it wasn't the place for me.

Maryland, New Jersey, Philadelphia and then on to New York's famed Madison Square Garden for two sold out shows. The two days in New York City were a whirlwind of activity including interviews, a radio station visit, and a photo op at the Statue of Liberty, which ended as soon as it began when a sea of fans swarmed the area and the band had to be rushed back into their limousine for safety.

"I wonder what would happen if we just left Lonny outside by himself?" Mitch teased as the limousine pulled away from the screaming girls.

"He'd probably get killed," Fuzzy mused.

"Maybe he'd finally get laid," Benji said, glancing at me.

My face burned fire but I kept quiet. I wasn't sure if he was insinuating I was a tease who was stringing Lonny along, or if Lonny needed to forget about me and live the rock star life. Fuzzy, who was sitting across from Benji, kicked his leg.

"What?" Benji said. "The kid needs to pop his cherry and obviously *she's* not helping in that area."

Now all eyes were on me, and nobody said a word. I was hoping Lonny would speak up and defend me but he sunk in his seat, nearly disappearing between Mitch and Butch. The uncomfortable silence was deafening and unable to bear it any longer, I got out of the limousine as soon as it stopped at a light. I could hear Lonny shouting for me, but I knew he wouldn't come after me. He *couldn't*. I needed to be alone, away from all those men. I needed to be able to think without someone constantly being at my side, telling me where to go or what to do. I was desperate to speak with Marilyn, or to have some female companionship. I couldn't take it anymore.

I wandered aimlessly through the city not caring what time it was, or where I was supposed to be. Obviously the safety of the band was more important, as no one got out of the car to follow me, or see if I was okay. And I was fine with that. I needed to be

308

alone, and I needed to clear my head. I made my way back to the hotel when I knew everyone else was at Madison Square Garden, and I missed the show that night. I watched some television, read my book and went to bed early, and it felt good.

I was sound asleep when I heard voices in the hallway, having no idea what time it was. I sat up and turned on the light next to the bed as the door opened. Lonny was the first inside the room, with Benji, Fuzzy and Mitch right behind him. Lonny made eye contact with me then turned around and punched Benji in the face, knocking him to the floor. Lonny was so angry it took Fuzzy and Mitch to pull him off their bandmate. Fuzzy held Lonny back as Mitch helped Benji to his feet and out the door.

"You okay, doll?" Fuzzy asked. "We were worried about you."

I nodded.

Fuzzy had a hand on Lonny's shoulder as he patted his chest with the other hand. "He deserved that," he said, "but you have to let it go." He said goodnight and left us alone.

I sat there stunned, waiting for Lonny to speak first. He angrily paced the room, running his hands through his hair.

"I was worried sick about you," he said. "And the worst part was I couldn't go after you. I had to stay in the fucking car!"

"I'm okay. I needed to be alone."

"Tonight was the biggest night of my life — *Madison Square Garden* — and you weren't there!"

"I'm sorry." I asked Lonny to sit down, and when he sat on the bed next to me I took both his hands in mine. "I'm not going to be there tomorrow, either."

Lonny looked like I'd just stabbed him. "Why not?"

"I'm going home."

Lonny stood up and started pacing the room again. "No Roo, you can't do that. Why? Why would you want to go home?"

"Because I don't belong here."

He sat back down and grabbed my hands. "Yes you do. You belong here with me."

"It's too hard," I said. "All the girls… I'm holding you back. You deserve to experience what it's like."

309

"Don't *I* get to decide what *I* want?" I nodded and he continued, "I come back to the hotel with *you*. I don't want to be with *them*. Even if you're not my girlfriend I choose to be with *you*. Doesn't that matter?"

"Yes, it matters."

"Who cares if Benji thinks I'm a virgin? And it's okay if they know you're not banging me on a daily basis. I don't want them to think any other way about you!"

I had no idea how to respond. Lonny was saying almost everything I wanted to hear.

"Everything I have is yours," he continued. "I want to share it all with you. Without you it means nothing."

My heart was ready to burst. I didn't think it was possible to love him more than I already did, but here he was proving me wrong.

"I don't know what to say," my voice croaked.

"Say you're staying with me."

I threw my arms around him and buried my face in his hair. "I'll stay with you."

"Promise you'll never leave me," he whispered desperately.

"I promise."

Butch had to sneak Lonny and me out a back entrance into a white van when we left the hotel to go to Madison Square Garden the next evening. It wasn't until we got to the venue that I realized the enormity of what I missed the night before. How could I have been so selfish? Lonny played The Garden and I wasn't there! Lonny held my hand as Butch led us through the building, and I was surprised when the band's security, stage and film crew all said they hoped I was feeling better and that it wasn't the same without me the night before. I didn't think anyone would notice I was gone, and it made me smile.

I was nervous as we entered the dressing room because I didn't like being the center of attention, nor did I like people being upset with me. After Lonny punched Benji out, I had no idea what

310

I was walking into. Fuzzy was the first to greet me, pulling me into a hug and away from Lonny. I struggled to see what was going on, as if Fuzzy were trying to protect me from something. I got a glimpse of Benji, who had a nice shiner where Lonny punched him, and I held my breath as they met in the middle of the room. Benji patted Lonny on the back and pulled him in for a hug, then let him go. Men were so different than women when it came to things of that nature, and I was thankful. Fuzzy loosened his grip on me as Benji walked our way. He wrapped his arms around me and apologized for everything that happened, then told me I was a good kid and I should never change for anybody. And neither should Lonny. I breathed a sigh of relief, because the last thing I wanted was for Lonny to have conflict in the band because of me.

As the band did their soundcheck I walked around The Garden taking photographs of everything, then walked among the seats at each level to get photos of the band from different perspectives. I eventually made my way back down to the stage area and sat a few rows back so I could see all the band members. As I snapped away, I felt someone sit in the seat next to me. It was Howard.

"Hey, Howard!" I greeted enthusiastically. "I didn't know you were going to be here!"

"Ruby, we need to talk about your photos."

My heart plunged into my stomach. "You don't like them."

"It's not that… you're doing an amazing job. But I can't have you taking photos of Lonny drinking alcohol, or photos of you and the band… half dressed. What you all do in the hotel is your business. I don't want pictures of it."

I swallowed hard, embarrassed that he thought I was fooling around with the entire band. As a group, no less! I was too humiliated to say anything, so I just nodded in agreement.

"And there's a lot of photos of you and Lonny together… you know I can't print those."

I apologized to Howard and promised to follow his rules. "How's Marilyn's mom?" I asked, desperately wanting to change the subject.

Howard hesitated, which caused me to fear the worst. "I think she's going to be okay."

311

"That's great! Will Marilyn be joining us soon?" I was ever so hopeful.

"I'm not sure. Fuzzy would be more helpful in that area."

Howard patted my leg, then got up and walked away. Now that he was gone my face burned fire, embarrassed that he thought I was sleeping with the entire band. Nothing could have been further from the truth! I was suddenly overwhelmed with feelings of homesickness, and needing a comforting hug from my mother. The lack of female companionship on this tour was beginning to tear my heart up.

That evening's performance was probably the best on the tour so far, and I wasn't the only one who thought so. The band knew it as they ran offstage and headed to the dressing room afterward, where they met with journalists from newspaper and radio, and celebrities of all kinds. I stayed out of everybody's way and did my job, taking photos and keeping my mouth shut.

Everybody wanted a piece of Lonny but knew they had to bide their time, opting to interview or schmooze the other band members until it was their turn. Lonny never got a break; it was no wonder he was exhausted all the time. I noticed a beautiful woman with jet black hair and striking green eyes standing next to Lonny, getting closer and closer as he was interviewed by one person, then another. She stood there as if she knew him, as if they were together in some way. She slid her arm around his and he flinched, looking to see who was touching him. He smiled at her and continued talking to the person interviewing him. Mitch happened to walk by me and I grabbed his shirt, pulling him back my way.

"Who's that with Lonny?" I asked him.

"I don't know, but I'm gonna find out," he teased, heading in their direction.

I could see Mitch talking to the woman, and she was gracious as she smiled and listened to him, answering his questions, but when he tried to pull her away from Lonny for his own benefit she declined, waving him off with her hand.

Mitch returned to where I stood on a chair in the corner of the room and said, "Sheila Birch, Playboy Playmate."

How could I ever compete with a woman like that?

"Wanna make Lonny jealous?" he asked with a wicked grin.

"Thanks, but no." As much as the idea appealed to me, I would never be able to go through with it. If Lonny was interested in the woman, there was nothing I would do to stop him. It was his choice.

Mitch walked off to talk with someone else and Fuzzy stood next to me perched on my chair, so I put my arm around his shoulders and leaned against him, watching the scene playing out in front of us. So many people, so much celebrity, so much arrogance and money. Definitely not a place I felt comfortable. I leaned closer to Fuzzy's ear and asked him how Marilyn's mother was doing.

"Day to day," he replied. "Mare's hoping to meet up with us in Cleveland."

I was so excited to hear this I hugged him as tightly as I could. Just knowing Marilyn might be joining us soon filled my heart with joy. I looked up to see Lonny waving at me, so I stood up straight and waved back. He was saying something to Sheila and pointing at me. She smiled and nodded and I waved again. It was quite strange, but whatever Lonny wanted.

Fuzzy said, "Lonny has his choice of all the ass in the world, but he turns it down at every turn. All because of you, doll. Don't forget that."

I hugged Fuzzy and kissed his forehead. "Thank you for always taking care of us," I said.

Lonny suddenly appeared in front of us with Sheila in tow, continuing her hold on his arm. "Roo, this is Sheila… Sheila, this is my girl, Roo."

Sheila smiled and shook my hand. "Nice to meet you."

Lonny introduced me as his girl… whatever did that mean? Was he trying to get rid of Sheila, or was he jealous of me being so close to Fuzzy? He was so hard to figure out sometimes.

"Roo? That's an unusual name," Sheila said.

"It's Ruby. Call me Ruby." No one else in the world was allowed to call me Roo. *No one.*

Sheila smiled and asked breathlessly, "Is there an after party somewhere tonight?"

"This is it," Fuzzy replied. "We're off to Boston tomorrow."

Sheila got as close as she could to Lonny, continuing to hold onto his arm, and now playing with his hair. "It's so crowded in here," she grumbled.

Lonny was frozen, seemingly unsure of how to handle the situation with Sheila. He never wanted to hurt anyone's feelings, and he was almost too shy to tell people to get lost. But maybe that wasn't it. Maybe he really was interested in her and just didn't know how to move things forward with me in the room. I decided to help him along, asking Fuzzy if he could maneuver me through the crowd so I could go into the hallway for some air. I hopped on Fuzzy's back and he plowed through like a bull, and once we reached the hallway I hopped off.

"What're you doing?" he asked.

"I needed some air. It's so crowded in there," I mocked Sheila.

"So you leave him in there with her?"

"I'm not his girlfriend," I reminded him. "He can do whatever he wants."

"He introduced you to her as his girl… what the hell else can that mean?" I'd never seen Fuzzy so frustrated.

"That's not what it means to him."

"God!" he shouted. "I want to take both of you by the neck and smash your heads together."

"Why?"

"I don't understand you two. You're together, you're not together, you're holding hands, you're kissing, but you're not his girlfriend… what the hell *are* you then?" Fuzzy was pacing and scratching his beard.

"Why are you so upset? I'm okay with our relationship."

"You are definitely *not* okay with it!"

"Why are you yelling at me?"

"I'm sorry doll, but I see the way you look at him. You loved him before the band, before the fame. You are *not* okay with the girls."

He was beginning to upset me. "No I'm not, but you can't force someone to love you. I can't force Lonny to love me."

314

Fuzzy was visibly upset, covering his mouth with his hand. I couldn't understand why my relationship with Lonny was so emotional for him. It looked as though he had tears in his eyes, but I knew I must have been imagining things. He pulled me into his arms and apologized, saying he would stay out of my business. "I just want you both to be happy, doll," he said, still holding onto me tightly. "You belong together." He was starting to sound like Marilyn.

Lonny poked his head out the door and said, "Please save me— oh, sorry…."

"No kid, it's cool," Fuzzy said with a laugh. Before he pulled away from me he whispered, "Go show that woman who Lonny's girl is."

I knew the rule about Lonny being unattached, but wondered what it really mattered. If he had a girlfriend, would the fans disappear? Maybe the crazy teenage girls… and maybe that would be a good thing for Lonny. Maybe then they'd leave him alone and he wouldn't have to be a prisoner everywhere he went. It was a pleasing thought, but I knew Howard was in the room and I'd already been scolded by him once that day. And he made it a point that people could not know about me and Lonny.

I took Fuzzy's hand and pulled him back into the dressing room, following close behind Lonny who was desperately trying to avoid Sheila. I caught Mitch's eye and yanked my head in Sheila's direction, hoping he'd understand what I was trying to tell him. And bless him, he did. I had one arm linked through Fuzzy's and the other around Lonny's shoulders as I watched him swoop in on Sheila like the lead singing pro he was. She kept looking our way and I just smiled and nodded. I finally got tired of her staring at me so I leaned close to Lonny's face and brushed my mouth against his ear, causing him to start laughing. He threw his arm around me and pulled me over to the food table for a drink. He leaned in close to my face and said, "Thank you," then kissed me on the cheek, not caring who may see him.

As Lonny and I left our room the next day to get on the bus, we saw Sheila leaving Mitch's room. She glared at me and smiled at Lonny as she passed us saying, "I'm not done with you, pretty boy," before disappearing into the elevator.

315

Lonny grumbled, "Whatever."

Since everyone figured out where we were staying, Lonny and I exited a back door of the hotel where Butch put us in a plain looking van that brought us to the tour bus a few blocks away. It was getting ridiculous, and I could see that it was beginning to wear on Lonny.

As we rushed onto the bus, everyone started clapping and whistling. Mitch tossed the entertainment section of the morning's newspaper at Lonny, speaking in his high pitched woman's voice, "He's simply a dream." We took our usual seats in the back as Lonny opened the paper to see what all the commotion was about. There was a photo of Lonny onstage during the encore, evidenced by his wearing of the necktie, and a photo of Lonny with Sheila Birch smiling next to him as if they were some hot love item. It was an article about the band's performance the night before, but it also talked a lot about the celebrities that happened to be in attendance and backstage. Apparently Sheila was asked what she thought about the young guitarist and her response was, "He's simply a dream." Lonny was never going to live that down. There was a small comment about the black eye Benji was sporting with a quote from him that said, "Ran into my hotel room door."

"You might be a dream kid," Mitch teased, "but she slept with me last night."

"We know," I replied. "We saw her leaving your room."

Everyone howled.

"You're welcome," Lonny laughed.

Boston, Buffalo, Cincinnati, and in Cleveland I was really hoping Marilyn would join us, but another disappointment. Fuzzy explained there was a setback and she wouldn't be able to leave. I missed her so much I wanted to cry when he told me she wasn't coming. He said she might make it to Chicago, so I hung all my hopes on that. I really needed some girl time with her.

Two sold out shows at Detroit's Olympia Stadium and then we were headed home to Chicago. Lonny and I were excited to see our parents and for the band to play in front of his home crowd. We also knew it was probably going to be complete mayhem once the bus pulled into town. Lonny and I talked to our parents often during the tour to keep them up to date and to let them know we were okay, but he was concerned after talking to his mom before we left Detroit that morning. Fans had already begun showing up at her house hoping for a glimpse of him, and several times she called the police to get them out of her yard. He suggested she stay with my parents until we left town, but she was stubborn. She wasn't going to let them run her out of her own home unless it was absolutely necessary. And she probably didn't feel comfortable drinking in my parents' house.

Lonny and I were hoping to sneak home to my parents' house after getting settled in our hotel, but it was not to be. Howard, who joined us in Chicago, said he couldn't risk it, but we would see them at the first show as he had tickets and backstage passes for all of them.

As Lonny and I sat down with the room service menu to decide what we wanted for dinner, there was a knock at the door. He tensed immediately, so I got up to look out the peephole. It was Howard.

I opened the door a crack and he said, "There's some people I think you and Lonny should see."

I looked at Lonny, who got up and stood in the corner of the room, trying unsuccessfully to hide. I unlocked the chain and let Howard into the room. Neither of us were prepared for what happened next, as our parents walked into the room carrying food trays and a cooler full of drinks. Both of us screamed and jumped into our parents' arms as soon as they were empty. We were hugged and kissed by all three parents and I started crying. I didn't realize how much I missed them until that moment. Lonny wiped tears from his face when his mother finally let go of him.

"We brought you a home cooked meal," my mom said, after wiping the tears from her own face.

Fuzzy, Mitch and Benji entered the room and Lonny was eager to introduce them to our parents. My father greeted them with strong handshakes, and both mothers hugged and kissed them all on the cheek.

"These two," Fuzzy teased, "are nothing but trouble. We've had to keep them out of jail a few times."

My dad laughed, but our mothers looked shocked until Fuzzy started laughing.

317

"Good kids," Mitch said. "Really good kids."

"We have enough food for all of you if you're hungry," Joanie said.

The guys were excited to be invited, and even though the room was small, we all found a place to sit and enjoy our home cooked meal together. I was quiet, taking in the conversation and energy of everyone who meant the world to me all in the same room. The only person missing was Marilyn, but I still held up high hopes that she would be joining us soon.

"Lonny, you look tired," Joanie said.

"Mom, we were on a bus for almost six hours," he replied.

"Don't talk back to your mother," Fuzzy playfully scolded.

"Will Marilyn be here soon?" I asked.

"Oh yes, we just love Marilyn," my mom added. "I would love to see her again."

Fuzzy smiled and waited to finish chewing and swallowing before responding. "I'm hoping she'll be here tomorrow."

Everyone cheered because everyone loved Marilyn.

After every last morsel of fried chicken, side dishes and chocolate cake were devoured, Howard and the guys disappeared to their own rooms to let us have some quality time with our parents.

"You're the talk of the town Lonny," my dad said.

"There are signs all over welcoming you home," his mom added.

Lonny grinned, embarrassed.

"Have you talked to Gina?" I asked my mom. "Do you know if she's coming to one of the shows?"

"I'm not sure. I assume she'll be going with Billy if she does."

I could feel Lonny tense up beside me at the mention of Billy's name, and then he slyly slid his arm around me, as if announcing to our parents that I belonged to him.

"Have you seen Billy?" I had to ask.

"He's working at the hardware store, so I see him fairly often," my dad joked. My mom always said my dad spent more time at the hardware store than at home. "He doesn't even ask about you anymore."

318

I smiled, relieved.

When it came time for our parents to head home they hugged and kissed us each goodbye, and my mother stopped and looked around the room. I knew what was coming.

"Are you sharing a room?" she asked.

"Yes, Mom. Two beds, see?" I thought it was obvious, but pointed them out anyway.

"I don't like it," she said.

"Don't worry Mom," Lonny said. "Roo is still pure and besides, it would be gross to sleep with my sister."

Everybody laughed and my mother seemed to be satisfied with that. After they left we closed and locked the door and got comfortable on the bed to watch some television. Lonny rested his head in my lap and wrapped his arms around my legs and I finger combed his hair, which was getting really long. I knew his mother didn't like it, but was thankful she kept it to herself.

"I don't care what Howard says," Lonny spoke quietly. "If I wanna have a girlfriend, why can't I?" I said nothing as he rolled onto his back to look up at me. "Do you wanna be my girlfriend?"

I thought my heart was going to explode right out of my chest. I smiled and nodded, then leaned over and kissed him. It was a sweet, soft kiss, and when I pulled away he said, "Whattya stopping for?"

I got up from the bed and grabbed my bag, pulling out my Polaroid. I started taking photos and said, "We need to have pictures of this moment!"

"Shouldn't you be in them?"

It was never easy to take a photo by turning the camera around backwards, but we managed to get a few decent shots to commemorate the moment Lonny asked me to be his girlfriend. And nobody in the world could have possibly looked happier than us. When the photos were dry, I wrote the date and time on them so we would always remember our special moment.

"We should go to bed," Lonny suggested. "We have a long day tomorrow."

I went to the bathroom to change into my shorts and t-shirt, and Lonny was already in bed when I came out. I crawled in beside him and turned out the light. We each scooted toward the middle

319

of the bed so we were as close to each other as possible, and his lips were so close I inhaled his breath as if it were my own. And without him breathing life into me, I would surely die.

Lonny touched my cheek with the tips of his fingers, rough and calloused from playing guitar. "I want everyone to know you're my girlfriend," he whispered. "But we'll have to keep it secret in public."

"I can do that," I whispered.

"Did you feel that?"

"I did!"

"When you breathe out, I breathe in… we're breathing for each other. It's like an invisible string that goes from your heart to my heart, binding our spirits together."

"Lonny," I whispered. "I felt it… I can feel your whispers in my lungs. I don't even need to hear them… I *feel* them."

I was so overcome with emotion my eyes burned with tears. Was it really possible to love someone that much? Was it possible he could love me with the same intensity?

Lonny kissed me softly then took my hand in his, intertwining his fingers with mine. With our lips touching, breathing into each other, we fell asleep.

When I woke up the next morning, I opened my eyes to see Lonny sitting on the floor with his acoustic guitar, writing something down in his journal.

"Good morning," my voice croaked. "Whatcha doing?"

He smiled as he looked at me. "I woke up with a song in my head. Wanna hear what I have so far?"

"Of course."

He plucked out a melody and sang, "So in tune, so in sync, when you're not here I can't even think. Breathe into you, breathe into me, an unbreakable bond only we can see. An invisible string from your heart to mine, our spirits entwined for all of time."

"Lonny, it's beautiful!"

"It's for you."

I jumped out of bed and flung my arms around him, careful not to crush his guitar in the process.

"How 'bout you take a shower and I'll order breakfast?" he said, smiling.

320

I kissed him quickly, then bounced into the bathroom to get ready for the big day ahead.

The first stop of the day was Vinyl Horse for an autograph signing. Butch led Lonny and me through a back entrance of the hotel to a waiting limousine that drove around to the front to pick up the rest of the guys. The number of fans hoping to get a glimpse of Lonny increased immensely compared to other towns we'd been in, due to Chicago being considered his home city. As the guys hurried to get into the limousine the screaming girls saw that Lonny was already inside and rushed the car. Butch was trying something new, but apparently his plan backfired. I was terrified as I watched girls throwing themselves onto the hood of the limousine trying to get a closer look at Lonny. I was fearful someone was going to get run over, but fortunately no one was injured. I couldn't begin to imagine what the scene was going to be like at Vinyl Horse. It was a small store, and I hoped Ricky had a plan on how to handle the amount of fans that would show up.

When we pulled into town there were signs, posters and giant banners everywhere welcoming Lonny home. I tried to get photographs of everything from inside the limo, but it proved difficult. The look on Lonny's face was priceless; I don't think I'd ever seen him smile like he did when seeing the love our rundown old town was showing him. And then we saw it… the end of the line of fans that led to Vinyl Horse. We were a mile away and could see the fans were still lining up. Not wanting to lose their place in line the girls screamed, jumped and waved at the limo as we drove by, the film crew recording everything from a vehicle behind us.

There were police cars patrolling the area and policeman keeping the crowd under control. We had to drive up a few blocks and turn around so we could enter the record store from the back alley, which the police were thankfully protecting for us. The film crew, cut back to just two men for this outing, went in first to take their places. We knew the moment they stepped into the record store because the chorus of screams was painful to the ears. I greeted Ricky with a huge hug and introduced him to the band, Butch, Randy and Howard. He shook Lonny's hand and welcomed him home with a hug and a slap on the back. Ricky then led me into the store where I heard my name shouted from several different people. I smiled and waved to people I went to high school with, who had never before acknowledged my existence. Ricky had a ladder securely set up in the corner of the store where I would have a great vantage point for photographs. I climbed up to my perch and looked at the crowd already gathered inside the store. I noticed Gina standing in line with Billy and waved when they made eye contact with me. She looked like she was ready to burst into tears.

The crowd inside the store screamed as Ricky led Fuzzy, Mitch and Benji to their seats behind the table, and when Lonny appeared with Butch close by his side, the cacophony of screams was so alarming I thought my ears were going to bleed. Butch, who was a large, imposing man, got the attention of the crowd and laid down the rules — if they could not control themselves and the safety of the band came into question at any time, the autograph session would be over and the band would leave and not return. The police relayed this information to the fans waiting patiently outside, and as the crowd increased in size every minute, they were forced to close down the street for several blocks. Butch announced that people were allowed to take photos of the band, but because they needed to keep the line moving due to its size, they could not stop and pose with any of the band members. Fans were also only allowed to get one item autographed, again to keep the enormous line moving.

And then it began... one by one the people in line were ushered to the table to have their item of choice autographed. Lots of young girls were wearing t-shirts with Lonny's picture on them and I wondered where they got them because I wanted one! Every once in a while a girl would faint before even getting to the table, and have to be carried outside where the paramedics were on hand to take care of them. Most of the girls were so young all they did was cry when they reached Lonny, who was conveniently positioned last at the table. He just smiled and talked to each of them, signing their album cover or the t-shirt they were wearing, and then they ran out of the store screaming.

I watched intently as Billy and Gina reached the table. Gina had tears on her face but she was smiling and talking to Lonny. He

322

took his time with her, talking and laughing, and at one point leaned over to whisper something in her ear. As she and Billy left the store, they both turned to wave at me before they were ushered outside.

Two hours later, there seemed to be no end to the line of fans waiting to get into Vinyl Horse to meet the band. I noticed Howard whispering to Fuzzy, who was shaking his head violently and didn't look happy. A few minutes later Butch announced that the band was going to take a fifteen minute break and would return shortly. I made eye contact with Lonny as he stood from his chair and he shrugged before disappearing to the back with the rest of the band. Howard motioned for me to follow them.

When I reached the back room, Fuzzy was two inches from Howard's face screaming, "We're here because of those fans!"

"I understand that," Howard said, remaining calm. "But we have to be at the radio station in two hours."

"Screw the radio station," Mitch scoffed. "Who's going to be more upset? The fans who don't hear us talking on the radio, or these fans who'll get turned away after waiting for hours to see us?"

"We're not leaving these fans," Benji added.

"There's nothing I can do," Howard replied. "We have a commitment to the radio station, and the fans will just have to understand that's how it works."

The realization that hundreds of fans who had been waiting patiently for hours to see the band were going to be turned away suddenly hit me. "You wanna see chaos? Turn all those fans away," I said. "Butch announced if the crowd didn't behave the band would leave and not come back. They've all been waiting patiently with no problems."

"We were brought here for an autograph signing," Fuzzy continued. "Those fans were never told we'd be leaving at a specific time. It's not *their* fault."

"It's not fair to the kid," Benji said. "It's his hometown, his first autograph signing. Most of those fans are here to see *him*."

"This is your event kid," Mitch said with a grin. "What do you think?"

I grasped Lonny's hand, reminding him I was on his side.

323

Lonny glanced around the room, making eye contact with everyone there, then said, "We stay."

Fuzzy told Howard, "Call the radio station and tell them plans have changed."

I smiled and ran back into the store to take my position on the ladder as the band returned to the table and took their seats. I had no idea what Howard was going to tell the radio station, but he was furious. I hoped it didn't end up falling back on Lonny somehow. I could picture Howard paying someone in the crowd to act like a lunatic, just to force the band to shut down the autograph session so they could get to the radio station as planned.

The band stayed until the last person was out the door, and then it was a mad rush back to the hotel so the guys could get their bags before heading to Chicago Stadium for soundcheck. We ran into our room and I swapped out the used film for new rolls, shoving those in my bag as Lonny grabbed his gear bag. I turned to rush back out of the room, but ran into him as he was standing right behind me, smiling.

"We're super busy the next two days," he said, sliding his hands into my back pockets and pulling me against him. "Lots of interviews and people backstage."

"I guess we'll have to be sneaky then." I leaned in for a kiss and Fuzzy popped in, urging us to get moving.

Lonny held my hand tightly as we walked through the backstage area of Chicago Stadium, a place we'd only experienced from the vantage point of audience members before that moment. We were all taken by surprise when a girl screamed and jumped into Mitch's arms, wrapping her legs around his waist and kissing him all over his face. He seemed to know her, so it didn't appear to be a security breech of any kind.

"Who's that?" I asked Fuzzy.

"Mitch's Chicago girlfriend," he whispered. "Well… she's everybody's Chicago girlfriend."

"What does that mean?"

"I'll explain later," he whispered, smiling as the girl greeted him with a big hug.

The blonde girl who wore too much makeup was tall on platform sandals, dressed in tight jeans and a tight, low-cut blouse.

She smiled at me and stared at Lonny a little bit too long for my liking.

"You must be the new kid," she said to Lonny. Then to Fuzzy, "I've got some friends coming later, one for all of you."

"I'm happily married Fawn, you know that," Fuzzy replied. "And Lonny's not available either."

She pouted. "Too bad. Oh well, at least I can still have fun!" She grabbed Mitch by the hand and disappeared around a corner.

"We've got soundcheck in fifteen minutes!" Fuzzy yelled after them.

The rest of us headed into the dressing room and I said, "So... Fawn?"

Fuzzy grinned but seemed reluctant to finish his explanation of the boisterous blonde girl hanging all over Mitch. Lonny sat on a chair and pulled me onto his lap, wrapping his arms around me. This made Fuzzy smile.

"Fawn is... she's a... she's a professional groupie," Fuzzy finally said. "She's what you'd call the head of the Chicago groupie circuit."

I had no idea what Fuzzy was talking about. "Groupie circuit? That's a thing?"

"Fawn is Mitch's girlfriend whenever he's in Chicago. And then when we leave, she's with the next band in town."

"And she's bringing her groupie friends for the rest of the band?" I asked, bile rising in my throat.

"Not for me," Fuzzy said, raising his hands in defense.

"No thanks," Lonny announced, his grip on me getting tighter. "That's gross."

"Groupies are everywhere," Benji chimed in. "You two are just too green to know what's going on around you."

"And that's okay," Fuzzy defended us. "Let them stay innocent as long as possible."

Howard poked his head in and said it was time for soundcheck, so everyone followed him. Mitch and Fawn had their arms around each other as they walked together, and I wondered if she was going to be a permanent fixture in the group while we remained in Chicago.

325

News crews had already set up inside the arena so they could get clips of the band doing their soundcheck, before the media circus that was going to unfold backstage when the soundcheck was over. I walked around to get photographs of everything going on during the soundcheck, including the people involved. I eventually sat down in the front row to take some soundcheck photos, but was quickly joined by Fawn.

"So you work for the band?" she asked, sitting next to me.

"I take photos for the fan club."

"And you're the new kid's girlfriend?"

"His name is Lonny."

"It's okay. Lonny's too young anyway. What is he, sixteen?"

"Eighteen."

"Oh." She seemed to think on this for a minute. "No, he's still too young."

"He's not available anyway," I informed her.

"Ruby!" I looked up to see Theresa Brooks heading my way. Happy to get away from Fawn, I excused myself and greeted the journalist with a hug.

"Are you coming backstage after the soundcheck?" I asked her.

"Yeah, but I'm small beans compared to the television crews that are already set up. Think you can help me out?"

Theresa was pivotal in helping Joanie after the teenage girls broke into her home and stole some of Lonny's belongings, and if anyone deserved time with him, she did. I took Theresa by the hand and brought her backstage, her photographer following close behind us. As the band came offstage Lonny walked to where I was standing and I introduced him to Theresa, explaining how she helped his mother after the break-in. Lonny was happy to give Theresa an exclusive interview, forever grateful for the way she helped his mother in a time of crisis.

I ran to catch up with Fuzzy, wrapping my arms around his waist as we walked. "Any word from Marilyn?" I asked, hopeful.

"Not today, but hopefully tomorrow," he replied, looking devastated.

There were news crews all over the place, most of them wanting a piece of Lonny, the hometown hero, but they were willing to talk to any band member they could get their hands on until it was their turn. As Fuzzy was approached by one such crew I pulled away and mouthed, "I love you," to him, which brought a smile to his face. He blew me a kiss and turned his attention to the person asking him questions.

I wandered around backstage taking photos and marveled at the controlled chaos that seemed to greet me at every turn. I noticed Fawn hanging back, speaking only to the roadies and venue security personnel. I assumed they must know her pretty well, considering she was the head of the Chicago groupie circuit. I wondered if that really existed or if it was something Fuzzy made up.

I took a photo of Howard as he walked toward me and he laughed, saying, "I found some people you might know."

Then I saw my mom, dad, Joanie, Billy and Gina. I jumped up and down excitedly as I hugged each of them, even Billy.

"I brought you a present, Ruby," Gina said, beaming. She handed me a t-shirt with Lonny on the front of it, just like the girls were wearing at the autograph session.

"I love it!" I cheered, putting it on over the shirt I was already wearing. "It's perfect, thank you!"

"It's crazy back here," my dad said.

"It's usually pretty busy," I explained. "But since this is Lonny's home city, it's really insane. The Golden Boy comes home," I laughed.

"All this for my boy?" Joanie asked.

"Yeah Mom, didn't you know he was famous?" She looked shell-shocked and I said, "Come on, I'll show you around."

I loved being able to show our parents what our life was like on the road, and I introduced them to the road crew, roadies and movie film crew as we ran into them. Billy remained silent the entire time, probably still shocked at how famous Lonny had become, and that I was part of his entire world.

Lonny appeared out of nowhere, scaring me half to death. He greeted our mothers and Gina with a hug then said, "I need to borrow Roo for just a minute. Band business." Holding my hand, he pulled me away to a secluded area where all the band's equipment transport cases were stacked.

"Is everything okay?" I asked, worried.

"I just needed a break," he said. He put his hands on my face and pulled me in for a kiss. When he pulled away he noticed my t-shirt and asked, "What are you wearing?"

"Gina gave it to me. Isn't it great?"

"My face really *is* everywhere."

I smiled and said, "You're what's hot."

"Do you think I'm hot?"

I giggled and covered my mouth with my hand. My face flushing I said, "Yes."

He hugged me tightly and replied, "You're all that matters."

"So how did Gina and Billy get backstage?"

"Gina told me she didn't have tickets to the show, so I asked Howard to take care of her. Unfortunately that meant Billy, too."

"He's been quiet as a mouse," I chuckled. "He knows he can't hurt me anymore."

Lonny kissed me slowly and deeply, sending the butterflies aflutter in my stomach. When he pulled away and began walking me back toward the media circus, I was lightheaded and grinning like a fool. I was deposited back with our parents, and Lonny ran off to do his next interview. I watched as our parents, Gina and Billy looked on in amazement, as if they couldn't believe it was the Lonny they knew; that it must have been someone else who had become so famous.

As we got closer to show time, the news crews and everyone else backstage disappeared quickly, allowing the band their time alone before hitting the stage. Our parents, Gina and Billy were in the dressing room with us, and Fawn was wrapped around Mitch over on the couch. It was nice that Lonny had this time to talk with our parents, Gina and Billy. At one point, Billy pulled me to the other side of the room to ask how things were going. I assured him I was having the time of my life and I couldn't be happier.

"What he did for Gina... he's a good guy," he said.

"I'm glad you can finally admit that."

Howard announced that anybody who wasn't in the band needed to leave the dressing room, and those with tickets should make their way to the arena to be seated. I walked out with the small crowd and told our parents to be prepared, that once the band hit the stage it was going to be really loud. They all hugged me and followed the security guard who would be leading them to their seats.

Fawn opened her mouth to speak, but I suddenly felt a hand pull me back into the dressing room. It was Fuzzy. "You're part of this band, doll."

"Where did you get that shirt?" Mitch howled.

"I think you need to wear it tonight," I suggested.

He held out his hand with a smile and I took off the Lonny t-shirt and gave it to him, insisting he give it back to me when the show was over.

I wasn't quite sure why Fuzzy pulled me back into the room when he did, unless he was trying to prove a point to Fawn and the other hangers on that waited outside with her. Lonny sat on a chair and pulled me onto his lap. I knew he was nervous when he buried his face into my back and started drumming his fingers on my legs. It was his first performance in front of the home crowd, and I could understand why he'd be nervous. Eighteen years old and playing sold out shows across America, including two capacity crowd events at home were a feat not many people could accomplish. Combine that with the number of fans who showed up for the autograph signing and the amount of media surrounding him that evening, he was probably the most famous person in town. If not the country.

"Time to go," Howard announced.

Everyone stood and Lonny stumbled, holding onto my shoulders for balance. I turned around and put my hands on his cheeks, pulling his face close to mine.

"You've got this," I whispered. "No one can take any of this away from you. You earned it."

I ran ahead of the band so I could get photos of them being walked to the stage, and I loved seeing Mitch wearing a t-shirt with Lonny's face on it. The crowd was going to love it, too. At the side of the stage the band waited for their cue, and the guys had already decided Lonny's entrance should be delayed, just to build up the crowd even more. Benji ran out first, then Fuzzy, then Mitch, who made sure to point out the shirt he was wearing to the audience, and they went absolutely mental.

It wasn't long before the audience began chanting Lonny's name, and it was deafening. Lonny pressed his lips against mine, holding them there as I whispered, "I love you."

He smiled, then ran onto the stage where the berserk audience roared so loudly it sounded like the building would collapse on top of us all. I was blinded by tears at first, so proud of Lonny and seeing our parents in the front row cheering him on. Gina was so sweet, singing along and sometimes screaming, while Billy stood like a statue with his arms folded in front of him.

"So you're part of the band?" I heard Fawn shout next to me.

Keeping my eyes on Lonny I leaned sideways and shouted, "I'm on the payroll!"

She said something in return, but the noise level between the band and the audience made it impossible for me to hear her. I was immensely grateful.

Halfway through the band's third song, a girl managed to get onstage and went right for Mitch, which was unusual on this tour. Then she began tugging ferociously at the t-shirt he was wearing, trying to rip it off him. She was quickly apprehended and tossed back into the audience. Mitch laughed and continued singing without hesitation. Lonny walked to the front of the stage and pointed at his mom, blew her a kiss, and performed the most blistering guitar solo of the entire tour. He had never looked more confident.

I held my breath when it came time for Lonny to sing "Take Me Home." As he opened his mouth to sing, a girl appeared out of nowhere and tackled him. Security was on her quickly as Mitch helped him to his feet. I began to fear for Lonny's safety and prayed the rest of the show wasn't interrupted with girls attacking him. Lonny's mother looked as if she was about to have a nervous breakdown, but seemed to relax when he was back on his feet and the band started the song over.

330

The band rushed offstage for their break before the encore, running to the dressing room where I was pulled inside, but Fawn was denied entry by Howard. I found myself grinning until I noticed Lonny was sitting on the couch holding his right shoulder.

"What's going on, kid?" Howard asked.

"Nothing," Lonny answered. "Just sore from being tackled."

Howard ordered him to ice it until they were ready to go back on.

I told Mitch I wanted my shirt back and he laughed, stripping it off and tossing the sweat drenched piece of clothing at me. I laid it over the back of a chair, hoping it would dry out before we left for the evening.

Fuzzy stood next to me and put an arm around my shoulders saying, "Pretty amazing homecoming, kid."

Lonny smiled and nodded but looked at me strangely, as if to ask why I was standing next to Fuzzy and not sitting with him on the couch. As they got ready to go back onstage, Lonny took off his sweaty shirt and I presented him with his tie — bright yellow with red polka dots.

"Did you steal this from a clown?" he teased, slipping it over his head.

"It's my favorite so far," I told him.

The band headed back to the stage and I hung back to take photos, noticing Fawn walking beside me.

"We should be friends," she said. "I mean, we're not in competition with each other."

Competition? Was this girl for real?

"Nope, no competition," I replied.

"I can see why Lonny's into you," she said, causing me to look at her. "He's new to all this, and he hasn't experienced women of substance yet."

She smiled brightly, but I was so dumbfounded I couldn't think of anything to say in return. Was she telling me that groupies who slept with every band in town were women of substance? Or was she insulting Lonny and me for being so much younger than the rest of the band?

"How long have you been a woman of substance?" I asked.

331

"I like you, kid, you're funny. I just turned thirty-three."
Thirty-three?

"So… how long?"

"Seventeen, in Detroit. Rolling Stones first American tour."
Seventeen?

"Don't you want to get married? Have kids?" I asked.

"If Mitch would settle down, sure."

"So Mitch is the one you'd choose?" I supposed it was possible for groupies to fall in love.

"Absolutely. He's sensitive, he's sexy… and under those clothes he's—"

"I've seen him."

Fawn looked at me with wide eyes. "You have?"

"Yeah, I beat him at strip poker. Saw *everything*." I could tell she didn't quite believe me. "Hey Mitch!" I shouted. "Have I ever seen you naked?"

He turned to look at me with a huge smile on his face. "Yeah baby, the full package!" All the guys howled with laughter.

I turned to Fawn and said, "He's no different than you, really. He has a different girl in every town."

"Shut up."

"He had a girlfriend back in L.A., but broke up with her right before the tour. Me and Lonny actually walked in on him with a girl in Denver. He had the wrong room key and—"

"Stop talking."

I looked at Fawn, who was visibly upset. I was astounded; I hadn't meant to hurt her feelings. She was the groupie after all… the woman of substance. Wasn't she supposed to know how rock stars worked? I was new to all this and I only knew what I'd witnessed with my own eyes. Didn't she say she wanted to be friends? What else could we possibly talk about? I had absolutely nothing in common with her.

"I love Mitch," I said. "He's a lot of fun, but he's only using you. Isn't that how it works with rock stars and girls? I thought everyone knew that."

"Know what I think? I think you're way out of your league here, kid. I think you need to go home and sell Girl Scout cookies, because that's where you belong."

332

And with that, we were at the side of the stage. I was a bit flustered by the way Fawn turned on me, but managed to do my job and get photos of the guys as they ran back onstage for the encore. For the last song, Lonny stood at the front of the stage the entire time, and at one point held his hand above his eyes, as if scanning the crowd. The lighting guys turned on the house lights so Lonny could see the crowd, and it was enough to take my breath away. I managed to take several photos of him standing in front of the crowd with his arm in the air as a thank you. It was pure magic.

As the band ran offstage after the show, I jumped into Lonny's arms and wrapped my legs around his waist. "Lonny!" I cheered. "That was incredible!"

Lonny was out of breath, smiling and laughing, holding on to me as tightly as he could. The hometown crowd of over 18,000 was not about to go anywhere without seeing their Golden Boy one more time, continually chanting Lonny's name.

"Go ahead kid," Fuzzy urged. "You earned it."

I let go of Lonny and Mitch gave him a gentle push back toward the stage. "Nah, that's okay," he said, not wanting all that attention on himself alone.

Mitch then made an over-exaggerated push so people could see it wasn't Lonny's idea to come back onstage. As embarrassed as he was the smile on his face could never be duplicated as he stood at the front of the stage, pointing at our parents and blowing them all a kiss, then waving to the crowd that was going berserk over him and him alone. He gave them one final bow and ran back offstage.

I was trying to take photos of Lonny, but the whole way back to the dressing room he was putting his arms around me and kissing my cheek, or sliding his hand into my back pocket and squeezing my behind. When we all got back to the dressing room he didn't care who was around, kissing me hard on the mouth for all to see. Everyone erupted into howls and applause and when Lonny pulled away from me, he wiggled his eyebrows and I covered my face, embarrassed. Happy, but embarrassed.

It wasn't long before other people began filing into the dressing room, including Fawn and our parents. Joanie immediately wrapped her arms around Lonny, crying and telling him how proud she was of him. It was a very touching moment between Lonny and his mom, and I made sure to get it all on film. As Lonny talked with my parents I noticed Fawn arguing with Mitch on the other side of the room. They were whispering quietly, but fiercely, and I wondered if she was relaying any of what I said to her before the show. I could see him laughing, which only seemed to infuriate her further. A few minutes later I saw her dragging Benji out of the room and wondered what that was all about. As long as she stayed away from Lonny, I didn't care what she was up to.

"Where's Gina?" I asked my mom.

"Billy didn't want to come back here again, so they went home."

I nodded in understanding. Billy couldn't stand seeing me happy; he thrived on me being miserable. As happy as our parents were to be a part of Lonny's new life, even briefly, they were soon headed home themselves, which worked out perfectly because they would never have approved of the champagne toast Howard presented us with.

Mitch made his way to where I was standing taking photographs and leaned close to my ear. "You really pissed her off," he whispered.

"I didn't mean—"

"It's okay, kid. You're right… I use her for what she offers. It's not like she's saving herself for me or anything."

"So you're not mad at me?"

"Only because now I probably won't get laid tonight," he joked.

"Where was she going with Benji?"

"Really kid?" He patted me on the back and as he walked away laughing, I figured it out. He obviously wasn't too broken up about it. He joined Lonny at the food table, and I watched their animated conversation for a while until Fuzzy stood next to me.

"Whattya think they're talking about?" I asked him.

"Judging by Mitch's hand gestures and facial expressions, I'd say sex."

"Really?"

"Plus Lonny looks terrified, so…."

334

I looked at Fuzzy and said, "Stop teasing Lonny. He's not a virgin, you know."

"Yeah," he said. "I heard all about it."

I was shocked. "He told you?"

"Yeah. What about you? Have you guys…?"

"Almost… I don't know what I'm doing."

"Trust me doll, he will love *anything* you do. He's a guy. As long as we're getting attention, it's game on. All you have to do is *tell* Lonny you're interested in sex and he'll be ready, if you know what I mean."

I giggled, embarrassed.

A few minutes later Benji and Fawn returned and she made a beeline right to Mitch, snuggling up to him as if nothing had happened. And he didn't seem to be bothered in the slightest.

"Hey Girl Scout!" she shouted at me. "I'd like to order four boxes of cookies, please!" She howled with laughter, but everyone else looked at her like she was nuts.

"What the hell is she talking about?" Fuzzy asked.

"She told me I should be home selling Girl Scout cookies because I don't belong here."

"She's such a bitch," he grumbled under his breath. "She used to be Joey's whore, but he dumped her a few years back. Mitch doesn't care about crazy as long as he's getting laid."

"And did you ever have your own?" I asked, grinning.

"Hey, ten years ago when we were starting out, we did it all. Groupies, drugs, orgies, you name it. Some of us grew up and became responsible adults, some of us want to stay rock stars."

"So everything changed when you met Marilyn?"

"Yeah doll, everything changed when I met Marilyn. She's the love of my life." Fuzzy smiled, but he looked so sad. I didn't have the heart to ask him about Marilyn anymore, so I assumed I would see her whenever she caught up with us. I could see tears in his eyes and knew how much he was missing her, so I stood up and pulled him into my arms, hugging him as tightly as I could.

Howard announced the band would be leaving shortly, as they had another big day tomorrow, so anyone who wasn't part of the band slowly made their way out of the dressing room. Lonny removed his tie and slipped it over my head, then took my t-shirt

335

with his picture on it and put that on. I took several photos of him smiling and pointing to his face on the t-shirt.

We all piled into the limousine, and I was surprised to see Fawn climb in with us. She grinned at me and said, "Hey there, Girl Scout."

"She has a name," Lonny defended me.

"I know, silly," she laughed. "It's just a term of endearment."

I knew better.

I leaned close to Lonny's ear, and cupping my hand for privacy whispered, "I'm ready." He turned to look at me, wide-eyed. He smiled and put his arm around me, pulling me as close as possible. Then he kissed my cheek and nuzzled his face against my ear, whispering, "You're on."

"No secrets, kids!" Benji teased. "Now you have to tell the whole class!"

I grinned and said, "I told Lonny I have a present for him."

The guys hooted and whistled, playfully slapping Lonny wherever they could reach him. He was laughing as he held up his hands for mercy.

"And Mitch," I said, looking right at him. "Stay out of our room."

Mitch winked and replied, "You got it, baby."

"It's about time," Benji teased.

"Thank you, Blow Job Benji," I joked.

Everyone howled with laughter, but I didn't like the way Fawn was looking at me. It was obvious she didn't like the relationship I had with the band, and jealousy didn't look good on her. She failed to understand that I *worked* with the band, I wasn't there to *sleep* with them.

By the time Lonny closed and locked the door to our room, I was kneeling on the bed waiting for him. He stood at the edge of the bed and gently tugged on the tie I was wearing to pull me against him. He softly kissed each of my cheeks, my forehead, then worked his way down to my neck where his breath was hot against my skin. He pulled away when I grabbed the hem of his t-shirt, letting me peel it off his body and throw it on the floor. I placed my palm against his chest, feeling his heart thundering beneath my

336

touch. He stared into my eyes as he slipped the tie off my neck and tossed it on the floor, then I lifted my arms to the sky so he could pull my shirt over my head. I reached for his jeans and unfastened the button, but as I touched the zipper he pulled away and began pacing the room, running his hands nervously through his hair.

"Are you sure, Roo?"

I smiled. "I'm sure." To show him how sure I was, I stood up and slid out of my jeans, then sat back on the bed.

"Are you nervous?" he asked.

"Very. But it's you, Lonny, so I know it's gonna be okay."

"I have a confession to make."

There I was, sitting in my bra and panties, feeling a little overexposed.

"Remember in the pool when your top accidentally came off?" I nodded, remembering it vividly. "You were topless, and when you... you know... pressed yourself against me, I was so turned on I lost it."

"You mean...?"

"Blew it. Right there in my shorts, in the pool."

I covered my mouth with my hand and gasped. "That's why you left me there? I thought it was because you thought I was disgusting."

"Roo, I would never think you were disgusting! I was too embarrassed to tell you what happened."

I got off the bed and stood in front of Lonny, wrapping my arms around him and pressing my face against his chest. His fingers caressed my shoulders, then my back, then he slowly slid his hands inside my panties and squeezed my behind. I inhaled sharply, looking up at his beautiful, innocent face. Never breaking eye contact with him, I unzipped his jeans and slid my hand inside. He gasped and bit his bottom lip as his eyes rolled back in his head. I had no idea what I expected it to feel like, but was pleasantly surprised by how soft the skin was, and I could feel it growing against my hand.

"I wanna see you," I whispered.

Lonny's hands were suddenly in my hair, his mouth hungrily kissing me as he walked me backward toward the bed, both of us falling in a heap once we got there. I wrapped my legs

337

around his waist as he writhed on top of me, ravaging my neck and groping my breasts over my bra. I brought his face back to mine and kissed his mouth, my breath coming in gasps and sighs. Lonny's hand slid inside my panties and he touched me… *there*. I stopped breathing, gasping audibly.

He immediately stopped kissing me and said, "Did I hurt you?"

"No," I managed to say. "Please don't stop."

There were strange sensations going on in my stomach and pelvic region, like being on a roller coaster with its ups and downs and twists and turns. I squirmed underneath him, not really sure what my body was experiencing, but it felt good and I wanted more. Lonny got up, and standing at the end of the bed he slowly slid my panties off. I got on my knees and watched his face as he reached behind me to unclasp my bra. Slowly, he pulled the bra away from my body and tossed it on the floor, grinning like a fool as he stared at my nakedness. I pressed myself against him, his hands exploring every inch of my body as I hungrily kissed his mouth. I ached in places his fingers probed and found myself yanking at his jeans, wishing he would just take them off. Finally he stepped back and slid off his jeans, allowing me to see him in all his splendor and as I reached out to touch him, he lifted me into his arms and lay me down on the bed. He gazed into my eyes as he hesitated, then gently thrust himself inside me. I held my breath and watched his face, unsure what I was supposed to be doing. Lonny was sweet, touching and kissing me so gently as if I were something fragile that might shatter underneath him.

I tangled my fingers through his hair and pulled his face close to mine so I could kiss him. I kissed him hard, letting him know there was nothing fragile about me and that he need not worry about hurting me. He groaned into my mouth as I grabbed his behind with both hands, and it wasn't long before Lonny's body moved quickly above me. I watched his facial expressions change with the rhythm of his movements until his eyes opened to look at me during his final thrust, and then he collapsed on top of me and rolled off onto his back. His chest heaved up and down as he tried to catch his breath, covering himself with the sheet and lighting a cigarette. I picked the t-shirt with Lonny's picture on it off the floor and put it on, then grabbed my Polaroid and started taking pictures of him.

"What are you doing?" he asked, appalled.

"Nobody sees my Polaroids but me," I assured him, climbing back on the bed and straddling the parts of him he covered with the sheet. I continued taking photos of his face; the face I loved, belonging to the boy I loved. He tugged on my shirt, trying to pull me down next to him, taking a drag off his cigarette.

I took the cigarette from him and put it in my mouth, having no plan to smoke it. I messed up my hair, leaned back against the headboard and closed my eyes. Lonny grabbed my Polaroid and started taking pictures of me. And I let him.

"You hungry?" he asked.

"Starving."

Lonny rolled over and picked up the phone to order room service. As he talked I ran my fingertips up and down his back, causing goosebumps to cover his skin. Just as I tried to slide the sheet down to peek at his bottom, he hung up the phone and flipped back over, pulling me down on top of him. I smashed his cigarette out in the ashtray, then placed both hands against his face. I kissed him softly on the mouth and asked, "Was it better than last time?"

Lonny smiled, sliding his hands under my shirt and caressing my back. "I don't remember a last time."

"I don't either." And it was true. All the thoughts that haunted me since graduation simply vanished.

When our food arrived we sat at the table to eat, and I grabbed a pen to write the date on the Polaroids. I gave Lonny the photos he took of me because I certainly didn't want them. Though I did have to admit I looked pretty good, for the simple fact they didn't look like me and I looked so much older.

"Did I do it right?" Lonny asked.

"Is there a wrong way?"

He grinned, his face blushing. "But did you... you know... like I did?"

I had just eaten the last bite of my cheeseburger, which gave me a minute to figure out exactly what he was asking me. I didn't want to hurt his feelings, but I had no idea what it took for *that* to happen.

"I don't think so," I finally replied. "I think it might be something women have to learn. You know, with experience."

Lonny looked confused, and it was adorable.

I shrugged. "It's not like I talk to my mom about this stuff. Or anybody else."

"So you'd do it again?"

I smiled and took a swig of my soda. "Only with you."

Lonny had a huge smile on his face as he shyly looked away. "We can learn together."

I got up from my chair and straddled Lonny's lap, facing him. I caressed his shoulders, then wrapped my arms around his neck. "You'll always be my sweet boy," I whispered.

"You'll always be my girl."

"Promise?"

"Promise."

I kissed his mouth softly, then began kissing his neck. He leaned his head back, exposing his throat to me. There was just something about his neck that I loved; his soft skin, his sexy Adam's apple… and when he threw his head back while playing guitar onstage, I lost control of my senses every time. I could feel his groans against my lips and his excitement growing underneath me, so I knew I was doing something right.

Lonny lifted his head and kissed my mouth, gently at first, then invaded me roughly with his tongue, which only sent me to the moon as my body began to tremble. I was still only wearing the t-shirt I put on, never bothering with my panties, and underneath me Lonny managed to slide his unzipped jeans down without missing a beat. I could feel him between my legs and my breath caught in my throat. My inexperience was evident, not quite sure what I should be doing at that moment, and my face burned with embarrassment.

Lonny smiled at me and whispered, "It's okay." He slid his hands underneath my legs and gently guided me on top of him, where I slowly lowered myself and we were one with each other again. I knew immediately I was the one in control in this position, and with Lonny's help found a rhythm that worked for both of us.

He slid his hands underneath my shirt, slipping it over my head and tossing it on the floor. I giggled, imagining it was a bit weird for Lonny to have his own face looking back at him while we were in the throes of passion.

Lonny kissed a trail from my lips, down my neck, to my throat, to my chest, where he hesitated, as if fearful of my breasts, small as they were. As soon as his mouth touched one of them I inhaled sharply, and when I felt the wetness of his tongue, I began to feel a pressure in my belly that expanded and deflated like a balloon, up to my chest and back down again. I tried to focus on Lonny, but could only close my eyes as everything around me faded into warm shades of greens and yellows. My breathing took on a life of its own, gasping for air as if I'd pass out at any moment, our bodies moving faster and faster in synch with each other. Every emotion I'd ever felt for Lonny came crashing down to where we were joined, where his body was one with mine, where an eruption of spasms happened at the same time for both of us and we collapsed into each other, trying to catch our breath.

Lonny's eyes met mine, our chests heaving against each other. I pushed his sweaty hair away from his face and he pulled me in for a kiss.

"That time," I whispered against his mouth, "I definitely did."

I took a cigarette out of the package sitting on the table and lit it, then placed it between Lonny's lips. He winked and nodded, thanking me. I got up and headed to the bathroom, and when I came back out he was still sitting as I left him, his pants around his ankles and smoking a cigarette. I cleaned up our food garbage and crawled into bed, exhausted. I watched him, sitting with his eyes half closed and a goofy grin on his face as he finished his cigarette.

My sweet Lonny.

With the cigarette pinched between his first two fingers, he pointed it at me and asked, "Do you know why I always have my back to you every morning when we're in bed together?"

"No."

"Because I don't want to poke you with my boner."

We both burst into uncontrollable laughter. We heard pounding on the wall and "*Shut up!*" from the room next door,

341

which caused us to laugh that much louder, knowing it was Mitch having a bit of fun.

As we settled into bed, Lonny pulled me into his arms and kissed me sweetly.

"How many girls wish they were me right now?" I asked with a laugh.

"Doesn't matter," he sighed. "You're the only one I want."

I smiled in the dark, my heart doing flip flops in my chest.

I woke up the next morning to Lonny standing next to the bed, trying to wake me up. He was pointing at the television and saying, "Roo, look! Wake up!"

I focused my eyes on the news and there was Lonny's face, all over the television! They were replaying portions of the late news from the night before, and it was their story about Lonny coming home to play Chicago Stadium. I sat straight up in bed and shouted, "You're on TV!"

Neither one of us knew his mom was interviewed, but there she was, telling everyone how proud she was of Lonny and that she couldn't wait to see him perform onstage that night. There were a few short interviews with girls waiting outside, telling the cameras what they loved about Lonny, then a short clip of the band doing soundcheck, and then the man himself, Lonny smiling away, his dimples as big as could be, talking about how excited he was to be in Chicago to perform for his home crowd. The whole thing was very short, but to see Lonny on the local news was unbelievable!

When it was over, Lonny turned to look at me with the biggest smile on his face I'd ever seen. "Right now," he said, "is the best time of my life. I'm part of the greatest band in the world, I've got my music, and I have my girl." He crawled on top of the bed and tried to kiss me, but I blocked him with my hand.

"Death breath," I explained.

"I don't care, move your hand."

He kissed me, gently pushing me down on the bed. Even through the bed covers and his jeans, I could feel his growing excitement. And then the phone rang. Lonny rolled his eyes and picked it up, said okay, then hung up again.

"Breakfast in Fuzzy's room half an hour," he told me.

Half an hour later we entered Fuzzy's room, where everyone else was just starting to eat. Lonny and I each fixed a plate and sat on the floor as Howard announced the radio station visit they cancelled the day before was rescheduled for early that afternoon. He excused himself, saying he had to make some phone calls and Mitch followed him out into the hallway. Fawn looked a bit sheepish as she watched them leave the room.

"Do you ever hear from Joey?" Fawn asked the room.

"No," Fuzzy responded immediately. "Have no use for him."

"The new kid's good," she chuckled. "But he's no Joey."

As Fuzzy was about to say something, Mitch came back into the room and told Fawn, "Sorry, it's a no go."

"What's the big deal?" she whined.

"Howard said no."

"What's going on?" Fuzzy asked.

"She wants to go to the radio station with us," Mitch explained. "Howard won't let her."

Fawn pouted and glared at me. "I bet she gets to go."

"Hey," Fuzzy growled, pointing a finger at her. "Ruby works for the band and she should be there. It's part of her job."

"Is fucking the kid part of her job?" Fawn hissed.

"Get out," Mitch ordered.

Fawn looked stunned.

"Get out," he said again. "You leave Ruby out of this. And Lonny too, for that matter."

Fawn stood up and tried to plead her case, saying she didn't mean any harm. I wanted to argue, but kept my mouth shut. Lonny whispered in my ear, "Ignore her."

The next thing we knew, Mitch was slapping money into Fawn's hand and pushing her out the door. "Take a cab!" he shouted at her before slamming the door in her face. He turned to me and held his hands in a praying position against his mouth. "Ruby, baby, I'm sorry about that."

"It's not your fault," I said.

"I'm done with that stupid bitch," Mitch said. After a moment of awkward silence, he said, "So Ruby, does Lonny make sex faces when he plays guitar?"

343

I pulled a face and laughed. "What? No…." I immediately realized I had just been outed, answering the burning question on everybody's mind that morning.

"Lonny, you dog," Fuzzy teased.

I covered my burning cheeks with my hands and shook my head. Lonny was too busy eating breakfast, wiggling his eyebrows at me and grinning.

The radio station visit that afternoon was interesting as the two disc jockeys on the air didn't make their entire interview about Lonny, which I could see was a relief to him. They gave each band member equal time, and it was nice to see them all engaged for a change. I gave them credit, because not a single one of them ever complained that Lonny got all the attention or took the spotlight away from them. They were all more than willing to let him be in the forefront, having never experienced it, and they'd all walked that walk years before.

No matter where we were that day Lonny couldn't keep his hands off me, stealing kisses and hugs wherever he could get them, and I certainly wasn't complaining. I couldn't wait until we were back in the privacy of our own room, and I could feel my face flush every time I thought about it.

In the dressing room before soundcheck, Howard let everyone know how happy he was with the tour so far, and how it exceeded even his expectations. "Ruby," he said, making me a bit nervous. "Everyone loves having you on tour, and the work you've been providing me is stellar. I don't want an answer right now, but I have two propositions for you."

Lonny, who was sitting next to me, squeezed my hand.

Howard continued, "I would like you to accompany us on the upcoming European tour, and I'd like to hire you as the official Livingston Monroe photographer."

The entire room erupted as Howard finished his words, and I still couldn't believe he was speaking them to me. Not only was he asking me to travel with them to Europe, he was offering me a full time job. That meant Lonny and I would never have to be separated again!

Howard left the dressing room and each of the band members embraced me, showing their excitement about having me around on a full time basis. One by one they headed toward the stage for soundcheck and as Lonny and I lagged behind, he held my hand and said, "Roo, we'll get to spend all our time together! We can get our own place and you'll never have to go back home!"

I couldn't wipe the smile off my face as I watched the band do their soundcheck from the side of the stage. Me? The full time personal photographer for Livingston Monroe? Going to Europe with the band? Getting to spend every day, every minute with Lonny? I didn't have to think twice about any of it, as the only obvious answer was yes!

"Hey there, Girl Scout."

My stomach lurched.

"You can't get rid of me," Fawn continued. "I know too many people."

"It has nothing to do with me."

"It has *everything* to do with you," she hissed. "I don't know what you have that makes those guys so protective of you, but you're just a skinny, ugly, freckled virgin that no sensible man would ever waste time on."

Her words slapped me so hard I had no response. I turned to concentrate on the soundcheck, trying to pretend she wasn't there. She wasn't telling me anything I didn't already know about myself, except I wasn't a virgin and Lonny seemed to like me okay. I knew she was just trying to get under my skin, and I wasn't going to let her win.

"You wait," she spoke close to my ear. "Once that kid sees what real women have to offer in this business, you'll be crying your ugly ass all the way back home where you belong, because you certainly don't belong here."

The band came bounding offstage and Lonny put an arm around me as we walked, and no one said a word about Fawn being there. I turned to look for her, but she was nowhere to be found. Her words shook me and the fact she disappeared so quickly before the band could see her caused me concern.

"Lonny!" Howard called from the area near the dressing room. "It's your turn to do the interview! You're the last one!"

345

Howard thought it would be fun to have the film crew record interviews with each band member. The questions were far from serious, meant to be tongue-in-cheek, and just for fun. The questions were the same for each guy and they were all interviewed by me, but I was always off-camera. I pulled myself together after the run-in with Fawn, not mentioning it to any of the guys. As I interviewed Lonny, the other guys did everything they could to distract him, whether it was throwing things at him or walking behind him and doing bunny ears behind his head. He laughed them off and interviewed like a pro, even though I had to stop laughing and start over a few times. When the interview was over, Lonny looked straight into the camera and said, "Gotta go find my girl."

After the film crew moved on I said, "Howard will never let that into the film."

"I don't care," he laughed.

He pulled me into a kiss that I interrupted by saying, "Fuzzy looks really sad today."

"I know."

"I'm going to pay special attention to him tonight, is that okay?"

Lonny smiled. "As long as you're in my room tonight."

I kissed him, he kissed me back, and we headed into the dressing room. I stood behind the chair Fuzzy was sitting in and wrapped my arms around him, kissing the top of his curly head. He patted my arms, then brought me around to sit on his lap. Lonny was plucking out a tune on his guitar while Benji and Mitch ate from the food spread.

"So doll," Fuzzy said, "you gonna take Howard up on his offer?"

"Oh I don't know," I said. "Europe *and* a permanent position with you guys? I don't know if I can handle all that."

"And being with Lonny every day," Mitch teased. "What a nightmare."

Lonny laughed, then I said, "I guess you'll all find out when I give Howard my answer."

"Lonny, your chick is brutal," Mitch grumbled playfully.

"Don't ever change, Roo," Lonny joked.

346

Lonny started playing "Got To Get You Into My Life" by the Beatles, and Mitch gladly provided the vocals. I loved it when they broke out into songs other than their own, and they gelled like they'd been playing together forever. Not a single one of them ever missed a beat, no matter what was thrown at them.

Mitch sang, "Ooh, you were meant to be near me… ooh, and I want you to hear me…."

And all four of them sang together, "Say we'll be together every day."

After spending so much time with these guys, I couldn't imagine being without them. Life on the road was tough and far from perfect, but they were my family. I couldn't imagine my future any other way.

The second night at Chicago Stadium was a carbon copy of the first, with Lonny getting all the hometown love he deserved from the crowd. As they were playing the last song before their encore, someone shoved me from behind. I didn't have to turn around to know who it was, so I ignored her. I tried to get Butch's attention, but he was too busy focusing on Lonny, which was his job. All of a sudden, I was yanked back by my hair and lost my balance, but managed to catch myself before falling. Face to face with Fawn, I wondered what her intentions were for being there that night.

"That kid is shit!" she yelled at me.

I laughed in her face. "How would you know? You don't care about the music; all you care about is your after party sleaze show!"

I turned my back on her to finish watching the show; she wasn't worth any more of my time. The guys finished their song and ran off the stage, Lonny first in line. Fawn stuck out her leg and tripped him, sending him crashing to the floor. Butch immediately ran to Lonny's side and I took off running after Fawn, who somehow managed to escape being seen by anyone but me. It wasn't hard to catch up to her as she tried running in her platform shoes, and once I reached her I realized Mitch and Benji were running after *me*. I was fueled by pure anger and adrenaline, tackling her to the floor. She kept trying to claw at me, but I was able to slap her hands away every time.

347

"Get off me, you stupid bitch!" Fawn screamed.

"What the hell's going on?" Mitch asked, staring down at her.

"She tripped Lonny!" I explained.

Security was soon pulling me off Fawn, and when they set me on my feet I saw Butch and Fuzzy gingerly walking a pained Lonny into the dressing room. I turned back to face Fawn, who was being held by the security guards.

"Why would you do that?" I yelled. "What's wrong with you?" I ran into the dressing room to see if Lonny was okay and the look on his face told me everything I needed to know. Howard barged into the dressing room with a couple of medics who began examining Lonny's right shoulder, which I realized was dislocated once they gingerly removed his shirt. I immediately headed out the door and lunged at Fawn, but Mitch caught me before I touched her, lifting me off the ground and holding me back.

"You stupid whore!" I yelled at her. "What the fuck is wrong with you?"

Howard came out of the dressing room and told the security guards that he wanted Fawn arrested and that they would be pressing charges against her. She screamed as she was dragged away by security, but Mitch didn't let go of me until we were safely back in the dressing room with the door closed.

"Just pop it back in," Lonny groaned in agony. The medics wanted to take him to the hospital to have him looked at by a doctor, but Lonny kept shaking his head. He finally had enough and yelled, "Just pop it back in!"

"Just do it," Howard said, "or one of us will."

Mitch turned me around so I couldn't see what was happening, and I'm glad he did, because the crushing sound of snapping bones and the agonizing scream that came out of Lonny almost caused me to throw up. Mitch lifted my head with his hand and whispered, "He's okay."

The medics soon left and while Lonny iced his shoulder Howard paced the room, running a nervous hand through his hair. "What the fuck just happened?" he asked. "*Someone* tell me!"

"It was Fawn," I said when I finally found my voice. "She tripped him."

348

"Why would she do that?" Howard yelled.

Nobody really knew why she would trip Lonny. "She hates me," I said. "She did it because of me."

"Why would she hate you?" Fuzzy asked.

"She thinks I'm keeping her from the band. She was here during soundcheck saying awful things to me."

Lonny, covered in sweat and white as a ghost, asked, "Why didn't you tell us, Roo?"

I shrugged. "I didn't want to bother you. I'm sorry." Lonny was hurt and it was all my fault for keeping my mouth shut. I apologized as I burst into tears.

Mitch pulled me into his arms and said, "Baby, it's not your fault. She hates you because we love you, and she hates Lonny for taking Joey's place. Simple as that. She's crazy!"

"But now Lonny's hurt and—"

"I'm fine," Lonny insisted. "Let's finish the show."

Everybody filed out of the room, but Lonny closed the door when it was just the two of us left.

"Lonny, I'm so sorry," I cried. "It's all my—"

He pressed his mouth against mine to shut me up. "It's not your fault."

"I love you," I cried. "And she hurt you because of me."

"Stop. I'm okay."

"What if Howard blames me? He won't hire me at all."

"Does that mean you're going to tell him yes?" Lonny was grinning from ear to ear.

I nodded as I tried to smile.

"You're my girl, Roo. We're in this together. Come on, let's go."

I wiped the tears from my face as we followed the rest of the guys back toward the stage, Lonny holding my hand tightly, letting me know he did not blame me for anything that happened. He kissed me and strolled back onstage like he owned the place, the crowd going wild when he reemerged. The band played their final two songs, and while I could tell Lonny was experiencing pain, he did not let it affect his playing whatsoever.

After the show everybody gathered in the dressing room as always, but Howard was beside himself. As Lonny iced his

349

shoulder, everyone was quiet as Howard paced, looking like he was going to explode.

"Do you have any idea… *any* idea how much we have riding on this kid?" he finally said. "One stupid move by a jealous groupie and it could've been all over. Do you even know what that means?"

Fuzzy moved to stand behind me, putting his hands on my shoulders and gently squeezing. I got the feeling I was going to be sent home.

"Do whatever you want at the hotel on your own time, but here… backstage… business only. If anything happens to Lonny, or any of you, we're fucked."

I understood what Howard was trying to do, and what he was trying to protect, but it made no sense. The venue is where the band should be at their safest. They could easily get hurt at the hotel, where they were more likely to do something stupid. But I kept my mouth shut.

Howard left the room and we were all silent for a moment before Mitch started laughing. He turned on his imitation girl voice and said, "You stupid whore! What the fuck is wrong with you?" He was imitating me yelling at Fawn. "Ruby baby, I had no idea you had it in you!" They all started laughing, but I wasn't amused. Fawn's actions caused Lonny to get hurt, and I knew he was trying to hide how much pain he was actually in.

Everyone became quickly silent as the door opened and Howard walked back in, with two police officers and Fawn behind him. For some reason I immediately felt the need to protect Lonny, pulling away from Fuzzy to stand in front of him.

"What's she doing here?" I asked.

Howard replied, "Fawn has something she'd like to say."

"After the speech you just gave us, are you kidding?" I hissed.

Howard didn't like it when people questioned him, but he especially didn't appreciate it when I did it. "Get her out of here," he said to the room.

Fuzzy took me by the arm but I yanked it away from him. "Why do I have to leave?"

"If Roo leaves, I leave," Lonny said.

350

"It's okay," Fawn said, her voice cracking. "She needs to hear this, too."

I folded my arms angrily and held my position in front of Lonny.

"I'm sorry," Fawn said. "I didn't mean to hurt Lonny, not anyone. It was an accident."

"Then why did you run away like a guilty coward?" I shouted.

Howard was done with me. "Get her out!"

Fuzzy had to physically lift me off the ground and carry me out of the room, and before the door closed on us I heard Howard shout, "Lonny, sit!" I struggled to get away from Fuzzy, and when he finally let me go I fell in a heap on the floor. He extended a hand to help me up but I slapped it away, standing on my own. I started walking. I had no idea where I was going, but I had to get away.

"Where are you going?" Fuzzy called after me.

"Anywhere but here!"

He jogged to catch up to me, blocking my path. "Look," he said, placing his hands on my shoulders. "In this world, groupies have their role. It's not pleasant for girls like you, or the girlfriends and wives left behind when a band goes on tour. But we can't change that."

Violently pointing back toward the dressing room I said, "*That* groupie hurt Lonny! She was supposed to be arrested and Howard said he was pressing charges. Why is she in there with Lonny right now, *lying*? It was no accident! She tripped him on purpose!"

"I imagine Howard doesn't want to deal with this after tonight, so he's probably going to let her apologize and let it go."

This made me furious.

"You need to calm down before we go back there," Fuzzy said. "The last thing you want is to piss Howard off. Besides, we leave tomorrow and you'll never see Fawn again."

"So she's just going to get away with what she did?"

"Most likely."

He put his arm around me as we walked back to the dressing room. I needed Marilyn so badly, but I knew I couldn't

351

ask Fuzzy about her anymore. As we entered the dressing room again, Fawn was crying and hugging Lonny. He seemed to take her apology as genuine, but I didn't like seeing her touching him. She hugged Benji, then hugged and kissed Mitch, saying thank you to everyone in the room. She looked like something out of a horror movie with the mascara running down her face.

Fawn made her way toward me but Fuzzy, who had his arms protectively around me, put his hand up and said, "You're done here."

I watched as Fawn was escorted out of the room by the police officers, and when the door closed I glared at Howard. He looked at me and said, "Ruby, are we okay?"

Fuzzy could feel my body tense as I wanted to tell Howard exactly what I thought about what transpired, but he gently squeezed me as a warning. "Yeah, we're okay," I conceded.

"Good," Howard said, clapping his hands together. "We're going out tonight." Everyone was quiet, thinking it was a joke. "You guys are headed to Kansas City tomorrow and I'm heading home until Seattle, and I thought you deserved a night out."

The guys cheered, but all I wanted was to go back to the room. After everything that happened with Fawn, and Lonny getting hurt, I wasn't in the mood to go out. I even offered to go back to the room while the rest of them went out, but Lonny wouldn't hear of it. If I was going to stay in the room, so was he, and I knew he really wanted a night out, so I agreed to go with them.

Howard brought us to a club where loud music thumped throughout for the people on the huge dance floor, with lots of private nooks and crannies and seating areas if you didn't want to be bothered by others. And no one questioned mine or Lonny's age, which was a huge plus. Mitch and Benji left to scope out the place, while the rest of us found a table and sat down. It wasn't long before people were coming up to our table to ask for autographs, or to simply chat with Fuzzy or Lonny.

"I'm sorry about Fawn," Howard said, leaning close to me. "But staying involved in a long, drawn out legal battle with her just isn't worth our time, or money."

I was still angry, but smiled. "I don't wanna talk about her anymore."

Howard laughed. "Good."

Howard left to get drinks and I noticed a group of girls talking with Lonny. It was refreshing to see nice, normal girls talking to him instead of trying to rip his hair out.

"Come on Lonny," one of them begged. "Come dance with us."

He kept saying no, but finally glanced at me for guidance. I just smiled and nodded, and he disappeared onto the dance floor. Fuzzy put an arm around me and said, "You're a good sport, doll."

"I don't hate the fans," I told him. "Just Fawn." We both laughed and I patted his leg. "Besides, I wanted to spend time with you tonight."

"Oh did you now? Well... I can't argue with that then."

Howard returned with drinks for all of us and I looked up at him when he placed one in front of me. "Long Island iced tea," he said.

"Drink it slow, doll," Fuzzy warned. "This one is enough for the night."

Howard and Fuzzy talked business as I people watched, but I was specifically looking for Lonny, who I couldn't find. Benji soon came back to our table, joining in on the business talk, and I craned my neck, still looking for Lonny. I decided to use the washroom, and while I was in one of the stalls I heard a couple of girls come in. I could see through the gap in the stall door that they were primping themselves in the mirror.

"Oh my God, he's so cute!" one of them said.

"But he's just a kid," the other said.

"He's eighteen. Only a few years younger than us."

"Too young for me. I'd rather have Mitch. He's a *man*."

"You can have him," the first girl said. "Lonny already told me I could come back to his hotel room tonight."

The girls left the bathroom giggling and I sat there stunned. Surely she had to be lying to her friend? I had to toughen up if I was going to be a permanent fixture with the band. There were going to be girls like this everywhere, and I couldn't keep Lonny

353

away from them. I finished my business, washed my hands and looked at myself in the mirror. Fawn was right; I was ugly.

When I got back to our table, Lonny was there and he looked happy to see me. We both knew we couldn't show any affection to each other in public, but it was difficult. I returned to my seat next to Fuzzy and took a long swig of my drink before Lonny was standing next to me.

Leaning over so he was close to my ear, he asked, "You okay?"

I nodded, and when he put his ear close to my mouth I said, "I just overheard two girls in the bathroom. One of them said you invited her to your hotel room tonight."

Lonny stood up straight with a look of horror on his face. "I did not!" He grabbed my hand and pulled me to a secluded corner of the club. "Girls *lie*," he said.

"I didn't say I believed her," I said into his ear. "But she was convincing."

Lonny brushed his mouth against my cheek as he said into my ear, "You're my girl. My *only* girl."

He snuck in a kiss that I was all too willing to risk being caught over. But I interrupted it over something that could've waited until we were back in our room.

"What did Fawn say to you?"

"Really, Roo? Now?"

"You were hugging each other when I came back in the room."

"I just wanted it over with," he said. "She was all crying and apologizing, saying it was an accident and I—"

"Do you believe that?"

"I don't think she meant to hurt me."

"Lonny, I saw her with my own eyes. She tripped you!"

Lonny looked annoyed. "Roo, we don't have to see her anymore. Can we just have a good time tonight?"

"Okay. I'm sorry."

"And later, when we're back in the room…." He gave me a tongue kiss I felt all the way to my toes, then as if nothing happened, we headed back to our table.

"Lonny!" Mitch shouted, pulling him away from me. "There's some people I want you to meet." And just like that, he was gone again.

"Everything okay?" Fuzzy asked.

"I think Lonny is too trusting."

"He still has a lot to learn, but he's learning quickly."

I wasn't so sure about that.

Anyone who wanted a piece of Lonny that evening got one, whether it was a quick chat, sharing a drink, having a dance, signing autographs or taking photos. By the time Mitch brought him back to our table, he fell into the seat next to me, laughing and rambling on about something none of us could decipher. It was late, Lonny was drunk, and it was time to go.

We all piled into the limousine, with Lonny practically face down in my lap. He flipped over onto his back, his legs splayed out over Mitch's legs. He was laughing and singing something nobody could understand.

"Feed the ducks with a bun," he sang, laughing hysterically. We then figured out he was singing "Itchycoo Park," by the Small Faces when he repeated over and over again, "It's all too beautiful."

Lonny grabbed the front of my shirt and pulled me down to his face, trying to kiss me. "Come on Lonny, not now," I said.

"Why won't you kiss me?" he asked.

"Nobody wants to see that," I explained.

Fuzzy had to help Lonny out of the limousine when we got back to the hotel, and fortunately it was late enough that there were no girls hanging out by the front door. Mitch helped Fuzzy drag Lonny to our room, and when I opened the door I asked if one of them wouldn't mind getting a bucket of ice for me. Fuzzy said he'd take care of it as Lonny fell face first onto the bed and didn't move. I turned on the light and Lonny flipped over onto his back, holding his arm out in my direction.

"Come here," he mumbled. I walked closer to the bed and he grabbed my hand, pulling me down on top of him.

"You're wasted."

"Don't tell my mom," he slurred, laughing.

"We've both been very, very bad," I replied, giggling.

Lonny flipped me over onto my back and crawled on top of me. He started kissing me, wet and sloppy, and someone knocked on the door.

"It's Fuzzy," I said. "We have to ice your shoulder. Let me up."

Lonny groaned, but didn't move.

"Just a minute!" I yelled.

It wasn't long before I realized I was trapped underneath Lonny as he had passed out and began snoring. I managed to squirm out from underneath him, patting his back and calling his name several times, but he was passed out cold. I grabbed my hairbrush from the bathroom and stuck it in the door to keep it from closing so I could get the ice bucket from Fuzzy, whose room was right across the hall.

"Sorry," I said. "Lonny passed out on top of me and I was trapped."

I followed Fuzzy into his room as he laughed, handing me the ice bucket. I thanked him and headed back to our room, noticing the door was closed and half the brush was sitting on the ground. The strength of the door must have been too much for my brush, snapping it in half and leaving me locked out.

I knocked, calling Lonny's name, but I knew it was probably a waste of time based on his condition when I left the room. I knew it was late and I didn't want to disturb everyone else in our hallway, but where was I supposed to sleep if I couldn't get Lonny to open the door?

"Lonny!" I yelled only once, pounding on the door. Nothing.

Mitch was soon opening his door. "Psssst! What's going on?" he whispered loudly.

"I'm locked out."

"Sorry baby, but I don't have room." He winked and closed the door.

I laughed, knowing exactly why he didn't have room for me. I continued tapping on the door lightly, but it was futile. I sat on the floor and leaned against the door, trying to figure out what I was going to do. I looked up just as Fuzzy opened his door, smiling at me.

"You can't sleep there," he said. "Come on."

I got up from the floor and went into Fuzzy's room where he pulled a t-shirt from his suitcase and handed it to me. I went into the bathroom to change into the shirt that was big enough to be a nightgown, then crawled into the second bed.

"Thank you," I said.

"No problem, doll."

Lying there in the dark I so badly wanted to ask about Marilyn, but decided against it. If there was any news he wanted to share, he would've told me. I felt bad for Lonny, knowing he was probably going to wake up in pain since he didn't ice his shoulder after getting back to the hotel. One thing was certain; I didn't like sleeping without Lonny. In fact, I didn't like being away from him at all.

I didn't sleep well that night, restless without Lonny, and wide awake around seven the next morning. I didn't want to disturb Fuzzy, who graciously let me share his room, so I lay there quietly with my eyes closed. As soon as Fuzzy started moving around, however, I hopped out of the bed and pulled on my jeans, anxious to get back to Lonny. I ran across the hall barefoot and still wearing the shirt Fuzzy gave me to sleep in. I knocked lightly calling Lonny's name, and my heart jumped as I heard him unlocking the door a few minutes later.

Lonny peeked out at me with his eyes half closed, grumbling, "Roo, what're you doing out there? Come back to bed."

I followed him into the room and watched his naked form walk back to the bed and crawl in, pulling the covers over his head. Something didn't seem right, and it wasn't long before I found out why. I thought I must be having a nightmare when she threw back the covers and said, "Hey Girl Scout." I *prayed* I was back in Fuzzy's room having a nightmare, because it couldn't be possible.

Fawn crawled out of the bed naked, picking up her clothes that were scattered all over the floor.

"Lonny?" was all I could manage.

"Roo, come on," he grumbled. "Get back in bed."

"It's a little too crowded, Lonny!"

357

Lonny peeked out over the blanket and as soon as he saw Fawn standing there, he jumped out of the bed and wrapped the blanket around him.

"What the fuck is she doing here?" Lonny asked, looking like he was about ready to throw up. I couldn't believe what I was hearing. My stomach churned and I could feel bile rising into my throat.

As Fawn slowly got dressed, Lonny struggled for something to say. "Roo, I don't… it's not… I can't…."

"Thanks for propping the door open for me," Fawn said with an evil grin.

I ran out of the room and pounded hysterically on Fuzzy's door, hollering for him to let me in. When he opened the door I pushed my way inside, locking myself in the bathroom where I collapsed on the floor, unable to catch my breath.

Fuzzy knocked on the bathroom door asking, "Why did Fawn just leave Lonny's room?" I couldn't believe he actually thought I would answer his question!

A few seconds later Lonny was pounding on the bathroom door, begging me to let him in. I ignored him, unable to move. I could hear Fuzzy and Lonny talking, but I couldn't understand anything they were saying. I didn't want to understand anything they were saying; I wanted everything that just happened to go away so I could enjoy the life I had with Lonny. But that was no longer possible. Not after the way Lonny betrayed me, and in the worst possible way imaginable. My head was spinning and I couldn't find a way off the horror ride I was stuck on. In just a brief moment my entire life came to a screeching halt, and it was never going to be the same. It could *never* be the same.

"Roo!" Lonny yelled, pounding on the door. "Please let me in!"

"Come on out, doll," Fuzzy calmly said.

I somehow managed to stand, my entire body shaking. My heart shattered, the shards of what remained stabbing my soul, every bit of happiness I'd ever known escaping and leaving me in complete blackness; I would never be whole again.

I opened the door to see Lonny standing there with tears running down his face, and he was still wrapped in the blanket. I pushed past him to stand next to Fuzzy on the opposite side of the room. I'm not sure why I felt the need to do that, but I didn't want Lonny anywhere near me.

"Roo, please don't hate me," he cried. "I don't know what happened."

I wiped the tears from my face, but new ones continued to fall. "You were dressed when I left the room last night. This morning you were both naked. You're *still* naked."

"I didn't touch her, I swear!"

I marched to where Lonny was standing and grabbed the blanket, pulling him close to my face. "You look me in the eye and tell me you know for a fact nothing happened with her."

He said nothing.

"You can't, because you don't know," I cried.

"Roo, please—"

"Lonny, go put some clothes on," I growled, turning my back on him.

As soon as I heard the door open and close, I collapsed to the floor sobbing. I gasped for air, unable to catch my breath. Fuzzy paced uncomfortably, having no idea what to do.

"I need to talk to Marilyn," I sobbed. "*Please. I need to talk to her!*"

Fuzzy sat on the floor next to me, taking my hands in his. "I can't do that, doll."

"Fuzzy, *please*," I begged. "I *need* her." I continued to sob, begging him to call Marilyn so I could talk to her.

"Look at me, doll."

I focused on Fuzzy's face, and he had tears in his eyes. "You can't talk to Marilyn," his voice croaked. "I don't know where she is."

I audibly gasped, not understanding what he was telling me.

"She left me, doll. She's gone."

Fuzzy, the strong, sensible leader of our dysfunctional group, broke down crying. I crawled onto his lap and held his face against my chest as we sobbed together.

"Why didn't you tell anyone?" I asked.

"I kept hoping she'd show up. I had to tell Howard because he knew there was nothing wrong with Mare's mom."

I buried my face in his soft curls and whispered, "I'm sorry. I'm so, so sorry."

"I wanted to have kids, she didn't. I asked her to stop drinking, and she went nuts. I just want her back," he sobbed.

There we sat, two broken souls holding each other and crying, each wanting to fix everything for the other, but having no idea how to make it happen.

Fuzzy pulled his head up to look at me. "Go talk to Lonny. You need to work this out while you still can."

Tears burned my eyes as I replied, "He was the one person who'd never hurt me, and now he's hurt me more than anyone else ever will."

"Do you love him?"

I cried as I nodded.

"Go talk to him."

I got up and walked across the hall, knocking lightly on the door. Lonny opened it right away and I walked in, making sure I didn't touch him. I sat on a chair as he sat on the bed, unable to look at me.

"Why are you wearing Fuzzy's shirt?" he finally asked.

"Are you serious?"

"Yeah...."

"I got locked out of our room last night, thanks to your groupie whore. Are you really gonna get on my case about this shirt after what you did?"

Staring at the floor he grumbled, "She's not my groupie whore."

"You were in bed with her," I cried. "I gave myself to you... and now... I want to throw up."

"Roo, you know I would never hurt you."

"Too late," I said, sobbing. "All I can think about is you... with *her*." I got up and grabbed my suitcase, tossing it on the table. I started throwing my stuff inside, choking on my tears.

"What are you doing?"

"I'm going home."

360

Lonny jumped off the bed and whirled me around to face him. "You can't leave," he cried. "You promised you'd never leave me."

"That was before you slept with someone else."

"But we don't even know what happened!"

"Lonny," I cried. "I can still smell her perfume." I picked up the phone and called my parents' house. I knew when my father answered that my mother was at church.

"Dad," I said calmly. "I need your help."

Lonny looked at me desperately, tears running down his face. "Hang up, Roo," he said. "You can't leave."

"Dad, I need you to come pick me up. The tour's over for me, and I need to come home now. Yeah, I'm at the hotel. Thank you."

Lonny grabbed the phone out of my hand and slammed it down. "You're not leaving!" he shouted. He tried to put his arms around me but I pushed him away. The thought of him touching me made my stomach turn.

I grabbed the bag of used film from the Chicago shows and said, "I need to tell Howard I'm leaving," I said, heading toward the door. He grabbed me before I opened it and held me against the wall by my shoulders.

"You can't leave," he cried, piercing my soul with his eyes. "I need you to stay."

"Why Lonny? What do you need me for?"

"Roo, I *need* you. You know I need you."

"You don't need me."

"I can't do this without you," he sobbed. "You know I can't."

"I'm just in the way."

"Roo, stop it. Please don't leave. I'll do anything to make you stay."

"Why would you want me to stay?"

"Please," he begged. "I need you."

"Why do you need me, Lonny? Why?"

"I just… I just do."

He tried to kiss me but I pushed him away, opening the door and heading to Howard's room. He was surprised to see me

361

when he opened the door. I handed him the bag with the used film and said, "My answer is no. I'm going home today. Thank you for everything."

As I turned to leave Howard said, "We still have five shows left on this tour. You're not done."

I didn't want to cry in front of Howard. I managed to say "I'm sorry," and walked away before the tears started again. When I got back to our room, Fuzzy, Benji and Mitch were all there with Lonny.

"Ruby, what's going on?" Mitch asked.

"Ask Lonny," was all I could say.

Mitch took me by the hand and pulled me into the hallway. Just as he did this, Howard came walking down the hall looking for me. I covered my face with both hands because I didn't want anyone else to see me crying. I didn't want to humiliate myself further by having to explain what happened; Lonny should be the one humiliated by all that. Howard went into our room, giving Mitch privacy to talk to me alone.

"Ruby, baby, what's going on?" he asked. "You can't leave. We need you way too much."

"None of you need me," I cried.

"Lonny's a wreck."

"He's the one who slept with Fawn last night."

Mitch stood up straight and stared at me, stone faced. "He did what?"

"She locked me out of the room. I found them in bed together this morning."

I'd never seen Mitch speechless before, but there he was, staring at me with his mouth open. Complete silence.

"That doesn't sound like Lonny," he finally said.

"She was just waiting for the perfect opportunity, and I gave it to her. Lonny was wasted, and I left the room for just a minute to get ice from Fuzzy…."

Mitch put his hands on my shoulders and said, "You need to think about this clearly. He made a mistake… that doesn't mean you have to leave. This is your job, a lifetime career Howard set up for you. Don't throw it all away because of some shit move by Lonny."

362

I pulled away from Mitch and went back inside the room where everyone was staring at me. "The bus leaves in two hours," Fuzzy said. "Why don't you take some time alone, doll, and get yourself together. We want you to stay with us."

"You're our sunshine, baby," Mitch said, smiling.

Of course all the men could just sweep the incident under the rug and expect me to forgive Lonny and let it go. They were a band; there was a code. I knew then and there I couldn't be part of their world any longer. And I could never forgive Lonny for what he did.

I threw my camera bag over my shoulder and grabbed my suitcase. "Thank you for everything, but I have to go." I bolted out the door and ran for the elevator.

"Rooster, wait!" Lonny called, running to catch up with me.

I jabbed the elevator button over and over again, praying the doors would open soon. I couldn't look at Lonny again. I didn't want to hear anything else he had to say.

"Roo please," his voice croaked. "Please look at me."

I turned to face him, unable to control my tears.

"Whatever happened was a mistake. Please forgive me. I can't live without you. *Please*."

The elevator doors opened and I stepped inside, turning to face him one last time. "I love you, Lonny," I cried, "but this is just too painful."

Lonny could barely speak as the tears choked him. "You promised you'd never leave me."

"That was when you were the one person who would *never* hurt me."

The last thing I saw was his panicked face when he realized I wasn't coming back.

I cried all the way down to the lobby, then wiped my face before getting out of the elevator, putting on my sunglasses. I walked through the lobby and out the front door, where a large group of girls gathered in the hopes of getting a glimpse of Lonny. As I waited for my dad I could hear whispering behind me, but didn't really care what any of the girls might have been saying. All that would be behind me and I'd never have to worry about silly girls or slutty groupies again.

As my father pulled up to the curb, I heard Lonny shouting at me from up above. "Roo!" he screamed. "Please don't leave!"

I looked up to see him hanging over the balcony and I felt sorry for him. I waved goodbye, threw my suitcase into the back seat, then got in front with my dad and closed the door. As he pulled away, I heard his favorite Bee Gees cassette playing, and it was on the song "To Love Somebody." When I heard the line "you don't know what it's like… to love somebody… the way I love you," I burst into uncontrollable sobbing.

"Honey," my dad said. "What happened?"

"I don't wanna talk about it," I sobbed.

"Are you hurt?"

I was, but I knew that's not what he meant. "No, nothing like that."

"Your mom will be home from church by the time we get back."

I knew he was encouraging me to figure out what I was going to tell her before we got to the house. My mom surprised me, though. She could see I was visibly upset and didn't press for answers. I asked both of them not to tell anyone I was home early from the tour. Not even Lonny's mom, because I knew he certainly wasn't going to tell her what happened. I told them I would explain when I was ready and escaped to my bedroom, where stacks and stacks of envelopes containing my photos from the tour were piled neatly on my bed. I pushed them all onto the floor with one swipe of my arm, then fell face first onto my comforter where I cried for the next several hours.

Early in the evening my mom came into my room to tell me someone was on the phone for me.

"Who is it?"

"I'm not sure, but I think it's one of your band friends."

I didn't want to talk to any of my band friends, but I got off my bed and dragged myself into the kitchen where I sat on the floor and closed my eyes before saying hello.

"Hey doll," Fuzzy said. "I just wanted to make sure you were all right."

Tears trickled out the corners of my eyes as I answered, "No."

"You have to come back," he begged. "The kid is a wreck."

"You need to tell them about Marilyn," I changed the subject. "They're family; they need to know. And you deserve their support."

"Yeah, yeah, I'll do that. What about you? When you coming back?"

"I can't," I cried. "Not after what he did."

"It was a mistake. Can't you forgive him for that?"

"Promise me you'll take care of him," I said, the words choking me.

"Come on, doll. You're the only one who can really take care of him."

"Promise me," I cried.

After a long silence he finally sighed and said, "I promise."

I got to my feet and hung up the phone, and as I attempted to go back upstairs to my room my mom called me into the living room.

"Ruby, are you pregnant?"

"Mom! No!"

"We just don't understand what happened. We saw you two nights ago and you were so happy. You were in your element and everything seemed to be in place for you. Now this….."

"Please Mom," I cried. "Not now."

I went back upstairs and crawled into bed, my refuge from the world. I pulled the covers over my head and cried myself to sleep. Sometime in the middle of the night my phone rang.

Lonny.

He was crying so hard I could barely understand what he was saying. "Please," he begged. "I'm so sorry."

"You need to sleep, Lonny."

"I can't sleep, Roo. Not without you. I can't do this without you. I need you."

"Lonny, I—"

"You promised you'd never leave me!"

I was quiet for a long time, listening to him cry. It was heartbreaking, but everything that was happening to him was

365

because of something he did. "You broke my heart," I cried. "How can I ever trust you again?"

"I'll do anything," he begged. "Please just come back."

"There's too many girls," I whispered, wiping the tears off my face. "They'll do anything to get to you, and I was just in the way."

"I don't want other girls," he said.

"You already *had* another girl, Lonny!"

"Roo, please listen to me. I was wasted. I don't remember anything!"

"Is that supposed to make me feel better?"

"How many ways can I say I'm sorry?" When I didn't respond he asked, "You're still my girlfriend, aren't you?"

I was so tired of crying, and my head hurt. "I left because of what you did, Lonny! No, I'm not your girlfriend anymore!"

I could hear his chest heaving before he found his voice again. "Come on Roo, don't do this. Please come back."

"You cheated on me with that *whore*. I can't stop thinking of you with her. I want to throw up!"

"Please Roo," he sobbed. "You're my only girl. I can't live without you."

"Why, Lonny?"

"What?"

"Tell me why you can't live without me."

"Because you're my best friend. Without you, nothing matters."

"But *why*?"

"Roo, I don't know what you want me to say."

"You know what I want you to say and you can't say it."

"Please come back and we can work this out. *Please*."

"We can still be friends, but it's over Lonny." I said goodbye and hung up on him.

2011

I sat up quickly and asked my mother to repeat what she just said to me.

"Lonny tried to stop your wedding."

I stared at her like crickets were crawling out of her ears. "What are you talking about?"

"I think it's time you knew the truth."

"I'm listening."

"Lonny's hotel information is on the table; take dad's car. And don't come back until you two have figured this out."

I grabbed my dad's car keys and rushed out of the house. It was like a bad dream as I drove, the same Bee Gees cassette tape playing through the speakers, the same song that broke my heart when he picked me up off the hotel curb thirty-one years earlier.

You don't know what it's like… to love somebody… the way I love you.

"God, Dad! Don't you listen to anything else?" I yelled to the inside of the car.

My eyes were blinded with tears as I drove to the hotel where Lonny was staying. It was well after midnight and he was probably asleep, but my mom's revelation about my wedding day changed everything. And she wasn't going to let me get away without talking to Lonny immediately.

I ran into the hotel lobby and got into the elevator, my stomach in knots. I stood in front of his door and hesitated just a moment before lightly knocking. I must have looked a wreck, but it didn't matter. Nothing mattered but whatever happened after he opened that door. I knocked again, a little harder the second time, and my stomach lurched as I heard him releasing the lock. He opened the door a crack to look at me, but said nothing.

"You tried to stop my wedding?" I asked, my voice cracking.

He opened the door to let me in, walking back to the bed and picking up his laptop. "Can I call you tomorrow?"

"Later, kid."

Lonny closed his laptop and sat on the bed, staring at me.

367

Was he going to answer me, or was he expecting me to keep asking questions?

"I'm giving you one last chance to tell me the truth for *once*. No more secrets, no more games. Or I swear to God, Lonny, I'm walking out that door and you will *never* see me again."

Lonny ran his hand through his hair, then vigorously rubbed his face. But he said *nothing*.

I turned and walked back toward the door, knowing this was it. I was done with Lonny. As my hand touched the doorknob he wrapped his arms around me from behind with such force I almost hit the door with my face.

"I love you," he said. "August 15, 1975," he continued, pressing his face against the back of my head. "You were wearing a red and white checked shirt with bell-bottom jeans, and those weird sandals with the bump under the toes... the blue ones. And you smelled like cherry lip gloss."

I inhaled sharply, resting my forehead against the door to keep from collapsing.

"I loved you the first time I saw you," he said. "And I've loved you ever since."

1980

My parents did as I wished, keeping my early return home quiet. I spent most of my time in bed, trying to figure out how I was going to move on with my life. Lonny's nightly calls became less hysterical when we talked, then they tapered off to brief, weekly conversations. Our relationship was irretrievably broken, but neither of us could completely sever the invisible tie that bound us together. I don't think either of us could have survived.

One morning my mother snuck into my room to wake me. She sat on my bed and waited for me to roll over and face her.

"Honey, the tour was over a month ago," she said softly. "You need to get out of bed." I didn't respond. "I wish you'd tell us what happened."

"It doesn't matter," I grumbled.

"Are you and Lonny okay? I mean, are you still friends?"

"Yeah."

"You need to face the world, Ruby. You can't spend the rest of your life in bed hiding from it."

"The world is an ugly place I don't want to be part of."

"This isn't the Ruby I know," she lightly scolded. "I knew going on tour with that band wasn't a good idea."

"It has nothing to do with the band. Please stop."

"Nothing to do with the band? Then why is all your mail from the tour still unopened? You haven't even unpacked your suitcase."

I rolled over, turning my back on her and pulling the covers over my head. I could never tell her the truth. As angry as I was at Lonny, I would never tell anyone what happened. It wasn't anyone's business, and he didn't need my parents angry with him as well. The truth was, I loved him with every breath I took. I understood what it meant to long for someone, to ache just to be with them. I'd think of our time together and the way he looked at me, or kissed me, or touched me. I'd think of our bodies one with the other and want to pick up the phone and call him, to tell him I was sorry and that we belonged together. But then thoughts of the other woman would creep into my head and my heart would

369

shatter all over again. I could never see Lonny's face without imagining him with *her*. At least when I was in bed asleep, my dreams didn't betray me.

I felt my mom's weight lift off the bed. "You need to get a job," she said. "You're almost nineteen, and you need to learn what it's like to be an adult." I rolled my eyes, knowing she couldn't see them. "You're going to start paying rent to live here. I'm giving you until the end of August."

Well, that gave me two more months in bed.

It was short lived, however, when on my birthday my mother exploded into my room, yelling at me.

"Ruby, you're going to get out of that bed and join us for dinner. Joanie is coming over, and you're going to eat pizza and strawberry shortcake like we do every year on your birthday. Do *not* give me any lip!"

And with that, she was gone again. I slid out of bed onto the floor and crawled over to my suitcase, opening it for the first time since returning home from the tour. I pulled out my clothes and tossed them in a pile; even though they were clean they'd been locked up for too long and smelled like it. I pulled out a few of Lonny's ties, which I must have thrown in by mistake when I was angrily throwing things into the suitcase to get away from him. I grabbed my camera bag, taking out my cameras and the giant stack of Polaroids. Slowly I looked at each photo, getting more and more choked up after each one. My mom burst back into my bedroom and I tossed the photos back in the suitcase, wiping my face.

"Well at least you're out of bed," she grumbled.

"Can't you knock?" I shouted.

"Dad wants to know if you're coming to the parade."

"No, I'm not."

As she walked back out she said, "Watch your mouth."

I rolled my eyes and gave her the finger, something I never imagined I'd ever do to my own mother. I dragged myself into the bathroom to take a shower, letting my tears for Lonny roll down the drain with the soapy tap water.

I greeted Joanie with open arms and a smile as she welcomed me home with an intense motherly hug. She handed me a bundle of giant papers and folded posters, saying, "Would you

370

mind putting these with Lonny's other things? I just can't keep anything at the house since those girls broke in."

It was all the signs and posters hanging up around town when Lonny came home to do the record signing at Vinyl Horse. Every single one of them! It seemed like a hundred years ago. I promised her I would keep them safe with Lonny's other personal things.

"When do you think my boy will be home?" she asked me at dinner.

"What do you mean?"

"When's Lonny coming home?" she asked again.

"Well, they took a few months off after the tour before they head to Europe in September," I explained. I didn't have the heart to tell her that Lonny had no intention of moving back home. Not only because he loved California, but because the band had so many things to do. Just because the tour was over didn't mean their career ended. There was a new record to write and record, interviews, photo shoots, television appearances… it never ended.

"So you don't know?" she asked.

"Mom, they're really busy. They're always working."

"Well, when will I get to see him again?"

"Soon, Mom. He misses you very much."

My mother decided to change the subject. "Did you hear Billy is learning how to tattoo?"

I wrinkled my nose. "Tattoo? Who gets tattooed?"

"He didn't quit his job at the hardware store, did he?" my father asked.

"No, no, he's still at the store," my mom assured him. "He's learning on the side. God knows what for."

Joanie kept bringing the subject back to Lonny, while my mom would change it to Billy. I wasn't quite sure what they were playing at, but I didn't like it. I would talk about Lonny, painful as it was, but I certainly didn't want to talk about Billy.

"Please stop talking about Billy," I said.

"Ruby, stop being so rude," my mom scolded.

"I don't want to talk about him, Mom. He's an asshole."

"Is this what you learned working with that band?" she hissed. "A foul mouth and filthy hand gestures?" I must have

371

looked shocked because she finished with, "Don't think I didn't see what you did."

"I just don't want to talk about Billy!"

I silently praised the Lord when the phone rang. My mom got up to answer it, giving me the evil eye the whole way there. "Happy birthday, Lonny!" she cheered. "Yes, yes, you're right, we're eating pizza right now. We only wish you were here to celebrate with us."

I sat there listening to everyone talk to Lonny while I nibbled on my pizza. My mom, my dad, then Joanie. I wondered if he had interest in talking to me. I got my answer when I heard Joanie say, "Okay honey, I'll let her know. I love you. Goodbye." She sat back down and smiled. "He said he'll call you later."

I nodded and smiled. There was really nothing else to do.

"Are you coming with us to see the fireworks?" my dad asked.

"I'll pass, thanks." I didn't want to go into town and see anybody I knew. I couldn't handle all the questions or assumptions, or people acting like my best friend when all they really wanted was something from the band. And they needed me to get it for them.

After dinner my father asked me to go outside with him. As he pretended to putter around in the garage he said, "I know things have been strained with your mom, but she's worried about you."

"I'm fine, Dad."

"Then why are you always crying?"

I guess I wasn't hiding it very well. "I'm just sad, that's all. Haven't you ever been sad?"

"Of course, but I didn't have the luxury of hiding in my bed for months on end."

"Don't worry, I'll be getting a job soon. Don't want you missing out on your rent money."

I could tell my father wanted to say something in response, but instead said, "We've never missed the fireworks. It's our thing, you know."

"Okay, okay," I conceded. "I'll go to the fireworks. But if Billy tries to sit with us, I'm coming home."

He nodded in agreement. "You miss Lonny."

372

It wasn't a question. I looked at my dad and tried to smile, but could only feel tears burning my eyes instead. I just nodded as he pulled me into his arms and gave me a big, comforting dad hug.

"It'll get easier," he said. "Broken hearts don't last forever."

As promised, by the time the end of August rolled around, I was back working with Ricky at Vinyl Horse, even though I would have preferred spending the rest of my life in bed. It was hard the first day walking in to all the Livingston Monroe merchandise hanging on the walls. Aside from the albums there were posters, t-shirts, photographs, buttons and everything else you could imagine. Everywhere I looked, I saw Lonny's face. It was pure torture. Ricky was so excited to have me back at the store he gave me a raise and any paid days off I wanted. Customers who visited the store often were happy to see me and welcomed me back, but they always had a question about my time on tour or about Lonny. Once the novelty of having me back in the store wore thin, the questions tapered off and I didn't have to answer quite as many. The teenage girls were the worst, however, coming in to giggle but too afraid to talk to me.

Gina would come in after school and do her homework in the back office and Billy would pick her up on his way home from work. She hated going home alone, and when their father came home he was angry and verbally abusive. I didn't blame her for not wanting to be in that environment, and I was glad Billy waited for her outside the store when he picked her up. The last thing I wanted was for him to worm his way back into my life.

In September, Ricky was playing *Desolation Boulevard* by Sweet in the store, and while I put price tags on David Bowie's new album, *Scary Monsters and Super Creeps,* I sang out loud to "Ballroom Blitz."

"Oh reaching out for something… touching nothing's all I ever do."

"I'd recognize that awful singing anywhere."

I looked up to see Molly, who had just walked in the door. I said hello, but didn't feel like engaging in conversation. The last time we talked she wasn't very nice to me.

I continued working while she browsed through records, then the magazines. "You don't have any magazines with Lonny hidden in the back, do you?" she finally asked.

I laughed. "Nope. Everything that comes in sells out the same day."

"I bet you get first dibs."

"One of my employee perks."

Molly flipped through the poster display, not really looking at anything long enough to be interested. Finally she stood in front of me at the counter and waited for me to look up.

When my eyes met hers she asked, "Can we go out for lunch or something? I want to apologize for the way our friendship ended."

"You just did. No need for lunch."

"Come on Ruby," she pleaded. "I'm not going back to school, so I thought maybe we could be friends again. I was stupid, and I'm sorry."

"If this is about Lonny, forget it."

"Hey," she sounded agitated. "We were friends before you ever knew Lonny. He's the one who stole you away from *me*."

"Then you went out with him and decided I was trying to steal him away from *you*."

"That was all a crazy mistake," she defended herself. "One I'm trying to fix."

I sighed. "I can do a late dinner tonight. I close at nine."

Molly smiled from ear to ear. "Great, I'll pick you up."

We went to the local burger joint and were seated in a corner booth. Once we ordered our food, Molly didn't stop talking. She told me how going away to college didn't work for her, and that she was going to stay at home with her parents and go to the community college until she figured out what she wanted to do. I also got to hear about the boys she dated while away at school, and that she really missed having a boyfriend.

"Is talking about Lonny not allowed at all?" she finally asked.

"Go ahead."

"How is he? Is he okay?"

"He's great," I assured her.

"I told people at school that I went out with him, but they didn't believe me. My mom finally sent me one of my prom pictures for proof." She laughed; I didn't. "What was it like being on the road with them?"

I smiled, because generally I had wonderful memories of our time on the road. "I can't even describe it," I said. "I had a great time, and I loved every minute of it."

"So what are they up to now?"

"They just left for Europe."

"You weren't allowed to go?"

I hesitated before answering. "I was only with them for the first tour."

"How amazing would it be to travel to Europe with them!" she exclaimed, clapping her hands together. "I saw your pictures in the fan club newsletter and they were amazing!"

I didn't have the heart to tell her that I hadn't seen any of my own photos. Everything Howard mailed to me sat in my room, unopened; the packages of photos he promised, and the fan club newsletters. I didn't have the heart to look at any of them.

Molly and I did a lot of catching up during dinner, and agreed that since we were both back living at home we should make more of an effort to see each other. As the waitress brought our bill I saw Molly looking past me, her smile disappearing instantly. It wasn't long before I knew why, as Billy and Seth Brown plopped down on either side of us.

"You girls leaving?" Billy asked.

"Yep," I answered abruptly, trying to push my way out of the booth.

"Come on," Seth said. "Stay and have sundaes with us."

"Ew," Molly groaned. "We have to go."

"So Ruby," Seth grinned, trying to put his arm around Molly, who kept slapping it away. "What was it like being on the road with a rock band?"

I had no tolerance for Seth, knowing full well he was going to find a way to insult me as he always did. I looked at Billy, pleading with my eyes to let me out of the booth. He slid out so I could escape, and Seth did the same for Molly, but as Seth stood near me he made pig noises and sniffed me.

"The stench of ugliness is in the air," he said. "I see being a road dog didn't improve your looks any."

I walked straight out of the restaurant and to Molly's car, and Billy never did anything to defend me. I was silent as Molly drove me home, and when she parked in the driveway she turned to me and said, "Seth is an asshole. Don't listen to him."

I looked at Molly and replied, "I know what I look like. I'm not stupid."

"Maybe I could help you learn to put on a little makeup." I rolled my eyes, and as I stepped out of the car she shouted, "I'll call you!"

I knew she was only trying to help, but it made me feel worse. My parents were already in bed, so I snuck up to my room and closed the door, changing out of my clothes and crawling into bed. I turned on my bedside table lamp, then pulled the Polaroids from the tour out of the drawer. I slowly examined each of them, missing Lonny more than ever. I thought about our conversation the night before they left for Europe, and he didn't once ask me to join them. It was obvious he'd learned how to live without me and didn't need me the way he thought he did. He just needed to grow up and be a man, and he did it. Now it was my turn to grow up.

It seemed Lonny's celebrity status wasn't as well known in Europe as it was back home, so he was able to leave his hotel room and explore the places they traveled to. I was happy for him, because for two people who never traveled before, all we saw on tour was the inside of our hotel room, the venues they played, or things passing by the bus windows. Lonny made sure to send me a little gift from every country they visited, and photos from his newly purchased Polaroid camera. He wanted me to experience Europe, even though I wasn't there with him. I loved seeing photos of the guys, and it was even better when one of them would write me a quick note. I missed them all so much.

They returned home from Europe the week before Christmas, and Joanie held out hope he'd come home for the holidays, even though he told her he wasn't going to make it. On

Christmas Eve, my father brought me out into the garage under the guise of a surprise for my mother so she wouldn't question it.

"If your mother knew I was telling you this," he said, "she'd kill me."

I suddenly felt sick. "Is something wrong?"

"Billy came to talk to us the other day. He asked our permission to marry you."

I stumbled back a few inches, shocked at my father's revelation. "But we're not even dating."

"I don't know when he planned on doing it, but Christmas is a good guess. I just didn't want you to be blindsided."

"Thanks, Dad. I won't say anything."

"Your mother seems to think it's a good idea. I told her you were way too young."

"Good idea? I *am* too young! And I don't even like him!"

Christmas came and went and there was no proposal from Billy. I never even saw him. It felt like I was holding my breath every day just waiting for the bomb to drop on me, but nothing. Molly and Gina both asked if I wanted to hang out at their house for New Year's Eve, but I just wasn't in the mood. I kept thinking about New Year's Eve the year before and the party at Marilyn and Fuzzy's, and was seized by depression.

I picked up my phone and called Fuzzy's house, something I'd never done before. I always let Lonny call me when he wanted to; I never tried to call him. Fuzzy answered on the third ring and seemed excited to hear it was me on the other end.

"What a nice surprise, doll!" he exclaimed. "It's great to hear your voice!"

"I was just thinking about the New Year's Eve party last year. Feeling a little sad."

He laughed loudly. "That was some party, wasn't it?"

"How was Europe?"

"Oh doll, it was fantastic! It wasn't the same without you, though. You would have loved it."

"I'm glad Lonny wasn't a prisoner there like he was here."

"The kid really blossomed, doll, he really did. And onstage… he blew it up! I wish you were there to see it yourself."

I could feel a sob get caught in my throat and changed the subject. "So is the divorce final?"

"Yeah," he sighed. "I love her to death, but she didn't want to work things out. Just wanted her freedom."

"I'm sorry."

"Yeah, well, that's life. I'll manage. It helps to still have Lonny at the house. Not so lonely."

"Is he there?" I held my breath after asking.

"Actually doll, he's outside, but…." He hesitated before finishing with, "He's not alone."

I tried not to show my anguish, swallowing my grief and saying, "Oh that's fine, don't even tell him I called. I just wanted to wish him a Happy New Year."

"Happy New Year, doll."

I hung up the phone and cried, not realizing I had cried myself to sleep until my mom entered the room to wake me up. It was dark outside and I had no idea what time it was.

"Is it midnight?" I asked, trying to get my bearings.

"No, it's only eight o'clock, but Billy is downstairs. He wants to see you."

"I don't want to see him."

"Ruby, don't be rude. At least just say hello."

"Mom, I don't want to see him. I don't have anything to say to him. Tell him I'm sleeping."

"I'm not going to lie for you. Go downstairs and tell him yourself."

I turned on the light next to my bed and said, "What's your problem? Why can't you just stay out of my business?"

"As long as you're in my house, your business is my business. Now get downstairs, and if you don't want to see Billy, tell him yourself." She left my room and I wanted to scream. Lonny was with a girl and Billy was downstairs. Wonderful.

I dragged myself into the kitchen where Billy was waiting for me. My parents were in the living room, but I knew they were listening.

"Hey Ruby," he said, fidgeting with his gloves.

"Hey."

378

"Would you want to go for a ride? So we can have some privacy?"

"I don't feel like going out," I replied, hoping he would just go away. "Did you want something?"

"I just wanted to wish you a Happy New Year I guess."

"Okay, well, Happy New Year." All I wanted was for him to leave. I couldn't stand being in the same room with him.

He moved closer, as if he were going to say something, then leaned in and kissed me. It was a quick kiss on the mouth, but it still repulsed me. I pushed him away and said, "Goodbye, Billy." I went back upstairs to my room and let him find his own way to the door, since he was more than familiar with its path.

It was around eleven-forty-five when my father knocked on my door, something he rarely did. He wanted to know if I was going to come down to ring in the new year with them, and in between sobs I told him no.

"Did he ask you?" he whispered.

"No."

"Well that's good then. I love you, honey."

"I love you, too, Dad."

He closed the door and let me be. Something I wished my mother would do without insisting on antagonizing me. At midnight I agonized over my New Year's kiss from Lonny the year before. It was short, but it was *Lonny.* I thought about Peter, and that made me smile. I always tried to remember what he told me about being a bright light, but believing that was harder and harder with every day that passed.

The next morning I walked into the kitchen to hear my mother saying, "What are those poor kids going to do?"

I didn't say anything as I pulled a box of cereal out of the cupboard.

"Ruby, it's awful," my mom said. "Just awful."

"What is?"

"Billy's father died last night, just after midnight. Heart attack," my father answered.

I sat down in disbelief, pulling my robe tightly around me. "What are they gonna do?"

"Right now their aunt is with them. She's their mother's sister. Very nice woman, never married."

"What does her never being married have to do with what's going on?" I hissed. It seemed that anything my mother did easily set me off.

"Ruby, how dare you talk to me like that!"

When my father scolded me under his breath, I knew I'd gone too far, but I didn't care. I took my cereal into the living room and turned on the television. My father was close behind, sitting in his chair and picking up the newspaper.

"You had a taste of what it's like to live away from home," he said, never taking his eyes off what he was pretending to read.

"I loved it," I grumbled. "I wasn't being bitched at all the time by *her*."

"Don't you think you're being a bit unfair?"

"She treats me different since I've been back. I don't like it."

"She could say the same about you."

"Aw Dad, don't you start too! I'm not a little kid anymore."

"Just calling 'em as I see 'em."

My mom came into the living room and announced, "Ruby, we're going to be cooking today so we can take meals over for Billy and Gina."

"I already have plans," I lied.

"With who?"

"Friends."

"Which friends, Ruby? You have no friends. You go to work and then you come home and lock yourself in your room. Lonny isn't coming back and you need to get a life!"

I turned to glare at my mother; something I would have been slapped for before I turned eighteen.

"You can't work in a record store your entire life," she continued. "You need a career, which you have no skills for. You can't live with us forever. You don't know how to cook or iron or even do laundry!"

She had pressed my last nerve. I stood up and shouted, "You never *let* me do those things because you have to control *everything*! And when I try, I never do anything right!"

380

We were both seeing red and my father got up to stand between us. "Ruby, go upstairs."

I ran as fast as I could to get away from my mother. Before I closed my bedroom door I could hear them arguing, but I had no idea whose side my father was on. I imagined if he wanted to stay peacefully married to my mom, it would be hers.

I ripped my robe and pajamas off and bundled up in my warmest clothes, then ran downstairs to put on my coat and boots. I heard my mother asking where I was going, but I left without answering. I needed to get out of that house and away from *her*. I had no idea where I was going on New Year's morning, so I just walked. I trudged through the snow to Joanie's house, hoping she'd be awake, but she didn't answer the door. I debated whether or not to let myself in, and the bitter cold made my decision for me. I quietly unlocked the door and kicked off my boots, then snuck into Lonny's room and climbed into his bed. I cried for the life I gave up by coming home. Everything was all set. I had a career handed to me on a platter, a life I loved, a man to spend it with, and I threw it all away because I couldn't forgive Lonny.

I woke up when I heard Joanie crawl into the bed with me. I turned to face her and she whispered, "Are you okay?"

I immediately burst into tears and cried, "I miss him so much."

She wiped the hair away from my face and kissed my forehead. "What's going on?"

I poured my heart out to her, explaining how things had been strained with my mother since coming home, and all we did anymore was fight with each other. I told her about the awful things she said to me that morning before I fled the house, and how I felt she was always pushing me to go out with Billy when I didn't even like him.

"I did my best," she whispered, her face so close to mine I could already smell her first whiskey of the day. "But I wasn't a good mother to Lonny. You still have a chance to make things right with your mom; I've lost Lonny forever."

My heart broke for her. "You haven't lost him. He loves you. More than anything else in the world."

"You're a sweet girl, Ruby, but I won't have another chance because Lonny isn't coming home."

"Mom, I know how much he loves you. He may not be coming back home to us, but that doesn't mean you can't go visit him."

"I'd like to see California." She smiled. "Would you go with me?"

"Of course. It'll be fun."

"You set it up with Lonny and we'll do it."

1981

I dragged myself to work on Valentine's Day and when I walked into the store, Ricky was playing Queen's "Somebody To Love." He teased that he was going to play songs with the word "love" in them all day long, but I begged him not to. He didn't listen. Lonny confirmed in our conversation the night before that he was seeing someone, even though he admitted to not knowing where things were headed. The fact that he had a girlfriend was all I needed to know; it didn't matter where things were headed.

Can anybody find me somebody to love?

By lunchtime I had more than my fill of love songs and told Ricky I was going to get food. He slapped cash in my hand and I went to the hot dog joint across the street to get lunch for both of us. On my way out of the small takeout place, I bumped into Billy.

"Hey," he said, out of breath. "Just the person I wanted to see."

"Yeah?"

"I have an extra ticket to see REO Speedwagon tonight at the Amphitheatre, do you want to go?"

"Thanks, but I don't really feel like it." I pushed past him out the door and onto the sidewalk.

"Seth can't go anymore and Gina doesn't wanna go," he explained, following me.

I did love REO Speedwagon.

"I don't know Billy," I groaned. "It's Valentine's Day, and I really don't—"

"It's not a date, I swear. I just need someone to go with me."

I chewed my bottom lip as he waited for an answer. "If you promise it's not a date…."

"I promise," he said, bouncing back into the hot dog place to get his own lunch.

Billy picked me up after dinner, and when I got into his car he handed me a bouquet of flowers. I got out of the car and walked back to the house, but he ran after me.

383

"It's not a date, I swear!" he said, grabbing my hand and spinning me around. "But doesn't every girl deserve flowers on Valentine's Day? Even from a friend?"

I pouted for a few minutes because I didn't believe him, then relented and followed him back to the car. He was a complete gentlemen the entire evening, and never tried to touch me or hold my hand, or even kiss me goodnight when he brought me home. To say I was relieved was an understatement. I walked into the house and threw his flowers in the trash.

I was starving for live music and Billy knew it. Somehow he managed to come up with Amphitheatre tickets to see Rush the following week, UFO in March, Judas Priest in June, and he gave me Van Halen tickets for my birthday in July. Gina accompanied us to every concert except for Van Halen, and when Billy took me home it became clear why.

I thanked him for taking me to the show, but as I reached to open the car door he took my left hand and held me back. I turned to face him, my stomach lurching and my skin prickling.

"I know things haven't been easy with your mom," he said. "Hopefully getting out of the house to do fun stuff helps."

"We can't even be in the same room anymore."

"At least you still have your parents."

"I'm sorry. I can't imagine what it's like for you."

"My Aunt Gert is cool; she basically let's us do whatever we want."

"But how are you getting by? Still living in the house, paying bills?"

"My dad wasn't a banker for nothing," he chuckled. "He had trust funds set up for *everything*. Me and Gina are taken care of until we're twenty-five, the house is paid off, and the bank takes the property taxes out of a fund set up just for that."

"So you're gonna stay in the house?"

"Why not? Aunt Gert doesn't really need to live with us, but I think she's lonely. And she takes good care of us."

We talked about how well Gina had done in school that year, and how she was getting involved in school activities and making new friends. Even though she lost her second parent at the beginning of the year, she truly found her voice with her art,

384

expressing herself beautifully in paintings and drawings. At sixteen, she was turning into a gorgeous girl with a personality to match. She was my bright light.

"It's all because of you," Billy said. "You're the one who brought her out of her shell. It means the world to me."

"She's like the sister I never had."

Billy became quiet and it looked like his eyes were tearing up, but I couldn't be positive. I prayed he wouldn't start crying because I wouldn't be able to handle it. I was already sitting in the car with him longer than I ever intended.

"We've been having fun, haven't we?" he asked. I nodded, staring straight ahead. "I like spending time with you."

"Billy, don't—"

"Hear me out." He tugged on my hand to get me to face him. "Marry me."

I heard the words echo through my head like a pinball machine, but I didn't believe I was actually hearing them.

"I don't want to get married," I finally answered.

"I love you, Ruby. This is something that would be good for both of us."

"How?"

"It'll get you out of your parents' house, and you can move in with me and Gina. Aunt Gert can move out, and we can live however we want. I'll take care of you, Ruby. Whatever you want, it would be yours."

The thick July air was beginning to choke me.

"Gina loves you, too," he continued.

After a long, awkward silence, I said, "I can't marry you."

"Give me one good reason."

"I don't love you."

I got out of the car and sprinted to the front door, but Billy was right behind me. He spun me around and said, "*He* doesn't love you!" I fought so hard not to cry, but lost the battle quickly. "Everyone knows you found him in bed with a groupie. He doesn't give a shit about you!"

Pain seized my chest. How could Billy possibly know that? How could *anyone* know that?

"You don't know what you're talking about," I hissed, wiping the tears from my face.

"He doesn't love you, Ruby, but I do. I always have. We were meant to be together… you and me. It's fate. If you were meant to be with him, you wouldn't be here, lonely and miserable."

I went into the house and ran up to my room, hearing my mother screaming at me about something but ignoring her. I closed and locked my door, then picked up the phone. I frantically dialed Fuzzy's number, praying someone would answer. Hot tears burned my cheeks as I listened to the phone ring, but nobody picked up.

"Please somebody answer," I begged the air. "*Please.*"

Deflated, I hung up the phone and cried myself into such a state that I ended up running to the bathroom to vomit. My mom poked her head in to see if I was all right, and as I tried to wave her off she sat on the floor next to me to hold back my hair.

She rubbed my back as I continued to retch, and her voice was soothing as she said, "Whatever it is, it'll get better."

I flushed the toilet and leaned against the wall, the tears still falling. "Billy asked me to marry him."

My mom tried to look shocked, then asked, "What did you say?"

"I said no."

"But honey, why? You've been spending a lot of time with him since his father died."

"We weren't dating! He promised we were just friends."

"Would marrying Billy be so bad?" she asked. "His father made sure he and Gina were taken care of, and he works so hard. He'd take good care of you."

"Do you hate me? Are you trying to get rid of me?" I sobbed.

"Of course not! Why would you say that?"

"I don't love Billy. I can't marry someone I don't love."

My mom pulled me into her arms and cradled me like a child. "Sometimes love isn't part of the equation. Sometimes it's a matter of circumstance. You were crazy about him at one time… I'm sure you'd grow to love him as your husband."

I couldn't believe my ears! Had my mother gone completely insane?

I went to bed in a daze, the words of Billy and my mother swirling in my ears like a bad dream. I tried calling Fuzzy's number one more time because I *needed* to speak to Lonny, or at least get a message to him, but still no answer. I cried myself to sleep, knowing everything that was happening was my own fault. If I hadn't left the tour, if I hadn't pushed Lonny away, if I'd just *listened* to him, we'd probably still be together. I was twenty years old and ready to die.

Gina came into the store the next day to see me, and she was in tears as soon as she walked through the door. I brought her into the back room for some privacy and she started bawling. I asked her what happened, and her response stunned me.

"Why don't you like my brother?" she cried.

"What? I like Billy okay."

"He asked you to marry him and you said no. Is it because of me?"

"No Gina, it has nothing to do with you," I insisted.

"I know he can be a jerk sometimes, but he really loves you. You're all he ever talks about."

"We're not even dating," I mumbled.

"I miss my mom!" she wailed, bursting into ugly, guttural sobbing. "I need you, Ruby… please don't leave me because of Billy."

I put my arms around Gina in the hopes of comforting her, but it wasn't working. She continued to cry, causing Ricky to poke his head around the corner to see what was going on. I just shrugged and looked at him wide-eyed for help, but he wasn't getting involved with a crying teenage girl. I eventually managed to get Gina calmed down and asked if she wanted to hang out with us in the store, which she did for a little while, but when she didn't find anything new with Lonny's picture on it, decided to go home.

I rushed home from work, and as I ran upstairs to my bedroom I could hear my mother screaming at me. I locked the door and called Fuzzy's house, my heart racing when someone picked up.

"Hey doll," Fuzzy greeted.

I didn't waste any time. "Is Lonny there? I really need to talk to him."

"Sorry doll, he's with Rhonda this weekend. Getting in some vacation time before rehearsals start for the September tour."

Rhonda.

"Tour?"

"Yeah, we're doing a shorter big city tour before the double live album comes out at Christmastime. You should hear it doll, it's out of this world!"

"Of course it is!" I tried to answer cheerfully.

"Do you want me to give Lonny a message when he gets back?"

"Nothing important," I replied. "Don't even tell him I called."

Everything I wanted to say to him sounded stupid in my head now that his girlfriend had a name. I imagined she was beautiful and making him quite happy. I wondered if she had any idea how lucky she was.

I changed into a pair of shorts and a tank top and went for a walk. I stood in front of Billy's front door and took a deep breath before knocking. Aunt Gert answered the door and told me he was in his room, so I made my way through the house and stopped in his doorway. He was lying on his bed with his eyes closed wearing a set of headphones. He had no idea I was there, and I realized I didn't have to do it. I could turn around and go home and he'd never know the difference. He must have sensed my presence because he opened his eyes and sat up quickly, tossing his headphones on the bedside table.

"Hey Ruby," he greeted softly.

I stood like a statue, unable to find words.

"You okay?" he asked.

Thoughts of Lonny with a girlfriend and sounds of my mother screaming at me whirled in my head, making me dizzy.

"Yes." He pulled a face and I said, "I mean, yes I'll marry you."

Billy agreed to keep our engagement quiet until I was ready to make an announcement. We decided not to make a big deal out of it and planned to get married at the courthouse the end of

388

August. He said he would do whatever I wanted, and what I really wanted was to announce our marriage *after* it happened. He wanted me to quit my job so I could take care of things at the house and he could send Aunt Gert packing, but I refused. I told him my job was the one thing that was my own, and I wasn't giving it up for anything. He said he admired me for that.

Ricky opened a new store in the city, Vinyl Horse Chicago, probably four times the size of the one I worked in. He split his time between stores, and I hated the days he was in Chicago because he was so much fun to work with. But that left me in charge and I hired Gina to come in and work after school and on weekends. Ricky was on the lookout to hire a store manager for Chicago, but he wasn't satisfied with anybody he interviewed.

It was miserably hot the middle of August, and the air conditioner Ricky had in the store window wasn't working, so we were sweating bullets. He ran to the hardware store to purchase a few fans, but all they did was blow the hot air around. I told him he needed to stop being so cheap and get central air conditioning, but he scoffed as he picked up the phone to call the repairman.

I fanned myself with an old crossword magazine Ricky had behind the counter, and my mind wandered to my upcoming wedding. Billy and I decided to tell my parents, Joanie, Gina and his Aunt Gert that we were going to get married at the courthouse and my mother immediately stepped in and changed it to the chapel of our church instead. I begged her not to do that, but she wouldn't listen to me. I just wanted something simple and quick; neither one of us wanted it to be a big ordeal.

I brought my attention to a poster of Livingston Monroe on the wall and stared at Lonny's face. I imagined it was him I was going to marry and I smiled. I remembered what it felt like when he kissed me, and even the passage of time couldn't fade that memory.

Ricky interrupted my thoughts by asking, "Would you consider being the store manager in Chicago?"

"Me? No way… I don't want to go to the city. I like working close to home."

"It would mean a big raise."

"I don't even have a car."

389

"The train stops a few blocks from the store."

"Thanks, but no."

Ricky ran his hands through his thinning hair and said, "Well, could you help me out with one thing at least?"

I smiled. "Of course."

"I need you at the store tomorrow for an autograph signing."

All I could think of was the chaos of Livingston Monroe's autograph signing and I immediately felt my stomach clench.

"Come on Ruby, you know how they work, and you're the only one I trust to do it right."

"Does the air conditioning work there?" I teased.

"Yes!"

"Okay, fine," I grumbled. "But I'm not going to like it. And I hate the train. And I want the weekend off."

Ricky laughed and said, "Deal. You can thank me later."

"So who's the mystery guest?"

"Peter Summersby."

Ricky closed Vinyl Horse the next day for two reasons — the air conditioning was still not fixed, and we both needed to be on hand for the Peter Summersby autograph signing. I knew it probably wasn't going to be as chaotic as Livingston Monroe's, but the store would be crawling with people nonetheless.

Ricky drove me in his car, and based on what I'd seen that one trip, I had no desire whatsoever to drive into the city every day, no matter how much I loved my job. He had several employees on hand for the day, and as soon as we walked in he told them I was in charge. Some of them were much older than I was and looked at me like I had sprouted horns.

Peter's latest album, *Bright Light*, was hanging all over the store, even from the ceiling. Posters with his smiling face graced the walls, and his management team sent over a stack of black and white photos for people to get autographed as well. I set up ropes

390

to keep the line of people contained throughout the store as they came in the front door and would exit through the side door.

Peter wasn't supposed to arrive at the store until two o'clock, but people started lining up before noon. As the clock snaked closer to his arrival time, my stomach did somersaults. I couldn't wait to see him, and I wondered what his reaction would be when he saw me. I wore a simple sundress to combat the heat, but I also wanted to look nicer than I did on a daily basis. It didn't go unnoticed by Ricky.

"I've never seen you wear a dress," he teased.

"I wanted to look nice... for the occasion."

He gave me a wink and a smile and said, "He should be here any minute."

I followed him to the back of the store and my heart thumped wildly as part of the security team Ricky hired for the day escorted Peter through the door. His agent introduced himself and Peter to Ricky, and I stood like a concrete block waiting to catch his eye. He was more beautiful than I remembered and his smile was even brighter than before, if that was even possible.

My heart stopped when he looked my way and he immediately pulled me into his arms for a warm hug, which was something I desperately needed. He held me at arm's length and smiled his million dollar smile as he took me in.

"Aren't you a sight for sore eyes!" he finally said. "I had no idea you'd be here!"

He hugged me again, giving me a chance to drink him in and enjoy the physicality of it all. I was truly happy for the first time since I could remember. He smelled so good and his hair was soft against my face, and he was suddenly ripped away from me by his agent, who said he needed to get started. Peter quickly introduced me as an old friend, but his agent didn't care. He looked at me like I was just another groupie waiting to get my claws in Peter. It was obvious he wanted to get in and out as soon as possible.

Peter signed autographs and took photos with his fans until the last person walked out the door at six o'clock. He was genuinely happy to meet everyone, and took his time with each person that stepped up to the table. As soon as Peter was finished, his agent was ready to rush him back out the door and off to who knew where.

"Brad," Peter said, patting him gently on the chest. "I'd like to catch up with my friend Ruby. You go ahead without me, I'll find another way back to the hotel."

Brad sighed and replied, "I'll leave the limo for you. I'll take a taxi."

"I'm starving," Peter said. "Would you like to have dinner with me?"

I smiled and nodded. There wasn't anything I wanted more.

"You'll have to help me out," he chuckled. "I'm not familiar with the territory."

"Yeah, sure! What are you in the mood for?"

Peter took me by the hand and walked me toward the door. "Don't wait up for us," he teased.

"Ruby, how will you get home?" Ricky asked with a sly grin.

"I'll manage."

Peter helped me into the limo and sat smiling at me. The limo driver asked where he wanted to go and he said, "Oh, I'm not sure. Ruby?"

"What do you have a taste for?"

Peter told the chauffeur to drive around, then raised the privacy window. He put his hands on either side of my face and whispered, "I have a taste for your lips, if that's all right."

He pulled me to him, his lips like velvet against my own, and I was floating high above the earth. His kisses were soft and gentle and my body was responding. I hadn't been with anyone since Lonny, and I was making Billy wait until our wedding night. As he continued to kiss me he whispered, "What do you have a taste for, sweet Ruby?"

"Room service," I whispered against his mouth, which quickly turned into a smile.

Peter lowered the privacy window and said, "We'll just be heading back to the hotel, please."

We sat quietly grinning like fools, his hand on my knee, stroking my skin so softly he gave me goosebumps. I watched his face as I slipped off my panties and shoved them in my bag; he bit

392

his lower lip, knowing perfectly well what my intentions were. I just smiled.

After helping me out of the limousine at the hotel, he grabbed my hand and we sprinted to the elevator. As soon as the doors closed he pressed me against the wall and kissed me with great urgency, his hands hovering at the hem of my dress, but never venturing underneath. As soon as we reached his floor, he pulled me quickly down the hallway to his room where he fumbled with the key. This made me giggle. As soon as we got into the room he had me up against the door, his hands pulling my dress up and over my head. I frantically unbuttoned his shirt, which he threw on the floor, then as he was unhooking my bra I unbuckled his belt and opened his jeans. I marveled at his flawless body as he peeled off his pants, then he lifted me up and plowed into me so forcefully I had to catch my breath. Anybody walking in the vicinity of his room would know exactly what was happening as we repeatedly banged up against the door, and that made it even hotter. We were both so worked up that sweet release happened quickly and he carried me to the bed, where we collapsed in a sweaty heap, our chests rising and falling heavily as we tried to catch our breath.

I rolled onto my stomach and propped myself up with my arms, looking down at him. "How long are you in town?" I asked, grinning.

He laughed his sexy, hearty laugh, exposing his perfect teeth and delicious looking neck. "I'm flying home to England tomorrow to see my mother."

I pouted.

Peter picked up the phone and dialed. "Brad," he said, "change my flight to Sunday. No, no, no, *you* work for *me*. Make it happen." He hung up the phone and asked if I was ready for dinner.

As we sat down to eat I asked, "Whatever happened to your television show? I looked all over for it, but never found it."

Peter rolled his eyes. "Never aired. The networks didn't think the public would be interested in a mind-reading veterinarian. My sidekick was a St. Bernard, and even he couldn't convince them."

"I'd be interested."

"Of course you would be, love. You like me." We both laughed and he asked, "Were you at my show last night?"

I gasped. "No! I didn't know anything about it! Where?"

"ChicagoFest. It was loads of fun; great crowd. I asked Lonny to mention it to you."

I frowned. "He probably forgot. His new girlfriend, you know. I don't talk to him very much."

"Working in a record store I'm surprised you didn't hear about it yourself."

I hesitated before saying, "I've been a little preoccupied."

"Everything okay?"

"I'm getting married next Friday."

Peter almost choked on the food he just put in his mouth. He stared at me with his gorgeous blue eyes and I tried to smile. "Aren't you a little scamp…."

"Would you have done anything different if you knew?"

He chuckled. "Not in the slightest."

"I didn't think so."

I got up and sat on his lap, running my fingers across his toned chest. "Will you teach me everything you know?"

"For your new husband?"

"For *me*."

I kissed him softly on the mouth and he slid his hands down my back and squeezed my behind. He kissed me deeply, and I could soon feel his desire growing underneath my leg. We hopped into bed for another romp while our dinner got cold.

I woke with a start and the room was pitch black. I frantically tried to turn the light on, causing Peter to pull the covers over his head once I did. He peeked out at me with one half-opened eye. "Problem?"

I picked up the phone and dialed my parents' number. "Mom, I'm staying in the city with friends from the store. I'll be home sometime Sunday, okay?"

"Do you even have clean clothes?" she asked.

"It's fine."

I wasn't listening to anything she said as Peter disappeared under the sheet, kissing my chest and working his way down the

394

rest of my body. When I felt his mouth wander between my legs, I said, "Gotta go!" and hung up the phone quickly.

I reached to turn off the light, but Peter threw off the covers and said, "Don't. I want to see all of you."

I suddenly became self-conscious of my body and tried to cover myself with my hands and arms. "I'm not sure about *that*...."

"You asked me to teach you."

"I know but—"

I must have looked terrified because he smiled and kissed my belly. "Tell you what," he said, stretching out next to me. "Let's take a shower. Maybe you're just not ready for that yet."

He nibbled on my neck and I asked, "Do people really like it?"

"It's one of life's greatest pleasures," he whispered against my neck. He got out of bed and I watched his perfection walk to the bathroom. A few seconds later he came back to the bed and took me by the hand, pulling me into the bathroom with him.

He turned on the shower and I said, "Oh... you meant together...."

The next morning I woke up to find Peter sitting in a chair strumming his guitar and smiling at me. "You sleep okay?" he asked.

"Yeah."

"Lonny told me what happened. Why you left."

I was mortified. "Why would he tell you?"

"Does it matter? I was happy the two of you finally figured things out."

"You were?"

"Of course. I know how you feel about him. What I don't understand is why you're going to marry someone you don't love."

"How do you know I don't love him?"

Peter laughed, setting his guitar down and crawling back in bed with me. "Because you're spending the weekend in a hotel shagging me."

I covered my face with my hands and groaned. "It's complicated."

"Does Lonny know?"

395

"His mom told him." I swallowed hard and asked, "Have you ever been in love?"

"Once. She didn't quite feel the same, but she loved my money." For the first time since meeting him, Peter looked devastated.

I touched his mouth with my fingertip and said, "Someday you'll find your true happy."

"You sound like Marilyn."

"Are you still friends with her?"

"Of course."

"Tell her I'll never forgive her for abandoning me. True friends don't just disappear and never talk to you again."

Peter was shocked at my statement. He fumbled over his words as he tried to come up with lame excuses about why Marilyn couldn't tell me she left Fuzzy, or why even after their divorce she hadn't reached out to me.

"You were working with the band," he explained. "She knew how close you were to Fuzzy and she didn't want you to think badly about him. Then with the passage of time... well, you know."

"I'm still mad at her."

"Look," he said, his hands beginning to wander into pleasurable territory. "We're in bed... naked... I don't really want to talk about Marilyn or Lonny, or anyone else for that matter. I still have so much to teach you."

By the time our weekend together came to an end, I was sad to say goodbye to Peter, but I was the happiest I'd been in a very long time. He insisted I accompany him to the airport in the limousine, which would then take me back home. We managed one last shag, as he called it, on the drive and it was the most intense connection we had the entire weekend. The limited time, the possibility of getting caught, our last moments together, and the way he forced me to keep my eyes fixed on his the whole time was so powerful we both erupted in a thundering climax that took a few minutes to recover from.

As we pulled up to the curb where his security entourage waited, he held my face in his hands and smiled. "My sweet Ruby," he said. "Thank you for a lovely weekend."

"Thank you. For everything."

He touched the turquoise pendant I still wore around my neck. "My mother would love you."

I grinned. "It's too bad we aren't each other's true happy."

"Indeed."

"You're my bright light, Peter. It's because of you I can smile now."

He kissed me sweetly for the last time, his mouth soft and velvety.

"Until we meet again." He lowered the privacy window to let the driver know he was ready, and in an instant he was gone. I watched as the security guys towered over him in height and size, their bulk swallowing him whole before my eyes. I gave the driver my address and my unforgettable weekend with Peter Summersby was officially over.

I didn't wear a traditional wedding dress, opting instead for a simple, ankle-length sundress my mother helped me sew just in time for the big day. I carried a small bouquet of wildflowers that matched the flowers I wore as a makeshift headband in my hair. As my father walked me down the aisle I could see Billy standing at the altar, looking handsome in his suit. Seth stood beside him as best man, and Molly waited for me as maid of honor.

The music from the organ seemed to be unusually loud, but that was due to the fact the chapel only had a handful of people on either side attending the wedding, probably about fifteen in total.

Every time I found myself feeling sick or wanting to run screaming out of the building, I thought about Peter. He automatically brought a smile to my face, making it easy for others to believe I was truly happy. And when I thought about the special time I spent with Peter, I was.

Before I knew it I was Mrs. William Downey, and my new husband leaned in for a quick kiss. Our small gathering of loved ones smiled and clapped for us as we headed down the aisle to the back of the church. We had a small receiving line as each person congratulated us before heading out the door, with my mother being the first in line.

"I have to get to the house for the caterer," she said, kissing me on the cheek and rushing out the door.

Everyone was soon coping with the blistering heat as they left the church, eager to get back into the air conditioning, whether in their cars or my parents' house, where our informal reception was taking place. Billy's car was decorated with streamers and empty cans and the words "Just Married" written in soap across the back window. He held my hand tightly as he walked me to the passenger side of the car, opening the door for me. It was then I noticed my mother hadn't even left yet, talking to someone in a car I didn't recognize.

"Who's my mom talking to?" I asked Billy.

"Probably someone we didn't invite to the wedding," he joked. "Come on, let's go."

I watched her a little bit longer, wondering who could have stopped her in her tracks the way she was rushing to get back to the house.

"My bride is sweating," Billy said.

I smiled as he helped me into the car and we were soon on the road, the sound of obnoxious empty cans hitting the pavement as we drove.

Most of us beat my mother back to the house and when she finally arrived, she was all out of sorts. I knew it was because her plans were interrupted by whoever was in that car, and she would likely not recover the rest of the day. That's how she operated — she always had a plan, and if things didn't go exactly as she intended, she was wrecked until she slept it off.

I went into the kitchen to help her organize the food and caught her crying. I touched her arm to let her know I was there.

"Mom, are you okay?"

She quickly wiped the tears from her face. "I just can't believe my little girl is married," she said. "Now get out of here and go be with your husband."

"Who were you talking to in that car?"

She smiled and said, "Mr. Riley, your grade school gym teacher. He happened to be driving by and sends his best wishes."

2011

I turned to look at Lonny, whose face was covered in as many tears as my own. "Why couldn't you ever just tell me?" I cried.

He placed his hands lovingly against my cheeks and whispered, "I didn't know how. That's why I kept begging you to read my journals. Everything I couldn't verbalize was written there for you."

He was right. He asked me to read his journals many times and I always refused because I felt it was too personal. Had I just listened to him, things could have turned out much differently for both of us.

He gazed into my eyes as his thumbs gently caressed my cheeks and I waited, breathless, for what he would do next. He leaned forward and brushed his mouth against mine, pulling me in for the kiss that would mend the pieces of my shattered heart. He tasted like cigarettes and cheap beer and it was the sweetest thing I'd ever known.

I opened my eyes when he pulled away, his hands still against my face. "You're the love of my life, Roo. I'm sorry. For *everything*."

"It wasn't all your fault," I cried. "So much of it happened because of me, and I'm so sorry. But I never stopped loving you. *Never.*"

"Happy birthday, Roo."

"Happy birthday, Lonny." I kissed him softly and whispered, "You tried to stop my wedding?"

Lonny took my hand and led me to the bed, where we sat facing each other.

"My mom told me you were getting married," he began. "But she was wasted and I didn't believe her. At three in the morning the day of your wedding, the phone was ringing off the hook. I ignored it, thinking it was for Fuzzy, and my girlfriend was with me."

Rhonda.

400

"Anyway, the phone kept ringing and I finally got up to answer it. It was Marilyn. I thought she wanted to talk to Fuzzy and told her to call back at a normal hour, but she yelled at me when I tried to hang up. She told me she had just talked to Peter, who told her you were getting married."

"Good old Peter," I said with a smile.

"How would Peter know you were getting married?"

"Please... continue."

"I hung up the phone and got dressed, then raced to the airport. I felt sick thinking you were going to marry Billy."

"But you had a girlfriend."

"If I could convince you that I was the one who loved you, it didn't matter. But I was too late."

I grasped his hands as I noticed his eyes were wet with tears.

"Just as I pulled up to the church I saw your mom running toward her car. I had to blast the horn to get her attention, and I thought she was going to ignore me at first."

"Was she surprised to see you?"

"She was pissed and told me you were already married."

"I saw her talking to you," I said, my own eyes tearing up. "But I didn't know it was you."

"She told me how happy you were, and that I better not even think about trying to talk to you. She said she loved me, but that I already ruined your life once and she wouldn't let it happen again."

"I'd have gone with you."

"What are you saying?"

"If you told me you loved me at any time during my marriage, I would've gone with you. You're the only one I've ever loved."

"Then why did you marry him?"

I looked down at our hands, my vision blurred by tears. "I agreed to marry him because I didn't think you'd ever love me. I would have never left the tour if you told me you loved me. It's all I ever wanted to hear."

He yanked me toward him, pulling me into an embrace so tight I almost couldn't breathe. "I was so immature," he mumbled. "And scared and stupid."

"So was I."

"Why didn't you tell me you were getting married? Why did I have to find out through Marilyn, who found out through Peter?"

I pulled away from Lonny so I could breathe and flopped on my back. I looked up at him and said, "I didn't think you'd care."

"But Peter knew and I didn't?"

"Peter did an autograph signing at the record store a week before the wedding. That's how he knew about it." Lonny lay down beside me and I turned to face him.

"I saw you when you came out of the church. You were so beautiful, and you looked so happy."

"I got really good at pretending to be happy."

"I'm so sorry, Roo."

"So are you saying my mom knew you loved me and kept it a secret all these years?"

1981

Billy called me at work one bitter day in December to tell me he had something special planned for the evening, and I asked Molly if she'd make me up to look nice. She was excited to play with my face even though I hated wearing makeup, but I decided to try and make an effort for my husband since he had gone out of his way to do something nice for me.

"You look really pretty," Gina told me after Molly left.

"Do you know where we're going tonight?"

She grinned. "I promised not to tell."

Billy rushed into the house to change his clothes, quickly kissing me before heading to the bedroom. "The limo will be here soon!" I heard him shout as he disappeared.

"Limo? Am I underdressed?" I was wearing a nice pair of jeans and my favorite soft, pink sweater with pearls around the neckline.

"No, it's perfect," Gina said.

Billy rushed back out, wearing a nice button-down shirt tucked into a pair of jeans, accented by a leather belt. He kissed me and told me how nice I looked, then saw the limousine pull up and the three of us rushed to put on our coats and get outside. I got into the limousine and found my parents and Joanie already inside. It was then I realized what was happening. We were on our way to the Livingston Monroe concert. Though my stomach clenched because I hadn't seen any of them in over a year and a half, I shrieked with excitement when Billy announced what the surprise was. I thanked him with a hug and a kiss, then tried to mentally prepare myself for seeing Lonny.

"Was it really a surprise, Ruby?" Gina asked hopefully.

"Big surprise," I answered happily.

I thought we were going to see the show and head back home, but I should have known better. We were immediately escorted backstage where the band was involved in a raucous game of ping pong — Lonny and Fuzzy against Mitch and Benji. My heart swelled when I saw them; so full of love and happy memories. I stayed in the back, not wanting to be the first person they saw. I didn't want anyone watching me, or my reaction to any of the guys.

Lonny immediately stopped what he was doing when he saw his mother, greeting her excitedly when he pulled her into his arms for a hug. Then he embraced my mom and dad, then Gina, and I found I couldn't look at him as he quickly said hello to Billy and shook his hand. I finally got up the nerve to look at him and my insides melted. He no longer looked like a boy; he was a man. His beautiful smile appeared and he pulled me in for a hug I never wanted to end.

I could feel tears pricking my eyes until I heard Fuzzy shout, "Is that my Ruby?"

I pulled away from Lonny and sprinted to Fuzzy, jumping into his arms as he lifted me off the ground, kissing me on the cheek. "It's so good to see you, doll," he said.

"My turn, my turn!" Mitch hollered. I rushed to his awaiting arms next as he kissed my cheek and said, "We miss you, baby."

I greeted Benji next and asked him how Wanda and Calvin were doing. "Calvin is growing like a weed, and Wanda is clean. I'm really proud of her."

I noticed the way my mother was looking at me, and she didn't look happy. It was hard to describe what she looked like, but Lonny interrupted my thoughts when he ushered everyone into the dressing room. I couldn't help craning my neck and looking behind me, wondering if any groupies would be making an appearance.

"So Ruby," Fuzzy said, handing me a can of soda. "I understand congratulations are in order."

My eyes found Lonny and he immediately began having a side conversation with his mother. "Yes," I finally found my voice. "Billy and I got married in August."

The guys congratulated us as Billy put his arm around me so tightly it hurt. Between my mother looking like she was going to throw up and Billy acting like a macho man, I wondered what alternate reality I was in. Lonny asked Gina if she wanted to take a peek at the stage and she jumped at the chance. Billy looked torn, unable to decide if he should follow his sister or stay with me. Billy trusted Lonny so little he chose to follow his sister, which was a relief for me because then I was able to breathe. Which made me wonder why Billy would go to all that trouble to bring us to the show despising Lonny the way he did.

I mentioned to the guys that my father was the ping pong champion his senior year of high school and Mitch jumped up and said, "Come on pop, show me what you got." Never one to back down from a challenge, he followed Mitch out to the table to show him exactly what he had. Benji followed, then my mother and Joanie.

"Mitch isn't that good," Fuzzy laughed. "You doin' okay, doll?"

I pasted on the smile that became so familiar and said, "Yeah, I'm okay."

Fuzzy was just about to say something when Howard entered the room. "I heard you were here, but I didn't believe it," he said.

I got up and greeted him with a warm hug. "I was hoping I'd see you."

Lonny returned with Billy and Gina and I purposely sat on the couch next to Fuzzy so Billy couldn't act like a caveman claiming his property in front of all the other men. Lonny stood as far away from me as possible, looking over the food trays.

"Lonny, how's Rhonda?" I asked, trying to make conversation, but way too curious about his love life.

Lonny popped a grape in his mouth and shrugged. "She dumped me."

I was shocked at first, wondering who in their right mind would dump Lonny, then remembered I did just that. Then I wondered if he cheated on Rhonda.

"Don't worry about this kid," Fuzzy said. "What's the new girl's name? Angela?"

Lonny turned several shades of red before saying, "Yeah, Angela."

"That's good," I said with a smile. "You deserve to be happy, Lonny."

He raised an eyebrow and nodded as if he didn't believe my sentiment to be genuine.

405

The rest of our group barreled back into the room, Mitch announcing, "Baby, your dad was on fire! Caught me on a bad day…."

"Well," Howard's voice thundered through the room. "Ticket holders should probably head to their seats now."

I gave all the guys a hug before we headed to the auditorium, but just before the door closed, I was pulled back into the dressing room. Howard poked his head out to say, "Ruby will meet you at your seats."

"We just wanted some time alone with you, doll," Fuzzy said, grinning.

"You're still part of the band," Mitch added. "You always will be."

We all gathered into a circle with our arms around each other, but Benji wiggled away from me to make sure I was next to Lonny instead. Howard gave a speech about the energy and spirit of the band, and how they were on top of the world because they were brought together by fate, making powerful music that transcended age groups and genres. Howard was the first to pull away and head out the door. I hugged Benji and he followed, then Mitch, then Fuzzy, who lingered much longer than the others.

"You belong with us, doll," he whispered in my ear. I smiled as he walked away.

Lonny stood in front of me, unsure what to do. "Are you happy, Roo?"

"I'm as happy as I deserve to be."

He pulled me into his arms and we held each other for what seemed an inappropriately long time. I closed my eyes and soaked up everything I could — his arms around me, the softness of his skin, the smell of his hair, the feel of his breath on my neck. I knew it would be a long time before I'd see him again, and I wanted to memorize everything.

"Angela's a lucky girl," I whispered.

He pulled away and said, "Yeah, well, I don't know about that."

As he caught up with the rest of the band, I made my way to the auditorium and sat in my front row seat next to Billy, who immediately put his arm around my shoulders and whispered, "What was that all about?"

"Band stuff. Like old times."

He didn't respond, and he didn't release his hold on my shoulders. The house lights went down and the audience jumped to their feet screaming. I did the same, forcing Billy to either let me go or join me. He stood up with the rest of us, but I knew he didn't really want to be there. The curtains opened and the band exploded into their first song, giving me goosebumps and a joy I hadn't experienced since my last show with them. It was indescribable.

Gina and I screamed and danced and cheered and everything else we could during the show, while Billy continually tried to wrap his arm around my shoulders or my waist too tightly. He hated that the band paid attention to me, but what did he expect? They were my friends, and I was in the front row! Even though we were in the front row, there was a barrier of about twenty-five feet between us and the stage, so it wasn't like they could reach out and touch me.

I thought it was odd that Lonny didn't sing "Take Me Home" before the encore and wondered if they decided to scratch it from their live set. I was disappointed, knowing it was a popular part of the live show. Gina turned and asked if I thought they would perform it for the encore. As I opened my mouth to speak, pain I couldn't describe seized my chest and I had to sit down.

"Ruby, are you okay?" Gina asked.

Billy was all over me. "Ruby, what's wrong?"

I clutched my chest and leaned over, trying to control my breathing. Something was wrong, but it wasn't with me.

"Ruby," Billy called, his hands all over me. "Tell me what's wrong."

"You're smothering me," I grumbled. He backed off and I continued to clutch my chest until the band returned to the stage, which took much longer than it should have.

I stood up as Lonny walked out slowly, wearing my favorite bright yellow tie with red polka dots, and sunglasses. The sunglasses told me he must have been suffering from one of his headaches. He pointed at me and smiled, and I realized my hand was still grasping my sweater, right over my heart.

407

Mitch introduced Lonny, and the band went right into "Take Me Home." It was such a popular song in their live set they decided to move it to the encore, which made perfect sense.

As the band came to the front of the stage for their final bow, Fuzzy leaned far over to say something to one of the security guards, who, after the band disappeared, came to give me a message.

"They want you backstage, miss."

"What the hell, Ruby?" Billy hissed. "Gina has school tomorrow!"

"I'm sure it's only to say goodbye."

The security guard led us all backstage and Fuzzy was quick to grab me and rush me into the dressing room, where Lonny was in a heap on the floor. I took off his sunglasses and the tie and tossed them on a chair, asking Fuzzy to help get him into the bathroom.

I could hear Joanie asking, "What's wrong with my boy?" as I followed Fuzzy into the bathroom.

"Hold him over the toilet," I instructed Fuzzy.

Lonny was covered in sweat and white as a ghost, and for the first time I'd ever seen, seemingly unconscious. I shoved my fingers down his throat in the hopes he would vomit, but nothing happened.

"Hey kid, Ruby's here," Fuzzy said. "She's gonna take care of you."

"Lonny, can you hear me?" I shouted.

I heard Billy say, "He's probably on drugs."

"Everybody out!" Howard bellowed, pushing Billy, Gina and our parents out the door and closing it behind them.

Lonny groaned then began vomiting into the toilet, much to my relief. Mitch brought me a bucket of ice and some towels and I sat on the bathroom floor with Lonny until he stopped throwing up. I leaned up against the wall and cradled his head in my lap, icing it as I always used to do. I wondered how he'd been managing his headaches without me around to take care of him. I imagined he always had a pretty girl around who was more than happy to take care of things.

408

I looked up when Howard opened the dressing room door to let everyone back in. Everyone in my group stood staring at me in disbelief, having no idea what was wrong with Lonny.

"He gets these headaches," I whispered, trying to explain.

"Ruby, we have to go," Billy said. "The limo is waiting for us."

I looked at my mother, whose mouth was hidden by her fingers. I thought I saw tears welling in her eyes, but I couldn't be sure from where I sat on the floor. "I'll stay with Ruby," she said. "You all go home; we'll take a taxi later."

I wasn't really surprised that Joanie didn't offer to stick around, knowing she was probably anxious to get home and have a drink before going to bed. They all said goodbye, and Billy made sure to squeeze in a kiss before they walked out the door. I was relieved that he was gone, unable to handle the angry looks he was giving me while I was only trying to help Lonny.

Lonny lifted his arm and weakly motioned for me to come closer so I could hear him. I bent myself in half to lean over as far as I needed to be close to his face.

"You knew something was wrong," he spoke slowly. "I saw your face... your hand on your heart...."

"I felt your pain. I almost collapsed."

"You belong with us," he whispered, so softly I could barely hear him.

"I have responsibilities here," I whispered just as softly back to him, wiping his sweaty hair away from his face.

"He doesn't love you."

But do you?

"I made a commitment," I whispered, tears stinging my eyes. "And I promised Gina I would take care of her."

I straightened my body and leaned against the wall, catching a glimpse of my mother. She was watching us and she was crying. I mouthed, "He'll be okay," but she didn't seem convinced.

When Lonny was feeling a bit better, Fuzzy helped him off the bathroom floor and put him on the couch. He sat crouched over, holding his head.

"Time to get this kid back to the hotel," Fuzzy said.

I asked Howard to point me in the direction of a phone so I could call a taxi and he said, "It's already taken care of."

"I don't want you to leave yet," Lonny mumbled.

I handed him his shirt and said, "It's late. You need to get some sleep before you hit the road tomorrow."

Fuzzy was brilliant and probably the only one in the world who understood the dynamic that was Lonny and myself, in whatever form it happened to be. We all strolled out the backstage door to the limousine and taxi that awaited us. Howard said goodbye and got into the taxi, followed by Benji, then Mitch, who gave me a long hug and a quick kiss before disappearing behind them.

The taxi took off and Fuzzy said, "Your chariot awaits."

Fuzzy sat on one side of the limo next to my mother and I sat on the other with Lonny stretched out and his head in my lap. I looked at Fuzzy, who was smiling at me and I mouthed, "Thank you." He winked and nodded, knowing how much I appreciated as much time with Lonny as possible.

I combed Lonny's hair with my fingers and noticed he was sporting sideburns. "Lonny, are those sideburns?" I asked.

He opened his eyes a little bit to look up at me and smiled. "You like 'em?"

"I didn't think you could grow them," I teased.

"I shave my face now, too," he quietly joked.

My sweet faced boy.

When we got to my parents' house, my mother kissed Lonny and myself goodbye and Fuzzy walked her to the front door. I looked down at Lonny, who was looking up at me with slits for eyes. He grinned and bopped my nose with his finger.

"I'm sorry," he whispered.

"For what?"

"Things didn't turn out like we planned."

"No they didn't, but promise you won't forget about me. I can't lose you."

"I could never forget about you, Roo. I—"

Fuzzy hopped back into the limo saying, "Your mom okay? She was bawling all over me before she went in the house."

410

"She's worried about Lonny," I assured him. "They've never seen one of his headaches in action. And this one was the worst I've ever seen."

I bent over and rested my forehead against Lonny's as the limo headed to Billy's house, stopping in front of the driveway. "Thank you for letting us spend time with you tonight," I whispered.

"It was my idea."

"You set it all up?"

"With Gina's help."

That bastard.

"Thank you," I whispered, kissing his forehead. His lips were so close, and the temptation to kiss them was far too great. I thought about my lying, manipulative husband, who was probably watching through the window at that very moment waiting for me to come in the house. My fingertips caressed Lonny's cheek as a tear fell from his eye. I leaned over and pressed my mouth against his, said goodbye, and got out of the limo.

"I'll walk you to the door," Fuzzy said.

I saw the garage door opening and replied, "It's okay. He's waiting for me."

I said goodbye to Fuzzy with a hug and made my way through the garage, into the kitchen. "I was wondering if you were ever coming home," Billy grumbled. "It's two in the morning."

"Lonny was really sick," I replied. "I've never seen him that bad."

"How convenient."

I pushed past him and went to the bedroom to get ready for bed. He was right behind me, and as soon as I went into the bathroom I saw him in the mirror as he grabbed the back of my head.

"Make sure you wash that whore makeup off your face," he said angrily.

I turned to face him, shocked. "I wanted to look nice for you," I explained. "For our special night."

"You wanted to look nice for *him*."

411

"I didn't even know I was going to see him!" He said nothing else, but glared at me with a look that scared the hell out of me. "You did it on purpose."

"Did what?"

"Brought me to see Lonny so you could torture me."

Billy reached back and slapped me across the face so hard I lost my balance, hitting the wall and crashing to the floor.

"And that's the *last* time you'll see him."

2011

I got up from the bed and paced the room. "My mom," I fumed, "knew how miserable I was all this time and *never* told me?"

Lonny sat up. "Roo, please don't be mad at your mom."

"She could have changed everything! So many things could have been avoided if she'd just told me what she knew!"

"Roo—"

"Being married to Billy... moving to New York... your *accident*! So many things didn't have to happen. We could've been together all these years like we were supposed to be!"

Lonny grabbed my hand and stopped me in my tracks. Sitting at the edge of the bed he pulled me toward him until I stood right in front of him. He looked up at me and said, "Hey. We can't change the past. We're together now and we have our whole future ahead of us."

"My mom stole our lives away from us," I cried.

"She was only trying to protect you."

"Protect me? I was living in hell! And what about everything you went through?"

"Roo, there was just too much love."

"What the hell does that even mean?"

Lonny sighed and asked me to sit down. "I don't know, Roo. I think we had deep love for each other, but we were so young we didn't know what it all meant. We didn't know how to process it. And when obstacles came up we got scared and backed down instead of fighting for each other. It was easier to push each other away. I think we needed to live through our trials and go through the pain in order to appreciate what true love really is. *Our* true love."

"Leonard Winter, you've always been my true happy."

"And you've always been mine, Ruby Winter."

I woke up to soft sunlight and Lonny snoring beside me, both of us on top of the bed and fully clothed. We had spent the rest of the after midnight hours kissing, cuddling, and enjoying each other's company. I looked at my phone and it was seven o'clock in the morning. I gently poked him until he was awake.

"My mother's going to kill me," I groaned.

"Isn't she the one who said don't come back until we figured things out?" he grumbled, never opening his eyes.

"Yes, but…."

"Go back to sleep."

"It's our birthday. My dad is probably already up and getting ready to make his red, white and blue pancakes."

Lonny's eyes flew open as he said, "Pancakes?"

"Same ones he makes every year," I said, knowing they were always Lonny's favorite.

He stretched as I got up to use the bathroom. When I came back out he was standing on the balcony smoking a cigarette. He came back in when he was finished and wrapped his arms tightly around me, kissing the top of my head.

"I'll hop in the shower and meet you at the house," he said.

He kissed me so passionately I didn't want to leave, and thoughts of joining him in the shower were overwhelming.

"I love you," I said when I pulled away.

"I love you, too."

I ran out the door and drove home, saying hello to my father as I sprinted past the kitchen on my way upstairs to my room. "Lonny joining us for breakfast?" he shouted after me.

"Yes!"

I took a shower and headed back downstairs, where Lonny was just wheeling his mom into the kitchen. Dad was making his annual Independence Day pancakes and eggs, and my mom was buttering the toast. Lonny kissed his mother on the cheek as he set her up at the table, then walked toward me with a huge smile on his face. He took my face in his hands and kissed me on the mouth, lingering long enough to let our parents know our relationship had taken a completely different turn. I could feel my face flush as he pulled away and I saw three sets of parental eyes watching us.

414

Joanie gasped, thankfully taking all the attention away from me. She had tears running down her face and Lonny rushed to her side, asking if she was okay. She nodded and grunted, trying desperately to communicate without words.

"I think she's overcome with joy," my mother said.

Joanie nodded, trying to smile. I wrapped my arms around her and said, "So am I, Mom."

My father cleared his throat and in an overly masculine voice said, "Lonny, what are your intentions with my daughter?"

Lonny was fixing us each a cup of coffee and answered, "Well... Dad, I'd like permission to date my sister."

We all burst into bellowing laughter. My mom passed out the dishes and we all sat down to eat breakfast as a family; something we hadn't done in many years. I looked around the table at my family — my parents smiling at each other and Lonny helping his mom eat before ever touching his own food. I was surrounded by so much love it was overwhelming. Lonny caught me watching him and winked, patting my leg under the table.

After breakfast I helped my mother clean up the kitchen while everyone else went outside to the patio. I washed the dishes as she dried and put them away.

"You guys should think about getting a dishwasher," I teased. "Get with the times."

"Your father keeps trying to talk me into it, but I honestly love washing dishes. It's relaxing for me."

I watched Lonny through the window over the sink and felt a lump forming in my throat. "Lonny told me everything. I can't believe you've been lying to me all these years."

My mom was taken aback, almost dropping the dish she had in her hands. "Ruby, you had *just* gotten married. I wasn't about to let Lonny go running after you and make a scene."

"Because you knew I'd go with him."

I watched as her face paled. "What?"

"He told you he loved me and you threatened him to stay away from me because you *knew* I'd leave with him."

"You were just kids. I thought it would've been a huge mistake."

"You were the adult; you could've made everything right."

"Ruby, I don't know what you want me to say. I can't change the past."

I turned to look her in the eyes. "No, but maybe you can explain to me why you robbed us of a life together."

"That's not fair."

"What's not fair is that I spent thirty years with Billy when you had the power to change it. You *knew* I didn't love him. You *knew* I loved Lonny."

My mother sat at the kitchen table and asked me to sit with her. I took the towel from her and dried my hands as I sat across from her.

"You have to understand the position I was in at the time," she began. "And as parents, we don't always make the right decisions. We aren't perfect."

"Please get to the point."

"When you came home early from the tour, all I could see was my broken little girl. Broken doesn't even cover it; you were shattered. You never told us what happened and we could only imagine the worst. Whether it was Lonny or the band, or some other thing, *something* destroyed you and I just couldn't bear it." I watched as her eyes began to tear up and she covered her face with the towel. "I didn't want you back in that environment. I didn't want you to get hurt again running off with a rock star."

"Rock star? It was *Lonny!*"

"I was only trying to protect you."

"Lonny and I deserved to be together," I cried. "You could've made it happen, and you chose not to!"

"You can't put all this on me," she said, wiping the tears from her face. "*You* could have told Lonny how you felt. Or for that matter, he could have told you himself before you got married!"

I looked up to see Lonny standing there staring at us. I didn't know how much he'd heard, but I knew he heard the last thing my mother said. I got up from my chair and went upstairs to my room, heading straight for my closet.

"Roo, what're you doing?" Lonny asked, standing right behind me.

I found the box I was looking for and brought it to the middle of the room, sitting on the floor with it. "I have so much anger," I said. "She's wrong. *She* could have saved us both so much anguish."

He sat on the floor next to me and held my face in his hands. "We're together now," he said. "Why can't you be happy with that?"

"I am happy, but—"

"No. No buts. Your mom is right. It should have been me to do the right thing, and I didn't. Please stop blaming her."

"But she *knew*," I cried. "All these years she knew how miserable we both were and she kept silent. All the time she stole from us. I can't forgive her for that."

"You have to let this anger go or it'll destroy you," he said, looking directly into my eyes. "It'll destroy any future we hope to have together."

I pushed his hands away from me and opened the box, watching his face as he peered inside. He pulled out the stuffed monkey that used to sit on his shelf, then a baseball, and then his journals. He ignored everything else in the box after he saw the journals. He ran his hands over their covers, traced the binding with his fingertip, and brought them close to his nose.

"Smells like our old house," he said. He opened one of the journals and flipped through the pages until he found what he was looking for. "August 15, 1975. I met a new girl today. I felt sick when I first saw her. Not sick in a bad way, but sick like I'll die if I never see her again. She's the most beautiful girl I've ever seen, with red hair like fire and freckles like the sun bent over and kissed her face a hundred times."

1983

Billy didn't lay a hand on me again after the incident following the Livingston Monroe concert. The next morning Gina was eyeing the bruise on my jaw and even though she said nothing, it was obvious she knew what happened. I saw the tears in her eyes as she left for school and that was the day she began distancing herself from the brother she once adored.

Gina entered her freshman year at the University of Chicago in the fall of 1983, and even though she could have commuted from home she chose to stay in the dorm at school. As sad as I was about her decision, I understood it completely. The house wouldn't be the same without her, and I would have to learn how to live without Gina there as a constant buffer.

As Billy left her dorm room to get the last of Gina's things from the car, she looked me in the eyes and said, "I know what you did for me."

"And I wouldn't change a thing," I said with a smile.

We pulled each other into a hug and she whispered, "You're free now. Please get away from him."

Something caught in my throat and all I could do was hold Gina close to me as she cried. "I'll be okay," I assured her.

She pulled away from me, our arms still intertwined. "You belong with Lonny," she whispered, tears streaming down her face. "I knew that when I saw you taking care of him after the show. Billy knows it, too… I know that's why he hurt you that night."

Tears stung my eyes as I pushed Gina's hair away from her face and pasted on my fake smile. "Things just aren't that easy," I said. "I made a commitment and Lonny has a different life now. And a girlfriend." Lonny *always* had a girlfriend.

"Lonny loves you, Ruby," she said. "I know he does. I could tell by the way he looked at you."

I wiped the tears from her face and replied, "It's a nice fantasy, but it's not reality. Not mine, anyway."

Billy returned carrying the last box saying, "That's the last of it, kiddo."

418

Gina stiffened as Billy tried to give her a hug before we left, but he barely seemed to notice. He did notice how she threw her arms around me and bawled uncontrollably, which caused me to start crying as well. For so many reasons. I told her she could come home whenever she wanted, and to call day or night if she needed anything. I could see Billy's arms folded across his chest and knew he was getting impatient. Gina and I finally parted, sending "I love you's" down the hall as we walked away.

Once we were on the road, I lost it. I cried all the way home, thinking about having to live with Billy alone and Gina's words about Lonny. Billy put a hand on my leg thinking it would comfort me, but he had no idea how it only repulsed me.

"I think we should have a baby," he announced.

"What?"

"I know you're sad Gina's gone. We've been married a couple of years now, it's time. I'm sure your parents would love to have a grandchild."

I continued to cry, knowing that having a child with Billy was the last thing I wanted to do.

I secretly began taking birth control pills to avoid getting pregnant, and Billy began his apprenticeship as a tattoo artist. He would finish his day at the hardware store at five o'clock, then drive into the city to the tattoo shop. It was nice for me because he was hardly ever home, and sometimes I was already in bed asleep when he got there.

Even after I got married I continued my Friday night rituals with Joanie, ordering pizza and watching television. Sadly, *The Midnight Special* and *Don Kirshner's Rock Concert* both ended in 1981 so I couldn't watch those anymore, but I had MTV and an endless supply of music videos. It was always exciting when a Livingston Monroe video came on, and I loved seeing Lonny on television.

Lonny tried to call me when I was at his mom's to be safe, and more often than not he didn't disappoint. We both knew we could talk uninterrupted when I was with his mom. If I was at home, there was always the chance Billy could come home at any moment and it wasn't worth the risk.

419

One Friday night Lonny and I were talking about the new Livingston Monroe album that was coming out and how four songs that he wrote were going to be on the album, and he would be singing lead on two of them. I wanted to tell Joanie the great news, but she was passed out cold in her recliner.

"So Mitch doesn't have a problem sharing the spotlight?" I asked.

"Nah, he's cool. He has no problem sharing it with me."

"Does the new album have a name yet?"

Lonny laughed. Oh how I loved hearing him laugh. "It's called 'Smoking In Bed' after one of my songs."

"I love it!"

"We've been talking about the album cover and I was thinking…."

He stopped and I waited for him to continue, but he didn't. "What about the album cover?"

"Remember those Polaroids I took of you at the hotel… the ones of you in bed with the cigarette?"

Panic seared my chest. "Yes…."

"The guys want to use one for the cover."

"Lonny, no!" I gasped. "Those pictures were for your eyes only!"

"I know, Roo, but all the other ideas have been shit. They really loved my idea."

"I can't believe you showed them those pictures!"

"Your hair is covering your face. No one will even know it's you."

"Wanna bet?"

"If you say no I won't let them do it, I promise."

I groaned. "Lonny, that was a private moment between us. I can't believe you did that."

"I'm sorry, Roo. I'll tell them they can't use it."

"Thank you. It's just… embarrassing."

"Why? You're hot."

My face flushed and I smiled like a fool. I found myself thinking about Lonny kissing me, touching me, giving me my first orgasm… I was quickly shaken from my thoughts when someone began pounding on Joanie's front door.

420

"Oh shit," I grumbled.

"What's the matter?"

"Billy's here. I gotta go."

I hung up the phone and opened the door, where Billy felt the need to push past me and into the house. "Who were you talking to?" he asked.

"What are you—"

"I saw you through the window. Who were you talking to on the phone?"

"Are you spying on me?"

"You were talking to *him*." He grabbed the front of my shirt and pulled me close to his face. "*Don't* lie to me."

"Keep your voice down," I pleaded. "You'll wake her up."

"She's passed out drunk. She can't hear me."

"I don't want her to see you here."

"Why not? I'm your husband. I have a right to be anywhere you are."

I swallowed hard. "You know she doesn't like people in her house." He pulled me toward the door but I dug my heels into the carpet. "This is my night with Joanie. I won't let you take that away from me."

"Your night with the alcoholic, or your night to talk to *him*?" He wouldn't even say his name.

"I don't come here to talk to him!" I whispered loudly.

"Let's go." He started to pull me toward the door again and I kicked his knee, causing him to buckle and fall over.

"I'm staying here," I insisted.

Billy's face burned red as he picked himself up off the floor. He grabbed my hair and pulled my face toward his. "You're coming home, and you're coming home now. Otherwise I'm going to tell your parents what he did to you."

While it probably wasn't a big deal to most people, I didn't want my parents to know what happened with Lonny. They treated him as their son, just as Joanie treated me as her daughter, and I didn't want them to think badly about him. It was the same threat Billy always used against me, and I let him. I was afraid if things got to the point where he told my parents what Lonny did, there would be no end to my suffering. I needed to protect myself, but I also felt I needed to protect Lonny.

"Let me just say goodbye," I said. He let go of my hair and I walked to Joanie's chair and adjusted her blanket. I leaned close to her ear and whispered, "I have to go home, Mom. I love you."

I locked up and as he pulled me down the sidewalk toward his car I could hear the phone ringing inside.

1984

In February, Ricky made me regional manager for his chain of Vinyl Horse record stores, five in all. I received a hefty raise and split my time between all the stores, loving every minute of my job. Billy claimed to be proud of me, buying me a car for the occasion so I had my own transportation, but wary of the fact I would no longer only be in our local store where he could keep an eye on me.

Ricky and I were together in the Chicago store the day before the new Livingston Monroe album was released, and we stayed after closing hours to price the albums, cassettes and CDs and to replace the cryptic advertising posters that looked like an album wrapped in a brown paper bag.

"You sneaky, sneaky girl," Ricky teased.

I walked to where he was opening the first box of albums and I thought I was going to have a heart attack. There I was on the cover, all sexed up in my white t-shirt, pulling it down between my legs because I wasn't wearing any panties, my after-sex hair covering my face except for my mouth, where a cigarette dangled. Somehow they took Lonny's face off the t-shirt and replaced it with the Livingston Monroe logo, and the album title "Smoking In Bed" written on the sheets.

"That little shit," I grumbled.

"You didn't know?"

"I told them no!" I paced the store, wringing my hands and wondering how I was going to explain this to my family. To my *husband.*

"Smoking in bed," Ricky said over and over again. "Nice double entendre."

I was embarrassed to ask Ricky what he meant. I had no idea what a double entendre was. After he explained it to me, I hadn't even thought of *that* interpretation of the cover and had to sit down, afraid I was going to pass out. "Billy's going to kill me."

"I think it's cool."

"Would you think it was cool if you were my husband?"

"I suppose not." Ricky hesitated then held up a poster and said, "These are going up in all the stores tonight. How are you going to handle it?"

I pulled an album out of the box and turned it over to see the back cover. Four individual live shots of each band member, Lonny wailing on his guitar shirtless with a tie around his neck. If he were standing in front of me I would have strangled him with his own tie.

"Do you think people will believe it if I say it's not me?" I asked my trusted friend.

"You can try…."

"I'm dead."

"Look, it's a hot cover. Embrace it. You're only young once."

Two days later I was working in our local store and went over to my parents' house for dinner, bringing along the new Livingston Monroe album for them as well as Joanie. My mother greeted me with her usual hug, but I winced and pulled away immediately. She was concerned about my pain, but I tried to wave it off.

"I fell in the shower yesterday," I lied.

"Did you go to the hospital?"

"No, I'll be fine." I handed her the album and said, "Please don't be upset with me."

She stared at the album in her hand for a long time before looking back at me. "You look… very nice dear."

"We were all joking around that day," I lied again. "I asked them not to use it."

My dad came into the kitchen and looked over my mother's shoulder at the album she still held in her hands.

"So this is what everyone's talking about," he said.

"Dad, I—"

"You're beautiful," he said, kissing me on the cheek.

Joanie entered the house and immediately wrapped her arms around me for a loving hug, pain stabbing me like a thousand knives nearly causing me to collapse. My mother insisted I go to the hospital and my father didn't hesitate to help me to his car and drive me there.

424

"Is there anything I need to know?" he asked as he drove.

"I fell in the shower," I lied.

"Ruby, are you telling me the truth?"

No.

"Yes, Dad."

"Lonny called last night because he's worried about you. Said he felt like you were hurt, but he couldn't get ahold of you."

"I went to bed early," I lied. "I guess I didn't hear the phone."

I had two broken ribs that the doctor told me would heal on their own in a month or two. He told me to ice them and take Tylenol for the pain, then sent me on my way. We went back to my parents' house so I could eat something, but I wasn't very hungry. All I wanted to do was go to sleep. And not wake up.

"What time does Billy get home?" my dad asked.

"Usually around midnight."

"Here are your options," he said, pointing his fork at me. "You're going to stay here tonight, or I'm going to take you home after Billy gets there."

I nodded. I was in too much pain to argue.

Lonny called around eleven o'clock, and while my parents were usually in bed at that time, my father was still awake and answered the phone. I took the receiver from him as he went back into the living room to watch television.

"I know something's wrong," Lonny said. "What happened?"

I was tired and in pain, and I didn't want my father to hear anything I said, so I spoke just above a whisper. "You promised me they wouldn't use my picture."

"I'm sorry, Roo. I was voted down."

"It's your fault for showing them the picture in the first place."

"I know, and I wish I could take it back."

Tears pricked my eyes as I thought about how that album cover led to me suffering two broken ribs.

"I wish you could, too," I whispered. "But you can't."

"What happened?" he asked again.

425

My voice shook as I replied, "I fell in the shower and broke two ribs."

He gasped loudly and yelled, "Roo, what the fuck? Did he do that to you? Tell me the truth!"

"I'm fine, honest," I lied. "I slipped in the shower and fell against the side of the tub. I'll survive."

"Roo, promise me you're not letting him hurt you."

Letting him?

"I'm fine, Lonny. I promise. How's Lorelei?"

Lonny hesitated then said, "She's fine, I guess."

"Listen, I have to go… my dad's taking me home."

"Roo, I—"

I hung up before I heard him say anything more. My dad drove me home and we waited in the living room for Billy to get there. He was surprised to see my father there when he walked into the house. Billy came over to where I was sitting and kissed me on the cheek.

"My daughter has two broken ribs," my father told him.

Billy feigned shock. "What happened?"

"She says she slipped and fell in the shower. Any reason why I shouldn't believe her?"

Billy looked at me and asked, "Are you okay? Why didn't you call me?"

"Billy, if I find out you had anything to do with this, I won't call the police. I'll take care of you myself." My dad kissed me goodbye and headed home.

As soon as he was gone Billy gave me a look that frightened me to my very core. I got up and went into the bedroom, feeling him right behind me. Pain stabbed me as I changed into my pajamas, but I fought the urge to cry. I couldn't let him see me cry.

As I climbed gingerly into bed he asked, "Have they seen their whore daughter on that album cover yet?"

I didn't dignify him with an answer, rolling over and turning my back on him, no matter how excruciating the pain was. I thought about Lonny's new girlfriend Lorelei and wondered what she looked like.

426

Livingston Monroe's "Smoking In Bed" tour brought them to Chicago that summer, and like the last time they were in town, Lonny secured front row tickets for us and sent a limousine to pick us up. Billy walked into the house just as the limo pulled up to the curb.

"What's the limo for?" he asked.

My father knocked on the front door and as I opened it told him, "Livingston Monroe concert tonight."

"Why didn't I know about it?"

I felt safe with my father standing there, and extremely bold. "You're working so hard, I never had a chance to tell you. I wish you could come with us, but I know you have to go to the tattoo shop tonight."

I made a big production in front of my father, hugging Billy and kissing him goodbye before heading out to the limo where my mom and Joanie were waiting for us. I didn't even try to look nice, dressed simply in a pair of jeans, an old Livingston Monroe t-shirt, and my favorite Converse. Lonny knew Billy wouldn't be accompanying me this time around, sending the limo extra early so we would all have plenty of time to see him before the show. It had been three years since we saw each other last and I couldn't wait to put my arms around him.

"Billy's not coming?" my mother asked.

"He has his apprenticeship at the tattoo shop at night," I answered. "You know that."

"It's not right. He should be with you tonight."

I made a face and ignored her. What did she think was going to happen without Billy there? I would actually enjoy myself, I knew that much. And I was going to enjoy myself to the fullest, because I had no idea which Billy would be waiting for me when I got home.

Howard ushered us through the backstage area where we found the guys playing a two-on-two basketball game with a hoop that was attached to the wall. From what I could tell it was Fuzzy and Lonny against Mitch and Benji, and Lonny was running circles around all of them. My heart caught in my throat when I set eyes on Lonny. They all stopped dead in their tracks when Howard's attention grabbing whistle pierced everyone's ears.

This time I stood at the front of the line with my arms folded angrily across my chest, hoping they'd get the message that I wasn't happy they chose to use my photo on the album cover after I explicitly asked them not to. The guys looked nervous, saying nothing and looking genuinely sorry, but the look on Lonny's face said something else entirely. He looked scared.

Lonny kissed both moms and shook my dad's hand, not wanting to get them all sweaty, but he picked me up off the ground and threw me over his shoulder like a rag doll and carried me to the dressing room. He smacked me on my backside before setting me on the floor and wrapping his arms around me for a long awaited hug.

Please don't ever let me go.

I could hear the rest of the group enter the dressing room, but I didn't care. I was going to hold onto Lonny as long as I could. He pulled away and tousled the top of my head with his hand like a brother would do to an annoying sister.

"Where's your husband?" Lonny asked, grabbing a towel to wipe the sweat from his face.

"Working," was all I would say.

Benji greeted me with a hug, Mitch kissed me quickly on the mouth and said, "Great to see you, baby," and Fuzzy pulled me off the floor in his usual bear hug, kissing me on the cheek. They all looked the same. Lonny was the only one who really changed, looking so much more like a man than even three years earlier. He was no longer my sweet faced boy.

We sat in the front row to watch the band do their soundcheck and I couldn't believe what I saw. On either side of the stage were gigantic cutouts of me from the album cover, where smoke billowed out from the edge of the cigarette in my mouth. I was embarrassed as it was to be sitting there with our parents, but then I noticed Lonny had a new guitar… one with my picture from the album cover on it. I was so thankful Billy couldn't be there that night.

428

When the soundcheck was over, Lonny called me onto the stage as our parents were ushered back to the dressing room. He knelt on the ground to tune his acoustic guitar and asked me to sit down. He sat in front of me and took my hands in his.

"You don't look good, Roo," he said, looking into my eyes.

"Thanks a lot," I huffed.

"You're starting to look like a skeleton."

"I'm just tired. I'm working a lot; Ricky's got me running between all his stores and——"

"Tell me the truth." He leaned closer and rested his forehead against mine.

Tell him!

"I was starting to get fat," I said.

According to Billy.

"You don't look healthy," he said. "I'm really worried about you."

Please ask me to come with you.

"Are you happy, Roo?"

"Are you happy?"

"I have a great life," he answered. "I wish you could be part of it, but yeah, I'm happy."

"Then I'm happy. All I want is for you to be happy."

Tell him the truth!

Lonny pulled his head back and smiled at me. "I'm glad Billy couldn't come tonight."

"Me, too." I laughed. "He wants me to have a baby."

Lonny's eyes grew large. "Roo… is that what you want?"

"No. He's been wondering why I'm not getting pregnant. He doesn't know I've been taking birth control pills behind his back."

"Please be careful, Roo. You don't want to piss him off."

"Yeah, I know."

He got to his feet and held his hand out to help me up. He held my hand all the way back to the dressing room, and when we walked in Fuzzy pulled me onto his lap but Lonny said, "Aw no, she's all mine tonight," and pulled me onto the couch next to him. He put his arm around me and stayed attached to my hip anytime they weren't onstage that evening. It was the first time in ages I truly felt loved.

When it came time for us to leave, I wasn't nearly ready. I didn't want to leave my friends and I didn't want to go home. Our parents said goodbye to the band, saving Lonny for last, and while they were occupied with him I said goodbye to my friends. First Benji, then Mitch, who hugged me so tightly I could feel the tears threatening. I couldn't even look at Fuzzy when he hugged me, but he forced me to by putting his fingers under my chin and lifting my face. As soon as my eyes met his I lost it, tears escaping as I tried to smile.

"I miss you, doll," he said, smiling down at me.

I could only nod in agreement, words failing me.

It came time to say goodbye to Lonny and everybody left the room. This surprised me, but I was certain Fuzzy had something to do with it. Lonny smiled at me and looked up at the ceiling, blowing air out of his mouth.

"It's always so hard saying goodbye to you," he said, his eyes wet with tears.

"Then don't say it," I cried. "Say something else instead."

Tell me you love me.

"You know you can tell me anything, right?"

"Yes."

"Please promise me you're gonna be okay."

I smiled and held up my hand, my pinky extended. "Pinky swear."

Lonny chuckled and locked his pinky around mine. "I miss you."

"I miss you, too."

He pulled me in for a hug and held his face against mine. It was soft and warm and I closed my eyes to imprint it in my mind forever. I drank in the scent of his skin and let my lips lightly touch his neck.

Please tell me you love me.

I finally pulled away, knowing everyone was waiting for me and probably wondering what was taking me so long. I also knew I would never hear Lonny say the words I was so desperate to hear, so I put my hands on his cheeks and kissed him on the

430

mouth. I held the kiss longer than I should have but it was perfectly innocent, just two mouths touching.

"I have to go," I whispered, exiting the dressing room and following behind our parents and a security guard.

"Roo!" Lonny called after me. I turned to face him one last time and he said, "I'll call you Friday!"

As soon as I sat down in the limo I leaned over and sobbed into my lap. Leaving Lonny was harder each time I had to do it, and the unrequited love I had for him stung deeper every time we saw each other.

I was so thankful Billy was already asleep when I got home. I tiptoed around the bedroom as I removed my clothes and put on my pajamas, then quietly slid into bed, my back to my husband. It wasn't long before I felt Billy's hand on my thigh, working his way inside my shorts and pulling them down just far enough to shove himself inside me.

When Billy was finished he said, "Go take a shower. You smell like *him*."

2011

Lonny and I drove into town for the fireworks that evening, getting comfortable on a blanket and listening to the live band that was performing. He sat behind me, holding me in his arms with his chin on my shoulder.

"You were pretty quiet at dinner," he said.

"I didn't have anything to say."

"Your mom doesn't deserve the silent treatment."

"Can we just enjoy the evening without talking about her?"

"Okay fine, sorry."

I just wanted to watch the fireworks, enjoy the fact that Lonny and I were together, and savor the feeling of his arms around me. I didn't want to talk about my mother and how she'd betrayed me most of my life.

"So whatever happened to Gina?" he asked.

"She's the curator for a very high end art gallery in Chicago, making six figures. Ten years ago she adopted the baby of her college roommate. His name is Max. She's an amazing woman."

"It certainly sounds like it. She always told me she never would have survived without you."

"Me? I didn't do anything."

"Are you kidding? You took care of her after she lost both parents. I bet you didn't know she was considering suicide before you got married."

I quickly turned to face Lonny. "I didn't know that."

"See?"

"How did you know that?"

"She told me. We kept in touch until sometime after she graduated college."

"Lonny Winter, did you sleep with her?"

"God no!" he replied, laughing. "Give me some credit!"

"I just know how crazy she was about you and—"

"She wrote me letters, and once in a while I'd give her a call. We never saw each other."

"She was going to kill herself?"

432

"Yeah but she didn't, because you gave her something she desperately needed. Hope. And love."

If my marriage to Billy was worth anything, it was that right there. If the pain and suffering I went through at the hands of my husband saved Gina, I had to find a way to get over the anger and resentment buried deep inside me.

Lonny put his arm around me and pulled me against his chest, kissing the top of my head. He started singing along to the song the band was playing, "I'll Be" by Edwin McCain.

"You're my survival, you're my living proof my love is alive and not dead."

I knelt in front of Lonny and hugged him tightly, kissing his whole face. "I love you, I love you, I love you," I said. "I survived because of you."

Patriotic music blared through the loudspeakers as the fireworks began. I settled into Lonny's arms as we watched the colors erupt in the hot, July sky above us. I couldn't remember the last time I was that truly happy.

We walked back to the car hand in hand when the fireworks were over, and before Lonny opened the door for me he pressed me against the car and kissed me deeply. When he came up for air he chuckled and said, "I always wanted to do that in high school, but I had no balls."

"You had no car," I joked.

Instead of driving back to the hotel he drove back to my parents' house, and I didn't ask why until he parked in the driveway and didn't turn off the car.

"Aren't we going back to the hotel?" I asked, confused.

"I am. You're going inside and working things out with your mom."

"Lonny, come on," I growled.

"I'm serious, Roo. Dinner was uncomfortable enough; you need to find a way to forgive her. You have a lot of bitterness and anger to work through, and your mom is the key."

"Thanks for ruining a perfectly nice evening."

Lonny turned to face me. "Are you staying here when I leave for Vegas, or are you coming with me?"

"Don't you want me to come with you?"

433

He rolled his eyes. "That wasn't my question."

"I'm going with you."

"Then you need to work this out before we leave. I'm not leaving here with you pissed off and not speaking to your mom."

"Why do you care so much?"

He lit a cigarette. "She's my mom, too. She deserves to be forgiven. Just like I do, just like you do."

I was incredulous. "What did I do?"

"For whatever, Roo. I don't mean anything specific. This is what you always do. You're so angry you're not even listening to what I'm saying."

I got out of the car and slammed the door saying, "You have *no* idea what I went through with Billy. You bet your ass I'm angry."

As I walked toward the front door he shouted, "I love you!" and I gave him the finger. I went into the house and straight to the living room where my parents were watching the news.

I turned off the television and said, "We need to talk."

"Why don't you sit down?" my dad said.

"I'm too upset to sit down." I stood there with my arms angrily folded in front of my chest. "Mom, why did you push so hard for me to marry Billy?"

I knew from the look on my father's face that he had no idea what was going on. "He loved you Ruby," she said. "He was a hard worker and I knew he would take good care of you."

"Take good care... take good care of me?" I was nearly blind with rage. "Do you know how well he took care of me? A couple of broken ribs... a few concussions...."

My mother's hand flew to her mouth, horrified at my revelation. My father sat motionless as I described the hell and suffering I went through during my marriage to Billy, and all because he *knew* I didn't love him. My mother had tears streaming down her face as she listened.

"You *knew* I didn't love him. You knew I loved Lonny, and you knew he loved me. But you still pushed me to marry Billy. *Why?*"

She cleared her throat and said, "I told you before, you came home early from the tour a shattered mess. I didn't want you going back to that life."

"I don't believe you!"

"Billy came to me and told me how much he loved you," she said quietly, wiping the tears from her face. "He was worried about you based on the stories you told him about being on the road. I can't say I blamed him."

"What stories?"

"About Lonny and the drugs."

My face burned fire as my hands balled into fists at my side. "Lonny didn't do drugs!"

"The *orgies*, Ruby! The thought of my little girl—"

"The what?"

She repeated the word orgies as if I didn't know what they were. "You and Lonny and the rest of the band...." She looked at me with disgust I couldn't begin to understand.

"That *never* happened!"

My dad was white as a ghost.

"He said you got pregnant and Lonny forced you to have an abortion. That's why you came home."

I stared at my mother blankly as the blood boiled in my veins.

She finished with, "I love Lonny as my own son, but I could never forgive him for that."

"So you believed everything Billy said without even *asking* me? It never crossed your mind that he was lying? You trusted his word over your own daughter!"

"Ruby, I—"

"Mom, *none* of those things happened. None of them!"

My mother burst into tears, trying to apologize but unable to speak the words. My father got up from his chair to sit next to her on the couch, comforting her with his loving arms.

"I *hated* Billy," I hissed. "And no, I wasn't a virgin when I went on tour with Lonny. Billy made sure of that graduation night when he forced himself on me."

"Why didn't you just tell us?" my father asked.

"I was humiliated, and I didn't think you'd believe me."

435

"Ruby, I'm so sorry," my mother cried. "I wish I could go back and change everything. I would never intentionally hurt you. I love you so much."

"But you thought it was okay to keep the truth from me? You robbed me of a life with Lonny and trapped me in a life with a man who beat the shit out of me because he knew I didn't love him."

"Ruby, I think you're being unfair," my father said. "Your mother may have persuaded you to marry Billy, but it was ultimately your decision. You're the one who chose the life you ended up with."

My heart fell into my stomach, bile rising in my throat. "After what I've just told you, how can you say that?"

"I don't understand why you would marry Billy if you hated him so much."

Tears choked me. "Because I didn't think Lonny loved me. And I promised Gina I would take care of her." I hesitated before adding, "And I just couldn't handle Mom screaming at me anymore."

My father looked at me like I'd just grown another head. "Ruby, I don't understand how this is your mother's fault."

I went on to explain how Lonny showed up to stop the wedding but we were already married, and even though she knew how much we loved each other she threatened him to stay away from me.

"So many times you could've said something and you stayed silent," I cried. "I saw the way you were looking at us when I sat on the floor taking care of him after that concert. You *knew*. You knew we belonged together and you said *nothing*."

"I thought I was doing the right thing," her voice cracked. "I was only trying to protect you, and I ended up hurting you even worse. I didn't know. I'm so sorry, but I didn't know."

I saw my mother crack. She was always the strongest woman I knew, and it broke my heart to see her completely unravel in front of me. *Because* of me. And she never once asked for me to tell the truth about why I came home early from the tour.

She sobbed against my father's chest as he held her tightly in his arms, pleading to me with the look on his face. I wanted to

436

go to her, to comfort her and tell her I turned out all right, that my life was finally going in the right direction, that I forgave her, but I couldn't move. So my father did the only thing he could; he brought her to me. My mother wrapped her arms around me and sobbed against my face, apologizing over and over again. My father wrapped his arms around me, pulling both of us tightly against him as we all cried together.

"I'm sorry, Ruby. I'm so sorry," my mother cried. "If we knew what Billy was doing, you know we would've stepped in. We would never have allowed it to continue."

"I know," I cried. "I'm sorry. I'm sorry for not telling you. I just didn't know how, and I was so scared."

It was late when we stopped crying and hugging and apologizing, and we went into the kitchen to finish off the strawberry shortcake and iced tea. My phone had been buzzing in my pocket the entire time but I ignored it, hoping it was Lonny and not my bastard ex-husband. I pulled it out and looked at the screen.

Lonny
Lonny
Lonny
Lonny
Lonny

I didn't realize I was smiling until my father said, "Are you happy now, Ruby? Are you going to be okay?"

"Yeah Dad, I'm happy, and I'm going to be okay. Better than okay."

I waited until I got into bed to read Lonny's text messages.

Lonny: I hope things are going well.
Lonny: You're too beautiful to be angry all the time.
Lonny: I love you.
Lonny: You've always been my girl, even if you didn't know it.
Lonny: Going to bed. I'll see you in the morning. I love you.

His last text was an hour old, and even though he was probably asleep I texted him back.

Me: All is well. I love you, too.

Twenty minutes later I heard something lightly tap my bedroom window, but I ignored it since it was windy outside. It happened again and I got up to look out the window, seeing Lonny in the back yard smoking a cigarette and waving at me. Throwing pebbles at my bedroom window, just like in high school. I smiled and snuck outside to the back yard where he gave me a hug and a quick kiss and sat down on top of the picnic table.

"I couldn't sleep," he said.

"Miss me?"

"Yeah," he replied with a laugh. "I don't want to be without you, even if it's just a few hours."

I sat next to him, leaning against his arm and resting my head against his shoulder. "It was awful," I said.

"But you and your mom are okay now?"

"You'll be happy to know I probably have no tears left to cry."

He put his arm around me and squeezed, but said nothing. I could tell he wanted to know what happened, but didn't want to ask. I lifted my head to see his face, staring straight ahead and blowing smoke rings out of his mouth. I turned to face him, crossing my legs in front of me, and he did the same. He smashed out his cigarette and took my hands in his, caressing them with his thumbs. I stared down at his hands and his beautiful, long fingers.

"My mom didn't think you were good enough for me," I mumbled. I looked at his face, shocked by my statement. "Billy told her he loved me, and he promised to take care of me. She didn't want me to be with you because she believed all his lies." He pulled a face and I continued. "Billy relayed road stories he claimed I told him, and she believed him."

"What stories?"

"About you doing drugs. About the orgies I had with you and the rest of the band."

438

Lonny jumped off the table. "*What*? You weren't like that! *We* weren't like that!"

"That's not even the worst part. He told her that I got pregnant and you forced me to have an abortion."

Lonny looked like he was going to explode. He paced with his hands grabbing the top of his hair. "She *believed* that bullshit?"

"She saw what a wreck I was when I came home… it all made sense to her at the time."

"It's all my fault."

"Lonny, don't."

"It's all my fault," he repeated. "Everything that happened to both of us is because of *me*. If you hadn't left the tour early none of this would've happened. And you left because of *me*."

"Lonny, come on. It's late, let's go inside and get some sleep."

Lonny wrapped me in his arms and crushed my face against his chest. "I'm so sorry, Roo. I can't even imagine what you went through being married to him… to that piece of shit."

"It's over now. I don't have to worry about him anymore."

Lonny pulled away from me and held my face in his hands, his eyes wet with tears as he looked at me with unrelenting guilt. "So many times I wanted to tell you I loved you… to beg you to come with me…."

"We were both stupid," I said. "But we can't change what happened. We can only start over and make a new life."

"I promise I will spend the rest of my life making it up to you."

I hopped off the picnic table, took Lonny by the hand, and led him back into the house where we quietly went up to my room and crawled into bed.

I smiled and whispered, "I really think you should kiss me now."

I woke up to the sun shining brightly outside, and Lonny squirming in bed beside me saying, "We didn't do anything, I swear!"

I lifted my head off his shoulder to see my mother standing there, looking a little startled. "It's okay," she said. "I'm not judging."

"It was late when Lonny came by, I didn't want—"

"Ruby, it's okay," she said. "I'm glad you're here, Lonny. I have something to say to you."

Lonny and I both sat up, which helped my mother see that we were both fully clothed.

"Lonny, as much as I've always loved you as a son, I've had a lot of ill feelings toward you that I found out last night were caused by lies."

"Mom, it's okay," he said. "Roo told me everything."

My mother burst into tears. "Lonny, I'm so sorry. All these years I knew Ruby belonged with you, but I was blinded by lies."

Lonny motioned with his arm for my mother to come closer to him. He put his arms around her waist and said, "Mom, it's not your fault. I'm the only one to blame. It should've been *me* to tell Roo how I felt and I blew it so many times."

"But Lonny," she sobbed. "I'm her mother. I should've seen what he was doing to her. I should've known something wasn't right."

"What do you mean?"

I looked at my mother and shook my head, biting my lip. I didn't want her getting into the details of my abuse with Lonny right then. She gasped at her indiscretion and stopped talking, causing Lonny to whip his head my way.

"Roo?"

My mother rushed out of the room saying, "I'm making breakfast if you're hungry."

"Roo?"

I smiled and caressed Lonny's soft cheek with my fingertips. "We'll talk about it some other time, okay?"

He nodded and kissed me. "Glad I didn't have to stand up," he joked, sending us both into a fit of laughter.

440

1984

Everyone in town was buzzing with excitement over the release of the Livingston Monroe movie, and I was no exception. John Cunningham, the owner of the small movie theater in town, made a big deal out of the occasion and hosted a pre-movie party with food, drinks and Livingston Monroe music for all to enjoy. I was thankful Billy had to work, and Gina came to share the experience with me and my family. Lonny invited me to California to see it with him and the rest of the band, but I declined because I knew it would only infuriate Billy.

Watching the movie was surreal, seeing myself more often than I would have liked, but reliving every moment because I was there as most of it happened. I wasn't on the European leg of the tour so that was all new to me, but I was surprised by some of the things the film crew captured that I never realized. For instance, when Lonny dislocated his shoulder and was screaming at the medic to pop it back in, I had no idea they caught that on film. I was so worried about Lonny that I didn't even notice. I cried through a lot of the movie remembering the amazing time I had with the band, but especially experiencing it with Lonny. It was the best time of my life.

Late that same evening I woke up around one in the morning with pain in my chest. I sat up and tried to slow my breathing without waking up Billy, who was snoring beside me. I quietly got out of bed and immediately collapsed, the pain in my chest so severe I couldn't move, couldn't breathe. When I focused my eyes again it was two o'clock. And then the phone rang.

I quickly picked up the receiver and said, "What happened to Lonny?"

"There's been an accident," Fuzzy said, his voice shaking. "They don't know if he'll make it through the night."

My heart jumped into my throat and choked me. "What happened?"

"Just get here, doll."

I hung up with Fuzzy and called my mother to let her know I was leaving, and to tell Joanie I would give her more information when I had it. The phone woke my father, who offered to take me to the airport.

I turned on the bedroom light, not even thinking about Billy, and he immediately started a barrage of expletives. I ignored him and pulled my suitcase out of the closet, throwing clothes and toiletries in as fast as I could manage.

"What the fuck are you doing?" he growled.

"Lonny was in an accident," I said, never looking at him. "They don't think he'll make it through the night."

Don't let him see you cry.

"He'll probably be dead before you get there," he hissed.

I don't know what came over me, probably the very real fear that I may never see Lonny again, but I walked to Billy's side of the bed and slapped him across the face.

"You shut up!" I yelled.

Billy jumped out of bed so fast I didn't have time to react. He knocked me to the floor so hard I hit the back of my head on the bed on the way down. He straddled me, holding my arms down with his legs as he squeezed my face with one hand.

"This could be the best day of my life," he said with a terrifying smile. "The little shit dies and I can finally have my wife to myself!"

"My dad is taking me to the airport," I said quickly. "He'll be here any minute."

Billy thought about it for a moment, then let me up. "I'll be here when you get home. When will that be exactly?"

Carrying my suitcase into the living room I said, "I don't know."

"Don't make it too long," he threatened.

I saw headlights in the driveway and ran to my father's car without so much as a goodbye to Billy. As far as I was concerned, I didn't care if I ever came home. And if Lonny died, I would die right along with him. Without Lonny I had nothing.

I took a taxi straight to the hospital when I landed in Los Angeles, where Fuzzy met me in the front lobby. He hugged me quickly and took me by the hand, leading me through the maze of hallways and elevators to ICU. Neither of us said a word, my heart pounding violently in my chest, my stomach threatening to lose its contents.

Fuzzy explained to the nurses that I was Lonny's sister, which I knew just made everything easier considering the situation. As we walked up to Lonny's room Mitch and Benji came out, as only two visitors were allowed in at one time and they wanted to let Fuzzy go in with me. They greeted me with gentle hugs and no words, but it was obvious both of them had been crying. I had no idea how to prepare myself for walking into that room.

Fuzzy put his hands on my shoulders and looked into my eyes. "Doll, you need to know that he doesn't look like himself. I just want you to be prepared."

I walked into Lonny's room slowly, feeling Fuzzy's strong hand on my shoulder as he followed close behind me. I stepped beyond the curtain and when I saw the person lying in the hospital bed, I immediately fell to the floor and began vomiting into the garbage can.

Fuzzy sat on the floor with me after I finished and whispered, "Let him know you're here, doll. Doctors say he can probably hear us."

"That's not Lonny," I cried. "That's not him. It's *not* him."

"I'm sorry doll, but it is. I don't want it to be him either."

Fuzzy helped me to my feet and I wiped out my mouth with a tissue. I took a deep breath before walking to the side of Lonny's hospital bed and taking a good look at him. His entire head was bandaged, his eyes were both swollen shut, and his face was purple and battered with bruises. His left arm was bandaged from his fingers to his shoulder, held up in a contraption that made it look like the wing of an airplane, bent at the elbow with long screws holding bones in place. His left leg was in a cast up to his hip and a chest tube was sticking out of his skin near the left ribcage.

My hand trembled as I brought it to my mouth, afraid Lonny might hear me gasp as I stood there staring at him in shock. This couldn't be my Lonny; there had to be some mistake. I looked down at his right hand, which seemed to be miraculously unharmed, knowing those were his long, beautiful fingers. He was in a coma and on a ventilator, and my heart shattered to see him in

443

that condition. What happened to my sweet Lonny? I still had no answers.

I pulled a chair up to the side of the bed and held his right hand in mine, desperate for some kind of connection, some realization on his part that I was there. That we were all there. His hand was cold and I held it against my cheek, hoping to warm it up some.

"Lonny," my voice cracked. "It's Ruby. I'm here for you. Fuzzy, Benji and Mitch are all here, too. I love you, Lonny. Please don't leave me."

I fell asleep with my face on Lonny's bed, still holding his hand against my cheek. Fuzzy woke me up when the nurses needed to come in and take his vitals, empty his urine bag, and change out his IV fluids. It was early afternoon. Fuzzy brought me to a private waiting room where Mitch and Benji sat silently.

"What happened?" I asked.

They all looked at each other, no one knowing who should be the one to speak. Mitch decided to take the burden off of Fuzzy and said, "We were at Howard's house for a party after we all saw the movie. Joey Buckingham showed up, accusing Lonny of sleeping with his wife." Mitch couldn't continue.

"Joey started pushing him around, but Lonny swore he didn't even know his wife," Benji continued. "They started fighting. We tried to pull them apart…."

The room became silent. I knew Lonny's injuries weren't all caused by fighting with Joey Buckingham.

"The next thing we knew," Fuzzy said, "Joey was throwing Lonny through a window. Second story. What you can't see are his broken ribs, collapsed lung and bruised kidney. He stopped breathing in the ambulance but they were able to revive him."

I felt like I was going to faint. "And where is Joey?" I asked.

"The police want to question him, but nobody can find him," Mitch answered.

I covered my face with my hands and began rocking back and forth in my seat. It was all impossible to take in, to believe. I had just talked to Lonny on the phone, and he was so excited about the movie he couldn't wait to hear what I thought about it. And he already died once in the ambulance on the way to the hospital.

My body began to shake uncontrollably as I sobbed into my hands. The love of my life was down the hall dying and I couldn't do anything to help him. There was no way I could survive without Lonny, even though he lived on the other side of the country. Lonny was my entire reason for living, the reason I was able to face each day in my abusive marriage, the reason I knew true love really existed. If I lost him, I would lose everything. I would lose my very soul.

Mitch sat next to me and put a comforting arm around my sagging shoulders. Somehow that made the situation much worse, and I could no longer control my sobbing. It was loud, ugly and guttural, as if my very life was being ripped from my body.

"The press has gotten hold of the story," Howard's voice was heard as he entered the room. "The vultures are going to want a piece of all of you when you try to leave."

"Do they know what happened?" Benji asked.

"They just know Lonny's been in some sort of accident, but that's all they know right now." Howard placed his hand gently on top of my head. "I'm glad you're here, Ruby."

"Maybe they should know the truth," I cried. "Maybe they should know what that bastard did to him."

"How's he doing?" Howard asked.

Fuzzy shook his head and said, "No change."

A nurse came in and told us we could go back into Lonny's room, but I couldn't move. I stayed where I was and let Howard go in with Benji.

Mitch never took his arm away from me, saying, "He's a strong kid, and he's already made it longer than they expected last night."

"Why would Joey do that to him? What sane person would hurt Lonny like that?" I just couldn't wrap my head around it.

"Joey's nuts," Fuzzy replied. "And very jealous and obsessive when it comes to his wife."

"So out of the blue he decides to attack Lonny, who may or may not have been sleeping with his wife?" I was incensed.

445

"That's the million dollar question, baby," Mitch said. "And only Lonny knows the answer. Well… and Penelope, but we haven't seen her."

"Fuzzy, he lives with you. Don't you think you'd know?"

"Lonny lives his own life," Fuzzy defended himself. "I don't monitor what he does."

"I'm sorry," I cried. "I'm just trying to understand all of this."

Fuzzy knelt in front of me and took my hands in his. "We're all trying to make sense of it, doll. I have so much anger in me right now I might kill Joey if I see him."

"I can't lose him, Fuzzy, I can't."

He leaned forward and held his face against mine, and I could feel the wetness from his tears. His voice broke as he said, "I can't either, doll."

A week later, Lonny's condition hadn't changed. His visible injuries were healing nicely, but he was still in a coma and on the ventilator, and wasn't responding to anyone. After a long and gut-wrenching conversation with Joanie, we knew he would not want to be kept alive that way, and the decision was made to turn off the ventilator. Fuzzy had his arms protectively around me as we stood in the room watching the doctor and nurses surrounding Lonny's bed.

Even though I couldn't see Lonny, I buried my face in Fuzzy's shirt. I tried to concentrate on the busy sounds outside the room, but all I could hear were the muffled voices of Lonny's medical team and the machines in the room beeping and humming and pumping oxygen into his lungs. It felt like life and death doing an agonizingly slow dance, trying to decide who was going to take the lead.

I heard sucking noises then something that sounded like Lonny was choking, and I ran. I felt hot and cold at the same time, covered in sweat and disoriented. I managed to find the private waiting room and sat on the couch with my head in my hands as I tried to get my bearings. I felt like I failed Lonny by running, but I couldn't stand there listening to him die. I begged him to forgive me as I sat sobbing into my hands, not knowing what else to do.

It seemed like hours before Fuzzy entered the room and knelt in front of me with tears in his eyes. My own eyes burned as I waited for the devastating news, but Fuzzy smiled.

"He did it, doll. He's breathing on his own."

I threw myself into his arms and cried for joy. My fingers found comfort in his hair as I gently squeezed his thick curls.

"He's not out of the woods yet," he continued, "but this is a huge hurdle."

"I failed him, Fuzzy. I ran when I should've stayed and faced the outcome."

"Don't do that to yourself, doll. You're running on little sleep or food; give yourself a break."

Fuzzy brought me back to Lonny's room and it was a relief to see him without the intrusive breathing tube sticking out of his mouth, but even though he was breathing on his own he was still unresponsive. This only sent me spiraling back into despair and the fear I would lose him forever. I pulled a chair up to his bed and held his right hand against my cheek as I watched his face. His bruises were fading and the swelling had gone down some, but it still didn't look like Lonny.

"You should come back to the house tonight and sleep in a real bed," Fuzzy suggested. "Have some real food. When was the last time you ate?"

I'd been sleeping on the couch in Lonny's room since arriving there, and I couldn't remember the last time I ate anything substantial. The nurses were so kind, bringing me drinks and snacks as they could and making sure I was comfortable. I'd only leave long enough to go back to Fuzzy's house to shower and then I'd come right back. Lonny and I had been apart far too long already; I couldn't be away from him in his greatest time of need.

"I can't leave him," I said.

"If there's any change the hospital will call us right away."

"I need to be here when he wakes up."

"Doll, you're a wreck. You'll be no good to him in your condition."

"I'll be okay, but I can't leave him."

Fuzzy exhaled loudly for effect. "I have to leave for a bit to take care of some things, but I'll be back, okay?"

447

I nodded as he kissed the top of my head and squeezed my shoulder. In a way I was glad he was leaving so I could finally be alone with Lonny, but Fuzzy had been my rock on so many occasions, I almost felt guilty for feeling that way. I continued holding Lonny's hand against my face, hoping by some miracle he would know I was there, know I was touching him.

About an hour later a nurse came in to change the dressing on Lonny's left arm and as I made to leave, she told me I didn't have to go anywhere. I watched as she gently removed the dressing that revealed grisly stitches beginning at the palm of his hand and snaking all the way to his armpit. I suddenly wondered if Lonny would ever play the guitar again. Judging by the visible damage I could only wonder if nerves and tendons may have been severed in the accident.

The nurse saw me watching her with tears running down my face and said, "This kid's a fighter."

After she left I whispered, "I love you, Lonny. I promise I'm never leaving you again." I felt his pinky twitch and my heart thundered in my chest. I didn't dare move or breathe for fear I was mistaken. I stood up and leaned closer to his battered face. "Lonny, can you hear me? I'm here, I'm here!"

I buzzed the nurse's station and heard a voice say, "Can I help you?"

"He moved!" I shouted back.

The nurse who just changed Lonny's dressing came back into the room and asked me to tell her what I saw, and I explained how I felt his pinky move. She checked his vitals then told me, "Sometimes coma patients twitch involuntarily, but let's not give up hope."

I sat back in my chair, deflated. Here I thought Lonny made a major breakthrough, but the nurse was telling me it was just something that happens with coma patients. I placed his hand gently on the bed and cried silently to myself. I felt so helpless. I grieved for the relationship we had in high school, for the love we briefly shared, and for the years we spent apart when we should have been together.

Fuzzy returned several hours later and as I tried to explain that I felt Lonny move his finger, I rambled on like a blithering fool and he had no idea what I was even saying.

"I felt Lonny move his finger," I cried, "but they don't believe me."

Fuzzy pulled me into his strong arms and said, "I believe you, doll. I do."

I began crying so uncontrollably I couldn't catch my breath.

"I don't think Lonny would mind if you had a nice dinner and got a good night's sleep, doll. You need to recharge. Come home with me tonight and you can come back first thing in the morning."

"I *can't*. I can't leave him."

Fuzzy turned me to face Lonny and said, "Hey kid, Ruby needs to eat and get some sleep. I'm taking her back to the house, but I'll bring her back first thing tomorrow, okay?"

I watched Lonny, hoping for a smile or a reaction of some kind, but there was nothing. Not even a twitch. I wilted and Fuzzy nearly had to hold me up as he led me out of the room.

I think I passed out in Fuzzy's car, because I don't remember the trip from the hospital to his house. It could've been exhaustion and lack of food, but it was probably a good idea he dragged me out of there when he did. I napped on the couch while he grilled some steaks, but a dream of Lonny being hurled through the window of a skyscraper shocked me awake. I went into the bathroom to splash cold water on my face then went into the kitchen to make a salad for dinner.

"Do you really think Lonny moved his finger?" Fuzzy asked, pulling two baked potatoes out of the oven.

"I do. I think he was trying to communicate with me."

"Then I believe you. Nobody knows that kid better than you do." Fuzzy placed a dinner plate in front of me and asked, "How did you know?"

"Know what?"

"How did you know something happened to Lonny when I called? I didn't even say anything and you knew."

449

"Lonny and I have this thing… it's hard to explain. We can feel each other's pain. Lonny calls it the whisper. I felt it about an hour before you called me."

He poured us each a glass of wine and said, "That's when the accident happened."

"So what's going on with you? Any girlfriends since Marilyn?" I desperately needed to talk about something other than Lonny's accident.

Fuzzy chuckled. "I've had a few, but nothing serious. I've pretty much just thrown myself into work, whether it's the band or the warehouse. I like to keep busy. What about you?"

"Regional manager of the Vinyl Horse stores," I said with a smile. "Ricky keeps me really busy."

"How's your husband handling you being here?"

I grunted. "I don't want to talk about *him*."

I hadn't spoken to Billy since I left the house. Anything I had to say to him I relayed through my mother, who seemed to be in regular contact with him while I was away. The thought of hearing his voice made me cringe, and I couldn't let him get into my head.

Fuzzy offered me Lonny's room to sleep in, but I felt it was too much an invasion of his privacy so I slept in the spare room instead. I slept fitfully for about two hours before getting up to take some aspirin for the headache I knew was coming. Before heading back to bed I sat on the couch and picked up a framed photo of Fuzzy and Lonny off the coffee table. It was a photo I had taken on tour and they both had huge smiles on their faces, arms around each other like the best friends they were. Lonny looked so young and innocent, which is exactly what he was at that time; clueless as to what awaited him.

I thought about Lonny lying unconscious in the hospital with injuries that would take him many months to recover from… if he survived. The tears started flowing again and I tried to stay quiet so I wouldn't disturb Fuzzy, but I soon heard him in the kitchen.

He saw me sitting on the couch and I asked if I'd woken him up.

"Just thirsty, doll. You okay?"

450

His innocent question sent me spiraling into an uncontrollable fit of tears. How could I be strong for Lonny when I was such a mess?

Fuzzy sat next to me and said, "We take for granted the people we care about. We go about our daily lives like they're always going to be there at the end of the day. That kid was always full of positive energy and gave me the strength to keep going without Marilyn. He's clever and he's funny. This house is dead without him in it."

I looked at Fuzzy and saw tears forming in his eyes. "What will we do if we lose him?" I cried.

He tried to smile. "I don't know, doll."

"We can't lose him," I whispered. "I'll never survive."

Fuzzy immediately burst into tears, covering his face with his hands. I petted his head, letting him know it was okay to show emotion, something I rarely saw him do. I pulled him into my arms and held him against my chest, rocking him like a child as we cried together.

"I can't get the image of him going through that window out of my mind. We should've been able to stop Joey, but it all happened so fast."

"Don't blame yourself," I cried. "Joey is the only one to blame for what happened to Lonny."

"I promised you I'd take care of him…."

I lifted Fuzzy's face so he could see mine and gently stroked his beard with my fingers. "This is *not* your fault."

"I'll never forgive myself."

I pressed my forehead against his as we continued to cry together. "I'm so lonely without him."

He wrapped his arms around my waist and pulled me against him, our lips crushing together in a desperate attempt to feel whole again, to make sense of what happened, to fill the void we were both experiencing in our lives. I'd never kissed a man with a ticklish mustache or beard before, and when I realized I was enjoying it far too much, he stopped. He apologized quickly as he got up and disappeared back into his bedroom. I followed him.

451

I could see him sitting up in bed by the light of the television, and he was still crying. I struggled to find my voice. "I'm sorry. I didn't mean to—"

"It's not you, doll. I shouldn't have—"

"Please don't leave me alone tonight," I whispered, my tears choking me.

He threw back the covers, inviting me to join him. I climbed in and got settled in his comforting arms as he wiped the tears from his face. We lay there silently until I thought about Lonny's battered body and my tears started all over again.

"I promised I'd never leave him," my voice cracked. "If I'd stayed, none of this would've happened."

Fuzzy rolled on top of me and I could see his eyes were still wet with tears. "Stop it," he ordered.

"Everything's my fault," I cried. "Everything that's happened to me, everything that's happened to Lonny."

He pressed his face against the middle of my shirt and said, "Don't do this, doll. Just... stop. *Please*."

He lifted his head to look at me, trying to smile, but we were both such a wreck we could only cry. He wiped the tears from my face as I weaved my fingers through his thick curls, then he kissed me with such desperation that in the depths of our despair we surrendered to each other.

I woke as the sun was rising and quietly snuck out of bed to take a shower and dress before Fuzzy got up. I was fixing breakfast when he came into the kitchen and stood behind me, resting his hands on my shoulders.

"Morning, doll."

"Morning."

"You okay?"

I nodded. "Yeah, I'm okay."

"Good." He kissed the top of my head, then poured himself a cup of coffee and sat down.

I turned to look at him and he was juggling some seashells he had taken out of a bowl sitting on the kitchen table.

"I didn't know you could juggle."

"There's a lot you don't know about me," he said with a wink.

I smiled as I watched him toss and catch the fragile objects with his hands.

"Lonny is obsessed with shells," he said. "Brings them home by the handful."

I had no idea Lonny was so fascinated by seashells. I looked at the collection of mismatched shells in the bowl, some perfect but most broken in some way, and asked, "Are those all his?"

"Yeah. He has them all over the house."

"Can I have one?"

"Take as many as you like. I'm sure he won't mind."

I took one perfect little conch shell, and a cockle shell with a hole in it that almost looked heart shaped.

"He likes the broken ones best because nobody wants those," he added. That sounded just like Lonny.

As soon as I cleaned up the breakfast dishes we were on our way to the hospital. Fuzzy stopped at the beach along the way so I could find a seashell worthy of bringing to Lonny, and I wasn't disappointed.

We walked into Lonny's room and he looked just as we'd left him the night before. I had hoped there would be some change, however small, but there was nothing.

"Good morning, Lonny! I brought you a present," I said brightly. I placed a seashell with a bluish hue in his right hand, closing his fingers around it. "I picked it out just for you."

I watched his hand, hoping for movement. A twitch, anything. But nothing.

"Lonny, I'm going to put your seashell on the windowsill, okay?" I was trying so hard not to cry, but my voice shook as I spoke. I pulled a chair up to the side of his bed and took my usual position holding his undamaged hand in mine. I had no intention of leaving his side again.

Fuzzy and I talked about good times while we were there, laughing about Marilyn's New Year's Eve party and about funny things that happened on the road. We included Lonny in the conversation because the doctors said he could hear everything we were saying and we wanted him to remember happy events in his life. I also told Fuzzy some stories about when we were in high school and would end each one by saying, "Remember that, Lonny?"

Fuzzy had to leave around lunchtime to take care of some business at the warehouse and hugged me fiercely before walking out the door. I caressed my cheek with Lonny's hand as silent tears escaped my eyes. I tried to be positive so Lonny wouldn't hear me crying the whole time, but it was extremely difficult. He was so damaged I didn't know how he would ever recover.

I knew how terrible my voice was, but decided to take a different approach and sing to him. Maybe it would be so horrible to his ears he'd wake up and tell me to shut up. I sang a few songs we loved in high school, including the songs we danced to at prom. I grew increasingly frustrated and rested my forehead on his bed, fighting the tears that insisted on burning my eyes.

I felt Lonny's finger twitch against my cheek and continued to cry. But then I felt it again. I instantly froze, waiting to see what would happen next. Lonny's fingers appeared to reach out and caress my cheek and I lifted my head to look at his face. His mouth closed and opened briefly, and I saw his tongue move. My heart raced but I didn't know if this was something to be celebrated, or just another twitching episode coma patients experience. I held his hand against my face and watched in agony, hoping for any sign of life beyond his breathing.

"Roo," he said, so softly I could barely hear him.

"I'm here," I said. "Lonny, I'm here."

He opened his eyes and it was as if he couldn't see me, his stare as vacant as a mannequin. "Roo," he said again.

I buzzed the nurse's station and yelled that he was awake as soon as they answered. Lonny's nurse was soon at his bedside checking his vitals.

"Welcome back," she said with a smile.

I stayed out of her way but watched Lonny's face as he realized something was seriously wrong. He didn't move, but his eyes darted around the room and he looked back at me in panic. I smiled at him, hoping to relieve his anxiety, but then I watched as he looked down at his broken body and his eyes became wet with tears.

"Roo," his voice croaked.

"It's okay," I tried to assure him. "You're going to be okay."

I wanted to shout from the rooftops that Lonny was awake, but I didn't want to walk away from that moment. He looked so terrified I didn't want to leave him. After the nurse left I held his hand and smiled, trying to reassure him that everything was going to be all right.

"What happened?" his voice cracked.

"There was an accident," I said. "About a week ago. We didn't think you were going to make it."

"Car?"

"How do you feel?" I changed the subject.

"Mom...."

"She knows. I've been keeping everyone updated."

"How long have you been here?"

"Fuzzy called and I came right away."

He closed his eyes, tears trickling down his cheeks. I wanted to pull him into my arms and comfort him, to tell him that the hard part was over, but I knew the hardest part had only just begun.

Fuzzy returned a couple hours later while Lonny was sleeping and I couldn't wait to tell him the wonderful news. He was ecstatic, pulling me into his arms for a celebratory hug.

"Best news ever," he whispered against my face.

"He's been sleeping a lot because of the pain meds, but he's out of the coma."

We turned toward Lonny who was staring at us blankly.

"Welcome back, kid!" Fuzzy greeted.

Lonny looked straight at Fuzzy and asked, "What happened?"

"You two talk and I'm gonna make some phone calls, okay?" I said.

I went to the private waiting room where I could call home. I was surprised that I burst into tears when my mother answered the phone. She immediately thought I was calling to tell her Lonny died.

"No Mom, he's awake. He's awake."

"What wonderful news!"

455

"He doesn't remember anything."

"What am I supposed to tell Billy?" she asked.

"Tell him the truth. Tell him Lonny just woke up and I'll go from there. I'm not hiding anything."

"He's a mess with you gone."

Because he can't control me. Or hurt me.

"Ruby," she continued. "You have a husband, a job, and a house that needs attending. You can't stay out there forever."

"Mom, Lonny just woke up. Give me a break, okay?"

"You need to come home. Now that Lonny is awake, there's no reason to stay."

Whose side are you on?

The next week proved to be exhausting as Lonny came to grips with the facts of his accident, but even worse the extent of his injuries. At times he was incoherent due to his pain medication, and at others he was angry and distant. It was understandable considering what he'd already been through, and staring an unknown future in the face had to be daunting.

I continued to sleep on the couch in Lonny's room and one night I woke to hear him sobbing. I sat next to his bed and held his hand against my face, letting him know I was there.

"I don't even know his wife," he cried. "I would never sleep with someone's wife."

"Don't think about him. Think about getting stronger and going home."

"What if I can't play guitar?"

"Don't think about what you can't control right now," I whispered. "Just concentrate on getting better."

"Look at my arm, Roo," he cried.

"I know it looks bad now, but it's gonna get better. I promise."

He pulled his hand away from me to wipe the tears from his face. "Thank you for being here."

I smiled and caressed his cheek with my fingers. "Hey, tomorrow is a big day, you know. You're moving to a regular room, and they're taking the staples out of your head."

"How long are you staying?"

"As long as you need me."

456

He grinned and said, "Don't make promises you can't keep."

"Lonny, I just want you to be whole again."

"What if that never happens?"

"Then I guess I'll have to stay until it does." I leaned over and gently pressed my mouth against his, letting him know I had no intention of leaving him again.

The next morning after being transferred to a regular hospital room, the bandage around Lonny's head was taken off and the staples were removed. They only shaved the side of his head where the wound was, so he was grateful not to be completely bald. Mitch told him he was going to bring a razor so he could shave the right side of his head to match. Lonny actually seemed to entertain that idea.

Now that Lonny was in a regular room he wasn't restricted to only two visitors at a time, so it was nice for me and the band to be there together. When his lunch arrived, Fuzzy brought me back to the house so I could take a shower. For some reason there was no hot water in the bathroom of the spare room where my things were unpacked, so he told me to go ahead and use the shower in his bedroom. I smiled as the hot water rained down on me, so thankful Lonny was on his way to recovery. He had a long road ahead of him, but I knew he was strong enough to do whatever he needed to make it happen. I was excited about scouring the beach on the way back to the hospital to find the perfect shell for his gift of the day. The warm sun, my toes in the sand, searching for a piece of nature that would bring a smile to my love's face... I couldn't have been happier. I decided then I was going to tell my mother I wasn't coming home. I was going to stay where I belonged. I was going to stay and take care of Lonny, and we were going to be together like we deserved.

I realized I was in desperate need of a shave, but my razor was in the other bathroom. I turned off the water, wrapped myself in a towel and ran out of his room saying, "Sorry Fuzzy, I forgot my—"

I stopped dead in my tracks when I saw Fuzzy standing next to Billy, who was glaring at me like I had just committed the crime of the century.

Fuzzy turned to face me and said, "Your husband seems to have followed us home from the hospital."

"What are you doing here?" was all I could think to say.

"I came to bring my wife home," he growled. "I can see now why you didn't want to leave."

"Billy, this isn't what it looks like."

"It never is, is it?" The look on his face shook me to my core.

Fuzzy held up his hands and said, "Look man, Ruby's been sleeping at the hospital every night. She only came here to take a shower, so don't get any stupid ideas."

"Get dressed," Billy ordered.

"I haven't even taken my shower."

"Ruby, get dressed."

I went into the spare room and closed the door. Panic filled every part of my body and my brain tried to quickly process everything that was happening. I dried myself off and got dressed, taking the cockle shell with the heart shaped hole in it off the bedside table and slipping it into the front pocket of my jeans. Billy burst into the room and started throwing my things into the suitcase that was open on top of the bed.

"We're leaving now?" I stupidly asked.

"Do you think I'm here for vacation?"

"You should stay a few days so I can show you around." I was doing anything I could to diffuse the situation.

"I had to take a day off work to come and get you. I'm not here to play around."

Billy grabbed my suitcase and headed out toward the living room where Fuzzy stood waiting with his arms folded across his chest. Billy looked so small and harmless standing next to him.

"I'm not leaving without saying goodbye to Lonny," I said, taking full advantage of the fact Fuzzy was there.

"Fine," Billy agreed. "Let's go." He grabbed my hand and pulled me out the door toward his rental car.

"Right behind you, doll!" Fuzzy shouted.

Billy had no idea where he was going, waiting for Fuzzy to pull ahead so he could follow him. He was eerily silent, which was far more terrifying than when he yelled at me. When we got to the

458

hospital Billy was holding my hand so tightly it felt like he was crushing bones. I entered the room first, followed by Billy and Fuzzy. Lonny's face lit up when he saw me, then immediately fell when he laid eyes on Billy.

"Hey Lonny," I spoke softly. "I have to go home now."

Lonny said nothing, his eyes darting back and forth between me and Billy. He shifted uncomfortably in his bed and cleared his throat. I walked to the side of his bed and held his hand, turning my back on Billy, hoping I was blocking his view of Lonny's face. I knew he wasn't going to give me any privacy, so I had to be careful what I said. And in Lonny's condition, I didn't want him worrying about me after I left.

"I can't do this without you," he whispered, his eyes filling with tears.

I smiled as tears burned my own eyes. "You're a fighter, Lonny. You can do this because your friends are gonna help you get through it."

Tears trickled out of his eyes as he whispered, "You promised you weren't leaving."

I ran my finger over the razor stubble on his chin and said, "I kinda like your scruffy look."

"Ruby, we have to go," Billy said.

I wanted to give Lonny a hug, to pull him into my arms and let him know how much I wanted to stay, but his body was still so broken I didn't want to cause him more pain. My heart thundered in my chest as Billy watched every move I made, but I knew what was coming once we got home and there was a good chance I may never see Lonny again.

I leaned over and placed my right hand gently against his left cheek as I pressed my face against his right cheek. "I don't know when I'll see you again," I whispered.

Lonny lifted his free arm and tried to hug me the best he could. "Please don't go," he cried.

"He will *never* understand our bond, but keep me in your heart and we'll always find each other there."

His body shook underneath me as he cried. "Roo, please…."

459

"I love you, Lonny," I whispered, kissing him on the cheek before I straightened up. I snuck the seashell out of my pocket and placed it in Lonny's hand, closing his fingers around it.

Billy grabbed my hand and started pulling me away from Lonny's bedside, but I never took my eyes off him. We watched each other until we could no longer see each other.

When we got in the car I asked Billy, "Does my mom know you came here to get me?"

"No." He turned to face me, shoving an angry finger in my face. "And shut your mouth. I don't want to hear another word."

"I just asked a question."

I saw stars when he popped me in the mouth with the back of his hand. "I said shut your mouth."

It was an agonizingly long trip. Billy's silent treatment meant I needed to prepare myself for the hell he would unleash once we were in the privacy of our own home. As soon as he parked the car in the driveway, I got out and started running. If I could just make it to my parents' house….

I was in the bathroom cleaning the blood off my face when the phone rang. Even though I could only hear Billy's side of the conversation, I knew it was my mother.

"Ruby's still in California," he lied. "I just talked to her a few minutes ago. She said she'll probably be there another week or two." He stopped to listen to whatever my mother was saying then answered with, "I wouldn't worry about anything Lonny says. Ruby said he's pretty drugged up and not making much sense."

Lonny knew.

I looked in the mirror and hated myself. Not because my eye was swollen shut, or because blood was trickling out of my nose, or because I had a fat lip, but for leaving Lonny, for being stupid, for being terrified to speak up, for being *weak*.

I crawled into bed after a long, painful day and wanted nothing but sleep, but unfortunately Billy had other plans. He spooned me lovingly and nuzzled his face against the back of my neck.

"I don't understand why you aren't pregnant yet," he whispered.

Panic ran through me as I feared he found out I was secretly taking birth control pills. "I don't know."

He kissed my shoulder and I knew I had to go along with whatever he wanted, no matter how repulsed I was. I closed my eyes as the weight of his body pressed down on top of me, my mind taking me to a happier place. A place where I actually felt cared for in the arms of a man who knew how to love a woman, even if it wasn't about love at all.

Peter.

2011

I dragged a box out of my bedroom closet and sat on the floor next to Lonny. He opened it and started pulling out envelope after envelope addressed to me, but never opened.

"What are these?" he asked.

"All the photos I took on tour."

"The ones Howard sent you?"

I nodded. "Yeah."

"You never opened them?" A look of pure shock covered his face.

"I never had the heart to look at them."

"I only saw the ones that made it into the newsletter."

I smiled. "I guess we both have some surprises waiting for us."

One by one we opened an envelope and went through the photographs inside, some of them causing us great sorrow, but most of them bringing a smile and laughter as we remembered the great times we had on Lonny's first tour with Livingston Monroe.

"The majority of these photos have never seen the light of day," Lonny said. "You have a goldmine here."

"What do you mean?"

"You own the copyright to these photos, which means you can do whatever you want with them."

I was skeptical. "I don't know…."

"Do you know how many people would love to see these? You could put up a website or something."

"I don't know about that stuff."

"I'll help you. People might be interested in buying some of these… you could probably make some pretty good money."

"Really?"

"You need to start thinking about your future, Roo. What're you going to do with your life now?"

I hadn't really thought about that. And what I really hadn't thought about was a response to the envelope Lonny opened next.

"Um… Roo…."

I took the photos he handed to me and felt my face flush. They were pictures I took of Peter's autograph signing at the record store, and then back at his hotel. There was nothing sexual or indecent about the photos from the hotel, but it was obvious by looking at them that we had been intimate with each other.

"Sorry," I said, embarrassed. "I forgot about those."

"Peter?"

"It's not what you think."

"It's exactly what I think," he retorted.

I tried to cover the smile with my hand, but I was busted. "You're right, it is."

"I don't want to look at those."

"There's nothing inappropriate. Are you jealous?"

He pouted and scratched his head. "I don't like thinking about you with other men."

I laughed. Loudly. "Other men? How many do you think there were?"

"I'm not having this conversation." He was acting like a spoiled child.

"What about you? Every time I turned around you had a new girlfriend. Big rock star... I wasn't stupid. I knew what that meant."

The awkward silence in the room was thick enough to chew, and my teeth just weren't sharp enough to break through.

"Roo, it's just... it killed me thinking about you being *married*. And now I find out you had an affair with Peter? When did that happen?"

I hesitated before answering, "The weekend before my wedding."

Lonny's mouth was agape and I didn't like the way he was looking at me. He stood up and said, "I need a cigarette," before storming out of my room.

463

1986

Lonny recovered completely from his superficial injuries, going through months of physical therapy and several surgeries on his arm, but due to extensive nerve damage his guitar playing was never the same. Rather than replace Lonny, the band went on hiatus until they decided what they wanted to do. In the two years since his accident, the band released a greatest hits album and an album of unreleased songs and demos. In conversations with Lonny I found out he was learning how to play the piano, drawing and painting on a regular basis, and indulged in horse track betting to pass the time when he was bored. I was relieved he didn't take the path of drinking and drugs, which he very easily could have considering his mother's alcoholism.

I hadn't seen Lonny since I left him at the hospital that day. Billy's aggression seemed to subside a bit as he quit his job at the hardware store and began working full time as a tattoo artist. He worked nights, so he allowed me to continue my visits with Joanie on Fridays, especially since Lonny was in a serious relationship with Isabella, his physical therapist. It was the longest relationship he'd ever been in, and if he was happy, I was happy for him.

Billy still didn't understand why I hadn't gotten pregnant yet, and I tried to convince him that maybe it just wasn't going to happen for us. I knew he didn't really want to have a child; he only wanted another way to control me. I knew what I had to do to keep him happy, and how to paint on the smile that everyone was used to seeing. I was dead inside, with only the happy memories of my past keeping me physically breathing. I had come to terms with the fact that this was the life I was destined to live; the life I deserved.

Billy had Sundays off, so we would go to my parents' house for dinner. Sometimes Gina would join us, but it was rare, and Joanie would be there as well. One Sunday that summer I was helping my mother clean up the kitchen when my father yelled for me from the living room. It sounded urgent and I ran to see what was wrong.

I saw the headline, "Livingston Monroe Plane Crash," and fell to my knees in front of the television. They weren't able to

464

announce which band members were on board, but everyone in the small aircraft was killed on impact. My skin prickled as I heard someone scream out in agony, then I realized it was me. Billy sat on the floor next to me and pulled me into his arms, comforting me in my grief. A few minutes later the phone rang and I could hear my mother saying, "Yes, she's here… h-hold on Lonny, please… Ruby, it's Lonny."

I rushed to the kitchen and took the phone from my mother.

"Roo," he cried. "They're all gone."

I almost threw up. "Everyone?"

"Howard was flying, Benji, Wanda, Joey… and Mitch."

I sunk to the floor. "Fuzzy?"

"He wasn't with them."

"Lonny, I'm so sorry," I cried. I had never forgiven Joey for what he did to Lonny, but Lonny had a big heart and never pressed charges against him and the two actually became friends. Part of me wondered if this was his punishment for the brutal attack, but it didn't explain the deaths of my friends.

"Roo, what am I gonna do?"

"I don't know," I cried. "Poor Calvin. What's gonna happen to him?"

"I don't know," he cried. "I wish you were here."

"Me, too. I wish there was something I could do."

"Fuzzy just came home. I'll talk to you later, okay?"

He hung up the phone but I kept my place on the floor, the receiver still in my hands. I stared at it in disbelief as tears blurred my vision. I hugged my knees to my chest as my mother took the phone from me and hung it back on the wall. It felt as though the roof had crashed down on my head. A dull throbbing began in my temples and the rest of my body went numb. Billy was soon at my side, hugging me and holding his face against mine.

"It'll be okay," he said. "Lonny's okay."

Billy had been so supportive in the days after the crash, loving and comforting in every way imaginable. I had every intention of going to California to attend the memorial service for my friends and to support Lonny, with or without Billy's permission. As supportive as he'd been, I wasn't even fearful of

465

telling him I was going. I was actually surprised when he said he didn't have a problem with it.

A few days before I planned on flying out, I went to the bank to make a withdrawal so I could purchase my plane ticket. The bank teller told me I couldn't make a withdrawal because my name was not on the account. This made no sense to me, since Billy and I merged our bank accounts after we got married and I had made withdrawals in the past. Rather than argue with the teller, I took it up with Billy when he came home from work.

"I tried to make a withdrawal at the bank today," I said carefully. "They told me I wasn't authorized because my name isn't on the account."

"I felt I needed to make some changes."

"It's *our* account. My paycheck goes in there, too."

"You know the trust fund payments have stopped. We need to be very careful how we spend our money."

"I never spend anything!"

"I'll give you a weekly allowance if you want, but I think it's best this way."

I could feel my stomach twisting. "I need money for a plane ticket."

"For what?"

"To go to the memorial service for my friends."

"I'm sorry Ruby, but we can't afford that."

"You promised me I'd be able to go."

"I'm sorry, but you just can't."

I could feel the rage burning inside me, ready to explode at any moment. I knew I had to tread carefully, but I couldn't even think straight. I wanted to be there to support Lonny and Fuzzy, but I needed to be there for myself. I needed to support my friends who were gone forever. The friends I would never see again.

I stood up and grabbed the lamp off the table and smashed it through the television set. I was going to smash it against anything else that got in my way, but Billy wrestled it away from me and pushed me onto the floor.

"They were my friends," I cried.

"You can mourn them from here for free. You're doing it already," he scoffed.

466

"You promised."

"You promised to love and obey me."

I curled up into a ball on the floor and cried, waiting for the beating I knew all too well, but it never came. Billy cleaned up the mess I made and went to bed.

The next night at Joanie's I dreaded getting Lonny's call. He was already distraught over the loss of his friends, and I had no idea how he was going to react when I told him I wasn't coming to the memorial service. He was a wreck when he called, and I waited as long as I could to tell him the news.

"Are you flying in on Sunday?" he finally asked. I was quiet for too long. "Roo? Are you coming Sunday?"

"I'm sorry Lonny, but I can't."

"Why not?"

"I can't afford it." I didn't even know if that was the truth. My gut told me it was a lie.

"But you have to come!" he shouted.

"Lonny, I'm sorry."

"I'll pay for your ticket. You can stay at the house with us. You can afford that, can't you?"

How could I argue with that? How could Billy? "Are you sure?"

"Roo, you need to be here. And I need you."

You always need me, but you never love me.

"Okay, yeah," I said.

"I'll have a ticket waiting for you at the airport."

"Thank you, Lonny."

"You have to be there."

On Sunday morning I started packing my suitcase and Billy asked what I was doing. "I'm going to the memorial for my friends."

"I said you couldn't go."

"You said we couldn't afford it. Lonny has a ticket waiting for me at the airport and I'm staying in the spare room at their house. No cost to us." I smiled like I was the most brilliant person on earth.

"You asked for handouts?"

"I didn't ask for anything. It was Lonny's idea."

467

"Lonny's idea," he repeated. "Does the filthy rich rock star think I can't take care of my own wife?"

"It's not like that," I insisted.

Billy grabbed my suitcase and threw it against the wall, sending the contents spilling all over the floor. Like a fool I fell to the floor and started putting my things back in the suitcase. He kicked it away from me shouting, "You're not going!"

I saw him lift his hand and immediately curled into a ball on the floor. "Please don't hurt me," I begged. "I'll stay home. I promise."

That night after dinner at my parents' house my mother answered the phone and held it out to me. Everyone went into the living room to have dessert and watch a movie, and I waited until they were all out of the kitchen before I said anything.

"Where the fuck are you?" Lonny yelled.

"Lonny, I can ex—"

"You promised me you'd be here!"

"Please don't yell at me," I whispered.

"I can't believe you're doing this. You're abandoning me when I need you most!"

"Lonny, that's not fair."

"Fair? Is it fair that our friends are dead? Is it fair that Calvin has no parents? What's fair about any of this?"

Lonny was getting hysterical and I didn't like the way he was talking to me. "Lonny please, I can't do this right now."

"I haven't seen you in *two* years! This is because of Billy, isn't it?"

"Please don't," I whispered.

"Fuck Billy! And you know what, Rooster? Fuck you, too!"

He slammed the phone down so hard I heard a bell ringing in my head.

2011

I slowly looked through the photographs of Peter and I smiled. I loved the photos of us together, both smiling happily and not having another care in the world other than the time we spent together that weekend. I was forever grateful for what he gave me, and I wasn't going to apologize for it.

I got up and walked to my bedroom window, watching Lonny sitting on the picnic table smoking a cigarette. He must have been on his second or third based on the time he was gone, so I went outside to talk to him. He sat with his feet on the bench, legs bent, the rips in his jeans exposing his knees. I drew circles on one knee with my fingertip, then leaned in and tried to nuzzle my face against his neck.

"Roo...."

"Aw what's the big deal?" I groaned, pulling away.

He shrugged and stumbled for words. "I don't know... it's you... *my* Roo... sweet and innocent and virginal... wearing cute sundresses and smelling like cherry lip gloss."

"Well *your* Roo spent a weekend naked in a hotel room with Peter."

He smashed out his cigarette and said, "A week before your wedding?"

"Do I need to remind you that you once dated twins? I never judged you."

"I tried to stop your wedding," he said, his hands talking more than his mouth was. "If I'd come home a week earlier, would you have spent the weekend in a hotel room with me?"

"It's not something I planned," I explained. "But Peter gave me something that helped me survive my marriage."

Lonny wrinkled his forehead. "What was that?"

"I was so desperate to feel adored... to feel love. Peter was the only one who ever told me I was beautiful. He gave me physical love that I was able to lock in my memory bank and think about when Billy was forcing himself on me."

"What about us? Wasn't that enough?"

469

"Lonny, you were my boyfriend for all of two days, and neither one of us knew what we were doing. Peter was experienced, and I asked him to teach me everything he knew."

"Everything?"

"Everything," I said with a grin. "But I played dumb with Billy. If it weren't for Peter, I would've been dead a long time ago."

Lonny took my hands in his and pulled me closer to him. "So you're saying you have a whole arsenal of tricks you've never used?"

"Maybe," I laughed.

He put his hands against my face and buried his fingers in my hair. "I'm jealous of anyone who was lucky enough to be with you," he admitted.

"For the record, I thought about you every waking moment, and I would have done anything for it to be you."

"For the record, I always thought you were beautiful."

Lonny leaned forward and pressed his mouth against mine, sweet and innocent like the first time he ever kissed me. A flood of memories came rushing back and I smiled.

"I love you."

He smiled back. "I love you."

1989

I hadn't heard from Lonny in three years, since the day he hung up on me so angrily for not going to the memorial service. Billy was certainly happy and it made my marriage a lot easier to deal with, but it broke my heart. Fuzzy would send me letters at my parents' house filling me in on what was going on with Lonny, and it wasn't good. Fuzzy described it as being in self-destruct mode, as he was depressed about the deaths of his friends and not being able to play guitar, and he was bleeding his bank account dry by feeding his gambling habit. I promised Fuzzy I would do what I could, but any call I made to Lonny begging him to talk to me went unanswered and he never called me back. I still spent Friday nights with Joanie, so Lonny made sure he called her when I wasn't there. I would ask if he ever mentioned me and she would cry as she said no. He had no idea the brutality I would have endured if I insisted on going to the memorial service, as badly as I wanted to be there. *Needed* to be there. It was the first time I begged Billy not to hurt me and he hadn't hit me after that, because Lonny was no longer disrupting his life in some way.

I was twenty-eight years old and the loneliest I'd ever been in my life. Without Lonny nothing mattered. I had no phone call to look forward to, no letters to read, no new photographs to enjoy. Joanie would show me any photos he sent her, but she kept his letters private and I respected that. I would never have asked her to share those with me. It had been five years since we'd seen each other and three years since I heard his voice, and in our last conversation all he did was yell at me. I couldn't get the sound of his anger out of my head. And now he was a complete mess, falling apart and deeper into a depression that no one seemed to be able to help him escape from.

The only good thing to come out of the plane crash was that Fuzzy and Marilyn reunited at the memorial service and ended up getting back together. Fuzzy had officially adopted Calvin and they were raising him together. Lonny moved out when Marilyn and Calvin moved in, stating it was time for him to find his own place. This made it difficult for Fuzzy to keep an eye on him, and only aided in Lonny falling deeper and deeper into a life of destruction. The last Fuzzy reported was that he had left the country and was in London somewhere.

I threw away my birth control pills in the hopes that I could create a child that I would love more than anyone else in the world, even more than Lonny. Even if it meant Billy was the father. As fate would have it, the result was the same and I still wasn't getting pregnant. I thought there was some small chance being pregnant would change the way I felt about myself, but worthless was the badge pinned to my heart.

In August we went to my parents' for dinner to celebrate our eighth wedding anniversary. My mother and Joanie went all out with the cooking and I thought they were making a big deal out of nothing. It wasn't like it was our tenth anniversary or anything. Before we sat down to eat my mother gave me an envelope that came in the mail that afternoon.

"Looks like an invitation of some sort," she said.

I tore open the envelope to reveal an invitation for Marilyn's surprise 40th birthday party. Everyone wanted to know what it was, thinking it was a wedding invitation... perhaps Lonny's.

I explained what it was and said, "I'm not going."

"Why not?" my father asked.

"No reason to see those people again after all this time," was my response.

"You should go," Billy said.

I almost shit myself. "I should?"

"Yeah," he said with a smile. "You've been working hard and keeping up the house, taking care of things... I think you should go."

I didn't know if this was a game Billy was playing in front of the parents or if he was being genuine, but I hadn't seen Marilyn in ten years and the thought of being in the same room with her again made me deliriously happy.

Three days before I was to leave for California I found out I was pregnant. Billy was overjoyed and couldn't wait to share the news with everyone. My parents were ecstatic and while Joanie seemed to be happy, I could tell she wasn't banging any celebratory drums.

Lying in bed that night Billy said, "I'm not sure you should leave now."

"Why not?"

"Because you're pregnant. I don't want anything to happen to the baby."

"My doctor said it was safe for me to fly."

"Are you sure?"

I hesitated before saying, "Okay, I won't go."

He kissed me and said, "Thank you."

"I'll cancel my flight and hotel room in the morning."

On Saturday I packed my suitcase and took a taxi to the airport as planned. Billy worked regular hours on Saturdays and could do nothing to stop me. I left a note on the kitchen table telling him I would be back Sunday night, as we originally agreed.

I was nothing but smiles on the way to my hotel. The sunshine, being away from Billy, knowing I was going to see Fuzzy and Marilyn... I hadn't felt that happy or that free in many years. I had plenty of time to kill when I got to my hotel, so I took a much needed nap before showering and dressing in the new outfit I bought especially for the occasion. I pulled the silky black bodysuit up over my body, then slipped into my black leather miniskirt, zipping it in the back. I put on my black zippered ankle boots and leopard print jacket and studied myself in the mirror. I definitely needed some makeup, so I put on a little bit of mascara and eyeliner to brighten up my eyes and a touch of pink lipstick to top it off.

I had taken the phone off the hook while I was napping, but as soon as I hung it back up it was ringing nonstop. I knew it was Billy and I knew he was angry at me for leaving after promising not to, but I would deal with him after the party.

The taxi pulled up to the address on the invitation and I could do nothing but smile like a fool. Even in the dark I could never forget Peter's house. I walked to the door, adjusted my skirt and rang the doorbell. I couldn't wait to see Peter and give him a big hug, and I nearly jumped in his arms when the door opened.

Only it wasn't Peter. It was a gorgeous woman with curly jet black hair and eyes so blue they almost looked fake.

"Come on in," she said with a smile.

I walked into the house behind her, a little bit nervous because I had no idea who she was as she never introduced herself. I looked around at the people who were already there and I didn't recognize a soul. I was relieved when Peter came out of nowhere and lifted me off the ground in a hug.

"Sweet Ruby, it's so good to see you!" he said, kissing me on the cheek. Peter hadn't changed much except for his hair, embracing the eighties with a loose, blond perm. "You look fantastic!" he exclaimed. "Absolutely breathtaking!"

My face flushed, but I thanked him with an embarrassed smile. "You haven't changed," I said. "I love your hair."

"I'd introduce you to my lovely wife, but she's divorcing me."

I didn't know he was married. After stumbling for something to say, I mumbled, "I'm so sorry."

He smiled his bright smile and said, "She's taking me for everything I have. But I have my horse rescue and my twin girls, so really, she can have the rest."

"You have children?"

He picked up a framed photo of himself with the most beautiful little girls I'd ever seen. "Katherine and Jacqueline — they'll be five years old in a few months. Love them to bits."

"They're beautiful. Tell me about your horse rescue."

Just as Peter opened his mouth to speak I saw Lonny across the room talking to the blue eyed woman. I didn't hear a word Peter was saying as I waited to see if Lonny would notice me. As soon as his eyes met mine I looked away, refocusing on Peter. Our last conversation was nothing but him yelling and cursing at me three years earlier and wasn't he supposed to be in London?

I could see out the corner of my eye that Lonny was making his way toward me, but someone yelled that Fuzzy and Marilyn had just pulled in so everyone froze and remained silent. I didn't have to see him to know he was standing behind me, sending my stomach twisting into knots. Peter opened the door to let Fuzzy and Marilyn in, and as soon as they turned the corner everyone yelled, "Surprise!" She genuinely looked surprised; you couldn't put anything over on her, so I was wondering how Fuzzy was going to pull it off. Even after ten years, she still looked young and beautiful.

Marilyn screamed with excitement, playfully smacking Fuzzy on the shoulder then kissing him. Then she saw me. It was as if no other person was at the party as she made a beeline straight to me, pulling me into her arms.

"Oh doll," she cried. "It's so good to see you. I've missed you so much."

We held each other for a long time, both of us crying. Realizing we were both probably smudging our makeup she took me by the hand and brought me to the nearest bathroom.

"You look fabulous, doll," she said.

"So do you!"

"Some days I feel like I'm sixty, but I'm doing okay," she joked.

"I was so happy to hear you and Fuzzy got back together."

"He's my true happy," she said with a smile, wiping the streaked mascara with her finger.

"Hey," I pouted. "I'm still mad at you!"

She pulled me in for a hug and said, "I was a selfish asshole. I had to learn a lot of hard lessons. Forgive me?"

I pulled away to look at her face and nodded. How could I ever stay angry with Marilyn?

"Have you talked to Lonny yet?" she asked.

"I thought he was in London."

"Came home last week. Have you talked to him?"

"Not yet. I'm not sure I want to. He was pretty awful the last time I talked to him."

"A lot of shit happened three years ago that we can't change. So much grief, no answers. After his accident Lonny lost his identity; lost himself. He was on a downward spiral, but it was manageable. Then the crash happened and his entire world was destroyed. The things he said to you were unforgivable... I would never defend him there. But maybe you can find it in your heart to forgive him."

475

We rejoined the party and Fuzzy picked me up off the ground for a loving hug. "I'm so glad you came, doll," he said. "It's great to see you."

I noticed Lonny was across the room talking to some other people and I breathed a sigh of relief. Peter took me by the hand and led me to the couch, where we talked uninterrupted about the work he was doing with his horse rescue. I knew how passionate he was about animals, specifically horses, and I'd never seen his eyes sparkle with so much fire before. Considering he was in the middle of a divorce, he was the happiest I'd ever seen him. And he never let go of my hand the entire time we talked. Peter always made you feel like you were the only person in the room when he talked to you. I was forever grateful that he was my friend.

It wasn't long before Marilyn joined us and said, "Remember when you two met at my New Year's Eve party? Wasn't it fabulous?"

We laughed, remembering it fondly. We talked about that party for some time, reliving some of its best moments. Peter was not only a great storyteller, but hilariously funny, and he added quite a bit of humor to the stories when he told them.

"Look doll," Marilyn said, tapping my leg. "Lonny keeps looking at you. Why doesn't he just come over and talk to you?"

"You keep out of it!" I scolded playfully, remembering how much Marilyn liked to meddle in other peoples' business.

No sooner had the words left my mouth, Lonny was on his way over to where we were sitting. Sure, because it wasn't obvious enough that we were talking about him. Even without meddling, Marilyn had a way of getting involved. Lonny grabbed five champagne flutes and handed one to each of us.

"To Marilyn," he said, holding up his drink.

"To Benji," Fuzzy said. "The best brother I ever had."

"To Howard," Marilyn said. "The best manager a band could ever have."

"To my wife," Peter said. "For divorcing me and making me the happiest man alive."

"To Mitch, the first penis I ever laid eyes on," I remarked.

Everyone howled with laughter, but it was the truth. My four companions sipped their champagne but I held onto my glass.

"Why aren't you drinking your champagne?" Marilyn asked, giving me her quizzical eye.

Shit.

"I'm pregnant."

Lonny nearly choked on his champagne hearing my response. Marilyn screamed so loud the attention of all other partygoers was focused on our little group.

"To Ruby!" Marilyn shouted, holding up her glass for another toast.

"Congratulations, doll," Fuzzy said, smiling.

Peter, who was still sitting next to me, gave me a hug and said, "You'll be a wonderful mother, love."

I hadn't planned on mentioning my pregnancy while I was visiting, but there it was. Lonny cleared his throat and walked away, avoiding me the rest of the evening.

As the party began to wind down, I asked Fuzzy who the blue eyed woman was that Lonny always seemed to be talking to.

"That's Penelope Buckingham."

"Joey's wife?"

"Yep. He wasn't sleeping with her when Joey threw him out the window, but he's been trying hard since he met her at the memorial service."

"Is she interested?"

"I think she's playing hard to get."

"For three years?" I joked.

Marilyn interrupted us and said, "We're taking you to the hotel to get your things. You're staying with us."

I knew better than to argue with her, but I knew I had to call Billy once I got back to the hotel. He was going to be furious as it was, and if I didn't call he'd probably hop on a plane and come to drag me home again.

I said goodbye to Peter, thanking him for a lovely evening. He hugged me gently and kissed me on the cheek. "It was good to see you again, sweet Ruby."

Penelope said goodbye to Marilyn and Fuzzy and walked out the front door, and I watched as Lonny gawked at her the entire time. As we reached the door, Lonny put a hand on my shoulder.

"Can I talk to you?" he asked.

477

"Lonny, it's late. You had all night to talk to me."

"Please?"

I was getting annoyed. "Lonny, I——"

"Let me take you back to your hotel."

I looked at Marilyn who nodded and smiled.

"All right," I said.

Marilyn and Fuzzy each gave me a hug and kiss, and I really didn't want to say goodbye to them. Marilyn promised to keep in touch and they drove away. As Lonny drove me back to my hotel, he was silent. He said he wanted to talk, yet he said absolutely nothing. This annoyed me more than anything. Here was my best friend in the whole world, the only man I'd ever loved, and I couldn't get out of the car fast enough.

Lonny pulled into a parking space at the hotel and stared straight ahead.

"Well thanks for the ride, Lonny," I said. "And the stimulating conversation."

He turned to face me and said, "Roo, I'm sorry. For everything."

"Okay." I turned to open the door but he reached out to grab my hand.

"I need to talk to someone."

"How about you give Penelope a call?"

"Why do you always have to be such a smart ass?"

"Goodbye, Lonny." I got out of the car and started walking toward the hotel door.

Lonny soon caught up and stood in front of me, blocking my path. "I'm sorry. I need to talk to *you*. I need *you*, Roo."

"You always *need* me, but then you drink your asshole juice and treat me like shit. I'm done, Lonny."

His eyes filled with tears as he whispered, "*Please*. I'm sorry."

I hesitated before asking if he wanted to come up to my room. He nodded and wiped the tears from his eyes as he followed me into the hotel. We were both silent in the elevator. As soon as we got into my room, I told him I needed to call Billy and that he had to remain completely silent. He sat in a chair at the table by the window and said nothing.

478

I kicked off my boots and sat on the edge of the bed, dreading the call I was about to make. The phone rang and rang and there was no answer. This worried me more than if he'd answered screaming at me. It was two in the morning there. I hung up the phone and tried to look unfazed.

"I'm going to get out of these clothes," I told Lonny. "I'd offer you a beverage, but I'm in a cheap room."

I went to the bathroom to change into a pair of shorts and a t-shirt, and when I came back out Lonny was in the same position I'd left him. Elbows on his knees, staring down at the floor. I got comfortable on the bed and waited for him to talk. His continued silence was making me increasingly uncomfortable.

He finally lifted his head and looked at me with eyes that hadn't seen life in a very long time. I felt compelled to repeat the words he once said to me.

"You don't look good, Lonny."

"I've lost everything, Roo."

"What do you mean?"

"I lost my career, my band... After my accident Peter would take me to the horse races to get me out of the house. But then it wasn't enough anymore. I found out you can bet on anything and everything, and I was winning. Big. I was a hot shot with a lot of money, I was in a long-term relationship with a beautiful woman who had a career of her own, and nothing could stop me."

Lonny shifted in his seat, running his hands nervously through his hair. "Then the plane crash happened. We lost our friends... my world was forever altered and I couldn't handle it. Isabella didn't like the person I had become and ended things. I begged her not to leave me, but she wasn't having any of it. The last time you and I talked... I really did need you. I was about to blow my brains out, but I knew if I could just see you, I'd be able to get back on track. But you didn't come."

Lonny had tears running down his face and I listened with such profound sadness I soon felt them falling from my own eyes.

"I was spiraling out of control. I couldn't play guitar, half my band was dead, and gambling took over my life. It's the only thing that made me feel good; made me feel alive. I didn't even

479

care about girls or sex anymore. Fuzzy warned me, Marilyn nearly slapped the shit out of me… Peter tried taking me to Gamblers Anonymous… I turned on all of them. They were the best friends I had in the world and I shut them all out."

Lonny wiped the tears from his face and cried, "But the worst part was losing you. So many times I wanted to talk to you… *needed* to talk to you, but I was so angry I just blamed you for everything that was wrong in my life. You were my best friend in the whole world, and you were the person I was most angry with. And you went on living without me and I hated you for that, too."

I wasn't living.

"Lonny, I'm so sorry," I whispered, shocked at his revelation.

"Roo, I just found out I have a three-year-old daughter." He bent over and began sobbing, rocking himself back and forth like a child.

My heart jumped so high into my throat I almost choked on it.

Lonny had a child?

"I got so wasted I couldn't even see straight and went to a hotel with a woman from the memorial service. How can I be a father? I can't even take care of myself."

Lonny fell onto the floor and I rushed to his side, pulling him into my arms.

"It's okay Lonny, you'll be okay," I whispered.

He held onto me for dear life as I tried to comfort him. "I have nothing left, Roo. I'm almost broke, and I lost my house."

"Where have you been living?"

"One of the empty rehearsal rooms at the warehouse."

"Why didn't you ask someone for help?"

"Because I'm a piece of shit. I can't ask for help. I deserve everything that's happening to me."

I gently pushed Lonny away so I could see his face. I put my hands on his cheeks and forced him to look at me.

"Lonny Winter, you are *not* a piece of shit. You made some mistakes, but you're still a good person. You're my favorite person in the world."

He managed to crack a smile. "Does that mean you forgive me?"

I pulled him close to me again and pressed my face against his as we cried together. I held him as tightly as I could without strangling him.

"I didn't want to turn into my mom," he cried.

"We'll fix this, Lonny, I promise. I don't know how, but we'll fix this."

"I'm so sorry," he sobbed. "I didn't ever want to hurt you."

I stood up and held out my hand, helping Lonny to his feet. I sat on the bed and he followed me. He reached out and touched my stomach.

"So there's a baby in there?" he asked.

"Yeah, there's a baby in there."

"What does it feel like?"

"I'm only about eight weeks, so I don't really feel anything yet. What're you going to do about your daughter?"

He rubbed his face and said, "I have no idea. I want to take care of her, of course. I'd like to meet her."

I smiled. "I bet she's beautiful."

"I don't even know what she looks like."

"One step at a time. You can't solve all your problems in one night."

"Fuzzy didn't tell me you were coming to the party."

I stretched out on my side and said, "He didn't tell me you were coming either." I patted the bed next to me and Lonny lay down, facing me. "How many times do you think we've faced each other like this?"

Lonny smiled. "Too many to count."

I reached out and touched his cheek and he placed his hand over mine, then kissed my palm.

"I'm scared," I whispered.

"About what?"

"Having a baby. Being a mom."

"Roo, you'll be a great mom. You deserve this."

"I never wanted to get pregnant, because I didn't want to have a child with Billy. But I was so lonely and realized I was only punishing myself."

"You'll be the best mom ever," he assured me. "And two grandmothers to help you."

"Can you imagine? Both of us having kids?"

He laughed. "No, not really. How has Billy been?"

I rolled my eyes. "He'll always be Billy. But since you haven't been part of my life the last three years he's mellowed out some."

Lonny made a face. "So now what?"

"You're going to call me… whenever you need to, whenever you want to. At *my* house. No more of Billy's bullshit. I'll tell him you're married or something."

After a long pause Lonny said, "I haven't minded being lonely. I knew that way I couldn't hurt anybody else, and the pain keeps reminding me I'm still alive."

I touched his chin with my fingertip as tears threatened. "You've had enough pain in your life, Lonny. You deserve to be happy."

"Roo, can you do something for me? It's okay if you say no."

"Anything."

He hesitated then said, "Please kiss me."

I pushed his hair out of his eyes and smiled, scooting closer to him until our noses touched. I lightly touched my mouth to his and he closed his eyes. I should have ended it there, but instead my heart got the best of me and I parted his lips with my tongue. Lonny needed to know he was still not only lovable, but capable of love, and I didn't feel a harmless kiss made me a marriage criminal. He returned the kiss… soft, deep and sensual, and when I felt my body aching for more, I pulled away.

"Thank you," he whispered.

"You're welcome."

"I should go."

"Stay."

I was not about to let Lonny go and sleep in the warehouse, and in the morning I was going to call Fuzzy and ask if they could meet us for breakfast.

The ringing telephone scared me half to death at six in the morning. Lonny grumbled next to me and I clasped my hand over his mouth as I answered it.

"I can't believe you left after we agreed you shouldn't travel!" Billy shouted.

"*You* didn't want me to travel. My doctor said it was fine." I was always so brave when I was on the phone.

"You listen to me you stupid bitch—"

"I'll see you tonight when I get home."

I hung up the phone and went to the bathroom. When I crawled back into bed Lonny asked, "Why do you let him talk to you like that?"

"Because I'm stupid."

He pulled me into his arms, squashing my face against his neck. I didn't mind, however, because it was nice to be close to him again, to feel his arms around me, to smell his skin, to feel his soft hair against my cheek.

"You don't deserve to be treated like that," he said. "He should be grateful he has you."

"He doesn't care because he knows I won't leave."

"Do you want to leave?"

He'd never let me leave.

"It's not that simple, especially now that I'm pregnant."

"I guess not."

"Leaving you at the hospital was the hardest thing I've ever done," I whispered. "I would have rather died than leave you there."

"Who knew that would be the easy part of the shitty life I'd make for myself?"

"When are you going to tell your mom about your daughter?"

Lonny sighed heavily. "I don't know. I have to see how things go first."

"What's her name?"

"Celia."

"That's a beautiful name. Where does she live?"

"Vegas."

"Well isn't that just shitty…."

He burst into laughter. "Yeah... not sure I'll be making too many trips to Vegas." We lay there silently for a few minutes before he asked, "Do you care if it's a boy or girl?"

"I'd like a little girl, but as long as the baby's healthy that's all I really care about." I rolled over onto my back and stretched my arms and legs. Lonny turned onto his side to face me, sliding his hand under my shirt and gently placing it on my stomach. My own husband hadn't even done that.

"Thanks for sharing your bed," Lonny said, smiling at me.

I smiled back then sat up and looked down at him, holding his hand. "You were thrashing a lot in your sleep."

"I have a lot of nightmares about the accident."

"Do you remember anything?"

"Only what comes to me in dreams."

"Can I see it?"

Lonny didn't respond at first, then slowly lifted the long-sleeved shirt he was still wearing over his head and tossed it on the floor. He tilted his arm so I could see the grisly scar that was a daily reminder of the hell he went through.

"Does it hurt?" I asked.

"Mostly numb."

"I'm sorry I didn't come for the memorial," I whispered, agonizing over the deaths of our friends. "I really wanted to be there... for you and for them... for *me*." Before I realized what was happening, I was sobbing over the loss of our friends as if I'd just heard the news. I'd never been able to properly mourn them, surrounded by their friends, family and people who were also feeling the depths of despair over their deaths. Billy wouldn't allow it, and I feared just how much he would hurt me if I insisted on going to the memorial without his approval.

Lonny gently pulled me down next to him, holding me tightly in his arms and petting my head. "It's okay Roo, it's okay. I know it wasn't your fault. I know it wasn't your choice."

"I'm sorry I let you down. I'm sorry I made you so angry. You don't understand what it's like—"

"Shhhhhh. It's okay. You don't have to explain anything."

"I miss you so much," I sobbed.

"I miss you, too."

484

"I should never have left you. At the hotel, at the hospital… Lonny, I'm so sorry."

He pulled me closer, my wet face pressed up against his, and I could tell by the way his body trembled that he was crying, too. A few minutes later he gently pulled away so he could see my face. He caressed my cheek and tried to smile.

"Promise me we'll always be together, even if we can't be together. I can't live without you, Roo. I just can't."

I closed my eyes and nodded as the tears fell from my eyes. He pressed his lips against my forehead and held them there. "I promise."

I called Marilyn as soon as we knew they'd be awake, and when I told her Lonny was in trouble she insisted we come to the house immediately. Not only did she have breakfast ready when we got there, she called Peter to join us as well. I loved being back in their beautiful home, even though my last memory of being there was when Billy showed up to drag me back home when Lonny was in the hospital.

"Where's Calvin?" I asked, not having seen him since he was a baby.

"Stayed over night with Grandma so we could go to the party," Fuzzy answered.

"So doll," Marilyn said with a smile. "How are you feeling?"

"I'm feeling great," I answered.

Fuzzy asked, "Are you hoping for a girl or a boy?"

After my meltdown earlier that morning, my feelings had changed. "I'm hoping for a boy. I'd like to name him after Mitch and Benji."

Fuzzy smiled and winked, while the others verbalized their joy and Lonny smiled and squeezed my leg.

We continued to make small talk while we ate, but as soon as breakfast was over, Lonny squeezed my hand under the table. I looked at him with my eyebrows raised, not knowing if he wanted to tell them his own story or if he was more comfortable having me do it. His eyes welled with tears as he gave me a nod, and I cleared my throat. I pulled his hand out from under the table and set it on top, holding it tightly so that everyone could see it. I slowly began to relay the story Lonny confessed to me, and all three of them were visibly shocked.

"Where have you been living, kid?" Fuzzy asked.

Lonny wiped the tears from his face and croaked, "An empty rehearsal room at the warehouse."

Marilyn got up and stood behind him, wrapping her arms around his shoulders and burying her face in his hair.

"My sweet boy," she cried. "My sweet, sweet boy."

Marilyn's reaction brought us all to tears and Lonny completely lost the composure he was trying so desperately to hold on to. He let go of my hand and clung to Marilyn as he sobbed against her. I wiped the tears from my face knowing that the three people Lonny and I trusted most with his secret would take good care of him, and I didn't have to worry about him once I went back home.

None of them scolded Lonny for not coming to them for help. None of them treated him like a pariah who needed to be thrown out on the street. All three of them immediately began discussing what they could do for Lonny, and how they could help him. I knew he was in good hands.

Marilyn went back to her seat as Lonny wiped the wetness from his face. "Lonny has one more thing to tell you," I said.

He stared at me like a scared child but I squeezed his hand and smiled, letting him know everything would be okay. He swallowed hard and drank down the rest of his orange juice before lifting his head.

"I just found out I have a three-year-old daughter. Her name is Celia," he replied softly.

Marilyn gasped loudly. "Oh doll!"

Fuzzy smiled and said, "Congratulations, kid."

486

"You'll move back in with us, doll, we'll help you with your baby, and—"

"Mare, he hasn't even met his daughter yet. Slow down," Fuzzy interrupted her.

Peter cleared his throat and said, "I think Lonny should move in with me. You guys have Calvin here now, and I could really use the company. And perhaps a bit of help with the horse rescue."

I smiled so big I thought my face would break.

"And we can go to G.A. together," Peter concluded. He gave Lonny a hug and patted him on the back. "We won't let you fall through the cracks again."

The five of us were able to spend some quality time together before I had to head to the airport, and even though Lonny volunteered to take me everyone agreed he shouldn't be left without a chaperone. I assured him I would be perfectly fine taking a taxi, and he reluctantly agreed.

I said goodbye to Peter first, hugging him tightly and thanking him for offering to take Lonny in. He promised he would do everything in his power to make things right and told me to call him any time. He wished me well with my baby and kissed me on the cheek, then brought my suitcase to the waiting taxi.

Fuzzy pulled me into his strong arms and kissed the top of my head. "I promise we'll take care of him, doll," he said. "Thank you for bringing him to us this morning."

Marilyn was crying by the time she wrapped her arms around me. "I wish you didn't have to go, doll. I wish you could stay here forever."

"Me, too," I whispered.

"He's lucky to have you," she whispered close to my ear. "He would've never come to us on his own."

"Please take care of him," I begged. "*Please.*"

"You know we will, doll. And you keep us updated with that baby!"

I promised I would. As soon as Marilyn let go of me, Lonny took me by the hand and led me toward the taxi.

"You're gonna be okay, Lonny," I told him.

"Thanks, Roo. For everything."

487

"You know I'd do anything for you."

"You know I'd do the same, right?"

"Yes," I agreed. "But right now you have to take care of yourself and be whole for your daughter."

"Promise we can talk to each other."

"I promise."

Lonny pulled me in for a loving hug that I returned all too willingly. I didn't want him to let me go. I didn't want to go home. I didn't want to ever leave his side but here we were, saying goodbye once again.

I soon felt Lonny's hands on my face, forcing me to look at him. His eyes were wet with tears but he was smiling. "I'm hoping for that boy," he whispered.

"Me, too."

He kissed my forehead but that wasn't enough for me. I pressed my mouth against his and held it there for all to see. I said goodbye and jumped into the taxi, waving goodbye to my friends as it pulled away. As soon as I could no longer see Lonny, I burst into tears.

Billy screamed and yelled at me when I returned home that evening, but he didn't touch me. I let him rant and rave and explained that I was feeling just fine without any complications. In the middle of his fury he disappeared into the garage and I could hear him smashing something to bits.

He quickly returned, face red and sweating, asking, "Was he there?"

"Was who there?"

"*Him.*"

"Yes, he just came back from London. Married, with a three-year-old daughter," I lied. Well, half lied.

He was so dumbstruck he just stared at me. I stared back, smiling only on the inside and not daring to do it with my face. I was exhausted from the day's events plus traveling, and told him I was going to bed. Before crawling into bed, I removed my wedding band as I did every night, and reached to put it on my bedside table but missed, sending it bouncing onto the floor. I got on my knees to retrieve it from under the bed and found something I wasn't expecting. I held the condom wrapper up just as Billy walked into the bedroom and he froze. We had never once used a condom.

"That must be an old one of my dad's," he stammered.

"Nice try."

I grabbed my pillow and went to sleep in Gina's old room. I was willing to give him this one because of the night I spent with Fuzzy, and I was more relieved than angry, but I couldn't let him know that. He didn't even try to apologize.

Several days later I was working in the local Vinyl Horse with Ricky and we were laughing and having a good time, stocking new merchandise and eating lunch, when I felt cramping in my abdomen that I'd not experienced before. It wasn't extremely painful, akin to menstrual cramps, so I ignored it. It occurred several times throughout the day but I assumed it was normal. I went to the bathroom as we were closing for the evening and knew something was seriously wrong when I saw blood in my panties. Ricky called my mother and told her to meet us at the hospital.

By the time my mother brought me home, Billy was there and pacing frantically, wondering where I was. She hugged me tightly and told me to call her if I needed anything, then kissed my cheek and headed for home.

"What's going on?" he asked.

I burst into tears as I tried to explain that I had a miscarriage, but the look on his face told me he had no idea what I was talking about.

"I lost the baby," I cried.

He stepped toward me and I flinched, but he put his arms around me and comforted me as lovingly as he knew how. He told me he would take care of me and all I needed to do was rest. He took my hand and led me to the bedroom, helping me change out of my clothes into my pajamas, then tucking me into bed.

"Do you need anything?" he asked, tears forming in his own eyes.

"Just sleep."

He kissed me softly on the lips then changed for bed and crawled in beside me. He held me in his arms as I cried for the loss of my baby, my Mitchell Benjamin, as I'd hoped. It was the most incredible grief I'd ever experienced and the only person I wanted to be with was Lonny. Even though my grieving husband was comforting me in our shared loss, Lonny was the only one I wanted to be with. To talk with. Lonny was my comfort and my joy; he was my true happy.

I don't know what time it was when Billy woke me up as it was still pitch black outside. I tried to focus my eyes as he pulled on my arm, ordering me to get out of bed. I was still trying to wake up when he turned the light on next to the bed. I could see the fury on his face and my stomach clenched.

"It's *your* fault our baby died!" he screamed. "I *told* you not to fly and you did it anyway!"

"The doctor said it had nothing to do with that," I argued.

"Shut *up* you stupid whore! Lonny, Lonny, Lonny, your whole *fucking* life nothing but Lonny! I hope your trip to see him was worth it!"

"Lonny wasn't even supposed to be—"

He shut me up with a backhand to my face. He then pulled on my arm, trying to drag me out of bed, but I held onto the wrought iron headboard with my free hand, begging him not to hurt me. He yanked my arm so hard he dislocated my shoulder, and I understood the pain Lonny felt when it happened to him. I hit the floor with a deafening thud and nearly vomited.

He dragged me across the floor as the carpet burned fire against my skin, and the whole while I begged for mercy. "Please don't hurt me," I cried. "I'll do *anything… please…*"

I woke up on the bathroom floor, my face pressed against the cold tile. I couldn't move my body, only my eyes. I had hoped I was dead, but the excruciating pain I felt told me that was not the case. My mouth began to water but I had no strength to get up and go to the toilet, so I vomited on the floor in front of me. I could feel the dried blood under my nose and my head was spinning. I closed my eyes and prayed I would die, begging God to take me and give Lonny the heart to forgive me.

The next time I woke up I could hear Billy using the toilet, but kept my eyes closed so he wouldn't notice. He flushed and walked over me to exit the bathroom, not even bothering to see if I was breathing. I waited a few minutes before I lifted my head, a million knives stabbing my skull as I did so. I struggled to lift

490

myself up with my good arm, knowing the other was dislocated at the shoulder. I managed to drag myself to the toilet where I was eventually able to pull myself into a sitting position. I was covered in urine and vomit as I dragged myself through both to get to where I was. My right foot was turned the wrong way, broken at the ankle, and my left arm was not only dislocated at the shoulder, but dangled at the elbow. I somehow managed to lift myself up onto my left foot and hopped over to the sink to look in the mirror. One eye swollen shut with dried blood and vomit crusted to my face. My pajama bottoms were soaked with urine and I realized I might have a few broken ribs.

This was the last straw. I could no longer spend my life as Billy's punching bag. I could no longer handle the yelling and screaming, the accusations, the name calling, or the Lonny hatred he spewed on a regular basis.

I opened the medicine cabinet, trying not to scream out in pain as it engulfed me. I pulled out the bottle of sleeping pills and swallowed a handful down with water. The dizziness caused me to lose my balance, but I managed to stay upright, swallowing another handful of pills. I didn't stop until every last pill was gone and I felt sweet release was close at hand. I was fourteen again, seeing Lonny at school for the first time. He was smiling at me, telling me how much he loved me and that we would be together forever. He leaned in to kiss me….

I woke up trying to focus through a fog that clouded not only my eyes but my brain. I didn't know if I was dead or alive, conscious or unconscious, dreaming or awake.

"Ruby? Are you awake, honey?"

Mom.

I turned my head in the direction of her voice and vomited, causing her to jump up and run out of the room. She ran back in quickly with a nurse right behind her.

Hospital. Alive.

The nurse smiled and asked me a lot of questions that sounded like incoherent mumbling and I stared at her blankly, unable to respond. She checked my vitals as someone else came in to clean up the floor and then I was again alone with my mother.

I looked around the dimly lit room. "Where's Billy?" Just saying his name caused my insides to clench.

"He went to get us some coffee."

I looked down at my body, mostly covered with a blanket, and saw my left arm was in a cast and when I tried to move my legs, I could tell my right ankle was in a cast as well.

"What happened?" I asked.

"Lonny called the house around four this morning… he was hysterical. He told your father that something was wrong and we needed to check on you. It was all a bit dramatic, so we assured him you were fine and hung up. But he kept calling back until we agreed to go to the house to check on you. Not call, but get dressed and go to your house."

Tears trickled out of my eyes with the realization that Lonny knew.

"It took a while for Billy to answer the door," she continued. "When he finally let us in he was a mess, saying he'd just called 911 because he found you at the bottom of the basement stairs. That you tried to kill yourself, Ruby."

I looked up at the ceiling as the hot tears burned my cheeks. I couldn't stand the way my mother was looking at me, the way she was *judging* me. But it wasn't nearly as bad as the way I was judging myself. I was even a failure at dying. I silently cried but didn't respond to my mother. Billy had already set up the lie, the story, the alternate reality, and I was the distraught woman whose word couldn't be trusted because I tried to kill myself.

"Lonny *knew*," she said. "How on earth could he possibly have known?"

It was one thing explaining it to Fuzzy, but my mother would never understand the bond between Lonny and myself. She would never understand or accept the deep love I had for him, and I just didn't have the strength to explain it to her.

As I wiped the tears from my face the door opened, and my entire body stiffened. I wasn't prepared to see Lonny rush in, out of breath and looking like he'd just run across the country to get there. The look on his face when he saw me caused me to start sobbing.

"Lonny!" my mother gasped.

492

Lonny put his hands against my face and quickly kissed my mouth. He gently pulled me against him and said, "I'm so sorry, Roo. I promise I'm not leaving here until I get to the bottom of this."

"You shouldn't be here," I cried. "Do they know you left?"

"Nobody knows I'm here, and I don't care."

"You have to let them know where you are."

"I will, I will," he whispered against my face.

"What the fuck is *he* doing here?"

"Billy!" my mother scolded. "Language!"

Lonny let go of me and lunged at Billy, sending the two cups of coffee flying through the air as he pinned him against the wall.

"*You* did this to her!" Lonny yelled. "I *know* it was you!"

Billy's face contorted in anger as he unsuccessfully tried to push Lonny away. A nurse rushed into the room after hearing Lonny yelling, asking them to keep the noise down or she was going to call security.

"He did this to her!" Lonny yelled, pointing at me.

Billy used the distraction of the nurse to catch Lonny off guard, shoving him onto the floor. Lonny was never a fighter, but he was so angry he got right back up and punched Billy in the face. The two started brawling and the nurse had no choice but to call security. I knew the damage Billy's anger could cause and I was worried for Lonny. I kept begging them to stop but they couldn't hear me. Nobody could hear me because I was only screaming the words inside my head, unable to verbalize anything once Billy walked back into the room.

Security stepped in and separated the two men, dragging them out of my room. I became hysterical because I was convinced Billy would kill Lonny if he had the opportunity. I begged my mother to go after them to make sure Lonny was safe, but she looked at me like I had lost my mind.

"Mom please," I begged. "He's going to hurt Lonny."

"Lonny is the one who's acting like a lunatic," she replied.

"You don't understand," I cried. "*Please.*"

She sat down and said, "Lonny deserves whatever he gets for coming in here and accusing your husband like that."

493

I began frantically pushing the call button for the nurse and when they answered I begged them to protect Lonny from Billy. I don't remember what happened next, but I could hear my mother telling someone that I was out of control and I soon fell into a deep sleep.

I opened my eyes and had no idea if I was dreaming or not, Billy sitting next to my bed, my mother sitting across the room, and Lonny leaning up against the radiator by the window with his arms folded in front of him. I closed my eyes again, praying I was in California with Lonny and we were together and happy and madly in love.

"I would like to be alone with my wife," Billy announced.

Lonny, please don't leave.

"I'm not leaving," Lonny protested.

"Get the fuck out."

"Billy!" my mother scolded.

"Please leave me alone with my wife," Billy said again.

I never opened my eyes but could hear the shuffling of feet as my mother and Lonny left the room. Once the door closed behind them I could feel Billy lean closer to me.

"Did you call him?" he whispered. "Ask him to come here?"

I kept my eyes closed and ignored him.

"He better stop messing in my business or he'll end up in a body bag," he threatened. My eyes flew open and he grinned.

"I'm going to tell everybody the truth," I said. "I'm going to tell everybody what you did to me."

He laughed. *Laughed!* "You may be stupid, Ruby, but I know you're smarter than that." He took my hand in his and squeezed, hard. "I know you would never want anything to happen to your precious Lonny."

I didn't want to give him the satisfaction of seeing me cry, but the situation at hand was too overwhelming. "You leave him alone," I said, the tears burning my face as they flowed down my cheeks.

"You were so upset about your miscarriage you wanted to end your own life, swallowing God only knows how many sleeping pills. You lost consciousness and fell down the basement

494

stairs, which is where I found you, bruised and broken. Your parents saw you there and that's where the paramedics retrieved you. It's all very simple."

I swallowed hard as I looked into his eyes, cold and calculating. I could barely even get the words out. "Don't hurt him."

"What's that?"

"Please don't hurt him," I whispered. "He's been through enough."

"We have an understanding then."

"Whatever you want," I cried. "Just leave him alone."

I wiped the wetness from my face as he got up and went into the hallway. As Billy led my mother and Lonny back into the room, I could read Lonny's face like a book.

"I have to go to work," Billy said. "Ruby, call me at the shop if you need anything." He leaned over and kissed my forehead, told me he loved me then whispered, "He better be gone when I come back tomorrow." He turned toward my mother and they hugged each other, then he pushed Lonny out of the way and left the room.

"Honey, I need to go home and fix dinner for your father, but we'll be back later, okay?"

I nodded. I wanted my mother to go away. I didn't like the looks she was giving Lonny, all the while thinking Billy was husband of the year. She kissed my cheek, gave Lonny a hug, and was gone.

"Please don't leave," I begged Lonny.

He pulled a chair next to my bed and took my hand in his. "I'm not going anywhere, I promise."

"Did you tell Fuzzy you were here?"

"I called Peter. They aren't happy with me, but they understand. They send their love." He watched me for a long time before asking, "Is the baby okay, Roo?"

I shook my head as the tears returned. "The baby's gone," I cried.

"I'm so sorry," he whispered.

"I had a miscarriage last night. Then I took... I took the sleeping pills."

495

The truth.

"Roo, why would you do that? So many people love you... why didn't you reach out for help?"

I looked into his eyes and saw great pain there. "Lonny I don't know... I just did it, okay?"

"I'm not judging you," he said, his voice shaking. "It's just the thought of losing you...."

"But you didn't. I'm still here."

"Did he do this to you because you lost the baby?"

Tell him the truth.

"Lonny, I'm so tired," I cried.

He smiled at me and said, "It's okay, you go to sleep. I'll be here when you wake up." He kissed my hand and held it against his cheek, and I finally felt safe. I didn't wake up again until sometime in the middle of the night when I thought Billy had come back to finish me off, crawling on top of me and smothering me with my pillow.

"Roo, I'm here," Lonny said, still holding my hand. "I'm here, it's okay."

It took me a moment to focus my eyes and realize I was only dreaming, but I was gasping for air and feeling every bruise and break on my body at the same time. It was as if Billy was beating me senseless all over again.

"Please don't hurt me," I whimpered.

"Roo, it's me. I'm not going to hurt you."

I was finally able to focus on Lonny's face in the dim light as he stood next to my bed. "Lonny...."

Lonny must have pressed the call button for the nurse because I heard a woman's voice speaking then he replied, "She needs pain medication."

My nurse was soon bedside, injecting pain medication into my IV. She checked my vitals and lifted the blanket away from my right leg to check my ankle, adjusting my leg so it was again elevated.

"Are you a relative?" she asked Lonny.

"Yeah, um, her brother."

"We can get you a cot if you want to go to sleep."

"No, that's okay, thanks."

496

"Let me know if she needs anything else."

Lonny caressed my arm as the pain meds worked quickly and I groggily turned my head to look at him. "Thank you for staying."

"Is your ankle broken, too?"

"Yeah," I grumbled.

Lonny held a cup with a straw to my mouth and said, "Have some water. You're really dehydrated."

I took a long drink and he put the cup back on the table, then walked toward the end of the bed to look at my leg. He looked back at me with tears in his eyes.

"Tell me the truth, Roo," his voice cracked.

I looked up at the ceiling, feeling groggy enough to spill the truth, but scared enough to know I didn't want anything happening to Lonny. Tears burned my eyes as I replied, "I took the sleeping pills because I wanted to die. I don't remember anything after that."

The truth.

"Please don't lie to me. If he did this to you, I'll take you back to California with me when you're well and we'll figure out what to do."

Lonny was telling me what I wanted to hear, but it was far too late. If I took off with him to California, there was no doubt in my mind Billy would come after me and we'd both be dead. I couldn't let that happen. I couldn't bear it if anything happened to Lonny at the hands of my husband.

"They found me at the bottom of the stairs. Everything that happened is my own fault."

The truth.

"All these injuries? They all happened from falling down the stairs?" Lonny leaned in close to me. "I'm only going to ask you one more time, then I'll let it go. Did Billy do this to you?"

I reached up and stroked Lonny's cheek with my fingers. "Everything that happened is because of me."

The truth.

"I'm worried about you, Roo," he said, a tear trickling down his cheek. "Seeing you like this breaks my heart." Lonny covered his mouth with his hand as he burst into tears.

497

Lonny was such a mess in his own life, I couldn't have him worrying about mine. "I'll be okay, I promise."

He nearly choked on his tears, sitting down and bawling into his hands. I needed to protect my sweet Lonny any way possible, even if it was painful to me. He had a daughter to think about and I only had to play Billy's game. I just needed to get better at following the rules and predicting the ones that were unwritten.

"Lonny," I whispered. "I could really use a hug."

Lonny stood up and gently pulled me into an embrace as we cried against each other. "I'm so sorry about your baby," he said. "You deserve to be a mom."

I wasn't sure I agreed with that. What kind of person would want to raise a child in a violent home with Billy? My mother tried to explain that my miscarriage was a blessing in disguise and I didn't understand it at first, but perhaps she was right. She just didn't realize in which way she was right.

"Have you heard anything more about Celia?" I asked.

Lonny pulled away and smiled, wiping the tears from his face. "The day you left I got a picture of her in the mail. Wanna see it?"

"Of course."

Lonny pulled his wallet out of his pocket and took out the photo, handing it to me. She had beautiful blonde hair that fell in curls to her shoulders, and a smile that could illuminate the darkest of places.

"She's beautiful," I said. "She has your smile."

"You think so?"

"Yeah. Did you tell your mom?"

"I did. She has mixed feelings obviously, but she's hoping to meet her one day. She's excited to be a grandma."

"You're gonna be a great dad, Lonny."

"Thanks, Roo."

"Does your mom know you're here?"

Lonny laughed. "She does now. She came with your parents after dinner to visit but you were zonked out. She wasn't expecting to see me when she walked in the room. And what's with the weird looks from your mom?"

I rolled my eyes. "No idea. Maybe she's going through menopause or something."

"You should get some sleep. You're slurring." Lonny sat down in the chair next to my bed, never letting go of my hand.

"What did it feel like when you knew I was hurt?"

"Thought I was having a heart attack. I couldn't breathe. I don't know how many times I had to call your parents' house before they took me seriously. As soon as your dad confirmed what I already knew, I took off for the airport."

"I love you, Lonny."

But he didn't hear me, because I didn't say it out loud.

2011

Lonny and I stuffed our boxes of memories into the trunk of the Mustang at morning light and prepared to continue our journey to Vegas to see Celia. He wanted to make it to Denver that day and it was going to be a fifteen hour drive, at least. He tried to talk his mother into coming with us, promising he would take care of everything for her there, but she wasn't interested. I tried to convince all of them that they should move to California to the warmth and sunshine and to be close to us, but they were all perfectly happy where they were. I don't think any of them were willing to pick up and move across the country at this point in their lives, and I understood completely.

Even though we had taken tons of pictures during the visit with our parents, Lonny made sure to take many more the day we left. I used my camera and he used his phone, and he took lots of selfies so we could all be included. The photos I took of Lonny and Joanie melted my heart; he loved and adored her no matter what his life with her was like growing up.

After all that had transpired since showing up unexpectedly on my parents' doorstep, it was a tearful goodbye for all of us because we didn't know when we would see each other again.

I gave Joanie the longest goodbye hug as she cried on my shoulder, and I heard my mother tell Lonny, "I love you as my own son, you know that. I hope you can forgive me."

"I love you, Mom. Nothing to be forgiven."

Lonny pulled my father away to say goodbye so my mother and I would have some privacy. "I love you, honey. I'm sorry for everything."

"I love you, too, Mom. All is forgiven."

She pulled me into a hug that reminded me of the way she would hold me as a child. "If you love him, he needs to know the truth."

"About what?"

"About Billy." I pulled away, and as she held me at arm's length she smiled. "He knew deep in his heart what Billy was doing, but you never told him the truth. He always *knew*, Ruby."

500

"I'm not ready to tell him."

"Promise me you will at some point."

I nodded half-heartedly, knowing I didn't want to have that conversation with Lonny. I knew he would figure out that nearly every beating I took was because of him and I didn't want that hanging over his head. I promised I would tell him. *Eventually.*

We got into the car and waved goodbye as Lonny pulled away, the next part of our journey still ahead of us. I pulled an old, tattered envelope out of my bag and showed it to him.

"Know what this is?" I asked.

He wrinkled his forehead, having no clue what it was until I pulled a wad of cash out and fanned it in front of him. "No way!" he exclaimed.

"Yep. Every dollar they gave us for graduation."

"I told you to spend that!"

"No way, Lonny. This was *our* money."

"You could've used that so many times," he argued.

"It was our money and it's still *our* money."

Lonny turned to grin at me, his eyes hidden by his sunglasses. He took my hand and kissed it saying, "So are you ready for our new life together?"

I broke into a smile so big I thought it might swallow my face whole. "I am."

"I love seeing that smile on your face, Roo. I used to dream about it all the time." I giggled, embarrassed. "Did you ever dream about me?"

I let out a heavy sigh, replying, "More than I'd like to admit."

He squeezed my hand lovingly and smiled. "I love you so much."

"I love you, too."

We stopped in Omaha to get gas and eat lunch, sitting outside so Lonny could smoke. I sat across from him and dug into my fries as I watched his long fingers pull the pickles off his cheeseburger.

"Why don't you just order your burger without pickles?" I teased.

He shrugged. "I don't know. I don't want to bother them."

501

That was my Lonny; never wanting to make waves.

He took a huge bite out of his burger and noticed I was still watching him. He laughed as he chewed. "What?"

"Nothing."

"Come on, Roo."

"I've always thought you had beautiful hands."

He swallowed. "These things?"

"Yeah."

"Why are you sitting all the way over there?" he changed the subject.

"Better to see you from over here."

He got up and sat next to me with a goofy grin on his face. "That's better."

I smiled and patted his thigh, then slid my hand between his legs as I bit into my cheeseburger.

"Better behave, or we'll never make it to Denver," he teased.

Lonny hadn't made a single move on me since professing his love and I thought it was a bit odd. Maybe it was age, maybe it was being home with our parents. My mom claimed she wasn't judging, but I knew she was and that's why Lonny went back to the hotel every night and I stayed in my old room. Maybe he was waiting for the right moment, or was planning something special. All I knew was being close to him awakened feelings in me that were long buried, and I ached for him.

"Did you ever write a song about me?" I asked, feeding him an onion ring.

"All of them."

"All of them? What does that mean?"

"Every song I ever wrote was about you."

I stared at him with my mouth open. "'Love In Slow Motion?'"

"Yep."

"'Ripped To Shreds?'"

"Yep."

"'Blue Eyed Fire?'"

He sang, "Take me in your arms and hold me tight, it's only my dream because it won't be reality tonight... I bet you're

502

sweet as candy but that I'll never know, my heart screams yes, but my head, my head, my head has done me wrong."

"Lonny, I had no idea."

"You never wondered?"

"Well I wondered, but I didn't really believe—"

He interrupted me with a kiss. "You were always my muse, Roo. Always my inspiration."

"'Smoking In Bed?'"

He laughed his loud, hearty laugh. *"Obviously."*

"Okay, that one I knew," I admitted, grinning.

We finished eating and Lonny headed to the bathroom before we got back in the car for the second half of our journey toward Denver. I leaned against the car as I waited for him and felt my phone vibrating in my bag. Maybe it was my mother trying out the new phone Lonny purchased for her. Or my dad — he seemed to understand the whole texting thing better than she did, but she promised to learn the new technology even while refusing to give up her landline.

I fished out my phone and looked at the screen.

Lonny: I love you!
Me: I love you!

I smiled as I felt my face flush, and as I went to throw my phone back in my bag, it buzzed again.

Billy: He doesn't love you. He never has. He might use you for a cheap lay, but that's all you'll ever be.

My entire body prickled and the bitter taste of bile covered the back of my throat. He started a new life and left me behind and he still couldn't let me be happy without trying to mess with my head. I threw my phone back in my bag and closed my eyes, silently counting to ten.

"You okay?"

I opened my eyes to see Lonny standing in front of me. "Fine," I said with a smile. "Let's go."

503

It was eleven o'clock in Denver when we checked into the hotel. Even though we switched off with driving duties, we were both exhausted and couldn't wait to go to bed. I went into the bathroom to brush my teeth and change into shorts and a tank top, and Lonny was already in bed snoring when I crawled in next to him.

I kissed him softly on the cheek and he whispered, "Goodnight, Roo. I love you."

"I love you, too."

Sometime in the middle of the night my phone buzzed in my bag and I ignored it. But it didn't stop. It kept vibrating against the desk it was sitting on and dim flashes of light disrupted our sleep. Lonny rolled over and grumbled something I couldn't decipher and I got up to turn my phone off.

Billy: I made a mistake.
Billy: I was wrong.
Billy: I shouldn't have left you.
Billy: I'm sorry. I'm sorry I hurt you.
Billy: You've always been the only girl for me.
Billy: I love you. I miss you.

My breath caught in my throat and I quietly tiptoed to the bathroom, closing the door behind me. I sat on the edge of the bathtub and stared at my phone. Why was he doing this to me? Why couldn't he just leave me alone and stay out of my head?

"Leave me alone," I whispered to the air. "Leave me alone, leave me alone, leave me alone."

Lonny and I were finally together, finally happy. That's what Billy couldn't stand. He couldn't handle the fact that I ended up with the man I'd always loved and that I was happy. Billy was only happy when he controlled me, when he made me miserable, or when he was beating me, and this had to be his way of doing that without even being part of my life. It was his way of reaching out and terrorizing me, messing with my head, sending me back to that dark place I almost never recovered from.

It wasn't long before Lonny tapped on the door and asked if he could come in. He poked his head in and said, "Are you okay? I can hear you talking to yourself."

I tossed my phone on the floor and chewed my fingers as I watched Lonny pick it up and look at the screen. He stared at me and said, "Roo, you don't really believe...."

I slid off the tub and sat on the floor, bursting into tears. "Why won't he just leave me alone?"

"It's my fault, Roo, I'm sorry. I should never have emailed him those pictures when I was drunk. Otherwise he wouldn't have even known about us."

I realized I was slapping my hand against my forehead like a lunatic. "It doesn't matter, Lonny. He's always in my head... always hurting me. He's *always* there."

"Do you trust me?"

I nodded, wiping my face.

"We'll figure it out together," he said. "He can't stay in there forever or he'll kill you."

"It was so much easier when he beat me."

"*Beat* you?"

I tearfully looked up at Lonny and cried, "All those times you thought he was hurting me, you were right."

Lonny fell to the floor next to me in a heap, staring at me with such pain in his eyes I couldn't look at him. "Roo, no... you promised me—"

"I couldn't tell you the truth because I was afraid he'd hurt you."

"Oh my God," he whispered, closing his eyes and leaning against the wall for support.

"I told him I didn't love him, but he wanted to marry me anyway. He knew I loved you, and he used it against me every chance he got. I didn't want you to find out; I didn't want you to blame yourself."

Lonny listed all the injuries he knew of and I had to admit the cause for each of them, and they all revolved around him. His face lost all color as the reality of my abuse hit him hard. He was visibly shaking as he looked at me with tears in his eyes.

"Did he kill your baby?" he asked.

"No, but he blamed me for the miscarriage. Said it happened because I traveled to see you, when I didn't even know you were going to be there. That was the worst beating he ever gave me."

Lonny pulled me into his arms as we cried together. "I'm so sorry, Roo," he said against my face. "I'm such an asshole, making that comment about how my nightmares were real and yours weren't. You had every right to be pissed off at me. I'm *so* sorry."

"You didn't know. And I didn't want you to find out like this."

"No more secrets," he said. "Can we promise each other that?"

"No more secrets."

Lonny helped me up off the floor and led me back to bed. As we got comfortable he said, "Tomorrow we run that phone over with the car and get you a new one. With a new number."

"I love you, Lonny."

"I love you, too. We're going to get rid of Billy once and for all, I promise."

He kissed me goodnight and I felt safe in his arms, knowing Lonny would do everything in his power to make sure Billy didn't destroy the rest of my life.

We were awakened in the morning by Lonny's phone buzzing on the table next to the bed. "Morning sweetheart," he answered sleepily. "That's okay, we needed to get moving anyway."

Celia.

"We're in Denver, so I'm guessing early evening sometime. Yes, I promise I'll text you as soon as we get in. I love you, too."

"I love your face when you talk to her," I said, caressing his chest with my fingers. "It's so beautiful."

"She's excited to meet you." I smiled as he kissed me. "We should get going. We already slept later than I wanted to."

Fifteen minutes later we were in the car, first smashing my phone to smithereens, then hitting the road. Lonny shuffled the

506

tunes on his phone, and "Hey Jealousy" by the Gin Blossoms blared through the air.

Lonny sang, "And you know it might not be that bad…."

I sang, "You were the best I'd ever had…."

Together we sang, "If I hadn't blown the whole thing years ago, I might not be alone!"

We were about an hour outside of Las Vegas when Lonny started to get one of his headaches. It was nearly eight o'clock and we were both exhausted and hungry. He insisted he was okay to finish driving, but he didn't look well. By the time we reached our hotel he was leaning out the open driver's side door throwing up in the parking lot. I sat in amazement as I realized we were going to be staying at the Bellagio. We eventually walked to the hotel, and he sat patiently slumped in a lobby chair as I checked us in. I helped him into the elevator and up to our room, which had a view of the famous Fountains of Bellagio.

"Lonny the view," I gasped.

"Only the best for my girl," he replied softly with a grin, then disappeared into the bathroom to vomit.

I left to get ice and when I returned, joined Lonny in the bathroom. I sat on the floor with him and lovingly went through our icing routine.

"Wouldn't you rather watch the fountains?" he whispered.

"They'll still be there when you're feeling better."

Lonny's phone began buzzing in his back pocket and I pulled it out for him. It was Celia trying to video chat with him.

"Hey sweetheart," he said, barely opening his eyes. "We just checked in."

"Oh no Daddy, you have one of your headaches," I heard her say.

"Unfortunately."

"Do you want to meet for breakfast tomorrow?"

"That'd be great."

"I can't wait to meet Ruby. I love you, Daddy."

"I love you, too." He hung up with Celia and put his phone on the floor.

507

I finger combed his wet hair away from his face and leaned over to kiss him on the cheek. "Have you ever read *The Beautiful and Damned*?" he whispered, his eyes closed.

"Can't say that I have."

"There's a line that says 'two souls are sometimes created together and in love before they're born,'" he recited. "That's us, Roo. I truly believe that."

"That's beautiful, Lonny. I believe it, too."

About an hour later Lonny picked himself off the floor and left the bathroom. He ordered room service and we sat on the floor in front of the window, taking in the view as we ate our late dinner.

"Lonny, it's breathtaking," I whispered. I turned my head to look at him and he was grinning at me. He was so pale and his eyes were glassy; his headaches took nearly everything out of him. "Thank you for saving me."

"I wish I'd done it a lot sooner."

"We're together now and that's what matters."

He smiled, his dimples making a welcome appearance. He leaned over like he was going to kiss me, but blew a raspberry on my neck instead. I howled with laughter and he pulled me into his arms and kissed the top of my head.

"Nobody laughs like you, Roo," he said.

"No one's ever made me laugh like you do." I pulled away to look at Lonny. "You're drained. Let's go to bed."

I was lying on my back when Lonny climbed into bed, snuggling up next to me. He placed his head on my shoulder and buried his face in my neck, then slid his hand under my shirt, letting it rest on my stomach as he stuck his pinky in my bellybutton. I waited to see if he would do anything else but he fell asleep quickly. Not surprising, considering his headaches wiped him out completely. I closed my eyes and listened to the soft purring of his breathing, so grateful for that moment.

When I opened my eyes the next morning, I could hear Lonny getting out of the shower. I picked my new phone up off the bedside table to look at the time and saw that he had sent me a text.

Lonny: I wanted your first text to be from me. I love you!

"What are you grinning about?" I heard Lonny ask as he emerged from the bathroom wrapped in a towel that hung low on his hips.

"Oh nothing," I said, stretching my arms and legs. "Just a text from some cute boy."

"Do I have to beat him up?"

"Maybe."

He flopped onto the bed next to me and gave me a quick kiss. "I love you."

I smiled. "I love you, too."

"I can't wait for you to meet Celia."

"I'm really nervous."

He made a shocked face then smiled. "No reason to be nervous. She knows *all* about you."

"Everything?"

"Well... I guess not every intimate detail, but she knows you're the love of my life and she was the first one I texted when I officially found my balls and told you that."

"Tell me the story about when you first saw me."

Lonny smiled and kissed me softly then whispered, "I think it's time to hear *your* version of that story."

I gazed up at him, looking deeply into his eyes and seeing nothing but love there. I whispered, "I think that's more suited for a bedtime story."

Lonny's eyes grew large as he grinned and said, "Looking forward to it."

We had just walked into the restaurant when a young girl came flying toward Lonny, throwing herself into his arms and hugging him fiercely. The look of pure love on his face was something I would never forget.

Lonny didn't even have a chance to introduce us as Celia flung herself at me next, hugging me and telling me how happy she was to finally meet me. She was a stunning beauty, with lots of curly blonde hair, chocolate brown eyes and a mega-watt smile. She held me by the hand as she led us to our table, sliding into the booth first and making sure Lonny was in the middle. Celia was nothing but fresh air and sunshine, talking a mile a minute with a smile on her face the entire time.

"Ruby, I can't believe I'm finally meeting you!" she cheered. "I was so glad my dad finally found his balls… sorry Daddy… and told you the truth!"

I howled as Lonny grinned, a bit embarrassed. "It wasn't entirely his fault," I told her. "I was partially to blame."

"Aw, who cares?" she said. "You're together now, right? We should never live in the past!"

Lonny and I nodded in agreement.

Halfway through breakfast Lonny said, "Sweetheart, I know you've been working hard with school and your job and never take handouts from anyone, but Ruby and I have a surprise for you."

Celia was all smiles and perfect teeth as she waited for what Lonny would say next.

"The car you're driving is old and unreliable, and tomorrow we're going to take you shopping for something new."

Something new?

"Oh Daddy I couldn't," she replied, her fingers covering her mouth. "You're already paying for school and—"

"I don't want you driving a car I don't trust. I want you to be safe."

Celia dramatically lunged at Lonny, thanking him and crying against his shoulder. I sat in wonderment, still finding it hard to fathom that Lonny, my best friend and love of my life, had a child. Yet here she was in all her glory.

Celia excused herself to the bathroom to freshen up after what she called her "gooey display of emotions."

"Kid should've been an actress," Lonny chuckled.

"You're not giving her the Mustang?" I asked, surprised.

Lonny kissed my hand and said, "That's our car Roo; I don't think I can part with it now. Besides, I want her to pick out her own car."

I smiled as it made perfect sense to me. "We have packed a lot of memories in that car in a short amount of time."

"Besides," he said, taking a swig of his coffee. "You'll need something to drive once we're home."

Home.

Lonny spent the rest of the morning playing tour guide, driving us around so he and Celia could show me the sights. Lonny surprised us both by announcing he had a very special evening planned, and that he was taking us shopping for dresses. We argued with him, not wanting him to spend money on frivolous things, but he insisted he didn't do it very often and the three of us together was a special occasion.

Celia and I tried on dresses and modeled them for Lonny, who sat back grinning at the private show. Celia was beautiful in everything she tried on, and settled on a flowing lavender mini-dress with a faux gemstone neckline, along with a purse and shoes to match. I thought I looked foolish in everything the sales clerk brought me to try on, even though Celia didn't agree.

Celia left and came back with a light blue dress and said, "Daddy said to try this one on."

I put on the dress Lonny picked out for me and wondered what he was thinking. The bodice was fashioned like a bustier with thin straps and intricate beading throughout, and the satiny A-line skirt fell just above the knee. I felt ridiculous until I looked up to see Celia and the sales clerk staring at me with their mouths open.

"Ruby it's perfect," Celia said breathlessly. "Daddy knows you so well. It brings out the blue in your eyes."

I blushed as the sales clerk found a purse and a pair of shoes to match, but I didn't let Lonny see me in the dress, telling him he'd have to wait until dinner. He coughed up his credit card to pay for our far too expensive attire and something he purchased for himself, but we couldn't see it because his was in a garment bag.

We dropped Celia back at her car and she promised to come up to our room and help me with my hair and makeup before dinner. Lonny made sure her car started and she was on the road before we headed back to the hotel.

"You spent entirely too much money today," I teased.

"You know me… I never spend money. I'm the luckiest guy in the world today, being able to spend it with my two best girls. It's worth every penny."

"I love you. And not because you took us shopping."

He looked at me and smiled. "I love you, too. What do you think of my little girl?"

"I love her, Lonny. She's just like you."

Lonny took us to Sinatra for dinner, one of the most expensive Italian restaurants in Vegas. I was uncomfortable with him spending so much money on us, but the look on his face when I emerged from the bathroom in my new dress was priceless.

"Isn't she beautiful, Daddy?" Celia squealed. And as she saw him putting his hands on my neck and leaning in to kiss me she giggled, "Don't ruin her makeup."

He kissed me on the cheek and whispered, "The most beautiful girl in the world."

I couldn't help staring at Lonny throughout dinner, dressed in a casual black suit with a black tie and shoes to match. He looked so handsome. And seeing the way he interacted with Celia made him even more so, with such pure love and adoration. He was definitely a proud father, and he deserved to be.

Celia was full of questions during dinner, wanting to talk about our time in high school but mostly about our time on the road with the band. She knew her father's version of things, but she wanted my point of view and mostly wanted to know what he was like. Lonny and I bounced stories and anecdotes off each other like a well-oiled machine, never missing a beat, as if we'd been doing it together for years. If Celia wasn't laughing she had a smile plastered on her face a mile wide. I could tell she didn't hear much about Lonny from her mother, a one-night-stand who probably knew very little about him at all. It was nice to finally talk about the good old days and relive the happy times without wanting to burst into tears.

512

After a wonderful meal we headed back to our hotel for cocktails. Lonny and I were standing at the bar waiting for our drinks and he leaned over and kissed my ear. His hand rested on the small of my back as he whispered, "I love you."

"I love you, too."

"Daddy, look who's joining us tonight!" Celia squealed.

Lonny lifted his face away from me and as he looked past my head I saw his face pale.

"Hey there, Girl Scout."

I immediately stiffened at the sound of her voice and the way she insisted on addressing me. But it couldn't be possible. I looked at Lonny, whose eyes spoke nothing but pure terror, and I turned to face her.

Fawn.

I looked at Celia, who was smiling brightly with her arms lovingly draped around the woman who ruined my life all those years ago. Time was not good to Fawn, but even through the plastic surgery, excessive makeup and sixty-five years of age, there was no mistaking the groupie I found in Lonny's bed.

My head spun and my stomach clenched as reality hit me hard. I looked from Fawn back to Lonny, waiting for him to speak, but he stood there like a statue and said *nothing*.

"Aw Girl Scout," she said with a taunting pout. "The kid still isn't man enough to tell you the truth."

A thousand knives pierced my heart as I turned and walked away. Out of the bar, out of the hotel, into the open air. My chest heaved as I alternated between trying to breathe and trying not to vomit. I must have been running because I could hear Lonny's voice calling me and he sounded so far away. He finally caught up to me and grabbed my arm.

I yanked my arm away from him so forcefully it hurt. "Don't touch me!"

"Roo, I'm sorry. I'm so, so sorry."

"Did it *never* occur to you that at some point you'd need to tell me that *whore* is Celia's mother? She ruined my life, and now I find out that not only did you sleep with her *again*, but fathered a child with her!"

"Roo, I didn't... I wasn't...."

513

"Out of all the shitty things you've ever done, this is the worst betrayal ever. Fuck you, Lonny!"

"This!" he screamed, violently pointing at me with both hands. "This is why I didn't tell you! I knew you'd never understand and you certainly wouldn't forgive me. Not that I need your forgiveness because we weren't even *together* when it happened!"

"Don't you dare blame this on me."

"I'm not blaming you for anything! But you need to stop being such a bitch when it comes to *my* life!"

He might as well have slapped me across the face, because his words and tone stung me like I'd never be able to recover.

"*You* made the decision to leave because *you* couldn't find it in your heart to forgive me," he continued. "I apologized and begged you for months to come back and you refused. *That's* on you!"

"You cheated on me. The thought of being in the same room with you made me sick."

"Roo, I'm not going to apologize for what happened. I was ready to blow my head off that day, and had I not gone with her that's probably what would've happened. You weren't there, but she was. She saved me, and I ended up with a beautiful daughter because of it."

I paced the sidewalk, wanting to lash out and make him hurt as badly as he was hurting me. I had one bullet that I knew would do the trick and I didn't care how badly it would hurt him, or that it could separate us forever.

"I slept with Fuzzy."

514

1991

In 1991, Billy's boss at the tattoo shop decided to sell his second business in New York and Billy jumped at the chance to buy him out. Everything was already in place — the shop, the equipment, the employees, the business, the apartment upstairs — all Billy had to do was come up with the money. And he did. All without my knowledge.

I was heartsick when he told me we were moving and I had no say in the matter. I told him I wasn't going with him and I wanted a divorce, but three broken fingers changed my mind quickly. He sold the house and split the profits with Gina and we sold almost everything we owned, taking as little as possible in a small trailer with us when we left.

Billy had finally managed to make it so that he was the only person in my life, and I was dependent on him for everything. I was forced to work in the shop with him which meant we were together all day, every day, seven days a week. I had no time to myself, which meant no time to talk to Lonny.

Lonny, on the other hand, was flourishing. Peter was still taking him to G.A. meetings and keeping him involved with his horse rescue. He was already a partner in Fuzzy's warehouse, but they decided to expand and now housed recording studios as well as rehearsal space. Lonny and Fuzzy were producing other bands on their own record label and making quite a reputation for themselves. Even though Lonny couldn't play the guitar the way he used to since the accident, he learned the piano quickly and was able to write songs for other artists and had become very much in demand. Lonny also continued drawing and painting, and some of his larger pieces sold for staggering amounts to celebrities who wanted the rare honor of having something of his in their home.

He was most proud of his relationship with Celia, whom he met not long after returning to California after visiting me in the hospital. He sent me photographs of the day he met her, and she instantly bonded with him. He had come to a verbal agreement with Celia's mother that he would take her every other month until she started school, then he would take her one weekend a month,

515

holidays and during the summer. It was an arrangement that worked for them, and I loved the photographs he sent with his letters. I had never seen him as happy as he was with his daughter.

Billy only softened on Lonny when I snapped at a customer who was giving me a hard time in the shop. We had already lost two employees that week because they simply couldn't stand Billy, and he was worried his investment was going to go down in flames quickly. I was desperately lonely and homesick and one evening when we made our way upstairs after closing the shop, I pulled a giant knife out of the drawer and threatened Billy with it. It wasn't difficult for him to wrestle it away from me, but it scared him enough that he agreed to let Lonny and I write letters to each other as long as he read them all first. He also allowed me to talk to Lonny on the phone twice a week. I was grateful, and Billy knew from reading Lonny's letters that his whole world revolved around his daughter, not me.

Billy let me spend time with Lonny once a year when he came to visit me for our birthday. It was the one day a year I looked forward to more than any other. Lonny would come into the shop and present me with a cupcake that held a single lit candle while singing happy birthday to me. Billy refused to close on the holiday, and since it was always slow that day, I was allowed to leave with Lonny so we could spend our birthday together. It was my happiest day of the year.

Lonny had an amazing support group in Peter, Fuzzy and Marilyn, and I was a bit envious of the relationship they all had with their children and each other. Celia was best friends with Peter's twins and she was extremely close to Marilyn and Fuzzy. I wondered if Billy would have insisted on moving to New York if our child had survived, and if that child would have made any difference in our volatile marriage.

Billy's abuse subsided for a long time after moving to New York. He was so focused on the business that I became less of an obsession, but he also realized that Lonny was no longer a threat. It wasn't until musicians began frequenting his shop that he finally took notice again, and if any one of them chatted me up while they were there I'd end up with some sort of injury that night after we got home. Never anything as severe as when I had the miscarriage,

516

but he let me know that I belonged to him and I shouldn't be getting any ideas. What he didn't realize was that I had no interest in any of the people who came into his shop. Not the famous ones, the semi-famous ones or the guys who still played in their garage. I loved meeting and talking with them and taking photos of them for the shop, but that's where my interest ended. And a plain, boring girl like me was of no interest to them; I was definitely not their type. It didn't matter to Billy though, because any other man was the enemy.

I got the feeling Billy was cheating on me when he wasn't forcing himself on me quite as often. Part of me was relieved, but the part of me he had brainwashed was jealous. By the time he finally left me, he hadn't touched me sexually in two years. It was as if his warped game had finally come full circle and he was bored with me.

2011

Lonny froze and glared at me. "You and *Fuzzy?* When did *that* happen?"

I folded my arms angrily in front of my chest and Lonny's phone rang.

"Yes, I found her. She's right here," he said, then held the phone in my direction. "Celia wants to talk to you."

"Ruby, my mom was an asshole. Please don't be mad at Daddy."

"It's not that simple."

"Please… it's my fault. I didn't know she's the reason you broke up! She said she has something to say to you both. She's not the same person she was back then. Please come back."

"Celia—"

I stared at Lonny as she interrupted me. "Please Ruby," she sobbed. "I know how much you love each other. Hate my mother all you want, but don't hate Daddy. He just got you back."

I handed the phone back to Lonny and stared at the ground.

"Okay sweetheart, calm down. Okay. I'll be right there." Lonny put his phone back in his pocket then leaned over to try and kiss me.

I pulled far away from him and scoffed, "Kissing me doesn't make any of this go away."

"Maybe not," he sighed heavily. "But right now my daughter is in full meltdown mode and we need to fix this."

"Fine," I grumbled, following him back toward the hotel. "But I'm going home in the morning."

"Run away. It's what you do best."

My stomach knotted as we walked and we were soon at the table where Celia and Fawn waited for us. Celia was in hysterics until she saw Lonny, and as soon as he pulled her into his arms she was calm. I sat down, crossed my legs, and waited for Fawn to speak.

"Drama queen," Fawn grumbled, rolling her eyes and taking a sip of her cocktail.

"Leave her alone," Lonny scolded.

518

Fawn whispered, "Daddy's girl," while pointing toward Celia with her thumb. I suddenly realized what it must have been like for Lonny to raise a child with this awful woman.

"Did you have something you wanted to say to us?" I finally asked.

Celia pulled away from Lonny, wiped her smudged eye makeup with her fingers and sat up straight, waiting for what her mother had to say.

"I've made a lot of mistakes in my life," Fawn began. "I was selfish and headstrong and I hurt a lot of people. Celia already knows this, but I have terminal lung cancer and I don't know how much time I have left, but I have apologies to make and some things need to be made right."

Lonny and I remained quiet; I felt no sorrow for her.

"Look, Girl Scout—"

"Her name is Ruby!" Celia shouted, causing heads to turn.

"Look, Ruby," Fawn started over. "I can't change the past. I was who I was, and while I'm not proud of some things, I enjoyed my life. I was living the dream and I lived it as long as I could. Forty years old and pregnant, it was time to make some changes."

"I'm sorry, but what does this have to do with me?" I growled.

"When Lonny joined the band all the girls were chomping at the bit to get to him. To be the first to bang the Golden Boy."

Lonny, who had his arm around Celia, said, "This really isn't appropriate—"

"Daddy, shhhhh!"

Fawn rolled her eyes. "Anyway, nobody could get anywhere near the kid thanks to you," she said, pointing at me. "The two of you were inseparable, attached at the hip. Green little teenagers afraid of their own shadow."

"Fawn, come on," Lonny scolded.

"I disliked both of you. Lonny for taking Joey's place in the band, and Ruby for being the one everyone in the band was so protective of. You were both so gloriously happy. The band was happy. It made me sick. That first night in Chicago when your parents and boyfriend were backstage—"

519

"Boyfriend? What boyfriend?" I quizzed.

"Your boyfriend, Ruby, the blond guy. Came with his sister or something."

"Billy?"

"Yeah, that's him."

"Billy was *not* my boyfriend. *Lonny* was my boyfriend."

"Okay, well... whoever he was, we got to talking backstage and I found out he hated the kid even more than I did."

My face burned fire as Billy became part of the conversation. Lonny shifted uncomfortably in his seat and I knew he had no idea what was coming either.

"He came up with this brilliant plan," Fawn said with a laugh. "I thought it was ridiculous, but realized it could actually work."

"Plan?" Lonny asked. "What plan?"

"I just disliked you both," Fawn said with a shrug. "But that Billy... he really *hated* this kid. So I went along with it."

"Mom," Celia whispered. "I don't like this. Not one bit."

"So I hung around the hotel waiting for everyone to come back the second night," Fawn continued. "I already knew which room you were in, and Ruby, you couldn't have made it any easier for me. As soon as you propped the door open with that brush and went to Fuzzy's room, I was in."

That's how Billy knew! It was his plan!

Lonny gave me the side eye and I knew he was wondering if that's when I slept with Fuzzy. Something caught in my throat as I watched the smile cover her face. I cleared my throat, hoping to dislodge whatever it was, but it was my life caught in there. My life, the one that Fawn ruined, and I was learning that Billy had a part in it.

"I'm sorry kid, but I never slept with you that night," Fawn chuckled. "I didn't even want to. I just wanted to piss off your girlfriend and it worked. Too well, apparently."

"Mom, how could you do something like that?" Celia gasped in horror.

Lonny looked at me with large eyes and an open mouth. I could feel the tears burning my eyes as he grabbed my hand under the table.

520

"But you were naked," I said. "You were both naked. In his bed."

Fawn howled with laughter. "It took me an *hour* to get his jeans off! He may have been passed out drunk, but he fought me every step of the way. Once that was done, I just got naked and went to sleep."

I sat there in stunned silence. All those years I thought Lonny cheated on me and it never happened. I left him behind because of a lie perpetrated by a jealous groupie and *Billy*. Both of our lives forever changed based on a trick.

I didn't want to cry in front of the woman who ruined my life. I shot daggers at her with my eyes but said nothing. My brain was so twisted I couldn't even form a rational thought or find the words that could honestly express how I was feeling.

"She left me because of you," Lonny finally broke the eery silence. "She was the only one who ever mattered to me and you destroyed everything!"

"Look kid, I'm not proud of what I did. But I thought it was time you knew the truth."

Lonny looked about ready to explode. He covered his mouth with his hand and closed his eyes. I could see his chest heaving violently and did the only thing I could. I reached out and took his hand in mine and waited for him to look at me.

"Lonny, I'm sorry. I should've listened to you. You were right. *Nothing* happened and it's my fault for leaving."

"I'm really sorry," Fawn said. "I'm not the same person I was. I feel terrible for what I did."

"Mom, you're an awful person," Celia said.

"I never hid anything from you, Celia. You always knew what I did and who I did it with. And you know I haven't been that person for a very long time."

Huge tears fell down Celia's cheeks as her voice croaked, "But you never told me you hurt Daddy like that."

Fawn took Celia's hand in hers and whispered, "I'm sorry, honey. Lonny and Ruby didn't deserve what I did to them. They were good kids and I ruined what should've been their life together. I'm trying to make things right."

"But you can't," Celia cried. "Why should they ever forgive you?"

Fawn focused her eyes on the napkin she was playing with. "I don't expect forgiveness. I just wanted you both to know how sorry I was."

"Maybe this is why you have cancer," Celia hissed. "Payback for what you did to Daddy."

"Celia, enough!" Lonny scolded. "You don't have to be cruel."

Celia glanced at her watch and said, "Shit! Daddy, I have to go to work. Will I still see you tomorrow?"

"Of course, sweetheart."

Celia kissed us each goodbye then turned to Fawn and said, "I hate you for what you did."

Once Celia was out of sight Lonny said, "We're done here. Let's go, Roo."

As Lonny and I stood to leave Fawn said, "That's it, Lonny? We have a daughter together and I don't even get a goodbye?"

Lonny didn't move.

"I thought I was doing the right thing," she said. "I guess your resentment only got worse."

"You robbed us of the life we deserved together," Lonny growled. "If you'd wanted to sleep with me it *might* have made sense, but it was all a game between you and Billy. Who, by the way, talked Roo into marrying him and spent the next thirty years beating the shit out of her."

Fawn's face lost all color as she looked at me. "Ruby, I'm so sorry. I never—"

"What Billy did was his fault, not yours."

"Roo, let's go." Lonny was getting impatient.

I looked at Fawn, the woman I loathed for over thirty years, and I actually felt sorry for her. She looked as rough as the life she lived and never seemed to experience the love Lonny and I shared, and now she was dying.

"Thank you for saving Lonny," I said. "And thank you for giving him such a wonderful daughter."

"Thank you for saying that."

522

Lonny was soon by my side, putting a loving arm around me.

"Please take care of our little girl," her voice cracked.

"Thank you for telling us the truth," Lonny said.

Lonny took me by the hand and led me out of the bar, outside into the night, and to the Fountains of Bellagio to enjoy the show from the ground level. We watched in amazement with Lonny standing behind me, his arms wrapped around my waist and his chin resting on my shoulder.

"Thank you for doing that," he whispered in my ear. "I couldn't have done it. I was ready to just leave her there."

"She's dying. She deserved a little compassion."

"Didn't expect that from you after what she did to us."

"It's still painful, but I did it for Celia. And for you."

He kissed me on the neck and we continued watching the show, complete with lights and music. It was so beautiful and romantic.

"So Peter... *and* Fuzzy? I'm running out of friends, Roo," he joked. I knew it was coming, I just didn't know when. He leaned over and rested his elbows on the railing and looked up at me.

"It was only once," I explained. "When you were in the hospital."

He looked shocked.

"You were still in a coma and we didn't know if you were going to survive... you were unresponsive and everything was so bleak. We were both so lonely and distraught over the fact we might lose you. He blamed himself for not being able to stop Joey, and I blamed myself for lots of reasons. So much guilt and despair... it just happened."

He watched me intently for a while before saying, "I'm glad you were there for each other."

"I never meant for anyone to find out, let alone that way."

"It's okay, I deserved it." Lonny stood up straight and pulled me against him, kissing me. "Marry me. Right now."

"Yes."

He immediately pulled out his phone to take a selfie of us in front of the magnificent fountains, taking several. I then watched

523

as he pulled up the photo he liked best, edited it to read "She said yes!" across it, then texted it off to someone.

"Who'd you send that to?"

"You!" The smile on his face was like a little kid on Christmas morning, and he just asked me to marry him!

The next thing I knew we were standing in a wedding chapel being pronounced husband and wife, and Lonny placed his hands gently against my neck and pulled me in for a loving kiss.

"I love you so much," he whispered against my mouth.

I looked deeply into his eyes and whispered, "I love you, too. More than anything in the world."

He wiped a tear from my cheek and asked, "Why are you crying?"

"Because I'm so happy."

The people who ran the chapel took several photos that we'd be able to see on their website in a few days, but they also obliged Lonny when he asked to take some photos with his phone. He held my hand as we walked out of the chapel, taking one last selfie of us in front of the chapel's brightly lit sign. He played around with his phone as we walked to the car.

"What are you doing?" I asked.

"Texting you the photos. It's late back home, so let's wait until tomorrow to tell the parents." He was grinning like a lovestruck teenage boy and I loved every inch of him.

Lonny opened my car door then leaned in to buckle my seatbelt, stopping to kiss me before closing the door and running around to the driver's side. He hopped in then turned to me with the biggest smile on his face I'd ever seen.

"Did you plan this?" I asked. "Is that why we're all dressed up?"

"No," he chuckled. "The moment felt right and I just went with it."

"I'm glad you did."

"Crazy in love," he said. "Now do you understand?"

I smiled as my skin broke out in goosebumps. "I always did."

Lonny leaned close to my ear and whispered, "And right now all I want to do is make love to my wife."

He kissed me softly, then buckled his seat belt and started the car, pulling away from the chapel. As he drove, he called the hotel to request a bottle of champagne be delivered to our room before we got there. I was giddy as we drove and Lonny reached out to grab my hand.

"You and me, Roo, just like we were meant to be."

I couldn't keep my eyes off him. Here was the boy I'd loved ever since he walked into my life at the age of fourteen, and now he was my *husband*.

"I love you, Lonny."

"I love you, Roo."

Lonny parked the car and ran around to my side to open the door. He held my hand as we walked into the hotel and took the elevator up to our room, where a bottle of champagne sat on ice waiting for us. I kicked off my shoes as Lonny threw his jacket over a chair and loosened his tie. He popped the cork on the champagne and poured us each a glass as we stood in front of the window watching the Fountains below.

"To my beautiful wife," Lonny said, clinking his glass to mine.

"To my hot and sexy husband," I replied.

I put my glass down and slid Lonny's loosened tie out from under his collar and over his head, then put it around my own neck. I slowly unbuttoned his shirt and kissed the middle of his chest when I was finished, then I walked away to close the curtains. I slipped out of my panties as he took off his shirt and chugged down the rest of his champagne, then I took his tie off of me and put it back over his head. He laughed.

Lonny turned me around and slowly unzipped the back of my dress, softly running his finger down the length of my spine. He kissed the back of my neck and removed the decorative hairpins one by one, letting my hair fall naturally until it was spilling down my back. He slid the straps of my dress down and kissed each of my shoulders, sending shivers throughout my body. I turned around to face him, my arms crossed in front of me to hold up my dress.

"I don't look the same," I whispered.

"Neither do I."

"I have scars."

"So do I."

I slid out of my dress, feeling overly self-conscious as Lonny took me in with his eyes and smiled. He reached out to trace a scar across my stomach with his finger. He looked at me questioningly with tears in his eyes and I simply nodded, letting him know it was another one of my marital battle scars. He lifted me into his arms and placed me on the bed where he kissed me softly.

"No one will ever hurt you again," he whispered. "I promise."

"I love you so much."

Lonny smiled. "I love you, too."

I giggled and said, "You have entirely too many clothes on."

Lonny laughed and began to do a goofy strip tease beginning with his shoes and socks, bending far over to remove them so I had to admire his backside. I got up and sat on my knees, giggling as he turned around to unbuckle his belt.

"Let me help you with that," I said, biting my bottom lip.

Lonny walked toward the bed and I grabbed the tie that was still around his neck, pulling him up against me. I slipped the tie over his head and tossed it on the floor, watching his face as I reached to remove the belt from his pants. He kissed me softly as I slowly slid the leather strap out from each belt loop, then dropped it. I unbuttoned his pants and he kissed me with more urgency, and when I unzipped them he ripped them off so fast I squealed as he flipped me onto my back and pressed himself on top of me. The moment we both waited decades for, when we physically became one with the other again, with a bond so strong no one, not even time could break it, was finally here. Lovers who were tragically torn apart by lies and schemes were now together as husband and wife, never to be separated again.

I watched Lonny's face as he thrust himself inside me and it was nothing but pure love. We watched each other as if we couldn't believe we were actually together, and things were so much different this time around. We weren't eighteen and inexperienced anymore; we knew what our bodies were capable of and what it took to please the other. Crazy in love, both of us finally knowing how the other felt, and no more secrets.

We spent our wedding night making up for lost time, coming up for air only to order room service to fill our grumbling bellies and to finish the champagne. Lonny and I couldn't keep our hands off each other, and I actually surprised him with some of the things I had learned but never tried. At one point he collapsed onto his back out of breath, but he was smiling. He had definitely learned some of his own tricks in the years we spent apart. I cuddled up next to him and pulled the covers over us, and we fell asleep.

I could hear a phone ringing in the distance and lifted my head to listen. The room was pitch black so I had no idea what time it was, but I could see it was Lonny's phone ringing on the bedside table. I nudged him and he grumbled, grabbing the phone and bringing it under the covers with him.

I heard his muffled voice say, "Hey sweetheart... what time is it? Oh shit, I'm sorry. We had a late night." He flung the covers off his head and rubbed his eyes. "Give us a few minutes, we'll be right down."

Lonny hung up his phone and said, "I told Celia to meet us downstairs at noon."

"What time is it?"

"Noon."

"Oops."

I groaned as Lonny turned on the light, then watched his perfect, naked form walk to the bathroom. When he came back he dove under the covers and climbed on top of me.

"I think you and Celia should do this on your own," I said, trying desperately to finger comb the giant knots out of his hair.

"You don't want to come with us?"

"You haven't had any alone time with her since we've been here."

"You just don't want to go car shopping," he teased.

I laughed. "I'd go anywhere with you, but right now Celia is waiting downstairs and there isn't much time."

"Fine," he said, kissing me quickly and hopping back out of bed. He ran into the bathroom to brush his teeth and take a quick shower and rushed to get dressed. I was impressed that he only ended up being fifteen minutes late, kissing me deeply before heading out the door. I stretched my arms and legs and smiled. I had to remind myself that it was no longer a dream, that Lonny and I were actually together and we were *married*. I jumped out of bed and dug in my bag for my phone, sitting up to read Lonny's messages. I loved the photos he sent before and after our wedding, and couldn't wait to tell our parents.

I was startled as my phone buzzed in my hands.

Lonny: I love you! Thank you for saying yes, my beautiful wife!
Me: I love you too, my hot and sexy husband!

I grinned like a fool all the way to the bathroom. I took a nice long shower, dressed comfortably for the heat and threw my camera in my bag, headed out for my own adventure. I spent the afternoon walking the Vegas strip taking pictures of anything and everything, enjoying being alone for the first time since I could remember. Not that I wanted to be away from Lonny for even a minute, but I was finally happy, finally whole, finally comfortable in my own skin.

I stumbled across an amazing thrift store and purchased something for Lonny and Celia, as well as myself. I stopped at an ice cream shop and bought a banana split, and just as I sat down to dig in, Lonny appeared out of nowhere and scared me half to death. He kissed me and sat down on the bench next to me.

"You gonna share that?" he asked, flashing his dimpled smile.

I handed him the spoon and he made sure to feed me first, then took a bite himself.

"So… what did Celia end up getting?" I asked.

He pulled out his phone and showed me a photo of Celia standing in front of a white 2011 Volkswagen Beetle. "I was offering her the world," he joked. "And that's what she wanted."

"At least she went with the convertible," I teased. "It's adorable and it fits her perfectly. Did she get anything for her old car?"

"Fifty bucks. I'm surprised they didn't charge us to take it off our hands." We both laughed.

"When are we going to tell our parents we got married?" I asked.

"Right now." I watched as he texted the before and after wedding photos to my mother and father, but didn't add any words.

"Did you tell Celia?"

"Not yet. I want us to do it together." Lonny grinned when his phone rang and he showed me it was my mother calling. "Hi Mom." Instead of putting it on speaker so everyone around us could hear, he leaned close to my head and held the phone between our ears.

"Lonny," my mother gasped. "Did you and Ruby get married?"

"We did!" he cheered. "Last night."

"Hi Mom!" I said.

"Oh my gosh, Ruby! I called because I don't understand this texting thing…."

"Did you see the pictures?" I asked.

"I did! I just showed your father and Joanie. Joanie is so happy she's crying. Your dad won't admit it but I think he's crying, too. We're all so happy for you!"

Lonny and I both replied, "Thanks, Mom."

"How's Celia?" she asked.

"Oh Mom, she's wonderful," I gushed.

"And she's crazy about Roo," Lonny interjected.

"Who wouldn't be crazy about our Ruby?" she teased.

"We've got some ice cream to finish before it melts," Lonny said. "We'll let you know when we get home tomorrow, okay?"

"Okay kids, congratulations! Love you both!"

"Love you," we said together.

Lonny hung up and put his phone back in his pocket then leaned over and kissed my mouth, not pulling away immediately.

"Are we really going to be home tomorrow?" I asked.

"Yep. It's about a four hour drive give or take, so we'll have breakfast with Celia and head out after that."

I smiled and said, "I can't wait to see your house."

"*Our* house," he corrected me. "It's pretty bare bones, so I hope you'll feel free to make it your own."

I took the bite of ice cream he offered me then remembered my surprise. "Oh! I bought you something!"

"You did?" He was grinning like a little kid.

I dug in my bag and pulled out a small box that I handed to Lonny. He was smiling as he opened it.

"I thought we should have rings, you know, since we're married now." I hoped he liked the rings as much as I did.

"They're beautiful," he said.

"Nothing fancy, but they spoke to me. I hope yours fits."

Lonny took the smaller gold band and slid it on my finger, looking up at me with a loving smile on his face. I slid the other gold band on his finger and it fit like a glove, sending a relieved smile across my face.

"They're perfect," he said. "Thank you."

He kissed my mouth softly, then brushed his lips against my cheek as he whispered in my ear, "We have some time to kill before our plans with Celia tonight."

My face flushed and I giggled as we finished up the banana split and walked hand in hand back to our hotel. I continued taking photos with my camera, only this time Lonny was my focus, and he obliged me with a smile.

No sooner had we finished our late afternoon newlywed romp, Lonny's phone rang. It was Marilyn trying to video chat him.

"You should answer it," I said. "Let her think she interrupted something." Lonny answered the call with his crazy bed head and the covers down to his bellybutton. I dove underneath the sheet so she couldn't see me.

"Hey doll," I heard Marilyn say. "What are you doing in bed at this hour? Are you sick?"

Lonny pretended to be annoyed. "Really? What does it look like I've been doing?"

I giggled as I heard Marilyn gasp. "I'm sorry, doll. Why on earth did you answer the phone then?"

"I was finished," he teased.

"When will you be home?" she asked, as if there was nothing awkward about their phone conversation at all.

"Sometime tomorrow. Then you can meet my wife."

"Wife?" she gasped. "You got *married*?"

"Last night." He grinned and held up his hand to show her the wedding band.

"Lonny! What on *earth*?"

Marilyn didn't sound happy.

"Shhhhhhh!" Lonny scolded her. "She'll hear you."

"I hope you know what you're doing, doll. Married? Fuzzy's going to shit."

"Relax, you'll both love her."

"I doubt that very much."

"Marilyn!" he scolded.

"Why didn't Celia tell me?"

"She doesn't know yet."

"Were you drunk? Are you *that* lonely, Lonny?"

I slid my arm out from under the covers and reached up to playfully pull on Lonny's bottom lip. He said, "I gotta go!" then hung up the phone, laughing hysterically.

I came out for air, laughing. "I see she still doesn't hold back. She's *pissed*," I said.

"You should've seen her face!"

"Still, she should be happy for you."

"Well, she knows I haven't been seeing anybody, so she probably thinks I got drunk and married Fawn."

That's a name I didn't need to hear while lying naked with my husband. I got out of bed and grabbed my phone, then plopped back down beside Lonny.

"I want to send our wedding pictures to Gina," I said.

"Tell her I said hello."

After my text was sent I said, "Celia is picking us up in an hour. We should take a shower." I got up and went into the bathroom and when I realized Lonny wasn't behind me, poked my head out and said, "Aren't you coming?"

He looked surprised. "Oh. Yeah!" He hopped out of bed so fast I thought he might injure himself.

531

Celia picked us up in her brand new Beetle, excited for me to see what her dad purchased for her. It couldn't have been the more perfect car for her, and the smile never left her face as she drove us to her favorite Mexican restaurant for dinner. We drank margaritas and ate chips and salsa while waiting for our dinner, and, sitting on the same side of the booth as Celia, Lonny put an arm around her and cleared his throat.

"Celia, Roo and I have some news we'd like to share," he said.

Her blonde curls bounced on her shoulders as she smiled and clapped excitedly, waiting to hear what he had to say.

Lonny grinned and said, "We got married last night."

Celia was speechless, her smile turning into a gasp as she covered her mouth with her hands. "Daddy!" she finally cheered, hugging him tightly. "I'm so happy for you!" She reached across the table to grab my hands and said, "Thank you for making him so happy. I've never seen him smile like this before."

"Don't tell Aunt Marilyn," Lonny said. "We want to surprise her when we get home."

"My lips are sealed!"

"Celia, I bought something for you today. I couldn't believe I actually found it, but I have one just like it." I pulled a t-shirt out of my bag and handed it to her.

Celia gasped and said, "Is that Daddy?"

Lonny laughed loudly when he looked at what she was holding — a t-shirt with his picture on it, just like the one Gina gave me at the show all those years ago. Mine was packed in my Livingston Monroe box.

"Thank you, Ruby! I love it!" She pulled it over her head and wore it atop the tank she was already wearing.

"One of my favorites," I replied, smiling at Lonny.

After dinner we went to the club where Celia worked as a bartender to enjoy our last evening together listening to live music. Celia introduced us to her co-workers on duty that evening, so proud of her father, telling them exactly who he was. Then she'd show off the shirt she was wearing to embarrass him further, but I knew he was loving every minute of it, and so was I.

532

After we got back to our room, I pulled my phone out of my bag and saw that Gina had sent me a text.

Gina: I didn't recognize your number. You & Lonny got married?! It's about time you two got together! I'm so happy for you!!!!
Me: Thank you! Give Max a hug and a kiss for me!

Knowing it was late in Chicago and Gina probably wouldn't see my text until morning, I gently pushed Lonny onto the bed and crawled on top of him, nibbling his neck. My phone buzzed in my hand.

Gina: Have you heard from my crazy brother?

I showed Lonny her text and he shrugged.

Me: No. I got a new phone and changed my number.
Gina: Beat the shit out of his girlfriend and put her in the hospital. She had him arrested. Loser tried calling me for bail money. I ignored him.
Me: Good.
Gina: Best part? She wants out of the business, so she's suing him for her half. So what did he do? Torched it!
Me: What?!
Gina: Burned it to the damn ground!
Me: Why would he do that?
Gina: Because he's crazy! Thought he could burn it down, get the insurance money, then pay her off with that. I'll email you the article. Enjoy your new husband! Give Lonny a hug for me! Love you!
Me: I will — love you too!

I showed Lonny our conversation and he lay there with his mouth open. "Karma finally found his address," he said.

Lonny and I were so tired we fell asleep as soon as we crawled into bed. In the morning we took a shower and packed our suitcases, checking out of the hotel and meeting Celia for breakfast. We took our time, wanting to enjoy every last minute before having to leave her behind. She didn't want us to leave, but I knew she especially didn't want to be separated from her father. Lonny let her know that she was welcome to visit any time, and if she decided to switch schools or make a permanent move, he would help her with the arrangements. Celia and I exchanged phone numbers so she could reach me whenever she wanted to, and I promised to send her all the photos I took during our visit.

We walked to the parking lot together and Celia was crying before we even reached our car. She wrapped her arms around Lonny's waist and cried against him as he kissed the top of her head.

"I know you hate it here," she cried. "But you're not that far away. Will you please visit me more often?"

"Yes sweetheart," he whispered against her head. "I promise. With Roo by my side, it'll be easier for me to manage now."

"Thank you, Daddy."

Celia pulled away from Lonny and put her arms around me. "I love you, Ruby. Thank you for making Daddy so happy. He never thought he was good enough for you, and I kept telling him he was wrong."

"I love you, too. Thank you for taking such good care of him."

It was harder than I thought it would be to say goodbye to Celia, but we finally managed to get in our car and drive off, waving until she became a blur in the distance. Lonny wiped the tears off his face and chuckled.

"Saying goodbye to her breaks my heart," he said, adjusting his sunglasses.

"Thank you," I said.

He smiled at me. "For what?"

"For everything."

He squeezed my hand and replied, "Anything for my girl."

We got to Lonny's house later that afternoon, and after he unlocked the front door he lifted me into his arms and carried me across the threshold.

"Welcome home, Roo," he said, placing me on my feet again.

The house was small, but bright, with three bedrooms and two bathrooms. The back yard consisted of a patio area covered with a pergola, and a small swimming pool with a separate hot tub. Lonny wasn't kidding when he said the house was bare bones, but I hoped we'd be able to decorate together. Above the sink in the kitchen was a small bay window that looked out to the pool area, and I noticed a handful of seashells sitting inside, including the cockle shell with the heart-shaped hole in it.

"Lonny, are these the shells I brought you in the hospital?"

"They are."

I walked into the living room and stood staring at a piece of artwork over the fireplace. I wasn't quite sure what I was looking at at first but then it slowly started to dawn on me.

"Are those your concert ties?" I asked.

"Yeah," he chuckled. "When Isabella and I were together, she took all the ties and had that made for me. Isn't it cool?"

"It's amazing!"

"I think there's a few missing though."

"I have them."

"You do?"

"Yeah," I replied sheepishly. "Apparently when I left the hotel that day, I accidentally threw some in my suitcase in my rush to leave."

"So they've found their way back to me, just like you have."

I turned to face him and he was smiling at me. I wrapped my arms around him and hugged him as tightly as my arms had strength. "I love you so much," I said.

"I love you, too. Let's get the stuff from the car."

After bringing in our boxes from the car, Lonny took me by the hand and led me to his bedroom. There was a huge bed and a couple of dressers, an attached master bath, and one piece of artwork hanging on the wall. It took me by surprise at first, but as I walked closer to the bed to see the painting hanging over it, I heard myself gasp.

535

"Yes, it's you," Lonny said. "I painted that about a year ago, right after moving into this house. You're the first person to see it."

"Lonny, I don't know what to say."

"Say you love me and don't think I'm creepy."

"I love you, and it's beautiful."

Lonny wrapped his arms around me from behind and rested his chin on my shoulder. He whispered in my ear, "As you can see, I basically just eat and sleep here. I'm looking forward to making a home here with you."

"I love it Lonny, and wherever you are, that's my home."

"I think we should go on our backpacking trip to Europe," he said. "For our honeymoon."

I turned to face him and he kissed me softy. "That would be wonderful!"

"Wanna try out the bed? I'm the only one who's been in it, I promise."

I laughed. "Hell yes!"

Our quick romp left us satisfied, out of breath and deliriously happy, lying facing each other with goofy grins. I reached out and pushed a strand of hair away from his face.

"Why didn't you tell me there was a Livingston Monroe display at the Rock and Roll Hall of Fame?" I asked.

He kissed me and said, "Fuzzy and I donated a bunch of stuff, but never knew what they did with it."

"I went there when we were stranded in Cleveland. There's an entire room dedicated to the band."

He kissed me again and said, "I had no idea."

"Your smashed up Flying V is there. What happened to it?"

Lonny visibly cringed, then sighed. "I lost my mind after the plane crash, but I was enraged when you didn't come for the memorial. It was the closest thing to me when I hung up on you... I smashed it to bits."

"Do you miss it?"

"As much as I hated the idea of playing for an audience when I was a kid, being onstage ended up being what I loved most. I miss it every day."

I could feel tears burning my eyes. "It's so unfair."

He gently grazed my mouth with his thumb then kissed me deeply. "No living in the past. It's over."

Lonny's phone started ringing and when he looked at it he laughed loudly. "Marilyn." He put the phone back on the table, ignoring her call and kissing me instead. A few minutes later his phone was blowing up with texts. We looked at his phone together.

> Marilyn: Are you home?
> Marilyn: Why are you ignoring me?
> Marilyn: I know you're home.
> Marilyn: We're in your driveway!
> Marilyn: Nice car… is it your wife's?

And then the doorbell started ringing. We howled with laughter as Lonny jumped out of bed to throw on a pair of jeans and a t-shirt. "You come out when you think it's the best time," he said, kissing me quickly before heading out of the bedroom and closing the door behind him.

I rushed to put my clothes back on and tried to listen to the conversation going on in the living room.

"Why didn't you tell us when you got back?" Marilyn asked.

"I was tired," Lonny replied. "Took a nap."

"Took a nap? I can tell by your hair you weren't taking a nap. Can't you keep it in your pants, doll?" she teased.

"It's been in my pants for over a year," Lonny said.

"Mare, please stop," Fuzzy begged. I could almost hear him rolling his eyes.

"So when do we get to meet the wife?"

Peter!

I smiled hearing the banter between Lonny and our friends.

"I don't know," Lonny replied. "Maybe she doesn't want to meet you."

"Why wouldn't she want to meet us?" Peter asked, sounding offended.

"God Lonny, I feel sick," Marilyn grumbled. "If you did what I think you did…."

I took this as my cue and tip-toed out of the bedroom and stood behind our three friends, who had their backs to me. At sixty-two, Marilyn and Fuzzy had both let their hair go silver, and at fifty-seven, Peter had a beautiful head of salt and pepper hair. I couldn't wait to see their faces; it had been far too long.

"So," Lonny said with a smile. "Meet the wife."

Marilyn, Fuzzy and Peter turned at the same time and were prepared to be shocked, and because they weren't expecting it to be me, they were. All three of them shouted loudly when they realized it was me, Marilyn screaming so loud she could have burst an eardrum.

"Lonny, you shit!" Marilyn yelled. "I can't believe it's you, doll! Oh my God, you *married* him!" Her smile was almost blinding as she pulled me into her arms and squeezed the breath out of me.

"Mare tried to get it out of Celia, but she was great. Ignored her completely," Fuzzy laughed. "You know how she hates being ignored." He pulled me into a hug that was almost as loving as Lonny's. "I love that you're here, doll."

"Good to see you, love," Peter said, hugging me and kissing me on the cheek. "You look absolutely breathtaking."

"It's all because of Lonny," I said, smiling like the newlywed I was.

"See, doll?" Marilyn squealed. "I *knew* you and Lonny belonged together. I didn't expect it to take three decades, but I know what I'm talking about!"

Lonny stood behind me and wrapped his arms around my shoulders, nuzzling my neck. I closed my eyes and smiled, taking in the scene surrounding me.

Lonny and I were finally *home*.

The End

"Whispers On A String – The Novel" Soundtrack
Available on Spotify

"You're My Best Friend" by Queen - 1976
"Mama Kin" by Aerosmith - 1973
"Surrender" by Cheap Trick - 1978
"You Take My Breath Away" by Rex Smith - 1979
"Lady" by the Little River Band - 1978
"Drift Away" by Dobie Gray - 1973
"Lovin' Touchin' Squeezin'" by Journey - 1979
"Band on the Run" by Paul McCartney & Wings - 1973
"I Wanna Be Sedated" by the Ramones - 1978
"C'Mon Everybody" by Humble Pie - 1972
"I'm On My Way Back Home" by the Partridge Family - 1971
"I Can See Clearly Now" by Johnny Nash - 1972
"At Seventeen" by Janis Ian - 1975
"Find Your Way Back" by Jefferson Starship - 1981
"Cool Change" by the Little River Band - 1979
"Dressed For Success" by Roxette - 1988
"What Is Life" by George Harrison - 1971
"Y.M.C.A." by the Village People - 1978
"Knock On Wood" by Amii Stewart - 1979
"Don't Stop 'Til You Get Enough" by Michael Jackson - 1979
"I Feel Love" by Donna Summer - 1977
"Boogie Fever" by the Sylvers - 1975
"Keep Yourself Alive" by Queen - 1973
"Second Hand News" by Fleetwood Mac - 1977
"Cherry Bomb" by the Runaways - 1976
"Shambala" by Three Dog Night - 1973
"Every Time I Think Of You" by the Babys - 1979
"Up In a Puff Of Smoke" by Polly Brown - 1974
"I Want You To Want Me" by Cheap Trick - 1979
"Everything I Own" by Bread - 1972
"Crazy Horses" by the Osmonds - 1972
"Bad Case Of Loving You" by Robert Palmer - 1979
"Could It Be Forever" by David Cassidy - 1972
"Speak To the Sky" by Rick Springfield - 1972

"Love Brought Me Such a Magical Thing" by the Bay City Rollers - 1978
"Hallelujah" by Jeff Buckley - 1994
"Gotta Get A Message To You" by the Bee Gees - 1968
"Bad Time" by Grand Funk Railroad - 1975
"My Maria" by B.W. Stevenson - 1973
"Roll On Down the Highway" by Bachman Turner Overdrive - 1974
"Fat Bottomed Girls" by Queen - 1978
"Accidents" by Thunderclap Newman - 1969
"Baby I Love You" by the Ramones - 1980
"Go All the Way" by the Raspberries - 1972
"We'll Never Have To Say Goodbye Again" by England Dan and John Ford Coley - 1976
"Got To Get You Into My Life" by the Beatles - 1966
"Itchykoo Park" by the Small Faces - 1967
"To Love Somebody" by the Bee Gees - 1967
"Ballroom Blitz" by the Sweet - 1973
"Because You're Young" by David Bowie - 1980
"All Out Of Love" by Air Supply - 1980
"Somebody To Love" by Queen - 1976
"Out Of Season" by REO Speedwagon - 1980
"Spirit Of Radio" by Rush - 1980
"Livin' After Midnight" by Judas Priest - 1978
"Breathless" by the Corrs - 2001
"Stone In Love" by Journey - 1981
"Whisper To a Scream (Birds Fly)" by Icicle Works - 1983
"Lorelei" by Styx - 1976
"I'll Be" by Edwin McCain - 1998
"Goodbye" by Night Ranger - 1985
"Winning" by Santana - 1981
"When I'm With You" by Sheriff - 1982
"I Will Be There" by Glass Tiger - 1987
"Hey Jealousy" by the Gin Blossoms - 1989
"New York Groove" by Ace Frehley - 1978
"Forever Unstoppable" by Hot Chelle Rae – 2011

ACKNOWLEDGMENTS

Thank you to my first readers, Lesa Beaty, Gretchen Hinkson, Marie Crouch, Pam Helke, Mary Gorleski, Patti Kalaytowicz and Lori Bruggeman. Your encouragement, honest feedback, editing and proofreading were invaluable!

Thank you, Jackie Byrka, for answering my call when I was in need of an old roll of 35mm film for my book cover. I couldn't have done it without you!

Writers are nothing without their readers. Thank you to everyone who has read my work and shared their opinions with others. As a tiny fish in an enormous ocean of famous authors, reader reviews and word of mouth are essential to getting the word out about my work. Every little bit helps, and I am thankful for each and every one of you! If you have enjoyed any of my books, please feel free to write a review on amazon.com or goodreads.com; I would be truly grateful.

WWW.KATHLEENSTONE.ORG

NOVELS

Head Case

"...the equivalent to Motley Crue's 'The Dirt'"
~ D*Rick, Amazon Reviewer

"Stone has an almost magical style that allows the characters to grow before a reader's eyes, in a sly yet efficient way."
~ R. Scott Bolton, RoughEdge.com

"Head Case is the first installment of the chronicles of Regi Sebastian, drummer of the rock group Pages. Written in a simple, easy to read narration that almost gives the effect of not reading a book at all, but instead getting the juicy low-down from a best friend over dinner and drinks. Head Case has a bit of anything you could possibly ask for from a rock and roll story, everything from both the glamour and grit of the rock and roll world, to sex, drugs, and even murder. It's a true page-turner that nags at you when you put it down because you want to know what's going to happen next. Quite a fun read for anyone who likes an action filled storyline, but for those of us who had our own dealings with rock and roll bands this is a must read... this book isn't as cliche as one might think, it's frankly quite relatable."
~ Melanie Falina, Unrated Magazine

Whiplash

"Stone's storytelling ability is flowing and captivating in an easy to read narration that's filled with... what else, but the heavy metal trinity — sex, drugs, and rock & roll! Whiplash offers a rock and roll fringed drama with a jaw-dropper at the end."
~ Melanie Falina, Unrated Magazine

"... a fast pace that never falters and a clearness and crispness that makes the book a pleasant, easy read. Again, the characters are so fully drawn and realized that it's never a problem remembering who is who — despite the book's necessarily large cast of characters."

"… the various rock bands and/or rock stars that Stone name-drops are well-placed reminders of the real rock world — and enhance the novel's realness as well."
~ R. Scott Bolton, RoughEdge.com

Haven

"Like Facebook and other social media sites today that allow us to reconnect with people from our past, in Haven, Kathleen Stone bridges the gap and brings Regi, Mickey and Jesse right back to us once again. The whole wild saga that began years ago in a quintessential whirlwind of sex, drugs, and rock and roll has now evolved with children and real-life situations that all Stone's readers can relate to, but they're all just fibers in the great membrane which holds them all together — the band. Kathleen Stone's tone and flow is a relaxed personal one — reading her words is like sitting across the table from a good friend at a cafe as she fills you in on everything that's been happening since your last meeting. Whether you're a musician, a music enthusiast, or simply a fan of literature, the characters in Stone's rock and roll chronicles become friends, and being able to catch up with them once again is an experience that runs the gamut of emotion, but overall, provides an abundance of comfort that only other really good things in life can."
~ Melanie P. Falina, Music Journalist & Poet

"When 'Haven' begins, a lot has changed in the world of Regi and the gang. The band is trying to put together a comeback tour but Regi feels it'd be better for her to stay home with her children who are, in fact, her very life. What follows is a story of jealousy and uncertainty that sometimes will make you angry, and other times will bring tears of joy to your eyes. There's people struggling with love (and lost love), children who are confused by their parents' unusual lifestyles, and the driving force throughout: Can Pages return to the road without Regi back on the drums?"

"It's an entertaining read from beginning to end, although sometimes you might be angry with Regi for all the chaos she seems to bring. That will all go away when she goes to bat for an abused child, a story arc that deserves a book all on its own. I'd love to see a movie about just that part: A famous rock star hiding a child from her abusive father to keep her from harm. It's my second favorite part of 'Haven.' The first is the very last page which will have you pumping your fists in the air."
~ R. Scott Bolton, RoughEdge.com

ANTHOLOGIES

(Published under Kathleen Strelow)

Secrets, Fact or Fiction Volume I & II

"Josie," by Kathleen Strelow will tug at your heart and most people will, at the least, have tears threatening to spill."

~ Armchair Interviews, Amazon

Made in the USA
Monee, IL
10 April 2021

65322753R00319